THE *AL-ANDALUS* CHRONICLE

Howard Headworth

ATHENA PRESS
LONDON

THE *AL-ANDALUS* CHRONICLE
Copyright © Howard Headworth 2004

ISBN 1 84401 271 9

First Published 2004 by
ATHENA PRESS
Queen's House, 2 Holly Road
Twickenham, TW1 4EG
United Kingdom

Printed for Athena Press

THE *AL-ANDALUS* CHRONICLE

To Katie

It's a shame you couldn't
be here today. It's a
glorious sunny morning yet
nice a cool.

with very best wishes

Howard

30 X 2004

Acknowledgements

I would like to thank several people who helped with the historical information for this book: Luisa Laynez Vallejo, for obtaining a beautifully illustrated promotional book, *La Espada en Toledo*, published by the Comunidad de Castilla-La Mancha; Luis Emilio Vallejo Delgada, the Director of the Arqueological Museum at Porcuna, near Córdoba, for information about the castle there; Ginés Pastor Medina, in Almería, an authority on marble from Macael in Almería; David Highley of the British Geological Survey, Nottingham, for information concerning the historic extraction of marble; and Jorge Lirola Delgado in the Department of Arab and Islamic Studies, the University of Almería, for providing details on Arab dress at the time of the Muslim occupation of southern Spain. I particularly thank my neighbours, Karen and Frank Villafana, for so diligently proofreading my manuscript, and for their helpful textual suggestions. Lastly, I am indebted to Mark Sykes, Chief Editor of Athena Press, for his enthusiastic support of this book and the care taken in its publication.

Howard Headworth
January 2004

Historical Setting

It is 1483. The Islamic empire of *Al-Andalus* in southern Spain is drawing to its close, while the Christian kingdom is about to enter its most glorious era. For nearly eight centuries the Muslim people have enriched the land with fine buildings, cool gardens, fountains and colourful dress; with art, poetry and music, and, above all, with their skills in using water to cultivate the hot and dry lands of southern Spain. Muslims, Jews and Christians have lived in harmony under a benign but firm governance. The marriage in 1469 of Fernando of Aragón and Isabel of Castile forges a royal partnership, *Los Reyes Católicos*, which turns the course of Spanish and European history and sets Spain on its path to fortune, glory and empire. By the end of the thirteenth century the Islamic Empire had shrunk to half its size, and by the middle of the fifteenth century it is a moribund shadow of its former glory, occupying only part of what are now the provinces of Almería, Málaga and Granada.

With great military skill, the availability of new engines of war, religious fanaticism, and financed by Rome which declares a holy war and, not least, by devious cunning, the Catholic Monarchs move to put an end finally to the decaying Islamic Empire. Opposing them is a weak, twenty-year-old sultan, Boabdil who, with feuding support, weak military forces and fortifications never designed to withstand the mighty guns now being forged in Germany and Austria, recognises that he cannot stem the tide. Gradually the borders crumble, sometimes by force, sometimes by treaty.

The events are seen through the eyes of a half-Jewish and half-Christian boy in the eight years from 1486 to 1493. His adventures take him on journeys across *Al-Andalus*, where he encounters many of the principal players at that time and witnesses many of the historic events. The story unfolds in three parts: *Ensnared by the Inquisition*; *Farewell, beloved Granada*; and *Ignominy and Glory*.

The Al-Andalus Chronicle
Part I: Ensnared by the Inquisition

Contents

Part I: Ensnared by the Inquisition

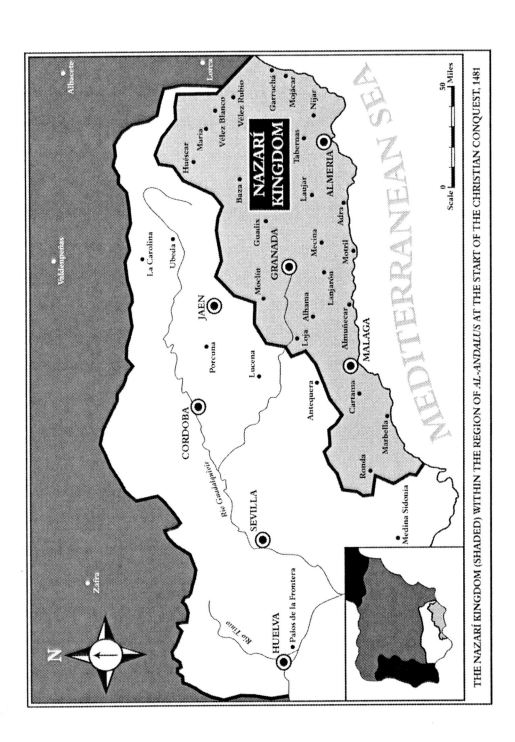

THE NAZARÍ KINGDOM (SHADED) WITHIN THE REGION OF AL-ANDALUS AT THE START OF THE CHRISTIAN CONQUEST, 1481

I: Pedro's Lair

October 1487

With his bloody sword in one hand and his scabbard in the other, thirteen-year-old Pedro Togeiro de Tedula ran and ran and ran. He zigzagged up through the steep streets and alleys of Vélez Blanco, through the open gateway in the wall which ran across the centre of the town and up through the Muslim quarter. Then out onto the open space next to the square-walled *alcázar* where he and his young Muslim friend, Yazíd, had rescued Mahoma Hamar from a thief some months before. He ran and ran. Down along the shallow saddle of the hill on which the town was situated, then across to the slopes of the mountains which led down to Velad al-Almar some miles away. Without thinking, he knew he had only one place where he could possibly go. Crossing the rocky valley which incised the mountain wall, he stumbled over the uneven boulder-strewn slopes below the limestone cliffs and soon reached the cover of the pine trees. But he did not stop even then. With his lungs at bursting point, he charged through the dead lower branches of the trees, tearing his arms and legs through his shirt and thin cotton trousers. But he felt nothing. With relief, he joined the path which he and Yazíd took from the lower gates of the town and tore up it towards the cliffs above him. The path soon ran out as the rocks became precipitous above the tree line but he ascended all the time until he came out below their secret hideaway beneath the high overhang. He climbed the last few feet onto the ledge, where he flung his sword and scabbard to the ground and collapsed, almost dying for breath.

He wished he had died there and then. In a pitiful state physically and mentally he just lay there sprawled headlong in the dust. He did not know how long he stayed like this, an hour, maybe two, maybe three. Eventually he rolled over and sat up. Mercifully, his knife was still in its sheath attached to his belt. His treasured sword lay at his side, coated with a dark dried stain along a third of its length. He reached over, picked it up and hurled it into the far corner of the shallow cave. It struck hard against the cave wall, ringing out as it did so. The scabbard followed.

This accursed sword! What misery had it brought on him. What terrible things had he done with it in his hand. His mind was in total turmoil; the picture he had of the horror in Marco's face that afternoon fought with his recurring image of the terrible happenings at Bédar six months before. His dear friend Marco, who had shown him such affection and understanding, now dead by his hand. Two other men dead, one in the most hideous agony as a result of his thoughtless action at the weir – all because of his accursed sword. Oh, how he wished he could have buried himself in his mother's arms. She would have understood. She would have stroked away the tears and eased his torment. But that could not be. She was gone. All he now had was an irritable and testy father who had no time for him or his sister, Cristina.

Crying out aloud in a mixture of anger, remorse, guilt and self-loathing, he climbed up and around the cliff from his hideout into the narrow crevice which held the boys' secret cache. It being not more than waist-high, he sidled to the very darkest recess. He threw himself down with his knees tight to his chest and his head bent low in his hands, sobbing. And thus he stayed as the sun set behind the mountains, through the chill of the night until the long shadows of the early morning sun started to creep up the valley over which his crevice looked.

He was spent. There were no more tears to shed, no more claws grabbing at his guts, no more strength to clench his fists and to grit his teeth. Just a deep, pitiful self-loathing. By mid-morning, as the sun began to warm the valley and shine directly into his narrow crevice he knew he could not stay there forever. He had to do something, go somewhere. Nothing would bring back Marco, who had become such a wonderful friend. Nothing would make amends for the tragedy at Bédar.

With a start he realised that it was not his sword which was cursed but himself. Whatever he had done to cause it, the devil had entered his soul and he was damned, maybe for ever. When he had ascended the town the previous afternoon he knew that he could never, never, go back home to his father's house, and he must strive for all he was worth to free himself from the devil's grasp. It might take him a lifetime and he might have to journey the rest of his life in search of freedom. But try he must.

With some vestige of calmness returning, he retrieved some of the packets of food which he and Yazíd had secreted in a corner of the crevice and clambered down to his den-cum-cave around the corner. The thick, fatty slices of smoked ham, the sweet dried figs and raisins, plus the salted almonds, all washed down with the water from the clay pitcher, soon started to energise and warm his lean body and rekindle his tormented spirit.

Something else was troubling him, but he could not put his finger on it. Then it dawned on him what it was. He was sure that his father would force Yazíd to disclose where he was likely to have gone to and make Yazíd bring him up to their hideout. Although his friend was smart enough to make sufficient noise as they approached the cave to warn Pedro or, more likely, lead his father to another one of the caves along the mountain wall, Pedro could not be absolutely certain. He had to remain vigilant and listen out for sounds of people approaching.

Gradually his spirits started to revive and he began to think more clearly. The muscles in his legs were still painfully tight from his fleeing so frantically from his home the previous day and his body was still limp and weak from the distress and tension he had endured. He knew that he could not possibly move from his hideout during the day. He had no alternative but to stay a second night to fully recover his energy. He would aim to move off just before sunset the following evening.

He removed David Levi's knife from the sheath at his left side. In its way, it was as beautiful as his sword. The man was truly a craftsman. Glistening in the sun, the blade had the same diamond profile and possessed a beautiful handle made from a deer's antler with a short, brass crosspiece. Like the sword, David's initials were handsomely engraved on one side of the blade just above the crosspiece.

Feeling guilty for throwing his sword away, Pedro got up and retrieved it and its scabbard from the corner of the rock overhang. Luckily it was not damaged, although the limestone wall bore the signature of the tempered blade. It was obvious that he could not risk taking it with him. For one thing he would be too noticeable; but more importantly, he feared what other evil he might perpetrate with it. No, better conceal it here.

He climbed up again into the narrow crevice and found the remnants of cotton material which Yazíd had pilfered from beneath the market stalls when the stallholders were packing up for the day. He tore them into strips, soaked them in olive oil from the earthenware jar and wrapped the strips tightly around the sword, tying the bundle tightly with twine. He did the same with the scabbard. Then, reaching as far as he could, he secreted both of them in the deepest dry crack in the crevice. He did not know how long it might be before he would retrieve them, but he knew that they would be safe there from harm's way. Even Yazíd would not find them unless told where to look.

Next he had to make their cache in the crevice shipshape and to clean himself up as best he could. Yazíd would guess that Pedro had been there since most of the food would have been eaten. No doubt he would work like a beaver to restock the store in the event of Pedro's return. But first, the cuts and abrasions; some were looking rather nasty. He climbed down from the crevice and searched for chamomile plants in the stony pasture above the tree line. Chamomile was well known as an effective antiseptic. After some searching he found some of the spindly plants with their sparse greyish-green feathery leaves. The clusters of white flowers had long since seeded and been blown away. He picked a few leaves from the tall stalks of several plants until he had enough. Against his better judgement, he collected some dry twigs and leaves as tinder, and in a clearing amongst the trees he soon had a fire going after a few strikes of steel on flint from his box of miscellaneous odds and ends. What smoke it produced would hopefully dissipate through the foliage above. He found a broken potsherd nearby and washed out the soil and stones before boiling some water on the fire and adding the camomile leaves. He stirred the brew with a stick until a yellowy green tea formed. He put out the fire, let the fluid cool and with a piece of cloth swabbed his cuts and abrasions, letting the medication soak into the wounds. Pedro scrambled back along the slope to the valley which he had crossed the previous afternoon. The late afternoon sun still retained some warmth. He stayed there until sunset, giving his wounds chance to heal in the warming rays of the sun.

He decided that it would be safer to spend the second night in the narrow crevice than in the bigger and more exposed cave overhang. In his state of mental torment the previous night, he had totally forgotten the woollen blanket which was concealed in the crevice. After another meal of ham and dried fruit, the boy spread out some straw over the uneven floor of the narrow cave, tucked himself into his blanket and quickly fell sleep.

The next morning, with the whole day to kill, he sat on the grass to think. What would he do? Where would he go? He could not go back home, that was certain; his short-tempered father would thrash him to within an inch of his life. Moreover, for a while at least, he needed to keep away from the highways; there was no knowing who would be searching for him. His options were few. I know, he thought. I'll run away to sea. That's what boys have always done when they get into trouble. The city of Almería traded around the whole of the Mediterranean and was a very busy port. Yes, he would head there. But first he would visit his big uncle Joshua in the village of María and explain things to him. He had always had a soft spot for his cheery uncle and knew that he would get a fair hearing.

An hour before sunset, Pedro set off. With his knife sheathed tightly on his belt, his shirt, trousers and sandals dry and his wounds already healing, he felt invigorated. With a spring in his step and his mind now clear as to what he would do, he headed off up the sloping valley which provided the only access through the limestone wall.

II: *Vélez Blanco*

March 1487

At an elevation of three thousand six hundred feet, Vélez Blanco was situated at the eastern end of the Sierra María range of mountains. This broad limestone range ran almost without interruption to Granada and beyond, well over a hundred miles to the west. The town lay on a spur running down from the limestone massif which rose high above the town in an almost continuous wall which descended south-westwards towards the hill-top fortification of Velad al-Almar, four miles away. Dominating the town and directly opposite it four miles away was the towering sentinel of Cerro de la Muela, aptly named 'the molar', being a precipitous, flat-topped mountain over five thousand feet high, with ribs of resistant limestone running down its flanks like enormously jagged walls. Below Muela to its right, the wide valley of the Río Vélez provided an easy route to the city of Lorca some thirty miles away. Indeed, it was this very route which the *alcázar* at Vélez Blanco was constructed to secure. The pale-coloured mountains behind and above the town were scarred by large caverns and overhangs, their walls stained by black seepages, and it was to one of these that Pedro would flee some six months later. Below them, ancient screes of rocks and boulders were populated and anchored in place by open, pine woodland. Pine needles, bare rocks and the impoverished soils supported a scant variety of plants.

Vélez Blanco's lower outer wall circled the saddle of the hill on which the town stood. It had three gates, to the south, east and north. On the south side this wall ascended the hill to join the *alcázar*, while a second inner wall ran across the town at a higher elevation to a tower near the north gate. Adjoining the *alcázar* on the higher side of the inner wall was the *mesquita*, or mosque, and the *aljibe*, the underground water storage cistern cut out of solid rock.

Young Pedro, now just turned thirteen, was a half-Jewish, half-Christian boy. His Jewish father, Abraham Togeiro de Tudela, was a successful apothecary and seemingly much older than his forty-one years. Abraham was of middle size, but hunched and somewhat bony. He was now a crotchety and irritable man. It was only through his renowned skill as an apothecary that he managed to keep his customers. Like most of his race, he wore his thinning and straggly hair shoulder-length and had an untidy, greying unkempt beard. A widower, he had not always been irked by petty things. Five years before, his dear wife Miriam, then only twenty-six, had disappeared while they were visiting the port of Aguilas, where Abraham was conducting business. Abraham had never seen his wife again or learnt what had become of her. As far as Abraham was concerned she was dead. Miriam had been the pride of his life, but theirs had been an unusual union. Miriam had been a beautiful young Christian woman, tall, slim with golden hair and pale blue eyes. She had a silky-smooth skin which she protected carefully from the fierce summer sun. She loved and respected Abraham, then an erect and upright man, for his skill and learning and, not least, his honesty, and she took no notice of the dire warnings against 'mixed-blood' marriages from her family or Abraham's family. Sadly, after their union her parents considered her tainted and not worthy of their continued affection and care. They never saw her again. Abraham did not fare much better either. His father, Isaac, now dead, disowned him and passed his import-export business in the city of Almería to the eldest of his three sons, Simón. The latter adopted his father's prejudices and had only met Abraham once since he had married Miriam. But nevertheless, he continued to send Abraham the spices and other commodities which he needed for his practice. To a Jew, trade came first. But with Miriam gone, Abraham had become a changed man. For Pedro, the loss at the age of eight of his sunny and sparkling mother was traumatic enough, but for his young sister, Cristina, then just five years old, it was a crushing blow.

At thirteen, Pedro was tall for his age. He had his father's dark features but possessed his mother's blue eyes. Like most boys he was lean and agile; the mountains around Vélez Blanco saw to that. At the time it caused considerable conflict between Miriam and Abraham, but Miriam had her way and Pedro was saved from Samuel Beneviste's circumcising blade when he was eight days old. Samuel, who was the authorised mohel for the town's small Jewish community, refused to speak to Abraham for years afterwards for not adhering to the strict Jewish rites. Abraham's rejection of this traditional custom alienated his brother Simón still further, and this more than the marriage was the reason why the two brothers had only met once since the wedding.

The family home of Abraham, Pedro and Cristina was situated in the small Jewish enclave between the outer town wall and the higher inner wall and was reached from the road leading up from the east gate. The house sat on a T-junction. Narrow cobbled streets rose steeply through the predominant Muslim quarter, criss-crossed with side alleys and dead ends. Two spring-fed pipes issued from the front wall of the house and cascaded into a stone water trough. To the left lay a small open space, and Abraham often used this small square to erect stalls on which to display his jars and bottles of medicines and palliatives. In the hot summer months he hung a canvas awning over the stone-flagged area. The coolness afforded by its shade, as well as the adjacent piped spring, made it a ready meeting place for Jew and Gentile alike. Abraham's dispensary looked out onto the small square. A door behind the counter led to the central living room, while a curtained alcove in the dispensary concealed a smooth marble-topped table, a stone sink and a battery of equipment and utensils for grinding, mixing, blending, distilling and extracting his medicines.

Above, and overlooking the water trough, were two small windows in which Abraham displayed his jars of herbs and spices which were supplied by his two brothers, Joshua and Simón. They were simply there for display. Not so those inside on the shelves behind Abraham's counter. In neatly labelled, matching white china jars were chamomile for everything from liver disorders to piles. There was black pepper as a stimulant and an aphrodisiac; powdered ginger for travel sickness and rue for sterility. There were balms for soothing; poultices for inflammations; ointments for stings and abrasions; sweet medicines for children; unpleasant medicines for hypochondriacs. There were creams, liniments, embrocation, syrups, sedatives, enemas, laxatives, purgatives, balsams and general elixirs. Everything was there for every possible need, collectively aggrandised as medicines, palliatives, antidotes and general cures. But Abraham was more enlightened than most of his contempories. Yes, he had leeches for bleeding, that was expected of him; but there were no birds' beaks, cockroaches, lizards, toads or rats' tails in his inner sanctum from which he might brew deadly potions. No customer ever managed to peep behind the curtain, and it was only in the last year that Pedro was permitted within this sanctum, as his father started to initiate him into his secret rites for the time when Pedro would succeed to the business.

Whatever motive Abraham had for concealing his professional practices from his family and customers it need not have been fear of being exposed for sorcery. For several centuries Jews had made a notable contribution to medicine in Spain, indeed in Europe as a whole, and were renowned for their knowledge and skills. Salomón Byton was a physician to Queen Isabel[1] of Castile, while King Fernando of Aragón was served by another Jew, Gento Silton. A hundred years before, Josef Orabuena de Tudela was physician to Carlos III in the northern kingdom of Navarra, where he founded a medical school. Abraham's grandfather, Aaron, attended this school and it was from there that he took the family name, de Tudela, which his son Isaac, and Isaac's three sons, Joshua, Abraham and Simón inherited.

The family's living quarters were sparsely furnished with a wooden table and chairs. An open grate and chimney provided much-needed warmth during the bitterly cold winter months. Symmetrically placed on each side of it were two of Miriam's beautiful tapestries, woven painstakingly from wools of soft browns, greens, mauves, greys and yellows; the dyes being produced from local plants and fruits. Along one wall was a low rug-covered divan which afforded comfort for Abraham's ageing bones. Against the opposite wall was a high pine dresser holding brown earthenware plates, bowls and dishes. Roughly-woven rugs from Níjar covered the centre of the floor. These were part of Miriam's dowry on her marriage. They were now faded and badly

---

[1] For consistency throughout the trilogy Spanish names have been used and not their Anglicised equivalents. Thus Queen Isabel and King Fernando are used and not Queen Isabella and King Ferdinand as they are commonly known in Great Britain.

worn, but with Miriam gone, Abraham felt little motivation to replace them. Off this central living room was his bedroom with a small window set in the thick stone wall. A waist-high brick oven protruded into the back yard from the kitchen, while a floor-level hearth and an iron griddle allowed earthenware vessels to be heated. From the kitchen a low door led out into a cobbled back alley at the end of which a latrine served a handful of dwellings. Abraham rarely ventured into the back alley. He had learnt to his cost more than once how treacherous the cobbles were there when it rained.

It was some six months before his flight to his mountain retreat when Pedro had met his Muslim friend, Yazíd, as arranged at the south gate of the town, the six-inch thick, iron-studded doors being swung open on their massive iron hinges at dawn each day. Both boys were barefoot. Pedro wore as usual his worn and patched-up woollen breeches, which extended to just below his knees, plus a thin, equally faded woollen shirt with baggy sleeves, tied at the wrist. On his head he wore a loose cap. As ever, Yazíd wore colourful, ankle-length baggy pantaloons tied by a cord around his waist and a sleeveless, unfastened coarse woollen waistcoat. Around his head was wound a dirty white turban, the end of which hung over his shoulder.

A year younger than Pedro, twelve-year-old Yazíd was a much smaller boy. Raven-haired with a dusky skin and flashing white teeth, he made up for his lack of height with a robust and strong body. When it came to wrestling and running, Pedro was no match for his Muslim friend. Yazíd could run like the wind and seemingly all day at that. Sometimes they descended the valley running down to Velad al-Ahmar, and it was a rare event indeed for Pedro to beat Yazíd back to the south gate. It was not just that Yazíd could run and run and run. He had a knack of disappearing and then suddenly reappearing from nowhere. On one occasion, Pedro waited for him for nearly an hour at an arranged spot, yet failed to see his friend a few yards away, sitting motionless in the shade of a gnarled olive tree.

'How long have you been there?' queried a startled Pedro.

'Since the shadow started to form beneath this tree,' came Yazíd's perplexing reply.

Despite their different languages and cultures, Pedro and Yazíd had been bosom friends since they were very small boys, and now they were inseparable. Yazíd was the only son of Yakub ibn Hayyan and his wife Fátima. Yazíd had four sisters, two older and two younger than him. Yakub was a leather merchant and he imported hides mainly from Valencia, higher up the Mediterranean coast from Almería. As a wholesaler, Yakub sold the hides – not only the very best quality oxhides, but also fine calfskins or pigskins – to local craftsmen, who fashioned them into shoes, saddles, thick breastplates for soldiers, and countless other essential and luxury items. Leather, like wool, was one of the vital commodities of both societies, Christian and Muslim.

But clothes and footwear were expensive. A woollen shirt cost one hundred and fifty maravedís, a pair of sandals two hundred maravedís, while a nobleman would pay nearly two thousand maravedís for a fashionable doublet. This at a time when skilled workers, such as carpenters or shipwrights, earned fifty-five maravedís a day, while a humble field worker in Andalusia earned just eighteen. Barely enough to survive, when a dozen eggs in the market cost twenty-four maravedís, a chicken twenty, and a quart of milk five. Those without work starved.

'Where shall we go?' queried Yazíd.

'Let's go up to the *alcázar*, we haven't been up that way for some time,' replied Pedro.

'All right,' said Yazíd, 'I'll race you there!'

Without waiting for a reply, Yazíd was gone, flying into the town and ascending the narrow streets and alleyways which wound up the steep slope like a rectangular maze blocked with dead ends and culs-de-sac. Pedro chose the easier but less direct route, out through the arched stone gateway, and up the path around the outside of the town wall, clambering over bare rock where the walls' foundations were exposed. Catching his breath, he stopped halfway up the path to watch a farmer working half a mile away below him. Inevitably Yazíd was there near the *alcázar* waiting when Pedro arrived twenty minutes later.

Although Yazíd's native Arabic was the most commonly-heard language in the town, its border location and the comings and goings of traders meant that Castilian was now becoming commonplace. In a similar fashion, only a few members of the small Jewish community now spoke only Hebrew, which was also being replaced by Castilian. Abraham and his two brothers sometimes conversed in their ancient language, but Miriam had insisted that their children should not be taught their father's tongue. Reluctantly, Abraham had complied. Instead they would learn to read and write Latin and Castilian and pick up what Arabic they could in the town. But Pedro's understanding of Arabic was much, much better than simple proficiency. He comprehended well what was said to him, spoke it sufficiently to be understood and could decipher the alphabet. Not even Yazíd knew why.

Soon after Pedro's and Yazíd's race up to the top of the town, Pedro's father Abraham called him into his dispensary. His mood was a little lighter than usual.

'Pedro,' he said, 'I promised you a long time ago that when you reached your thirteenth birthday I'd have a sword made especially for you.'

'Yes, I remember, Papa.'

'Well, it was your birthday last month and the time has come.'

'We live in difficult times you know, Pedro,' he continued with unusual cheeriness, 'our world is changing around us, but, regrettably, not for the good. You'll need to carry a sword and know how to use it. David Levi, my blacksmith friend in Lorca, has offered to forge you a Toledo sword, the very best. I really can't afford the time to go there, but I'm a man of my word. Next week we'll go there and see David complete it.'

'But Lorca's a long way away in Murcia, isn't it?' asked Pedro excitedly. 'And isn't it in the Christian kingdom of King Fernando and Queen Isabel? Will we be safe to go there?'

'Yes, but your uncle Joshua is coming down from María to accompany us. The three of us on horseback will be safe enough,' Abraham replied.

'Can I come too?' pleaded the long-legged Cristina, the first signs of womanhood starting to blossom under her thin dress.

'No, you can't,' replied Abraham, harshly dismissing her request. 'Your aunt Ana is coming down from María with Joshua to look after you while we're away.'

Abraham was right. They were indeed troubled times. Their hillside town of Velad al-Abyadh, later known as Vélez Blanco, lay on the Muslim side of the ill-defined borderland between the Islamic kingdom of Granada to the west and the Christian kingdom of Murcia to the east. The valley of the Río Almanzora roughly defined the border further south. This river, like all of the rivers in this part of Spain, was dry for most of the year, although it was flowing weakly now. Lorca, some thirty miles away to the east and with a population exceeding six thousand, had for two hundred years been an important Christian city attracting several religious orders to found abbeys, convents and seminaries, all of which helped to establish its key location guarding the eastern frontier. That had not stopped Muslim forces from retaking the city time and time again. However, after a short spell in Muslim hands it was taken by the Christians just twenty-five years before, on St Patrick's Day, and had remained in their hands ever since. Yes, the borderland was a dangerous place, yet the tension along the border had relaxed after the Sultan of Granada and the Governor of Murcia had re-established trading links between the border towns. This augured well for the future.

If only this trend were reflected to the west. The reality was that the whole of the Islamic kingdom, or what now remained of it, was crumbling around its edges as the Christian armies took, lost and retook towns and cities which often changed hands several times in a year. Most they held on to, consolidated and refortified.

It was still quite early when Abraham, Joshua and Pedro set off on their long day's journey to Lorca. Little did Pedro realise that the journey would bring his boyhood to a premature end and change his life for ever. Abraham had nowhere to stable a horse, so, when needed, he hired one from 'Old Moses' in the town. Financially shrewd, as well as mean, Abraham had long ago realised that it was better for someone else to feed, house, groom and saddle an animal than to do so himself for his infrequent use.

They rode out of the south gate turning down off the Velad al-Almar road and descended onto the more frequented road to Lorca. None of their mounts could be described as a white charger. Even if Abraham had been willing to pay for one, 'Old Moses' could not have provided such a noble beast; in fact, he might not have even known one if he had seen one. No, Abraham got just what they paid for: two aged but reasonably sturdy mares, whose girth showed that they had enjoyed a winter of ease in Moses' stable, plus a smaller more nimble mount for Pedro. Pedro had only been in the saddle a couple of times before, but felt quite at ease on the responsive animal. Each mount was equipped with a high-backed saddle and broad leather stirrups which provided protection from thorns. The two men were appropriately dressed for the journey with calf-length riding boots, leather breeches and heavy dark brown riding coats over their tunics and broad-sleeved white blouses. The only weapon they carried between them was Joshua's heavy dagger, which was sheathed on his belt, and which provided him with token security on his travels around the towns and villages he visited. More usefully, however, each saddle held a long oak stave swinging from a leather holder. For each of them this was a much handier weapon to fend off thieves and villains.

With the snow-capped, flat-topped Muela towering over them on their left, they travelled at a steady trot. A short distance on to their right, seemingly stretching up into the sky, was the imposing castle of Xiquena. Built by the Muslims, it closed a blind spot from Vélez Blanco as it guarded the route to Lorca. Set back from the road on a high rock outcrop, the castle's red sand-stone walls, constructed on parallel rock spurs, rose to a square tower set on the summit, while the lower ground between the spurs descended to a grassy field. There, animals grazed, tended by a shepherd. A forked standard streamed brightly from the top of the tower, while masons could be seen replacing some fallen stones in the lower walls.

'Whose standard is that?' asked Joshua.

'It must be that of the Marquis of Villen,' replied Abraham.

'A Christian?' asked Pedro.

'Yes, it's been in Christian hands more or less since the thirteen hundreds. Although Yáñez Fajardo took it for the Muslims some forty years ago, the Marquis recaptured it eighteen years ago and he's strengthened it even further. He's closed off its weak point behind the hill so it's pretty impregnable now.'

'So if this castle is in Christian hands, Papa, our town must be close to the frontier between the two kingdoms?'

'Los Vélez more or less forms the boundary between the two kingdoms, my boy! Before I was born, our town, plus some other villages, were handed over to the Christians under treaty, but they were soon recovered and have remained in Muslim hands ever since. But things are very unstable, Pedro, and I don't think they can stay as they are for much longer. That's why David Levi has offered to make this Toledo sword for you. I'm too old myself to learn how to use swords, lances, let alone the new firearms, and in any case I would be no match for a trained soldier; but you have your life ahead of you and you must learn to defend yourself.'

Pedro then rode ahead, totally at ease now on his pony, and the two men caught up on their news. They met only half a dozen times a year and, while very different in physique and temperament, they were good friends as well as brothers.

'How's business these days, Abraham?' was the usual opener from the amiable Joshua, five years Abraham's junior.

'So-so,' was Abraham's guarded reply. 'Jhi, next door, by the square where I put my stalls when the weather's nice, continues to moan about the noise and disturbance, but he doesn't complain when I give him ointment for his boils or for Ada's veins. Samuel, the mohel, is at last talking to me again. But that's only because his wife Martha's got a nasty goitre and he wouldn't take her to see Abel, the doctor…'

'Well, you know, Abraham,' interrupted Joshua, 'you stuck your neck out in not conforming to our normal rites with Pedro. What do you expect of your community's mohel?' He paused. 'Are you still getting your supplies of eastern spices from Simón in Almería?'

'Yes, as regular as the sunrise. Every six months a supply arrives via Aguilas, but they cost me a small fortune,' he moaned.

'I'm not surprised, Abraham. Just think how long the journey takes and the number of traders involved, each making a tidy profit.'

'So how's your business doing?' Abraham asked, changing the subject.

'Things are thriving, Abraham. In the winter I only keep a handful of workers on, but in the summer I employ a dozen or so twelve- to sixteen-year-olds since they've got the keenest eyes and are more nimble in the mountains. They collect for me sage, thyme and rosemary which like the thin limy soils on the hills, but they also collect juniper whose berries you distil for essential oils. They grow in the rock crevices.'

'So how far afield do you go to sell your herbs now?' continued Abraham.

'Apart from supplying you with those medical herbs for your stalls in the summer, I sell my herbs in the markets as far away as Cúllar, Baza and Huéscar.'

'Goodness, I didn't know you went that far! Is it safe to travel that far afield?'

'So far, yes. I encounter squadrons of Muslim horsemen from time to time and occasionally I hear cannon fire across the plain towards Granada, but as yet I've had no problems. Small bands of soldiers are the biggest threat, since they are less disciplined, but so far I haven't been molested.'

'Rather you than me, Joshua!' was Abraham's closing remark.

By now it was well past midday and becoming very warm. They were almost halfway to their destination. All three had removed their heavy clothing and were glad to let the breeze blow through their loose blouses. Abraham decided that they should press on and just make do while in the saddle with a drink from their leather bottles and a bite to eat from the delicious buns which Ana had brought down with her from María that morning. They rode on in silence, each in his own thoughts.

Eventually they entered the bigger valley of the Río Luchena, as the road turned south-east towards Lorca. In contrast to the abandoned fields which they had passed earlier, the flat valley floor was cultivated with neatly arranged orange and lemon groves watered by irrigation channels. Each small farmstead was picked out by a small white, single-storey farmhouse – and a barking dog.

With aching limbs and sore backsides they entered the north gate of Lorca in the early evening. The double-gated arched entrance was guarded by two helmeted soldiers, each leaning on a stout, eight-foot ash staff, tipped with a broad, heavy spearhead. Luckily the guards were not unfriendly.

'Good evening, gentlemen,' the taller of the two said. 'And who might you be?'

'Good evening, officer,' Abraham replied. 'My name is Abraham Togeiro de Tudela. This is my brother Joshua and that is my son Pedro.'

'You're Jews, eh? Where have you come from?' he asked, eyeing their weary horses.

'We've ridden from Vélez Blanco…'

'Today?'

'Yes.'

'Quite some ride!'

'Yes, it's been a long way.'

Abraham rose stiffly from his saddle and rubbed his aching back. 'We're here to see someone on business. An old friend of mine, in fact.'

'Well, that's good,' said the soldier. 'We're instructed by the Governor of the city to encourage trade, so we wish you well. How long will you be staying?'

'Just a day or two,' conceded Abraham.

'Then enjoy your stay, gentlemen. One word of advice though. Don't make yourself conspicuous. Jews are suffered rather than welcomed here, and there have been cases of beatings and house lootings, although I gather that it's a lot worse in other towns in the kingdom. So take care.'

'Thank you for your words of warning,' replied Abraham.

They passed through the gate exchanging waves. They had gone some thirty yards when the guard shouted to them. 'I should have said, Don't forget your mellow badges.'

Abraham waved in acknowledgement without really hearing what the soldier had said. '*Your mellow badges?*' He frowned, trying to puzzle out the words shouted to him. Joshua interrupted his thoughts.

'Do you know Lorca, Abraham? Do you know where we're going?'

'Roughly, Joshua. It's a long time since I was here, but I think I can find David's place.'

'What do you know about the city, Father?' chipped in Pedro, whose eyes were darting everywhere, studying the fine stone buildings around. Normally he would have held his tongue with his father. Anything could precipitate a sharp retort or a clip around the ear, but with Uncle Joshua around he felt more relaxed and protected from his father's wrath.

'I don't know much, Pedro. But I can remember someone telling me, and for some reason the date stuck in my mind, that in November 1243, Fernando

III took Sevilla in the west from the Muslims and, can you believe, on exactly the same day his son, later known as *El Sabio*, took Lorca here, hundreds and hundreds of miles away. Now isn't that an incredible coincidence! I do know that Lorca developed as a Moorish town a long time ago. They built the *alcazaba* on the summit which you can see up there and a long surrounding wall. With livestock on the meadows and with its own salt pans on the coast, it became a very prosperous town with an important bazaar. Then it expanded down the slope onto the plain where most of the town now lies. But the old district still lies on the hill leading up to the *alcazaba*.'

'Where are we going now?' asked Pedro.

'I think we're best to find some cheap lodgings down here in the centre of the city before looking for David's smithy tomorrow. I know it lies below the *alcazaba* but I may need to search for it.'

It did not take them long to find a modest hostelry in the road leading up to the Plaza de España, the central square. Leaving their horses in the stable attached to the inn, they were taken up some stone steps to a balustraded balcony off which various small bedrooms led and which looked down internally onto a square central courtyard. Little was said by the innkeeper, who seemed very surly to them, if not aggressive. However, they made themselves as comfortable as they could, washed off the day's dust and tucked into a large, if poorly cooked, meal in the vaulted refectory below.

Although David Levi was a blacksmith by trade and relied on this for most of his income, he was also a highly skilled swordsmith. As a young man he was apprenticed to a master craftsman in Toledo, called Josef Aboah. Toledo was already long-renowned for its swords. For a hundred years or more craftsmen from all over Europe came there to learn how to make the weapons, which were prized for their strength, flexibility, balance and, above all, their beauty. David trained under Josef for ten years. But times were becoming very unsettled for Jews. Just forty years earlier, Pedro Sarmiento, Mayor of Toledo, fermented violent anti-Jewish feelings, promulgating a repressive statute against the community. Jews were dragged from their houses and severely beaten. Houses and shops were looted and burnt and many citizens forced to leave the city. Amongst those affected was Josef Aboah, David Levi's tutor. He had to close down his sword-making business and move south to the Islamic kingdom of *Al-Andalus* where Jews, Christians, Muslims and even *gitanos* – the gypsies – lived together in reasonable harmony. So Josef Aboah and his family moved to Granada, the largest city in *Al-Andalus*, and this was where he struck lucky. He soon established himself near the main bazaar to work alongside Julian del Rey, known as *El Moro*. He was the most famous swordsmith in all Spain. As his nickname suggests, he was a Muslim; but later, under pressure, he moved to Toledo and some years later was baptised into the Christian faith.

When Josef Aboah had to leave Toledo those years before, David Levi, then in his mid-twenties, lost his living and all his possessions, and he and his young wife, then pregnant, moved to Lorca, where anti-Semitism had not taken hold. Sadly, what happened in Toledo was being repeated in almost every corner of Spain; nowhere was immune. Just nine years earlier the papal bull *Exigit Sincerae Devotionis* authorised the establishment of the feared Spanish Inquisition. Soon heretics were being put to death and burnt all over Spain: eighty in Toledo in the years immediately following, and twice that number in the following decade. In many towns and cities the tight-knit Jewish communities were declared ghettos, and strict rules laid down on the movement of the citizens in and out of them. City by city, Jews were required to wear brown clothes and carry a yellow X or patch on their clothing, with the result that they were easy targets for robbery, beatings and physical humiliation.

It was against this background that Abraham, Joshua and Pedro found themselves in a Christian city, unaware of the true scale of the religious intolerance then taking root in the kingdoms of Spain.

Since David Levi's house and smithy were only some ten to fifteen minutes' walk away towards the top of the town, Abraham and Joshua decided to leave their mounts at the stables attached to the inn. A hundred yards away they saw a man being dragged into a three-storey house by two black-robed and hooded men. The poor man, clearly already badly beaten, wore on his coat a large yellow 'X'. Being curious, Abraham and the other two ventured down the road to discover what house it was. It was marked *Casa del Inquisidor*. Two other men, one whose fingers were bound with blood-soaked bandages and trying to support a second, were thrust out from the a heavy oak door onto the cobbled street. Both wore yellow patches on their clothing. Now suddenly the shouted message from the gateway guard the previous evening made sense to Abraham. 'Don't forget your yellow patches!' That's what he was saying, he realised.

They continued up the hill, and found David Levi's house along a row of low dwellings below the castle. The sound of hammer on red-hot iron greeted them from the open door of his smithy as they arrived. Now in his late fifties, David was a stocky and balding man who, as a true smith, had muscular shoulders and hairy, scarred arms.

'*Shalom!*' he said warmly when he saw Abraham in the doorway. 'It's good to see you, my friend. This must be your brother, Joshua, and, my word, this must be young Pedro, who I'm making the sword for. Welcome all of you. Come next door and meet Magdelena. We've been expecting you.'

'*Shalom*, Magdelena,' Abraham kissed her on both cheeks. 'You're looking well, my dear. I won't ask you about your swollen legs but you do look really fit.'

'Thanks to you, Abraham, I am. You've no idea how grateful David and I are to you. I was almost a cripple. I couldn't stand being on my feet for more than a few minutes and my legs were like tree trunks, red and swollen! If it hadn't been for the soothing balm which you sent me, that fool of a doctor here would have bled me to death like a sacrificial lamb. Oh, I'm so indebted to you.'

She skipped across the room and gave him a big hug. The others laughed.

'What was so pleasing, Abraham,' said David, 'was how quickly your oint-ment arrived. Within three days of leaving here, the rider who I employed was back with your package and within a week Magdelena's legs were showing an improvement. All thanks to our fortuitous meeting fifteen years ago in Mojácar! I still marvel at my luck in bumping into the finest apothecary in all *Al-Andalus.*'

'Oh, come, come, David,' responded Abraham, not used to flattery.

'No, it's true, Abraham. You're a miracle worker. But now, thanks be to God, I have the chance to repay your kindness to Magdelena and me. I promise you, young Pedro's sword will be the finest in all the land...'

Pedro's grin reached from ear to ear.

'Come, I'll show you how far I've got with it.'

'Before we go, David, things seem to be bad here in the Jewish community. How long have things been like this?'

'Ever since the Inquisition took hold here two years ago. We're all supposed to wear yellow markings on our clothing and we're not allowed to ride on horseback. The Jewish enclave in Lorca has almost become a prison, and we're only meant to leave the city during daylight hours and we must return by nightfall. You won't believe the things which some of our people have been charged with by the *Inquisidor*: like lighting candles on Fridays but not other days; reciting Jewish prayers; not eating pork; giving alms to our community here – and, can you believe, changing our underclothes on a Saturday! If it all weren't so life-threatening one would have to laugh. Really though, Abraham, you can count yourself lucky you live on the Muslim side of the border.' He sighed. 'But come,' he continued, 'enough of the gloom. Let's go around to the smithy.'

III: Disaster at the furnace

David Levi's smithy was, true to tradition, dark and hot with everything covered in soot and iron dust. The characteristic but indefinable smell of fresh iron pervaded the workshop. He handed Pedro the dull, half-finished sword, still warm to the touch. The haft end was thinner and had a rougher feel to it. In the youngster's hands, the whole thing seemed very heavy and cumbersome. David saw the disappointment in the boy's eyes.

'Don't be downhearted, my boy,' he said. 'I've still to temper it and complete the haft, the pommel at the end and the hand guard. When I've given it a final burnish to make it as bright as a mirror, it'll be ready for you. I've already prepared the scabbard for you.'

'Your father said that you'd like to see how I've made the sword? Well, I'll show you. I've put aside some of the short lengths of the metal which I used for it.'

Abraham interrupted him. 'David, I think we'll leave you two to get on with it. We'll catch up with you later.'

Pedro was bubbling over with questions.

'Where does the iron you use come from, Señor Levi?' he started.

The swordsmith, a bit shorter than the lanky thirteen-year-old, roared with laughter.

'Hold on, young man,' he said, 'and do please call me David. The only person who calls me Señor Levi these days is the Rabbi, and only then when he is after me for money.'

He went over to the forge and handed Pedro a long leather apron, donning his own much thicker one which reached his ankles. He slid his hands into a pair of thick worn leather gauntlets.

'Now, to answer your question…'

'It occurred to me, Abraham,' said David the next morning, 'that I need to make a journey to Bédar shortly to fetch some more iron. Why not let me take young Pedro with me? He can see how iron is made in the furnaces there. It's not far from Vélez Blanco, and I'll ensure that he gets home safely. What do you say?'

'Pedro?' asked his father, raising his eyebrows questioningly.

'Oh, yes please, Papa,' pleaded Pedro. 'That would be wonderful.'

'Well, that makes things easy, David,' confirmed Abraham. 'I think we'll leave Pedro in your safe hands to complete the sword, and Joshua and I will head back home today. If we leave now we can still get back before dark and save ourselves the expense of another night in that rat-infested inn. What do you say, Joshua?'

The two men agreed and proffered their farewells to their Lorcan friends.

'Come, Pedro,' said David. 'Let's finish your sword. Then we can go to Bédar tomorrow.'

'Now to explain how these special Toledo swords are made,' David said after Pedro donned a leather apron and heavy gauntlets. 'There are three stages in making a Toledo sword, my boy. The first is to forge the steel blade and shape it to its right length and thickness. I've already spent the last three days doing this. Then the blade is tempered, which we'll do today. What's interesting, young man, is that a few years ago the swordsmiths in Granada examined some of the fine swords produced by Arab craftsmen in Damascus and Baghdad. To their amazement they found that their blades were not just made of the finest steel, but they had a central core of soft iron which enhanced their flexibility without in any way impairing their strength. This technique has now been adopted by the Toledo craftsmen and I have decided to use it on your sword.

'I've just had an idea, Pedro!' he then said. 'Before we temper your sword, why don't I make you a dagger with these leftovers. Then you'll have a proper Toledo sword and a dagger to match and you'll be the envy of all your friends!'

So, David turned a short piece of round bar and a length of flat steel over and over in the blazing coals of his forge to heat them through. Then like lightning, when each was just below white heat, he snatched up the iron bar, plunged it into a tray of fine sand, and in an instant placed it along one side of the flat steel lath. As quickly as he could he folded the steel over the iron core and then hammered the soft seam closed. He put the single piece back in the fire and very quickly hammered it along its length, gradually flattening it until the iron blended with the outer steel sheath of the dagger. As it cooled to red heat he continued striking the bar until the gooey molten sand was squeezed out of the joint. Then when it had cooled to a dull red colour he plunged it into a vat of cold water to cool.

'So there we are, Pedro. The makings of your dagger! I'll finish it later. Now let's go back to your sword over there and temper the blade to impart its hardness so that it will retain its cutting edge for a very long time. Have no fear, Pedro, this blade will cut through a soldier's body armour just like butter. Then, I'll fix the crosspiece of the hand guard, as well as the finger guard to the rear, which I've decided to add for you. I have all these ready here,' he said. 'Then, lastly, and the bit which we swordsmiths enjoy doing most, is to fix the handgrip onto the haft. Because this is a sword especially for you, I'm making the grip of alternate hoops of white and red brass.' He grinned. 'Now watch.'

David put the sword blade into the dull fire and left it there for fifteen minutes, turning it over and checking all the time that it did not heat beyond a dull violet-blue colour. When the sword was evenly heated to this lowish temperature he plunged it into a vat of tallow which smoked and hissed. He left it there as the blade cooled slowly. Next, he pushed along the haft the short hand guard with its two forward-facing protective loops, and the backward-facing finger guard. He placed it in the fire for a minute and then hammered the whole unit tight onto the haft. Then he carefully tapped onto the haft alternate thick oval rings of white and red brass and heated it in the fire again. The centre brass rings were slightly thicker than those at each end. With a wooden mallet, scorched black through use, he gently shaped the rings until they were fixed firmly onto the steel shaft.

'Right, that's enough for one day, Pedro,' he said. 'Tomorrow we'll decide what weight pommel to fix to the end of the haft to make the sword perfectly balanced for you. You will need to help me with this. Then finally, we'll hone the cutting edges of the sword and polish it until it gleams.'

The next morning after Abraham and Joshua had set off home on their horses, David took Pedro again to the forge. While he tested how the sword felt in his hand, David tried out various pommels at the end of the haft until the sword's balance lay a short way in front of the cross guard. Pedro tried it out, sliding his forefinger inside one of the forward steel loops for greater control, with his remaining fingers being protected along the haft by David's special finger guards.

'This is truly amazing, David,' he said. 'Yesterday I couldn't move it in my hand because the sword felt so heavy. Now, all of a sudden, it seems as light as a feather, and as easy to wiggle in my hand as a stick!'

David laughed. 'That's because we've got the balance just right, Pedro. It's so important, and it's the care one takes over this which helps make these swords so special.'

He shaped the selected pommel on the anvil, hammering it onto the remaining inch of the haft. Finally, he fixed it in the fire, saying, 'Nearly there, Pedro.'

Lastly, with Pedro turning the handle, he ground the point and the edges of the sword on his large fine-grained millstone which turned through a trough of cold water, ensuring that the sword did not overheat and thereby lose its temper. Finally, he bound a leather strap around the millstone, pulling it aside from the trough of water, and for almost an hour burnished the blade until it shone like a mirror.

Proudly, he handed it to the boy.

'Done – it's finished, Pedro. It's some while since I fashioned a Toledo sword, but this is as good a sword as I've ever made. How does it feel?'

'Wonderful, David. It feels so light in my hand, and yet I know it's really quite heavy.'

'In fact, Pedro,' David concluded, 'it's a little shorter than a normal sword because you are still not fully grown. If I'd made it full-length, with the extra weight needed in the haft to balance it, you would have found it too heavy. But don't worry about it being a little shorter than usual. It will be your skill in using it which will be important, not its length.'

With Pedro the proud owner of a beautifully-crafted Toledo sword and a matching dagger, he and David Levi set off on the fated journey to Bédar to collect the iron from Álvaro Rodríguez. It took two days for them to reach Bédar, which lay just off the main highway to Almería. While David walked alongside the four-wheeled wagon pulled by his donkey, Rosa, Pedro rode Moses' sprightly pony which his father had left behind for him at the inn where they had stayed in Lorca. David carried blankets and plenty of food and water for the journey, and for the first night the two of them were content to light a fire and roll out their blankets between the wheels of the wagon.

The iron ore was mined from the sides of the steep mountains around Bédar, which itself was located high on the hillside overlooking the coastal plain and the ancient hilltop town of Mojácar in the distance. Rodríguez's furnace was cut into the bank of a dry river bed a mile below the village. David and Pedro arrived just before sunset on the second day soon after a sharp storm. Puddles lay in the road and water trickled along the roadside ditches. David stopped his wagon at the entrance to the track leading to the furnace. They could see its chimney half a mile away.

'Pedro, I need to go up to Bédar to fill up the water containers at the fountain there and get some fresh bread, fruit and meat. Why don't you stay here and look around? There's no need for both of us to go. I'll only be an hour or so. I'll meet you back here at this entrance.'

Pedro dismounted and sat on the side of the track watching the sun set over the mountains behind him. He secured his pony and ambled around absent-mindedly, taking his newly made sword with him. Thrusting and slashing, cutting and parrying with it, sometimes as Richard the Lionheart and as sometimes Saladin, he found himself on higher ground above the track to the furnace. A short distance on he encountered a small stream, a foot deep and not much wider, ponded back by wooden boards held in place by a post driven into the stream bed. The channel below was dry and choked with weeds, while just above the weir, a side channel led off at right angles into an equally weed-choked ditch. Only a dribble found its way into it from the larger stream.

Pedro noticed a small fledgling caught in the brambles on the bank of the stream struggling to free itself. He leant down the bank to release it but slipped on the wet grass. His prized sword flew through the air as he slid unceremoniously on his backside down the bank, kicking over the post supporting the wooden weir. The post broke off and, with a rush of water, the boards were swept away. Within minutes the flow had abated until only a trickle remained. Pedro ran along the bank, retrieved the boards and replaced them as best he could, hammering the post back into the soft stream bed with the pommel of his sword. With his hands he pulled out the weeds clogging the overflow channel, then used his heel to clear the debris along its bed. Well, he thought to himself, at least it's in a better state than when I found it. By the time he got back to the roadside entrance, David was waiting.

'Been practising your swordsmanship?' he asked with amusement. 'How many Christians did you slay – or was it Moors today?'

It was starting to get dark as they headed down the track towards the furnace. Suddenly there was a loud explosion. The sky ahead became lit by orange flames and black smoke. A terrible commotion greeted them as they approached the furnace some hundred yards further on. Men, blackened by smoke and dust, rushed past them, oblivious to David's wagon taking up most of the width of the track. Sparks shot through the darkening sky while bursts of flames pulsed upwards. A man on horseback galloped past, struggling into his saddle while gripping his shirt in his hand, such was the haste with which he had evidently left. Others were rushing pails of water along the track to the furnace which lay around a bend, dug into the bank. Shouting, screaming – awful screaming – and the striking of iron on rock and iron on iron filled the night air. Pedro was terror-struck by the sights and sounds ahead of him.

David Levi pulled Rosa and the small wagon into the side and Pedro tied his mount to it, trying to calm them down. He stayed back as David tore along the track. The boss of the furnace, Rodríguez, saw David approach but barely gave him a glance. A huge man, he was kneeling beside another man stretched out on the cinder track. He was writhing in agony and screaming in terrible pain. Thirty yards away three men were furiously shovelling grit and cinders to form a small retaining bank as molten iron, now dull red with a scoriaceous crust, flowed in a treacly stream, already congealing. Two other men, their arms and faces blackened, sat with their heads between their knees, coughing and retching, struggling to breathe the sulphurous air. A third man lay nearby, clearly dead, his shirt burnt from his smoking back.

David himself was not unused to the sight of serious iron burns, his own arms bearing the scars of a lifetime's work, and he joined Rodríguez alongside the stricken man. Pedro stayed where he was with the animals, appalled by the carnage a short distance away. The poor man lying on the ground was clearly dying. His hair had been burnt from his head and the side of his face and neck was so blackened that he was barely recognisable as a person. But worse, far worse, what remained of his chest was a mass of charred red flesh, still smouldering. The acrid stench of barbecued meat hung in the air. A dark grey lump of iron smoked in the cavity it had calcined inside his body.

Rodríguez glanced at David at his side, knowing there was nothing which he could do for the poor man whose screams filled the night air. David nodded towards a heavy hammer lying on the bank nearby. David got up from his knees, walked back to Pedro and led him quietly around the corner out of sight. Two dull thuds followed. The man's screaming ceased. Mercifully he was at rest.

Leaving Pedro where he was, David returned to the scene of the disaster. He half-guessed what might have happened, but tomorrow would be soon enough to enquire. The two coughing men were by now sipping water and although they were wheezing with lung-wrenching gasps they were evidently going to recover. The other three men plus Rodríguez, and with David's help, carried the two dead men some distance from the blown-out furnace. Silently, they dug a deep grave in the soft stony soil, wrapped the men in what spare garments they could lay their hands on and quietly buried them. Rodríguez mumbled some words. They said 'Amen' and walked back, heads bowed, towards the desolate scene.

Hoof beats thundered along the track joining the road down from Bédar. An elderly man, smartly dressed in a black coat, stopped abruptly alongside the five men, his horse's hooves imprinting deeply in the soft cinder path. A second man arrived, this time wearing the shirt he was clutching in his hand as he hurtled past Pedro and David forty minutes earlier.

'I'm afraid it's too late, Doctor Juan. Poor José died twenty minutes ago. There was nothing you could have done. The man was terribly injured, struck by a mass of molten iron. He was in the most terrible agony. I'm relieved he passed away.'

Rodríguez' eyes met David's. Nothing was said.

'Martín, the other man, who had only been here a week, died of his burns, or from inhaling the fumes. I'm not sure which, but luckily he died quickly. We've just buried them over there. I'll place crosses on their graves tomorrow. I'll go and see their wives shortly and give them what wages their husbands were due, and what little more I can afford. José's wife has a young baby. It's terrible. He was such a hard-working fellow, too.'

Rodríguez paused, his mind reliving the tragedy. 'I'm sorry you've made a wasted journey, Doctor. All rather in vain.'

'Can't be helped, Rodríguez, can't be helped. But while I'm here I'll take a look at those men over there.' He could see the two other figures in the light of the receding flames getting to their feet.

David looked up into the man's face, pale but ghoulish in the flickering light of the flames of the furnace.

'I apologise for our arriving at such a terrible time, Álvaro,' said David. 'We'll come back tomorrow for the iron.'

'Please don't apologise, David, I'm glad you turned up when you did,' he replied, 'I doubt if I'd have had the courage to do what I had to do if you'd not been here.'

Pedro had witnessed all this from the corner of the path where David had left him. They said nothing as David headed down the valley turning off into the tributary *rambla* where they made camp on the soft grey sand. They released Rosa from the wagon and unsaddled Pedro's pony, giving them water from the ample supply which David now had, and allowing the animals to graze on the grassy bank. They lit a fire with the dry canes of the tall rushes which hung over the bank, using as kindling the dried twigs and bark strewn along the dry watercourse. David brewed up a thick broth in an earthenware pot using beans, lentils and the fresh lamb which he had bought that afternoon. The fresh bread was delicious but their shattered nerves were barely calmed by the watered wine.

Sitting cross-legged around the fire with their bowls between their legs, they were both in sombre mood, unconsciously avoiding dragging their spoons across the rough bottom of their earthenware bowls and so disturb the silence. David could not forget the writhing agony of the dying man and the glistening lump of hot iron burning in his chest. He would never be able to forget the odour of his sizzling flesh. Pedro's mind saw as pictures the shadows of the men from fifty yards away moving around in the dull red light of the furnace then still-glowing, accompanied by the victim's agonised cries and the gasps for breath from the sulphur-choked men beyond.

Their campfire slowly dimmed and the noisy grazing of the animals ceased. Pedro looked up at the black moonless sky. 'I wonder what Jupiter made of it all…' he mumbled.

'What?' said a startled David Levi.

'I'm sorry, David, I was talking to myself. I was wondering what Jupiter made of the terrible things we saw tonight.' He pointed to a shining star above them.

'That's Jupiter?' asked the elder man.

'Yes, the very bright one to the south. And there's Mars a bit lower to the right, the orange star. Both doing their backward loop.'

'Doing what?' puzzled David.

Pedro didn't answer.

'Do you know a lot of stars, Pedro?' David asked after a few minutes. 'I can find the Pole Star and I know Sirius. But that's about all.'

'Yes, I know all the main stars, and the constellations too.'

'How? Who taught you?'

'An Arab taught me.'

'In Vélez Blanco?'

'No. Somewhere else,' he replied vaguely.

'So do you understand Arabic, Pedro?'

'Yes, I understand most of what is said to me; but I don't speak it too well.'

'The same Arab?'

'Yes, and Yazíd.'

'Yazíd?'

'My young Arab friend, Yazíd. We play together.'

'And you speak Arabic with him?'

'Oh yes. Most of the time. And Yazíd's father, who's a leather trader and who always speaks Arabic to me.'

They lapsed into silence. Soon they were asleep.

Rodríguez was standing on the bank above the furnace with his hands on his waist when David and Pedro arrived the next morning. He waved to them to join him. He looked grim and dishevelled, and obviously had not slept that night. In a monotone he explained what must have happened. In order to avoid too much excavation when they built the furnace and to provide it with insulation, the furnace was constructed in a narrow gulley which joined the broad sandy *rambla* below the bank on which they stood. The furnace was constructed of unmortared foot-size blocks of black volcanic rock which came up the coast from Cabo de Gata, near Almería. The locally mined crushed ore was loaded in when the furnace was ablaze. It took two whole days to reduce the grey ore to iron and, once lit, Rodríguez would make batches on consecutive days. The molten metal was released from a clay-plugged hole at the base of the furnace into damp sand. This was so channelled and shaped as to produce ingots of iron of different shapes and sizes to meet the various needs of blacksmiths, who would forge them into implements.

The swordsmith and Pedro listened to Rodríguez' explanation in silence. His massive frame and sombre mood did not encourage interruption. Although the chimney had remained intact, Pedro could see that the top and the front of the furnace had been blown off.

'So what caused yesterday's explosion?' asked David.

'Water, my friend, water,' came the grim reply.

The simmering anger of the huge man was barely contained.

'Yesterday we had a sudden, short storm. We didn't notice it, but a short burst of water must have poured down the gulley and some must have seeped through the dry stone walls of the furnace. The effect of cold water on molten iron is disastrous…'

'…as you can see,' he added, pointing to the ruins below them. 'I've been to look,' he continued. 'Some wretched vandals had removed the boards across the stream and diverted the storm water into the side channel but then replaced them, because I can see that the post holding them in place has been hammered back in.'

His fists clenched by his side, the big man was shaking, trying to contain his rage.

Pedro was stunned, mortified. His mind was in a total whirl. What had he done? Yesterday two men died because of him, one in such appalling agony that Rodríguez had to put the man out of his misery with hammer blows. The man left a young widow with no means of support and a young child to raise. Rodriguez' livelihood had been destroyed. All this because of him. Appalled, he was sick on the ground.

'Are you all right, Pedro?' David said as he placed his arm around his shoulders. 'It must have been that meat I got in Bédar yesterday,' he added. 'It didn't look too good when I bought it. To be honest, I didn't feel too good last night myself. I'm sorry, young man. It's my fault. But bring it up, and then you'll feel better.'

David's sympathy, and his taking the blame for Pedro's sickness, just added to the boy's discomfort. What could he do? What could a thirteen-year-old be expected to do?

As the implication of what happened soaked in, Pedro realised that he could never, never, admit to the terrible thing which he had done, however innocently he had dislodged the post holding the boards. The big man alongside would literally break him in two with his enormous hands.

'I expect you're right, David, it must have been the meat. But I feel better now,' was Pedro's lame reply.

It was too late anyway, he realised. The time to admit to what he had done had passed. From now on he would have to bear the guilt of what he had done alone and for the rest of his life.

'Well, David,' said Rodríguez, 'there's nothing to be gained by brooding here over what happened. You came here to buy some iron from me, so let's go and load your wagon. How much did you say you wanted?'

They walked to the hut where the big man stored his iron ingots. Pedro, quiet and withdrawn, followed several paces behind, relieved that the action had moved on. Luckily, neither of the men saw that he was still in a state of absolute shock. But he was glad to be able to help the two men lift up the heavy bars into David's wagon.

David paid Rodríguez for the iron bars. He said all the right things to the ironmaster by way of condolences and best wishes for the future, and promised to continue to bring his business to him when the furnace was rebuilt. He and Pedro left, returning along the track down to the main highway. They travelled together in silence. The swordsmith could see something was troubling Pedro deeply, but after much soul-searching he decided not to ask what the reason might be. Luckily for his future dealings with Rodríguez, David had no inkling of the true reason. When they reached Pedro's turning off the Huércal Overa road to Vélez Blanco, Pedro parted to ride the twenty or so miles home, making the long climb over the 3,000-foot summit of Santa María de Nieva. But his overwhelming shame and grief over what he had caused to happen the previous night were more than he could contain. Within a couple of hundred yards of leaving David he burst into a flood of tears and long, breath-choking sobs which continued with little abatement until he ascended the summit and could see the hill fort of Velad al-Almar below him. He pulled himself together to stop at a roadside fountain and rinse his eyes and face before riding the final few miles home.

Still agitated beyond belief, he arrived home safely that evening. His father's cheerfulness had evaporated and he showed little interest in Pedro's return.

David Levi's anvil might have helped forge Pedro's Toledo sword, but it was the disaster at the furnace which would irrevocably shape Pedro's future.

IV: First Blood

Summer 1487

Abraham's cheerful mood during the journey to Lorca quickly evaporated and he returned to being his irritable and cantankerous self; in fact, more so. Maybe it was the fewer number of customers who visited his dispensary during the spring and summer months; maybe it was the June anniversary of his marriage to Miriam fifteen years before and the recognition of how lonely his life had become since her disappearance. Whatever the reason, his cussedness had worsened. Little that Pedro or Cristina could do pleased him, while the frequency with which he struck them or lashed out at them with his hands or leather belt increased. Both began to live in fear of his moods.

However, Abraham could not be faulted for keeping faith with Pedro's acquisition of his Toledo sword, or for that matter with his continuing education. Ten-year-old Christina, being a mere girl, was deemed not to require an education except a basic ability to read and write Castilian. But from the age of eight Pedro attended lessons with three other pupils with Rabbi Halib, from whom they learnt to read and write Latin, although with little enthusiasm, and Castilian with Rubin Manrique who was the ritual slaughterer in the Jewish community, the sole person authorised to supply its kosher meat. Pedro attended each of these one morning a week, while on Wednesdays and Sundays he learnt mathematics and science, geography and history.

Soon after Abraham and Pedro returned from Lorca, Pedro was put in the hands of Marco Arana, who was a retired soldier and one of some seventy Christians living in the predominantly Muslim village. Marco was fifty years of age and had seen service in many countries bordering the Mediterranean Sea. By the time he returned home from his exploits he had little interest in marriage and lived instead with his sister, Rachel. Shorter than Pedro, Marco's ample paunch and slow speech disguised a nimbleness of foot and speed of reflexes which belied his age and made him a superb tutor in swordsmanship. This was in spite of his missing left hand, his proud testament to his years as a soldier. Pedro soon came to love this man and found in him the kindness and understanding which was so lacking in his father. Put simply, he was fun to be with. Marco's round face and ruddy complexion perfectly fitted his loud, boisterous manner and generous spirit. Pedro's twice-weekly sword lessons were the highlight of his week, as were the experiences which Marco related to him when the hour-long sessions were over. Despite a lifetime of fighting and using every sort of weapon then in use, Marco had never handled a sword as fine as Pedro's. Toledo swords were made for the wealthy and for nobles. For a plain soldier, a distant sight of one was all one could normally aspire to.

So Marco felt privileged to teach swordplay to someone bearing a Toledo sword, while Pedro felt honoured to learn from a worldly and experienced old soldier. Theirs was thus a perfect match.

'I'll teach you to defend yourself against all types of arms and against all types of adversaries,' was Marco's opening remark. 'Remember, your sword is a little shorter than most which you'll confront. Also, it's essentially a sword for thrusting and not slashing, as is the case of cutlasses, scimitars and sabres. You'll need to learn how to block attacks from each of these. You'll need to develop a strong right arm and you'll need to do exercises for this each day. But don't worry, I'll show you what you must do.'

'One other thing, Pedro,' he added, 'swordsmanship is a chivalrous and graceful skill and you must dress properly if you're to conduct yourself with dignity. So I want to see you in a clean, long-sleeve blouse tight at the wrists, ankle-length trousers and leather sandals. You can choose yourself if you want to wear that floppy cap of yours. And, by the way, wear that beautiful Toledo knife David Levi sent to you. It's good training to be as encumbered – as you're likely to be – so that you'll have learnt not to get your scabbard mixed up with your sheath!'

With Abraham's increasing black moods and bursts of violence, the dispensary house was becoming more of a prison than a home for Pedro and Cristina. More and more Pedro sought solace in the limestone mountains above the town. For a long while he and Yazíd had made the caves which abounded in the rock wall their boyhood dens, and it was to these which Pedro frequently returned during the summer months of that year. Sometimes alone, sometimes with his Muslim friend, he would clamber over the large boulders which formed the lower slopes of the mountainside, up through the cover of pine trees with their spiky dead lower branches, and finally climb up to the caves and overhangs in the vertical rock wall. But Yazíd's reasons for ascending to their hideout were different from Pedro's. His home life was joyous in comparison with Pedro's, but he could rarely stay still for more than a few minutes and would head off into the mountains without as much as a thought. His father, Yakub, had long ago guessed that his only son had the wanderlust in his soul, and, he realised that to constrain the boy was as futile as bottling the wind.

After a while, both boys had got into the habit of taking some food up with them to share the peace and seclusion of the caves which, facing east, provided shelter from the winds which were rarely absent in these mountains, and from the winter rains. Before long their supplies grew into a small cache of food. Without knowing exactly why, they set aside in a deep and narrow cavity in the rock, above and around the corner from their rock-overhang den, a small jar of olive oil, a pitcher of spring water and some bags of dried fish, dried fruit and salted nuts. Pedro also sequestered from his house a woollen blanket, while

Yazíd contributed some strips of cotton cloth which he picked up in the market after the stalls had been cleared. A small wooden box with a sliding lid contained odds and ends such as a flint and steel to light a fire with, some linen twine and a blade. Lastly, a few bags of straw helped fill up the hollows in the uneven floor of their main den.

Pedro's lessons with Marco started in the cobbled back alleyway which ran behind Abraham's house. First he was taught how to hold the sword wrist-up with the heel of his hand snug against the pommel. This provided the maximum wrist flexibility. Then he was taught how to stand sideways for balance and to obtain maximum reach, as well as offering the narrowest target to his adversary. He was taught to thrust at full arm's length, to withdraw, to thrust again aiming for the opponent's neck, often the least protected area, even with body armour. He was taught to use a shield to parry blows to his left side and to strike his opponent off balance; to use a coat or cloak bound around his left hand and arm to stifle blows while he thrust with his sword; to have faith in the strength of his sword's steel to block opposing blows – steel which, more often than not, would break inferior weapons in two. He was taught to cope with downward slashing strokes from his foe's curved weapons which could cleave a man in two from shoulder to groin. Against this threat, agility and anticipation were the only defence. During all this training Marco used a variety of weapons to teach Pedro the appropriate defence.

'What army did you fight in, Marco?' Pedro asked while they were relaxing with a beaker of cool spring water after a particularly strenuous session.

'Well now…!' was the lead-in to an old soldier's favourite pastime: talking about scars, trophies, conquests and battles won and lost.

'My father enrolled me to serve with the Marquis of Tarragona when I was just fourteen. He got paid fifty maravedís for this, a tidy sum in those days, so I can see now why he was so keen to get rid of me. The Marquis was beholden to the Count of Barcelona, whose ancestors had always been crusaders…'

'Like Richard the Lionheart?' interrupted Pedro.

'Yes, how do you know about him?'

'Yazíd and I play crusaders and infidels, and I'm always Richard the Lionheart.'

'Who's Yazíd?'

'My young Muslim friend,' was Pedro's reply. It was now becoming quite rehearsed. 'You must have seen him around the town? He runs everywhere.'

'Yes, I have. He seems a right little scallywag to me. Anyway, Pedro, the Count's grandfather served in the last fatal crusade four years before the end of the last century at the Battle of Nicopolis when, as usual, the Christians were annihilated. But can you believe this, Pedro? From then until now *six* papal bulls have been issued calling for yet more holy crusades, but not one has started out, not a single one. Maybe at last we Christians are learning!'

'Nevertheless,' he continued, 'when the Turks started to rampage through the Balkans and threaten Constantinople, the Count despatched the Marquis with his followers to join the forces there in repelling the infidels. So the Marquis, with a couple of hundred men, including me just turned sixteen, set sail from Barcelona and landed in Constantinople. After the fall of Kosovo, the Emperor Constantine knew that it was only a question of time before the Turks took his city. After Sultan Murad II's death, his son Muhammed put all his effort into its conquest. He was no fool. He made treaties with Venice and other neighbouring states to ensure that they didn't become involved in the struggle. Then on March 25th in '53 the Turks started a bombardment which lasted forty whole days. Their forces were enormous. We had only six thousand soldiers defending the city, and the Turks had ten times that number. They also had far more and far bigger cannons and a much superior fleet.'

'Where were you all this time, Marco?'

'Hiding, Pedro Togeiro de Tudela, hiding!... Well, not quite hiding, but none of us was looking to be at the front of the inevitable battle and end up with our heads on pikestaffs displayed on the tops of the walls. So I was on the walls near the Aurea Gate, near the seaward end, trying not to be seen. I heard afterwards that the Sultan had no wish to destroy the city and simply wanted to make Constantine a vassal prince of Morea. But Constantine was determined to become a martyr, and it's said that before the assault he pledged his spirit to his soldiers. But I can't say that I felt particularly "inspirited" at the time, I can tell you!

'The Turks opened up three great breaches in the city walls and on the night of the 29th the Sultan's personal guards forced an entrance through the central gate...'

'The Gate of Saint Roman?'

'Yes, I think it was called that, but it was a long time ago now.

'And then they stormed the city. Constantine, who was wearing purple shoes so as to be nice and conspicuous, died in this first assault – luckily, I might add – and his principal lieutenants quickly surrendered.'

'So how many were killed?'

'Only a few hundred in the assault, but a couple of thousand overall during the bombardment from the sea.'

'What happened then?'

'A number of us, rashly I suppose, ran around the south walls to the side of the narrows overlooking the Bosporus and down the steps leading to Saint Sofía, the main cathedral. Later that day, the Sultan entered the cathedral and recited the Islamic Koran from the pulpit and then defiled the altar by walking on it in his bare feet.'

'Did you catch sight of him, Marco?'

'Yes I did. I remember he had a high forehead under his enormous turban, a long hook nose, a full well-trimmed beard and a weakish jaw. Frankly, he looked a pretty typical Turk to me!'

'What happened afterwards?'

'The Marquis and all the Christian kings, princes and lords defending the city were taken prisoner to be held for ransom. This happens everywhere, you know, but I've no idea what became of the Marquis or any of them, frankly. Whether the Count of Barcelona paid the ransom for him I don't know. I somehow doubt it.'

'So when did you lose your hand Marco?' asked Pedro.

'Ah, Pedro,' he said proudly, 'that's another story. But it was fighting, and it was during the civil war in Cataluña, which lasted almost ten years. I'll tell you about it another time.'

By September Pedro was becoming quite a proficient swordsman, able to anticipate the moves of his instructor and avoid or parry his blows. He had learnt the strengths and weaknesses of weapons he might face and the vulnerable points in body armour which his adversary might wear. Helmets, visors and body armour all restricted and slowed the movements of soldiers and, since Pedro would not be encumbered by any of these, his speed of foot and quick reflexes were his best defence. By now teacher and pupil were practising moves with bared swords; the cloth bindings they had used earlier on and the protective caps on the blades having been set aside.

One afternoon in the middle of the month, later than usual because of a short downpour of rain, Marco was trying to teach Pedro a particularly tricky sword thrust. The dialogue was very one-sided.

'No, Pedro, you must get really *low* and stretch out as far as you can… No, not like that,' he chided.

Unusually, Marco was getting annoyed with his pupil. 'You've got to get down low and thrust upwards with the point of your sword!' he shouted.

'Yes – now do it again!' he shouted once more.

Abraham, attending the stove in the kitchen, lifted his head at the raised voices outside, not making out quite what was said.

'That's better,' Marco continued. 'But turn your wrist up, otherwise you can't get the angle.'

This time Pedro did what he was told. With his front leg well forward and bent low he lunged at full stretch, his sword aimed upwards at Marco's well-padded and protected chest. But at that very instant Marco's leather sandals slipped on the wet cobbles, and with a look of total horror on his face he fell forward onto Pedro's sword, his loud cry becoming a choked gurgle as the blade passed straight through his neck. As he fell mortally wounded to the ground, Abraham appeared at the kitchen door to witness Pedro removing his sword as a fountain of blood gushed from the stricken soldier's wound. Marco slumped dying onto the wet cobbles.

Seeing his father at the doorway, guessing that he had been drawn there by the shouting, and terrified as to his reaction, Pedro grabbed his scabbard from the window sill, careered along the short alleyway at breathtaking speed and, bloody sword still in his hand, bounded over the wall at the end. He tore along the next passage into the streets leading up to the top of the town, and did not stop until the town lay well below him.

Pedro heard his father shouting at him from the kitchen doorway as he disappeared over the wall. He was not to know that this was the last time he would hear his father's voice.

Pedro continued to run and run...

V: Escape to María

...and run, to the one place he felt he would be safe. There he stayed for two long days and nights, traumatised beyond belief by what he had done to Marco, and haunted still by the sights and sounds of the terrible happenings at the furnace.

Yazíd knew nothing of the death of Pedro's sword master, Marco Arana, until two days later when he called on his friend. Cristina told him how in a bitter argument during a training session two afternoons before, Pedro had plunged his unguarded sword through the old soldier's throat and how her brother had run off and had not returned home. Yazíd was stunned to learn of the dreadful event and could not believe that Pedro could have done it intentionally, yet Cristina had taken the word of her father that the incident was no accident but the spiteful killing of the trainer by her brother in a fit of temper. She had had to suffer Pedro's moodiness ever since he returned from Lorca with his fancy sword. Deprived of a mother's love, coping with her father's increasing black moods and now Pedro's fitfulness, the young girl had become desperately lonely and was withdrawing more and more into herself.

Unsure of the loyalties of the young girl, Yazíd said nothing to her, but guessed immediately where Pedro would have gone. He wanted to run to join Pedro in their hideaway there and then, but could not get away until he had finished the chores his father had given him. He did these as quickly as he could and just before sunset headed off as fast as he could towards their secret den. However, as he crossed the broad, high valley through the mountain ridge he saw the dark figure of his friend silhouetted against the bright skyline over which the sun had just set. Pedro was in view for less than a minute before passing over the crest and Yazíd knew that it would be an impossible task to catch him in the growing darkness. Reassured that Pedro was, at the very least, alive and well, Yazíd returned thoughtfully to his home, determined to replenish their cache with whatever Pedro had consumed during the days he must have been there.

After two miles trudging up the rocky valley, Pedro bore right, ascending up onto the mountains of the Sierra de María, which rose to over six and a half thousand feet to his left. The ensuing darkness did not worry Pedro unduly. He knew these mountains and the paths through them like the back of his hand and with his eyes accustomed to the light provided by the half-moon he could find his way. After nearly two hours of strenuous trekking he started to descend, reaching the tree line of the extensive pine forest which lay above María. He was glad to do so. He was chilled to the marrow. Exacerbated by the wind that perpetually raced around these highlands, the mountain air at five thousand feet during these October nights was little above freezing. It was after midnight when, nervously, he knocked on the door of his uncle's small house not far from the square.

'Who's there?' came a rather weak, squeamish response. Not without reason. At the door might have been the henchmen of the Inquisition, the Sultan's personal guard or outlawed soldiers of the Christian king.

'It's me, Uncle Joshua, Pedro.'

'Pedro, Pedro Togeiro, Abraham's boy?'

'Yes, yes, please let me in. I'm absolutely frozen.'

The door opened a fraction. Joshua's round stubbly face appeared, lit scarily from underneath by a tallow candle. His floppy nightcap with its bobbled end was slewed down over one eye, and his bare feet protruded beneath his long woollen nightgown.

'Come on in, for God's sake, my boy. What are you doing here? Are you in trouble? Have you left home? Are you on your own?'

'Hold on, Joshua!' came Ana's scolding voice from within the house. 'Let the boy in, he's not here on a social call at this time of night.'

'Yes, come on in, young Pedro. I'm sorry to be so discourteous, come on in.'

Ana appeared from their bedroom, a blanket around her shoulders and over her nightgown. Between them, she and Joshua stirred the embers of the fire and threw on some small pine logs which quickly caught light.

'Come over here, my dear,' said Ana. 'Get close to this fire, you look frozen through. Where have you been? Oh, I'm sorry. There's time for explanations later. First things first, I expect you're hungry and you'll need something warm inside you.'

Ana was totally in her element coping with domestic emergencies, being busy, ordering Joshua around.

'Josh, go and get some of that mulled wine and put it on the fire. It's just what he could do with, I'm sure. And bring in the new loaf and the cheese. And the knife, you always forget the knife.' She turned to Pedro.

'Now put this blanket around your shoulders, and take those sandals off your feet… Oh, my word, look at the scratches on your legs! Where have you been? What have you been doing?'

The fussing went on until the fire was ablaze in the grate, the mulled wine had been warmed and poured out and Pedro had demolished the first thick slice of Ana's delicious white bread and goats' cheese. He was only thirteen and a half, after all. Pedro felt overwhelming relief to be beside a warm fire with these loving people. Ana tried to conceal her joy at being able to succour her young nephew, whom she had treated as a son ever since Miriam's disappearance six years before; while Joshua was thrilled to see young Pedro again, as he'd always had a very soft spot for him.

'So tell us what happened, Pedro. Why you're here.'

The warmth, the food, the mulled wine and, not least, the relief from the stress he had been under for two days was all too much for Pedro. As he sat by the fire he put his head in his hands and for the penultimate time in his young life he sobbed his heart out, failing totally to make any coherent sense with his explanation.

The elderly couple looked at one another anxiously.

'Take your time, my dear. There's no rush. Let it all come out. Here, dry your tears with this.'

Eventually the sobbing ceased and Pedro could explain what happened two days before, how he had accidentally killed his sword master, Marco Arana, and how he had fled into the mountains above the town. Even in front of his understanding aunt and uncle he could not bring himself to tell them of the tragedy at the furnace at Bédar. The shame of this still haunted him, and the images of the silhouettes in the flames were never far from his mind.

'But it was an accident, Pedro! The poor man fell on your sword, didn't he?'

'I killed him, Uncle Joshua, it was I who killed him! Papa came out of the kitchen thinking that we were arguing, and in that very instant I thrust my sword through his neck, and he fell to the ground bleeding terribly.'

'Your father will understand, surely? I'll come back with you and help you explain.'

'You don't understand, Uncle. Papa's black moods have been getting worse ever since we got back from Lorca, and I'm afraid he'll flay me alive if I return home. No, I can't go home.'

He paused, wondering whether to tell them.

'I've… I've decided to run away to sea.'

'*Run away to sea?*' came the response in unison from the couple.

'Yes,' said Pedro looking up at them. 'My mind's made up. I'm going to Almería to join a crew on one of the ships that trade around the coast.'

'And leave your family and friends behind here?'

'I'll return one day – when I'm sure that the devil's hand is lifted from me, and when I can carry my Toledo sword honourably without posing a threat to those around me. My mind's made up,' he said with finality.

Joshua and Ana looked at one another, a new respect for the determination of the young man starting to blossom with a recognition that, within his youthful frame, glowed a spirit which would eventually see him through his troubled times.

They sat in silence for several minutes, Pedro barely able to keep awake by the warm fire after his adventures, while his uncle and aunt pondered his plan to run away to sea.

'If he's determined to go, Josh, we'll need to make sure he's got something warm to put on and some food to take with him. Poor soul…'

With that they went back to bed.

It was mid-morning before Pedro rose. Ana was busy sweeping the house and Joshua was outside stirring his summer's harvest of plants and herbs in their baskets, endeavouring to make the most of the autumn sunshine for their drying. They sat together while Pedro devoured some breakfast.

'If you're still determined to go, my dear, you'll need some warm clothes and some food to take.'

'Yes, Aunt Ana. I suppose I will. But I haven't changed my mind. I'm still going to Almería.'

'Do you know how far it is, my boy?' said Joshua. 'It would take several days on a nimble horse! It must be well over a hundred miles through Huércal Overa and Níjar.'

'That's the long way around, Uncle. I'm going to go over the mountains. I've heard there's a road to where they quarry the marble, and then a good road which climbs over the mountains and then runs down to the Tabernas turning.'

'But there are some mighty mountains to cross, and the winter will be setting in soon.'

'I know, but I've lived in these mountains all my life. They don't worry me. I'll be all right. It might take me a month to get there, but that doesn't matter.'

'Hmm,' was Joshua's uncertain response.

Ana rustled out one of Joshua's worn woollen shirts. Although far too big for Pedro, it was not noticeably so when worn over his cotton blouse. She found a leather jerkin with short sleeves around which he could tie his belt. She found some linen trousers which would go over his thin cotton trousers, and with some socks for his feet when it got cold he would be reasonably clad. She removed the blanket which he had slept on that night and tied the ends of the roll together so that he could carry it on his shoulder across his back. In the meantime Joshua had been searching for one of the canvas shoulder bags which his workers used for collecting herbs and plants, and he put a few useful things in it for Pedro, while Ana stuffed it with some fresh bread, dried ham, goats' cheese and fresh fruit. Lastly, Joshua filled a leather bottle with fresh water which Pedro could carry over his other shoulder. He could refill it on his journey from springs and seepages which he would encounter.

He was ready to go.

'I think you're making a great mistake in trying to cross these mountains, Pedro. But I can see you've made up your mind. I visit nearly all the places around here, at least this side of the Sierra de María and the Sierra de Orce, where you're heading for, so I've drawn you a rough map.'

Joshua laid it out on the table.

'You'll need to take the Orce road running west from the centre of the village and then turn off around Casablanca a short distance on, whichever spot has the easier access over the mountains. You'll get there today. If you can find your way over this first range of mountains, then I'm told paths exist across the sierras from then on. But take care. There are deer and wild boar in these mountains and I've heard people talk of black bears too. Your knife will be of little use against any of these.'

'I'll be all right, Uncle Joshua,' said Pedro, folding the map carefully. 'Remember, I've grown up in these mountains and they're home to me.'

So, after much hugging from Ana and big Uncle Joshua, Pedro pulled the strap of the canvas bag over his head to swing at his right side and did the reverse with the blanket roll. His water skin was last.

Joshua accompanied Pedro to the door.

'Now, when you leave the village continue for some eight or nine miles until you approach a farmstead called Casablanca where Abdul Ibn Hazm lives with his family. A hundred or more years ago there was a community of several families there, but the plague wiped them all out.'

'The Black Death?'

'Yes, the Black Death. They say that it entered Europe through Italy after being carried across Asia by the Mongols. It wiped out almost a third of the populations in the south and the year later did the same in the countries in the north. It was truly disastrous. According to Abdul all the families at Casablanca died, and it was his father fifty years ago who put new roofs on some of the abandoned houses and raised him and his two sisters. Now Abdul lives there with the both of them, neither of whom married, plus his two wives.'

'Two wives?'

'Yes, Nurul and Azizah. Azizah was his first wife.'

'Abdul and four women? Under the same roof?' queried Pedro. 'It must be a madhouse.'

'It's worse than that!' exclaimed Joshua. 'Abdul is naturally the head of the family, but his elder sister, Irena, thinks that she is head of the household – as does Azizah his first wife. But his second wife, Nurul, has the strongest personality and the loudest mouth, so she in fact rules the roost.'

'And what about Abdul's younger sister?'

'Rayya? Rayya, whom I have always felt sorry for, is by far the most attractive of the bunch, and sensibly keeps herself out of harm's way in the kitchen where she produces the most delicious dishes.'

Joshua kept up the discourse, not really wanting Pedro to leave. At the back of his mind was the nagging thought that he would never see him again.

'Yes, I know them all well,' he continued. 'Abdul's a charming man and he and Azizah would make you most welcome if you told him who you were. But unless you're careful he'll have you helping him muck out his animals! So I wouldn't go as far as his farm. Just this side of it there's a low, isolated whale-back hill, and nearby there's a gap through the mountains which may be what you're after. It appears to rise reasonably gently.'

Little more could be said, so with a final shaking of hands and another mighty hug from his uncle, Pedro set off.

This, his first journey alone through *Al-Andalus*, would take him a very long way and to distant parts, and many would be the threats to his life.

VI: Meeting with the Mullah

October 1487

Setting off late morning, better equipped and in a much better state of mind than when he fled from Vélez Blanco a few days earlier, Pedro strode with a real spring in his step. He soon passed the almond orchards outside María and entered the extensive open forest of Mediterranean pines through which the road led and along which barely one person travelled a day. With yet other limestone cliffs topping the mountain range to his left, Pedro entered a widening plain with smooth and gentle slopes rising to each side. The road curved gently around to the right and, far away, encircling the plain, another distant range of mountains came into sight. Fields of wheat, recently harvested, formed a patchwork over the pale brown limy soil of the plain. Goats munched the stubble, attesting to the nearness of Abdul Ibn Hazm's farmstead, now a short distance on. Joshua was right. Ahead, to his left, a whaleback hill stood out from the softening profile of the hills, and a number of valleys invited easy access into them.

The first looked as good as any other. Within a short time Pedro was ascending high into the hills. It was now early evening and deep shadows were forming in the valleys. In one, Pedro found a shepherd's circular stone shelter and decided that this would do for the night. Being barely more than five feet across and three feet high and open to the elements, it at least had some dry, wiry grass spread over its rough base and offered some modest protection from the elements.

The next morning was chilly but bright when Pedro continued on his way. With no path to follow during his journey across this mountain range, he was faced with the problem of finding his way. He knew from what people had told him and from maps he had seen that the city of Almería lay more or less due south from where he had turned off near Casablanca. Using the sun as his guide he was certain of his southerly direction around midday when the sun reached its zenith.

Although it was only some ten miles as the crow flies to the next major valley he would reach, Pedro must have walked two or three times that in ascending the hills and weaving his way through them. More than a few times he had to double back when faced by a blind gulley. While he had food enough in his shoulder bag, he was able to refill his water skin from small springs which supported small oases of greenery in some of the narrow valleys. One tight ravine with some spindly lentisc bushes provided a meagre shelter for the night, although the cold mountain air and the twelve hours of darkness hardly added to the comfort.

On the morning of the third day the horizon in front of him disappeared, to be replaced by a distant line of hazy mountains. Soon he came to the edge of a cliff overlooking a broad valley. A straight road ran left to right below him. He found a gap in the cliff and descended to it. But where exactly was he?

A quarter of a mile away a goatherd sat on a tree stump supervising his wayward flock of independent souls. Pedro approached him. The Arab greeted him in his own language, his missing front teeth not aiding Pedro's comprehension of the rough dialect he spoke. The bony little man was dressed in an ankle-length grey – but once blue, woollen *camis*, over which he wore a coarse calf-length, dark-brown goat-hair *yallabiyya*, open at the front. A white turban was wound around his head, and his feet padded along on thick esparto grass sandals tied loosely to his feet with leather thongs. The age of the man was indeterminate. He had a long, unkempt grey beard. His teak-coloured skin was creased and furrowed from a lifetime spent outdoors. He could have been thirty or seventy.

'*Msa el-jeir*, good afternoon,' said Pedro with great courtesy in Arabic.

'*Msa el-jeir*,' replied the goatherd warmly, rising to his feet and bowing low, sweeping his right arm in front of him over the ground. He offered his hand in welcome.

'My name is Hisám, good sir.'

'And mine is Pedro Togeiro. Can you please tell me where I am?' asked Pedro.

'Hmm. That depends on your viewpoint. Come, young sir, join me while we eat some oranges and I will do my best to enlighten you and, if I am so inclined, I might even tell you where you are!'

With their hands sticky with the juice, the man spoke again.

'Now where are you, you ask?' Hisám began, clearly glad of some company and not wishing to see his new friend continue on his way too quickly. 'It depends on where you've been. You've just travelled through these mountains behind us, yes?' He jabbed his thumb over his shoulder.

'Yes, that's right.'

'So for several days your world was no more than a moving vista of hills around you, sometimes a long way away and sometimes very close, but always changing.' He raised his eyebrows questioningly.

'Yes, I suppose so,' replied Pedro, none the wiser.

'So for two or three days that was your world and that was all you knew?'

'Yes, I suppose so,' he said, puzzled.

'Now my world here is like a lily pad floating on a big pond, except it keeps changing its shape; like a film of olive oil on water. The lily pad's my herd of goats which I lead or, more often than not, am obliged to follow in and around this wide valley. Sometimes the animals are bunched together and my lily pad is small. At other times they are stretched searching for food and then my lily pad is large. But it's always really the same, and that's the extent of my world.'

Pedro continued to look perplexed.

'What I am saying to you is that where you are is of no consequence if your horizon is limited. You simply carry your own personal world around as you travel around. It will change its shape but it's your personal possession and you can feel contentment within it.'

He tried to amplify the philosophical point he was making.

'What does an ant know beyond a range of a dozen or so yards? What does a lizard know beyond a hundred yards? Those are their horizons and they live within them unaware of anything beyond.'

'And you are content on your own small lily pad, so to speak, Hisám?' countered Pedro. 'I mean not wanting to move further away? Discover new places? Meet new people?'

'I am a simple soul, young sir, I am content with what Allah deigns to give me. I have all I need: food to eat, clothes to wear, these innocent animals to keep me company. What more should I need for a contented life?'

Pedro sat there for a while, perplexed yet stimulated by this man who was clearly not as simple as he professed. Was his own father any happier with his struggles to make his business successful and maintain his reputation as an apothecary? Was Rodríguez at the Bédar furnace a content and happy man – not now, obviously. And what about Boabdil, defending his kingdom manfully against the Christians?

After a while Hisám broke the silence. 'Where are you heading for, my boy?'

'Almería.'

'Why'?

'I'm running away to sea.'

The penny dropped in Pedro's head as suddenly as the smile which spread across the goatherd's face.

'So! Tell me if I'm wrong, but I'd guess that something's happened in your young life to cause you to run away. I'm not asking that you to tell me what it is, that's your business, but I'd say that you must have broken out of your own personal boyhood world and encountered something you couldn't handle. Am I not right?'

Pedro thought about his happy boyhood days with Yazíd in and around the mountains above Vélez Blanco.

'Yes, you're right, Hisám. How shrewd you are. I'd not thought about it that way.'

'But now, young Pedro, you feel that you must continue your travels to put your troubles behind you. Until your spirit finds new contentment?'

Pedro nodded slowly, thoughtfully.

'Now I'll tell you where you really are! Two miles down the road is the village of Chirivel and beyond, a good day's walk, high on the hill is the hill fort of Velad al-Almar. In this other direction,' he waved his arm to the right, 'the road leads to Baza, Guadix and eventually to the fabled city of Granada.'

'Have you ever been to Granada, Hisám?'

'Oh no,' the goatherd laughed. 'I've only once been as far as Baza, and that's only some thirty miles away!'

'It looks a busy road judging by its ruts and hoof marks,' commented Pedro.

'It is. Only two days ago a squadron of light horse galloped past...'

'Muslim riders?'

'Yes, of course, we're in the Sultan's kingdom here. They must have been important horsemen. They all rode fine, black Arab horses and crimson cloaks streamed from their shoulders over their studded cuirasses. All wore large blue turbans and the leaders held aloft long lances with white streamers. Each of them had a curved scimitar jangling at his side. They were a fine sight.'

'And foot soldiers?'

'Three hundred went past yesterday. But a real ragbag of men. No good ever comes of large numbers of soldiers on the move. Nothing is safe from their marauding hands. Neither man nor beast; neither wife nor daughter.'

Hisám pointed to some bloody carcasses of his animals by the roadside. 'Look what they did to my herd,' he said angrily. He spat contemptuously on the ground.

'Ugh, they needed food for their camp that night so they killed three of my finest goats, cut off the best bits of meat they wanted, and left the remains of the animals there for the crows.'

'And they were Moorish soldiers?'

'Yes, but they're not much different from the Christians.'

'However, at least there's some meat left over for you, Pedro, since you'll need to eat tonight if I'm not much mistaken!'

Finally he said, 'I've detained you long enough, Pedro, and I can see my leading goat, Mars, is getting agitated and wants to move on. So cut off what meat you can find from the animals and we'll go our separate ways. Oh, by the way. I forgot to say. If you head for Chirivel you'll find a road on your right, but it's potholed and not frequented by many. It'll lead you over the Sierra de Las Estancias to the next valley. But I've never been there either!' He laughed.

'*Émshi bes-saláma*,' said Hisám in Arabic, wishing him a good journey.

'*Hasta luego!*' replied Pedro in Castilian, 'see you soon!'

By now the sun was setting directly over the Baza road. Pedro strode along purposefully, and within a short time the village of Chirivel was in sight. Before it, a track led off to the right, and this was his route for the morrow. He needed to have had little worry about finding somewhere to stop. The main road to Chirivel ran aside a dry river channel which was lined each side by rows of tall white poplars, their arrowhead-shaped leaves gleaming autumn gold in the setting sun. After the bleak mountains he had left behind him they were a beautiful and enriching sight. Fifty yards along the river bed the high bank had collapsed, creating a deep hollow beneath the roots of the trees. He scooped up several armfuls of dry leaves from the bank and heaped them into the hollow to lie on. With his steel and flint he lit a fire on the river bed. When the wood had burnt down to red embers he skewered his pieces of goat meat on some twigs and placed them over the fire on some stick supports. There would be enough left over to take with him on the morrow. With a full stomach and the fire still aglow at his back, Pedro rolled into his blanket in the hollow beneath the tree roots, cushioned by the thick mattress of leaves. This was how the life of the wanderer should be.

The region of *Al-Andalus* is high and mountainous. Aeons ago, Earth forces had crumpled the land into sierras or mountain ranges which ran east to west across the country. The land had been compressed by the northward movement of the African continent and southern Iberia fractured along distinct east-to-west cracks, either moving sideways or riding one over another. Sometimes the forces were so enormous that the rocks folded over on themselves like a cloth pushed across a table, with the top of the fold breaking away to be carried many miles forward. The scale of the land movements was prodigious, with the vertical displacement along some of the biggest cracks reaching several thousand feet, while the horizontal movements carried one side as much as thirty or forty miles relative to the other.

However these mountains were lifted, broken up, overturned or moved sideways. They had one thing in common to distinguish them from mountain chains elsewhere. The rocks themselves were left more or less unaffected. Not being remoulded deep in the earth's crust, they were neither melted or recrystallised. Granted, mudstones were altered to shales and slates, and limestones sometimes to marbles, but beyond that the process of physical change did not progress.

Two other features in the make-up of the landscape of *Al-Andalus* were evident. The intense compression which raised and deformed its mountains released pressures deep in the earth which caused high-temperature fluids to rise up through the cracks to precipitate as minerals in veins and lodes. These were later exploited by the earliest inhabitants of the land: lead and silver in the Sierra de Almagrera around Cuevas de Almazora and in the Sierra de Gádor, north of Almería; iron around Bédar in the convoluted mountains north of Mojácar; and iron, mercury and some other minerals in the Alpujarra to the west.

On the coast of Almería a second phenomenon occurred. Sometime in the recent past towards the end of the phase of mountain building, Africa 'stood off' from Iberia and swung to the right. In this 'stand-off', tension rather than compression became the dominant force. Rocks were melted and mobilised, erupting to produce a narrow and rugged line of volcanic mountains running north-eastwards along the coast. This volcanic activity did not occur as one single cataclysmic event but as a spasmodic series of eruptions along a weakness, the focus of which moved northwards. Such was the enormous volume of lava and ash spewed from the volcanoes that three collapsed in on themselves. Where one cut across another, gold rose from a great depth in several vertical pipes of pink earthy rock. As Africa returned to thrust against mainland Spain, one additional relic of those ancient times was still evident in this corner of Spain: that was the region's susceptibility to earthquakes. Imperceptible tremors occurred almost daily, but several plate-rattling tremors lasting tens of seconds occurred each year. A major cataclysm always threatened.

Pedro headed off across the broad valley which comprised one of the in-filled, east-to-west clefts which separated the mountain chains in the region. The ground rose slowly onto a higher plateau made of softer brown and lustrous grey shales interspersed here and there with hard bands of yellow marble. It took Pedro two days of easy walking to follow the dusty road as it meandered its way to the village of Oria and beyond to the Macael valley.

Oria lay at a junction of a cross-route to Baza, by a minor stream which flowed southwards. Although predictably dry at this time of year, the fertile valley floor supported a wealth of crops and thus a thriving community. Surmounting the walled village on a flat-topped, steep-sided hill was a square tower, with the old village built in tiers around the southern slope of the hill. A squat mosque stood on one side of the plaza or village square.

Pedro turned into the village, surprised to find such a large settlement seemingly in the middle of nowhere. He needed to buy some provisions to take on his journey. He still had the five hundred maravedís which Uncle Joshua had given him for the journey. He filled his water skin at the fountain in the square. As usual, it was a gathering place for villagers, for whom the young traveller provided some curiosity.

'Where are you heading, young sir?' asked a woman filling a large earthenware pitcher. She was of similar age to his mother, Miriam, at the time of her disappearance when he was eight years old and, although she had dark features, something in her poise instantly rekindled a vision in his mind of his mother. Over her white, ankle-length *camis* she swore a warm, olive-green woollen *durra'as* with an attractively embroidered collar and hem.

'I'm heading for Almería, madam,' he replied courteously in Arabic.

'That's a long way to go! Where have you come from?'

'From my home in Vélez Blanco, up near the border with the kingdom of Murcia.'

'I think I know of it since I've heard of a Jewish apothecary there who's famous for his cures.'

'He's my father!' exclaimed Pedro in amazement. 'Abraham Togeiro de Tudela is his name. I'm amazed you should have heard of him.'

'Oh yes, his medicines and ointments are well known around here. So what's your name, young man?'

'Pedro Togeiro, madam.'

'Well, Pedro. If you're going to Almería, you'd do well to visit Abu Bakr at the *rábita* along the road from here. He's a mullah or holy man, and came to this village from Almería many years ago. He's wise and scholarly and you'll learn much from him. Tell him that Sabyán sent you to him. I know and respect the man a great deal, as all of us do in Oria.'

'How should I address him, madam?' asked Pedro. 'I've never met a mullah before.'

'Here in the village we call him "the learned master" or "master" for short. He's not a man for titles but he doesn't demur at either of those forms of address.'

Pedro thanked Sabyán for her advice and searched out the *rábita* along the road. On the left side was a narrow field with a rich variety of crops growing amongst olives, figs, vines and almonds.

Rábitas were Muslim sacred places or shrines and were often located at holy springs or the site of a venerated saint. Many were founded by religious hermits. Frequently they were no more than tiny, thick-walled buildings sited in isolated places such as on the tops of hills. Unusually, the *rábita* at Oria lay only a short distance from the village near the roadside. With its high walls and buttresses and a single small window set high in the end wall, the tiny building could have withstood a siege for as long as water and food lasted. A large, broad-rimmed clay container attached to a length of bleached rope stood outside a well set within a stone dome structure. The whitewash of both the building and well were flaking badly. Pedro knocked on the thick door.

'So you're heading for Almería, are you?' the man said, after Pedro's introduction. 'I can understand why Sabyán sent you to me. Do come in. You're very welcome.'

The tiny building comprised just two rooms. One, essentially was a small chapel with no more than a prayer mat, a roughly hewn pine table at knee height, which was now almost black with age; some dusty shelves with tall books in one alcove, and a second low table near the entrance supporting a candle. The small room at the end served as the living room. It was almost as spartan as the chapel, with a blanket over a thin mattress on the floor, an open hearth with a low chimney venting through a hole in the wall, a shelf with the two earthenware cooking pots, a few jars and some wooden spoons and ladles, and a large covered pitcher of water in the corner.

By now Pedro's eyes had become accustomed to the gloom and he could examine the man more closely. He was some six inches taller than Pedro with a long head and high forehead. He was clean-shaven. He wore a simple long white woollen *zihara* or cloak pulled together at the waist, and cork-soled sandals on his feet. On his head he had a close-fitting red felt *sasiya* or skullcap, with his greying hair protruding beneath it. Pedro noticed how long and unmarked his fingers were; so different from the ordinary village people with their rough, scarred hands and grubby, broken nails. His uprightness, calmness and serenity all leant credence to the image Pedro had of a scholarly priest.

'Firstly, some introductions,' the mullah said with a smooth, deep voice in beautifully clear Arabic. 'I think you said your name was Pedro?'

'Yes, learned master, Pedro Togeiro. Pedro Togeiro de Tudela.'

The man looked very surprised. 'And you speak Arabic?'

'Some, yes. I live in a Muslim village and have learnt a little Arabic from my friend Yazíd and his family.'

'Hmm, very interesting.' He paused. 'But I speak some Castilian, Pedro, and since I have little opportunity to practise it here, would you object if we spoke your language?'

Pedro concurred.

'De Tudela, you said? I know that name from somewhere,' replied the learned man, now speaking Castilian.

'Yes, the lady Sabyán at the fountain said that my father's medicines and cures reach this village. He's an apothecary in our village of Vélez Blanco. My uncle Joshua, in the village of María collects and sells plants and herbs from the mountains there. I also have a second uncle in Almería called Simón, whom I've met only once, who's an importer of spices from the East. Both of them provide my father with the herbs and spices he needs for his medical preparations.'

'Quite a family business!'

'Yes,' replied Pedro proudly. 'My great-grandfather Aaron was a famous doctor and came from Navarra and established the business which has been in the family ever since.'

'Well now, Pedro, as Sabyán may have said, my name is Abu Bakr al-Jaldún but people here call me "the Mullah".' He laughed.

'Why do you laugh?' asked Pedro.

'Because I am not sure that I am a mullah or a particularly scholarly man. But it's what the simple folk here called me when I came here, and ever since it's stuck. I don't really mind. Now Pedro. Why don't you tell me your story and why you're here in Oria, and afterwards if you wish I will tell you mine; although I fear it will not hold much excitement for you.' He added, with a sense of pleasant anticipation, 'If you wish to stop the night in my humble abode and share what little food I have, then you will be most welcome. In fact, Pedro, you will do me a great honour if you do so, since as a devout Muslim I have a duty to offer hospitality and succour to travellers.'

So, excluding reference to the explosion at Bédar, Pedro settled down on the mat with Abu Bakr in the small back room and described his life story and what led him to run away from home.

'And now you're aiming to go to Almería to board a ship, are you? Well, in that case I'll tell you a little about the city and its history. Unfortunately it's not the place it was. But let's leave that until tomorrow, eh?'

Soon afterwards, after asking Pedro to refill the water containers from the well, the mullah excused himself, retiring into the small chapel where he washed and then knelt on the prayer mat, chanting in a low voice some of the teachings from the Koran. Glad to be of help to the learned man, Pedro carried the water pitchers to the well, which he found to have only a couple of feet of crystal-clear water. There had been no rain for several months. It was yet another beautiful October evening. The sun, just minutes before dipping below the horizon, backlit the dark grey cumulus clouds with a blazing golden rind; the sun's rays fanning out through the gaps between the clouds.

As Pedro returned to the dwelling with the pitchers, he observed that the top of the towering cumulus was already shearing away into an anvil-shaped projection. The holy man invited Pedro to help him prepare the meal for the evening over the open fire which he had lit in the corner hearth. While Pedro sliced the aubergines which were grown locally, Abu Bakr chopped some mutton and raisins, boiled some rice and added some salt and spices for flavouring. Within half an hour they were sitting together cross-legged on the mat in the living room, warmed by the open fire, enjoying a delicious *mosaka'a*. With the last of the season's fresh figs and almonds, it was the best meal Pedro had eaten for some time.

That evening, with both of them warm and replete, Abu Bakr explained how he had come to Oria and how he founded the *rábita*.

'I was born in the old city of Fez in Morocco, Pedro, where I trained as a cleric in the Great Mosque there. When I was twenty I came to Almería. The chief lawyer of Fez was worried by the plight of the Muslims living in infidel Spain. However, several years of famine and hunger in Morocco meant that it wasn't a very propitious time to entice our people to return home to North Africa. Morocco had become a backwater of literature and philosophical thought and at that time the finest poets and writers were living in *Al-Andalus*. I set my heart on studying their great works. To me, becoming an initiate in the *Mesquita Mayor*, the central mosque in Almería, seemed the perfect means of doing this. My duties there were lowly but I didn't mind that. I led the prayers at the Friday *oración* and helped in the administrative duties of the mosque. As with Christian cathedrals, they have many visitors and there's much to do, just to keep the place functioning smoothly.'

'So what went wrong, learned master? What brought you here to Oria?'

'All in good time, Pedro! I'm just coming to that.'

As he was speaking Pedro's sharp ears picked up the distant roll of thunder, muffled by the thick walls of the building.

'I soon learnt,' continued the mullah, 'that the Imam there, who was the head of the mosque, was an ascetic and was devoted to a life of rigorous personal discipline and self-denial. In fact, he was more monk than priest. Now in my view the main mosque in a large city is not the place for a monk practising abstinence and narrow religious beliefs. The Great Mosques, as in Fez or Almería or Córdoba, like the Christian cathedrals, are the centres of the community and serve an important function as such.'

The mullah stopped as the small living room was lit up by flashes of lightning to be followed several seconds later by claps of thunder.

'As I said earlier, my interest was Islamic literature and philosophy and, although I was content to live a celibate existence and abstain from physical pleasures, as I have done all my life, I have never seen this as an end in itself, or at odds with the teachings of our Prophet, Mohammed, or the Muslim code of conduct laid down in the Koran.'

As he spoke, concurrent flashes of lightning filled the room with bluish light for a couple of seconds, accompanied almost at the same instant by enormous concussions of thunder. Intense rain started to beat down onto the roof.

'Nothing I've learnt or experienced since then dissuades me from believing that Islam is the true religion. It provides a complete way of life for its followers and a code of conduct in personal cleanliness, family life and behaviour. As you will know, the Koran is our sacred book. It is the word of God recited to our Prophet Mohammed by the Archangel Gabriel. We believe that Mohammed was the last of the prophets through the ages. The one hundred and fourteen verses of the Koran or suras are written in classical Arabic, and we Muslims have to memorise these. By the time I was six I knew them all by heart, and it was this precocious ability which my father believed I possessed which convinced him that I should devote my life to the Faith. Now the Hadith record the deeds of the Prophet, and are the source of our law. That and the suras stipulate our way of life through the five maxims of the profession of faith, prayers preceded by ritual washing five times a day, giving alms to the poor generously, keeping the fast during Ramadan and, once a lifetime if possible, making a pilgrimage to Mecca, the holiest city of all.'

'Have you been to Mecca, learned master?' asked Pedro.

'No, I haven't. To be honest, Pedro, it seemed the least important of the obligations.'

'So, learned master, if you followed the suras and the Hadith as a young man, and went far beyond its requirement from what you have said, why did you need to leave the mosque in Almería and come here?'

'The problem, Pedro, was that my view of Islamic teaching differed fundamentally from the Imam there. As I said earlier, he was an ascetic who saw Islam as a closed sect, inward-looking, narrow and defensive. My view of Islam differed diametrically from his. I saw its tenets as a framework for ordering a sound and stable community in which people could live in harmony within God's law. I have never seen our Koran as a rigid set of rules designed to suffocate the people and put them in fear of how they conduct their daily lives. The Muslim world has gone through these phases of fanaticism before, and inevitably they end in rifts and bloodshed.

'So I stayed there for ten years, devoting myself to the writings, poetry, philosophy and science of our great literary figures. But my feelings against the Imam were so strong that it was impossible for me to continue further.'

The storm grew in intensity as thunder reverberated through the building with the flashes of lightning diffused into an even light by the low cloud and rain.

'By then I had devoted myself to studying the literary giants who had strode the Islamic world of *Al-Andalus*. Such figures as the most famous of the Arab historians, Ibn-Jaldín, who was born in Túnis and who wrote his *Universal History*; Ibn al-Jatib, who in the middle of the last century wrote a history dedicated to Granada but was, in fact, a true scholar of poetry, medicine, science, philosophy and history; Ibn Ben Zamrak, at about the same time, and vizier to the Sultan, who promoted the famous epigraphic decoration in the Alhambra with verses from the Koran; and the court poet of the same period, Ibn al-Yayyab. But one of my favourite writers was Ibn Luyún, with his book on horticulture which set down how the perfect garden should be laid out. You'll see many examples of these in your travels, and particularly in the Albaicín district opposite the Alhambra in Granada. Come with me, I'll show you. I have his writing in the next room.'

But Abu Bakr didn't get time to show Pedro his prized collection of learned works. As the storm overhead paused to gather its breath, Pedro and the mullah heard a deep rumbling from outside. They ran through the small chapel hearing cries and shouting outside. As they opened the door the rumbling became a roar. With the moon appearing fleetingly between the clouds which were starting to break up, they witnessed a frightening sight. Below the river terraces across the road, the dry river bed had become a raging torrent. Some ten yards wide, the channel was full to the banks and the river was starting to flood into the fields. Fifty yards downstream, the river swung sharply right below the bluff above which the village rose in tiers. The shouting grew more desperate.

Pedro was yards ahead of the mullah, even before the latter turned back to don his dark brown hooded *yallabiyya* made of camel hair. Pedro sped from one terrace to another, reaching the bend in the river. The water was racing past at a terrifying speed. Its velocity was too great to allow its smooth passage along the river channel, and its surface had given way to a mass of frothing white foam and standing waves as it tore through and around obstructions. Everything was being swept before it. More than ten months of channel detritus, fallen and uprooted trees, household rubbish, all were being propelled in a turmoil of mud and stone-laden water.

Pedro saw all this in an instant as he reached a group of hysterical villagers on the left bank of the river amongst the tall white poplars. The wall of a house had collapsed into the river, taking with it a poplar tree on the river bank, causing the level upstream to rise even higher behind the obstruction. The river level dipped to form rapids through the narrow gaps on each side of the collapsed wall, reaching breathtaking speeds.

Clinging like grim death to the large slab of masonry in the centre of the river were two small figures whose cries for help were quenched as waves of water broke over them, threatening at any moment to propel them into the maelstrom around them. Half a dozen people were running up and down the river bank, waving and shouting at the stranded youngsters, who could never have heard them over the roar of the water.

As Abu Bakr reached Pedro's side, the thirteen-year-old plunged into the stream, gripping the fallen tree which straddled the river, finding some footing on the river bed. He reached the demolished wall, grabbing it with all his might to prevent being carried away in the current. He struggled against its power and reached the youngsters, who were clearly almost spent. Pedro could not guess their ages, but he pulled his way along to the younger of the two and shouted to her to put her arms around his neck. With her grip as sure as it could be, Pedro pushed himself off into the dark water, glad to get a better footing with the additional weight of the young girl on his back. He shouted to her to hold on tightly. Arms leaned out as he reached the bank and grabbed the little girl.

Pedro turned back into the current, this time making the crossing more confidently. He was only just in time; the second child, a boy, had reached the end of his tether and his grip was loosening on the wall as Pedro grabbed him by the collar of his nightshirt. He pulled the lad's head out of the water and put the boy's arms around his neck. He pushed off, and in ten strides was across the river. Hands took the boy from him, and Abu Bakr pulled Pedro up the bank out of the fury of the floodwater. Pedro sat with his head between his knees coughing the brown water from his lungs and gasping for breath. The mullah knelt beside him and put his arm around the boy's shoulders, while behind them the wailing had been replaced with cries of relief and tears of joy.

The worst of the storm had abated but a light drizzle continued to fall from the broken clouds. The full moon started to gain the upper hand. It was only then that Pedro noticed who was holding the two children closely to her and sobbing deeply with gratitude for the safe delivery of her children from the torrent. It was Sabyán, the woman whom Pedro had encountered that day at the fountain. She passed her children to a couple on the river bank and ran over to Pedro, who was getting to his feet.

'Your saving my two children from drowning,' she explained, with tears streaming down her handsome face, 'is something for which I'll never be able to thank you enough. After my husband died four years ago, six-year-old Sara and eight-year-old Wasím are all I have left. If they'd died tonight my life would not have been worth living and, craving Allah's mercy, I would have followed them into the black water. Pedro, you know that I'll never be able to repay you for your courage and bravery.'

There was nothing that Pedro could or wanted to say. Abu Bakr, with his arm around her shoulder and those of the two children, led Sabyán away to her neighbours' house. Nothing more could be done that night.

'You go back to the *rábita*, Pedro,' instructed the mullah. 'Take those wet clothes off and get warm by the fire. I'll be along as soon as I can.'

Pedro went back and took off all his wet things. Shivering uncontrollably, he rinsed them through in the darkness in the water trough opposite the well. He hung them up near the fire in the living room, wound his blanket around him and was fast asleep when the mullah entered the room, having completed his fifth and last devotion of the day in his prayer room next door.

VII: Sabyán's feast

The sun was well up when Pedro roused the next morning. The mullah was out, but he had left some buns and peach jam for him for breakfast, and some warm, sweet mint tea was idling in a pot by the fire.

'I promised to show you the books in my small library,' he said to Pedro when he returned. They went through to the chapel and the elderly man took down an armful of the thick, leather-bound tomes; his lifetime's work.

Pedro was awe-struck when he turned the pages and looked at the Arabic script of the great historic figures which the mullah had studied and copied over so many years.

'These are beautiful, learned master, I've never seen anything so beautifully done as these. I can only make out some of the words, but the flowing style of the Arabic text and your clear black writing are truly lovely. They are so different from the blocky script of the holy books in Christian churches.'

'Yes, their Gothic style is very angular, but still very beautiful I think. Unfortunately, I cannot emulate their fine, illuminated manuscripts which are such an act of devotion. Even if I had the materials and the skills, Islam prohibits such decoration.'

'Nevertheless, your books are truly very beautiful, master.'

'Thank you, Pedro. But I promised to show you one in particular, because it's my favourite. Here it is. Would you permit me to read a little of it to you? Maybe you can follow the Arabic as I read it?'

'This is the work of Ibn Luyún on horticulture, and here he describes his ideal home and garden.' The mullah ran his finger along the text as he read slowly in Arabic.

'Can you follow what I am saying, Pedro?'

'Yes, master, most of it.'

'Good.'

'The old text reads:

To locate a home with gardens one needs to select a spot which is safe and secure. Orient the house so that the entrance faces the sun at midday and place the *pozo*, the well, and the *alberca*, the storage reservoir, at the highest point which is available so that the *acequia* can channel the water to all parts of your garden. The dwelling needs to have two doors for comfort, but no more, for reasons of protection. Close to the water tank one places plants which remain green and pleasant to behold throughout the year. Further away one needs colourful flowers and perennial bushes laid out in square beds. One surrounds all this with arbours of vines arching over the paths through the garden. The garden needs to be encircled by a path to separate it from the rest of the estate. Around its edges one plants figs, oranges or other fruit trees suitable for the locality. The biggest fruit trees should be planted at the northern end to provide a wind screen. In the centre of the garden one needs to site a secluded pavilion with seats where one cannot be overheard. The pavilion is surrounded by a trellis with roses to provide privacy with a broad fruit orchard around it. On the lower floor of the house one constructs rooms for one's guests with a separate entrance, while branches of trees overhead conceal it from view from the higher rooms above. And last of all, one cannot go wrong by having a dovecote with white doves!

'Isn't that delightful, Pedro? Oh, to have a house with gardens like that, eh!'

'Yes, master. It would be wonderful. I like the idea of the pavilion in the centre, where you can be alone.'

'Yes, Pedro, we all need our own privacy at times, don't we. But you're not going to get any peace for the moment, young man!' he chided. 'You and I have to go along to the village. It's market day.'

'Before we go, master, you didn't tell me why you settled here in Oria and chose this spot for your *rábita*.'

'No, I didn't. I said last night that I felt no alternative but to leave the *Mesquita Mayor* in Almería and search for a place where I could continue my literary studies while still obeying the Koran in the manner in which I believe the Prophet intended. So I decided that I'd take my books and as much writing material as I could transport on a couple of mules and "follow my nose", so to speak – much as you're doing, Pedro, on your way to Almería – until I found somewhere suitable to spend the rest of my life.'

'But what made you stop here?'

'I liked the isolation of this village in the mountains and I liked the friendliness of the people here. To me, they led the ideal existence combining obedience to the tenets of Islamic law while enjoying life to the full.'

'So you moved into this building?'

'Oh no!' laughed the mullah. 'There was, indeed, a building here but it was a ruin. In fact, I think that there's been a building of sorts here for hundreds of years. At one time it might have been a Visigothic holy place or shrine. Who knows, maybe the bones I uncovered beneath the floor might have been one of their saints. In any case, I took the precaution of interring his remains in as fitting a way as I could!

'For two years, with the help of the villagers, I rebuilt the walls, cleaned out the well and put a new roof on the building. So that's how I came to be here. But now we must go to the market before the stalls are taken down. We're already quite late as it is.'

It took them only a few minutes to get there. The river to the right, across the smallholding, had already ceased flowing. Only pools of water in the river bed, the rack caught in the overhanging branches of the trees and the flattened grass on the bank, bore witness to the torrent the previous day. Not so the outside wall of Sabyán's house, which exposed for all to see the austerity of the rooms within.

Some twenty stalls were laid out around the perimeter of the square with a line of them down the centre: fruit stalls, stalls selling nuts and raisins, vegetable stalls, and clothes stalls with rolls of colourful cotton, silk and linen. There were simple or cotton *camis*, *yubbas* and *durra'as* for ordinary folk, women's headscarves or shawls, the *lifafas*, *miqna'as* and *jimars* and beautifully embroidered *ziharas*, *gilala* and *taylasanas* for the better off. There were stalls with earthenware pots and dishes of every shape and size, iron pots, copper pans, wooden bowls, knives and spoons. In one corner Pedro could see live animals in cages; chickens and chicks dyed different colours, pigeons, rabbits and mice. In another corner, fresh-baked bread, buns and sweet cakes were enticing customers with their delicious smells, while next to the mosque, mouth-watering aromas emanated from a stall selling steaming-hot kebabs with chunks of charcoal-grilled lamb, kofta of grilled, minced meat balls and *shawairma* with chunks of lamb roasted on a vertical spit from which thin slices were cut and served with a bun or with rice on lettuce leaves. Over the whole market rose the truly deafening sound of the villagers gossiping; of their bartering and arguing with stallholders for the best price; of laughter and leg-pulling; of small children scurrying around under people's feet. As the learned master said, it was the sound of a people enjoying life to the full.

But if Pedro thought that he was going to wander around the market quietly amongst the stalls he was mistaken. No sooner had he and Abu Bakr entered the noisy throng than he was lifted onto the shoulders of two men, both dressed in their best clothes. Long white ribbons were tied around his wrists and two children, the children he had saved from the floodwater the previous night, led him through the crowd, dancing, laughing and giggling. Behind the small party walked Sabyán in her very best turquoise *durra'a* and a white *mandil* or scarf encircling her fine features. A gold pendant hung around her neck. Her oval face glowed with a radiant smile and all the villagers clapped and cheered as Pedro was conducted around the market, through and between the stalls. Many stretched up to touch him.

Eventually he was put down in front of a robust man who he took to be the elder of the village. He was standing on a box in front of the gathering crowd.

'Pedro Togeiro de Tudela,' he said in a loud voice, 'today is your day and you have the freedom of the village. Last night, Allah be praised, you saved the life of young Sara and Wasím and, maybe, even the life of our precious and beautiful Sabyán. You are indeed a brave young man and blessed by your God.

'We are a humble people here and there's little we can do to properly express our gratitude to you. But visit the stalls and whatever you wish is yours. We will all be offended if your modesty prohibits you allowing us to express our joy at having you amongst us. But first, Sabyán wants to give you a personal gift.'

Sabyán, glowing in the bright sunshine, came forward bashfully, knelt down and very solemnly kissed Pedro's hands. The crowd fell silent as she said a short prayer and got up slowly. Again, her graceful poise and the way she held her head brought back strongly to Pedro the image of his lost mother.

Sabyán stepped forward and placed a magnificent oval ruby ring on the middle finger of Pedro's left hand. It was set in gold.

'This ring belonged to my late dear husband. We were betrothed when I was just nine years old. His memory is fading from me now since he was killed fighting alongside our brave sultan at the battle of Lucena four years ago. I'd like you to have it, Pedro, as a memento of your brave actions last night. When I think of his ruby ring in the years to come I'll always be reminded of you and what you did.'

Without another word Sabyán got up, kissed Pedro gently on both cheeks and retired quietly into the crowd.

'What do I do, learned master?' Pedro whispered to the mullah, who had kept in the background through this ceremony. 'I can only carry a few things with me on my journey and can't possibly receive all the things which people might wish to give me. How do I avoid offending them?'

'You must visit each stall and praise the beauty and the craftsmanship of the gifts they want to bestow on you. For those items you choose to keep, thank them generously. For those you cannot possibly keep, explain your predicament and they will understand. After all, these are country people and many have travelled far to get here today, and they themselves will have carried heavy loads on their backs. But first, let's enjoy the delicious foods on the corner stalls, then I will leave you alone.'

Not wanting to offend the kind people of Oria, Pedro wandered slowly through the market. Sara and Wasím held his hands tightly, not wanting to let him go. He selected one or two things which he felt would not prejudice the stallholders' meagre takings for the day and made sure that he dwelt at each stall long enough to avoid causing offence.

A few days later Sabyán arrived at the *rábita* with a bundle of clothes. All were washed and pressed.

'These are for you to try on, Pedro,' she said. 'They were my husband's clothes. I've kept them all this time since he died, in case… well, in case…' She looked at the ground, her face flushing slightly.

'I'd like you to have them. He was about your height, although fuller in the chest, so they should fit you reasonably. I noticed at the market that your clothes are looking worn and you need something warmer now the winter months are nearly upon us.'

She laid the bundle down on the table in the living room of the mullah's abode and picked them out one at a time. She giggled with embarrassment as she held them against Pedro. Pedro was equally embarrassed and, although he would not have wanted to admit it, he was beginning to love the close contact with this gorgeous Muslim woman. His Aunt Ana fussed over him in a kindly but bullying sort of way, but Sabyán had his mother's grace and he was captivated by her.

'Here you are,' she said, 'a thick pair of green woollen *sarawils*, they're a bit baggy but they'll keep your legs warm; a maroon *zihara* for your body, which is warmer than a cotton *camis* and it has a wide belt so you can keep it warm around you. And here's a brown camel-hair *yallabiyya* to go over the top of all of them, with a nice hood to keep the wind out.'

'Sabyán!' exclaimed Pedro. 'With all this warm clothing I'll probably melt in the sun!'

'You've got some high mountains still to cross, my dear,' she said with feeling, 'you'll need all of these in the early morning and in the evening when the sun goes down.

'Now here,' she said again. 'Here are some really robust leather sandals and some long, warm woollen *yawrals* for your feet and legs when it's cold. The sandals will last you for years.

'And you'll need some underclothes. Here, take these. These have never been worn but I've washed them anyway.

'Lastly, Pedro, you'll need an *'imama* for your head. A spotless white one will look nice on you. Do you know how to wind it around your head?'

'Yes, Yazíd showed me.'

'Yazíd?'

'My Muslim friend back in Vélez Blanco… Yes, yes,' Pedro answered in anticipation, with a roar of laughter. 'It was Yazíd who taught me to speak Arabic!'

It wasn't totally true, but it made an easy explanation.

Sabyán lingered a while. She was clearly at home in the *rábita* and Pedro was becoming boyishly infatuated with her. She could sense his deep-seated need of a mother's love, and as a young woman alone in the Muslim world she herself felt growing fulfilment by their closeness.

Abu Bakr watched all this with a compassionate smile, recognising in both of them their mutual need for warm affection from someone close to them.

'There's some good news for both of us, Pedro,' he exclaimed. 'Sabyán is coming around tomorrow evening to cook us a special meal.'

Sabyán nodded with enthusiasm.

'I can tell you, young man, that her cooking is really special.' The mullah winked at Pedro, adding, 'But it's only because you're here that she's going to do it!'

'Oh no, learned master,' she said in consternation. 'I love coming here, as you know. Serving you is as much a privilege for me as it'll be for me to serve our young guest here. But maybe, Pedro, you'll help me prepare the meat and vegetables which I'll use?'

So it was all agreed, and the next evening at sunset, after Sabyán had joined the mullah for prayers in his small private mosque, she prepared the meal with

Pedro's help, each joking and teasing each other about everything and anything. Abu Bakr just sat there, stirring the fire, warmed as much by the growing bond between the Muslim widow and the Jewish-Christian boy as by the fire.

Pedro joyously did what he was told. He chopped up the chicken into pieces, did the same for some onions, stirred some spicy sauce over the fire. He diced several sorts of vegetables and turned into them some oil. The last item he was not allowed to see, but it smelled superb. Sabyán had prepared it earlier and brought it wrapped in a cloth. After nearly two hours' preparation all was ready.

'So what delights have you made for us, Sabyán? No, I should say Sabyán and Pedro?'

'Well, let's see, learned master.'

'First we'll have *wara'inab'mahshi* which is grape leaves stuffed with rice and minced meat. Then we'll have *kishk bil firakh* which is pieces of boiled chicken, which Pedro chopped up, braised in a spicy sauce made of yoghurt, chicken broth, onions and butter.'

'It sounds gorgeous!'

'With that we'll have *laban zabadi wa khiyar*, which is a salad made with diced cucumber, yoghurt, garlic, olive oil and mint.'

'And finally… well, you can wait for the "finally",' she chuckled. 'That's a special treat. I know how you men like sweet things!'

Sitting together cross-legged on the floor in front of the fire, Sabyán served her culinary specialities. To drink they had *romman*, pomegranate juice. If the mullah's meal on Pedro's first evening was the best meal he had eaten in weeks, this was the best he had eaten in years. When they were full, nearly to bursting, she served some unsweetened mint tea to rekindle their palates, and after a respectable interval she undid her cloth bundle and served the last course – *baklawa*, thin layers of pastry with almonds and pistachios steeped in syrup. It was dessert, pudding and sweet all rolled into one sumptuous extravaganza.

Pedro saw a lot of Sabyán over the next week or two. At the mullah's request, Pedro repainted the outsides of the *rábita* and the well house.

'Where does the whitewash come from?' shouted down Pedro from the roof.

'If you ask a priest that sort of question,' the mullah shouted back, 'you know you'll get one of only two answers.'

'What's the first?' shouted Pedro.

'If he knows where it comes from he'll tell you. But I don't know where this whitewash comes from.'

'So what's the second answer?' Pedro shouted down again.

'God provides those in need!' was the learned master's response.

Sabyán would come around to see how Pedro was getting on, sometimes with Sara and Wasím and sometimes alone, always finding an excuse to walk down the road from the village. Invariably she brought some treat for him.

When Pedro finished the painting, he helped the men in the village rebuild the wall of her house. However, after three weeks in Oria he realised that he was getting restless. He was afraid of becoming settled in this delightful community and looked forward too much to Sabyán's company. He had to move on.

On his last evening there, before setting off the next morning, the mullah fulfilled his promise of the first evening and, at length, narrated to Pedro the long history of Almería, the city where he was still aiming to go.

'As I will try and explain to you, Pedro,' he started, 'the city of Almería has had a chequered history, full of ebbs and flows, just like the sea to which its fortunes have been so closely tied. The city's location at the south-east corner of *Al-Andalus*, separated by high mountains from the great cities of Granada and Córdoba, means that Almería's origin and development has been quite distinct from theirs.'

The holy man then detailed the history of the sea port, founded originally by Yemen's settlers, and described its magnificent tower, the Torre de los Espejos, which allowed communication with ships out in the bay by means of mirrors.

'At Almería,' the mullah explained, 'the open exposure of the wide bay prevents the unloading of ships in bad weather, so a breakwater was built adjacent to the al-Hawd district and this affords shelter for the merchant ships and the fleet of warships. Such was the commercial importance of Almería at that time that more than eight hundred looms operated in the centre of the city turning out the most exquisite brocades, cotton damask, lace, velvet and silk, and beautiful carpets with intricate designs which were sent to all parts of the Muslim world. Many craftsmen, working in iron and copper, fashioned all manner of essential and luxury items for the rest of the kingdom. At that time over nine hundred hostelries, all paying taxes, served this bustling city. Merchants, envoys and ambassadors came from all the corners of the Mediterranean to trade and seek patronage from the Sultan's court.

'Unfortunately, Pedro, this amazing prosperity couldn't last forever. Inevitably other kings and other peoples became envious of its riches. In 1091 a new, austere Islamic dynasty called the Almorávides came to power, and an army from North Africa arrived at the Pechina Gate. The ruler, al-Matasím, died of sadness at the threat to his beautiful palace and thriving city. Under the ruling Almorávides the city succoured a nest of pirates who rampaged as far afield as Italy and even along the Atlantic seaboard.

'This could not be tolerated for long by the bordering Christian countries, and a mighty army and navy were assembled under Alfonso VII, the King of Castile. After a series of battles, Almería finally capitulated in October 1147. Alfonso died a few years later, and the Christians could not prevent a new Muslim dynasty called the Almohades retaking the city just ten years subsequently.

'However, under the Granada-based Almohades, Almería could not recover its former glory and the city declined to the point where the population is now little more than three thousand. The once rich al-Hawd precinct was totally abandoned and many areas of the Musalla precinct became open spaces. In 1309 Almería was besieged yet again, this time by Jaime II, the king of Aragón, but after several months the siege was lifted without any payment of tribute. The city suffered further ravages as a result of the Black Death, but fortunately, under Nazarí rule Almería has regained some of its lost splendour and prosperity. Maritime trade with the cities of Valencia and Murcia has returned to re-establish the skills in metal and weaving which had been so badly affected. But now, I fear, matters are coming to a head. As Christendom starts to gather itself for a final showdown with our brethren in the Levant, King Fernando of Aragón and Queen Isabel of Castile are nibbling away at what remains of our kingdom of Granada. Soon I fear all will be lost and we will be extinguished for good.

'So I'm afraid, Pedro,' concluded the mullah, 'that you will find Almería a mere shadow of its glorious self four hundred years ago. I suspect I'd get some shocks too, if I were to go back there now – after only twenty years!'

VIII: Hot Springs

November 1487

Pedro was mistaken if he thought he could set off from Oria on the last stage of his journey to Almería unnoticed. Although he'd only told the mullah and Sabyán the evening before that it was time for him to leave, Sabyán and her two children, her neighbours, who were with her on the river bank during the flood a few weeks earlier, plus the elders of the village, were all by the roadside as he left. Abu Bakr, the mullah, joined them, and with tears in Sabyán's eyes and much sadness on all sides, Pedro bid his last farewells and strode down the road looking every bit a Muslim boy in his new clothes and white turban. He was more loaded down than ever. With his dagger sheathed at his side, his blanket across his shoulder, Joshua's clothes washed and tied into a bundle, his water skin and a big bag of food handed to him by Sabyán that morning, he was more like a soldier going to war than a boy travelling across the land. The ruby ring on his finger which Sabyán had given him in gratitude for saving Sara and Wasím from drowning was a fitting memory for the happy time he had spent with the mullah and the villagers and the restitution of his physical and mental well-being which it afforded. However, the stay in the village had unsettled him. While he set off again with the purpose of reaching Almería and joining a ship, his resolve was starting to wane, and exactly how he was going to convince a boat's master to take him on as a member of crew was starting to play on his mind.

Nevertheless, he strode back through the plaza and past the mosque, joining the road heading south to Macael, Tabernas and eventually Almería. He soon passed through Partaloa, with its gigantic stone perched precariously on a brown sandstone promontory overlooking a fertile valley floor, where vegetable crops were competing for space with chestnut, almond, fig and olive trees. Beyond the village the country rose into high, rolling hills, the soft outlines of which contrasted with the lands to the north which he had left behind some weeks before. The soft grey shales forming the hills yielded little goodness in this barren country.

After a night in an abandoned dwelling, he headed west. Deeply incised along one of many clefts between the mountains, the Pechina valley was filled with pale, limy marls which themselves had been worn away to leave flat dissected terraces. Numerous cave houses were cut into the sides of the bluffs between the terraces, and pomegranates, oranges, figs were tended on the flat valley floors between. The occasional small stream trickled through choked vegetation, whose greenness providing a refreshing contrast to the brown fields and the gloomy mountains in the distance.

By the afternoon the castle of Purchena appeared in the distance guarding the major route ahead to Baza and Granada. Pedro turned south some distance before it, down into the bustling town of Macael, before starting to ascend the unbroken 6,000-foot-high barrier which constituted these sierras. Square stacks of neatly cut slabs of white marble, compounds with room-sized blocks of sawn stone and conical piles of glistening broken rock debris, signified the importance of the locality. As he turned south off the main road, six enormous wagons, four of them loaded with single blocks of marble and two of them with rough-cut marble columns wedged tightly with baulks of timber, turned up onto the main road from the village to head west towards Granada. Each was pulled by a team of eight oxen, whose muscular bodies shuddered under the strain as they drew the wagons up and around the tight bend onto the main road. How many days it would take the wagon train to reach Granada – if indeed that was their destination – Pedro could only speculate.

Macael was full of bustle and noise. White dust swirled in the air as the sound of sledgehammers, saws, chisels, driven wedges and straining pulleys filled the air. Pedro paused in the village to fill his water skin but pressed on. There was a harsh, aggressive air about this industrious town which unsettled the young traveller and he continued on without stopping.

People had told him that this would be the most strenuous part of his journey. As he looked up at the mountains ahead he could see why. Although not rugged, they seemed simply to go up and up and up. Three days' hard slog was ahead of him to the Tabernas junction. He put his head down determined to make as much headway as he could before dark. The sun had already sunk below the hills to his right and, free of its glare, Pedro could see Venus higher in the sky as it followed its steady course to the right, when, after disappearing for a while, it would reappear to the right of the sun as a bright morning star. As on the previous night, Pedro eventually found a ruin, and after eating he bedded down under a black clouded sky.

The next morning he climbed higher and higher up the steady incline. Soon he joined a wagon train like the one he had seen the previous afternoon. As before, eight oxen each pulled four wagons loaded with marble blocks, although in view of the mountain ahead, these were smaller than those of the previous day. As Pedro came alongside the leading wagon, the driver beckoned to him to climb up alongside. Pedro did not require a second invitation.

'Where are you heading, lad?' the driver shouted over the noise of the heavy wheels on the stony road, plus the clatter of thirty-two mighty hooves and rattling harnesses and chains.

'I'm on my way to Almería, sir,' Pedro replied in as loud a voice as he could muster.

'So are we, but I'll warrant you'll get there a long time before us!' said the driver. 'What's your name?'

'Pedro Togeiro de Tudula, but you can call me Pedro!' said Pedro cheekily.

'Tudula? That's in Navarra, isn't it? My name's Marwan, and I own the marble quarry back there. And how old are you, Pedro?'

'Thirteen, Marwan. I'll be fourteen next February.'

'So soon time to start earning your living then, eh! Good. So I'll expect to see you sometime next year, Pedro.'

Pedro shook his head and laughed.

They said little else during the next half-hour as the animals heaved their cargoes to the crest of the road.

'This is where we stop to give the animals a breather,' the quarry owner said as he guided the animals onto the side of the road.

'We now have to put four of the oxen at the back of the wagon to control its descent down the hill. It's a gentler slope going down to Tabernas, but it's still a very long way to go. So it's best, Pedro, if you continue on your own, since you'll get there long before us. You'll need to spend another night in these mountains, but there are plenty of sheltered places. If you turn off down to one of the Tahá villages you can get a bed for the night and a hearty meal.'

They shook hands warmly and parted company. Pedro had been glad of the ride up the hill from Macael, not least because the strongly-made leather sandals which Sabyán had given him in Oria were starting to give him blisters.

Some dozen separate settlements made up the defensive and administrative grouping of Tahá villages. Several, such as Benitagla, Benizalón and Benitorafe, revealed all too clearly their Berber origins. It was these mountain people from the High Atlas mountains of Morocco who settled here several hundred years before following the Arab invasion. But Pedro did not take Marwan's advice to go to one of these villages for the night and after some hours, he found an abandoned farm to spend the night in.

Pedro travelled through the driving rain all the next day. He pulled the hood of his thick camel-hair *yallabiyya* over his head and wrapped his blanket around his shoulders. He reached Tabernas at nightfall, soaked through, tired and very cold. The town was an old settlement and lay on a key Roman road which linked Murcia and Almería. High above the town in a dominating situation was an imposing *alcázar* with a broad square tower and a castellated wall around the crest of the hill enclosing the old town. Wet through, with blistered heels and sore feet, Pedro was little inclined to look for another ruin and instead found a modest tavern in the lower part of the town for the night. It being a wet night in November there were no other visitors, so he could spread his things out to dry. The meal of stewed rabbit and seasoned rice, dried fruit and warmed fruit juice went down a treat.

He was now only a couple of days away from Almería and he was becoming increasingly uneasy about the wisdom of running away to sea. Too many people along the way had warned him of the dangers and rigours of life at sea where sadly, privation, harsh punishment and physical abuse were a way of life.

By mid-morning the next day, limping noticeably, Pedro was back on the road. It was by far the busiest highway he had encountered in his journey over the mountains. Big, four-wheeled wagons lumbered past, laden with stone or timber for construction, gypsum for cement and wall plaster, cut blocks of alabaster for ornate friezes, all pulled by four to eight oxen. Smaller, two-wheeled wagons pulled by mules or donkeys carried farming produce, tied bundles of cut esparto grass, hay or hides to local markets. Amazingly, clomping noisily past was a camel train of some twenty beasts, some light fawn in colour, some dark brown, some big, some small, some clean, some dirty, all tied together in a long line, like beads on a string. The temperamental animals grizzled and grunted as they were coaxed and cajoled fore and aft by two drovers on foot, each armed with long swishes which they wielded generously but not uncaringly. Rolling from side to side as they loped past, some camels had big wooden crates roped to their sides, some carried sacks and some rolls of sailcloth. Pedro sat by the side of the road, fascinated, and watched them go past. As he did so a troop of some fifty Muslim cavalry rode by. Clad in light armour and mounted on their swift Arab horses, they looked decidedly the worse for wear. There were no banners or streamers. Dishevelled, with some riders in bandages, they rode past mechanically with their heads lowered.

The innkeeper had told Pedro of the startling scenery he would encounter as the road turned south to follow the course of the river on his last stretch to the coastal city. As a former sailor, the innkeeper had traded along the Arabian coast and had once journeyed on a camel train into the Sinai Desert. It was the similarity of the angular, desert landscape in this corner of *Al-Andalus* to those scorching lands which drew him to Tabernas to settle down and run an inn.

The previous day's rain had given way to a clear blue sky and hot sunshine, even though it was early November. Pedro joined the course of the Andarax river, which drained the Alpujarra region to the north-west and in winter received meltwater from the Sierra Nevada beyond. Although the river channel was sixty yards wide, only a meagre stream, barely five feet wide, flowed against the opposite bank. As the innkeeper had said, the landscape was indeed desolate and inhospitable. Steep, brown sandstone cliffs hung over the road on the left bank. Immense, inclined slabs capped many of the cone-shaped hills, seemingly ready to slide into the deep wadis and ravines which wound up and into the ascending khaki-coloured hills. Great cracks and rents in the rocks, often thrust or downslid at angles one with another, showed the stresses and strains to which the land was still subjected. Across the river, traced on each side by tall canes waving in the breeze, fluted, conical hills rose straight from the valley floor. These ascended, as far as the eye could see, in a jumble of rugged, dung-coloured hills, bare and featureless, devoid of vegetation, habitations, roads, man or beast. It was not a place to tarry.

Soon he was overtaken by a squadron of six Christian horsemen under the command of a sergeant and an officer. Like Pedro, they were heading towards Almería. More heavily armed and armoured than the Muslim soldiers, their unshaven and stern appearance did not bode well for the object of their journey.

What are they doing here in Muslim country? thought Pedro. What mischief are they up to? Did they have a skirmish with the Muslim riders I saw back up the road?

By the afternoon he reached the outskirts of Pechina, the earliest Yemeni settlement set on a low rise above the valley of the Andarax. As the mullah had explained in his discourse on the city of Almería, it was an incredibly fertile locality. The flows of the river there were augmented by copious springs which were fed via *acequias* or irrigation channels to fields and orchards across both sides of the valley floor. Orange trees laden with ripe fruit held pride of place in the centre of the valley, with orchards of lemons interspersed here and there between them.

Pedro stopped for some water and to soak his sore feet in a roadside channel before turning down into the town. His thoughts wandered back to his home in Vélez Blanco. It was now nearly a month since he had left home. For the first time since he ran from his house after killing Marco in that last and terrible training session, he felt homesick. Would his father have forgiven him by now? How was his sister Cristina, and how was she coping with their bitter and vengeful father? How was Yazíd? What other friend had he found to play with in the mountains since Pedro left? Pedro began to doubt his own resolve to run away to sea. Should he go back and face the wrath of his father? Should he go back to Oria and settle down in the village there where he had made so many friends? Sitting there in the warm afternoon sun, the doubts started to prey on his mind. Should he go back home?... Should he go back home?... Should he go back home? The single question kept going round and round in his head.

His soliloquy was abruptly broken as a beggar stopped alongside him as he went stumping past with the aid of a long staff. He was clad in a dirty ragged *zihara*, and his equally dirty *'imama* lay partly unfurled around his shoulders. His long, straggly beard, matted grey hair and stooping posture all pointed to an old man who had been on the road for a very long time. With his one eye focused on Pedro, his opening rejoinder was predictable enough.

'Have you got a bite for eating for a fellow traveller, my lord?'

Pedro retrieved the last of Sabyán's tasty buns from his bag and handed it to the man, with some of the cheese which was left over.

The beggar sat down alongside Pedro. His thin, bony legs differed only from his crooked staff by their deep mahogany colour.

He smelled. Pedro moved a yard away.

'You sore feet got, eh?' he croaked through toothless gums. He spoke a sort of pigeon Arabic.

'Yes, blisters too,' said Pedro, lifting his feet out of the water, showing the man his raw heels.

'Ah, you wan go up at al-Hamma.'

'Where?'

'*Baños*. Them *baños* up the road at al-Hamma. They most famous is in all *Al-Andalus*.'

'Why?'

'Why, ask you? Well, is famous there for its heat spring and curations. You worth trying,' he added.

Clenching it in his claw-like hands, he munched the second half of his bun noisily with his gums.

'Got money too, have you?'

Pedro gave him a hard look, got up, turned his back on the beggar and retrieved five maravedís from what little he had left of what his uncle Joshua had given him for the journey. It was enough for some food in the market.

'There you are,' he said.

'That all?' the beggar challenged.

'Yes, that's enough. Now how do I get to al-Hamma?'

'Up that road go, no is far. Tell them that Ibn send you.'

'Ibn who?' queried Pedro.

'Just Ibn. My mother, Allah be praised, not know who father of me was. So she call me just Ibn. That all the name I got!'

Pedro thanked the old man for his advice and headed off up the hill. It was a longer slog than he expected and it took him a good hour to reach the famous thermal spring. All the way he passed or was overtaken by couples or groups of people, mostly well-to-do and finely dressed, either on their way up to al-Hamma or on their way back down. Some greeted him warmly. Others acknowledged him perfunctorily as not worth the time of day. One could not blame them. His clothes were now in desperate need of washing, as he was himself.

The mountains between Pechina and al-Hamma were even wilder than those along the main river valley from Tabernas. The skyline was jagged with high turrets, sharp peaks and overhangs. Everywhere was the same greyish-brown barren landscape, the clumps of greyish-green esparto grass doing little to lessen its bleakness. In the foothills, volcanic rocks were jumbled up piecemeal with the brown limestone. Higher still, the mountains towering above were smashed by vertical rents leaving enormous blocks seemingly hanging in the air ready to crash into the valley below. Near the *baños* themselves, the deep clefts in the mountains were stained red, black, grey and pale yellow, where copper, iron and lead minerals and sulphur had permeated the cracks from depth. Thick veins of white quartz criss-crossed with white calcite as if in some primeval challenge for supremacy.

Directly opposite the set of buildings which comprised the Baños de al-Hamma, a series of sumptuous and verdant terraces ran steeply down to the valley floor well over a thousand feet below. Tall date palms, with clusters of yellow dates hanging from their branches, bordered the road, while others provided welcome shade over the terraces below. Fig trees, now stripped of their purple fruit and with their ugly branches largely denuded of leaves, competed with pears and apples. In the distance below to his right, Pedro could see the outskirts of Pechina. To his far left was the narrow coastal chain of volcanic mountains of Tarre Qabita. But for him the most thrilling sight was that of the city of Almería in the far distance, some nine miles away, with the deep blue Mediterranean sea beyond. The shimmering heat of the late afternoon made it difficult to distinguish the details of the city, but its Alcazaba stood out high above the heat haze on its rocky promontory close to the sea. Maybe a hundred lateen masts poked through the haze in the bay. This is where he was to seek his fortune.

The *baños* were alive with people milling around. It was clearly a place for the wealthy. Whatever Ibn might have said, it did not seem the place for a grubby, limping, thirteen-year-old, half-Jewish and half-Christian boy dressed as an Arab. Dozens of Muslim men, nearly all with carefully-trimmed black beards, stood around chatting. All were dressed in beautiful and ornate, brocade *yubbas* over spotless white, ample *ziharas*, carrying curved scimitars on their belts, secured in jewel-encrusted scabbards. Some form of headgear was mandatory, and for many of them it comprised a large pumpkin-shaped *'imamas* seemingly more cushion than hat. A couple of the new arrivals stood alongside beautifully-groomed Arab stallions which had bright red tassels strung across their foreheads, with black leather harnesses emblazoned with brass ornaments. But most of the horses were corralled nearby in a shaded enclosure cosseted by two attendants who seemed more concerned about catching the eyes of the gentry for favours than attending to the needs of their horses. The cluster of dwellings making up the settlement of al-Hamma lay close by.

The hot spring at Baños discharged from the baths inside the building into a roadside carrier before being channelled below the road to the terraces on the other side. Several women from the village dressed in faded blue-grey *yubbas* were busy washing clothes in the steaming water of the carrier, all oblivious of the crowd in the road outside the baths. Pedro commandeered the far end of the channel, stripped off what clothes he could decently remove and soaked them in the hot, mineral-rich water, before pummelling them on the stone wall of the carrier. Pairs of dark eyes turned towards him, scowling, as a plume of dirty water passed down the channel to where the women were washing their clothes and sheets. Pedro draped his own clothes over the wall to dry in the sun. He then clambered onto the back wall of the channel and dangled his legs into the warm water. It was hot enough to cause him to catch his breath. He coughed as the acrid vapours emanating from the stream caught in his throat, but it was just these dissolved salts in the water which he hoped would ease the aches in his feet.

As he sat there wriggling his toes in the water he became more and more puzzled by the animation and restlessness of the dozens of immaculately-attired men there. Oddly, their voices seemed somewhat high-pitched and the conversations between them seemed perfunctory as their black eyes darted around the crowd, searching for something somewhere. But what was it? Two Muslim lords arrived together on horseback; one was followed meekly by three finely-dressed women and the other by four. All the womenfolk were dressed in the most beautiful silk *durra'as* Pedro had ever seen in his life and all wore silk, shoulder-length *mandils* and, tantalisingly, most had diaphanous *jimars* concealing the lower parts of their faces. At the same time, leaving the entrance to the baths, were groups of two, three, four or more women, all in equally fine and brightly coloured silks. All were quickly gathered up by their menfolk, as if they were under threat of being carried off by the Mongol hoard.

'Puzzled, are you?' a voice said.

Startled, Pedro looked around. One of the gardeners from the terraces opposite, more fittingly clad in a simple white cotton *camis*, had walked across the road to see what the half-naked boy with his legs in the carrier was up to.

'Puzzled, are you?' he repeated. 'By all these people here, I mean,' he said by way of clarification.

'Yes, I am,' replied Pedro. 'I don't understand it. Why are there so many men standing around, and why are they behaving so oddly?'

The gardener laughed loudly.

'It's because it's Thursday. That's why,' he answered.

'What's so special about Thursdays?' Pedro queried.

'Because it's women's day!'

Pedro still looked puzzled.

'You see, on Sundays, Tuesdays and Thursdays the baths are used by the women and the other days of the week by the men. Our Koran forbids us bathing together, so we have to use the baths on alternate days. Friday, being the Muslim holy day when the mullahs give the *oración* is, of course reserved for men, so Thursdays are for women. The men accompany their wives and concubines here to the baths on these days, and they're watching to see which of the other men gathered here are eyeing them. It's really very funny.'

'But what do you expect?' he added scornfully. 'These peacocks have little else to do.'

'Do you want me to show you around?' he asked. 'I guess you've walked here to see the famous *baños* we have here. I'm told that they're the finest in all *Al-Andalus*.'

'That's what Ibn told me, too.' Pedro replied.

'Ibn? That old one-eyed, toothless rogue? You know him?'

'Yes, I met him by the turn-off from the main road.'

'And I bet he asked you for money? Did you give him any?'

'Just five maravedís for some food.'

'Good, I'm glad you didn't give him more. He's got more money hidden away than many of the wealthy nobles here today! But before we go we'd better tend to your feet; I can see you've got some nasty blisters on your heels. Wait here a minute. I'll borrow that fine dagger of yours a minute, if I may. My word, where did you get it from? It's beautiful.'

With Pedro's horn-handled knife, the gardener disappeared into the crowd, returning – after some alarming moments – and offering it to its owner. It was covered in sticky-looking amber gum.

'Here, I've got some pine gum from one of the trees opposite.'

He ran some of the gum over the blisters, tore off two pieces from the end of Pedro's turban and tied them around his feet.

'Sit still for a minute,' he instructed.

The gardener examined each of Pedro's tough sandals and used the dagger to scrape the burr from the inside of the leather. Then he softened them with some olive oil.

'Rub some of this into your feet, and leave them in the sun for a few minutes,' he said.

'How do you know about these treatments?' Pedro asked, trying to recall if he had seen his father use them.

'Aha,' he laughed, 'if you'd been a gardener all your life using hoes, spades, rakes and sickles you'd soon know how to cope with blisters on your hands. You should have seen my hands after my first day's work here! Every finger was raw and bleeding.'

'Come, I'll show you around. You can put your sandals on now, but leave the bandages on as long as you can.'

The gardener led Pedro around the back of the building along an alley to where the spring issued. The mineral waters rose from considerable depth below the mountains and issued through a broad fissure in the rock. They were stained ochre by iron oxides. The spring water in the collector tank was crystal clear, although saturated with many health-giving natural salts. Whether genuinely health-giving or not, the waters had been used since Roman time to aid digestion and respiration, reduce liver inflammation from intoxication, act as a sedative and relaxant and help the body's circulation. The flow of the spring was prodigious, and its temperature, while not boiling, was hot enough to make you gasp when you entered it.

Pedro could see through the entrance gate the enclosed, rectangular courtyard in the *baños* with its ornamental marble floor, its Macael white marble columns supporting the surrounding balcony to the upstairs rooms and the fountain playing into a fluted marble basin. Palms and ferns provided extra shade for the seats placed around the perimeter. All were occupied by the womenfolk there that day. Others stood around chatting animatedly, since this was one of their few chances of catching up on news from their circle of friends and neighbours. It was an opportunity not to be missed. Through the crowd of women, the gardener pointed to the steps running down to the baths themselves.

He winked at Pedro.

'Follow me. Although it's a women-only day today, I'll show you what the baths look like inside.'

Furtively, he led Pedro around to the side of the building and down a short flight of stone steps, ensuring that nobody saw them. Near the bottom was a narrow skylight containing thick, greenish glass. This let light in but kept prying eyes out. However, by some miracle, one of the small panes was broken and the gardener beckoned Pedro to peep inside.

The baths contained two large *albercas* or tanks, each some three yards long by three yards wide. The floor of the whole room was slabbed in brown marble with white marble lining the insides of the baths. A row of coloured patterned tiles ran around the baths just above the level of water. Brick arches around the sides, supported on square columns, concealed deep recesses, some of which contained bench seats. The recesses themselves were walled with more patterned tiles. The roof was a single brick barrel vault.

Some dozen naked women stood talking, laughing and giggling in the chest-deep water, or sat neck-deep on submerged benches along one side of them. Steps led down into the baths. If the thirteen-year-old was seeking titillation then, regrettably, he had to make do with a few dimly-lit bare bottoms descending the steps. Other women in white cotton *camis* sat on the benches in the recesses. Their lustrous black hair, cascading down over their shoulders, stirred the boy's senses more than he would have wished to admit. Even through the broken pane Pedro could smell the pungent fumes which emanated from the water.

The gardener took a quick peep through the cracked pane to see if he was missing anything and, with a shrug of disappointment, led Pedro around to the far side and some more steps down.

'As well as the two *albercas*,' he explained, 'there are seven baths along the passage which are carved from solid marble. These are for washing rather than the ritual cleansing for which the *albercas* are used, and which are so important to our faith. I expect you know that. You Christians are a dirty lot, I might tell you.'

'I'm half Jew, and that half of me gets washed as regularly as you Muslims,' retorted Pedro.

'Yes, I suppose it's true,' replied the gardener. 'In many respects we've similar traditions.'

They returned back up the steps.

'Where does the water go after it leaves the baths?' asked Pedro.

'It comes out here along this channel for the villagers to wash clothes in it. It's still very hot. It then passes below the road and goes into that large stone tank where it cools down before we can use it for watering our crops. So it gets well used.'

'As you would expect for the most famous hot spring in all *Al-Andalus!*' Pedro commented wryly.

'Of course! What else?' he replied. 'Now I must be going, I've got some new plants to water before I leave tonight. On Thursdays, most of us gardeners work late and afterwards we roast some meat on an open fire on the top terrace. It's wonderful, we have it all to ourselves. If you want to join us, you're welcome. I can guarantee the food, and there's plenty of it.'

Pedro did not need a second invitation, and his mouth already started to water at the thought of some spicy, Arab food akin to that which Sabyán had cooked for the mullah and himself in Oria. Yet the meal was still three hours away! So he killed time, wandering around as the sky darkened in the November evening. He had leant over the terrace wall. Just along from a shallow well he spotted two chambers in arched recesses which would be an ideal place to spend the night.

He and his feet felt good. His anxiety over the morrow's final journey to Almería and possibly his last day on dry land for weeks or months had withdrawn to the back of his mind.

It was approaching midnight when Pedro finally wriggled under his blanket and thick *yallabiyya* in the arched chamber looking out over the top terrace towards the city of Almería. The embers of the open fire had long ceased to glow and the evening breeze blowing from the sea had died down. The young traveller, well accustomed to the dark nights by now, felt a growing sense of foreboding as inky blackness and total stillness descended on the land. It seemed as if he were being enveloped in black cotton wool which stifled the senses and absorbed all sound. There was a nothingness in the air; not a single ray of light, not a single smell, not a single cry of an animal, not even the sound of scurrying insects gathering up the spoils of the day.

He pulled the blanket over his head as ghostly images and sounds echoed in the confines of the chambered recess. Silhouetted by red flames and the bright sparks of the exploding furnace, the awesome figure of the ironmaster Rodríguez stood over him with clenched fists shaking with rage; behind him his sword master Marco, shouted his very last instructions to him over the wet cobblestones: *Thrust upwards with the point of your sword!* Pedro rolled away screaming as Marco fell headlong over him, blood frothing from the fatal wound through his neck. The frightened face of his mother appeared at his feet as she was pulled from his grasp. Her face faded into that of Sabyán, whose lovely features were gradually replacing those of his mother in his memory.

Pedro forced his eyes open in an attempt to escape the nightmares but there was simply nothing in the black void to focus on. He closed his eyes tightly, but the ghostly images and sounds kept recurring in a jumbled frenzy.

'Pedro, Pedro... Pedro!' cried his mother, her forlorn voice trailing into the distance as she was carried off. 'Thrust upwards, thrust upwards!' shouted Marco. 'Water... it was water that killed them!' raged the giant Rodríguez.

He put his hands over his ears but the voices all around him did not abate. He fought to bring these nightmares under control, trying to concentrate on Sabyán's comforting words. Gradually, the voices receded into the blackness of the night and all was still. Eventually, through sheer exhaustion he fell asleep. But it would not be for long.

IX: Shock Waves

November 1487

Less than two hours later Pedro was awakened by the stirring of leaves on the ground outside. They scuffed the ground, sweeping up the dust as they swirled in eddies in the lightest of breezes. Then all was silent. To Pedro's great relief the suffocating blackness had vanished and the waning moon, now in its last quarter and rising in the south-east, was shining fitfully like a candle in the breeze as low clouds flitted across it. The breeze returned, this time more noticeably, blowing the dust into the open entrance to the recess.

Pedro arose and stood at the entrance of his shelter. The south-westerly breeze of the afternoon before had swung to the south-east but it was noticeably backing further towards the east as its momentum increased. Branches high above him bent under the wind's burgeoning force, swishing back and forth as the positive thrust of the wind alternated with the suction between the gusts. Within fifteen minutes, a gale was blowing, increasing in crescendo, tearing through the trees, raining hard yellow dates down onto the ground like hailstones. Pedro's ears started to pop as the air pressure continued to fall. Within twenty more minutes the gale increased in its fury to full storm force, gusting to a screaming hurricane. It tore up the steep slope from the valley below, carrying all manner of debris before it: leaves, twigs, palm fronds, fencing and boxes.

A branch crashed to the ground along the path to the terrace and with a loud, tearing noise the upper half of a nearby palm broke away and slammed through the other trees around it, falling directly over the road behind him. Pedro was glad he was under the stone roof of the alcove. Another tree to his left was uprooted bodily, tumbling head over heels down the tier of terraces, reaching the fourth one below before pitching head first into the soft, tilled ground. In being torn from the ground, it took away part of the bank entraining the spring overflow from the *baños*. Released from centuries of efficient containment, the water spilled down into the terrace, its gentle trickle giving way to a roar as the clay and stones of the retaining bank gave away. The water sped on across the top terrace, carving out its own narrow channel through the carefully tended rows of plants as it did so. It paused at the terrace boundary to form a small pond and then, with renewed energy, it cascaded over into the second terrace and then down and down towards the valley below.

Then as quickly as it appeared the gale slackened. Pedro's ears popped several times as the centre of the low-pressure cyclone passed over, with the sky momentarily clearing. He found himself standing in water. Twenty yards to his right, the water in the shallow well, relieved of its restraining atmospheric loading, overflowed, gushing water along the pathway.

Within minutes, the gales returned, this time blowing from the north-west behind him. It was noticeably chillier, and Pedro pulled on his thick brown *yallabiyya* around his shoulders. Trees that had managed to resist the earlier forces were now confronted by others from a different direction. Several succumbed and crashed to the ground. The well ceased to overflow and its water started to withdraw into its brick-lined shaft. The building opposite, now more exposed to the winds, did not escape the fury. Pantiles scalloped along the top wall around the flat-roofed building were dislodged and hurled into the road; several clattered onto the roof of the twin alcoves where Pedro was sheltering, splintering into fragments and then flying onwards in the wind.

Then, as quickly as the winds started, they abated and the air became still, warming perceptibly. The crescent moon, lit from the left by the sun still several hours below the south-eastern horizon, rose higher in the sky and brightened. Except for the night creatures, clearing the wind rack from the entrances to their earthy abodes and harvesting any spoils to be found around them, all was silent again. Like the day creatures disturbed in their slumber, Pedro returned to the warmth and comfort of his bed.

The sun was well up when Pedro stirred, but it was still quiet. This would be one of the momentous days in his life when he would begin the life of a sailor. He put on his Christian clothes, Sabyán's warm socks and sandals. His heel bandages were still in place and he pulled his socks carefully over them. The soreness of his heels had largely gone and the soles of his feet felt altogether better. He donned his old familiar floppy red cap and felt good; he was a Vélez Blanco boy again. He tied up his Muslim clothes tightly in a bundle, tucked his dagger deep into his canvas shoulder bag and after getting his other things shipshape he gathered some fallen fruit from the terraces below, a handful or two of fresh, crisp yellow dates from the ground around him, and went across the road to the hot spring carrier emanating from the *baños*. He washed the sleep out of his eyes, freshened himself up and sat on the wall to eat his breakfast.

All was devastation. In both directions, trees lay across the highway, their roots high in the air, mounds of earth piled around them. Broken tiles, branches, palm tree fronds, bunches of dates, vegetation and plants uprooted from the terraces filled the road between the fallen trees, to the extent that it was impossible to determine its true course. The terraces below were in a sorry state. Running diagonally across the top terrace was a foot-wide muddy channel, along which the water from the hot spring still flowed, splashing quietly down into the terrace below as if in a bid for permanence, and thence downwards to those below. Reining it in after its few hours of freedom would be the first task the terrace workers would do that day. It was truly a sad sight. Yet nature has no memory. Within a few weeks when all was cleared away and order restored, one would not be able to discern the former glory of what had been the verdant oasis of al-Hamma.

Pedro took in all the mayhem around him in only a few seconds. What grabbed his attention was the distant vista of the coast. The afternoon haze of yesterday had disappeared to give way to a beautifully clear day. With the early morning shadows highlighting its features, the city of Almería stood out clearly, with the towers and walls of the Alcazaba winding around its rocky promontory close to the sea. So did much of the city wall, with its many gateways, although a hill on the outskirts of the city blocked parts of it from view. The breakwater beyond the Alcazaba was visible, as were the multitude of ships tied to it, moored on the beach or at anchor in the bay waiting to load or unload their cargo. Lateen-rigged Arab dhows, which traded around the coasts of the Mediterranean, were dominant, but there were also scores of Christian caravels with their three masts, rounded prows and high sterns.

Pedro had been studying this fascinating scene for some while with a sense of growing anticipation when a dog started barking in the village. Others joined in. But it was not barking for attention or to frighten; more a whining in fear of the unknown, of the intangible. As Pedro listened, baffled by this discordant canine choir, he felt a jolt beneath him and he was pitched headlong from the wall onto the debris-strewn road. He tried to get to his feet, but within seconds the ground started to shake forward and back violently and he found it impossible to hold his balance. Jagged rifts opened up in the road and a low rumbling came from deep down in the earth. Tiles were propelled from the roof of the building behind him. Those palm trees left standing after the passage of the cyclone that night started to vibrate as if the hands of a giant were trying to throttle them. Branches broke off piecemeal with such force that they rent the trunks of the trees in two.

A continuous roll of destruction came from al-Hamma, as the poorly constructed flat-roofed dwellings collapsed like packs of cards. Within not much more than thirty seconds only a few of the sturdier dwellings and isolated walls remained standing. Men, women and children ran screaming from the ruins searching out open spaces for safety. Many of those emerging, coughing and covered in dust, immediately scrambled back into the ruins, searching for those who remained buried under the masonry and timber, or their animals or most precious belongings. The cries of those trapped mixed with the terrified screams of the survivors and the badly injured. An instant later, the same thing happened with buildings a short distance on. Walls of the few houses which remained standing succumbed and toppled over into the ruins around them, extinguishing many of those clinging to life and hope. While he was trying to hold his balance, Pedro was horror-struck to see in the distance an enormous pall of reddish-brown dust rising over Almería. The city and the coast beyond disappeared from view.

A new roar ascended from the valley as the sound of the destruction of Pechina reached Pedro. Another crevice opened up between Pedro's feet and he scrambled to one side, only to fall over again as the shock waves continued. Other cracks gaped wider, one side of them subsiding or grinding sideways relative to the other. With a thunderous crash the barrel-vaulted roof of the *baños*, supported by the inflexible stone walls of the building, collapsed piecemeal into the *albercas* below. The outer wall of the water carrier on which Pedro had been sitting earlier gave way as several rents appeared in it but, amazingly, when the channel had dumped its contents into the road, where it quickly disappeared down a crevice, there was nothing more. The famous hot mineral spring, a feature of *Al-Andalus* for at least a thousand years, had ceased to flow.

Looking along the road to his right, Pedro witnessed an unforgettable sight. As the secondary up-and-down shake waves took over from the first push-and-pull waves of the earthquake, successive ripples tore along the road, bucking and heaving it, just as a carpet might if shaken violently at one end. He himself was pitched up and down as the waves passed below him. All around him were the sounds of destruction, collapsing roofs, crumbling walls, rents in the earth, the whip-like crack of trees breaking in two, of people screaming in terror, pain and fear. Surmounting all these sounds was the deep, continuous roar of the Earth God, fully aroused now from his slumbers. The third-phase rotational waves took over from the shaking waves, and the sound of the ground itself being fractured miles below the surface added to those filling the air. A new rent appeared in the road. The twin barrel-vaulted shelter, from which Pedro had witnessed the cyclone, collapsed, much of the top terrace sliding into the one below. Half the road was carried away leaving a sinuous 20-foot-high bank. Forty seconds after Pedro was first pitched off the wall, the distant roar of the wholesale destruction of Almería hit him. It had no peaks or troughs, just one vast cacophony of overwhelming noise. The dust cloud above Almería had already reached a thousand feet in the otherwise still air, but was itself being blotted out by smaller clouds of destruction from Pechina to the right and the smaller villages along the Andarax valley.

The shaking continued for a full minute more before ceasing. But the angry Earth God was not yet spent. High, high above, the shaking had worked free two enormous, house-sized blocks of rock from the mountain side.

The release of the earth's crustal forces by the lowered atmospheric loading with the passage of the cyclone over the land that night was the straw which broke the camel's back. The earthquake had reaped its terrible reward. It was by far the worst such event in living memory in this corner of the sultanate. Yet nothing would compare with that which would occur twenty-five years later.

Pedro stood there, numbed by the terrible destruction around him. The rumbling and roaring of the earthquake had been replaced by an eerie silence. It was broken only by the spasmodic crashing of roofs and walls, the barking of dogs, the cries of those trapped in the ruins and by the shouts of the searchers.

Drawn to his ultimate destination, Pedro was in two minds about what to do; make haste to Almería to witness the destruction, or help rescue those trapped in al-Hamma. His mind was made up for him.

'You there… you with the red cap. Come and help me get my husband out!' shouted a voice in Arabic along the road.

Pedro ran along the road, or where he assumed the road was, keeping well away from the crumbling edge of the 20-foot slip. He clambered over the branches and foliage strewn across the road from the cyclone and ducked under fallen trees as if he were taking part in the village obstacle race.

A stocky, elderly woman with a green headscarf and torn and worn clothing which looked as if it had been handed down from mother to daughter for generations, was heaving fruitlessly at a wooden beam which was loaded down with a mass of masonry. A man's left arm stretched out from under the beam, the hand open in pitiful supplication. Low muffled moans came from within the ruins.

'Please help me,' the elderly woman pleaded.

Pedro could see at a glance from the trapped, claw-like hand and the mound of masonry loaded onto the man's chest that his chances of survival were slim. But while there was life there was hope. He eased the woman away from the beam she was tugging at, indicating the futility of her actions. He climbed onto the ruins and pushed blocks of masonry away, lifting them when he could, levering them sideways when they were at the limit of his strength. All the while, the cries from beneath the building became weaker. After half an hour, with the elderly woman helping, Pedro partly uncovered the roof beam which lay across her husband's chest. Blocks of stone still pinned his legs. He pointed to her to prop something beneath the beam if he lifted one end. A broad-chested man appeared from nowhere, and with all their strength he and Pedro heaved the beam a few inches, enough for the woman to wedge the stone under one end.

'Again,' the strong man said.

They heaved again and managed to raise it a few more inches, and again the woman managed to prop a stone under the beam. Pedro clambered over the ruins and retrieved a thick, broken-off piece of wood.

'Here,' he said to the woman in Arabic. 'One more time should do it. When we lift, push the stone away and push in this piece of wood. This should hold it more firmly.'

Pedro and the man heaved again with all their strength. The man's face reddened under the strain as he gritted his teeth and the veins stood out on his neck. Pedro did his utmost but knew that his effort was puny compared with this powerful man. Slowly the beam rose, a quarter of an inch, a whole inch, two, then finally three inches.

'*Now!*' shouted the man. 'We can't hold it much longer.'

The woman was not to be found wanting, with her husband's life in the balance. On her hands and knees in front of them, oblivious of the broken tiles and bricks cutting into her knees, she swiftly wedged the sturdy lump of wood under the beam which Pedro and the man were supporting. She shoved it in as far as she could, making sure that it would not slew away sideways when the beam was released.

'Slowly now, young fellow,' groaned the man, now at the limit of his strength.

Carefully, they lowered the beam onto the piece of wood. It held. Jerkily, an arm slowly withdrew into the ruins, the hand clenching as it did so.

Oblivious to the risk of it collapsing and crushing her as well as her husband, the woman dived under the beam into the dark rubble-filled hollow which concealed him. Her ample frame filled what little space there was. Another moan came from the cavity, this time more loudly now that the beam had been lifted from his chest.

'He's alive. Praise be to Allah!' cried the woman. 'He's alive!'

Pedro and the big man exchanged glances and shook their heads, knowing that even now the chances of getting the injured man out safely from the ruins were minimal. They persuaded the woman to extricate herself from the cavity. Being the smallest, Pedro crawled in head first to see how the man's legs could be freed. He could see the trapped man in the dusty gloom. His face was pallid and deathly. His right arm, although free, was broken, and blood was oozing from the exposed bone at the elbow. He felt the man's face and left arm, now freed.

'How are you getting on, young fellow?' cried the powerful man repeatedly, concerned as much for Pedro's safety as for the trapped man.

'I think I've freed his legs now!' Pedro shouted from the darkness. 'But they are in a sorry state.'

He extricated himself backwards from the hole and the man went in. Leaning over the still body of the woman's husband, he lifted his shoulders. Carefully, he eased him out of the hole, ensuring as best he could that the man's body did not twist sideways. With Pedro assisting from outside, the man was pulled from the ruins into the light of day. The poor woman flung herself prostrate on her husband, brushing the dust from his face, kissing and hugging him, oblivious of his broken arm and broken and crushed leg. Pedro and his helper, both covered in greyish dust and looking ghostly, looked on silently, panting breathlessly. They knew without speaking that the man was dead and the earthquake had added one more widow to its deathly toll.

'*Simón, Simón!*' the woman cried as she lay on the broken body of her husband, not wanting to believe that her husband had perished in the earthquake.

Pedro started at hearing the name and realised that he had completely forgotten that his uncle Simón, his father's estranged elder brother, lived in Almería, and might have also died in the earthquake. He had done all he could for the woman in al-Hamma. It was time to move on. He nodded to the man, who was trying to console the distraught woman, and left the scene.

X: Caught in Almería

Pedro arrived on the outskirts of Almería early evening. He was exhausted and dead on his feet. The nine miles had seemed like twenty and he had hardly stopped to eat or drink all day. From the *baños* he had found a short cut down into the valley which skirted Pechina to its left. Scenes of destruction lay all around. The famous rounded cupola of Pechina's mosque was no more. Along the Andarax valley into Almería it was much the same story. But inexplicably, as in many earthquakes, the scale of destruction was patchy; some communities were totally flattened while others close by were largely untouched.

Not so the third largest city in *Al-Andalus*. Wearily, he entered the city through the Pechina Gate, its principal entrance on the north side, having passed the city's main cemetery a quarter of a mile outside the walls. This was a hive of activity as hundreds of people milled around it. A hundred or more bodies wrapped in white sheets already lay on the ground in two neat rows as their final resting places were made ready. The arched entrance way of the Pechina Gate itself stood – but only just. Much of the wall running to his right towards the Alcazaba and to his left down towards the Rambla de Belén and the sea beyond had collapsed. The easy-to-build, rubble-filled Muslim walls had been the source of their own destruction. Along to his left inside the gateway, the timber stalls of the early morning market, re-erected each day, had all toppled over; the vegetables, fruit, clothes and pots strewn across the road piecemeal, many interred under the collapsed canvas awnings of the stalls.

By now starving hungry, Pedro collected some loaves of bread from around one of the stalls and, oblivious to the dust and grit covering them and their staleness, he devoured them, along with a length of hard mutton sausage which he found from beneath another. He headed left into the Musalla precinct, avoiding for the moment the narrow, but principal thoroughfare of Calle de las Tiendas, which ran down through the heart of the city joining the Calle Real de la Almedina in the central Medina precinct. The course of the narrow streets in the city were only discernible by the line of rubble, by those houses left standing and by the hundreds of people scrambling over the ruins.

He found a fountain still dribbling water and slaked his thirst, washing the day's dust from his throat and from his face and arms. The area, once a beautiful garden, had been given over to vegetable plots and animal pastures, but what orderliness there might have had was largely destroyed by the earthquake. Goats and sheep, finding themselves unconstrained by enclosures, were eating their way steadily through the vegetables, with chickens and other feathered fowl scurrying between their feet. Horses and the odd camel stood around, bemused, not knowing what to do with their newly acquired freedom.

Pedro passed the oratorio. Its high stone walls still intact but with its roof collapsed. By good fortune, the earthquake had struck in the early morning well before the Friday *oración* when thousands would have gathered to hear the imam. He passed several schools, some flattened, some inexplicably intact, yet of similar construction. The streets in this part of the city were deserted. Not so the more populated central Medina precinct. Pedro passed through the Puerta de los Aceiteros, one of two open stone gateways in the eastern wall of Rahman III's first walled precinct. The gateways with their broad, stone lintels remained intact, as did most of the walls either side, well constructed with enormous blocks of dressed stones, no worse for wear after being recycled time and time again for building.

By now it was nearly dusk. This, the oldest and most populated part of the city, was severely damaged. Everywhere, men and women were wearily picking through the wreckage of their houses searching for those still buried, retrieving furniture, carpets, cooking utensils, personal belongings and what riches they might have concealed in hidden corners. Bodies lay everywhere, some looking serene and at peace, others pitifully disfigured and maimed by the destruction. Wives and mothers were bent prostrate over the bodies of their menfolk and children, rocking back and forth, wailing laments. Pedro worked his way through the throng, aghast at the scale of the damage. Eventually, he found himself beneath the walls of the Alcazaba, itself seriously damaged.

Pedro started up the zigzag path to the main barbican gate leading to the lower enclosure, but his way was blocked by dozens of helmeted Muslim soldiers struggling with laden chests from the palace within. Like worker ants, a line of soldiers ascended the steps empty-handed, passing a line of heavily laden soldiers descending. Pedro had no idea where they might be going but guessed it was to ships waiting at the breakwater. Evidently, the palace of the Prince of Almería, Ibn Salim Ben Ibrahim al-Nagar and his son Cidi Yahya al-Nagar, who was mayor of the city, must have been badly damaged to warrant such an evacuation.

He turned around and headed towards the poorer Al-Hawd precinct lying to the west of the city. It was here, or at least what remained of the area after its abandonment two hundred years before, that his uncle Simón had run his spice-importing business. As Pedro reached the Puerta del Socorro, a well-dressed and evidently wealthy man beckoned him over. Erect and bearded, dressed in a broad-sleeved purple *yubba*, now-soiled, and black *'imama*, he stood in front of his two-storey dwelling, the ground floor of which was, or had been, his jeweller's shop. Much of the upper storey had collapsed and the front wall of what remained of it leant precariously over the road. The man was on the point of breaking down.

'Please help me, my boy,' he murmured apologetically as Pedro reached him. 'My dear wife and my two sons are dead...'

He paused and sobbed, shaking his head as his shoulders heaved in his overwhelming grief.

'My two young boys are lying over there; I managed to get them out but they were dead, crushed by the collapsed roof.'

Without looking around, he gesticulated to two enshrouded corpses lying neatly side by side against the wall at the end of the building.

'But my wife's still inside, dead, pinned under a beam. I simply cannot go in there with her lying there. Inside is a chest with all our life's savings. Please young man, I can see from your face that you're an honest fellow, please will you retrieve it for me? I promise I'll reward you handsomely.'

Pedro could see that the poor man was at his wits' end. His wife, sons, house and lifetime's business – all gone.

'I don't need a reward, sir,' he said. 'Just tell me where I can find your chest. I'll do what I can to help you.' Pedro thought he felt a slight jerk under his feet.

'You're very kind. If only there were more young people like you around… My chest is through in the back room. You'll find it at the back of the cupboard on the lower shelf. It's behind some books. The doorway's collapsed and you'll have to crawl under it as best you can. You'll have to scramble over the body of my…'

'I understand,' said Pedro sympathetically. 'Please try not to upset yourself. I'll find it.'

A few flecks of dust fell onto his face from the unstable wall above.

'But tell me,' Pedro added. 'Where will you take your chest? It's probably very heavy, and you can't wander the streets carrying it. There are villains and ruffians everywhere, ransacking and looting everything in sight.'

'I'll go to my friend, Simón.'

'Simón?' Pedro's ears picked up.

'Yes, Simón Togeiro, he's a merchant and lives three streets away on the other side of the Socorro Gate, just along there. He's a very good friend of mine.'

'And he's my uncle too!' added Pedro with glee.

'Your uncle?' The man was dumbfounded.

'Yes. My father, Abraham Togeiro, is his younger brother, and we live in Vélez Blanco. It's a very long story, but I'm on my way to find Uncle Simón now, although I've only a vague memory of where he lives.'

'So you must be Pedro?' replied the stunned jeweller. 'Simón has often spoken of you and your father, although I gather they don't speak to one another now. You've a sister too – Cristina, isn't it?'

'Yes, that's right,' replied Pedro, warming to the man.

'And you've a second uncle too? The youngest of the three brothers?'

'Yes, yes – Joshua. It's amazing that I should meet you!'

Pedro looked up as a piece of cement fell at his feet.

'I'll accompany you to Uncle Simón's,' he volunteered, 'but first let me retrieve your chest from the house.'

Pedro handed his clothes bundle to the jeweller and dumped his shoulder bag by the doorway. Without seeking a reply, Pedro stepped over the debris in front of the half-collapsed house and found his way to the back room in the growing darkness. The wooden lintel of the doorway was cracked but it still managed to prop up much of the ceiling. On both sides of the door, the beams hung down to the floor, their laths and plaster filling spewing out like white entrails. On the floor inside the door, the feet of the jeweller's wife protruded from beneath a pile of debris. From the other side of the debris, part of her face was exposed, her left eye stared at him as if from an alabaster mask. Gingerly he stepped over her body. More by feel than sight he felt his way to the cupboard at the back of the room. Its doors were blocked by fallen debris. He pushed it away with his feet, reached into the lower shelf, pulled out the neat row of bound ledgers, the accounts of a lifetime's work, and dragged out the chest. It was eighteen inches across and made of a dark, solid wood. Thick brass straps ran across its barrel-shaped lid to two latches at the front. Pedro made no attempt to look inside the box, but whatever the contents were, it was heavy. It was as much as he could do to lift it off the ground.

As he struggled with it to the door, a secondary tremor shook the building and for the second time that day he felt the ground moving under his feet. The aftershock lasted only ten seconds, but to Pedro, inside a half-ruined house, it felt like a lifetime. The remaining walls creaked and groaned, and more plaster rained down on his head. Clutching the box to his chest, he managed to get across to the door frame as the remains of the ceiling caved in behind him, smashing down on the cupboard opposite. With a final tremor, a thunderous crash occurred outside in the road. Pedro waited for a full minute in case there was a further tremor. Then, grasping the chest tightly, falling and tripping over debris in the dust and near darkness, he struggled out into the street. Outside, against the house, was an enormous heap of rubble. The remains of the upper floor wall had finally crumbled. Still clutching the heavy box to him, Pedro squinted into the gloom, looking for his newly acquired friend, the jeweller.

A mailed glove reached out and grabbed him roughly around the neck and a harsh voice spoke in Castilian. It was the first time Pedro had heard his native tongue since his stay with the mullah in Oria.

'Got you, you scoundrel! Thought you could get away did you? Stealing jewel boxes, is we?'

The mailed fist struck him behind his ear. Pedro fell to the ground. Standing over him was a Christian soldier, pulling his right gauntlet tight at the wrist with his left hand, ready to strike a second blow.

'Well, you've been caught red-handed…'

'No, I was…' Pedro started to explain in Arabic, then changed to Castilian.

'No, I was retrieving this box for this man…' Pedro looked around, bewildered.

'Speak Arabic, does you?… What man?'

'He asked me to retrieve this chest.'

'What man?'

'The man who owned this house, he's here – somewhere!'

Pedro got up and looked around in the near darkness. There was nobody. Just the pile of rubble, himself and this soldier. The soldier was in his mid-thirties, unshaven and about Pedro's height, with a thickset, ruddy complexion and a low forehead. Half his left ear was missing.

'Ha, ha, fine story!' retorted the grizzled *militar*. 'We've heard that before more than once today, haven't we, Gaz?'

A second soldier appeared. Like the first, he wore a steel cuirass over a chain mail shirt which extended to his thighs. They both wore tight black leather trousers and iron-studded boots. Both had steel helmets with high 'keels' which were now becoming fashionable. While the first carried a long spear, this second soldier carried a sword in his hand.

'Another looter, Zak?' the second said scornfully. 'They start young these days, eh?'

'How old are you?' spat the first, named Zak, at the same time striking Pedro on the mouth with his fist. He fell to the ground again, wiping the blood from the corner of his mouth.

'Please listen to me. I'm trying to tell you. I was only—'

'Quiet, scoundrel! I asked you how old you is?' He kicked Pedro viciously in the stomach while he lay on the ground.

'Thirteen,' Pedro spluttered.

'You looks more like fifteen or sixteen to me!' The soldier lashed out again.

'I'm fourteen next February,' groaned Pedro.

'What's you got in that satchel?'

Without waiting for a reply, Zak tipped out the contents on the ground. Pedro's spare sandals, socks and woollen coat fell out, with a few oranges he had picked that day. The man gave the bag a shake, it seemed too heavy. Out fell Pedro's Toledo dagger in its sheath. The brass stud securing the bone handle glinted in what little light remained. The second soldier, Gaz, pounced on it.

'Oh no you don't!' shouted Zak furiously. 'That's mine! I caught this rogue. Hand it over.' He grabbed the dagger angrily from the taller man.

'No, you don't, Zaquera. I'll take that,' said an authoritative voice from behind.

A lean man in his late twenties appeared. He was wearing a padded, short-sleeved tunic of dark green cloth over a chain mail shirt which extended to his wrists, itself over a cotton undershirt. A poorly-woven emblem of a cross made of the knobbly branches of a shrub was sewn onto one arm of his tunic. He wore a floppy maroon velvet hat with a feather stuck in it. A long sword swung in its scabbard at his side. It had a beautifully engraved haft. Sullenly Zak handed over Pedro's fine dagger.

'So!' the captain said. 'Something else you've stolen today! This is worth a ducat or two, I can tell you!'

He tucked Pedro's dagger into his sword belt.

'Sir, that dagger's mine. It was made for me by a swordsmith in Lorca…'

'Huh! Fine story. And I suppose you were invited to take this jewel box too, eh?'

'Yes, that's right,' Pedro said with relief. At last someone would listen to him.

'The man living here…' Pedro tried to explain.

But the captain was not interested. He poured the contents of the box into a coloured scarf which he removed from around his neck. Jewels, gold rings, earrings, bracelets and as many as a hundred gold *doblas* cascaded from the box. He threw the box into the ruins. He cross-knotted his scarf and tucked his heavy booty into the top of his tunic.

'You two, Gázquez and Zaquera. Take him away.' The captain spat the words out dismissively.

'Yes,' Zak replied in an insolent tone, still aggrieved about having Pedro's beautiful dagger taken from him.

'Yes *sir*, you cur!' admonished the officer. He added, 'We'll hang this young rogue tomorrow with the other vermin we've caught.'

It started to rain. Just odd drops at first, then more continuously. Small posies of reddish-brown dust formed on the helmets of the soldiers as the dust from the earthquake returned to earth. The rain, as it started to fall, was bitterly cold. Forming in the upper atmosphere as ice, it sucked the warmth out of the air in melting. What arrived at the earth's surface was freezing cold rain.

Pedro made one last attempt to explain, drawing his warm *yallabiyya* tightly around his shoulders. 'But sir…'

This time the thick ash haft of Zak's spear caught him across the back. Pedro cried out in pain as he sprawled onto the pile of debris.

'One more word from you and we'll string you up here and now. Do you hear me?'

Zak leaned over Pedro, ready to thrust the spear into him, then thought better of it. He removed a pair of iron manacles dangling from his belt. The two thick iron hoops moved around in rings which were joined by a short bar. Zak unfastened the manacles and thrust Pedro's hands into them. As he did so, one caught against the edge of Sabyán's ruby ring on his little finger.

'What's this?' Zak said, pulling Pedro's hands close to his face to get a closer view in the near darkness.

'Something else we stole, eh? Robbing corpses now, is we?'

He cuffed Pedro viciously to the ground again. He leaned down and yanked the ring from his finger.

'I think I'll look after this for you, my little sweet, never know who might steal it from you. It'll be safer with me,' he sniggered. 'But you let on that I'm looking after it for you and I'll cut your tongue out. Do you understand?' he threatened.

'Now get going!' he shouted, prodding Pedro with his spear again.

Pedro managed to scoop up his shoulder bag and his few belongings as he got to his feet.

The rain increased to a steady drizzle, driving in from the mountains behind the city, as they walked to a house in the Musalla precinct.

'Another looter for you, Sergeant!' shouted Gaz over the patter of the rain as he pushed Pedro through the door.

'Jiménez!' the sergeant shouted to the third soldier. 'Put him in with the others. There's a handy roof beam across the street we can use in the morning… for all of them.'

Pedro was shoved into a stone-floored room. The door was slammed behind him. A key turned. A groan rang out as he tripped over some feet. He pitched against the stone wall opposite. The room was pitch black, musty, but at least dry.

'Who's there?' croaked two voices together.

Pedro didn't reply. He lay there silently, motionless, his wet *yallabiyya* pulled around him as well as he could with his manacled hands. After little sleep the night before during the cyclone, and labouring fruitlessly to help save the man from the ruins at al-Hamma that morning, after walking nine miles along the earthquake-ravaged Andarax valley to Almería, and finally, after the beatings at the hands of the soldiers, he was utterly physically and mentally exhausted, hungry and desperately thirsty. It mattered little to him if he were hanged on the morrow.

The rain continued outside unabated.

It was a truly nightmarish night, one which would be played out in his bleakest hours for years to come: lying on an icy stone floor with his hands manacled in front of him, wrapped in his wet *yallabiyya*, which at least had the virtue of a generous hood, hungry and thirsty, alongside at least two men whose tortured groans disturbed the deathly silence. With his limbs jerking uncontrollably from chronic tiredness, visions of the jeweller's face appeared through the rubble of the outside wall of his shop, under which the poor man must have died. As his face appeared, white and ghostly, whole houses spun through the air, careering towards the young prisoner, growing by the second, shrieking.

As soon as one image passed another loomed up as black clouds tore across a darkening sky. Trees got caught up in the maelstrom as the cacophony raged around him. A head rotated on a scrawny neck within the rubble, changing its horrible features as if being moulded by some invisible hand; first the jeweller, then Pedro's morose, straggly-bearded father, then horror-struck Marco, then thunderous Rodríguez. The head spun faster, the wailing grew louder until, sweating, Pedro shot bolt upright from the stone floor, bloodying his nose with the iron connecting bar of his manacles as he tried to put his hands over his ears. In due course the torrent of images and sounds diminished and, mercifully, through total exhaustion, he passed into slumber.

XI: The Darkness Deepens

All too soon he was roused as his foot was kicked.

'Here you are, boy. Here's some water and something to eat. You look a bit the worse for wear.'

It was the third soldier, Jiménez, who was in the house-cum-prison when they arrived the previous night in the drizzle. He spoke Castilian, but in an odd way.

Pedro stirred, stiff, cold and shivering. Dim grey light entered through a high square opening in the wall. He looked around. The room was small, only some eight feet square. Lying cramped against the opposite wall were two men dressed in blood-soaked rags. Their faces were haggard with two or three days of stubbly growth, and they had clearly been badly beaten. One had a closed, blackened eye; the other had a swollen jaw and bloody mouth from which several teeth had been knocked out. While Pedro was still too numbed by his nightmare to react to the sight of these other prisoners, he was startled when he looked to his left to find two bodies lying alongside him. They were two dead soldiers, one still wearing a steel breastplate which had been buckled inwards. Pedro surmised that both must have been killed in the earthquake. All of a sudden he remembered the six grim-faced Christian soldiers, the sergeant and captain who rode past him two days earlier on the way from Tabernas. He'd now encountered four of them. These two made up the six. But what were they doing in Almería, a Muslim city?

Jiménez lingered for a second or two by the side of Pedro, mouth open to speak, then thought better of it and left. He did not even bother with the two men opposite. It was as if they did not exist. What he brought Pedro were only some crusts of dried bread, some hard pieces of dried salted meat and a large jug of murky water, but it was what Pedro's body cried out for and he devoured and consumed them all within a minute.

An hour later the first soldier, Zak, burst into the cell in the house. Civility was not part of his make-up.

'You two, you fornicating scoundrels!' he shouted at the two prisoners lying against the wall opposite Pedro. 'On your feet. And you,' he said to Pedro. 'Don't think you're going to escape what's coming to you.'

He pushed them out of the cell and out into the street. The two men seemed resigned to whatever fate might befall them. The day was brightening and warming. The city was shrouded in a low, humid haze as steam rose from the waterlogged ruins. The three prisoners were pushed and prodded at the point of Zak's spear to the side of the building. The sergeant and the remaining three soldiers were there.

The young officer, Captain Ortíz, clearly had a specific agenda.

'You! Jiménez and Matute, collect the bodies of Ruíz and Ortega and take them to the open space over there. I'll go and mark out the graves for the poor fellows. Sergeant Luque, take Zaquera and Gázquez and these two scoundrels... and this young looter. You know what to do. One hundred of them for each. Understood?'

Pedro and the two fettered men were pushed towards a post conveniently left standing at a nearby ruin. He saw Zak lick his lips at the prospect of the treatment he was about to mete out. The wrist and leg irons were removed from the two men. The man with the blackened and closed eye was pushed forward first. His coat was removed and his shirt pulled from his back. His hands were strapped to the post above his head. Gaz tore a piece off the man's shirt, rolled it in a wad and stuffed it in the man's mouth.

'One hundred lashes,' instructed Sergeant Luque.

'One hundred and fifty, I says,' demanded the evil Zak. 'Fifty for looting, fifty for raping the women and her two young daughters and fifty more for strangling them afterwards. Not that I care one way or the other. Them was only Arabs anyway.'

'One hundred, I said,' retorted the sergeant. 'They're going to be hung for the murders afterwards. Now get on with it!'

Both Zaquera and Gázquez held cat-o'-nine-tails with their rough knotted cords. Being left-handed, Gázquez stood conveniently opposite his fellow flogger.

'We'll do twenty each in turn, right?' shouted Zak. 'I'll go first.'

With relish he struck the man with the greatest force he could summon. The lashes caught the man across the shoulders and he shuddered under the blow, letting out a muffled gasp. Weals appeared on his back. Further blows were inflicted, the brutish soldier making sure that no part of the man's back, from his neck to backside, was omitted. He leaned forward to ensure the tails of the whip lapped around to the far side of his body. By the time he finished his twenty lashes the poor man was crying in one continuous, gasping sob. His back was cut by bloody striations. Pedro turned aside. He could not watch any more. He buried his ears in his hands, trying to blot out the sound of the man's muffled cries. He was beyond fear at the thought of this punishment being exacted on him. Gaz took over from Zak, more through duty than relish. But he had seen what these men had done to the woman and her young girls. He saw no reason to show any mercy. By the time he had finished the man could barely stand and his back streamed with blood.

The sight of the blood was all the incentive Zak needed to savour his second bout of flogging. His arm was now loosened and he fell to his task with glee. After sixty lashes the man's back was just red pulp. Strips of flesh hung down exposing the muscle and sinew beneath. By now the man hung limply against the post hanging from his bound hands. He ceased to cry out, just shuddering silently as the fearsome blows struck his body. When it was over he was cut down from the bloodied post. He fell to the ground in a heap, rolling over, the dirt and grit of the road sticking to his bloodied flesh. Zak yanked him away roughly by the arms, kicking him in the groin for good measure.

'You next,' said Sergeant Luque. He had seen hundreds of men flogged in his time, and had received his fair share of the punishment as a young miscreant, but he could never get accustomed to this scale of brutality.

The second man had witnessed the flogging of his co-rapist and murderer. Resigned, he was led to the post, stripped and his hands tied. The flogging was no less severe, nor was the shredding of his back to bloody pulp. As before, Zaquera went first. It was a right he was not going to concede. As before the man was cut down semi-conscious and dragged away unceremoniously.

'Now you, my little lamb. Let's see what you're made of,' sneered Zak. Sweating and panting he combed the bloody cat-o'-nine-tails through his hand as if it were the softest wool. Bits of flesh squeezed from his hand and fell to the ground.

Utterly terrified, Pedro was hauled to the post. His shirt was pulled down to his waist. The sergeant looked at his white, unblemished back, saddened.

'I'll do this,' he instructed.

'Oh no you doesn't, Sarge! He's mine. I caught the young tyke, I claim the punishment!'

'Stand aside, you vermin! If I had my way it would be you strapped to this post, not this lad.'

Zak spat on the ground as sloped away, sulking. He turned around.

'You listen to me, you young whippersnapper. I'll get you. Just be warned. You won't escape me… *ever.*'

Relieved of the task, Gaz searched out a puddle to clean his blood-soaked scourge.

With only enough force to carry the cat-o'-nine-tails across his back, the sergeant imparted the first blow. Pedro cried out and tried to twist away from the knotted tails as they struck his back. By the tenth blow deep weals were appearing. Here and there small punctures appeared in his flesh where the knots had bitten in. By the fifteenth blow, his back was starting to cut up and blood started flowing down his back.

'Stop, that's enough!' shouted the captain as he appeared from around the side of the ruin, followed by Matute and Jiménez. They had obviously finished burying their two dead companions. The sergeant was visibly relieved.

'That's enough, Luque,' he repeated as he came alongside the sergeant. He added after a pause, 'Who was it who told me that this boy spoke Arabic…? That's curious. Maybe I'd better find out a bit more. But maybe we should leave it to the ministerings of the holy friar…?'

He stood musing for a minute. 'Yes, I think that's what we'll do. We must be on our way shortly, Sergeant. Take Gázquez and that bastard Zaquera and hang these two rogues here from the high beam over there.'

The officer cut the bonds holding Pedro's hands to the post and helped him down onto the ground. Jiménez soaked a cloth in water and cleaned his back gently. Once the blood was washed away the injuries did not seem too severe.

'You'll have some scars for the rest of your life, but the cuts and weals will soon heal up,' he said in his peculiar Castilian.

'What's your name?' asked Captain Ortíz.

'Pedro Togeiro,' he replied. He croaked the words out. He was still in a state of shock from his ordeal.

'Well, Togeiro. You were caught red-handed stealing the jewel box from that shop and you know what happens to looters these days. Because of your youth I was lenient. Be thankful that you're alive. Someone else can decide what to do with you.'

'But…' interjected Pedro.

'Be quiet, boy. We've heard quite enough of your protests. You were caught good and proper.' After a pause he added, removing Pedro's knife from inside his officer's tunic. 'And what were you doing with this fine dagger? You must be an accomplished thief to have an eye for such things.'

'That knife…'

The officer coloured with annoyance and cuffed him. 'I don't want to hear any more of your protests, do you hear me? Do you hear me?' he shouted a second time.

Sullenly, Pedro lowered his head and fell silent.

'What are you going to do with me?' he asked timidly after a pause without looking up.

'We'll be taking you with us.'

'Where to?'

'You'll find out soon enough. Be glad I saved you from that thrashing.'

But Pedro's ordeal had barely begun.

Passing through what remained of the principal gateway on the north side of the city, the party of seven horsemen reached Pechina late morning. Destruction was everywhere. The extensive orange groves, with trees laden with fruit and ready for picking, had been badly damaged by the gales two nights ago. Worse, the extensive network of irrigation channels, fed by the numerous springs arising in the valley, and which drew the original Yemeni settlers there in the eighth century, had been breached in several places by the earthquake and many of the orchards were flooded. Dozens of farmers were struggling to repair the earth banks of the irrigation channels so that they could get into their orchards and start harvesting the fruit.

In very sombre mood, their hats pulled down close over their eyes as they peered through the driving drizzle, the horsemen pressed on through the town without pausing. Riding very upright in his saddle, looking every part the officer, Captain Ortíz led, setting a good pace. Zaquera and Gázquez, slouched in their saddles, followed behind riding side by side. A short distance behind were Jiménez and Matute. Pedro followed, his manacled hands tied to the pommel of the high saddle. He was already in some discomfort, with his wrists cut by the tight iron hoops placed around them, and the chafing of the insides of his thighs. Moreover, his backside was sore, since it was the journey to Lorca in March when he was last in the saddle. Sergeant Luque made up the rear with the packhorse trotting alongside on a loose rein.

They turned off left along the right bank of the Andarax through the richly cultivated valley towards Gádor. Caves were cut into the sands and gravels of the river terraces above. Noisy, half-naked children squabbled outside those caves occupied by the poorest people, while piles of boxes, bundles of poles and miscellaneous junk showed those used as stores for farm implements or farm produce. Desolate khaki-coloured hills extended several miles to the north, rising slowly into dissected escarpments and then into the mountains proper.

Captain Ortíz pulled off the road below some trees which afforded some shelter from the rain. The others followed. They all dismounted, stretched their legs and rubbed their backsides.

'Time for a bite to eat, Sergeant,' Captain Ortíz announced in a loud voice, addressing everyone. The four soldiers delved into their saddle packs and retrieved some provisions, finding tree trunks or large stones to sit on.

'Hold on, young fellow, I'll give you a hand down,' said Sergeant Luque to Pedro. He untied his wrists from the saddle and helped him off his horse. 'You're a bit sore, eh?' he laughed. 'Not ridden a horse before?'

Pedro nodded his head sullenly.

'But not for some time, eh?'

Pedro nodded a second time.

'Well, you'll soon get used to it again… You'd better. We've got a very long way to go.'

He handed Pedro a lump of bread and dried ham. Despite his lack of appetite he was glad of it. With the sergeant and the captain keeping an eye on him from a short distance away, Pedro ambled to a spot to sit as far away as he could.

They were soon on their way again, but not before Zak and Gaz had sneaked over to where Pedro was sitting.

'Don't think that you're going to escape us, you squirming little toad,' said the unshaven Zak, his eyes glinting. 'We'll have you before long, and then you'll have something to be sore about. Eh, Gaz?'

'You bet your life!'

They both laughed lasciviously.

As the sun started to poke through the clouds and the drizzle stopped, they turned off the valley road, starting the gradual ascent to the pass running above the Nacimiento valley, which lay below them to their left. It was a long and strenuous ride through featureless hill country, and the horses were clearly getting fatigued. By early evening they reached the Gérgal road which ran westwards to Guadix and Granada beyond.

Jiménez dropped back to ride alongside Pedro. It was he who gave Pedro the food in the cell that morning, but had had second thoughts about speaking to him.

'Finding it tough?' he said. In fact, more as a statement than a question.

'What's your name, lad?' he continued.

'Pedro.'

'Pedro? Well, mine's Jiménez, Abel Jiménez. But people call me Jim. You can call me that too.'

Pedro nodded with a weak smile, unable to fathom out the unusual accent of the horseman alongside him.

'Where do you come from, Pedro? Come on, lad, I'm not going to eat you!'

Slowly Pedro thawed and explained in a low faltering voice where he was from and what he was doing in Almería the day of the earthquake.

'So you say that you didn't steal that jewel box from that shop then?' Jim asked when Pedro was done.

Pedro nodded.

'I thought not. You've got an honest face, I can see that.'

'Well, Pedro,' Jim continued. 'I don't know what the captain intends to do with you. Although he's a bit devious at times, he's not a bad man, not like that Zak there, or that Gaz, who isn't much better. So you could be worse off. Just think of it, Pedro, you could have been hung for looting like those murderers this morning or, from what you said, you might be aboard a ship by now with a brutal bo'sun and with no means of escape. So look on the bright side, and think yourself fortunate.'

'I suppose you might be right, Jim,' replied Pedro, cheering up a bit.

'That's the spirit, my boy. Keep your pecker up. I'll keep an eye on you, don't you worry. So will Mat. Although he doesn't say much because of his terrible stutter, he's a huge chap, as you can see, and immensely strong. He's not one to meddle with. But you must beware of those two up ahead. They are full of real mischief. The sergeant—' he nodded his head over his shoulder – 'the sergeant hates them.'

'Where are we going, Jim?' asked Pedro hopefully.

'I'd better not let on where we're heading, Pedro. But it's several days' hard riding away. That's all I'd better tell you.'

'Where do you come from, Jim? I can't place your accent.'

'A long way away, Pedro, that's for sure. I come from Galicia in the far north of the country. It's a poor part of Spain. I came south looking for work. I tell you,' he chuckled, 'I didn't expect to join the army of the King! But at least the pay's regular and there's plenty of food. I could be a lot worse off.'

Jiménez leaned forward in his saddle, patted Pedro on the shoulder in a friendly gesture and rode forward to rejoin Matute.

It was already getting dark as they topped a rise and reached the Gérgal road. Captain Ortíz fell back to ride alongside Sergeant Luque. Pedro, riding just ahead, picked up some of the conversation.

'What shall we do, Luque?' asked the officer. 'Shall we press on towards Abla or head back along the top road to Gérgal?'

'Gérgal's only a few miles back along the road. I think we're best to go there. The horses are pretty well spent.'

'What shall we do, sir?' continued the sergeant. 'Shall we commandeer a house for the night as we normally do?'

'I think not, Luque. We have to be careful on this journey, particularly between here and Guadix. We'll be all right once we reach the Christian kingdom to the north. That troublemaker, Mohammed Abu Abdalá, is busy strengthening the Muslim towns and villages between Baza and Guadix ready for another showdown with us, and we need to keep away from the towns as much as we can.'

'He's *El Zagal*, isn't he?' the sergeant asked.

'Yes, *El Zagal* – the Valiant One... Boabdil's uncle. He's a spirited fighter and the one true military leader the Moors have.'

'So what shall we do? Find a ruined house or farmhouse to bed down in?'

'Yes, that's best. We've got provisions to last us for days and with all this rain there'll be no problem in finding water for the horses. I'll ride on shortly and see if I can find somewhere suitable this side of Gérgal.'

'Have you heard what happened at Málaga, Captain? The last I heard it was being besieged by the King and Queen's forces.'

'Yes. My brother was there with the King and he told me what happened when I returned to our farm in September. My cousin, Ricardo, was also there, but he was killed in the fighting. It was a really nasty affair and one which I'm not proud of. On May 7th Fernando assembled an enormous army of 12,000 horsemen and 50,000 soldiers and quickly closed off the port at Málaga. He had sufficient forces to totally surround the city, plus massive artillery, and was looking for a quick end to the siege. But the Muslims refused to hand over the city to the King, and withstood the siege and the bombardment of the guns, which made absolute mincemeat of their city walls. They ate everything: all their food, their horses as well as dogs, cats and rats. But they couldn't hold out for ever. On August 18th the King and Queen entered the city. My brother said that over 20,000 people had died of starvation, and the 15,000 left were sold by the King for 56 million maravedís, either into slavery or prostitution. The city was ransacked and then razed to the ground. Tragic, really.'

'But it'll serve as a lesson to Boabdil, *El Zagal* and the rest of them, not to trifle with the King. He's merciless, as he's shown before.'

'But *El Zagal*'s no better, is he? Do you remember what happened in May '79 when he killed all the Christian inhabitants of Alhama and put their heads on spikes around the city wall?'

'I do, but you're forgetting what prompted it, my friend!' replied the captain. 'The Marquis of Cádiz had laid siege to Málaga and other towns around it on behalf of the King, and then laid siege to Ronda. After cutting off the water supply, the city capitulated and much bloodshed ensued.'

As the six horsemen turned towards Gérgal, Captain Ortíz rode on at a gallop to locate a suitable shelter for the night. In a short while they met up with him outside the village. In what little light remained, Pedro could see that the walled settlement lay on the flanks of a broad defile in the unbroken Sierra de los Filabres, which rose to nearly seven thousand feet behind Gérgal.

Ortíz pointed the way and the rest followed him to an abandoned dwelling a short distance from the village. Such ruins were commonplace. Close by were other farmhouses and cottages outside the town wall, and all occupied, judging by the smoke rising from their chimneys and the candlelight flickering through the tiny windows. Pedro was pushed into a small outhouse at the back. After placing his lantern on the ground, Sergeant Luque removed the manacles from the boy's wrists, rubbing some feeling back into them for him. He brought ample food and water and, with an understanding nod, he locked the door behind him. Although it was now pitch dark, Pedro had had sufficient time to make out the layout of the small shed. It was better than he could have expected. The roof was intact, the floor was dry, and straw was heaped in one corner. Judging by the sweet musty smell in the room it had recently housed horses. Better still, there was sufficient space to pace from one side to another so as to stretch his legs. He did this for a while before sitting in the straw to eat the food he'd been given. The sounds of voices in other parts of the abandoned house subsided and he was soon asleep. It seemed several hours later when he was awakened by a door creaking open, low whispered voices and the quiet scuffling of feet.

Early next morning he was aroused by Jiménez as it was starting to get light. There was a rumpus outside. They had to leave at once. Pedro was told to get his things together and the manacles were put on his wrists as he went outside into the biting, cold morning air. Coming down the road was a group of men looking menacing. One was middle-aged and the other three younger, presumably his sons. All were dressed in their nightclothes and brandishing an array of heavy and fearsome-looking farm implements. The father's voice was heard above the others.

'What are they saying, Luque?' cried out the officer across to the sergeant.

'I've no idea, sir.'

'You lad – you understand Arabic, don't you? What are they shouting?'

Pedro had been too busy looping his own bags over the saddle to take much notice. He peered over his horse into the greyness. The Arab farmers were now only thirty yards away but, in reality, posed little threat to a group of soldiers in body armour and with their swords ready drawn.

'I can only make out some of their words,' shouted Pedro across to the captain, 'but I think they're saying that two of your men violated his seventeen-year-old daughter last night. She was betrothed to be married, but now no man will have her.'

'Damn it!' exclaimed Ortiz. It's those bastards Zaquera and Gázquez! Mount up, we'd better be going. I'll sort you two out later,' he yelled across to the two men, who were grinning in mock innocence.

They rode off at a gallop for a mile or more until they were well clear of Gérgal. The officer drew the party to a stop and dismounted. He drew his sword and went up to Zak and Gaz who remained mounted. Luque joined him.

'Well,' he said, prodding Zaquera with his sword, 'what have you two got to say for yourselves?'

'It wasn't us, Guv, honest,' replied the evil Zak. 'We was tucked up in our blankets sound asleep all night, wasn't we Gaz.'

'Yeah, that's right, Zak. We was too tired after all that riding to be thinking about much else but resting our bones. Must have been one of those Arabs from Gérgal. Poking around under women's skirts is all they think about.'

Ortíz looked around at Jiménez and the mighty Matute.

'Did anyone hear anything last night?'

'No, nothing, Captain,' said Jiménez, 'not a thing.'

Big Matute shook his head in agreement. Ortíz looked at Pedro, but did not really expect any response. There was none.

'I don't believe either of you,' he said to Zak and Gaz, 'and I don't trust you any more than I can see you. If I find that you were the rapists, or if I catch you up to any more mischief, then be sure you'll get a flogging – or worse! Do you understand?'

'Yes,' they replied together in a surly manner.

'Yes, what?'

'Yes, *sir*,' they spat in unison.

The next two days' riding were largely uneventful. By midday on the first day they passed through Ocaña. They entered the narrow defile winding around an enormous isolated block of dark brown slate, then down to Abla with its square blockhouse at the entrance to the village. Everywhere there were signs of reconstruction and repair; holes in walls were being filled, battlements being reconstructed, iron-studded doors being rehung on gateways. Blacksmiths were busy in every village, making and sharpening swords, lances and maces. The more skilled craftsmen were refashioning body armour and breastplates, 'letting them out' for former soldiers anticipating a call to arms anytime. Where they could, Ortíz and his men skirted the villages, often detouring into the foothills to avoid them. Where this was not possible they rode quickly and silently through them. By the end of the first day they reached Fiñana, a large town built on two hills and famous for its fine, rich, ornamental brocades.

They set off again early the next morning. The mountain range of the Sierra Nevada on their left, rising higher as they travelled westwards, was snow-capped and made a beautiful sight in the morning light. For eight miles the road rose steeply through a defile before spilling out onto the high altiplano of Calahorra. The flat valley, three miles wide, extended as far as the eye could see, flanked by high unbroken mountains. Set back on the left on a conical hill was the castle of La Calahorra, later to be rebuilt by the Christians as a formidable fortress.

The city of Guadix, ten miles further on, was to be avoided at all costs. It was the principal base of *El Zagal*, who was styled 'king' of this part of the sultanate, which ran from Baza in the east and over the sierras to the Alpujarra to the south. The *alcázar*, in the centre of Guadix, housed *El Zagal*'s court, while it, the *mesquita*, later converted into the Christian cathedral, and the large town itself, were surrounded by an extensive wall and numerous gateways built by Abderran III in the eleventh century. Muslim poets wrote of its *ramblas*, gardens and the numerous water-mills on which its economy was based; its silk, saffron and base metals. The landscape around the city was spectacular, composed of a deep network of valleys, gorges and ravines, with sharp-walled mesas and buttes rising above and, standing like sentries, high isolated pillars of rock, sometimes capped with flat 'helmets' of stone. It was into this terrain that Captain Ortíz was obliged to lead his party late on the second day so as to avoid the city. Enough militia was present in Guadix to pose a real threat to his party.

The captain had studiously avoided Pedro during the first two days riding. But on the third day, remembering that it was Pedro's understanding of Arabic which had helped him out of a difficult situation at Gérgal, he pulled alongside the youngster and engaged him in conversation. Zak, riding ahead, reined back a little so as to try and catch what was said. Ortíz was beginning to suspect that he may have been too precipitate in arresting the boy without giving him a fair hearing.

'Pedro, isn't it?' he began.

'Yes, sir,' replied Pedro dutifully, now riding without manacles, but always under the watchful eye of the others.

'Where did you learn your Arabic?'

'Where I grew up, sir, in Vélez Blanco. It lies on the frontier between the two kingdoms but is basically a Muslim town. My friend there, Yazíd, is an Arab, so I picked up the language from him and his family.'

'So what were you doing in Almería on the day of the earthquake?' the captain continued.

Gradually thawing and realising that a full explanation might facilitate his release, Pedro narrated his story to the officer.

'So you claim that you didn't steal the treasure chest from the jeweller, but were retrieving it at his request?'

'Yes – as I've explained. The poor man was waiting for me outside in the road and must have become buried by the wall of his house after it collapsed in the aftershock. Don't you remember the huge pile of debris outside his shop? The man must have been buried beneath it.'

'Yes I do, come to think of it.'

'I was going to accompany him to my uncle, Simón, who lives, or lived, nearby and who, by an amazing chance, this jeweller knew. He even knew of me, my sister and my father, since my uncle had spoken to him about us. He was going to leave his treasure box with Uncle Simón for safe keeping while he saw to the burial of his wife and two sons.'

'Hmm,' said Ortíz, stroking his well-trimmed beard, 'I must say your story sounds very plausible.'

'It's the truth, I assure you, Captain,' said Pedro, looking the man in the eyes. 'What would I do with a heavy treasure box which I could barely lift?'

'Hmm,' the officer murmured again after some thought. 'I must admit I am inclined to believe you.'

He retrieved Pedro's dagger from his saddlebag.

'And you say that this beautiful knife was made especially for you by a swordsmith in Lorca?'

'Yes, that and a Toledo sword. Oh, you should see it, sir! It's magnificent, with a beautiful hilt made from alternate white and red brass rings. The swordsmith, David Levi, is a true craftsman trained by one of the best swordsmiths in Toledo, although the man practises now in Granada, working alongside the famous Julian del Rey.'

'Yes, I've heard of him. He's known as *El Moro*. You're right. He's said to be the finest swordsmith in all Spain.'

The horsemen worked their way to the north of Guadix through the tortuous, incised terrain. In the early evening they heard the distant sound of cannon, the blast of trumpets and loud cheering from the city.

'Sounds like *El Zagal* has just returned from one of his forays,' shouted the captain over his shoulder.

'It was lucky we weren't around,' replied the sergeant. 'We would have been easy meat for his band of cut-throats.'

After sheltering in some natural caves that night, they turned off the Granada road the next morning, taking the higher road to Íznalloz and Estepa. The landscape changed dramatically, opening up into vast, rolling country and immense, craggy limestone mountains. The hard, well-drained road afforded easy riding and they made good time. But the weather took a turn for the worse. Sleet drove into their faces, while snow covered the mountains to their left, drifting into the re-entrants cut into their sides. By the fourth day they had entered the no man's land between the two kingdoms where many settlements had been abandoned, although villages like Benelina and Alcala gave testament to their Muslim origin. Ortíz and his party could now afford to relax; they were well out of reach of Arab horsemen. But if he and his men could take comfort from this, not so Pedro. He was being taken further and further away from Almería into country totally foreign to him. Moreover, he had no idea where his final destination would be, or what would become of him. True, Captain Ortíz seemed well disposed towards him now, but he had not released him or told him where, or to whom, he was being taken. Pedro grew more anxious by the hour as they travelled north through the mountainous terrain.

The fifth and, although Pedro did not know it, their penultimate night, saw them within a short day's ride of Jaén, some seventy miles north of Granada. As on their first night at Gérgal, they were fortunate to find an abandoned farmhouse adjoined by a set of outbuildings. Pedro was allotted one of them, which stored some heavy wooden furniture. As was the custom now, his hands and legs were freed. But he slept fitfully. It was to be the most traumatic night of his life.

He was awakened by his door being unlocked and slowly opened. Boots scuffed quickly across the dusty floor, lit by a lantern swinging from someone's arm. He was grabbed roughly. Before he could cry out a rough hand was pressed hard against his mouth. He was lifted to his feet and dragged across the room.

'Thought you might escape us, did you, my sweet?' said the villainous Zak, pointing a knife into his face.

'Well, we've got a little lesson to teach you, haven't we, Gaz? We've been waiting for this for days, my little lamb. Oh yes. We've been very patient.'

A piece of cloth was roughly bound across his mouth to stop him crying out. Gaz grabbed his shoulders and pulled him bodily, face down, over the rough table in the centre of the room.

'Now we'll see what you're made of,' said Zak in a loud whisper, the lamp on the floor lighting his face in a ghoulish leer.

He yanked up Pedro's *camis*, which served as a nightshirt, Gaz pulling it up over his shoulders. At the same time Zak opened his trousers, which were bursting under the strain of lustful anticipation, and thrust his thick, veined shaft into Pedro's rectum. Pedro screamed in agony, his cries not wholly suppressed by the gag around his mouth.

'You enjoying this, my little friend?' cried Zak, as he thrust and thrust deep into Pedro's body.

Pedro, bleeding profusely, twisted and squirmed, but it only exacerbated the terrible stabs of pain while, at the same time, enhancing the pleasure of the evil man who still held Pedro's hips, pulling his body onto him in rhythmic jerks.

'Hold him tight, Gaz,' he said. 'Your turn will come in a minute.'

Captain Ortíz burst into the room, holding aloft a lamp, followed by Sergeant Luque, also with a light. Jiménez and Matute, both tucking their shirts into their trousers followed a couple of paces behind.

Zaquera was pulled from Pedro, a mixture of semen and blood oozing from the latter's behind. He slumped whimpering to the floor. Zak was grabbed by Matute and held in a rock-like grip, while the sergeant held a sword to the chest of Gázquez. Jiménez helped lift Pedro to his feet and took him over to a corner of the room.

'You evil bastards!' Ortíz said to Zak, looking across the table to Gaz. 'I should have guessed that you'd have your eyes on this boy here, ever since your rape of the farmer's daughter. I shouldn't have listened to your pleas of innocence but dealt with you there and then.' He paused. 'Well, now, I'm going to put pay to your lustful antics once and for all. You'll never want to dally with women or boys again. And you, Gázquez. You're in this too. If we hadn't come when we did you'd have had your way with this boy too.'

'No, I was only…!' he protested.

His pleas were cut short by Zak.

'What is you going to do?' screamed Zaquera in terror.

'You'll find out soon enough,' replied the captain, extracting a knife from his pocket.

'Matute, tie Gázquez's arms onto that iron ring on the wall. We'll deal with him later. Sergeant, Jiménez – tie this man's hands to the legs of this table.'

'What is you going to do?' screamed Zak again with rising terror.

The captain did not answer immediately. He found a flat stone on the floor, spat on it and honed the edge of his knife until it was like a razor.

'So,' he said eventually, 'you want to behave like a horny ram…? Well, I'll treat you like a horny ram, just as I used to do when I helped the shepherds on our farm when I was a boy.'

'No, no, you can't,' moaned Zak. 'Not that, sir! Give me a flogging. But not that.'

Equally aghast at what the captain was intending to do, Luque and Jiménez were instructed to hold the man's legs down firmly.

'I almost forgot,' said the captain. 'Matute, unravel a few strands of that sacking over there, then come over here and hold this man's chest down.'

With Zak whimpering like a puppy, not capable of squirming around even if he wanted to, Captain Ortíz cut the still-open trousers away from Zak's legs.

'Hold his cock up nice and straight, Matute,' he ordered.

'Oh no! Please not that,' cried out the terrified Zak, convinced that his manhood was going to be removed in one stroke.

Ortíz had other ideas. With one swift cut he sliced open Zak's scrotum, then used the flat of his blade to pull out his two testicles attached to their white cords. He took the short lengths of string from the sacking from Matute and quickly tied off each testicle. Then, with a snip, each was removed. The pain endured by Zaquera was indescribable. Sweat poured from his forehead as he squirmed with agony in the vice-like grip of the powerful Matute.

Ortíz waved the bloody, nut-like objects in front of Zak's face.

'Be thankful I didn't take off your cock too, you fornicating scoundrel,' he said with his face poised directly over the stricken man. 'But this will stop your pranks.'

'Jiménez, release that other rogue, Gázquez. Let's…'

'No, no, not me!' cried out Gaz in fear, 'I didn't do nothing. It was that Zak. He made me—'

'Be quiet! I'll decide what to do with you later. Come over here. You can sew up your comrade. Here's a few strands of thread from the sacking and a needle. If you do it well he should live. If not… well, who cares? It's up to you.'

Zak was holding the open and bleeding wound of his scrotum in his hands as he writhed and twisted on the floor.

Pedro witnessed all this with the same horror he had witnessed the disaster at the furnace at Bédar eight months before. Using his *camis* he cleaned himself up as best he could. The stabs of pain which shot through him gradually subsided until he was left with a dull, numbing ache.

'Are you all right, lad?' asked the captain, watching with undisguised amusement the attempts of Gázquez to perform minor surgery on Zak with his left hand while on his hands and knees and in the shadowy light of the lantern.

'Yes, I'm all right,' answered Pedro, still sobbing.

'It's my fault,' admitted Ortíz. 'I should have put you in with Jiménez and Matute. You would've been safe with them. I should've foreseen what those bastards were going to do. I'm sorry, Pedro.'

The captain beckoned Pedro and the other three men to follow him out of the outhouse. 'We'll lock them both inside,' he said. 'Gázquez can finish what he's doing. I'll decide what to do with him in the morning.'

It came as an enormous relief to Gázquez when early the next morning he was sentenced by Captain Ortíz to fifty lashes. Cooped up during the night with the now not-so-brave Zak, who moaned and rolled around the floor incessantly, all he could think of was the threat of suffering the same fate as his companion. He lay rigid with fear all night long, terrified of being castrated and terrified of the pain which would be inflicted in the process. He nearly wept with joy when Sergeant Luque told him of the punishment and hardly made a whimper when the flogging was inflicted. In truth it was justice; since, as Matute realised, Gaz would not have assaulted Pedro on his own accord.

With the punishment completed, the two villains were told to pack their things and disappear.

'If I so much as catch sight of either of you again, as sure as God is my judge, I will have you hanged,' were Ortíz' final words to them.

Despite the pain and discomfort both of them were in, with much grunting and grimacing, they mounted their horses and rode off into the gloom of the morning.

Still unaware of his final destination, it came as a great surprise to Pedro when, four hours later, the group of riders reached the top of yet another high pass. The city of Jaén appeared in the distance. No words were needed. Pedro pointed to the city three miles away situated on a mountain side to his left and looked around at Jiménez. He guessed the unspoken question from the youngster ahead of him and nodded his head.

The former Muslim city of Jaén had been in Christian hands for some two hundred years but bore all the signs of its Moorish ancestry. An *alcazaba* crowned the city. Poised on a long, high ridge, it dominated the settlement situated on the hillside below. The recently completed Christian cathedral with twin high bell towers dominated the lower slopes.

The final hour's riding for Pedro shot past rapidly as he anticipated excitedly their arrival in Jaén and his release from captivity. Matute and Jiménez showed equal excitement at the thought of returning home after the long and tiring journey to Almería through the Muslim kingdom. Even now it was not clear to them what the purpose of the journey had been or what it accomplished. Pedro was not too downhearted when, as they passed through the principal gate at the bottom of the city, the captain put the manacles back on his wrists.

'Just a precaution, young man,' were his reassuring words. 'Until I can hand you over to my commanding officer.'

'What commanding officer? Why should you want to do that?' asked Pedro with sudden anxiety.

'Don't you worry, my boy,' was the reassuring reply. 'You can explain your story to him and I'm sure everything will then be all right.'

Nothing more was said as they rode through the largely empty streets of Jaén and up to a guardhouse in the city centre. Pedro was led inside. Jiménez, Matute and Sergeant Luque were keen to report in so that they could take their leave and make their way home. All three shook hands with the manacled boy and bade him farewell. They could not have foreseen Pedro's fate. While Ortíz spoke to his commanding officer, a guard pushed Pedro down a dark corridor and thrust him into a small cell, clanging the iron door behind him and locking it with a key. Pedro never saw Captain Ortíz again.

There he stayed with no food or drink until the next morning when, without a word, he was pushed out of the guardhouse into the street and pulled along tethered to a horseman he had not seen before. More than once he nearly lost his footing on the wet slippery cobblestones. It was as well he did not, since there was little doubt that he would have been dragged face down over the stones.

After some twenty minutes they reached a house which was built into a hillside. The horseman knocked on the thick studded door of the building. The door was answered by a tall, hatchet-faced man dressed in black monk's garb. Pedro's belongings and a large packet were handed to him, and the youngster was beckoned inside. No words were spoken.

As he passed through the door, Pedro noticed the insignia carved on a panel by the doorway. It was a cross made of the branches of a bush. Although such a badge had been worn by Captain Ortíz on the tunic, it had not really registered with Pedro. Now he knew where he had seen it before. It was in Lorca, several months before, when he, his father and uncle had seen Jews being bundled into a large house bearing the same insignia.

He realised that he was now in the hands of the feared Spanish Inquisition, and had been conducted to Jaén by soldiers in its service. Flogged, sodomised, his ruby ring stolen and his dagger confiscated, his world continued to crumble around him.

XII: Inquisition

November 1487

The hatchet-faced monk in black closed the heavy door of the building behind him and passed Pedro over to a short, corpulent and ruddy-faced man, from whose leather belt clanked an iron ring bearing a set of heavy keys. The monk said not a word.

'Follow me!' instructed the jailer.

'Where are you taking me? What am I doing here?' cried Pedro, scared out of his wits.

'I don't know why you're here any more than you do, sonny,' replied the jailer as he started down a corridor. 'But I can tell you where I'm taking you, and that's to a cell where you will be out of harm's way. Just follow me! You'll find out soon enough why you're here.'

Pedro knew little to nothing about the machinations of the Spanish Inquisition, but he had experienced enough imprisonment in the last week or so to fear the worst.

Holding a lantern above his head, the jailer led the terrified youngster down some stone steps which gave way to others cut into bare rock. At the bottom of the long flight of steps, Pedro was shown into a cell and the door clanked behind him. Pedro stood on tiptoe to peer through the iron grating in the door at the dark figure disappearing back up the steps lit by a small and receding pool of dim, yellow light. The sound of his iron-studded boots on stone and the jangle of his keys finally abated. Pedro had had no time to look around the cell before the jailer closed the door, but as his eyes grew accustomed to the darkness, he started to make out the outlines of the cell, which was lit by a foot-wide opening in one wall bisected by a single vertical iron bar.

Pedro stayed alone in that cell through the four cold, cheerless months of winter. He soon found that the window was cut through rock a few feet thick so that, although light entered the cell, he could see nothing of the outside world. The back wall and the window wall were solid rock, wet in parts where seepages occurred, while the door wall and the other side wall were made of blocks of cemented stone. Four paces took him across the cell one way and three the other. He soon found that he was not totally alone. Black rats ran along the back wall into its deep recesses, while loathsome red-brown cockroaches scurried in and out of the cracks and crevices of the rock and stones. Bats hung in the window aperture during the day, flying out at night to forage for food. The bony remains of mice and other small prey littered the stone window sill. Luckily the bats never entered Pedro's cell.

Twice a week, on Sundays and Thursdays, Pedro was provided with provisions, when the jailer asked him what he wanted. Whatever deprivations were imposed by the Inquisition, food was not one of them. Each day at midday, as regular as clockwork, a plate of hot, meaty food was put on the floor of his cell through a small, hinged opening in the door, and to this he added some of his twice-weekly provisions. How he eked out his rations during the week was up to him, but he soon got into a routine, ensuring that he kept sufficient food to last. Twice a week on these same days, the tall monk in black, referred to by the jailer as 'Number Two', searched his cell, presumably looking for prohibited items, which included eating utensils. A wooden pail stood in the corner of the cell, and once a day Pedro was let out of his cell to empty its contents. No contact was permitted with any other prisoner, if indeed there were any others there.

The deprivation was absolute. No light was permitted throughout the fifteen hours of darkness during the long winter days; neither was any heating provided in the freezing cell, high as it was in the *Al-Andalus* mountains. Books were totally forbidden as was any writing material. No personal or written contact was permitted with any member of one's family or with friends or representatives, all of whom were kept totally unaware as to the arrest and incarceration of their loved one by the Inquisition. The isolation was total and the boredom unbearable. The destruction of the human spirit by these means was decreed at the highest echelons of the organisation and set down in the very first Code of the Inquisition written by the Dominican friar, Tomás de Torquemada, the first Inquisitor General of Castile. He was appointed by Los Reyes Católicos themselves four years earlier after the Spanish Inquisition was established by them in November 1478 under the authority of a papal bull. If this isolation did not break the spirit of the unfortunate detainees directly, it softened them up for the interrogations which followed.

Pedro realised that he had to take regular exercise if his body were not to deteriorate. Each day he paced a thousand times back and forth between the side walls of his cell and a similar number between the door and the back wall. He stretched and bent his head, shoulders and limbs, trying to keep his arms strong in the way which Marco, his former sword master, had taught him. To prevent his brain atrophying, he practised remembering the exact location and contents of the medicines which his father had stored on the shelves in his dispensary. He tried to remember the names of the herbs which his uncle Joshua collected from the mountains around María, and exactly where they were found. He made up sentences to himself and tried to translate them into Arabic, and he tried to remember the details of the journey to Lorca with his father and uncle; in fact, anything to keep from going insane. But remembering the minutiae of the hours spent some nine months earlier with David Levi in his hot, iron-smelling forge while he made Pedro's sword brought him the most-needed comfort.

It was almost into the fourth month of his isolation, indeed a week after his fourteenth birthday on February 26th, that Pedro made contact with a prisoner in an adjacent cell. Over the years the scurrying of rats had widened a floor-level fissure in the rock wall which passed into the adjacent cell behind the stone wall against which it abutted. It was via this crack that a voice beckoned him. By each crouching in the corner of their respective cells, Pedro and his neighbour could carry on a conversation in low voices.

'My name's Alfonso de Castro. What's yours?' the voice said.

'Pedro Togeiro,' Pedro replied eagerly, keen not to lose contact with the man.

'What are you doing here, Pedro?' asked Alfonso.

'I don't know. I simply don't know,' replied Pedro, starting to sob with self-pity. 'I've been here over three months now and I still don't know why I'm here.'

'Are you a Jew, Pedro?' the man asked.

Pedro was taken aback. With all the time he had had to contemplate what had caused him to be imprisoned by the Inquisition, it had not entered his mind that his Jewishness – or half-Jewishness – was a factor.

'No,' he answered, not sure what to say. 'Well, yes, I suppose so. At least half-Jewish. But that can't be the reason why I'm here,' he added, somewhat uncertainly.

So by this means, Pedro and his neighbour exchanged their stories as to what brought them to their present plight. What Pedro learnt from Alfonso de Castro made him wish that he had never heard of what had befallen Alfonso, or what he was able to tell Pedro about the ways of the Inquisition.

'I was a cleric in the church of San Pablo in Úbeda which is an easy day's ride from here,' he explained. 'It's a beautiful town. I was responsible for the historical records of the church and preparing an inventory of the extensive archives there. It was a modest living yet rewarding.'

'So what happened to bring you here?' asked Pedro.

'My brother was a noted scholar. Some years older than me, he was under the patronage of the Marquis de Jabalquinto in Baeza, the town nearby. He had had a long interest in the heavens and had translated some of the words of the twelfth- and thirteenth-century Arab scientists, notably Ibn al-Jatib.'

'Yes!' interjected Pedro excitedly. 'He was a famous poet too. The mullah told me of him.'

'The mullah?'

'Yes, yes. When I stayed with him in Oria last autumn. But please go on, Alfonso. I'm sorry to interrupt you.'

'As I was saying, my brother was interested in the writings of these learned Arabs. He had long observed the movement of the planets around the earth and was familiar with the brightening and dimming of Venus as it moved towards the sun and the peculiar loops which Mars, Jupiter and Saturn make in the sky as they travel around the earth. Then, one summer evening, he was riding around the outside of a large, circular olive grove. Along the top of a rise a mile or two away, moving in the same direction, a farmer was slowly ploughing a field behind some oxen, while on a far mountain top a tower stood out against the bright sky. My brother noticed that as he rode up the left side of the field, the distant farmer traversed to the right in relation to the distant tower. But as my brother rounded the top of the field the farmer's position seemed to move left against the tower, yet returned to being right once my brother headed back down the other side of the olive grove. This puzzled him for days until he realised that it was exactly how Mars – and to lesser extents Jupiter and Saturn – appear to move each year in the southern night sky. In a flash of inspiration he deduced that the earth must move in a smaller circle than Mars and that could only mean that both were moving around another object, obviously the sun.

With great excitement he turned to the works of Ibn al-Jatib, and saw that all this was known hundreds of years ago. He realised that all the inexplicable things in the night sky could be explained by the sun being at the centre of the universe and not the earth. He wrote a hasty letter to scholars at Cracow University in Poland with whom he was corresponding, since already detailed observations of the motion of the planets were being made there. Unfortunately, my brother's letter was intercepted and passed to the archbishop. That night, soldiers of the Inquisition broke into his house and arrested him. He was thrown into prison, accused of heresy. That was four years ago, soon after the Inquisition really got underway in this part of Spain. For three years he was detained in a cell in total darkness with no contact permitted with the outside world – just like us here. Indeed, it was only much later that I knew of his imprisonment. My brother was examined by the Inquisitor in Baeza and under the pain of the rack...'

'The rack?'

'Yes, I'll come back to that,' said Alfonso.

'On the pain of the rack he confessed his heresy. All his belongings at the Palace were confiscated, as well as those of our father, who was a wealthy man living nearby. Our father was arrested as a conspirator but took poison soon after his imprisonment. He was in his late seventies and could not have survived the hardship. He took his own life because he was unable to stand the shame of what had befallen his sons.'

'Sons?' interjected Pedro.

'Yes, I was arrested too. My house and all my possessions were also confiscated. Nothing was spared.'

'But why? Why you?'

'Because the Inquisition is relentless. They assume every member of a heretic's family must also be of the same view, as must his close friends and associates. So all are arrested and treated as equally guilty as the prime suspect.'

'But that's terrible!' exclaimed Pedro.

'Yes, Pedro, it is. But the reality is that the Inquisition is only really concerned with confiscating your property and private wealth. Now by law, the belongings of heretics pass into its hands, so the wider it spreads the net the more wealth it acquires.'

'So what happened to your brother?' asked Pedro.

'He died in agony on the rack.'

'And you?' asked Pedro, fearful of hearing the answer.

'I spent two years in a rat-infested cell at Llerena, much like this. No warmth, no light, absolutely no contact with the outside world. As far as I know, none of my father's wider family has any inkling of what happened to him, my brother or me. This is how the Inquisition operates.'

'Why were you brought to Jaén?'

'To be examined by the Inquisitor here.'

Alfonso's voice started to break up as he began to narrate the ordeal which he had been through.

'Inquisitor Diego Rodríguez Lucero here is a young Dominican friar but he has little to learn from his peers about how to extract confessions in the most terrible way.'

'Is he the tall man in black who inspects my cell twice a week?' asked Pedro.

'No that's his assistant, that's why he's called Number Two. Lucero is a much smaller man with a pockmarked face. He's already become notorious for his cruelty, and I gather hankers after the more prestigious position at Córdoba. Judging by results I have no doubt he'll fulfil his ambition.'

It was the next day before Alfonso could speak of what he had been through. In a faltering voice with long pauses he told Pedro what had happened to him.

'I was not allowed any food or drink for more than a day. The following night I was led into the chamber of confession, which is nothing more than a torture chamber. I have heard many stories of such places but nothing prepared me for the horror I found there. There was no light in it except smoking torches on each wall, which threw eerie shadows everywhere and added to the terror. The rough stone walls were black with soot, grease and dirt. Along one wall was the rack…'

Alfonso's voice started to break up again. But he would not listen to Pedro's pleas to stop.

'It is the most evil contraption ever devised by Man. Just the sight of it is enough to extract a confession from the unfortunate victim. Made of heavy oak timbers, iron gears and levers, the whole thing is strewn with thick leather belts, leather thongs and iron rings to strap the prisoner to and stretch him. On the other side of the room was a long wooden plank, hinged along one end and again, festooned with leather straps. I was soon to find out what it was for. In the centre of the room, hanging from the ceiling was a pulley with a rope through it attached to a winding drum. A hook dangled from the free end of the rope.'

'I was stripped naked and led to the long hinged plank, to which I was strapped with leather belts around by body, arms and legs. My head was placed in a depression in the headrest and a strap fixed around my forehead.'

Alfonso's voice was now barely audible, but again he dismissed Pedro's pleas to desist.

'The tall friar, Number Two, spoke gently to me, saying how all my suffering would be over if I were to confess my sins. But I now realise that this was just a ruse to soften me up. Thin cords were tied around my arms, legs and ankles. The cords were slowly tightened in tourniquets with rods until the cords cut through the skin and deep into my flesh. I cried out in pain but it made no difference. Then the plank to which I was fixed was raised until my feet were higher than my head. An iron point levered my mouth open, then a funnel was pushed into my throat and a jug of water poured down it. I coughed and sputtered, unable to breathe, unable to turn my head, unable to eject the water. Jar after jar of water was poured down the funnel until I could breathe no more and knew that I was drowning as surely as if I were thrown into the sea. Within a whisker of dying, I was released from my bonds and turned over. You cannot believe how much water poured out of my body. This was clearly only the start of what they had in store for me…

'I was dragged into a chair and bound to it. There the interrogation started. Lucero posed the standard questions of the Spanish Inquisition – Do you believe in the resurrection of the flesh? And so on. These I quickly confessed to, since I have no quarrel with the basic tenets of the Catholic Church. But then he waved a piece of paper in front of me and asked if I confessed to its contents.

'"What is it?" I croaked, doubled up in the chair and still coughing up the contents of my stomach.

'"*Do you confess*?" he shouted, striking me across the face.

'"To what?" I groaned. "What is that piece of paper?"

'"This is your brother's letter to Cracow proclaiming that the sun and not the earth is the centre of the universe – a heresy against the teachings of the Holy Church."

'"I have no knowledge of my brother's letter. I rarely saw him and he never mentioned writing to Cracow before he disappeared."

'"You lie, you swine!" Lucero screamed. "Repeat the treatment."

'I pleaded with him that I knew nothing of my brother's beliefs, but thrice more I was subjected to the water treatment, twice refuting knowledge of my brother's beliefs. How could I confess to something I knew nothing about? Finally, after the third dose of treatment, when an even greater volume of water was poured into me, I mercifully passed out, knowing that I was at last dying at their hands. The next thing I knew I was back in this cell. That was five days ago. I have no idea how long I'll stay here, or what more they'll do to me. I would rather die here and now than face any more at the hands of Lucero.'

Alfonso's voice trailed away until there was silence. The frightful ordeal he had gone through and which he had narrated to Pedro clearly exhausted him, but the youngster hoped that in some way it eased his torment and allowed him to rest. However, it hardly assuaged Pedro's nervousness about how long he would be kept in the cell, or what punishment would befall him.

Late the next day Pedro called to Alfonso through the crack in the corner of the wall.

'Are you there, Alfonso? Are you all right?'

'Yes, I'm all right, Pedro. My voice finally gave up on me and I was totally exhausted. I'm all right now... I know for sure, Pedro,' he continued, 'that if I'm placed on the rack I'll confess to anything they ask and suffer whatever punishment they impose. I have no fight left in me.'

'I'm fearful of asking,' said Pedro, 'but what is the rack? What does it do?'

'Pedro,' replied Alfonso in a low voice, 'it's the vilest and most cruel torture ever devised. The inquisitors say that they're men of God, but they are truly agents of the devil himself. I can't think that you'll want to hear what I'll tell you about the rack, but I pray that you'll not come to any harm here, even at the hands of the likes of Lucero.'

'How old did you say you are, Pedro?' he asked.

'I'm just fourteen,' replied Pedro. 'In fact my birthday was only two weeks ago. Why do you ask?'

'Oh, nothing,' replied Alfonso, wishing he had not raised the matter.

'No, tell me,' insisted Pedro.

'I'd best not to have raised the matter. It's just that a new edict from Rome has lowered the age at which the Spanish Inquisition can carry out examinations for heresy to fourteen years of age. But please don't be concerned. I'm sure you'll be released very soon now.'

'So what about the rack?' Pedro asked.

'If you insist I'll tell you.'

'It takes three forms. In the *vuelta de trampa* the knees are placed between the rungs of the rack, one rung of which is removed, and over a bar with a sharp cutting edge. Cords are tied tightly around the ankles and toes. The cords are attached to a windlass which is turned to stretch the victim's legs and toes. The *mancuerda* follows. With the victim still stretched in this position, other cords are passed around his arms and the torturer places his feet against the rack and pulls the cords taut with all his strength. The cords cut deep into the victim's flesh, right down to the bone. This is repeated several times to different parts of his arms and the victim, not able to cope with the terrible pain being inflicted, generally faints. After this gentle warm-up, the victims – women as well as men – are subjected to the full rigour of the *potro* or rack. The victim is released from the *trampa* and *mancuerda* and laid over the eleven rungs of the rack with his head fixed in a depression in the end piece with a strap. They pass three cords around the arms, two around each thigh and one around each calf. These twelve cords are passed through rings fixed to the sides and ends of the rack, or to rings in the side walls, and then attached to the *garrotte maestro*, the windlass, which is turned very slowly with a long spar. This device allows any or all of the cords to be tightened at any one time. After each half-turn the stress is relaxed to accentuate the agony. Each half-turn stretches the limbs of the victim by some three inches, and six or seven such half-turns is not uncommon. But, in fact, there is no limit to the amount of torture inflicted. Inevitably the victim's limbs are dislocated and his joints and bones are broken. Most are crippled for life.' He paused.

'Have you ever heard of anything so terrible in all your life, Pedro?'

'No, it's impossible to comprehend,' replied Pedro.

Neither spoke for a long while. Then Pedro asked: 'What do you think will become of you, Alfonso – or for that matter, me?'

'I know not. Two hundred lashes? Eight or ten years in the galleys? Banishment? Or, God forbid, the *auto-de-fé*.'

'What's that?'

'The public trial and judgement of the condemned, often in front of thousands of people in the city square. The audience sit in specially erected tiered seats and galleries; not infrequently with the King and his court present. Invariably it's followed by the victims being burnt at the stake.'

Pedro heard no more from his friend in the adjacent cell. The next day he called to him but there was silence. The cell was empty. Alfonso had been taken away, maybe to be interrogated on the rack. Pedro never heard of him again or what became of him.

For the next week he returned to normal solitude, only broken by the midday provision of food and the emptying of his pail. Pedro hoped and prayed that his friend was correct in that he would be eventually released without any physical punishment. But the thought of the rack, the water treatment or being hung by the wrists from the iron ring, put the fear of God into him. What worried him most of all was the notion that the inquisitors were as much concerned to confiscate one's wealth and that of one's family as to extract a confession. Pedro determined there and then that whatever they did to him he must try and shield his father, sister and uncles from the clutches of the Inquisition.

Then one day no plate of hot food was pushed through the bottom opening in his door; nor was he let out of his cell. For the rest of the day he sat on his mattress, numb and shaking with apprehension as to its significance. His very worst fears were realised the following morning when the cell door was opened and the assistant inquisitor, Number Two, beckoned him to follow him up the flight of stone steps. Pedro's heart began to thump with fear. The door into the interrogation chamber was opened and he was pushed into the poorly lit room. It was just as Alfonso had described it. Two men stood there waiting for him dressed in black habits. One he recognised from the deep pockmarks on his face as the young and ambitious inquisitor at Jaén, Diego Rodríguez Lucero. But if his eyes were full of malice and ill intent, they were nothing to those of the second, taller man, with his sallow, gaunt appearance.

He must have been approaching seventy years of age. He had a bearing of one who demands and always gets his way, but worst of all he had cold, sunken, merciless eyes. His black habit with the cowl pulled back, was of the finest quality wool and around his neck on a gold chain hung a gold *Cruz Verde*, the insignia of the Spanish Inquisition. On his hands were several rings set with glistening stones. Pedro soon found out who the man was.

'I'll carry out this examination, Brother Rodríguez,' he said authoritatively.

'Yes, yes of course, Father Tomás,' conceded the younger man.

Pedro knew then and there that he was in the hands of the Inquisitor General of Castile himself, Tomás de Torquemada, who was feared throughout the whole land for his mercilessness.

'Sit down,' he instructed.

Terrified as to what was in store for him, Pedro sat down on the wooden stool opposite the two friars, who took their places behind a table. As he did so he noticed a brawny figure in the corner dressed all in black and wearing a mask over his eyes and upper face.

'What is your name,' he was asked without any ceremony.

'P – P – Pedro T – T – Toldera,' he replied falteringly.

'Toldera? That's not the name Ortíz reported you as having!'

'It's my name. Pedro Toldera. He must have misheard me.'

'We'll come back to that. Where do you come from?'

'From Almería, I—'

'Almería? You told him you come from Vélez Blanco, near the border of the kingdom.'

'No, I come from Almería. I told Captain Ortíz that I'd travelled from Vélez Blanco, but my home is in Almería.'

'Who is your father?'

'My father is dead. He died in the earthquake, together with my sister…'

Pedro was annoyed with himself. He realised that he need not have mentioned his sister. He went on, 'The earthquake was terrible. It totally destroyed our house and its furniture and contents. Over two-thirds of the houses in Almería were destroyed in the earthquake. It was frightening. There were—'

'Enough. Why were you not killed too?'

'I explained. I was returning from Vélez Blanco and arrived in the city the afternoon of the earthquake.'

'What were you doing in Vélez Blanco, which is a Muslim town, and what were you doing stealing a treasure chest from a jeweller's on the afternoon of the earthquake?'

'I didn't steal the treasure chest. I was on my way to see my uncle in another part of the city to see if he was still alive. The jeweller pleaded with me to retrieve his treasure chest, since his wife lay dead inside the house.' Pedro explained about the second tremor and his arrest by Captain Ortíz and his men.

'What became of the treasure chest?' asked the elder inquisitor.

'Captain Ortíz took it. He poured its contents, the jewels and the hundred or so gold *doblas* into his red silk scarf and tucked it in his tunic.'

'Did he now!' exclaimed the Inquisitor General, looking aside at Lucero. 'We must speak to Ortíz, mustn't we, Brother Rodríguez?'

'Indeed we must, Father Tomás.'

'What does your father do?'

Pedro wasn't to be caught out.

'I told you, he died in the earthquake. He was just a poor baker. We had a small house above the bakery and my father sold bread and pastries from there and also in the *zoco*, the street market, two days a week.'

'And your mother?'

'My mother died many years ago. I was brought up by my father, he…'

'Enough, you stupid boy! Do you think we're going to listen to any more of your cock and bull stories? Do you take us for fools?'

Tomás de Torquemada got up from his chair and leant forward over the table, glaring into Pedro's face.

'You're a Jew and the son of a rich Jew living in Vélez Blanco. And your name's not Toldera but Togeiro. Confess it!' he demanded.

'I'm not a Jew,' insisted Pedro under the withering gaze.

'We'll soon see about that,' the Inquisitor leered. 'Strip him!'

The muscular interrogator in the corner pulled Pedro from his chair and stripped him naked, standing him on the chair opposite the two friars.

'Now we'll see,' said the hook-nosed man.

Torquemada took a lantern and held it in front of Pedro's groin. He took hold of his testicles roughly.

'But you're not circumcised!' he said with a start. 'A Jew who's not circumcised?'

'I told you I'm not a Jew,' replied Pedro, squirming on the chair trying to conceal his embarrassment at the attention of the two men. How glad he was now that his mother had insisted that he was not mutilated by the mohel's blade soon after he was born.

Torquemada looked confused. 'Something's being concealed from us, Brother Rodríguez. I think we must speed things up a bit, don't you?' he said. He wrung his hands in anticipation.

'Interrogator, tie his hands behind him. We'll get to the truth. *El Strappato*, if you please.'

The hooded man pulled Pedro off the chair, forced him to the ground on his face and bound his wrists tightly behind him with several windings of cord.

Torquemada nodded to him as if to say, '*Go ahead! You know what to do.*'

The interrogator dragged Pedro over to the centre of the room to beneath the suspended pulley and the rope hanging from it. He placed the hook at the end of the rope under the bindings around his wrists and yanked Pedro to his feet. The torturer went over to the drum and cranked the handle to pull

Pedro's arms up behind his back, and then hoisted him until he was on the tips of his toes and supporting only some of his body weight. Pedro screamed in agony as excruciating pain shot through his arms and shoulders.

Expressionless, Torquemada nodded a second time. Pedro was lowered onto his feet, still with his arms behind him attached to the hook.

'Brother Rodríguez,' he instructed, 'no more nonsense. Start the questioning. Let's see what this so-called Christian boy believes.'

Lucero stood before Pedro holding a well-thumbed card with the Vatican-approved questions.

'Do you believe that in the Sacrament, the bread is the body of Jesus Christ?'

Pedro did not answer. He didn't know what on earth the man was talking about.

'Do you believe that Jesus Christ was born of a virgin?' came the second question.

Pedro tried to raise his head as his body was bowed forward under the strain of hanging by his arms. Lucero took this as an affirmative answer.

'Good,' he said. 'Do you believe in the resurrection of the flesh?'

Pedro could not hold his head up any longer and it slumped again onto his chest.

'No?' he said. 'Maybe a little persuasion, Master Interrogator, if you please!'

The burly torturer standing behind Pedro pulled on the rope so that Pedro was pulled up onto his toes again. He shrieked in pain again.

'Do you believe that Jesus Christ was made man from the bowels of the Virgin?'

Pedro was thoroughly confused, not understanding what was being asked. Why were they asking him these questions?

'I tried to explain,' he mumbled, in such agony that it was difficult to think of the words coherently.

'I tried to explain before,' he repeated, his voice barely audible, 'My mother died when... when I was eight... I have had no... no... I never received any... cathlic... Catholic instruction... I don't understand your qu – questions.'

Frustrated that he was getting nowhere with his questioning, Torquemada strode around the table and grabbed the handle of the windlass from the interrogator. He released the pawl anchoring the gearing of the ratchet, turning the handle to raise Pedro's feet clear of the ground. Pedro shrieked as his wrists took the full weight of his body, straining his shoulder joints to the point of dislocation.

'Now confess!' screamed the Inquisitor General into Pedro's face. 'Your name is Togeiro. Your father's a Jew and he's a rich apothecary in Vélez Blanco. Confess it!'

At that very instant the door of the interrogation room flew open and Lucero's assistant rushed into the room.

'What is it, Brother Juan?' Torquemada asked with some annoyance. 'You can see that we're busy.'

'I'm sorry, Father Tomás, but Don Gonzalo Fernández of Córdoba is here to see you. He says—'

'Tell him to wait! I don't have time for him now.'

Without any ado, the visitor stormed into the room, brushing Number Two out of the way with the sweep of his arm. He was a robust man, not yet forty, clean-shaven and dressed in a jewel-studded, scarlet doublet which extended to his thighs. His knee-length riding boots covered white woollen stockings, and the dark blue woollen cloak hung from his shoulders by a gold chain across his neck. A bright feather adorned his floppy velvet cap. The long sword on his belt rang against the stone doorway as he entered the chamber.

'Well, you'd better *make* time! I'm not waiting for you to complete your grisly work,' he said.

He took in at a glance the naked boy suspended by his wrists from the pulley with Torquemada standing by the windlass with his hand poised on the handle. Alongside him was the half-hooded interrogator, with Lucero still seated behind the table. Four paces brought the visitor across the room to Pedro. He pushed the Inquisitor General away unceremoniously, lifting the pawl off the ratchet. Pedro slumped heavily to the ground, crying out again as his shoulders hit the stone floor. The man from Córdoba drew his sword.

'Stand aside, both of you!' he shouted, addressing Torquemada and his henchman. He transferred his sword to his left hand and withdrew a razor-sharp dagger from his belt. Quickly, he sawed through the cord bindings around Pedro's wrists, releasing him from the rope which went over the pulley suspended from the ceiling.

'What are you doing here, Torquemada?' Don Gonzalo demanded, transferring his sword back to his right hand and swinging it around to cover the two standing men. 'This is outside your jurisdiction. You have no right to be here!'

'I was passing through Jaén, and Brother Rodríguez requested that I assisted him in the questioning of this boy. I operate with the Queen's warrant and can go where I choose.'

'Your warrant does not extend to torturing fourteen-year-old boys,' the Córdoba man retorted.

The tall inquisitor leered. 'I have every right, Fernández. You should acquaint yourself with the truth before you make false accusations. The Pope has lowered to fourteen the age at which heretics can be questioned.'

'You are wrong, you bloodthirsty swine! It is you who need to acquaint yourself with the facts. The Pope has lowered to fourteen the age at which *witnesses*, not suspects, can be questioned. This boy cannot be accused of heresy since he is deemed by law to be too young to know its full meaning. I have my own warrant from the King, and he shall hear of your barbarous deeds. You and your Dominican henchmen are a curse upon Spain and a disgrace upon the Holy Catholic Church.' He turned to the prisoner.

'Collect your clothes, Pedro, and follow me. The sooner we're out of this den of wickedness the better.'

He levelled his sword at the others in the chamber. 'Don't any of you move or you'll get a taste of your own medicine.'

As the visitor stormed out of the room, followed by Pedro clutching his clothes, he grabbed the bunch of keys from Brother Juan, who was still standing in the doorway.

'Which is the one for this chamber?' demanded Don Gonzalo. 'Quickly, man!'

Fumbling, Brother Juan found the requisite key on the heavy ring.

'Lock the door!' he instructed.

Shouts of protest came from within as the door banged to, its thickness blocking out their voices.

'Now find me Pedro's belongings. Be quick!' Don Gonzalo clouted him across the back with the flat of his sword; Number Two looked confused.

'You know what I'm talking about. Fetch the Toledo dagger which was sent here in a package when Pedro was brought here.'

'Oh yes, I remember the package, but I didn't know what was inside… truly, Don Gonzalo!'

Don Gonzalo and Pedro hurried after the friar down the corridor into Lucero's study at the front of the building. He found the appropriate key on the ring and opened a large oak cupboard. It was a Pandora's box of confiscated personal belongings and instruments of confession: shackles, sharp-pointed iron bars, thumb screws, pincers, manacles, fetters, levers, hooks, iron pokers with wooden handles for heating in the fire, and goodness knows what else for the most bestial acts. The friar quickly found Pedro's bundle. The boy, still only half-dressed, was thrilled when his treasured dagger, taken from him by Captain Ortíz in Jaén, fell from the package as Don Gonzalo undid it.

'Good,' Don Gonzalo said. 'One last thing, Brother Juan…'

The man was visibly relieved that his personal ordeal was nearly over and that he had actually been addressed properly by the gentleman from Córdoba.

'Certainly, Don Gonzalo, what is it you wish?'

'Where was Pedro's cell?'

'Down those steps.'

'Right! Go down to his cell and retrieve his personal effects.'

'There aren't any there, Don Gonzalo.'

'Go and check. He brought with him his travelling bag with his spare clothes. Fetch it!'

'Yes, Don Gonzalo. At once.'

The tall friar disappeared down the stone steps holding the lantern above his head. Pedro would never forget the sound of the clatter of feet on those steps.

'I'll explain how I came to be here in a minute, Pedro, but first we must get out of this terrible place.'

Pedro had managed to get his trousers on but his arms and shoulders were so painful that he could not lift them to shoulder height.

'I fear that your joints and tendons have been badly strained, my boy. A minute more hanging from that ring and your shoulders would have been dislocated from their sockets and you might have been maimed for life. Thank heavens I arrived when I did. Here, let's help you on with that shirt.'

'What are these marks on your back? You've been flogged too?'

'Not here, sir. That was four months ago in Almería when I was arrested by Captain Ortíz and his men.'

'God, what's the world coming to?' responded the well-dressed man. 'You've certainly been through an ordeal.'

He helped Pedro on with his shirt and then his warm *yallabiyya* which the friar had retrieved from his cell.

'I think you'll be fine, my boy,' he said. 'I don't think you've suffered any permanent ill effects, although it'll take two or three weeks before your shoulders and arms get back to normal. Now come with me!' He turned. 'Brother Juan, here are your keys back. You can release that lackey of Queen Isabel, but not for fifteen minutes. Is that understood?'

'Oh, yes, Don Gonzalo. Not for fifteen minutes.'

Pedro followed the man from Córdoba out of the building into a light shower but bright sunshine of early spring. His eyes squinted in the unaccustomed glare. The warmth of the midday sun on his back was wonderful, as was the fresh rain in his face. They strode down the road and around a corner into a small square where a soldier waited with three horses.

'Mission accomplished, Antonio!' Don Gonzalo shouted to the man as they joined him. 'And not before time I can tell you. Another minute and young Pedro would have been maimed for life by that tyrant, Tomás de Torquemada.'

'Torquemada? What's he doing here?'

'You may well ask. He said that he was passing through Jaén and Lucero asked him to help in the questioning. But the truth is that he sniffed a rich picking at the expense of this boy's family.'

'Pedro, this is Antonio Manzano, my personal attendant and bodyguard. I'll have to entrust you to him since I must continue my journey to Murcia. I'll see you when I return. You can trust and confide in Antonio totally. He's a military man, and nobody will dare challenge him. I know that you've had a terrible time, but you must believe me that all this is now behind you.'

'But how did you come to hear of my imprisonment, Don Gonzalo?' Pedro asked.

'Antonio will explain, but it was your Gallego soldier friend, Abel Jiménez. He wrote and told me that you were in the hands of the Inquisition.'

'You see,' he said as he climbed into his saddle, 'Not all soldiers are bad!'

'I'll drink to that,' said Antonio with a laugh. 'Come my boy,' he said as he started to put his arm around Pedro's shoulders, then saw the pain he was in. 'We must be on our way – away from this hellhole of a town.'

'See the rainbow, Pedro?' Don Gonzalo shouted as he neared the corner of the square, pointing to the sky behind Pedro and Antonio. 'It shows that your fortunes are at last changing for the better!'

And so indeed they were.

XIII: Deliverance

March 1488

Pedro chose to walk for a few miles. Never could he have imagined that the simple act of walking freely in the fresh air with the sun on his back and the warm spring rain on his face could be so wonderful. For the first time since his stay in Oria he felt on the top of the world. Antonio, seeing the pure joy on the boy's face and his head held high, chose not to break the mood by talking.

'Where are we going, Antonio?' Pedro asked in due course.

The old soldier laughed.

'Why do you laugh?' asked Pedro.

'Oh, nothing,' he chuckled. 'I guessed that would be your first or second question!'

'So what's my second?' challenged Pedro.

'Let's deal with your first, young man, and then we'll see if I'm right with your second. But first, climb up on my horse in front of me. I expect your arms are too sore to manage to ride on your own. Lavender is quite happy chugging along behind us on a loose rein.'

He stopped, got down, helped Pedro up in front of his high saddle and climbed up behind him.

'My gosh!' he exclaimed. 'You smell like a pig's latrine. The sooner we get you out of these filthy clothes and clean you up the better! However, right now, we're going to a village called Porcuna. It's halfway between Jaén and Córdoba. It's a long ride. But it's a nice day, the road is firm and we'll be there before nightfall.'

'Why are we going there?' asked Pedro.

'Yes, I thought that would be your second question, Pedro! There are a number of reasons and you'll discover these when you get there. Suffice it to say that you need to be somewhere where you can get treatment for your arms and wrists and where you can get over your ordeal. Don Gonzalo thought that Porcuna would be an ideal place for you.'

'But what's at Porcuna?' queried Pedro.

'There's a small castle there which is quite commodious. In fact, the new tower there was only rebuilt fifty years ago, and it's comfortable and spacious.'

A dark thought suddenly crossed Pedro's mind.

'Will I be imprisoned there?' he asked anxiously.

'Of course not,' Antonio laughed. 'Don Gonzalo wants to keep you there for a while for reasons you will learn. But you will be well cared for and there's a brilliant young doctor at Porcuna who will look after you.' He added, 'No,

Pedro, from what Abel Jiménez said in his letter to Don Gonzalo, you've had a bad time. A few months in the tranquillity of Porcuna will be just what you need. It will set you up for your next journey! Now, no more questions.'

'Just one please, Antonio. Who is Don Gonzalo who rescued me?'

'Don Gonzalo Fernández of Córdoba is a fine, honourable gentleman. I would happily lay down my life for him. King Fernando of Spain appointed him as his intermediary or ambassador to Boabdil – or, to give him his full name – Abu 'Abd Allah Boabdil.'

'The Muslim Sultan in Granada?'

'Yes, you've heard of him?'

'Yes, the mullah in Oria mentioned him in passing. But I don't know much about him.'

'You'll soon find out a lot more about the man. In fact, five years ago, he was imprisoned in Porcuna for three months, but was then released by the King and Queen. They considered him more use to them free but, at the same time, beholden to them. They're a cunning pair, I can tell you! And to keep tabs on him, they appointed his lordship as intermediary. He and Boabdil have become quite close since then.'

'Do you like the Muslim people, Antonio?'

'That's an odd question, Pedro! Yes and no,' he answered after some thought. 'I like them individually. They are some of the finest people I know. Warm, courteous and devoted, once you are their friend. But as a people, the Moors are devious and treacherous, and they can be very cruel.'

'Yet,' interjected Pedro, 'I don't recall seeing one of them in the torture chamber alongside Torquemada!'

Antonio gave him a funny, sideways look, then continued. 'They were once a fine people. They built magnificent palaces and civic buildings, made the dry lands fertile, and wove the most sumptuous cloth you can ever imagine. But now they've degenerated into a squabbling, narrow-minded tribe, always bickering among themselves, forming family factions, changing sides at a whim, until you have no idea who's good or bad, friend or foe, ally or enemy. They will depart this land one day and, as far as I am concerned, it cannot be soon enough.'

'Where does Boabdil fit into things, then, Antonio?' Pedro asked.

'Boabdil is a sad figure and I feel terribly sorry for him. He's a small, weak man. That's why he's nicknamed *El Chico*. He's caught between an incompetent and mischievous father, a powerful but treacherous uncle, cousins in Almería who are too big for their boots, and King Fernando – who can beat all of them into a cocked hat with his own brand of deviousness. Poor Boabdil, who is still only twenty-five, doesn't stand a chance.'

'And you said he was imprisoned at Porcuna?'

'Yes, he lost a crucial battle at Lucena in April five years ago…'

'Ah, yes!' interjected Pedro, 'that's where Sabyán's husband was killed – fighting alongside the Sultan.'

'Sabyán? A Moorish woman?'

'Yes, I met her at Oria soon after I ran away from home. She gave me her husband's ruby ring… well, it was her ring which he gave her when they were betrothed… I saved her two children from drowning, and…'

'Hold on, Pedro,' Antonio laughed. 'All in good time. It all sounds very exciting, and there'll be plenty of time later to tell me about all your adventures.'

'Now,' he continued, 'getting back to the battle of Lucena. I remember it as clearly as if it were yesterday since I was there and I can show you my wounds! In fact, I helped save Boabdil's life. It was the last battle I fought in!'

'What happened?'

'Well, Boabdil and his forces approached the town of Lucena with a view to laying siege to it. It was soon after our own siege of Málaga, and I imagine the Moors thought they would get their own back. Frankly, they deserved to.'

'So were you at Málaga, Antonio?' chipped in Pedro.

'Yes, of course, there was hardly a soldier in Spain who wasn't. But I left before the final surrender, and I'm glad I did so. What happened to those poor people who survived all those months of deprivation was shocking beyond words.

'But to return to Lucena, Pedro. After the failed siege of the town, our Christian forces turned and faced the Moors and a bloody encounter ensued. The confusion in the drizzle and smoke of the battle was terrible, but it was soon evident to me that the Moors were being forced back by our more experienced and better-disciplined soldiers. I then caught a glimpse of some-one who I later learnt to be Boabdil, standing next to his standard-bearer and evidently undecided whether to sound the retreat or to rally his men. His father-in-law was pleading with him to leave the field. I could see his pointing to the rear, but Boabdil refused to go. At the same time, fresh cavalry and foot soldiers joined our forces from the surrounding districts. The cheer which went up from our side reverberated around the hills. This spelt the end of the Moorish resistance, and their forces fled in total disorder, making easy meat for our horsemen who overtook them and cut them down. Boabdil became isolated from his entourage and was confronted by three or four *peones* waving spears, pikes and daggers. I could see Boabdil trying to keep them at bay with his scimitar, but the peasants from Baena were bent on robbing him of his fine armour, weapons and helmet and his horse and saddle. Luckily for Boabdil, to shouts of "Lucena, Lucena!" I and another horseman arrived on the scene ahead of my young lord. When my lord arrived he asked Boabdil who he was and he shouted in Arabic, "I am the son of Aben al Hajar, the Sheriff of Granada and Prince of the Realm."

'My lord dismounted, disarmed the Moorish knight and instructed me to bind his hands as our captive. The peasants who were still poking and pushing with their spears and pikes were sent packing, with much muttering and cursing. "Take ten lancers, Antonio, and accompany this so-called 'Prince of the Realm' to the castle in Lucena! I will fetch the count who's still chasing the Moors from the field."

'As we crossed the now quiet, but bloody scene of the battle, our *peones* were busy stripping the body armour from the dead or dying Moorish soldiers, searching out especially the fallen horsemen, cutting off fingers to get at the rings, turning over the bodies to find hidden money purses and then finally stripping the bodies bare of all their clothes. Such, Pedro, are the bounties of war, I'm sorry to say.'

'What happened then?' asked the boy.

'With all haste, my lord dispatched his butler, Luis de Valenzuela, to Valladolid to inform the King of the battle and to receive his instructions as to what to do with this celebrated Moorish prince. In the meantime, I led a troop of fifty lancers to Córdoba, where Boabdil was paraded around the city in chains and with an iron band tight around his neck. He was then placed under the authority of Don Gonzalo Fernández who interned him in his mansion until a reply was received from the King. As the officer who took Boabdil captive in the battle, my then lord of Lucena was permitted to keep Boabdil's personal belongings and weapons.

'I'd been accidentally speared in the arm by one of the overexcited Baena *peones* and decided that I was getting too long in the tooth for more fighting. Don Gonzalo asked me to join him as his equerry-cum-bodyguard, and with no family ties it was an offer I could not refuse. I have been in his service ever since.'

'But Boabdil ended up in Porcuna?'

'Yes. I was forgetting that's where we started. A few weeks later I was charged with accompanying him there, and that's how I and Don Gonzalo became associated with this Moorish Sultan. I might add that we have always shown him the respect and courtesy which his royal rank deserved, and he has always respected us for that.'

'And what was the outcome of the Battle of Lucena?'

'There were two outcomes. The battle was a total disaster for the Moors. Over one thousand of their finest light cavalry had been killed or captured as well as more than four thousand of their foot soldiers, including your Sabyán's husband, by the sound if it; that's around two-thirds of their force. But worse still for Boabdil, his uncle, Mohammed Abu Abdalá – *El Zagal* – joined forces with his father, Abul Hasán Alí, known as Muley Hasán, who was occupying the Alhambra in Granada; while his stepmother, the scheming Soraya, with Boabdil's younger brother, Yusuf, and his first minister, Aben Comisa, went to join Boabdil's cousin, Cidi Yahya al-Nagar in Almería.

'So, you see, Pedro, Boabdil lost his personal belongings, his freedom and his kingdom. A real tragedy for him,' concluded Antonio.

'But he's not at Porcuna now?'

'No, no. He was released soon after, but that's an even longer story and had better wait for another time. Now, no more questions, please, my boy. We've dawdled long enough. We've got some serious riding to do if we're going to get there by nightfall.'

So the old warrior spurred Sable, his mount, into a gallop and sped along the Córdoba road through the gently rolling country. Later, they stopped for a bite to eat from the food which Antonio had brought with him, drank some red wine from his leather bottle, changed horses and sped on their way once again.

It was, indeed, dark when they arrived at Porcuna. All were tired from the ride. Antonio led the horses at walking pace up the long slope which led into the village from the Córdoba road. This straddled the long whaleback hill on which the village sat. Topping the crest of the hill was a high rock and on this rock sat the new eight-sided tower. Running from the tower along the 'tail' of the rock was a small cobbled courtyard bounded by modest curtain walls, and these turned into a pair of single-storey gatehouses. The gatekeeper was on hand to open one of the sturdy gates to let them through. Antonio helped Pedro from his mount. A groom led the horses away to the stables, while Antonio took Pedro into the left of the gatehouses, both of which had a number of rooms.

'Here you are, my boy,' said Antonio as he led Pedro into one room. 'This is where you'll be for a while. There's a comfortable couch to sleep on there, and you've got your own table and chair. If it turns cold, old Ben can bring in a brazier with hot coals, but the worst of the winter weather is now passed, I'm glad to say. Ben will be along shortly to give you a warm drink and some hot food. Now relax and make yourself comfortable. But one thing: your door will be locked at night in case you try something silly like running away. You're truly better off here than anywhere else for the moment, and your time will come to return to the world outside. So just take it easy.'

Soon old Ben came in with a steaming plate of juicy mutton and carrots, with a big lump of bread, plus a tankard of hot spiced wine and water, flavoured with honey. After four months of lonely privation in the Inquisition cell, it felt wonderful.

The next morning, soon after receiving a couple of slices of fresh bread and jam, old Ben came in and beckoned Pedro to follow him.

'Bring all your things with you, boy,' he instructed as he waddled off.

He led Pedro into the gatehouse kitchen, which was warm and cosy and smelt of the fresh bread which he had just savoured.

'Take off all your clothes and put them in a pile over there with the rest you've got in your bag. And your thick *yallabiyya*. It stinks to high heaven!' he grimaced. 'There's a tub of hot water there to bath in and a scrubbing brush. Get yourself cleaned up and make sure you wash your hair and behind your ears. You can dry yourself on this cloth.'

While Pedro undressed, old Ben measured against him a clean loose-sleeved white woollen shirt and a dark red, sleeveless woollen jerkin with a leather belt. They fitted him well enough. He laid out some brown woollen trousers, some knitted socks and a pair of new leather sandals.

'I'm going to burn all these old clothes of yours, Pedro,' he said. 'They're disgusting and half-rotten.'

Pedro did not protest.

Soon after he had returned to his room, washed, scrubbed and clad in his new clothes, the door, now unlocked, opened and a thinnish young man with a receding forehead and collar-length dark hair entered. He was dressed in black and carried a broad, leather bag which was fastened over the top with a brass catch.

'Good morning, Pedro,' he said rather stiffly. 'My name is Jacob, and I'm here to administer to your injuries. I expect Antonio mentioned me to you.'

'Is Antonio here?' asked Pedro.

'No he's gone back to Córdoba. But you need have no fear. You are in good hands here. He'll be back quite soon to see you. Now, let's have a look at you. Take off your jerkin and shirt and lie on the couch on your stomach.'

Pedro winced as the doctor's long fingers probed deep into his flesh around his shoulders and shoulder blades, feeling the swollen and half-torn sinews within them. His hands ran down his back, examining the barely-closed wounds from the flogging he had received after the Almería earthquake four months before. Some of them were deep red and festering. The occasional 'Hmm' was all he uttered. He turned Pedro over and examined his shoulders and neck, again probing his fingers deep into his joints. Lastly, he examined the boy's arms and wrists, deeply incised and still weeping blood from the cords by which he was hung in the Chamber of Examination the day before.

'You can put your clothes back on now, Pedro,' said the young doctor.

He sat on the chair which he had pulled up alongside the couch and remained silent for a minute or too, stroking his chin thoughtfully.

'Well, it's clear,' he said in due course, 'you've had a very rough time. But I'm glad to say that all your injuries will eventually heal up. The ligaments around your shoulders are badly extended and swollen. I don't know how long you hung from your wrists, but another few minutes and your shoulders would have dislocated from their joints, with the most incredible pain, and you could have been crippled for the rest of your life. It was lucky Don Gonzalo and Antonio rescued you when they did. They're good men, the both of them. But the wounds on your back from the flogging are really nasty, and regrettably you'll be scarred for life, although the marks will fade. All your injuries will take a few months to heal. What we'll do is rub healing balm into your back and wrists and massage your shoulders and arms with oils. The manservant, Faiz, will do this daily, and I will visit you also to check your progress. Faiz will be along later this morning.'

'Now, if you want to go outside into the sunshine you can. But the gates will be closed, and we'd rather you didn't try and leave the castle. I'll see you again tomorrow.'

Later that morning Pedro was sitting against the wall outside, enjoying the bright sunshine and its warmth. He was puzzled by the warnings he had received, however gently proffered, about not trying to escape from the castle. Why were they so keen that he should stay there? As he sat there he caught the glimpse of a small face looking at him from a side window high up in the tower opposite him, some forty yards away. Then the face was gone.

Faiz located Pedro and they returned to his room. The boy removed his shirt again and the servant gently soothed warm oils into his shoulders and arms with his soft hands. He rubbed liniment into the weeping marks of the lashes and bound a broad piece of cloth around his chest, fastening it with a couple of pins. Pedro had never met anyone like Faiz before. Short and podgy, his smooth skin and pink complexion were matched by a high-pitched boyish voice.

'I expect you're wondering who I am?' Faiz said with a little chuckle after Pedro had put his shirt back on.

'I'm a eunuch, in the service of my lord Boabdil,' he stated quite proudly.

Pedro had heard of such people and how they came to be like they were.

'Why are you here?' asked Pedro.

'Normally I work with Nasím, Boabdil's personal manservant, who's also a eunuch. He helps look after the women of the harem in the Alhambra. But I'm here for a spell at his lordship's request looking after… well, if you haven't met him yet, you soon will.'

'Is the doctor, Jacob, in Boabdil's service too?'

'I suppose you could say that, yes,' the eunuch replied. 'He is the third son of Ibrahim, who is Boabdil's personal physician and is a Jew, of course. Ibrahim has more sons than the tribes of Israel and is so meticulous with his examinations as to be tiresome. But he's truly brilliant. He swears by the therapy of mineral waters and insists that his patients make frequent trips to the hot curative springs at Alhama in the mountains to the west of Granada, where he himself spends a lot of his time. Boabdil's mother, Fátima, spends much of her time there too for her sciatica, which is so excruciatingly painful.'

'Does Ibrahim live in the Alhambra too?'

'No, it would be against his religious principles. And imagine all those sons of his living next door to the Sultan's harem! No, he lives with his family in the Jewish quarter of the city.'

'So Jacob takes after him as a doctor?'

'Most of his sons have, or are doing so. I should imagine that there are enough of them to service the whole city! Jacob has his father's skill and takes his profession very seriously.'

'So I noticed!' commented Pedro.

'Oh, he'll melt a bit when he knows you better.'

As he was talking, Pedro noticed the small face again, peering over the ledge of the narrow window of a room which overlooked the courtyard. Then it was gone again.

'Now I must leave you, Pedro,' said Faiz rising from the chair. 'I'll be along the same time tomorrow. You can then tell me a bit about yourself.'

This routine continued for nearly a week, with the rest, the sunshine, the oils and liniments all contributing to a speedy improvement in the boy's physical state. However, he was starting to get restless.

That afternoon, Antonio Manzano showed himself into Pedro's room.

'Hello, my boy. I gather you're making good progress. I'm sorry I had to rush away last week, but I had an urgent note to deliver in Córdoba for Don Gonzalo, and I was unable then to introduce you to the little fellow with whom we want you to spend some time here. Can I introduce you to Cidi Ahmad, the son of Boabdil?'

Antonio looked around, darted back through the door and retrieved a small, darkish boy skulking around the corner.

'This is Ahmad.'

'Ahmad, this is Pedro Togeiro. He's here to be your friend.'

The boy hid behind Antonio's back, burying his face in his soft woollen cloak. The man laughed and ruffled the boy's hair behind him.

'He'll be all right in a few minutes, Pedro. He's terribly shy and that's partly why you're here. What I didn't explain last week on our way here was that although Boabdil was released by the King and Queen after being held captive here for three months, they soon had second thoughts about the wisdom of his being free to start up hostilities again. So as a condition of his release they took as hostage young Ahmad. He was then only three years old.'

'But that's terrible!' exclaimed Pedro.

'Yes, I know,' replied the old soldier, 'but that's the way things happen, I'm afraid.'

'So, Ahmad's been here for nearly five years?'

'Yes. The boy speaks Arabic, of course, but his Castilian is poor and, what's more, he has nobody he can readily converse with or with whom he can play.'

'Well, I'm not exactly his age,' responded Pedro, feeling a seven-year-old was a bit below his dignity.

'I know, Pedro, but you're a lot closer to him than either Don Gonzalo or me, and apparently you speak good Arabic. I'm sure that after he gets to know you the poor boy will loosen up a bit and learn some Castilian, which must be in his future interests. His father speaks it quite well now.'

'So that's why you brought me here?'

'That, and to get over your injuries. We didn't deceive you about that, did we?'

'No, I've been wonderfully looked after, Antonio.'

'Very well,' Pedro continued, 'I'll do my very best to help Ahmad. Do we have the freedom of the castle and its grounds to play?'

'Of course, of course. But no scaling the walls. Agreed?'

'Agreed!'

'I'll leave you two together to get to know one another, but I'll be around for a while if you have any problems.'

Pedro looked at the young prince and grinned at him. The boy blushed and turned away. This is going to be some task, thought Pedro.

'*Sabahil kter, Ismi Pedro, tasharafna.* Hello Ahmad, I'm Pedro. I'm pleased to meet you,' he began, trying to break the ice.

There was no response.

'*Hael tatakallarni asparni?* Do you speak any Castilian?'

The small boy shook his head.

'*La ta'la. Kol she 'alar mayoram.* It's all right. Don't worry.' He paused. 'Come on,' he continued in Arabic. 'Let's go outside in the sunshine.'

The boy shied away as Pedro tried to take his hand but he followed meekly down the short corridor and out into the courtyard leading up to the high tower. The elder boy sat against the wall and beckoned the younger boy to join him. Pedro picked up a small stone. He concealed it in his left hand and placed his fists together, knuckles up, in front of Boabdil's son.

'Which hand's the stone in?' he said again in Arabic.

The boy pointed to his left hand.

'Correct.'

This time, with his left hand turned palm upwards, Pedro placed the stone between his thumb and forefinger. He slid his right thumb beneath the stone, transferring it rather obviously into this same right hand. He made fists of his hands again and turned them towards Ahmad.

'Now which hand?' he said.

Ahmad slapped his right hand.

'Right again. Now we'll do it again.'

Pedro did it a second time, but this time letting the stone slide past his thumb to fall back into his upturned left palm. He put his fists up again.

'Now which hand?' he asked.

Ahmad slapped the right hand once again.

'Wrong,' he laughed. 'It's in this left one!'

The young prince looked perplexed and a smile crept onto his face.

'Now again,' said Pedro, laughing.

They played this simple game of sleight of hand for a while longer, the young boy gradually getting more excited.

'Now,' Pedro said, again in Arabic. 'You see that white boulder over there. I bet I can throw this stone closer to it than you can.'

'That's not fair!' cried Ahmad aloud in Arabic.

These were the very first words he spoke to Pedro.

'Why not?' asked Pedro.

'Because that's a magic stone.'

'Oh yes, of course. I forgot. Well, you have this magic stone and I'll throw another one.'

They each threw stones at the white boulder in the yard, Pedro ensuring that Ahmad won the first try and plenty of the remaining ones.

'That's enough for now,' said Pedro after half an hour or so.

'Can't we go on?' pleaded the smaller boy.

'No, we'll play some more tomorrow.' Then switching from Arabic to Castilian, he said, 'I'll teach you some of the games which Yazíd and I played in the town where we live.'

'Town… where… you… live?' repeated the prince slowly.

'That's right, Ahmad. Good for you. Tomorrow we'll play some more games and I'll show you my dagger.'

'Your… dagger?' His eyes brightened.

'Yes, and some of the time we'll speak your language and some of the time we'll speak mine. All right, Ahmad?'

'All right,' he replied confidently.

So this was how Pedro broke down the young prince's chronic shyness. Bit by bit he introduced more Castilian, until after a month the boy understood much of what Pedro said. But most of all, and to the delight of Faiz and the young doctor, the boy was starting to come alive for the first time since he had been held captive at Porcuna.

Pedro gradually spent more time in the boy's rooms instructing the prince in Castilian as well as in many of the things he had learnt in his school two days a week: mathematics, science, geography and history.

It was easier said than done. While Castilian had already become the dominant language of Spain, it had no order or structure and people pronounced it and wrote it much as they pleased. Moreover, depending on where you lived, everyday conversation could include bits of Catalan, Valencian, Basque, Galician, Latin, Hebrew, Arabic, and – particularly in the markets of *Al-Andalus* – the obscure language of the gypsies. For teachers it was a nightmare, and for that reason formal learning was still done in Latin.

One evening in late April, during another brief visit by Antonio Manzano, Pedro asked about the prince's family.

'Ask Faiz to bring us some fruit juice flavoured with cinnamon,' said Antonio, 'and then I'll try and do so. Luckily, I don't need to return to Córdoba until the morrow. But, Pedro, it's a sad tale of intrigue and family quarrels. You'll get utterly mesmerised by it all!'

'But I'm right in saying that Boabdil's mother is called Soraya?' started Pedro.

'No you're wrong!' replied Antonio. 'Boabdil's mother is Fátima.'

'Fátima? Is she of royal blood too?'

'Yes indeed. She's the daughter of Mohammed the Ninth, who was known as *El Zurdo*, the Left-handed. He was Sultan off and on for over thirty years.'

'How do you mean "on and off"?'

'This is where the story becomes complicated, since the sultanate has chopped and changed around family members depending on who is in or out of favour.

'For instance, I'm told that amongst the thirty-one Sultans in the last eight hundred years there have been thirteen Mohammeds, and Boabdil is number twelve! That's because there was a Mohammed before there was a Mohammed the First!'

'So how many Fernandos, Carloses, Alfonsos and Enriques has Spain had?' challenged Pedro, siding with the Muslims.

Antonio scratched his head and thought for a minute.

'The last Alfonso was Alfonso XI. But don't interrupt my boy. This is serious business!'

'Now, when Boabdil's grandfather, Said', he continued, 'relinquished power in '64, he was succeeded by Boabdil's father, Muley Hasán, who had been held captive in Segovia by us as a hostage for several years, but then released – foolishly, of course, since he then went on to triumph in a battle near Estepa over the redoubtable Ponce de León, one of the King's best commanders. Muley Hasán, Boabdil's father, was then the sole Sultan for twenty years, but he was not liked.'

'So is Boabdil Sultan now, Antonio?'

'Yes, he is – at least in name. He was reinstated as Sultan when he was released finally by the King and Queen two years ago. But he's really their vassal king and depends on their patronage to retain his position. But it will do him no good. When it suits them, but not before, the King and Queen will depose him and take over his kingdom.'

'And you think not before much longer?'

'Yes, it's inevitable now.'

'But,' concluded Antonio, 'you're likely to meet Boabdil shortly, since he's coming here to see Ahmad, as he does from time to time.'

'What makes you so certain, Antonio, that the Muslim empire will soon come to an end. You seem so sure of it!'

'Because, leaving aside the total disorder amongst the ruling Nazarí family, all the odds are becoming stacked against them. With the fall of Constantinople to the infidels forty or so years ago, after a prolonged and bitter siege, and following that of Kosovo three years before, Christendom lost the whole of its eastern empire. It has little prospect of ever recovering it. Where else can one halt the expansion of the Muslim empire but in *Al-Andalus*, where the rump of a decaying sultanate still survives? For three hundred years Spanish kings have been slowly rolling back the Moors across Spain, con-structing lines of magnificent castles across the country to consolidate their hold over the land. Now, with the marriage nineteen years ago of Isabel of Castile and Fernando of Aragón, the two main kingdoms of Spain are united for the very first time and they have joined forces to expel the Moors once and for all from our land.

'But there's another factor too. The King and Queen are pious and devout. Not for nothing are they called the Catholic Monarchs. With his blessing and the Vatican's considerable financial backing, the Pope in Rome has declared a Holy Crusade to finally put an end to the Muslim occupation of Western Europe. All the monarchs in the Western world are enjoined in the campaign.

'In fact, there's a bigger factor still, and that is the overwhelming might which Spain and its allies can now bring to bear against the Moors here. I have heard Don Gonzalo warn Boabdil of this, and he understands it. Unfortunately his uncle, *El Zagal*, doesn't, and despite his undoubted successes against us at the battles of Aljarquía, Madroño and Vega and many more besides, this formidable warrior, (for whom I have a sneaking admiration) will cause needless bloodshed and suffering to his people. But all to no avail. The Moors simply cannot match the number of light and heavy cavalry which we and our allies can now field against them, nor the tens of thousands of well-drilled and well-armed infantry who can be assembled. We now have powerful cannons which can fire enormous stones, a foot and a half across, for nearly a mile. Walls, towers and gateways cannot withstand their destructive power. These guns come from Italy, Germany and France, and the miser Domingo Zacharías is the master gunsmith behind them. We have all the material, labourers and techniques for waging modern warfare; hundreds of wagons to transport the stone cannon-balls, food, tents and clothing, as well as the new engines of war. All to move and support an army of eighty thousand infantry and twenty thousand cavalry drawn from across Europe. It moves slowly, remorselessly, without surprises, but nothing can stand in its way.

'What have the Moors got to oppose this? A few thousand brilliant yet lightly armoured horsemen, and several thousand poorly led and ill-disciplined foot soldiers. Even their castles offer them no protection, with their thin, rubble-filled walls, which are easy meat for modern artillery. But, in any case, Pedro, cavalry are becoming superfluous on today's battlefields. Soon massed ranks of well-trained and well-armed soldiers, equipped with long heavy bills, supported by artillery, will be more than a match for any number of horsemen, however valiant.' He paused, looking reflective but at the same time resolute.

'No, Pedro, the Moors don't stand a snowball in hell's chance against us now.'

XIV: The Sultan

May 1488

It was nearly two months after Pedro arrived at Porcuna when, one morning, a fanfare of trumpets sounded outside the castle walls, accompanied by the clatter of horses' hooves and the jangle of bridles and harnesses. Pedro and Ahmad ran to the window of the elder boy's room to see the gatekeeper run outside and heave open the gates of the castle. He was only just in time. As he did so six horsemen rode in with much clamour, pomp and ceremony. Pedro immediately recognised the corpulent and upright figure of Don Gonzalo Fernández on his fine chestnut stallion. Alongside him was a sumptuously dressed bearded man on a white horse. His gorgeous, scarlet *taylasan*, the tunic of a nobleman, had deep sleeves and was finely embroidered in silver and gold thread. He wore a bulbous, cushion-like white *'imama*, the larger the size denoting the higher the rank, and his black polished riding *ajfafs* were tucked into high stirrups, Arab-style. Long black tassels swung from his lightweight ornate saddle, while a red tassel swung on the forehead of his beautiful horse.

Two pairs of horsemen followed and drew to a stop behind Don Gonzalo and his colleague. They formed a troop of Arab cavalry. At one and the same time they looked both magnificent and menacing; magnificent in their burnished steel breastplates over dark red *gilalas*, long white *burnos* held by silver clips onto the shoulders of their breastplates which stretched over the flanks of their jet-black steeds, and generous, deep red *'imamas* wound tightly around their heads, the ends of which hung loosely over their shoulders; yet menacing as well, with their dark complexions, full black beards; each was armed with a long curved scimitar swinging from his belt, and each held upright in his right hand a long lance.

'*Ab!*' cried Ahmad through the open window, and ran to the door.

'*Besorc'a*! Pedro,' he shouted in Arabic. 'Hurry! It's my father. He's come to see me.'

Pedro knew that it was nearly a year since the young prince had last seen his father and he had been waiting for weeks and weeks for him to come. Pedro stayed at the window, not wishing to disturb the family reunion. The young boy ran across the cobbled courtyard to Abu 'Abd Allah Boabdil, who had just dismounted. The Muslim Sultan was indeed small. He barely came up to Don Gonzalo's shoulder and was almost totally hidden from view by his bodyguards. Ahmad pushed through the high-spirited horsemen to his father, who crouched down to hug and kiss him. Both wept with joy at their reunion. Ahmad pulled away from his father's embrace and pointed to Pedro watching the scene from the window. He shouted and waved to him to come down into the courtyard to meet his father. Don Gonzalo spotting the focus of the boy's cry, also waved to Pedro to join them.

'My word, Pedro,' Don Gonzalo said with a laugh when he joined the group, 'I thought for a minute you'd left us on one of your travels! It's good to see you looking so well, my boy. A bit different from when I plucked you from the clutches of that tyrant, Torquemada, eh? How have they been looking after you? How have you been getting on with young Ahmad? How's his Castilian coming on? Is he still as shy?' He checked himself. 'Heavens, I'm sorry, my boy! All these questions, and we're barely off our horses. You must tell me everything later, but first you must meet the young sultan; I have been telling him all about you.'

The good-natured ambassador led Pedro to meet the Muslim king. The young prince got in first.

'*Kanqaddem lek* Pedro,' said young Ahmad to his father.

'I'd like you to meet Pedro,' said Don Gonzalo to Boabdil, in exact unison with the youngster.

All four burst out laughing at the jumble of words.

'*Mtsharfin*, Pedro, *kif'entsa*?' said Boabdil to Pedro. 'I'm pleased to meet you, Pedro. How are you?'

'*Lena sh-sharaf sharyib*,' replied Pedro. 'I'm very well, thank you, Sire.'

'You are right, Gonzalo,' Boabdil said in faltering Castilian to the ambassador. 'He does speak good Arabic. You must ask him to tell us where he learnt my tongue.'

'All in good time, Boabdil,' said the Córdoban man. 'First, let's wash the dust off ourselves and take some refreshment out of this sun. It's already starting to burn. You two – go along and play for a while. We'll catch up with you and your news later in the day.'

That evening, after Boabdil had put his young son to bed on the second floor of the New Tower, Pedro sat with Don Gonzalo and the Sultan in his quarters on the floor below. They were those which he had occupied five years before during his three months' imprisonment there after the battle of Lucena. Now they were more lavishly decorated and sumptuously furnished with Moroccan drapes on the walls and low sofas and cushions on the stone floor. A finely-woven, crimson patterned carpet lay over it. An L-shaped screen across two corners of the octagonal room concealed the low couch which he used at night. There was little accommodation available in the tower, so Don Gonzalo slept in a room in the right-hand gatehouse, while the four horsemen found rooms and stables for their horses nearby in the town. Their Arab presence unsettled the townsfolk but the horsemen were on their best behaviour. They knew that the comfortable sinecure of being bodyguard to the Sultan would be quickly quashed if there were the slightest trouble with the Christian community.

'For the sake of Don Gonzalo,' Boabdil began, 'we shall speak Castilian, but you will excuse me if I stumble over some words. Firstly, Pedro, I want to thank you from the bottom of my heart for what you have done for my son, Ahmad. I'll not forget it. He's a changed boy. Your two months with him have transformed him from a chronically shy and moody child into a playful and entertaining youngster. He now understands and speaks Castilian well and, amazingly, he seems to have an understanding of geography, science and astronomy – although what history you have taught him seems to differ from our Arab understanding of events! You must let me correct you in this regard! But I am truly surprised that a young man of just fourteen years has so much knowledge, and I am keen to learn how you came by it.'

'Boabdil,' said Don Gonzalo, slowly sipping from a goblet of red wine, 'Pedro has, indeed, much to tell us. Apart from the harrowing events which have befallen him, which I hope he'll feel able to tell us about, I sense that he conceals a deep sadness in his soul. I don't think tonight, which is such a happy occasion for us all, is the right time to ask our young friend to unburden himself. Maybe in a few days' time he'll eat with us, and over a goblet of wine tell us his story. By then, my man Antonio will be here, and I know he'd also like to hear Pedro's story.'

'I'm flattered and honoured that you should invite me to dine with you, Don Gonzalo,' replied Pedro, 'but I'm not sure that my story is one which you'll wish to hear. I've done some shameful things and you may not be so disposed to look so kindly on me when I tell you of them. But, Sire,' he said turning to the Sultan, 'you offered to tell me the history of your peoples. I'm keen to learn of it. I know a little from what the mullah in Oria told me last year, but—'

'The mullah?' interrupted Boabdil.

'Yes,' answered Pedro. 'He's not a mullah now, it's what the people in the village call him, but many years ago he was a mullah in the *mesquita* in Almería before he left the city to live in his *rábita* in Oria. It's north of Macael, where the marble comes from.'

'Yes, I know it. Why did he leave the *mesquita*?'

'He said he found the imam there was more monk than priest and too devoted to a life of personal discipline and self-denial. The mullah thinks that the main mosque in a city is not the place for narrow religious beliefs, but should be the heart and soul of the community, as many of the Christian cathedrals and Jewish synagogues are. He believes that your religion should not be inward-looking and narrow, putting the people in fear of how they conduct their daily lives, but should provide a framework for a stable and ordered community living within the tenets of the Koran.'

'You put that very eloquently, Pedro,' interrupted Boabdil. 'Excessive religious fervour has been the curse of my people from time to time through our history. But carry on with your story… So your mullah left the mosque in Almería?'

'Yes, he had no particular plan as to where he would settle, but he came across the village of Oria while travelling north and liked the people there and the way they lived their lives. He renovated an old *rábita* there and settled down as the elder statesman of the village. Everybody is devoted to him.'

'He sounds a fine man, Pedro, and I should love to meet him. Why don't we sit in the shade of the castle wall tomorrow afternoon and I shall tell you about my people, and how we came to this land?'

As agreed, the next afternoon Boabdil, young Ahmad, who would not leave the side of his father, and Pedro sat on cushions under the shady wall of the castle. In a mixture of Arabic and Castilian, Boabdil told of his people.

'It's said that my ancestors came to the Iberian peninsula in the year 108; that is the Christian year 711. Tariq landed at what is now called Gibraltar, but which means *Jabal Tariq* in my language, the "Rock of Tariq", with some ten thousand followers – a mixture of Berbers, Yemenis and Syrians. This was not many years after the first followers of our prophet, Mohammed, had penetrated across North Africa from their lands to the east. In that year, 711, they overcame the Visigoths, who occupied the Peninsula when the Romans departed, at the battle of Janda. Eighteen thousand more arrived from Morocco the following year and under the command of Muza they conquered the regions of Granada and Murcia. Soon the influence of Islam had reached Galicia in the north-west of the country, and spilled over the Pyrenees into southern France. They administered their conquered lands through Tariq based in Astorga, near León, the convert Fortún in Aragón, and Muza in Zaragoza. However, the fall from grace of Tariq and Muza transferred power to Muza's son, Abd al-Aziz Ibn Muza. At his death a few years later, only the north-east part of the country remained outside Islamic control.

'At that time the caliphate in Damascus was the centre of Muslim power, but links with it were broken when in 755 Abd al-Rahman the First, fleeing from the killing of his ruling Omayyad family by the victorious Abbasids, disembarked at Almuñécar, near Málaga, with a small band of followers. He proclaimed himself emir and initiated the first hereditary dynasty. Based in Córdoba, he set in train three fundamental changes: the creation of a mercenary army in the service of the Emir; the re-establishment of public administration; and the use of our religion, Islam, as a means of binding the community together. By the time of his death in 788 he had conquered the northern domains and secured the land with a defensive arc based on Zaragoza, Toledo and Mérida, much as the Romans had done. However, his death opened the way for factions to develop which have plagued my people so often, leading to Barcelona falling to the French some years after, and it wasn't until Abd al-Rahman the Second ascended to the throne in 822 that power was reasserted in Córdoba. He had to cope with rebellious tribes in different parts of the emirate as well as attacks on Sevilla and Cádiz from Norman raiders. Rebellion amongst the Christianised Arabs in Córdoba, known as the Mozarabs, plus hunger and plague, and Christian resurgence under Alfonso the Second, after the amazingly well-timed discovery of the tomb of the Christian saint, Saint James, all augured ominously for our Islamic state.' The Sultan paused.

'However, the coming to power of the great Abd al-Rahman the Third...'

'The mullah said that it was he who founded Almería?' interrupted Pedro.

'Yes, that's correct, Pedro,' replied Boabdil patiently. 'And many other places too. His coming heralded a century of true splendour. His adoption of the title of Caliph confirmed once and for all our independence from Damascus. From his immense and splendid new royal palace on the banks of the Guadalquivir at Córdoba, the Medina Al-Zahra, he presided over a group of viziers or ministers through a *hayib*, or prime minister. He stabilised the borders by placing his most loyal followers as governors and instigated proper rights and justice for Christians and Jews alike. This has been a hallmark of our governance throughout our rule in Spain. Finally he settled the troublesome northern borders, recognising the independence of the kings of León and Navarra and the counts of Barcelona and Castile, all who then paid annual tributes to the Caliph.

'Trade flourished with the countries bordering the Mediterranean, so that the *zocos* or market places in all our cities were filled with the fruits, wines and exotic produce from all these lands. Córdoba, with one hundred thousand people, was by far the biggest city in the land, but the other *Al-Andalus* cities of Almería, Granada, Málaga and Sevilla all exceeded twenty thousand people. Valencia, Toledo and Zaragoza were the other largest cities in the rest of the caliphate. It was the time of *Al-Andalus'* greatest prosperity, and it was based on the olive, and the growth of cotton, flax and esparto, with the white myrtle sustaining the vital silk industry. Our animal herds flourished with the introduction of new breeds from North Africa, while the mining of gold, silver, iron, mercury and lead, the manufacture of glass, leather, wood engraving, silks, and marbles all made our land a prime focus for trade. *Al-Andalus* became by far the most advanced cultural society of Western Europe, and was renowned for its sciences and arts.

'However, Pedro, with the death of Almanzor, the Omayyad dynasty started to disintegrate. In your Christian year 1031, following a civil war, an assembly of nobles, called the Taifa princes, dissolved the caliphate and set up separate courts to rival Córdoba in splendour. None of these new rulers was mightier than the legendary warrior-king and poet, Al-Mutasím, who made Almería one of the most important centres of the empire. But their constant infighting led to the Christians conquering Toledo in central Spain in 1185. The Taifas sought the help of Yusuf Ibn Tasufín, leader of the Almorávides, which had extended their rule over North Africa and had their capital in Marrakech. Stoic and ruthless, these new peoples stopped the Christian advance southwards across Iberia in its tracks, but finished by deposing the Taifa princes.

'The Almorávides only lasted some fifty years. The Christian conquest of

1147 under Alfonso the Seventh, supported by the Genoese and Venetians, took Almería, which was seen as a threat to their dominant trading position in the Mediterranean. Thousands of its citizens fled to Murcia and Granada and the surrounding mountains. The city of Almería never recovered from its sacking by the Christians. The western part of the city was largely abandoned thereafter. However, a new ruling dynasty, the Almohades, retook Almería ten years later. They became the new rulers of the Islamic empire, choosing Sevilla as their new capital. But the glorious years of Abd Al-Rahman the Third were sadly long past. The new rulers were also Berbers from North Africa and believed in austerity. They had total contempt for the luxurious life of their forebears. Religious intolerance became rampant, and the consequential disenchantment of the inhabitants sowed the seeds for further Christian advances. The crucial defeat of our forces in 1212 at Navas de Tolosa, near La Carolina, at the crucial pass of Despeñaperros, opened the way for the Nazarí dynasty, which is my family, and we have ruled this country ever since.'

Boabdil took a much needed gulp of fresh orange juice. Even in the shade of the wall it was very warm.

'Our founder, Mohammed the First, did his best to stem the relentless southward push of the Christians with their third great advance against us. Barcelona and Valencia fell to Jaime the First, the King of Aragón, while around the same time in the west Fernando the Third of Castile and León took Jerez and Mérida and then finally Sevilla in 1243, while parts of Murcia fell in the same year to his son, *El Sabio*, later Alfonso the Tenth. By then, our beleaguered kingdom had shrunk to little more than the regions of Almería, Granada and the eastern part of Málaga. Even then we were in danger of being driven totally from all our lands. Aware of this, in 1246 Mohammed signed the Treaty of Jaén with the Christians.

'It has plagued us to this day. It recognised our kingdom of Granada and provided a basis of peace between our two peoples, Muslim and Christian. We saw this treaty as a truce between the two sides so that each could trade and prosper. After all, the Christians were desperate for our lead, iron and marble, as well as the oil from our olives, and we needed their woollen cloth and corn, and free passage for our boats to trade along the Mediterranean coast. However, as Don Gonzalo explained to me some time ago, the Christian kings from then to this day saw this treaty as making us a vassal kingdom of Castile – militarily subordinate to them. Whatever the truth of this, I know that our Nazarí kingdom has paid a high price for our alliance with the Christians. Do you know, Pedro, that under that treaty almost half our annual wealth continues to be paid as paria or tribute to Castile? Every year Castile demands more and more from us, and my people are impoverished and starving under this burden.

'One hundred years ago our dynastic succession started to break up and this had a debilitating effect on the stability of the kingdom. Success, then failure in battle, lands won and then lost, local treaties signed and then ignored, was enough for the sultanate to pass to brother, to son, to uncle, to nephew and then back to one or other in a desperate search for a great leader. In the last ninety years, can you believe, eleven different Sultans have ruled in eighteen separate reigns – sometimes three different Sultans in a single year. This is not the way to run a kingdom.

'Six years ago, as Don Gonzalo has confided to me, King Fernando and Queen Isabel initiated a new holy war against us. There seems little doubt to me that they will not cease until we are finally extinguished. Who then will pay their parias? Now my uncle Abu Abdalá is waging war with them around Baza, but what good will it do? How can we stem the tide of their encroachment into our lands? If we stand firm, as we did at Málaga last year, thousands die of starvation, and thousands more are sold to prostitution and slavery. If we capitulate through signed treaties, within months the terms of the surrender are broken and my people are expelled from their houses and land and they forfeit what little they possess. Is this how the self-professed Catholic Monarchs, anointed by their God, should conduct their stately affairs?'

The small man sat there on the ground sieving stones absently through his fingers. He looked desolate and remained silent for several minutes, oblivious to the presence of Ahmad and Pedro. When he eventually looked up he had tears in his eyes. Pedro tried to break his sombre mood.

'Sire, you started your discourse by saying it is said that your ancestors came to the Iberian peninsula in the year 711. What did you mean by that? Is there some doubt about it?'

Boabdil seemed glad of the question.

'Oh yes, at least as far as I am concerned. I think the idea of the Arab conquest in little more than three years is a fiction propagated by the Christians to cover their own weaknesses at that time, and to justify what they like later to call their "re-conquest"!' He smiled wryly. 'How could thirty thousand people conquer a mountainous land the size of Iberia in three years and achieve an assimilation which has lasted close to eight hundred years?

'The truth is that the inhabitants of the Iberian peninsula were essentially Hispano-Roman who had remained uninfluenced by Visigothic rule. A power vacuum existed which was filled by Tarik, who was probably a renegade Visigothic prince, and his invading army; they did not so much conquer the country as take advantage of the lack of opposition from the indigenous populace. Only afterwards did the Arabs arrive here, following in the footsteps of Tarik, infusing *Al-Andalus* with their own language, traditions and customs. Their distinctive architecture was essentially pre-Arab and Byzantine. The Christianised Hispano-Roman population was slow to respond to this new culture spreading across their land. They failed to match the religious zeal of our Muslim people until, can you believe, the bones of Christ's saintly brother, James, were miraculously found in Galicia and holy crusades were mounted to oppose us...

'By then we were too well established, and it has taken them more than seven hundred years to force us back across Iberia. It's been an unremitting struggle. My father, who was held hostage in the castle at Segovia thirty or so years ago, told me that the plaques on the walls in the throne room denoting each of the Christian kings, have brief citations beneath them. Nearly all of them laud successful campaigns or famous battles won against us: such has been the importance they have placed on driving us from our lands.'

It was almost a week later when Pedro joined Don Gonzalo, Antonio Manzano and Boabdil for dinner on the comfortable first floor of the tower. The meal could not match the sumptuous Arab offering which Sabyán prepared for Pedro and the mullah in his *rábita* the previous October. However, the spit-roasted partridges and quails stuffed with rice, chopped apricots and nuts with fresh vegetables were fit for a king, if not a sultan, as were saffron cakes soaked with warmed honey afterwards. Rather deviously, in order to help loosen Pedro's tongue afterwards, Don Gonzalo persuaded him to sample the local red wine. True to his faith, Boabdil desisted from alcoholic beverage and drank pomegranate juice instead.

'Now, Pedro,' said the King's ambassador, 'you promised to tell us your story. We are all replete with partridge and quail, so we'll be more than content to listen to you without interruption… well, not too much!' he added jovially.

'Firstly, tell us how you came to be in Almería and what happened to you there?'

'I left Vélez Blanco, where I come from last September,' Pedro began, 'and journeyed over the mountains on the way to Almería. I was bent on running aw– I was bent on joining a ship as a cabin boy. My journey took me across the mountains through the small village of Oria, which lies on the route to Macael. I happened to mention to a woman in the village square that I was travelling to Almería, and she said that I should meet Abu Bakr, the mullah, who hailed from the city. This is how I came to meet the holy man. He kindly offered to put me up for the night. It wasn't my intention to stay longer. That night there was a most terrible storm. The river across the road from the *rábita* and which ran below the hill on which the village stood became a raging torrent. Hearing screams, the mullah and I ran outside and we saw some villagers on the river bank with the waters raging past them in the darkness. We ran to them, and seeing the cause of their cries I managed to rescue two young children clinging like grim death to a slab of masonry in the middle of the torrent. The flood had carried away the side of the house which stood on the bluff. The two young children whom I rescued belonged to the woman standing on the river bank, whom I had met that day in the square. I only did what anyone would do in saving her two children, but I was treated like a saint and showered with kindness and gifts by the villagers, since the woman, Sabyán, was much liked in the community. So I stayed on in Oria for a few weeks helping the mullah clean out his well and repaint his house. He told me how he came to Almería from Fez in Morocco, and also narrated the history of

Almería from its founding. My stay there was amongst the happiest times I have had in my life, but I knew that I had to leave. The woman Sabyán – whose husband fought with you, Sire, at Lucena five years ago, and was amongst those killed – showered me with kindness. In all honesty,' said Pedro, colouring up, 'I realised I was developing a terrible crush on her. She was very beautiful, and her poise and gracefulness reminded me of my mother, who… well, reminded me of my mother. So I tore myself away and continued my journey.

'I walked on through Macael and down to Tabernas. Then on through the desolate, desert landscape along the Andarax. I'm sure you all know it well. I met a beggar on the way named, can you believe, Ibn. He said his mother couldn't think what to call him so she just called him "Ibn". He directed me to the *baños* at Al-Hamma some miles higher in the hills. Being Thursday it was women's day in the baths, and all the Muslim lords and nobles were standing around in their finery watching each other suspiciously to see who was eyeing up their own womenfolk. It really was quite amusing!'

Pedro paused to sip some wine. He was still describing the nice parts of his journey and he was enjoying himself. The other three sat there laughing and giggling, thoroughly enjoying the tale.

'One of the workers there, attending the wonderful terraced gardens watered by the hot spring, showed me the *baños* through a broken window with the women bathing in them. I had little doubt as to how the window came to be broken! That evening I joined him and the others for their feast, which they were treated to every Thursday. That night was pitch black and had an eerie feeling which muffled all sound, but there was no mist or fog and I could see the lights of the distant city. Then all of a sudden a fierce gale sprang up from nowhere. It started from the sea and moved right around until it blew from the mountains behind me. A well nearby overflowed, and the water channel through the gardens was cut by a fallen tree, spilling the water across the terrace and then down into the valley miles below. My ears popped continually. Then as quickly as the gale sprung up, it stopped, and all was deathly quiet again. It was all very strange.

'Early the next morning, I was sitting on the *baños* wall eating some breakfast when the ground shook beneath me. The hot spring ceased flowing, and terrifyingly, the ground along the road rippled up and down like a carpet being shaken. Then a great red-brown pall of dust rose from Almería and Pechina to my right, followed a half-minute later by a deep muffled roar. Around me, buildings collapsed and, as the shaking came to an end, an enormous rock became dislodged from the mountain above and came crashing down to my right, carrying more mountainside with it. Dogs barked and people screamed. Children ran from fallen houses. A woman called out from one collapsed building. With a neighbour I crawled into the ruins of her house to extricate her trapped husband. But by the time we had pulled him out of the ruins he was dead. He had been terribly injured.

'I was too tired to stay and help other villagers there who needed assistance and, in any case, I remembered that I had an uncle in Almería and I wanted to see if he was still alive after the earthquake. So I hurried down into the Andarax valley, past Pechina which was largely destroyed, and by the evening I reached Almería. I was exhausted, I can tell you.'

'Was that when you were arrested?' asked Antonio.

'Yes. I worked my way through the ruined city. There was death and destruction everywhere. A lot of the city wall had collapsed and most of the houses in the city also. It was getting dark. I passed an elderly man standing by his ruined jeweller's shop. His wife and two sons lay dead, and he implored me to go into the ruins to locate his jewel box. While I was inside, there was a second tremor, and when I came out the man wasn't there – just a pile of rubble. At that instant I was pounced on by two rough-looking soldiers. That's when my problems started. But I think you know the rest from what Abel Jiménez told you in his letter.'

'No. He said very little, Pedro. Just that you were in the hands of the Inquisition in Jaén. Please tell us what happened.'

Pedro's voice lowered into not much more than a whisper, as the events of that terrible time came flooding back into his mind.

'The one soldier was called Zaquera – Zak for short. The other was Gázquez, Gaz for short. They were evil men. They beat me to the ground and took the jeweller's treasure box from me. Zak saw the gold ring with the large ruby which Sabyán had given me for saving her children's lives and tore it from my finger, threatening to cut it off when it proved difficult to remove. Captain Ortíz arrived. It was already dark and raining. He confiscated the contents of the treasure box but would not listen to my story about what had happened. I was arrested and thrown into a freezing cell where there were two other men lying there in the darkness, groaning in pain. The next morning the three of us were taken outside. The two men, already badly beaten, were flogged with one hundred lashes by Zak and Gaz. Sergeant Luque was appalled by the brutality of it all. The two men were then taken away and hanged for having violated a Muslim woman and her two young daughters and strangling all of them afterwards.

'I was given the same sentence of one hundred lashes for looting. Still, nobody would listen to my explanation of what really had happened. Zak wanted to inflict the punishment himself, but Sergeant Luque snatched the cat-o'-nine-tails from him and did it himself. He saved me from permanent disfigurement. He wielded the scourge as lightly as he could so that the knotted tails barely cut into my back. I still screamed in pain. Then, after only fifteen strokes, Captain Ortíz intervened and stopped further beatings. He said that he'd decided to take me with them and that the "holy friar" could decide what to do with me.

'I had no idea where they were going to take me. We rode out of Almería and travelled several days through the mountains in weather which got progressively colder until it snowed. One of the soldiers, Abel Jiménez, befriended me, and was the only one to believe my story or show me any understanding. The fourth soldier, Matute, was a giant of a man but said very little. On the night before we reached Jaén, when I still had no idea where they were taking me, the two evil soldiers, Zak and Gaz, broke into the farm outbuilding in which I was locked. While Gaz held me down, Zak threw me face down over an old table and… and he sod… sod…'

'Sodomised you?' said Don Gonzalo, helping out.

'Yes, that's the word Antonio used.'

'Fortunately, Captain Ortíz burst into the shed with Sergeant Luque and the other two soldiers before Gázquez could have his way with me. While the powerful Matute held Zak down, Ortíz sliced open Zak's scrotum with a knife and cut out his… testicles. There was blood everywhere. He screamed the place down. Gaz begged that the same wouldn't happen to him. Instead, Captain Ortíz gave him a needle and thread and told him to sew Zak up! Captain Ortíz had already tied off the ends of the tubes. He said that he used to watch the shepherds on his father's farm do it when he was small. The next morning Gaz was flogged for his part in their assault on me and then they were sent packing. I've no idea what became of them afterwards.'

'No, nor have we,' added Antonio.

'That morning I was delivered to a building in Jaén, held in a cell, and dragged by a horseman through the streets to the house of the Inquisition. You know the rest of the story, Don Gonzalo. I was confined in a cold, dark cell for four months and then interrogated by the Inquisitor of Jaén, Diego Rodriguez Lucero, and the Inquisitor General of Castile, Tomás de Torquemada, whom a man in the cell next to me had described. What became of that poor man after what he had been through I have no idea. I think he must have been tortured on the rack. As they hung me by my wrists which were tied behind me, demanding that I tell them who my father was, you, Don Gonzalo, burst into the interrogation chamber and rescued me. I dread to think what more the inquisitors would have done to me if you had not saved me. Then you brought me here, and under the care of Jacob and Faiz I have recovered from my wounds.'

Antonio was the first to speak after Pedro finished his story.

'You've certainly had a lifetime's experience in the last six months, both good and bad. But what made you leave home in the first place? And why did you want to run away to sea?'

Pedro knew that his attempt at avoiding telling of the reason for his running away from home would not succeed.

'My father had a beautiful Toledo sword made for me for my thirteenth birthday. He said that we lived in troubled times, and that I should learn to defend myself. There was a retired Christian soldier in the town and he gave me sword lessons. He had fought at the fall of Constantinople when he was just sixteen years old… Marco Arana was a wonderful man, and I loved him.

He was warm and kindly and full of fun; so different from my brutal father with his black moods. One day, after a rainstorm, we were practising with bared blades in the alleyway behind our house. Marco was teaching me to make low upward thrusts and he got annoyed with me, shouting at me to get lower still and thrust upwards hard with my sword. As I thrust upwards as he instructed, Marco slipped on the wet cobblestones and fell onto my sword, which passed through his neck.

'My father had come to the back door having heard the shouting, and at that instant saw my upward thrust at Marco. There and then I ran from the yard to the mountains above Vélez Blanco. I hid my accursed sword in a crevice and decided that I couldn't return home. I'd done something wicked and in some way I had to atone. Running away to sea seemed one way I could do this.'

'But I don't understand, Pedro,' queried Don Gonzalo. 'Surely your father would've understood what happened if you'd explained it to him? He would've realised that it was an accident, surely? Is there something else? Something else you don't want to speak about? You said last week that you had done some "shameful things". Is there something else?'

'I hoped not to tell you,' replied Pedro, 'but you seem able to see inside me.

'Yes,' he said after a pause. 'There is something else, something worse, far worse which I did before Marco's death. The two things together made me realise that I was cursed by the devil himself and couldn't stay at home and risk a third terrible accident.'

'So what happened? Can you tell us about it?'

Slowly, very deliberately, Pedro started his confession.

'I mentioned that my father gave me a magnificent Toledo sword for my thirteenth birthday. As a treat, he and I, and my uncle Joshua who lives in María nearby, rode to Lorca where David Levi, a swordsmith, lived. My father had successfully treated the swollen legs of his wife, Magdelena, and David promised to make a sword for me in appreciation of his wife's recovery. David Levi was trained years before by a Toledo swordsmith but both of them had to leave there as a result of the attacks on Jews in the city. David came south to Lorca. He was only in his mid-twenties then. I watched how David fashioned the sword in his forge – and also my dagger here, which you have seen and admired. Both were made the same way with a core of soft iron welded inside the steel of the blade. This is the secret of Toledo swords. David had to take his wagon to Bédar, near Mojácar, to collect some more iron from a furnace there which belonged to his friend Rodríguez. My father agreed that I could go with him.

Pedro went over the grim details of the disaster at the forge: the flooded stream, the explosion, the man with iron burning in his chest, and Rodriguez putting him out of his misery with a sledgehammer.

'The next day I should have owned up and taken my punishment,' he went on. 'It was all my fault – and now I have the blood of three men on my hands.

I'm still haunted by this event, and can't get the images of the explosion and the injuries to the stricken men out of my mind. I couldn't bring myself to tell David Levi or anyone else what had happened. You gentlemen are the first people I've told about this terrible event. Now you can see that after I'd killed Marco three months later I felt that my very soul was damned, and that I had to run away until I could purge the evil from me.'

'My dear Pedro,' said Don Gonzalo, slowly and deliberately, 'if all this time you've been carrying around this burden of guilt for two accidents which were clearly acts of God, however terrible the consequences, it's no wonder that you've felt weighed down by them. They are more than a grown man could bear, let alone a fourteen-year-old boy. I do, indeed, feel truly sorry for what you've gone through.'

'Yes, it's unimaginable, Don Gonzalo,' added Antonio. 'And not to have confided in anybody. I cannot imagine that. After all this time…'

'Well now,' said Don Gonzalo, trying to lighten the mood. 'Look on the bright side, Pedro. You said that you needed to purge your soul for the accidents you caused. Well, since then you have had Sabyán's ruby ring torn from your finger by that blaggart, Zak. You have been flogged, sodomised and finally tortured by the Spanish Inquisition. Don't you think that's enough penance for any one person?'

'Yes, maybe it is,' responded Pedro thoughtfully.

'Pedro,' asked Boabdil. 'You mentioned that your father cured your swordsmith's wife's legs in Lorca. Is he a doctor? And you still haven't told us how you came to speak Arabic so well. Is your father an Arab? Maybe an Arab doctor?'

'No, no, Sire,' laughed Pedro. 'My father's an apothecary, in fact, a Jewish apothecary. And quite a famous one, I think. At least, the people in Oria knew of his medicines. My grandfather started the business years ago, and my father and two uncles are all, more or less, in the same trade. My father prepares his medicines and ointments from herbs and spices which are known to have curative powers. My uncle Joshua, whom I mentioned lives in María just a few miles above Vélez, has a team of young people who collect selected herbs and plants from the crags and woods above the village. These he dries out and sells in the markets of neighbouring towns and villages. He also supplies my father with those he needs.'

'And spices?'

'I have an uncle, Simón, who lives in Almería – or did. I don't know whether he survived the earthquake or not. I was on my way to find him when I was stopped by the jeweller who, as it turned out, knew Simón and knew of me and my family. I was going to accompany him to my uncle's house when the man disappeared under the rubble of his house after the second tremor. Anyway, my uncle Simón obtains, or obtained, spices from India and the countries beyond and, again, supplies my father with those he needs.'

'Your family name is "de Tudela". That's in the north of the country in the kingdom of Navarra. Why is that?' asked Antonio.

'My great-grandfather, that is my father's grandfather, Aaron, trained under the famous Jewish doctor, Josef Orabuena, who was physician to Carlos the Second. He practised in Tudela, but for reasons my father has never explained to me, my great-grandfather moved down here to *Al-Andalus*. Maybe it was because Jews are more tolerated here amongst the Muslims than amongst the Christians?'

'That's certainly true, Pedro,' said the Sultan. 'But you still haven't explained where you learnt your Arabic?'

'Ah,' said the youngster, giving his standard answer. 'My best friend is an Arab boy called Yazíd. We played together nearly every day after my lessons and I learnt what Arabic I know from him.'

'No, that can't be, Pedro!' said Boabdil reproachfully. 'Your Arabic is not that of a street urchin. It is more cosmopolitan. You learnt it somewhere else, not in Vélez Blanco.'

'Your features – they are not those of a Jewish boy,' interrupted Don Gonzalo. '*Is* your mother Jewish?'

'No, she was Christian, and…'

The three men looked at each other, then at Pedro and together said:

'Was? How do you mean *was*?'

Pedro's face darkened and he cupped his hands over his eyes as he started to weep. He couldn't stop.

The three men knew that they had touched the darkest spot in Pedro's short and eventful life.

He sobbed and sobbed and sobbed.

XV: Pedro's Secret

It was several minutes before Pedro could bring himself to continue his story. The others sat there in embarrassed silence. He did not get very far before there was an interruption.

'My mother…' he had begun.

There was a knock on the door and Faiz, Boabdil's servant, entered.

'My lord,' he said, 'our vizier, Abul Kásim Benegas, has arrived hotfoot from Granada. There's some urgent business he wishes to discuss with you. He says that it's too delicate a matter for him to have sent you a letter.'

'Oh dear,' sighed *El Chico* wearily. 'I expect my uncle has been causing grief somewhere, or Fernando wants more money from us because he can't pay his army. It'll be the same old story. Carry on, please. I'll return as soon as I've seen Kásim. He can join us when I return if he wishes.'

'Yes, carry on please, Pedro,' urged Don Gonzalo. He guessed that Pedro had reached the telling of some terrible event in his life which he'd bottled up for a very long time.

'My mother disappeared when I was eight years old,' Pedro continued. 'My young sister Cristina and I loved her dearly and will never forget her. She was tall, taller than my father, and had blue eyes. Her long fair hair reached down to her shoulders. She spent hours brushing it in front of the mirror. Our house was a happy place and was filled with her laughter. She always had time to play with me and Cristina, who's three years younger than me. My mother used to take us for picnics into the hills and woods above the town. It's why they're still so special to me and why I go there when I get into trouble and need to get away. My mother was a Christian and insisted that Cristina and I were brought up as Christians and not as Jews. But in all honesty I cannot say that the Church played much part in our upbringing. I think my mother just wanted us not to become Jews. I think my father went along with this due to the growing number of attacks on Jews in many cities around Spain. He admitted to me recently that he felt the days of the Jews in Christian Spain were numbered.

'To my father, my mother…'

'What was her name, Pedro?' enquired Don Gonzalo softly.

'Miriam. Her name was Miriam, Don Gonzalo,' he replied, then continued.

'My mother was the apple of my father's eye and he'd do anything for her, even giving in on the matter of our religious upbringing. He loved taking her down in the town because she was so beautiful and he enjoyed making his friends envious. She held her head high and moved in a way that was very distinctive and made her very graceful. Sabyán, the Muslim woman I met in Oria, whose children I saved from drowning, is strikingly similar to her in grace and poise. My mother had long, slim fingers and was a wonderful needlewoman. She wove cottons, wools and silks in intricate patterns adorned with the most gorgeous embroideries. She designed all these herself, and made the dyes for them herself. Our house was filled with her handiwork.

'I tell you,' he chuckled, 'what with my father grinding, mixing or distilling his medicines and ointments from his herbs and spices and my mother collecting, drying and boiling her plants and flowers to make the natural dyes she used, and fixing her yarns with alum as a mordant, the house was like a distillery! Our kitchen and back yard were always filled with dozens and dozens of big earthenware pots in which my mother dyed her yarns.'

Pedro's voice lowered as he looked at the floor.

'Then one day when, as I said, I was eight, my father took me and my mother to Aguilas. She was then twenty-six. My father had to go there to collect a retort for his dispensary and he wanted to treat us to a day out. Aguilas is the nearest large harbour to us, and he said that it was always an exciting place to go. There is so much bustle and activity with dozens and dozens of boats of all shapes and sizes from far away being loaded and unloaded. I'd never been there before and was so excited to go. Cristina was only five so my aunt Ana came down from María to look after her. My mother wore her favourite sky blue dress and with her long, fair hair she was truly stunning. I will always remember her in that dress. How I wish she'd worn her ordinary clothes that day.'

'What happened, Pedro?' asked Antonio, leaning forward in his chair.

'My father took us to the quayside so we could watch everything going on. He said that he'd be back in a few minutes after he'd collected the retort he was after. That's the last we saw of him.'

'We?' questioned Antonio, startled.

'Yes. We!'

'As my mother and I stood there hand in hand, joking and laughing and pointing to all the things happening around us, two burly black Africans shoved me away. One grabbed my mother around the waist and clamped his other filthy hand around her mouth to stop her from crying out. The other man grabbed her ankles, sliding his hand up her legs. She struggled like mad and tried to scream as they ran with her along the quayside, pushing through the dense crowd of people. But they quickly disappeared from sight. We never saw her again. My last memory of her is of her kicking and struggling to free herself from the two kidnappers.'

'You say you never saw her again?'

'No, never. We've no idea what became of her. My father thinks that she was taken to a slave market to be sold or maybe taken as a concubine of a wealthy Arab. But he believes that it's more than likely she'd now be dead. He hopes she is. He can't bear the thought of what terrible things might have been done to her.'

'Didn't your father look for her?'

'Of course. He told me later that he searched for her and asked after her until it was dark in every waterside tavern and dwelling, and on every boat moored there. He returned the next day, and the next day, for four days, looking everywhere in the roughest and dingiest places, but finally he had to give up.'

'So you two returned home without your mother? It must have been…'

'No, I didn't return home…'

'How do you mean?'

'Just after my mother was torn from my hand by the two Africans, and as I was just about to chase after them, I myself was grabbed from behind by a man with one eye and a deep scar down his face. He stank. He threw me over his shoulder, and despite my kicking and shouting he ran until he reached an old tavern at the edge of town. Without a word, a refined Arab in a spotless white *zihara* and dark blue *'imama* paid him a few gold coins. The man who grabbed me ran off. The man in white pushed me by the scruff of the neck into a dark room and bolted it from outside. I shouted for help but it was all in vain.'

'What happened then?'

'Some time later – I don't know how much longer, but it was dark outside – another man came and let me out. He was clearly a seaman, big and gruff. His name turned out to be Ali. He had a gold ring in one ear and a full, black beard. His face was weathered brown like old leather. He said something to me in Arabic which I didn't understand and took me through the dark streets to a dhow, and I was made to climb up over the side onto the deck. I never left that boat for well over a year.'

'So you were taken as a slave on board the boat?'

'Yes, as a cabin boy. I've learnt since that it's common for boys to be snatched as slaves by Berber pirates in all the ports of *Al-Andalus*, and throughout the Mediterranean. My uncle Joshua warned me of this last October when I left his house in María, determined to run away to sea.'

Pedro paused to take a sip of red wine. He had got off his chest what became of his mother and he felt a lot better. He had told nobody of the nature of his mother's disappearance since that time.

'My father blamed himself totally for losing my mother. He chose to tell people that she'd died of a fatal disease after visiting the port. He was a changed man afterwards: withdrawn, miserable and cantankerous.'

'What happened to you when you boarded the dhow? Were you mistreated?' asked Don Gonzalo.

'For a dhow, the boat was quite large. It had two masts and was lateen-rigged with big slanting triangular sails. It traded around the Mediterranean coast as far as Egypt. Ali was the captain, and there were just four other crew besides me. But they weren't always the same four. Two were always there, they were inseparable. The other two crew changed from time to time. One or both would vanish when we reached a port and Ali would take on two more. That seems the way with seamen.'

'Did they beat you?'

'You seem very concerned how I have been treated, Don Gonzalo!' laughed Pedro. 'Looking back,' he continued, 'I was fortunate to have been under Ali's protection. He was a rough and ready man and for the first few months he would cuff me hard around the ears if I didn't do what he said. But once I understood what he was saying in Arabic there was little problem. In fact, after I returned home I was punished by my father far more severely than by Ali. Ali just used his hands to clip me around the ears, but Father used a leather belt. But that was after my mother disappeared and he had become crotchety.'

'What about the other crew members?'

'Mo and Abul were as good as gold. They were always together, and being a young boy it took me a while to guess what they were up to. They always seemed to have their hands in each other's baggy *sarawils*, since that's all we wore most of the year; that and an *'imama* to keep the sun off. But they were harmless and very good to me, and saved me from the preying hands of other crewmen on more than one occasion.'

'Where did you live? What did you do on board?'

'There was no cabin above deck. Ali had a small space below deck at the bows and I shared that with him. It was only about five feet high and I could just stand up in it. The other crew had an even smaller space aft on the other side of the hold, but more often than not they would find somewhere on the deck to sleep, although there was never much room. At first I was not much use. I could barely keep my feet on the slippery deck, let alone shin up the masts to secure the lateen sails when we were in port or sheltering from a storm. So I brewed the strong, sweet-scented tea which Ali liked almost every hour of the day and night, and helped Mo and Abul prepare the meal at sunset, and I swabbed the decks and generally kept things shipshape. I found it very hard at first and cried most nights, as much for my lost mother, who was never very far from my thoughts, as for feeling alone and sorry for myself.

'Ali had his own wife and sons in the Al-Hawd district of Almería. He explained later that he didn't want to take me on board but the ship's owner, the man in white with the dark blue *'imama* who bought me, insisted that he take me onto his ship.'

'So were you always "cook and bottle-washer"?'

'Yes, I always had those chores, after all I was the cabin boy and only eight years old. After four months or so I was able to understand much of what Ali and his crew said to me. I was lucky because a sailor joined us in Barcelona who spoke Castilian and good Arabic. Initially, I learnt the hard way by Ali pointing at things and saying what they were in Arabic. But with Paco explaining what things were in Castilian and Arabic I picked things up very quickly. People are always asking me, "Where did you learn your Arabic?" but it was Paco and Ali who taught me most of what I know.'

'Well, Boabdil says that you speak it very well.'

'That's kind of him, but I still don't understand a lot of what is said to me.'

'Anyway, after four or five months Ali took me under his wing. I think he'd got to like me. He started to teach me how to navigate around and across the Mediterranean using his hourglass and compass…'

'How do you mean, Pedro? I've never understood these things,' asked Antonio.

'For Ali a compass was mostly sufficient. He'd been plying these same coasts since he was ten and knew them like the back of his hand. He understood the vagaries of the winds, and even in a gale, I never had any fear of the ship foundering. Ali was a brilliant sailor. However, to return to the navigating. One of my tasks was to keep the hourglass, and woe betide me if I forgot to turn it over on time!'

'Did you have to do this at night?'

'Yes, at night Ali or I would still turn them over. But if we forgot then we would have to reset them the next day at midday when the sun was at its highest point in the sky. This always took some time, so if I ever forgot to turn them I would get a sharp clout from Ali. After a few of these I rarely forgot! The hourglass was important, since it was the only way to keep a check on the movement of the sun in the sky. With an hourglass and the sun one hardly needs a compass.'

'What happened at night?'

'Whenever he could, Ali would anchor in a sheltered bay. If we were on the open sea then we could navigate by the stars. In many ways it's easier navigating at night since, depending on the season, there are many stars you can choose from. Ali was very patient with me and taught me to recognise all the bright stars and the main constellations. I think it was because I was the first person he'd had on board who'd shown any real interest.

'Did you know, Don Gonzalo, that stars' names such as Rigel, Pegasus and Aldebaran and very many others are all derived from Arab names, and that there have been a whole host of great Arab astronomers, from al-Khwarizmi in the eighth century to al-Zarqali in the twelfth? It was he who invented the astrolabe.'

'Not only did I not know that, Pedro,' replied the ambassador to the King with some consternation, 'but Sirius and Orion are the only two I can find at night. I'm amazed that you know so much about them.'

'I came to love the stars in the sky, Don Gonzalo. Some nights when it was pitch black I'd lie on a blanket on the deck just looking at them, trying to make out which stars formed which constellations, which Ali said are mainly of Greek or Roman origin. Some I've been unable to fathom out even to this day. Ali was no wiser.'

'What ports did you visit, Pedro?'

'Most of them. Ali traded around most of the Mediterranean coasts of Europe and North Africa; silks, brocades and marble from Almería, rice and oranges from Valencia, ceramics from Barcelona, wine and iron from Marseilles, cotton and sailcloth from Alexandria, and beautiful woven carpets and brassware from Tunis.'

'Didn't you go to Constantinople?' enquired Antonio.

'You mean Istanbul?' corrected Pedro. 'The Turks changed its name to Stanbul, or Istanbul –"Into the city"!'

'All right, Istanbul.'

'Yes, I forgot Istanbul. We went there three times during the eighteen months I was kept on that boat.'

'Heavens. That long? It must have seemed like a lifetime?'

'It seemed so at times. Istanbul was the only place I was allowed off the boat.'

'Just the once?'

'Yes, just once. Ali said that it was too dangerous for a small boy to be loose in any of the Mediterranean ports. Judging by what I'd learnt I think he was right. But the last time we visited Istanbul he took me ashore himself and showed me around the city. By that time he was treating me almost as his own son.'

'And what was it like?'

'It was fabulous. I loved it. Visiting there almost made my whole spell of captivity worthwhile. As I'm sure you know, the city lies at the entrance to the Black Sea. The main part of the city lies on the north side of the Bosporus straits and is split into two by a fast-flowing river which forms a channel called the Golden Horn. It's a wonderful natural anchorage and is several miles long and nearly half a mile wide. It was filled with two-tiered oared galleys like centipedes, big high-castellated carracks, square-sailed and lateen-rigged caravels, graceful feluccas from the Nile with beautiful triangular sails, and countless other merchant ships of all shapes and sizes.

'It was my task to keep a tally of the number of amphorae of wine we were unloading and not to get distracted. This is a common ploy by the Genoese traders who seem to dominate every port of call and would cheat their grandmothers out of their last ducats. Ali made me sit on the angled spar against the foremast so that I had a clear view of what was happening. The slaves unloading the amphorae were brutally treated by their Turkish masters. All had iron hoops around their necks and most seemed deeply branded on one shoulder. Many seemed to be Christians, judging by their pale skin and brown hair and the extra severe beating they received. Ali said that most of them would have been castrated and badly abused by their Turkish overlords, such is the hatred which exists between the two peoples. I tell you, I didn't wander far from Ali when he took me ashore!'

'What was the city like?'

'You can't forget Istanbul. The city is enclosed by a great defensive wall one hundred feet high, built and rebuilt over a period of a thousand years, which closes off the peninsula and runs around the southern coastline. This wall is truly immense, with dozens of square and rounded towers and massive gateways. The main city sits on six hills and by the time I was there, high turquoise and gold cupolas and minarets were already dominating the skyline. It had been only thirty years since the Turks took Constantinople from the Christians and everywhere churches were being converted to mosques, with long slender minarets being built onto them at their sides or corners. It is said that soon after the fall of the city as soldiers started to hack at the walls of St Sofia's cathedral, Sultan Mehmed had them arrested and admonished them by declaring, "For you, the treasures and the prisoners are enough. The buildings are mine!"

'On top of all these changes, new mosques were being constructed everywhere. Bazaars were springing up everywhere too; the Grand Bazaar had eleven entrances, it was so large. Across the river were the gentle slopes of the Pera district with even more new mosques being constructed amongst the tightly grouped houses, and with the palace of Pera on the crest of the hill. From the hills of the main city, the district of Scutari was clearly visible on the Asiatic side of the Bosporus. The rose-coloured houses there glowed brightly in the afternoon light, while away to the right on another slope was the city cemetery, with tall, slender cypress trees poking through the other trees. Boats of all sizes and from all nations tacked hard against the strong current of water to enter the Black Sea to the left. It was an awe-inspiring sight.'

'What was Alexandria like? You said you went there too.'

'Yes, a couple of times to take on rolls of sailcloth. It's the best to be had anywhere. I wasn't allowed off the boat, but it was strikingly different from Istanbul. Whereas Istanbul is now a Muslim city, Alexandria is essentially Roman still. A causeway links the mainland to the Island of Pharos, at the end of which is the stub of the incredible Roman lighthouse which was said to be over five hundred feet high, and at night could be seen from forty miles out to sea. The causeway separates the two harbours. We always anchored close to the beach of the Port of Eunostro, but most of the old city lies opposite the main harbour. From it could be seen the ruins of the Palace of Tolomeos with its parks and gardens, those of the Temple of Neptune, the Timoneon palace constructed by Mark Antony, and the columns and library of the Caesarean built by Octavius Caesar. Pompey's one-hundred-foot red stone column lay higher in the city, close to the city wall. It was very exciting to see it all.'

'As a matter of interest, how long did it take to sail from Almería to Alexandria?' enquired Don Gonzalo. 'I imagine it takes months.'

'It depends on the wind, but thirty or so days was normally enough. Coming back was less easy since it required a levanter wind from the east. April and October were best for this. So once Ali was in the eastern Mediterranean he would trade between the ports there during the summer months – maybe between Genoa, Istanbul, Alexandria and Tunis – before returning to our coasts here in the autumn. Even then it took seventy days or so to return.'

'So how did you come to get ashore again and return home?'

'I said that Ali began treating me like a son and he knew that I longed to return home to see my mother. You must realise that I'd no idea what became of her after she was snatched from me by the two Africans. I lived in hope that my father found her later that same day unharmed, and that she was now back home in Veléz Blanco. After some eighteen months Ali felt that the owner had had his full money's worth out of me. So one day as we approached Almería, and quite out of the blue, he said that he was going to set me free and drop me ashore in a rowing boat. Within an hour I found myself in the small port of Garrucha, not far from Mojácar. It took me just two days to get home from there.'

'It must have been an awful shock to find that your mother wasn't there?'

'It was truly terrible, far worse than being taken as a cabin boy on board the dhow. That happened all so quickly. But I'd had a year and a half to build up my hopes of my mother being at home. After a time my hopes became a certainty and then a reality. As I ran up the road from the city gate to our house I had not the slightest doubt that my mother would be there, sitting in the doorway in the sun doing her embroidery in a silent vigil, watching patiently down the road for me to return home. I knew my father would be pleased to see me but would pass it off with something like "You home then, Pedro? You took your time!"

'You simply cannot believe my disappointment when I found that my mother wasn't there. My father didn't seem to care whether I'd returned home or not. I barely recognised him. He seemed like an old man. His hair was unkempt and greying. He walked with a perpetual stoop and was bad-tempered and moody. Cristina said that he'd been like that from the time our mother disappeared and he had hardly spoken to her for months and months afterwards. It must have been truly dreadful for her to lose her mother and brother and suffer her changed father all at the same time. Nevertheless, after a few weeks he warmed a little and listened attentively to my adventures. It was then when he promised to have a Toledo sword made for me when I was old enough to handle it. I'll say that for him, he kept his word.'

Pedro sat back in his chair, thoroughly exhausted from the two hours it had taken him to narrate his story to Don Gonzalo and Antonio.

Abu 'Abd Allah Boabdil returned accompanied by his first minister, Abul Kásim Benegas.

'You won't believe the story which young Pedro has told us, Boabdil,' said Don Gonzalo. 'It's staggering to me that he could have been through so much. What with being taken as a slave on an Arab boat for eighteen months, losing his mother, causing the horrible death of two ironworkers at the furnace, accidentally killing his sword master who fought at the fall of Constantinople; then in the last few months having Sabyán's ruby ring torn from his finger, being flogged, sodomised and then tortured by the cursed Inquisition. Can you believe a more terrible set of experiences to go through?' He looked at the Sultan, whose shocked expression told his feelings.

'It's now clear to me, Boabdil, that we have to get him home safe and sound as soon as we can. Would you not agree?'

'Yes, certainly, Don Gonzalo. Indeed it's most opportune. Kásim has just told me that King Fernando wants us to move young Ahmad to Moclín, which lies between Córdoba and Granada. Maybe we can all leave together and then see Pedro on his way home from there?'

'But we need to plan this carefully, Boabdil. Having brought him here, it's our responsibility to ensure his safe return home. But it's getting late; I suggest you and I discuss this tomorrow. I think this young man here is in need of his bed. And so am I, for that matter!'

XVI: Mohammed the Valiant

The journey back through the mountains and past Guadix was deemed out of the question because of the unrest in the area. The most direct way was to travel due south to the west of Granada to Almuñécar or Salobreña on the coast and put Pedro on a boat going east to Almería. But this also was easier said than done. The whole of the mountain area to the west of Granada, running northwards from Málaga and Vélez Málaga to Loja and Lucena, almost to Córdoba, had been the scene of the bitter battles and skirmishes between Muslim and Christian forces over the last twenty to thirty years. Moreover, since that time, and not least at this moment, who held which town, village, lookout tower, olive grove or waterwheel changed by the week if not by the day, and there was no knowing who would be guarding the roads and passes.

'So how can we do it?' Boabdil asked Don Gonzalo.

'We need to think of someone who is known to both sides. Someone with standing who's instantly recognised by Christian and Muslim alike, and held in sufficient esteem to be allowed through unmolested.'

'Someone like King Fernando, you mean?'

'Hardly!' replied Don Gonzalo. 'He'd be taken hostage by your Muslim soldiers, and after being stripped naked of his possessions and fine clothes, he'd be offered as ransom for a tidy sum. Something approaching your annual paria payment I would guess!'

'So who then?'

'I've been giving a lot of thought to this, Boabdil. There's only one man I can think of who could travel speedily and unmolested through this territory with Pedro and then put him safely onto a Muslim merchant boat sailing east.'

Don Gonzalo leaned forward and whispered into Boabdil's ear.

'You can't be serious, Don Gonzalo! I've no idea where he is at this moment. But if you can persuade him to act as your courier for Pedro then I don't want to be around. You know how it is between him and me.'

'I know. But can you think of anybody better?'

Boabdil thought for a few moments, his lips pursing and his eyebrows frowning in concentration.

'No, I admit I can't. There's nobody better to guarantee Pedro's safety as far as Almuñécar.'

'Very well. The Big Man owes me a favour for holding off the King's army when he was beleaguered with his men at Archidona two years ago. The King is always ribbing me about that. I'll send Antonio post-haste to Granada in the hope that your people there will know where he is.'

'Antonio can go with one of my bodyguards,' said Boabdil. 'Yakub speaks quite good Castilian and it'll ensure Antonio's safety. I suggest we use Moclín as our point of rendezvous.'

'So be it. Antonio and Yakub can leave on the morrow. I'll prepare a letter. You'll need to write it in Arabic for me.'

It took two weeks to get a reply. The die was cast. A day's hard riding saw the party arrive at the *alcazaba* of Moclín, now in the hands of the Christians. The castle was threateningly close to Granada, which lay less than thirty miles to the south. The group was headed by Boabdil's most senior and trusted bodyguard who had been at his right hand through many battles and skirmishes with the Christians. Boabdil and Don Gonzalo followed, with Faiz and Pedro behind. Young Ahmad rode with his father. Boabdil's remaining two bodyguards brought up the rear. Helmeted, and with lances and their streamers held aloft, they looked imposing on their black steeds with their long white cloaks billowing in the wind. Only Boabdil had been to Moclín before when it was in Muslim hands. They worked their way up through the village, ascended the long, steep drive up to the main gate which was open ready. They turned right and continued aside the main wall before arriving in the castle grounds. The main living quarters in the big square tower lay ahead, close to the guardhouse. The northern wall to their right, patrolled by a sentry, followed the crest of the upper ridge, below which a scree slope fell away steeply. The castle of Moclín was substantially bigger than Porcuna and offered spectacular views to the east and south. The patchwork of roofs in the village far below provided a colourful and homely scene.

'Why is the Sultan so reluctant to meet your friend?' asked Pedro of Don Gonzalo, while they travelled there.

'He's hardly my friend, Pedro!' remarked the King's man. 'But you know by now the divisions which exist amongst the Muslim hierarchy. The Big Man has aligned himself with his brother Muley Hasán, who's Boabdil's father, and Soraya, who is Muley's principal wife, as well as the prince of Almería, Ibn Salim Ben Ibrahim al-Nagar and his devious son, Cidi Yahya al-Nagar. Yahya's a man I detest and don't trust for one minute. No woman is safe from his clutches. I think misguidedly that this group see themselves as defenders of the Empire. Boabdil, on the other hand, has for some reason aligned himself with the mischievous Abencerrajes, who are the Nazarí family line coming down through Yusuf the Third, Boabdil's great uncle. They've forcefully promoted themselves as sultans over the years.'

'Which group do you think is right, Don Gonzalo?'

'Take your pick! I admire the Big Man and his allies for making a last stand against us. But Boabdil is far more realistic. He knows that the days of the Moors are numbered and that further fighting will only lead to unnecessary suffering for his people. Málaga has left a terrible scar on everyone, even with me. I think it was unforgivable what we did there.'

As they entered the courtyard a smartly dressed young man came down from the castle wall where he had been looking out for them. He was fair, round-faced and clean-shaven. A silver medallion swung on his chest. His open white shirt provided more appropriate dress for early evening in June than the heavy clothes worn by Don Gonzalo and Boabdil.

He greeted them warmly. 'Good day, gentlemen. Welcome to Moclín. I trust you had a good journey. I'm Martín of Alarcón. The King has charged me with looking after Ahmad from now on – until such time as he is returned to you, my lord Boabdil. I trust that will not be too long.' He paused. 'So you must be Ahmad?' he said, approaching Pedro, who had just dismounted.

'Hardly, Martín!' called Don Gonzalo. 'That's Pedro Togeiro, who's been Ahmad's companion for a couple of months and who's been teaching him Castilian; and very well too, I may add. Ahmad's over there, hiding behind his father. He's still very shy... Ahmad,' he called out. 'Come over here and meet your new master, Martín of Alarcón.'

The courtesies and pleasantries were worked through and, in due course, they all entered the castle tower to freshen up, leaving their horses with the grooms who led them to the stables. Boabdil was aware of the new arrangements for Ahmad. What misgivings he might have had were quickly dispelled as he talked with Martín, who appeared to have a pleasant and open manner. He was sure that his son would warm to him very soon. But Boabdil had to be on his way. He didn't want to be around when the guide arrived who would accompany Pedro to the coast. This could be any day now. So early the next morning the Sultan bade a sad farewell to his tearful son and with his three bodyguards set off for Granada. He would arrive there by midday. It would be a year before he saw Ahmad again.

Pedro's excitement about returning home had been growing ever since Don Gonzalo had made his promise two weeks earlier. Now that he had left the confines of Porcuna and had started his journey home, he could barely stay still a minute and spent all the next day patrolling the battlements, watching for his guide to come. Don Gonzalo had not told him who the man would be, but he knew that he must be important if he could travel through both Christian and Muslim lands unmolested. He didn't have to wait long. In the afternoon of the second day, on June 4th, four men rode through the main gate and up the steep drive into the castle grounds. Hearing the sounds of horses hooves, Don Gonzalo ran out of the tower to meet them. Pedro ran along the battlements of the eastern wall, around the corner tower and along the northern wall, then tore down the steep flight of stone steps into the courtyard. Ahmad and Martín appeared in the tower doorway of the courtyard. Pedro recognised Boabdil's bodyguard, Yakub, as well as Antonio, who waved to him.

'Welcome to Moclín, Mohammed,' greeted Don Gonzalo to the tallest of the men as he descended from his horse. 'Did you have a good journey?'

'Thank you, Don Gonzalo,' he said rather testily. 'It was hot, tiring and dusty, and we met a squadron of the King's soldiers who made a nuisance of themselves, but your man, Antonio, soon put them in their place. Other than that the journey was largely uneventful. It's a long time since I was here. I can see that there have been a lot of changes.'

He introduced his party in faltering Castilian. He spoke it less well than his nephew, Boabdil.

'You know your man Antonio, of course, and Boabdil's bodyguard, Yakub. This youngster here is Nasr, the nephew of Ibrahim al-Nagar in Almería. He's acting as my standard-bearer and groom.

'Now, who's this?' he said to Don Gonzalo, pointing to Pedro running across the courtyard. 'He seems very anxious to meet us!'

'That's Pedro Togeiro, Mohammed. He's the young man you've agreed to see onto a boat at Almuñécar.'

'Hmm, just a sprite of a lad. He must've done something very important to warrant this special treatment,' he replied grudgingly.

'It's what he's been through, Mohammed, not what he's done. At my instigation he's been at Porcuna for two months teaching Ahmad Castilian. Now it's time he returned to his home at Vélez Blanco on the eastern border of your kingdom. I want to be absolutely sure that he'll get home safely.'

'Pedro,' said Don Gonzalo, as he reached them somewhat breathless. 'Meet Mohammed Abu Abdalá Ibn Sa'd…'

'Not *El Zagal* – the Valiant – lord Boabdil's uncle?' said Pedro, open-jawed.

'So you've heard of me, young fellow?' said the tall Muslim, puffing out his chest. 'I can see we're going to get on splendidly.'

Pedro looked up at the man as he brushed the dust from his tunic. He must have been close to fifty. He was tall, erect and strongly-built, with a dark, sunburnt and lined face. He had an imposing presence. He was clearly a leader of men and was used to being obeyed. A meagre beard followed his jawline, but it was his black slanting eyes which Pedro was most struck by. What did they convey – bravery and valour, or cunning, treachery and ruthlessness? Maybe a mixture of all of them. Was this the man who could lead his men into battle while negotiating terms of surrender? Was this the man who had the heads of all the Christian inhabitants of Alhama stuck on poles along the castle walls?

His thoughts were interrupted.

'Where's that weakling nephew of mine, Don Gonzalo? Why isn't he here to meet me? I've ridden all the way here from Guadix, leaving my men there strengthening the fortifications in the villages around. I expected him to be here to greet me.'

'If you mean Boabdil? He left yesterday. He didn't want to be here when you arrived.'

'Hmm. I'm not surprised. I would have probably wrung his neck. What's an honourable fellow like you doing being his protector?'

'I'm acting for the King, as you well know, Mohammed. However, Boabdil isn't as you describe him. He may not be a firebrand, but he's intelligent and thoughtful, and I believe has his people's best interests at heart.'

'What, by selling them down the river to Fernando and that pompous wife of his?'

'No, by trying to arrive at an accord with us which will safeguard your people's homes, livelihoods and beliefs.'

'You don't seriously believe that, do you, Don Gonzalo? Surely not. Fernando's not to be trusted. The only thing which he responds to is force. Like with like, that's what I say.'

'But you don't have the power now, Mohammed. You can't match the overwhelming numbers of our forces or the power of our guns. In the end you'll have no choice but to treat with us. This is what Boabdil recognises.'

'Huh. The man's a weakling and should never be sultan. Now if I were sultan...'

'But you're not, Mohammed. The people of Granada chose Boabdil in preference to his father.'

'What, my brother Muley Hasán? Ugh! He's no better than his miserable son...'

'Possibly. But maybe your people are wiser than you give them credit for. Maybe they've had enough bloodshed...' Don Gonzalo stopped, realising that they were not really getting anywhere. 'Come, come, my friend. We can't stand here in the sun arguing about the future of your peoples and mine. You know my views – this is your land and you should be allowed to live in it peacefully. You deserve to do so. You have terraced the mountains and watered the desert. We should leave you in peace.'

'Well said, Don Gonzalo! If only Fernando held your views.'

'He knows my views well enough, Mohammed, I assure you. But he believes that it's his destiny to drive you from his lands and he has the formidable support of the Queen.'

'You can say that again. Pompous she may be, but I've seen her influence on your armies when she arrives on the scene. Then we know that we're in for a fierce battle! But you're right. Let's go inside and wash the dust from our throats. Then we can plan our journey to Almuñécar. When shall we set off, young fellow?'

'Can we go this afternoon?' queried Pedro.

'This afternoon?' roared *El Zagal*, laughing. 'We've ridden three days solidly to get here, Pedro. I think tomorrow will be soon enough, don't you?'

He ruffled Pedro's hair with his callused sword hand and led the boy towards the cool shadows of the tower.

El Zagal, Nasr and Pedro were ready to set off early the next morning. Don Gonzalo, Martín of Alarcón and Ahmad were all there to see them off.

'Good luck, Pedro,' said Don Gonzalo. 'I've enjoyed meeting you. If I'd had a son and not three daughters, I would've been more than happy if he'd been like you.'

'Thank you, sir,' replied Pedro. 'You know that I can't thank you enough for rescuing me from the Inquisition and for bringing me to Porcuna. The spell there with Ahmad was what I needed to get over my wounds.'

'In mind and body.'

'Yes, I was in a terrible state, wasn't I?'

'You had cause to be, Pedro. Now be on your way. We'll meet again. Of that I'm sure.'

'I hope so, Don Gonzalo, I do hope so,' said Pedro.

'*Ma'al salama*, Ahmad,' shouted Pedro over his shoulder as they set off, waving to the youngster.

'*Ma'al salama*, Pedro,' came the reply.

El Zagal set off at a good pace on his big, black stallion. Pedro had to ride hard to keep up with him. The Muslim's black turban and crimson cloak, streaming out behind him in the morning breeze, made him instantly recognisable. If that were not enough, Nasr, riding effortlessly alongside, held aloft his master's banner, a black forked pennant bearing the image of a white falcon. *El Zagal* decided to skirt Granada, which lay a morning's ride to the south-east, and instead headed south-west for Illora and then southwards across the Río Genil and the main Granada-Sevilla road to the strategic town of Alhama de Granada. *El Zagal* was instantly recognised in all the villages through which they passed. More than once the three horsemen were forced to stop and dismount to partake of refreshments urged upon them by spirited womenfolk. However, not everyone saw him as a returning hero. In many places, conspicuous by the number of crippled or maimed former soldiers, and women trapped in poverty without husband or son to care for them, he was shunned and spat at.

They covered the forty or so miles to the key town of Alhama well before sundown. Alhama was the western gateway to Granada. Whoever held Alhama held Granada. For the moment it lay in Muslim hands, and was very much home to the big Muslim leader. With the town only a mile or two ahead, he cut back to the right, down a short winding ravine through which the Río Alhama descended. Pedro was puzzled why they turned off the road, but all became clear a few minutes later when they rode down a short track to a hostelry on the banks of the river as it left the gorge. A short distance below, dozens of naked children were splashing around in the water from which steam was rising.

'Do you know where we are, Pedro?' asked *El Zagal*.

'No, but we must be near Alhama.'

'These are the famous Baños de Alhama. I know the innkeeper here and he'll make us comfortable and give us rooms for the night. We've travelled enough for one day, but we made good time to get here before sunset. A prodigious quantity of hot water emanates here from these rocks and you can see there are several watermills above and below these *bañeras*. A soak in these rich mineral waters will do us the power of good after our riding.'

'Are these like the Baños de Al-Hamma, not far from Almería?'

'You know them?'

'Yes, as I mentioned earlier today when I told you how I came to meet Don Gonzalo, it was where I witnessed the earthquake which struck Almería last November and which led to all my problems.'

'Yes, these *baños* are very similar, but there are more of them here, and being at the end of a gorge there are watermills here too, as you've seen. It's why Alhama is such an important town.'

The innkeeper greeted them warmly and showed them to some rooms. The Muslim lord was given the most sumptuous rooms in the dwelling, with rich carpets and furnishings. Pedro and Nasr were shown to a modest and cramped room at the end of the corridor, but the hospitality afforded by the innkeeper was no less bounteous. Soon they were all relaxing in one of the hot-water baths, Pedro's companions seemingly less afflicted by the sulphurous, steamy atmosphere than he.

The next day, after a generous breakfast of fresh-baked bread and home-made savoury sausages, they set off again and soon entered the formidable southern gate of Alhama. The town lay on the slopes of a limestone escarpment and overlooked two narrow and very deep gorges along which lay yet more mills. With the narrow streets rising steeply all around, a compact, maroon-coloured, square-walled *alcazaba* with a single squat tower occupied a flat open space. A high but unpretentious mosque stood a short distance behind. At first baffled as to what they were, Pedro was suddenly shocked to discover that the blackened objects stuck on poles on the walls of the *alcazaba* were the desiccated remains of those Christian heads which had not decomposed in the hot sun and which *El Zagal* had had placed there as long as five years ago after his fury over the loss of Ronda. He had been hoodwinked by the wiley Marquis of Cádiz into believing that Loja and not Ronda would be the focus for the attack. The big man saw Pedro staring at them, but said nothing.

The road southwards out of Alhama continued to rise through rounded hills graced by holm oak trees with their dark green leathery leaves, yellow-flowered gorse, scented rosemary, pungent thyme and fragrant rock roses now in bud. Eventually, a broad flat valley opened up below them, its fertile soils, once the bed of a lake, supporting a rich variety of crops. By far the most important of these was the meadow saffron crocus, the anthers of which provided the much prized orange-yellow food flavouring, an important export from Almería.

Across the flat valley floor, the road rose a short distance to the high, strategic U-shaped pass of Ventas de Zafarraya, which was flanked by rugged crags. High on the left abutment of the pass a lone figure stood looking out from a watchtower, such was the importance of this gateway from the coast to the south.

'Is he friend or foe?' asked *El Zagal*, squinting up into the bright, midday sky at the silhouetted figure.

It mattered little. As he spoke, two Christian soldiers appeared from a stone guardhouse concealed behind a fallen rock. They were helmeted, clad to their knees in link mail, and were heavily armed with pikes, swords and evil-looking maces. They ran to the road and blocked the way with crossed pikes. Pedro was glad to be with the great *El Zagal*. The man was not noted for his patience or tolerance.

'And who are you?' one of the soldiers called out.

'And who are you asking me who I am?' replied the big Muslim with venom in his faltering Castilian. 'You're obstructing the Sultan's highway. Be gone before you have cause to regret your insolence!'

'We're here at the King's command. I repeat, who are you? Declare yourself!'

'Stand aside, I say. If I get down from this horse then your verminous entrails will cover these rocks like camel dung. Now, out of my way.'

The Muslim lord rode forward but the two guards were defiant and the pikes remained firmly where they were. *El Zagal* drew his broad, curving scimitar from his scabbard and dismounted. His young standard-bearer, in no way cowered by the threats, did the same. Pedro remained on his horse. He just wished he had his Toledo sword with him. What a tale he could tell, for generations of how he fought alongside the greatest Muslim warrior.

Fearlessly, *El Zagal* strode towards the two Christian guards. Their pikes started to waver.

'Do you not know who I am?' he challenged, raising his scimitar to shoulder height and pointing at his standard still held aloft by Nasr.

'W – w – would you be Abu Abdalá, the Sultan's uncle?' the second soldier stammered.

'Insolent swine! To you I'm Mohammed Abu Abdalá ibn Sa'd. Some know me as *El Zagal*. Now for the last time, stand aside and crawl back into the verminous holes you came from. By nightfall I'll have a squadron or two of cavalry here to clear you and that man up there from this pass. This is Muslim territory, and you'd better not forget it. Tell that to your accursed King.'

'Not any longer, my illustrious lord,' sneered the first Christian soldier insolently. 'You haven't been this way for a while, I can tell. All the land and villages from here to Vélez Málaga and almost as far as Nerja are in the King's hands. Soon Almuñécar and Motril will be ours and then...'

'Never Almuñécar. Not while I'm alive!' roared the Muslim.

With sword raised high, he ran forward with every intention of slicing the soldiers in two from shoulder to hip. The two guards lowered their heavy pikes and ran. In their desperate haste one of them lost his helmet and his pike caught between his legs, causing him to sprawl headlong onto the rocky ground, bloodying his nose. In doing so his pike slewed around, slamming into the back of the other guard who fell heavily onto his mace, the long spikes of which punctured his mail and chest. He yelped in pain, holding his hand to his body. Blood started to gush through the iron links and his fingers.

'Allah be praised!' mocked the big Muslim. 'Call yourself soldiers! I haven't laid a hand on you and yet you're bleeding like stuck pigs.'

He chased after them and clouted them with the flat of his sword. He stood there laughing, turning around to Nasr and Pedro.

'Note, you two. These are the King's men who we're supposed to fear. Huh! Let's be on our way, we've wasted enough time here as it is.'

With that he turned and with no more ado climbed into his saddle. Without even looking back he started down the long descent from the pass, the sea clearly in sight in the distance, some thirty miles away.

However, *El Zagal* was suddenly subdued. The bravado had evaporated. What the Christian soldier had said clearly troubled him.

'Why are we stopping, my lord?' asked Nadr.

'If Vélez Málaga is in Christian hands as well as all the villages down to the coast, we could have problems. There's a little-used track here which cuts through the mountains to the east and eventually joins the Almuñécar road from Granada near Lopera. It means that we won't reach our destination until tomorrow, which is a shame. However, there are plenty of farmsteads on the way where we can stay the night, and they're sure to be Muslim. If the worst comes to the worst we've food and water with us and a night out under the stars in June won't do us any harm.'

In any event it was not needed. They rode the rest of the day on a rough, difficult track, which even *El Zagal* had difficulty following. They crossed a 6,000-foot pass and were well down towards the Almuñécar road when they came across an isolated cottage where they found a ready meal and shelter for the night. They reached their destination late in the morning of the third day.

The luxurious palace or *alcázar* at Almuñécar lay on a rocky promontory jutting out into the sea from the long sandy beach. The walled town lay around it. The cool sea breezes there were a welcome relief from the sweltering summer heat of Granada, and it was the ideal location for the summer residence of the Granada sultans. If *El Zagal* had a home then it was here.

As they entered the main gate to the *alcázar*, an aide came running breathlessly down the path to meet the Muslim lord. He took the aide aside out of earshot of Nasr and Pedro. An animated conversation followed with much pointing over the mountains towards Granada. The aide nodded his head in agreement and sped back to the palace. Worried, *El Zagal* strode across to his standard-bearer and Pedro.

'King Fernando is mobilising substantial forces around Baza, which lies less than a day's ride from Guadix. I should never have left. I knew I was taking a risk. We must be on our way, Nasr – immediately. Ahmar is fetching us new mounts and some food and water which we can take with us. We must be in Granada this nightfall.

'Don't look so worried, Pedro. I won't let you down. In fact, everything's arranged. Before leaving Guadix I sent a message to the captain of a small dhow, whom I know well, to be here to meet us. He should have arrived yesterday and should be moored somewhere off the beach.' He pointed with his thumb over his shoulder. 'I'll get Ahmar to take you to him and see you safely on board. I've know the captain for years and I'd trust him with my life. Ahmar will pay the man half the sum he demands for taking you to Almería, or wherever you want to be landed.

'Here's a ring.' He pulled a silver ring off his little finger. 'Conceal this in your shoe or around your neck. When you arrive at your port of call, and if you're content with how you've been treated – and not otherwise, mind you – give the captain this ring. Only if it is returned to me or Ahmar will he receive the second half of his wages. Is that clear, Pedro? Ahmar will explain all this to the captain.

'Now we must be on our way. Good luck, young fellow. You are a spirited youngster and we need the likes of you on our side.'

'Thank you, my lord,' said Pedro as the man took up the reins of his fresh horse. 'Good luck against the King!' And he meant it. He was in little doubt where his sympathies lay.

In a short while Pedro was taken along the beach to the single-masted dhow which was anchored a short distance offshore. The formalities were agreed between the captain and Ahmar.

'So where do you want to go?' asked the captain after he had received the first instalment of his wages.

'I think Aguilas, please. I can get home from there easily. Do you know it, sir?'

'Know it!' the captain retorted. 'I know every harbour, anchorage and sheltered cove between Gibraltar and Alicante. And if I don't know the way, my boat surely does! Now make yourself comfortable. There's a corner over there you can bed down at night. The grub is basic but there's plenty of it. I'm not going to fuss over you. If you want anything, just shout.'

With that, he and his mate raised their single sail into the afternoon breeze, weighed anchor and set off.

Pedro couldn't wait to get home.

XVII: The road home

On June 11th 1488, Pedro disembarked from the boat in Aguilas. It was here that his mother had been abducted six years earlier and where he had been taken aboard as a slave boy. Such was his excitement at returning home, he had barely slept a wink on board. As he hastened along the quayside, the awful memories of that horrific day six years earlier came flooding back with startling clarity. He sat down stunned on the quayside, realising that in his keenness to return home, he had totally overlooked its emptiness without his mother there and the misery of living with his vindictive father. He saw his father's angry face in the kitchen window as he withdrew his sword from Marco's neck, and his father screaming at him as he fled from the yard. Yet there were Cristina and Yazíd. Both would be thrilled beyond belief to see him and hear about his amazing adventures, and there was loving Aunt Ana and big jovial Uncle Joshua too.

His mood lightened. Yes, it would be all right. Of course, Uncle Joshua by now would have explained to his father what had really occurred on that fateful day last October with Marco. Moreover he concluded that when he described the traumas which he had been through, his father would consider that he had served his penance for the things which he had done and be truly glad to have him back home safe and sound. Yes, all would be well. He was on his own again, free to come and go as he wanted, travel at what speed he chose, stop where he liked and savour the sunshine and countryside around him. Without doubt, it would be good to be home.

Pedro reached the outskirts of Puerto Lumbreras that afternoon. He skirted it on the south side and carried on some hours before finding the shelter of an abandoned farmhouse for the night. The boat's captain had provided him with food for the journey. He was well over halfway there. However, he was puzzled when he passed the Muslim town. Flying from the tower of the *alcazaba* in the centre of the town, two miles away, was a standard he could not identify. He had not seen such colours before. Broken by the odd trumpet call, a buzz of sound was emanating from the place, but it was due neither to the exuberant bursts of revelry nor the angry clashes of discord; just a drone, as if a hive of bees had been disturbed. What Pedro had no way of knowing was that when *El Zagal* had left Almuñécar to continue fortifying Baza and Guadix, Rodrigo, Ponce de León, titled the Marquis of Cádiz – the very same Ponce de León who'd taken Ronda from under the nose of the Muslim lord several years earlier – had, on the orders of the King, threatened an assault against Vera at the head of five hundred lancers, forcing its capitulation without loss to either side. The effect was devastating and like a pack of cards collapsing. With the acquisition of Vera, which was strategically placed at the lower end of the Almanzora valley, fell all the towns and villages for miles around, including: Vélez Blanco, María and Oria. The whole of the north-eastern corner of the crumbling Muslim empire – some fifty towns, villages, fortifications and watchtowers – had been lost in one single strike. What little regard these communities might have felt for their Sultan, Boabdil, had now totally evaporated.

But this time King Fernando was gracious. The inhabitants would remain free to go about their business unmolested and retain their properties and possessions. All were accorded the status of Mudejares – Muslims living in Christian territory – and would be permitted to live normal lives and practise their religious beliefs and customs. Pedro knew nothing of this and, indeed, would not find out what had happened for several days.

No matter. Soon after sunrise the next morning, still puzzled by the sounds he had heard from Puerto Lumbreras the day before, he set off once again. He would reach home this day. He passed below the hill fort of Velad al-Almar and angled up into the limestone crests above his home town. He was determined to retrieve his treasured sword first since he was concerned that its hiding place might have been discovered. He climbed into the rock crevice where it was hidden. Once removed from its wrapping and cleaned of the oil with which it was smeared, it gleamed like a mirror in the sun, just like new. The scabbard, separately wrapped, was also in pristine condition. He sat on the soft carpet of pine needles overlooking Vélez Blanco a mile to his left on the hillside. Excitedly, he could see the town walls climbing up towards the square *alcázar* on the hilltop, from which the same puzzling standard was flying as he had seen when passing Puerto Lumbreras. He could also make out the south gate of the town and the road up to his house on the corner with its water trough and fountain on the outside wall. Maybe his father would have his stalls erected in the small square opposite the house; and, who knows, Uncle Joshua might even be there with his array of herbs collected from the mountains above María…

Proudly he held his gleaming sword in front of him and recalled the devotion and skill which David Levi had exercised in forging it. Remembering the lessons which Marco had instilled in him, he arose, adopted the correct stance and balance, and for half an hour went through the routines of striking, thrusting and parrying, concentrating hard on imagining a variety of adversaries with different weapons. Possibly his wrist lacked the suppleness which it then had, but his grip was stronger and he felt he moved with equal facility. He slid the scabbard onto the left side of his leather belt, slotted in the sword, balanced his Toledo dagger on his right side and, with a jaunty stride, he set off for home whistling loudly.

It was just twenty minutes away. It would be wonderful to be back to his own town, his own mountains, his own family. Whatever his father might say or do he knew that Cristina would be overjoyed to see him again. And Yazíd? He would race him up to the *alcázar* at the top of the town, and this time he would win. But maybe Cristina, always fleet of foot and now a long-legged eleven-year-old, would beat them both!

The Al-Andalus Chronicle
Part II: Farewell, beloved Granada

Part II: Farewell, beloved Granada

I: A Cruel Homecoming

June 11th 1488

Fourteen-year-old Pedro had approached his home in the hilltop town of Vélez Blanco in high spirits, looking forward to returning to his apothecary father, Abraham, his leggy eleven-year-old sister, Cristina, and his Arab boyhood friend, Yazíd. Pedro hoped and prayed that his father, so miserable and cantankerous, would now be in better spirits and welcome him home. But for Pedro, the last eight months, since he had run away from home after the death of Marco Arana, had been terrible and traumatic. The happy weeks he had spent with the mullah and the lovely Sabyán in Oria had quickly given way to the horrors he had endured in November after the earthquake in Almería. There, he had been set upon by renegade soldiers and, after an ordeal at the hands of two of them, Zak and Gaz, he had spent four lonely months in a freezing cell of the Spanish Inquisition in Jaén. He had been rescued from the hands of the Inquisitor General of Castile himself, the sadistic Tomás de Torquemada, by Don Gonzalo Fernández of Córdoba, the King's ambassador to Boabdil, the Sultan of Granada. Pedro spent two months in Don Gonzalo's care in the castle of Porcuna, helping Ahmad, the Sultan's young son, learn Castilian. There, one evening, Pedro had unburdened himself to Don Gonzalo and Boabdil of the terrible things he had done which had led him to run away from home in order to expurgate the devil from his soul; of the awful events at the blast furnace at Bédar and the accidental killing of Marco Arana, his sword master. He told them of the disappearance at Aguilas of his beautiful fair-haired mother when he was just eight years old, and the eighteen months he was enslaved as a slave cabin boy on board an Arab dhow.

On hearing his story, Don Gonzalo and Boabdil were determined that Pedro should be returned forthwith to his home in Vélez Blanco. Don Gonzalo and Boabdil then summoned the legendary Muslim fighter, Abu Abdalá ibn Sa'd, known as *El Zagal*, to see Pedro safely onto a boat at Almuñécar. Disembarking at Aguilas, where he and his mother Miriam had been snatched by slavers all those years ago, Pedro set off for home in high spirits.

Pedro reached the outskirts of Puerto Lumbreras that afternoon, finding shelter in an abandoned farmhouse for the night. However, when passing the Muslim town he had been puzzled by a standard on the *alcazaba* which he could not identify. Moreover, broken by the odd trumpet call, a buzz of sound was emanating from the town as if a hive of bees had been disturbed. What Pedro could not know was that two days before all the towns and villages for miles around had fallen to the Christians, after Ponce de León had threatened to take Vera by storm. Some forty Muslim towns, villages, fortifications and watchtowers had been lost in one single strike.

Pedro knew nothing of this when soon after sunrise the next morning he set off once again. Today he would reach home. He angled his way up into the limestone crests above his home town of Vélez Blanco to retrieve his treasured Toledo sword, which he had concealed in a rock crevice eight months before. Once removed from its wrapping and cleaned of the oil with which he had smeared it, it gleamed like a mirror again. Then, sliding the sword into its scabbard and with a spring in his step, he set off for home, just twenty minutes away.

Pedro followed the path down along the outside of the wall to enter the east gate at the bottom of the town. But the gate had been left ajar and unattended. Why? The streets were silent and almost deserted, yet it was Wednesday – market day. Had a new outbreak of the plague hit the town? Where was everybody? High above him to the right, the same standard was flying on the *alcázar* as he had seen at Puerto Lumbreras the day before. Something was clearly amiss, but what was it?

Thoroughly puzzled, he pressed on up the road from the gate to his home two hundred yards away. It lay at a T-junction. He could hear the familiar sound of water gushing into the stone water trough which was set against the front wall of his house below his father's dispensary. Suddenly, when he was eighty yards away, as the small square to the left of the house came into view, he was horror-struck to see two Christian soldiers throw his father bodily onto to one of the tables which he erected in the summer to sell his medicines and cures. One of the soldiers held his father down by the shoulders, but out of the corner of his eye Abraham caught a glimpse of Pedro ascending the road. The other soldier, using both hands, pulled his sword down hard into his Abraham's chest with all his might. Then he took it out and, with murderous glee, drew it slowly and deeply across his father's throat. But even worse, a third soldier stood nearby, trousers down around his ankles, thrusting between the bared legs of Christina who, screaming loudly in terror and pain, lay prone over a second table, her skirt flung high above her waist. Then in a flash, a dagger appeared in his hand, and with one slashing stroke her life was extinguished.

Pedro witnessed all of this in the few seconds in which the small square came into view. Shouting with rage, he drew his sword from its scabbard and, holding it high above him, stormed fearlessly up the road at the three soldiers. A glint of red flashed in the sunlight. The soldier who had slain his father turned and reversing, his grip on his own weapon, hopped awkwardly down the road to confront the youngster. He bore on his tunic the cross-branched emblem of the Spanish Inquisition. The second and third soldiers followed a short distance behind. There was another flash of red in the sunlight. Pedro instantly recognised the loathsome Zak. Swinging on a chain around his neck was Sabyán's ruby ring. The murderer recognised Pedro in the same instant.

'So it's you, my tight-arsed friend,' he leered as he hopped down the road. 'You thought we'd never find your measly father and your juicy little sister, did you? Well, you've arrived home in the nick of time. We've got rid of another filthy Jew and one of his progeny. Now I can get rid of a third, and pay you back for what you done to me.'

Still obviously in pain, he hitched up the groin of his trousers with his hand as he reached Pedro.

As he did so, he thrust his bloodied sword at the boy's chest. But, encumbered by a chain mail jerkin over a heavy tunic, he was no match for Pedro's agility. Zak's direct thrust was just what Marco had trained Pedro to parry. He slammed Zak's sword away from him, breaking it above the hand guard and, with a second stroke, he slashed the sword across Zak's face. The evil man drew back to avoid the mortal blow, but he was not quick enough. The blade sliced diagonally across his face, opening it up from below his right eye to the jawbone. He fell to the ground holding his dissected cheek, through which his rotten back teeth were exposed.

Zak bellowed with pain as his blood flooded onto the street. Pedro stepped over him, sword held high in both hands, ready to sever his head from his body; but the other two soldiers arrived, sword and pike ready to strike. The second soldier, with his trousers still open, who had raped and murdered Cristina, was Zak's partner in crime, Gaz. The third, who had held Pedro's father down while Zak slew him, Pedro did not know. He had no option but to run.

'Your evil friend has got his just desserts and will not see out the day,' Pedro shouted over his shoulder as he turned tail down the road. 'One day,' he added, 'I'll catch up with you two, and you'll pay with your lives for what you did to my father and sister!'

II: The Rainbow Man

June 12th 1488

Although they lived in the upper town, Pedro's friend, Yazíd, and his leather-trader father, Yakub Ibn Hayyan, heard the commotion coming from the lower town. Father and son glanced at each other, and without so much as a word they rushed out of their house and down through the rectangular maze of streets in the direction of the disturbance. They both guessed that it was coming from the direction of Abraham's corner house. Yazíd hung back, keeping pace with his father. When they got there, no more than three minutes after the tragedy, the road was deserted. Abraham lay on his back on the table, dead, his head barely attached to his body. There was blood everywhere. Worse in many ways, Cristina lay spread-eagled on the table alongside, naked from the waist down. Her agonising death throes were set like a mask on the poor girl's face.

Sickened by what he saw, Yakub hastily pulled Cristina's skirt down over her bruised and fouled body, but not before Yazíd had taken in the horrifying scene. Neighbours arrived. The men carried Abraham and Cristina into the house and laid them on the floor, covering their bodies with what sheets and rugs they could lay their hands on. It would be the womenfolk, as ever, who would clean and dress the deceased.

'Do you know, Papa,' said thirteen-year-old Yazíd, 'I'm sure I heard Pedro's voice… I'm going to take a look around.'

He skirted Abraham's blood-smeared tables in the small square and glanced up the road ascending from it. Then he turned tail and headed down to the east gate, discovering a large pool of dried blood smeared across the road. He returned to his father with the news of what he had found.

'If it were Pedro you heard,' his father said, 'where would he have gone?'

'I know, Papa. I know exactly where he's likely to have gone.'

'Where, Yazíd?'

'I can't tell you, Papa. But I'll go and see if I can find him.'

'Good. Tell him to stay out of harm's way for the moment. Poor lad. If he were here, he could only have just returned, since if he'd been home more than an hour I know that he'd have been around to see you. Fancy returning home to face such a horror! If that's his blood on the road then he'll be dead by now, even though he managed to run away. But let's pray to Allah that he's safe. You must take food and drink to him and whatever else he needs.'

'Don't worry, Papa, there's already food hidden there for when he returned.'

'Very well, Yazíd, be on your way. If you find Pedro safe and sound, tell him that we're here to help him in every way we can. First he loses his mother and now his father and sister... it's terrible, truly terrible.'

Yazíd missed the last few words. He was already flying up through the town, taking care to set off along the road by the water trough and not directly up from the small square. He did not want his father to know the direction of their secret hideaway.

Nobody was more suited to such a pursuit as Yazíd. As he sped up the stony track to the limestone crags beyond the town he caught the odd glimpse through the pine trees of someone ahead running for all he was worth. It had to be Pedro.

'So it was you!' he said in his native Arabic as he reached the top. He ran up to his friend and literally threw himself at him, hugging him as tightly as he could.

'Oh, it's wonderful to see you again... I never thought I would... Where did you go...? Where have you been...? Your uncle Joshua in María told Cristina that you'd run away to sea and none of us would ever see you again. What brought you back?'

Pedro drew himself away from his friend.

'Are my father and sister dead?' he said quietly.

'Oh, I'm so sorry, Pedro. How could I carry on like that? Please forgive me. Yes, I'm afraid they're both dead – murdered – and Cristina...'

'Yes, I know. I prayed that I might have been mistaken in what I saw from down the road, but I knew I couldn't have been wrong. Not when those villains Zak and Gaz are concerned.'

'Zak and Gaz? You know them?'

'Yes, but it's a long story, Yazíd. I'll tell you about it all later. Was Zak still lying there, down the road from our house? I thought he was dying.'

'There was nobody there. Just a big dried pool of blood and a long red smear across the road. Was that what you meant?'

'Yes. As I came up the road towards our house, my father's small market square came into view and I saw this vile Christian soldier, Zak, who I've cause to truly loathe, thrusting his sword into my father's chest. Another soldier was holding him down. I yelled at the evil man to distract him. He saw me and chased down the road at me. Fortunately, I'd collected my sword from our hideout here on the way home. I fended off Zak's thrust, just as Marco taught me, and slashed him across the face. I wish I'd taken his head off. But it was a murderous blow through his cheekbone and jaw, and I'm sure he'll die. I hope he's dead already. The other two, his henchman, Gaz, who... who... attacked and killed Cristina, and another one, came down the road with pike and sword and I had to run for it. But there was no way they were going to catch me. They all wore body armour and helmets.

'I must go back and take their bodies into the house,' he added with urgency, making to set off down the path back to the town.

'Don't worry, Pedro. Your neighbours came out just as Papa and I arrived and they carried your father and Cristina into the house. The women are washing their bodies and dressing them in new clothes.'

'But I must go and see them.'

'No, you mustn't. Papa says that you must stay here…'

'Your father knows about our hideout?'

'No, I told him I knew where you'd be. You see, I thought I heard your voice, and that's why I came up here; but I didn't tell him where. He said that if you were alive you were to stay here and we'll… no, I mean… I'll bring you everything you need. Papa is distraught, Pedro. I've never seen him like that before.'

The two friends sat on the ground at the entrance to their hideaway, the high but shallow cave overhang. They were quiet for a while. Both had exhausted their immediate news. Pedro's brain was numb; Yazíd's mind was in a total whirl. What with Pedro returning home and the murder of his friend's father and sister, there was simply too much to take in.

It must have been twenty minutes or more before Pedro spoke.

'What I can't understand, Yazíd,' he said slowly, 'is what Zak, Gaz and the other fellow were doing in our town. Zak said he'd found my father and sister, but what brought them here?'

'Haven't you heard, Pedro? The news in the town is that two days ago the Marquis of Cádiz—'

'I know of him. He's one of the Kings' chief commanders…'

'Yes, he made a lightning attack with his forces on Vera, and Vera and all the towns and villages for miles around are now in Christian hands.'

'Including Vélez Blanco?'

'Yes, yes. Vélez Blanco, Mojácar and María, where your uncle Joshua lives.'

'Puerto Lumbreras?'

'Yes, everywhere.'

'Ah! That would account for the strange buzz which came from the town and the strange standard on the *alcazaba* tower when I passed by yesterday from Aguilas.'

'Why Aguilas?'

'It's all part of the story of what became of me.' He was surprisingly calm after the awful events of just a short while earlier. 'I promise I'll tell you everything tomorrow. It's a very, very long story. But everywhere's in Christian hands?' he repeated. 'I don't understand it,' he added after a moment's reflection. 'Boabdil and *El Zagal*…'

'Boabdil and *El Zagal*? *The* Boabdil and *the El Zagal*… the one we pretend to be when we play Christians and Muslims…?'

'Yes, him… them. I've been with them the past few weeks. They said nothing about Vera being under threat. How could it happen? When I left *El Zagal* just a few days ago…'

'A few days ago?'

'Yes – stop interrupting, Yazíd,' admonished Pedro. 'I promised that I'd tell you all about it tomorrow…'

'When I left the Muslim warlord…' he repeated.

'When I left him a few days ago, he'd just been called away to Granada because King Fernando was threatening Baza.'

'Where's Baza?'

Pedro ignored him. His brow puckered with a further thought.

'And what was Zak doing with the insignia of the Spanish Inquisition on his tunic? It wasn't there before. Ah! Come to think of it, he did have a mark on his faded tunic of where a badge once must have been. He must have had a new badge sewn on… Now it all starts to make sense…'

'You said the Spanish Inquisition?' Poor Yazíd was thoroughly bewildered by all this.

'Yes, I was tortured by them in their dungeons in Jaén and then rescued by Don Gon… No, that can wait until tomorrow. Look, Yazíd. We must decide what to do. I don't think I'm in any danger from Gaz and the other soldier. They must have carried Zak away. Even if he's alive he won't be going very far for a long time. However, for all that, I'm better off up here. Here's what I'll need…'

'Don't worry. I'll get some supplies. I'll be back this evening. I can't wait to tell Papa that I found you here safely.'

'By the way, Pedro,' he added. 'Your Arabic has improved no end.'

With that he was gone. Just the dry leaves, swirling off the ground in the eddies, marked his disappearance. Pedro chuckled. The same Yazíd as ever.

He returned mid-evening. The sun had long since gone down behind the crags above him, but the town below was still bathed in slanting golden light. It was the best part of the day. Yazíd struggled up the slope with a sheet over his shoulder containing enough to feed an army for a week. He dropped it on the ground and stood there panting.

'I only wanted some food and fruit to last me a day or two!' said the elder boy. 'What have you got there?'

'Well, let's see. Mama and Papa bundled it all together for you. There's a few loaves of bread, a batch of scones which she only baked this morning; there's plenty of fruit, including your favourite – dried figs; then there's some currants, and last year's almonds which I filched from the fields around Casablanca above María; and there's a lump of cured ham. Mama wanted to put in a sharp knife but I said that you had your Toledo dagger; there's a piece of hard tasty cheese, the sort you like; olive oil, salt, pepper and cinnamon; and there's this leather skin with a couple of gallons of water, plus some orange juice with which to flavour it. Oh yes, and there's a flint and striker to light a fire – to keep the wolves off, Mama said!'

'What wolves? Where does she think I am? But truly, Yazíd, I'm grateful to you all. This will keep me going for days.'

'You and me, Pedro. Papa said that I can stay the night with you. It'll be like old times, won't it? And you can tell me about your adventures.'

'I knew there'd be a catch!' replied Pedro. 'But what are all these?' he added seeing some bulky items on the ground.

'Mama put in some cushions which we could lie on and a couple of blankets. She said it might get cold tonight.'

'It's June!'

'Well, you know what mothers are like... oh, I'm sorry, Pedro. I shouldn't have said that.'

'That's all right, Yazíd. Your mother's treated me like a son for years, ever since we've known each other.'

The boys spread out the sheet as flat as they could and laid the food out on it. Vélez Blanco was now in near darkness along the slope to their left. Pedro watched as the sun's glow ascended the steep slopes of Cerro de la Muela, turning to red and then violet. Then it was gone. As their eyes grew accustomed to the near darkness, they scooped up some dry twigs and dead branches which carpeted the ground around them and in a short while had a nice fire going. It produced very little smoke; the wood was tinder dry. Neither had eaten since early morning and they quickly made a large dent in their provisions. Afterwards they put everything back into its wrappings, placed it in the sheet and lifted the sheet onto a ledge at the back of the overhang, away from animals.

Pedro fell quiet. A full stomach, the warm fire, the soporific effect of the woodsmoke and above all, over-tiredness, all brought on a moroseness as he relived the horrors of the morning. As his dulled brain mulled over the terrible events, he realised with a start that he was an orphan. He had become used to being without a mother. Now his father and sister were gone and he was alone in the world.

He stared into the embers of the fire and pulled a blanket around his shoulders.

'Are you going to tell me about your adventures, Pedro?' ventured Yazíd.

'What? I'm sorry, Yazíd, I was miles away...'

'Thinking about your father and Cristina?'

'Yes, I am.'

'I shouldn't have asked. I'm sorry. I expect what happened to them is only just sinking in.'

Pedro turned his head slowly towards his friend, one side of it lit by the flickering remains of the fire. He merely nodded slowly. Yazíd moved a yard or two away, puffed up the cushions and was glad to pull the blanket over himself. Pedro continued staring into the fire, trying to focus his thoughts on what he should do. The full shock of the brutal killing of Abraham and Cristina was only now striking home. The schism which had grown between himself and his father, and indeed between his father and Cristina, had grown too wide for him to feel great sadness over his father's death, although the manner of it involving the odious Zak and Gaz were so abhorrent as to make him simmer with unremitting fury. Not until he had avenged their deaths would his fury abate. For Cristina, though, he felt overwhelming remorse and sadness. What a desperate life the young girl had had! To lose her mother at the age of five, plus his disappearance at the same time for a year and a half, were traumatic enough for her. But then to be brought up by an uncaring and spiteful father, and then die in the most ghastly way imaginable. What a tragic waste of a lovely spirited girl on the brink of womanhood.

The sun was well up when Pedro stirred the next morning. It lay due east and was directly above the road to Lorca, which he had taken with his father and uncle Joshua fifteen months before on the way to see David Levi finish his Toledo sword, a thirteenth birthday present from his father.

The cave shelter was warmed by direct sunshine for just a few hours. Yazíd had gone. Pedro was incredibly thirsty and drank half of what remained of the water his young friend had carried up the previous evening. But his mind was on other things, weighing the pros and cons of what he should do now that he had no family. His ideas were starting to crystallise.

Out of the blue Yazíd was standing by his side, yet the elder boy had not heard him approaching up the stone track littered as it was with dried twigs.

Pedro looked around startled.

'Where did you come from?' he asked. 'I didn't hear you come up the path… and you're not even out of breath. How do you do it?'

'I don't know, Pedro,' Yazíd answered in all seriousness. 'Sometimes I start running and have no idea where I get to. Only last month, I set off down through the east gate and the next thing I knew I was standing on the crest of a high hill with a town in one direction some miles away and the sea on the horizon in the other!'

'Where were you?'

'I had no idea at the time, but a shepherd went past with some sheep and I asked him where I was. He was taken aback and said, "At the crest of Sierra María de Nieva."'

'But that's beyond Velad al-Almar on the way to Huércal Overa! I've been that way myself. It's miles away. At least fifteen miles, and nearly four thousand feet up. It's a real climb!'

'I know. I had to ask the shepherd the way home. I had no recollection of passing through the small hamlet below the hill fort. I wasn't at all out of breath or tired when I got to the crest of that long road over the mountain to Huércal Overa; but when I was aware of the journey back I barely made it home.'

'I think you must fly on a broomstick like a witch!'

'Yes – but people see me dash past, sometimes.'

'And you've no recollection of getting to these places, only the journey home?'

'Yes, that's right. I'm only tired when I consciously retrace my steps back the way I came. Then I'm thoroughly exhausted.'

'I don't understand it, Yazíd,' said Pedro. 'How far do you think you could go?'

'There's no saying. Maybe fifty or more miles? I don't know. I've tried talking to Papa about this but he just shrugs his shoulders and threatens to punish me if I run off, as he's done before. But it won't do any good.'

'If it weren't for that man who said he saw you running past his house I'd believe that you just disappear into thin air and reappear out of the blue somewhere else.'

'That's what I was beginning to believe. I wish it was as easy as that.'

Yazíd decided it was time to change the subject.

'Have you eaten, Pedro?' '

'No I wasn't hungry, but I drank a lot of the water you brought up yesterday. All the springs are dry here now. It's one thing these mountains can't provide in the summer.'

'I've been speaking to Papa. He asks if he can come up to see you. He says there are lots of things he must tell you about and discuss with you about your father and Cristina and the house. If you agree I'll go and fetch him now.'

'Yes, it's best, Yazíd. I think our hideaway here has served its purpose anyway. But have a rest a minute. You must be exhausted.'

'It's all right. I'll have a swig of water and be off. Papa says there's a lot to be done today and he's waiting for me to return.'

He sipped some water and was gone, just as he arrived, in a flash.

Yakub and Yazíd, each with a water skin on their shoulder, returned within forty minutes. The elder man greeted Pedro solemnly, expressing his commiserations over the death of his father and sister. They sat down on a big rock outside the cave.

'Pedro,' said Yakub in a businesslike way. 'I met Rabbi Halib yesterday evening. He and Samuel Beneviste, the Jewish mohel, Rubin Manrique and others, took Abraham and Cristina to the synagogue where they were laid overnight. In the circumstances it was not possible to bury them yesterday, as is the Jewish custom. We know that your mother, Miriam, brought you and Cristina up as Christians, but under the circumstances I agreed with Rabbi Halib that it's best if Cristina is buried with your father. I'm sure that this is what your mother would have wanted. God rest her soul.'

'Yes, I'm sure it is, Ibn Hayyan,' replied Pedro.

'After the ceremony in the synagogue this morning they will be interred in the small Jewish cemetery which lies adjacent to ours on the far side of the town. The rabbi says that there are two sarcophagi available side by side. I hope you are agreeable to this. I know that this is all being done in a rush, but it's June and…'

'Yes, I understand. The dead must be interred.'

'Exactly, we've sent a message to your uncle Joshua in María, and I'm hoping he'll get down here in time for the ceremony. I know he'll try.'

'I hope you're happy with this,' he concluded, 'but there's little alternative, really.'

'Yes, of course. I must thank you and Rabbi Halib sincerely for doing all this. Will I be able to come down to see them and pay my last respects? I feel terrible that I saw them being killed but wasn't with them when their guardian angels received their departed souls. You see, I'd no alternative but to run when Gaz and the third soldier came at me. They were only yards away when I fled.'

'We understand, of course,' sympathised Yakub. 'And so will Abraham and Cristina, Allah have mercy on their souls. I know, and they know, that you were there in spirit, Pedro. And you did avenge their deaths.'

'I'd like to think I did. Zak was the most wicked man who ever walked this earth,' he said.

'Good, that's settled then. I'll return shortly to attend the ceremony in the synagogue with some of your Muslim neighbours. Rabbi Halib has given his blessing to this. He's been wonderful over this terrible affair. I hope Joshua will be able to get down from María. Just a couple more things, Pedro. Then I must be gone. The three soldiers, if you can call those swine that, ransacked your house, but luckily, they didn't do much more than break jars and bottles. I think your father kept his money chest under the stone floor in the corner of your living room. He once retrieved it to pay me for some new shoes I'd made for him.'

'That's right.'

'One of your neighbours has stayed in the house since yesterday to guard it. What I suggest is that Joshua retrieves the money chest and all the most valuable belongings which can be easily packed and takes them back to his house in María. That's, of course, until such time as you want them. After all, everything's yours now.'

'One thing please, Ibn Hayyan. Will he take with him the wall embroideries which my mother made? They're all we have to remember her by, and they're very precious.'

'Yes, of course. I'll ask him. Have you any idea what you'll do now?'

'Not yet,' replied Pedro hesitatingly. 'I'm still mulling over what to do, but I'm pretty certain now.'

'Good. I'll be back this afternoon after the interment. Maybe we can discuss it then? I have some ideas on how I can help you but it can wait until later. Now I must be gone. By the way, Pedro, I like your hideout. I wondered whether you were in these caves. I used to play up here too when I was a boy. And we also hid food up here for a rainy day!'

'Rather than you come up here again, Ibn Hayyan,' said Pedro, 'why don't I come down at dusk to pay my last respects to my father and Cristina before the sarcophagi are sealed? I don't think I'm in any danger now, and in any case I've learned to defend myself. I can then see Uncle Joshua. We can recover the money box, roll up my mother's wall hangings and collect the other valuables.'

'That's a good idea. Why not meet in the cemetery at sundown? You know where it is?'

'Yes I do. I'll see you and, I hope, Uncle Joshua there.'

It took Pedro nearly two hours to narrate his adventures to Yazíd, who sat there with his mouth agape, as the tale was told.

'I can't believe that all those things could have happened to you in little over eight months,' commented the Muslim boy. 'It's incredible!'

'By the way, Pedro,' he said, getting up to stretch his legs. 'I've often wondered what the markings on the cave behind us are. Do you know what they are?'

'No. Many of the caves around here have these cave paintings of deer and horses and other animals, but what these are here I've no idea.'

'One looks like a flock of birds, that's easy, and this other one looks like two people carrying something, and this lower one looks like antlers. How long do you think they've been here, Pedro?'

'I've no idea. Maybe hundreds of years. Maybe thousands. Who knows?'

'And look at this one, down here in the corner just above the ground.'

'It looks like a man with his legs astride with his arms clasped above his head.'

'Or possibly a man with the sun rising behind him?'

'Or even a man with a rainbow over him,' added Pedro. 'It might represent an ancient rainbow god.'

'I like that. That seems the nicest of the explanations to me. I tell you what, Pedro. If you decide to go off on your travels again without telling me, why don't you leave signs on gateposts and trees so I can find you? You may need rescuing!'

'I hope I won't have to be rescued again, Yazíd! But what sign could we use?'

'Why not use the Rainbow Man? It'll be easy to draw.'

'All right, we'll use that one. And when you see it you'll know I passed by that way. I'll draw it on a wall or tree in the direction I'm heading. If it's upside down, I need rescuing urgently!'

'I'll be there, Pedro. You can count on me,' replied Yazíd, with absolute sincerity.

Pedro was at the cemetery waiting when Yazíd's father and Joshua arrived. Big uncle Joshua, his father's younger brother, embraced Pedro for a long while, relieved and delighted that he was home safe and sound. He had learnt of his nephew's journeys from Yakub, who had himself been told by an excited Yazíd, who got most of the story right. Pedro was left alone while he paid his last respects to his father and sister, who were both neatly wrapped in linen shrouds and placed feet first in the middle tier of small arched niches. When he was done, a man waiting patiently nearby sealed the sarcophagi with a shaped slab of stone and cemented it in place with wet plaster. With his arm around his nephew's shoulders, Joshua led Pedro back to Abraham's ransacked house. Yakub joined them.

'So what will you do, my boy?' asked Joshua fondly. 'You know that your aunt Ana expects you to come and live with us now. We're all the immediate family you have.'

'Isn't Uncle Simón alive then, Uncle? Didn't he survive the Almería earthquake?'

'Yes, he did. But his house was destroyed and he'd only just started sending Abraham his spices again. However, we're your nearest relatives and Aunt Ana is terribly fond of you, as you know.'

'I know,' replied Pedro. 'I can't come to live with you. I love Aunt Ana dearly, but…'

'She'd smother you?'

'Yes. That's about it, really.'

'I can understand how you feel. She smothers me too!'

'So what will you do?' chipped in Yakub.

'I think I'll continue on my way. Until my troubles started in Almería I was starting to enjoy the freedom of travelling where I liked, when I liked. I suppose one day I'll want to settle down, but not for a while. I'm told the Alpujarra on this side of Granada are very beautiful, and the Muslim people there are very warm and friendly. I may go there and see for myself.'

'It's a shame. Ana and I will be heartbroken to lose you again so soon. But first things first, Pedro. Let's retrieve Abraham's money chest, take down your mother's embroidered wall hangings and box up what else is particularly valuable. I brought my cart down with me, so we can load it up in the morning. Maybe you'll come back to María with me and say hello to your aunt? If you want to stay, if only for a short while, we'd both love it.'

'There's one other thing, Pedro,' said Yakub. 'If you're to continue the life of a wanderer, as I thought you might decide to do, then you'll need a proper knapsack to carry your belongings in. I'll ask Abel Benal, who's the best saddler in town, to make one for you. I've got an idea for a design which should be just what you need. And I'll get you a sturdy pair of shoes made too. It'll take a few days, but Yazíd can bring them up to María. He know where your uncle's house is.'

'A most generous offer!' roared Joshua with gusto. 'Now you'll *have* to stay with Ana and me until Yakub's knapsack and shoes are ready! Right, now where's this stone slab we have to lift?'

Joshua took Yakub's arm and led him to a corner and whispered to him. Pedro caught the words 'just the job'. Then Joshua slapped him on the shoulder jovially and Yakub left.

Ana was indeed thrilled to see Pedro the next day when Joshua and he arrived at María. She hugged him, kissed him, shed tears over him, fussed over him and overfed him. Joshua just shrugged his shoulders as much to say, 'Well, what can I do?'

'I've been thinking, Uncle,' Pedro said, as they placed Abraham's money chest alongside Joshua's in a concealed chamber beneath the floor of his house. 'Rather than leave the house empty, why not see if Simón would like to move there? If he's lost his house he might be glad to do so. He could import his spices to Aguilas almost as easily as he can to Almería. Aguilas can be reached easily in a day on horseback from here. Failing that, Yakub's elder daughter, Salome, got married last winter, didn't she? Why not let her and her husband, Alí, have the house to do their silk fabric printing in? There's running water in my father's dispensary, and all the jars and pots left in the back yard which my mother used for dying her yarns. It would be perfect.'

'On condition that the house remains yours and reverts to you on Simón's death, or as and when you return?'

'Yes, that seems fair.'

'It's a good idea, Pedro. I'll write to Simón today. I have to write to him about the death of your father and sister. We always got on well and it'll be nice to have him close by. Failing that I'll speak to Yakub. I'm sure the young couple would be delighted. The place they're living in now is terribly cramped and it's along the narrowest alley you've ever seen.'

Yazíd didn't appear at María for over two weeks. Pedro was becoming anxious, but then remembered his uncle's whispered conversation with Yakub the day of the interment. Maybe they were conspiring to keep Pedro in the clutches of Aunt Ana.

'Here you are, Pedro,' said Yazíd with glee. 'Here's the knapsack which Abel Benal has made for you, and a sturdy pair of shoes which papa had made for you too. He hopes they fit. The shoemaker says to rub this soft wax into them every week or two to make them last and to keep the water out.'

Pedro undid the package with the knapsack, not knowing what to expect.

'Abel Benal said that he made the knapsack out of sturdy canvas,' explained Yazíd, 'since leather would be too heavy and would go stiff when it gets wet. It's got lots of pockets and lots of leather straps sewn on to it.'

'But what's this?' said Pedro, turning it around.

'He's made it so that you can carry your Toledo sword in it. He said that your sword would be very cumbersome to carry on your belt all the time and in any case it would attract the attention of young sprites with more bravado than sense. He's fixed the knapsack onto a frame so that you can carry it on your back with these two shoulder straps. Your arms will then be free. The top of the frame has a slot which will take the scabbard of your sword, and you can tie it in place here at the top and here at the bottom. He's left a space behind the frame so that you can use your bedroll to cushion the sword against your back. He showed me how to fit it. The idea is that when you need to draw your sword, you simply lean forward and draw it out of its scabbard from over your head... like this!'

Yazíd demonstrated as if he had the knapsack on his back.

'Abel Benal says that by the time you've strapped your winter *yallabiyya* on the back, a water skin and all the other things you will need to carry, your sword will be barely visible and you shouldn't be hassled. He says to keep your dagger on your belt at your back. Again, he says, it's best not to let it be too conspicuous.'

Pedro opened the knapsack with its roomy central compartment and its two flapped side pouches. The iron frame gave it a sturdiness which he liked. He slid his sword and scabbard into the slot in the top of the frame, flattened his bedroll against it, strapped it in place and pulled the knapsack onto his shoulders.

'Fantastic! Abel Benal is truly brilliant. I was wondering how I could carry my sword with me without it swinging around my legs. This is a very clever solution. With everything else I've got to carry it will be barely visible.'

'It was Papa's idea!' said Yazíd proudly.

'Yes, I know, please thank him profusely for me. And for the shoes. By the look of them they'll outlast my feet!'

'You'll need to break them in slowly,' interjected Joshua. 'No more than half an hour for the first few days, otherwise you'll get blisters.'

'And then I'll have to go to the Baños al-Hamma again to soak my feet in the hot spring water!' remarked a very happy and relaxed Pedro. He laughed, recalling the sight of the naked Muslim women in the baths through the broken window pane.

'So when will you be off, Pedro?' asked Joshua. 'I don't suppose you'll want to stay around here much longer, will you?'

'Maybe tomorrow, Uncle Joshua. I can't wait to set off with this new knapsack.'

'Make it the day after tomorrow. It'll give your Aunt Ana time to make some meat pies and sweet buns for you to take. You know what she's like. Unless you're laden down with food, water and spare clothing, she won't believe you can survive more than a day or two – even in June.'

Yazíd hung around, not wanting to leave his friend whom he might never see again. But the evening was drawing in.

'I have to go, Pedro,' he said with tears in his eyes, putting his arms around his bosom friend and placing his head on Pedro's chest. Then he handed Pedro a thick black wax crayon which he'd been saving in his pocket for this very moment.

'You promise me you'll mark your route with our secret sign, won't you?'

'You mean the Rainbow Man?' laughed Pedro, standing with his legs astride legs astride and with his hands joined over his head.

'Yes, Yazíd. I promise. Every few miles and every time I change direction.'

'And upside down if you are in danger?'

'Yes, Yazíd. And upside down if I'm in danger.'

'Good. And then I'll come and rescue you! Goodbye Pedro.'

'Goodbye Yazíd. I'll be expecting you!'

'Two things before you set off tomorrow,' said Joshua the following evening.

You'll need some money to take with you. I've taken the liberty of taking five hundred maravedís and one hundred *doblas* from Abraham's chest; after all, it is your money now. Place it safely in the sealed pocket which Abel has sewn into the inside of your knapsack. However, that won't last forever. Last week I made an arrangement with Moses Nuñez, the moneylender in Vélez Blanco whom I've know for years, for you to have a dozen letters of credit, each for the value of five hundred maravedís, and I've deposited that sum with him from your father's money chest. You can cash these with official moneylenders in any of the big towns and cities. You'll need to give them Moses' full name – Moses Nuñez de Herrera – his full address and his listed number, 548. You must not, on any condition, disclose these details to anyone, and you must guard the letters of credit with your life. They're almost as good as real money. Do you understand?'

'Yes, Uncle. I understand fully. Thank you for making these arrangements for me.'

'Now repeat his name, address and listed number to me.'

Pedro did so successfully.

'Lastly, Pedro. Please write to us from time to time. Just so that we know you're alive and well. You can seal them with this sealing wax held over a candle. Address them to us via Yakub in Vélez Blanco. The riders never get as far as here. They'll cost you fifteen maravedís to send and they'll take a couple of weeks to transit from one town to another. Nevertheless, they will arrive at Yakub's eventually.'

'Very well, Uncle Joshua. I'll do my best to let you know where I am and how I'm getting on. But you know, you can always ask Yazíd! He has a sixth sense for knowing where I am. He's truly amazing!'

The next morning, with a handshake and a bear hug from his uncle, and a tearful soaking from Aunt Ana, Pedro set off on the second stage of his adventures. It would be a long time before he returned to this corner of the kingdom.

III: Riddles from a Hermit

July 1488

Pedro set off in the same direction from María as he had the previous October. From the outset he knew that he would be drawn irresistibly to the beautiful Sabyán and the learned mullah in Oria. It mattered little how he got there or how long it took. He walked with a jauntiness and spirit that was in sharp contrast to his previous journey; so much so that he missed the turn-off into the hills on his left and passed the farmstead of Casablanca where Abdul ibn Hazm lived in glorious isolation with two sisters and two wives.

Within a mile Pedro knew he had gone wrong; but, no matter, he would continue towards Orce a short distance on. It was about the most westerly of the forty or so Muslim settlements which had been surrendered to the Christians some three weeks before. From Orce a track rose south into the sierra, and this seemed as good an option to take as any. As he started up the track he remembered his promise to Yazíd and marked their Rainbow Man sign with his friend's black wax crayon on a corner stone. He toyed with the idea of inverting it and waiting for Yazíd to appear out of nowhere to save him, but after laughing to himself he thought it better of it. Best not to tempt fate...

It was early evening when he was getting tired and looking for somewhere to rest for the night when a voice called out from somewhere not far away in clear and beautifully-spoken Castilian. The speaker was evidently not from these parts.

'Laddie, I've been expecting you! Can you come and help me fix my roof, please?'

Pedro looked around and saw no one. Then the voice came again, this time in Hebrew, his father's tongue which he just about recognised; then in Latin and finally in Arabic.

There was still no sign of anyone. Pedro leaned forward and drew his Toledo sword from the scabbard secured in his knapsack. Better safe than sorry.

'Where are you?' called out Pedro.

'Over here, behind the trees.'

Pedro strode over to a small copse thirty yards away, sword in hand. Out jumped a scarecrow of a man, almost onto his sword point. He was all skin and bone with long, unkempt white hair. He had a stooping gait and loped from side to side with his spindly legs shod in furry moccasins. His clothes were nearly in tatters, but clean. Arthritis had closed his hands into angular claws. His teeth were surprisingly even and complete, if yellowed through lack of care. Most strikingly, however, his eyes were clear and bright blue. They had a sparkle and radiance at odds with the rest of his appearance.

'You have no need of that,' he said scornfully, pushing the blade away with his hand. 'Now, my young swordsman. Shall we speak Hebrew, Latin or Castilian?'

Pedro looked around to see who else was nearby who spoke so beautifully and clearly. It could not possibly be this hermit.

'Please have the courtesy of replying, young sir. Which language do you wish to speak, or are you dumb?'

'No, I'm – I'm… I'm not dumb,' stammered Pedro, replying to the man while still scanning the trees.

'Are you expecting someone else?' questioned the hermit. 'There's only me here, you know. Now, in which tongue shall I address you?' he said very correctly.

'I'm sorry, sir,' replied Pedro, at last concluding that he and the stranger were alone. 'Castilian is my native tongue, but I speak Arabic quite well and can read and write Latin moderately. I only know a few words of Hebrew, though. My mother prevented my father conversing to us in his own language.'

'So you're a Jew?' he said with undisguised interest.

'My father was…'

'*Was*? Now I know. If I'm not mistaken he died at the hands of soldiers – recently. Yes? I saw the blood… frightful… frightful. His name was Ab… Abel…'

'Abraham.'

'Yes, that's it. And you must be P… Pablo… no?'

'Pedro.'

'Of course.'

'How did you know?'

'I saw you coming this way several days ago and other images formed around you. Your mother was tall and fair to give you your blue eyes. So she was a Christian?'

'Yes. But how did you guess?'

'Ah, that was easy. We Jews tend to be dark and small in stature. You are neither, despite your youth, so it is fair to deduce that your mother had contrasting features. Sadly though, as far as she's concerned I just see darkness. She is no longer with you?'

'No, she was abducted by African slave traders several years ago.'

'Hmm,' he pondered a moment or two.

'However, Pedro,' the hermit continued, 'I see darkness, not death.'

Pedro was too confused for this comment to register.

'Sir, who are you?' asked Pedro, totally perplexed by this learned person in the guise of a hermit.

'Later, my boy. First, will you help me with my roof? I've been waiting all day for you to come, you know.'

He loped away. Pedro had to scamper to keep up with him. A hundred yards away they ascended through a narrow wood onto a low, gravelly plateau. On it stood several tumbledown stone circles some ten feet across. Little of them remained standing above the ground, except one. This had been excavated so that the inside of it lay a foot or two down from the narrow entrance, from which stone steps had been laid. The walls had been rebuilt. A thick high pole stood erect in the centre of the circle. Other narrower poles leant against the walls. The hermit's few clothes and belongings were spread out neatly on the low walls of adjoining huts.

'What are they?' asked Pedro.

'Why, this is my home!'

'But what are these stone circles? I've never seen anything like them before.'

'I came across them by chance three years ago when I came here and I rebuilt one as my home. A whirlwind two days ago blew the roof away.'

'These huts look like they've been here for years!'

'More like hundreds! Look, Pedro,' he said, holding some objects in his hands. 'I found these when I dug down into some of the huts. They were all green and corroded, but some vinegar and sand soon cleaned them up. I think they're made of copper.'

'They look like knives and clasps?'

'Yes, I'll show you other things later, including some bones. But first, please help me to raise these poles against the central trunk.'

For the next few hours the hermit lifted the side poles against the central trunk while Pedro tied them in place with thick esparto cord; his fingers were nimbler with the knots. The side poles overhung the sides of the circular wall by a foot or so.

'What do you cover them with?' asked Pedro.

'With turfs. I'll have to cut new ones tomorrow. The wind blew the others away. Will you help me?'

'Yes, of course,' replied the willing youngster. 'Look,' he said, 'why don't we stop and light a fire and have something to eat. I've loads of food with me. In all honesty, I'm very tired since I set out from María this morning.'

'Why not!'

Pedro unpacked his knapsack while the hermit lit a fire with a flint and striker. There was an abundance of dead wood around.

'We don't need to eat all your food, you know, Pedro!' shouted the hermit as he blew gently on some dry leaves from which a wisp of smoke started to rise. 'I caught and skinned a rabbit today while I was waiting for you to arrive. We can roast that. What do you say?'

'Wonderful. We can have some of my aunt Ana's fresh bread to go with it too. And a sweet bun or two afterwards.'

'Sounds like a feast to me!' replied the hermit, rubbing his hands together in anticipation. 'I live almost solely on rabbits here, you know.'

'How come?'

'This stony plateau sits on sand, which accounts for the belt of trees around the rim of the plateau. It's perfect for rabbits and there's several warrens full of them here. In fact, there are so many burrows I think one day the whole plateau will collapse into them. I move my snares around from one burrow entrance to another and catch two, sometimes, three rabbits a week.'

'What do you do for water?' enquired Pedro, something always in the mind of a traveller in southern Spain.

'The second benefit of being here is that the layer of sand sits on clay at the bottom of the slope, and several springs emerge from the contact between them. All but one goes dry in the summer, but that one does keep flowing, although it gets a bit brown. I've dug a small catch-pit into the clay and it provides a nice supply of cool, clean water. I'm very lucky really; all the water and food I want, and plenty of firewood to keep me warm in the winter. There's stacks of berries in the summer too, and wild strawberries. We can pick some tomorrow if you wish.'

It took the two of them a full week to complete the reconstruction of his circular stone hut. It was not just the cutting, transporting and laying the turfs. They had to be watered and bedded in. Dry clay had to be wetted and kneaded before it was sufficiently soft to be worked into the poorer joints. A hole was left in the roof to evacuate the smoke from winter fires, although most still swirled around inside. A doorway was then made out of branches tied onto cross-poles with cord to keep animals out, the floor was cleaned and the hut was finished. But it would be the home of the hermit for only a short time more. After Pedro's departure, a band of ruffians would come, discover the isolated dwelling, mock and humiliate its sole inhabitant, abuse him and finally hang him aloft from the central pole. There the body would swing until the structure collapsed in on itself. Over the years the beams would rot, dust would rise over the rubble until one day a man, equally bearded and as unkempt as the hermit himself, would dig away carefully at the circular stone mound. He would remove the earth with a trowel and soft brush and uncover the bones of an arthritic man surrounded by carefully laid out copper objects of a bygone age. The bones which would have been discovered would be announced to the world as being those of an important local chieftain who was accorded a fitting burial by his kinsfolk on his death...

It was on the second evening as they were eating that the hermit, whose name was Moses Santángel, replied to Pedro's question as to where he came from. The hermit's appearance had greatly improved. The youngster had cut his long unkempt hair with his sharp knife and straightened it out with a bone comb. He donated to Moses the set of Joshua clothes that Ana had tied to his knapsack as he was leaving. Altogether, the old man looked a different person.

'I can tell by your clear speech that you don't come from around here,' the boy remarked.

'You're right, Pedro. I come from Valladolid, the principal city of Castile, where the King has his court.'

'What brought you here?'

'Persecution – the curse of Spain. I was Chief Rabbi in the synagogue there. The youngest they had ever had. I was still in my thirties then.'

'You must have been a remarkable scholar to achieve such eminence at such a young age.'

'I suppose I was. I was brought up in Salamanca where I attended the university. Learning came easily to me. I was soon fluent in several languages and read all the books I could in Latin, Greek and Hebrew, as well as the few written in Castilian. Being a Jew, and myself the son of a rabbi, it was natural that I should follow in my father's footsteps, and I obtained a position in the main synagogue in Valladolid. Within three years I was made Chief Rabbi. By then, that is in the Fifties and Sixties, vicious attacks were being made on Jews in many, many cities. Under the threat of being charged with heresy and of confiscation of their property and belongings, my people were converting to Christianity. But, paradoxically, it is the converts rather than those who were true to their faith who are the most persecuted, and are now the real target for the feared Spanish Inquisition established seven years ago.'

'Under the Inquisidor General of Castile, Tomás de Torquemada?'

Moses Santángel sat bolt upright, startled.

'You know of him?'

'I know him!' replied Pedro. 'I was tortured by him.'

'When? How? Why?'

'Later. I'll tell you later. First, finish your story about how you came to be here.'

'Very well. By the way, Tomás de Torquemada also comes from Valladolid. He was born there in 1420. His uncle, Juan de Torquemada, was a cardinal and was himself a convert to Christianity. So it hardly becomes his noxious nephew to lead the persecution against my people!' Moses paused reflectively.

'The time came,' he continued, 'when I had to leave. My position in the synagogue was untenable. Many of my devotees were converting, and most of the rest simply stayed away for fear of being arrested. So I did what many Jews have done, and that was to come south to the Sultanate of Granada. Here we can live our own lives and worship Jehovah in our traditional way.'

Pedro looked perplexed.

'You look worried, Pedro,' Moses laughed, and sucked a rabbit bone. 'Be patient. I'm getting to the point of why I came here to Orce.

'At about that time, I realised that I had a certain gift for foretelling the future – "soothsaying" if you prefer. It wasn't that strong. At the very best the images I see are murky. However, my warnings, or prophecies – although I hate to call them that – turned out sufficiently close to reality on enough occasions for people to begin to make muttering noises that I had supernatural powers, which I certainly don't have. By that time I'd moved down here from Valladolid and settled in as Rabbi in Orce. There was no Chief Rabbi simply because the community is too small to warrant one. Now, people are the same everywhere. When one person is seen as different from the rest, whether he or she is seven feet tall, has six fingers on one hand, has two nipples on one breast or, in my case, an ability sometimes to foresee future happenings, then that person stands out from the crowd, and is deemed a threat. The stake is where most of us unfortunates end up.'

'Is that what brought you here?'

'In short, yes. Three years ago my position in Orce became impossible, and I decided that I'd leave the village and lead the life of a hermit where I wouldn't be troubled by visions.'

'Excuse my inquisitiveness, Moses, but what form do your visions take?'

'They're not really *visions*. That's just a convenient word to describe them by. They're more like ghostly shadows moving around in the background. Mostly they are indecipherable, and I have learnt to ignore them. Sometimes the images in the background clear for a moment or two and I see a future incident or place. It might be a house on fire, or someone falling from a high building, or on one occasion, twins for a supposedly infertile woman.'

'But you also see past events?'

'Yes, sometimes. Sadly, they're mainly those involving pain and suffering. It's as if they stimulate the air, as happens above a fire, and I seem to be able to sense this. People and events appear to me out of the blue, sometimes quite clearly. Often their names too.'

'As in my case?'

'Yes. I could sense air tremors coming towards me. They seem stronger when they're moving towards me than when they're moving away. That's how I knew you were coming.'

'That's amazing. Can you foretell my future, Moses?'

'All right,' he conceded. 'But first, let's see what I can deduce about your past. Come and sit in front of me and look at me. Place your sword alongside you.'

Moses took Pedro's hands, turned his palms upwards, and studied them. Then he looked closely at his face and into his eyes.

'Hmm... you have had a lot of sadness in your life, no doubt connected with the loss of your mother. But other things too. I see some tragic events, not long ago, involving your Toledo sword. You're half Jew and half Christian, but you're not circumcised – as I've observed when you've been washing at the spring – and that suggests conflicts in your upbringing. Recently you have been flogged; I have seen the marks on your back, and yet they are not severe. You speak excellent Arabic and not the Arabic of village traders. Your hands and shoulders are strong for your age and you have unerring balance when you move. The fleshy pads of your hands are thick, which suggests that they were once horny and hard through rough work.

'So, what does my intuition tell me?' he continued. 'You said that you lost your mother to African slave traders? I think you must have been taken onto an Arab boat, a dhow, which traded across the ocean. Why? Because the knots you used to tie the side poles onto the central trunk of my hut were not ordinary knots; they were seaman's knots. Moreover, when you helped me secure the turfs against the side poles you held them in place from inside, whereas most people would have pushed against them from the outside. It was then that I saw an image of you along a spar furling rough canvas sails and I knew that you'd been to sea, balancing on wet decks against a rolling swell, gaining strength as well as getting calluses on your hands. Somehow you must have returned home. Your father had this superb Toledo sword made for you, but in its wake there were tragedies. Maybe because of these you left home. That I cannot tell. You did something to fall into the hands of Christian soldiers and they flogged you with a knotted scourge, but someone intervened. Somehow also you fell into the hands of Torquemada, whom you told me about... and yet you must have escaped his clutches.'

'That's incredible!' said a stupefied Pedro.

'No, not really, my friend. You see, most of it was intuition from what you've told me and what I've seen of you. But I did see something of the sea in your eyes, and I do sense some terrible events surrounding your sword here.'

'You're right in all these things, Moses. Tomorrow after supper I shall fill in the gaps, and you will see how close you were to what really happened.'

The following evening he was part-way through telling the former Rabbi about his adventures when a man arrived on foot from Orce.

'Good evening, Rabbi Moses,' the man said respectfully, doffing his hat to the learned man.

'Good evening, David. It's lovely to see you. How are your dear wife, Beth, and your children? Well, I hope?'

'Yes, we're all very well in health, Rabbi. But...'

'Before you go on, David, I'd like you to meet Pedro Togeiro. He was passing by here a week ago and stopped to help me reconstruct my house after the whirlwind last week. Without his help I could never have done it. It looks fine, doesn't it?' he said proudly, leaning over and patting Pedro's hands in acknowledgement of his efforts.

'I'm pleased to meet you, Pedro,' said David. 'Yes, Rabbi, it looks better than it ever did. Really spick and span. However, apart from bringing you some provisions as usual from our community, I bring you some disturbing news.'

'What is it, David? What's happened?'

'You know that Orce, like dozens of other towns and villages around here are now in Christian hands?'

'Yes, Pedro told me.'

'Well, we're all classed as Mudejares and therefore should be allowed to live in peace without interference from the King.'

'Yes, Pedro told me that he made that promise.'

'Yesterday a troop of twenty lancers descended on the town and took a dozen of our young Muslim women, girls really, into the fields and… well, you can guess the rest.'

'That troop must be part of the contingent of five hundred lancers who took Vera on the tenth of this month,' commented Pedro.

'Yes, that's right, Pedro. Apparently, groups of them are visiting all the places which passed into Christian hands that day.'

'What became of the girls in the village?' Moses enquired anxiously.

'They all returned, each having taken a vow to say nothing of what took place. Can you blame them? But we can guess what took place. Three have already hanged themselves for the shame and humiliation they suffered. Others will no doubt follow suit. They know that if they admit to what the soldiers did to them then they'll be branded as whores and, at the very least, will never find a husband anywhere around here. News like this gets around. So they are doomed to live out their shame unmarried for the rest of their lives.'

'How utterly terrible, David! And I expect this will be repeated everywhere else the lancers go. Whoever thinks that soldiers' swords, daggers, maces and lances are their only weapons must be mad. Their most potent weapon lies inside their trousers. That's always been the way with soldiers and always will be. Nothing ever good comes of them.'

Pedro remembered that the shepherd, Hisám, at Chirivel, nine months earlier, had made exactly the same comment.

July had arrived; hot and baking as ever. Moses was becoming irritable and it was obvious that he wanted to be on his own again. Likewise Pedro was restless and wished to resume his journey. They were of accord that on the morrow Pedro would depart. Knowing that each would enjoy just their own company the next morning, they were relaxed and savouring their last evening meal together. The sun had set and it was cool and pleasant.

'You promised to guide me on my way, Moses, with some of your insights. Before I go tomorrow, will you peer into my shadows and tell me what you see?'

'I have looked already. There are no deep shadows. I see nothing unpleasant in your path. Nothing which you cannot handle.'

'Can you direct me where I should go?'

'No, you must choose your own path, your own destiny. Trust your own judgement. It will not fail you.'

'How long will I journey?' pleaded Pedro, seeking some guidance.

'Pedro,' the soothsayer said slowly in a quiet and sombre voice. 'You will be journeying through a people who, I regret to say, are coming to the end of their time. Their days are numbered. So tarry awhile amongst them. Learn of the crafts, skills, learning and wisdom with which they have enriched this harsh land. See how they have watered the desert with their ingenuity, how they have made the desert bloom and tamed the wild and rugged mountains of

Al-Andalus. Once they have gone from here the wilderness will return. Villages and towns will disappear forever. So stay with them, live with them. You have learnt much in your short life. Let them enjoy a little of you in return.'

'But will my journey take months or years?' pressed Pedro, still seeking guidance.

'I know not.'

'Look, my friend,' Moses said with a sigh. 'My time is different from yours. You are a young man, the time frame in which you live moves quickly, while mine moves slowly because I'm much older than you.'

Pedro nodded his head as if he understood.

'We all turn as if we were millstones, but at different speeds. That is until the stone ceases to turn and it is still.'

'And then we are dead?'

'Yes, exactly. Stone dead.'

'Is that where the expression comes from? I mean being "stone dead"?'

'Yes, of course, where else?'

'I thought…' started Pedro in reply, but stopped.

'I will give you just four clues for your travels, Pedro. Four riddles if you like. These might help you to know when it's time to move on from one place to another. But don't feel constrained by them.'

'That will be very helpful, Moses,' replied the fourteen-year-old with some relief, glad at last to have some real guidance about his future movements.

After a few moments' reflection, Moses said very deliberately, 'Remember these very carefully, Pedro.

'The first riddle is this: **when the river pebbles fly, vacate your sarcophagus.**' He glanced at Pedro quickly.

'The second riddle is: **when your seed is sown, lose no time in following the swirling tree.**'

There was a pause while he brought the next ones to mind.

'The third one is this: **follow the hunter's sword when tears fall on twinkling sapphires.**'

'And the fourth one?' asked a thoroughly confused Pedro.

'The fourth one is the most important of all: **you have reached both the end and the beginning of your journey. You must choose your destiny now as you look down on yourself with wings spread wide over a blazing cross.**'

'Moses, these riddles mean nothing to me.'

'Maybe not now, but they will when the time comes, and not before.'

That was all he would say.

IV: Sabyán's Harvest

Pedro arrived in Oria two days later, mid-morning. The air of tranquillity which he remembered from his previous visit still pervaded the village, but the village seemed deserted: even the dogs were silent. Puzzled, he wandered along a side street towards the main plaza next to the mosque. Filing ahead of him was a silent column of women, heads bowed and moving slowly. He spied a cripple some distance behind struggling along on a single crutch. He approached him.

'Who is the funeral for?' Pedro whispered.

The small man looked up and squinted into Pedro's face. Maybe he was partly blind too.

'You don't know?' he asked. 'It's for Abu Bakr al-Jaldún.'

'The mullah?' exclaimed Pedro.

'Yes,' replied the cripple. 'Sadly, he died last night. Why, do you know him?'

'Yes, I do, or I did,' replied Pedro, shaken. 'I stayed with him in his *rábita* for a while last year. I was on my way to see him.'

'He died last night… very sad… very sad…'

Pedro joined the women at the rear, reluctant to push his way through to the men who trooped silently ahead of them. The crowd stopped at the entrance to the mosque. Four men bore a stretcher on which the body of the mullah lay covered by a white shroud. They lowered it onto stools at the doorway. Then he glimpsed his mother, Miriam, or at least, her likeness. A sixth sense made the woman turn in Pedro's direction. Her body melted into softer lines when she saw him through the throng of people. White streaks marked her cheeks after a night of weeping. She smiled, recognising him, then lowered her eyes, embarrassed that she should exhibit happiness at such a sad time. She turned as the imam started to read verses from the Koran. Eventually, the short service came to an end. The four stretcher bearers reappeared and carried the mulah's body slowly along the road which led out of the village. The crowd dispersed, the villagers talking freely now amongst themselves. Their duty was done. A handful followed the procession out of the village.

Sabyán and her children stayed behind, looking around for Pedro. Her children, Sara and Wasím, spotted him and ran to him. He knelt down and clasped them to him, one at each shoulder, their small arms hooked tightly around his neck. Sabyán, as graceful and radiant as ever, wiped her cheeks with her sleeve and came over. She bent down and placed her hands on the sides of

Pedro's face and kissed him tenderly. Then, lingering, she hugged him close. What tears remained in her body finally flowed afresh down her face. This time with joy.

'Come,' she said. 'We must follow the mullah back to his home. He's to be buried there. We can talk later'

When they reached the small buttressed *rábita*, the mullah's body was lowered into a grave behind the building after a short prayer by the imam. Then the grave was filled in and a simple, unmarked flat stone laid over the spot. The group dispersed, heading back to the village.

'It's wonderful to see you again, Pedro,' said Sabyán when they were alone, embracing him again. 'But what brought you here today of all days? The mullah only died last night. How could you have known?'

Pedro drew some cool water from the well and they sat in the shade sipping it from a mug he found hanging inside the windlass.

'I didn't know, Sabyán. Maybe fate brought me here today.'

What happened to the holy man, Sabyán?' he asked after a while. 'When I saw him last he was full of beans and enjoying life. Was his death sudden?'

'Yes, I suppose it was. Two weeks ago he developed a fever and took to his bed. By yesterday he was incoherent and didn't recognise us and his breathing became fainter. There was nothing any of us could do. While I was with him last night he passed away. Some months ago, as if anticipating his death, he asked to be buried here at the *rábita*. He said he wanted to be buried alongside the remains of the Visigothic saint. You'll remember that he liked to joke that he unearthed his bones when he settled here. The village will never be the same again without him, Pedro. The mullah was so wise and his judgement was so sound. Many a time farmers in dispute over something or other would agree to submit to his judgement. Always his decisions were just, fair and so beautifully expressed in our language that not even the most aggrieved farmer would dispute it. What will the villagers do without him?'

She became quiet and pensive.

'Well, the poor man's gone, Pedro, but…' She turned to face him. A smile flooded her lovely features. 'But I've got you now. You've come back on the very day that the mullah passed from us. Allah be praised. But you must tell me how you come to be here. Come and eat with us at sundown and tell us. I can't wait to hear your news. Oh, it's so lovely to see you again, Pedro,' she repeated.

'And I'm thrilled to be with you again, Sabyán,' he said tenderly, 'and finding you and the children so well. You've never been far from my thoughts, even in my blackest hours – and there have been plenty of those!'

'That's settled then. We'll see you later and I'll put a mattress down for you upstairs. By the way,' she said as an afterthought, 'we start cutting tomorrow. We could do with your help!'

'Cutting what?' he asked.

'You'll soon find out,' she giggled.

Promptly at sundown he arrived at Sabyán's small house.

'I'm afraid,' she said, 'we still haven't finished rebuilding the house after the flood last year but, nevertheless, take your things upstairs, my dear, the meal's almost ready. We eat quite early so that I can get the children off to bed and have some peace and quiet. In any case, I want to hear your story in full with no disturbances...!' she reiterated, laughing.

'This looks delicious, Sabyán,' remarked Pedro when they were all seated cross-legged on the floor. 'What is it?'

'It's *abesha gomen*, a very simple dish which Sara and Wasím enjoy. It's very good for you with a lot of fresh vegetables which I bought today in the market. It's got diced cabbage, finely chopped small red onions, crushed garlic, rice and grated ginger root, salt, ground black peppers and, of course, olive oil – all you need for a day in the hills tomorrow, cutting.'

'Cutting what?' repeated an exasperated Pedro, wondering what he was letting himself in for.

'Tomorrow will be soon enough for you to find out. I don't want you running off in the night!'

With lumps of fresh bread and watered lemon juice to wash it down, the meal was consummated with thick pancakes and golden honey.

So Pedro told his story once more from the time he left Oria the previous October and set off for Almería. He told her how he came to lose the ruby ring which she had given him.

'I can't believe what you've been through, my dear,' she confessed. 'To arrive home and witness your father and young sister being butchered in cold blood is truly beyond comprehension. I don't know what I would have done if I had been in your shoes.'

'I did the only thing I could do, and that was to run!'

'But you did strike down one of the murderers.'

'I know, but it was hardly enough! One day I'll encounter those disciples of the accursed Inquisition and they'll get their just rewards. That I swear.'

'You must be careful, Pedro,' she said placing her hand on his. 'These men are killers.

'Well now,' she continued, brightening the mood, 'tomorrow you must show me your Toledo sword and dagger. My late husband's sword was a sorry affair: blunt, brittle and bent. It's no wonder the poor man lost his life at Lucena defending that no-good Sultan of ours.'

'Boabdil means well, you know, Sabyán. He's not a fighter like his uncle, but he genuinely does care about his people and wants to do the best for them.'

'Hmm. We'll see,' she said doubtfully.

They were up early the next morning, yet Pedro still had not learnt the reason why.

'What crop are you talking about?' asked Pedro, getting quite agitated.

'Why esparto grass silly, what else?' she joked. 'Come, we must be on our way. We've a long way to go before we can start work. I'll explain all about it on the way. Now put on your strong shoes. Here's an esparto hat to keep the sun off; you'll need it. It's going to be a scorcher today.'

The cultivation of esparto and its fabrication into a multitude of articles was by far the most important activity in Oria. Bartered, or sold for cash in the market, or sold to travelling dealers acting for distant *esparteros*, the craftsmen who wove it, it provided the major livelihood and income for the community. Now a widow, Sabyán had no choice but to earn her keep to feed and clothe herself and her two young children. The work was hard on the hands and the back, but she enjoyed the camaraderie and the rough humour of the workers.

The day was hot and they worked well into the evening with just a break at midday under the meagre shade of a gnarled olive tree for some water and some well-earned bread spread with olive oil. It was the staple diet of the country people. Basic though it was, it provided much of the daily nourishment they needed. At the end of the day, the esparto, which was to be macerated, was bundled up and tied onto the back of a donkey belonging to Abak, the manager of the cooperative. Then the field workers, hot and tired, trooped back to their homes in Oria, four miles away, with the laden donkey.

'Are you tired, Pedro?' asked Sabyán sympathetically when they arrived home.

She didn't wait for a reply. The look on his face said it all.

'Now you can see why I didn't want to tell you where you were going today! Never mind. You'll soon get used to it, that's if you decide to stay with us awhile. We hope you will. Cutting esparto's not as hard as it seems once you get into the swing of things. Now, what shall we have to eat. I expect you're famished.'

The routine continued each day, except Fridays, throughout July and most of August. Each evening bundles were loaded onto the donkey and returned to the village where they were stacked in a cave which served as a storehouse. In the autumn it would be entwined into cord, rope and other things. By the end of August the cave was filled with separate stacks of *esparto macerado*, the bleached and cured *esparto blanco*, and the cruder *esparto común*. Being bulkier, this occupied most of the cave.

The end of the harvest and nearly two months of back-breaking work in the sweltering heat called for celebrations. In the cool of the evening at the turn of September all the villagers gathered in the main plaza for their annual harvest fiesta. Sabyán and all the other women worked for days preparing delectable rice dishes with onions, almonds, and eggs, flavoured differently with garlic, ginger, coriander, cardamom, parsley and yoghurt and a thick meat. Two dozen chickens were killed and spitted ready for barbecuing, while the shepherd, Muin al-Adil, as was customary, generously provided one of his flock for the occasion. After its ritual slaughter the day before, it was spitted for roasting over the open fire.

Celebrations started at dusk. It was the one time in the year when the women were able to vie with one another to look the most fetching in their best and brightest long *durra'as* and what little jewellery they possessed. Sabyán was stunning in her long royal blue gown with a gold chain around her waist and gold earrings. Both were family heirlooms. When the women of the village arrived they had their heads and faces covered in silk *miqna'as* to draw the inquisitive gaze of the menfolk. It was truly a time for merriment. Abak and his three sons provided the music with their drums and pipes which, if not always melodious, was loud and rhythmic.

The revelry continued to the early hours until the bounteous fare was consumed and all were replete to bursting point. Many villagers there remembered Pedro's part in the saving of Sabyán's children from the flood the previous year. He was treated as a celebrity. His sword which Sabyán had persuaded him to wear, was passed around to men and women alike. They gasped at holding such an exquisite and beautiful piece of craftsmanship. One feckless youth did approach Pedro with an iron from the spit but he was quickly sent packing by Uzmán ibn Yakub, the village elder, who had anticipated his motives.

Historic events were unfolding not much more than thirty miles away. Furious at the loss of Vera and all the communities around to his old adversary, Rodrigo Ponce of León, *El Zagal* launched himself from Guadix against the Christians. Fernando reacted by putting the formidable Ponce in charge of all his forces on the frontier: *El Zagal* was to be destroyed once and for all. After taking Baza, Fernando then moved on *El Zagal*'s stronghold, Guadix, thirty miles to the west. Further Muslim resistance was clearly in vain. *El Zagal* made a secret treaty with Fernando, aware that it would cause fury in Guadix. To save the Muslim lord from embarrassment, Fernando promised to keep the terms of the treaty under wraps.

Fernando and his forces passed through his newly conquered but devastated lands. He stayed the night in Fiñana, twenty-five miles away, camping his army outside the walled town. The townsfolk of Guadix were in ferment over the surrender of their town to the Christians, but *El Zagal* managed to calm them down. On December 3rd 1488 the keys of all the towns, castles, towers and fortifications in the locality passed into Christian hands. All were surrendered simultaneously. Soon afterwards the King toured his new territories, finding its twenty thousand souls impoverished and living from hand to mouth.

Yet contrary to the promise made to his former adversary, Fernando, perfidious as ever, made public the terms of surrender with *El Zagal*. These declared that the Muslim warrior who had taken Pedro from the castle of Moclín to Almuñécar only six months before, would concede all his lands and possessions to Fernando, with the exception of two districts in the Alpujarra, one near Laujar in the east and the other near Lanjarón in the west. In addition, he would receive all the local taxes levied, twenty thousand Castilian *doblas*, plus free passage to North Africa if he chose to leave the country.

With the esparto festival at Oria over, traders arrived to negotiate the purchase of the bulk of the *esparto macerado*. They'd been to several villages around Oria already and knew its market value from the quality and the abundance of the crop. While the visitors could drive a hard bargain knowing they had other villages up their sleeves, they could not drive a wedge between the Oria growers who sought a single price for their produce. Abak and the other cooperative leaders haggled with the traders throughout the day and well into the evening, pausing and tugging their beards with airs of grave circumspection, knowing that their produce was in great demand. Finally both parties shook hands and clapped each other on the back. They had agreed a price for the esparto of 125 maravedís per bushel. It was the same price as the previous year, and the year before that, but they had bartered fiercely from their starting positions and honour was satisfied. The next week the traders would return with a team of mules and carry the esparto away to distant markets.

Pedro had only remained in Sabyán's house a week before moving into the then empty *rábita*. His deep affection for the Muslim woman brought home to him forcibly how much he had missed the loving devotion of his mother since her disappearance six years before. But his thoughts inevitably turned to poor Cristina and how much she would have responded to Sabyán's warmth and understanding.

A few days after the sale of the best of the high-quality *esparto macerado* to the travelling dealers, Pedro helped Abak load what remained of it onto two mules and accompanied them to Taki ibn Isa's home a mile away. After unloading and storing this year's crop, his wife, Halima, showed Pedro how they wove this type of esparto. Pedro was amazed at the dexterity and speed with which they worked.

The next day Pedro himself started work as an esparto weaver working alongside Sabyán and Abak. During a break at midday, as they sat outside in the shade of Abak's workshop, Pedro asked what items were made from *esparto común*.

'As big a range of things as Taki and Halima make,' he replied. 'Maybe more. We don't make all these things ourselves, Pedro, but *esparto común* is used to make all types and sizes of baskets, for women to go to market, for side-panniers for donkeys and mules, stronger ones for mining and for carrying sand, gravel and *yeso*. It's used to make nose-bags for horses, beehives and cages, griddles for winnowing corn, traps for river fishing, thick ropes and hawsers for boats and thick round filter mats for olive and grape presses.'

The months passed. Gradually Pedro got the hang of producing neat plaited cord and doubling it back and forth on itself to produce doormats and under-mats for bedding. By the turn of the year he was producing thick, round filters for the olive presses which would soon be in full swing in the villages nearer to Granada and Jaén. His fifteenth birthday in February came and went with just a modest celebration, yet, as Sabyán noted, it was a far cry from the dungeon of the Inquisition at Jaén in which he was interned the previous year. Spring turned to summer as Abak's store of esparto was consumed. Soon it was the blazing months of July and August and harvest time again.

Pedro had not been further than Taki ibn Isa's house, just a mile from Oria, in the whole time he was there, and he was feeling restless. He thought about the riddles of the hermit, Moses Santángel, but nothing had occurred to match any of them and thereby signal his time for departure. However, he need not have worried. At the harvest festival in September 1489, a stranger arrived who nobody had seen before. Tall, dark with fine aquiline features and a haughty if not noble bearing, all eyes followed his movements. He strode slowly and majestically through the crowd in a spotless white, ankle-length *zihara*, picking with his long fingers at one dish or another, examining this and that, his long curved scimitar swinging slowly in its jewel-encrusted scabbard. Nobody knew his name. Some whispered that he had said that his name was Sahlan, others said Shanan, while others said Salah. Who was he? Where did he come from? What was he doing in this backwater of a village?

Pedro watched as the tall stranger gravitated towards Sabyán who was resplendent in a new turquoise *durra'as* and her gold jewellery. From the other side of the village square Pedro noted an immediate effect on Sabyán. She seemed bewitched by the man as much as he was enchanted by her. They disappeared like shadows from the gathering. Nobody saw them go. Over the next few days and weeks Sabyán and the tall stranger were seen repeatedly together but still nobody knew from whence he had come, or who he was. Pedro found Sabyán fading from his life and he knew that he had lost her to another who, unlike Pedro, would savour her bed as well as her love.

With the esparto harvest over it was a good time to depart. Pedro said his farewells to Abak, who thanked him for his hard work over fifteen months, to the village elder, to the imam and finally, with much sadness, to Sabyán and her children. She had rekindled his faded memories of his mother, Miriam, and as far as he travelled he would never forget this lovely Orian woman.

V: The Stones of Justice

September 1489

Marking his way with the sign of the Rainbow Man, Pedro caught up with the traders who were returning with their loaded mules to Níjar.

'Which way are you going?' said Pedro to the leader, whose name was Messud.

'We could go through Tabernas or even over the Sierra de Los Filabres past the marble quarries, and then up over the Sierra Alhamilla to Níjar, but climbing up and descending mountains is tough on these animals, loaded as they are, so we're going around them, cutting across from here to Huércal Overa and down the busy route to Almería.'

'But these places are now in Christian hands. Won't that be a problem?'

'We had no trouble coming, Pedro,' he replied. 'We passed a few squadrons of the King's cavalry but they were all very civil and well behaved. But for all that, I'm glad you've joined us with that sword of yours concealed in your knapsack. It'll avoid inviting trouble and at the same time we'll have you to protect us if something nasty happens. That can't be bad, can it!'

It took five days to reach the prosperous town of Níjar which lay at the lower end of a steep valley running down from the hamlet of Huebro high in the mountains. These curved around westwards to Baños de al-Hamma where Pedro has witnessed the earthquake. Approaching Níjar, the crest of a foreland ridge had been cut by several sharp, V-shaped re-entrants, below which outwash cones fanned out onto the dry stony plain.

White stone structures, some dome-like and some barrel-vaulted, were scattered over the scrubby plain. The traders stopped at the nearest barrel-vaulted one. Messud opened the slanting half-broken, sun-bleached wooden door, for which esparto cord acted as its hinges.

The *aljibe*, at the most five to six feet deep, was half-filled with water, and like most of them collected rainwater from the land surrounding them. Occasionally they were filled by hand from an adjacent deep well or *pozo*. Shepherds and goatherds used them to water their animals as they passed by. Messud lowered the large clay pot lying by the doorway into the water on its length of rope and poured the contents into a long water trough outside. The three animals needed no invitation to slurp up the cool water.

'What's that?' queried Pedro as they reached a complicated-looking wooden apparatus at the lower part of the town.

'It's a *noria*, a form of waterwheel,' replied Messud. 'We'll stop and look. I'll ask old Ben to show you. He's there with his daughter. It looks like she's washing their clothes.'

Pedro peered over the edge of the waist-high stone wall which surrounded the device.

'How does the water rise from the well?' he asked with a frown.

'Look more closely. Around the outside of the waterwheel there's a thick rope with a number of earthenware pots tied onto it. This rope loops loosely down into the water, and as the waterwheel turns, the pots come up to the surface and pour their contents into this wooden chute and thence into the stone trough by the side.'

'It produces a lot of water.'

'It certainly does. Enough for two dozen women from the town to wash their clothes in running water at the same time, or to water a big flock of sheep and goats.'

'Clever, eh?' commented Messud.

As the trader continued up into the centre of the town with his loads of esparto, Pedro said his farewells and set off for Almería, only some thirty miles distant. Low clouds started to drift in from the sea, immersing the mountains above him in mist. The wind picked up, gathering the summer's accumulation of dust and dead leaves in swirling eddies. In a few minutes it started to rain; cold rain at first. The sky darkened, and as the rain increased in intensity to a real downpour, drops splashed high off the road. Pedro loved it. He took shelter under the roof overhang of a farmhouse and revelled in the smell of the rain and the freshness it brought. Lightning forked across the sky and thunder rolled around the valley, the time between them shortening as the storm got closer. Small streams started trickling down each side of the road, picking up twigs, leaves and dust, stirring it all into a reddish-brown soup that swept down the road, gathering momentum and joining other trickles to tumble through a gap in the roadside bank.

As the storm started to abate and then stop after just half an hour, a rainbow formed across the sky to the east, directly opposite the evening sun. Pedro marvelled at it as he did at all things celestial. Was it any wonder that the ancient peoples worshipped a rainbow god? He remembered Yazíd and their Rainbow Man sign and scratched the mark on a tree trunk as he entered the village. One could never be sure when the little imp might appear.

He entered Almería two days later. He needed to find a money-lender to cash one or two of the letters of credit which Uncle Joshua had arranged for him. He had little left of the five hundred maravedís with which he set off. Sabyán's gorgeous turquoise dress, which he had bought her for the September esparto harvest festival, had taken a large chunk of it, but he had no regrets about spending it. She had been the first person who had captured his adolescent heart and he hoped that she would find happiness and fulfilment with the tall dark stranger who had entered her life at the fiesta.

The Pechina Gate, the main entrance to the city, had only been partly rebuilt since the earthquake just over two years before. One gate remained tilted at an angle and permanently open, such was the security which the gateway afforded the city. He wandered along largely deserted streets, through the gate-less Puerta de los Aceiteros situated near the mosque, into the central Medina precinct. There were a couple of Jewish moneylenders there and he stopped at the first he came across. The man's building had barely survived the destruction and the roof was still covered in a sheet of sailcloth held in place with ropes and stones. The buildings either side of it had collapsed and weeds had almost covered the ruins of the buildings. This scene of random destruction amongst undamaged buildings was evident everywhere. The registered moneylender eyed him suspiciously. He was elderly, with a grizzled beard.

'What did you say was the name of your creditor, and where did you say you came from?' he asked.

'I come from Vélez Blanco and…'

'Where?'

'Vélez Blanco, near the Christian border. In fact it's now part of their kingdom.'

'Damn their souls,' he growled.

'My creditor is Moses Nuñez de Herrera.'

The Jew looked through his ledger, running a fingerless mitten down the page.

'Huh. And what's this Moses fellow's address and number?'

Pedro gave him the full address and his number, 548.

'Well, my boy,' he said ringing his hands. 'This letter of credit's worth five hundred maravedís. Let's see, taking off the interest of twenty per cent and my modest commission, that leaves you three hundred and twenty-five maravedís. Oh, and then there's the postage and—'

'Postage!' Pedro exploded. 'Moses Nuñez said nothing about interest or commission let alone postage. I want the full five hundred maravedís which I'm entitled to…'

Pedro leaned forward and started to withdraw his Toledo sword from its sheath strapped into his knapsack. The bright steel of the blade caught what little light entered the dim premises.

'Now, my boy…' stammered the moneylender, shying away from his counter. 'There's no need for…'

'I'm not your *boy*, you vulture! My name is Pedro Togeiro de Tudela and you can…'

'Who did you say?'

'Pedro Togeiro de Tudela, and if you don't…'

'Well now, Pedro. You can put your sword away. There's been a bit of a misunderstanding.'

His tone and manner changed. Now he was grovelling. 'Are you on your way to see your uncle Simón by any chance?' he said.

'You know him?'

'Oh yes. And I know of you, and your sister and Abraham, your father.'

'Well, you don't know as much as you think, since my father and sister Cristina are dead. Dead at the hands of soldiers of the Inquisition.'

'Now I recall Simón telling me. I'm so sorry, my son.'

'So where can I find my uncle Simón?' queried Pedro.

'His house was ruined and he moved across the street and lives there. I understand he's thinking of moving up your way.'

'Yes, my other uncle, Joshua, wrote to him to see if he wanted to take over our house in Vélez Blanco, since it's now empty.'

But Pedro had had enough of talking to this tiresome man. 'Please give me the money I'm due and I'll be on my way.'

The moneylender counted out the five hundred maravedís slowly as if they were solid gold ducats, then directed Pedro through the city to the al-Hawd precinct and bade him farewell.

'Oh, by the way, Pedro,' he shouted as the youngster started through the door. 'Will you be here for the entrance of the King and Queen?'

'How do you mean?'

'Didn't you know? I thought that's why you're here. Ibn Salim Ben Ibrahim al-Nagar, the Prince of Almería, signed a surrender treaty with them last month, handing over the city and the land and villages around to the royal couple. They're coming at the end of the month to formally receive the keys of the city. It will be quite an occasion.'

Pedro found Simón's house quite easily. There were not many left standing to choose from. But the Simón he found was not the Uncle Simón he remembered. The eldest of the three brothers, he could have been the others' grandfather, so great was the change which Pedro found in him. Hunched and unkempt, ten years of being a widower living alone had made him sullen and miserable, out of touch with things around him. Since the collapse of his house he barely had summoned the will to move across the street into an undamaged but deserted building. He had done nothing to make the building liveable let alone comfortable. He welcomed Pedro perfunctorily, not caring if he were there or not. Moreover, the invitation from Joshua to move to Vélez Blanco seemed to add to his indecisiveness, and his fifteen-year-old nephew harboured no doubts that he would never go there. Indeed, it were best if he did not. Joshua, all life and vitality, would not recognise his eldest brother now, and would not relish having him as a neighbour. Pedro was given an upstairs room in which to live and he did his best to clean it up and make it presentable. He decided from the outset that he would be in the house as little as possible and fend as much as he could for himself.

December 26th was the day appointed for the King and Queen to officially receive the city from the Muslims. While the terms of the surrender treaty made over the treasury of Ibrahim al-Nagar to the Catholic Monarchs, a belated element of pride made the prince decide to use as much of the city coffers as were needed to clean up the city for the handover. Bulletins were posted in the several squares of the city inviting citizens to join teams of workers to clear away debris still left in the streets, start the restoration of the mosque, repair some of the walls, and re-erect the many external gates to the city. The Pechina Gate, the main gateway, had priority. The necessity for this frantic effort, two years after the earthquake, was a sad reflection of the inertia into which the Sultanate of Granada had descended.

Pedro volunteered his efforts, pleasantly surprised by the wage of forty maravedís per day being offered. This was over double that of a farm worker. Three weeks remained to get all the work done. Three hundred or more workers, grouped into task forces, were assigned to different parts of the city. Pedro was allocated to the Pechina Gate, where the handover of the city keys would take place. With twenty others, of all ages and abilities, they lifted and realigned the main stones, set up wooden scaffolding to rebuild the central and two side keyhole-shaped archways made of blocks of alternating yellow and red sandstone. Massive iron hinges for the gates were forged afresh and cemented into the gateway. At the top, dressed coping stones were put back, the walls to each side of the gateway were rebuilt and, with just three days before the arrival of the monarchs, all was ready for the re-erection of the enormous iron-studded gates.

Cidi Yahya al-Nagar, the son of Ibrahim and mayor of the city, a lascivious, degenerate and corpulent figure now in his thirties, arrived on horseback with some of his followers to inspect the works. He expressed his surprise and delight at the rebuilding of the gateway and showered handfuls of jewels onto the ground for the workers. The foreman scooped up the agates, emeralds, garnets, bloodstones, sapphires, rubies, and all manner of other precious and semi-precious stones, to hand out later to his workers. Pedro was delighted to receive a deep-blue sapphire and a mid-green emerald. If only he still had Sabyán's ruby to complete the set!

The morning of the entrance of the monarchs was dull and overcast with a spit of rain in the air. Pedro decided that he would see more of the procession outside the gate than within, and took up a position a few hundred yards up the road. Promptly at midday, to the shrill of trumpets, a squadron of the King's own lancers rode ceremoniously by. They were magnificent on black mounts, sitting upright in their high-backed saddles. The horses were draped in the colours of the King, and the riders wore burnished breastplates over long-sleeved crimson woollen undershirts. They wore plumes on their helmets and their long pointed lances flew forked streamers. Following the lancers, drummers announced the two monarchs immediately behind them.

Although an accomplished rider, the Queen rode her white mare side-saddle to show off the fine green velvet dress she wore. A heavy golden necklace to match the bejewelled gold coronet on her head hung low around her neck. As she passed by she pulled back the hood of her cloak, despite the rain which was now falling steadily. Pedro had time to see that her face was comely rather than pretty. Her posture had an air of authority; she was not a person to be trifled with. To her side rode the King on a stately black stallion. A long maroon cloak hung from his shoulders by a gold chain around his neck and it largely concealed his dark blue doublet and hose picked out by gold thread. Like his consort, he wore a gold coronet with precious stones set in the apices and cornices along the upper rim. His hair was dark brown and trimmed straight to above the collar of his doublet. His round face looked stern. Pedro hoped for Yahya's sake that everything was in place and ready inside the gateway.

'He looks a bit severe, Pedro, doesn't he?' said a familiar voice behind him.

Pedro turned around as his brown *yallabiyya* was tugged.

'Yazíd!' he exclaimed. 'What are you doing here?'

'I couldn't miss the fun, could I?'

'How long have you been here?'

'Not long,' was all he would say.

'How did you know about the ceremony today? Was it announced in Vélez?'

'No, I just knew and came...'

'Did you follow my Rainbow Man signs?'

'Some...'

'When did you leave home? Does your father know you're here?'

'I don't know when I left. It might have been a few days ago or a week ago. Something brought me here. I didn't come looking for you.'

Pedro was as puzzled as ever by the vagueness of his young friend.

'Well,' he said, 'it's good to see you, Yazíd. Look! They must be the King's commanders.'

He was right. Immediately after King Fernando and Queen Isabel came their three principal army leaders, the Marquis of Cádiz, the Count of Cabra and Hernando del Pulgar, riding abreast. Following them was the portly figure of Don Gonzalo Fernández of Córdoba riding his familiar chestnut stallion. Pedro nudged Yazíd to point him out and waved frantically at his friend and saviour. Don Gonzalo waved back but Pedro doubted if he recognised him through the rain. Following behind were some two dozen lords and gentry dressed in their finery and displaying their personal coats of arms on the flanks of their horses. Following them came well over two hundred soldiers dressed in chain mail over woollen vests and wearing brown jerkins over their iron shirts. All wore the fashionable keeled steel casques. Taking up the rear were one hundred or more heavy cavalry mounted on sturdy horses. All were clad in heavy body armour and carried thick-staved halberds with long spikes and cross-sickles at their pointed ends. These heavy weapons were supported by a socket attached to a foot stirrup. Multi-pronged maces and long sabres dangled from their high saddles. The mailed soldiers and heavy cavalry were clearly there as a show of strength and not simply to guarantee the safety of the monarchs.

'Come on, Yazíd. We won't get through the crowds at the gate. We'll head down past the market, through the Puerta al-Marba – which still hasn't been properly repaired – and double back to the inside of the Pechina Gate. Follow me, I know the way.'

They arrived as Fernando and Isabel entered the Pechina Gate. A fanfare of trumpets blared out. Once inside they dismounted and walked through the light drizzle towards a small mosque inside the gate. From nowhere the mercurial *El Zagal*, now titled King of Almería, appeared alongside his Nazarí family ally, Ibn Salim Ben Ibrahim al-Nagar and his son, Cidi Yahya. Pedro waved frantically to his tall friend, who had secured his safe passage home from Moclín, but *El Zagal*'s slanting eyes were elsewhere. Fernando reached out his hand to him, palm downwards. Rings glistened on several fingers. *El Zagal* came forward solemnly and took his hand. Then Fernando lowered it, forcing the Muslim lord to his knees. Humiliated, he kissed the King's hand in supplication, as he had done at the surrender of Guadix a year before. Pedro glimpsed a fleeting, cold smile on the King's face. The Muslim lord stood up and said in faltering Castilian:

'We welcome Your Majesties to our city. You will see that the ravages of the earthquake two years ago caused terrible damage to Almería. Fewer than eight hundred of the city's three thousand dwellings remain from the disaster, and the commerce of my people has been severely prejudiced. Many people died and many more have departed. Grass grows over ruins which were once homes. Dogs roam over fields which were once gardens and orchards. Nevertheless, we welcome you to our midst and hope that Allah will show benevolence on those who remain and that Your Highnesses will look kindly on the poor and needy who have lost their families and their possessions.'

El Zagal bowed, sweeping his hand from his forehead to his ankle in a gesture of homage. He took a pace back. Ibn Salim Ben Ibrahim stepped forward, presented to the King the keys of the city on a velvet cushion. He repeated *El Zagal*'s graceful gesture and stood back.

'I thank you, my lords Mohamed Abu Abdalá, Ibrahim and Yahya for your greetings,' replied the King. 'On this momentous day, the twenty-sixth of December in the year of our Lord, fourteen eighty-nine, we humbly accept the keys of your tortured city and promise you that we'll do all within our power to return it to its former splendour and to relieve the suffering of your people.'

The Queen, a more than equal partner in the monarchy, added: 'And we are pleased to waive all taxes levied on the citizens of this city. May this stimulate its rebirth and rekindle the well-being of its people. We hope, moreover, that this gesture will encourage those who left the city to return and re-establish its prosperity.'

The trumpets sounded again, signifying the end of the handover ceremony. A cheer went up from the King's courtiers around him, and a louder cheer followed from his men-at-arms who raised their weapons in salute. The King took the arm of Ibn Salim, gesturing to him and *El Zagal* that they should mount their horses and undertake the inspection of the city with him. The five royal personages, followed by their officials and courtiers set off. Most of the spectators dispersed, shaking their heads questioningly over the promises made by the King and Queen. They had cause to. What they were not aware of were the attractive incentives being offered to Christians to induce them to colonise this Muslim city following its surrender. Some citizens followed the cavalcade on foot in its tour of the city. This proceeded down through the main business thoroughfare, the Calle de las Tiendas, to the mosque, still badly damaged. Then up the steep approach to the *alcazaba* where a reception had been laid on.

Pedro had seen enough. 'Well, what did you make of all that?' he said, turning around to Yazíd. 'Did the see the mighty *El Zagal*, who I told you about?'

'Yazíd?' he called out aloud, searching amongst the crowd. The youngster was nowhere to be seen. His friend had disappeared once again. He shook his head in stupefaction. Where and when would he turn up next?

It was time to move on and leave this moribund city behind. The Alpujarra beckoned. He took the side streets to Simón's house, packed his things and left a short note for his uncle. He was glad he was not there. Next time he wrote to Joshua he would tell him that he should forget Simón and let Yazíd's sister and her husband take over his house.

The Alpujarra was the name given to a beautiful region straddling what remained of the Almería and Granada parts of the sultanate. A deep, broad valley, it lay along a major east-west structural tear in the earth's crust. At the Almérian end of the Alpujarra, attractive white *Al-Andalus* villages lay on the north-facing side of the river valley; while in contrast, at the Granada end of the one-hundred mile valley system, the villages lay mostly on the south-facing side.

Each segment of the Alpujarra had its own distinctive landscape, land use and traditions. But the one thing the region did have in common was its strong Muslim tradition, established by the Berbers who settled there soon after the Moorish occupation. It was into this distinctive region that Pedro set off to explore.

He had no particular plan in mind. With the bitter memories still fresh in his mind, he followed the same road out of Almería as he had after being taken prisoner following the earthquake two years before. He turned off at Benahadux towards Gador, following the course of the Andarax, which was now flowing well. There he stopped for the night. White villages abounded on the fertile valley floor and the hillsides as he passed through them the next day. Oranges, lemons and figs grew abundantly on the loamy soils, although they conceded pride of place to market crops in the tidy smallholdings there. Across the valley a low range of yellow-brown sands were eroded into deep interlocking ravines, their barrenness due to their infertility and their being in the rain shadow of the mountain ranges each side. Well to the north, the high Sierra de Filabres towered above Gérgal, Abla and Fiñana, which lay in the parallel and higher valley leading to Guadix. Pedro continued on, not disposed to stop in any of the villages.

It was a day or two later when a major tributary valley opened up to his right and he approached the small town of Canjáyar, perched on a hill in front of him. A river flowed strongly below terraced slopes, tumbling down the valley from the village of Ohanes several miles higher in the mountains. Fields above and below the road, some with low stone terrace walls, were irrigated via a high-level *acequia* which took off from the river via a narrow earth channel some distance above. The course of the river by then was twenty feet below him.

As he crossed the stream at a ford, he heard the frightened cries of a horse. Down in the bottom of the tree-lined river, a mare was trapped in deep mud, and worse, her head was trapped in the fork of a sturdy branch. The poor animal could not move and, with her head stuck high in the air, she could not see either. Pedro ran down the river bank to the stricken beast. She had reins and carried a fine saddle, so it was evident that she must have bolted from her master. The boy threw off his knapsack and unsheathed his sword. He slithered down into the mud alongside the terrified animal. Pedro talked to her to try and calm her down. Then, reaching up high over the back of the mare, he hacked away the offending branch, which came away still caught around the animal's neck.

Holding her head firmly by the reins, he pulled the branch away from her bleeding neck. Without letting go he slithered out of the mud, helping the mare extricate herself from the glutinous mire. He led the mare up the bank, both horse and boy thoroughly exhausted and covered in the brown slime. As he did so, a man wearing riding boots and a thick riding coat came puffing down from the town, which lay half a mile higher up. He saw the state of the animal and the lacerations on her neck as she had striven to free herself from the tree. Pedro was cleaning his sword as the man arrived breathlessly.

'Thank you, my boy! My mare bolted when the village blacksmith touched a nerve re-shoeing her. I am indebted to you. She may well have throttled herself in that tree. You must come back to my house and clean yourself up. Are you new here? I haven't see you around in these parts before. You must allow me to repay you for your brave deed.'

The man was so relieved that his mare had not suffered any lasting effects that he could not stop talking. Pedro was bemused – if not amused – too. With the horse quietened down and clearly glad to be under the care again of her master, the three of them walked up the hill to Canjáyar. Jibril Fadl took Pedro to his big house in the upper part of the town, below a *rábita* perched on a rocky spur.

Jibril Fadl's wife took Pedro's clothes away to wash while her husband lent him some clean ones to put on while his dried. Sipping a cup of hot, very sweet mint tea, Pedro explained who he was, where he came from and how he found himself in Canjáyar. His wealthy host sat back and listened attentively without interrupting. He expressed surprise at some of the adventures which the teenager narrated, and was truly appalled by the killing of his father and sister. But he was particularly interested by Pedro's enthusiasm to learn of his people's use of water.

'You've come to the right place, Pedro,' he acknowledged, 'if you want to learn how we control the water so that all the farmers can use what there is to irrigate their fields. I've been looking for some time now for an intelligent youngster to manage its distribution amongst the growers here. If you'd care to stay, I'll pay you well, and I can let you have a snug little abode to live in… although,' he added, 'you'll always be welcome in this house too.

'What do you say? Oh, one thing I forgot to mention, Pedro. I'm a couple of men short, so until I can find some new workers you'll have to double up and help out in the fields. I hope this is acceptable to you.'

Pedro was flabbergasted. A wealthy patron, a job, a daily wage and a home – all in one day for saving a horse from a muddy river bed! Of course, he agreed, and that evening Jibril Fadl took him down the road on the way out of the village to one of a group of *cuevas* dug into the hillside below the *rábita*.

'These all belong to me,' he said, 'but few of them are occupied. If you'd care to have this one you're welcome.'

The cave-house was as old as the hills themselves. The whitewash on the bare sandstone walls inside was peeling off. Warm in the winter, cool in the summer, it had one room and a small alcove with a raised platform to accommodate a mattress. A tiny window opened out onto the street. A square chimney from the hearth was cut up through the rock above, while a glazed basin drained water to the outside. A piped spring lay literally yards along the road.

Apart from helping in the cultivation of the various crops grown on the *huertos* or market gardens, Pedro had the responsibility of administering the allocation of water. Traditionally, irrigation water to the *huertos* from an *acequia* was allocated alternately to left and to right during the days of the week. The arrangement was controlled by an *acequiero*. Pedro met some resistance at first from the dozen or so farmers belonging to the system but this soon abated once they respected his capacity for hard work and his quick grasp of the system involved. The arrangement was rigidly enforced. It was the responsibility of each farmer at the end of the working day to seal off with earth or boards the inlet to his fields, and for the next farmer downstream to make ready his inlets for the next day. In the summer and at times of drought the *acequiero* had the task of rationing the water equitably amongst the farmers. A council of elders arbitrated when there were disputes between the farmers over the allocation of water, or when they felt unfairly treated by the administrator.

Pedro was in his element working in the fields each day, helping opening and closing inlets as and when required, and digging and shaping the clever system of ridges and furrows called *surcos* which circulated water around a smallholding via a rectilinear network. In the evenings he kept a ledger of the hours each farmer had used the water. Jibril Fadl was delighted with the way things were running, the tidiness of the records which Pedro was keeping, and the unusual harmony which existed amongst his tenant farmers. It was partly in recognition of this that Pedro's sixteenth birthday was celebrated in such a munificent way in the mansion of his patron.

Then one day in the autumn of 1490, Jibril Fadl received a request from the head village elder in Ohanes for Pedro to assist in arbitrating a difficult case of water rights which had arisen in their village. The wealthy landowner from Canjáyar agreed with alacrity but Pedro, although flattered by the request, had misgivings about getting involved in another community's dispute, not least because of his youthfulness. Nevertheless, the hearing was scheduled to take place in Ohanes the following week. Situated at the head of the valley high above Canjáyar, Ohanes had been visited by Pedro more than once. He had sensed an aggressive air in the village. Everyone seemed to be looking over his shoulder at his neighbour, waiting to complain about encroachment onto his land or disturbance or whatever else. Pedro was not surprised, therefore, when a water dispute arose there.

The village itself lay high up on the hillside, such was the steepness of the valley on which it was perched. Terraces tiered way below it, as many as a hundred lay one above the other on the slopes of the mountain side at one point. They were watered by a system of channels and offtakes much as existed below at Canjáyar, except that the crops grown at Ohanes were market garden crops and not vines, olives or figs.

Pedro sat as a member of a tribunal to hear the dispute, which had arisen between the farmers of three smallholdings. The duty of the tribunal related only to the dispute over the allocation of water between them, and they were kept in ignorance of more serious issues which existed. These would be dealt with later by a hearing in front of the council of village elders themselves. The three members of the tribunal sat cross-legged on cushions on a step while the plaintiffs, having accorded the customary salaam to the tribunal, sat in similar fashion on the stone floor in front of them. A scribe sat apart recording every word said. Each plaintiff was called in turn, firstly to describe the facts at issue.

'You see,' said the first, Afdal ibn Ayyub, 'my fields lie near the end of the system several terraces down from the rest. So,' he complained, 'whatever goes wrong above I always suffer. Last spring, late one evening when it was nice and cool, I planted out some cabbage seedlings ready to receive the water allocated to me that night, and I set the boards at my inlet, as I'm required to do, ready to receive the inflow. As you know, your lordships, every now and then the rota allocates us water from nine o'clock when the last evening allocation ceases until six the next morning when the first one starts. In this way, every now and then we each receive nine hours' water. So this is a good time to plant seedlings and saplings. However, when I arrived the next morning, having tended the swollen arm of my dear wife, the sun was high in the sky and all my plants were shrivelled up and dying and my field was dry as a bone. I followed the *acequia* up through the other smallholdings and found that Abak Bujari at the top of the system had taken my allocation and watered his field of beans.'

This same man, Abak Bujari, was called next.

'My smallholding, your honours,' he started, 'lies near the top of the system so that I'm always having to consider the farmers below me and all their complaints. One morning last spring, when I went to attend my crop of beans at a very sensitive stage in their growth, I found my field flooded and the soil washed away from their roots. I did my best to salvage my poor plants but, can you believe, the following day when I arrived there, I found that they had all been trampled down.'

The third and last plaintiff, Kamil Zayd was called.

'You see, your highnesses,' began the farmer, 'I manage a small plot neither at the top nor at the bottom of the system. I am at the mercy of the people above me and I have to have due regard to the needs of those below me. What is more, I have the worst soil on the hillside. Little will grow in it and I have to labour all day to scratch a living. One day last spring, I was minding my own business, toiling in the heat of the sun, when Abak Bujari, who tends the fields above me, came storming onto my land shouting at me and abusing me for ruining his field of beans. I told him that I hadn't been on his land but he upbraided me and threatened to strike me. I am only a small man and he is a big man and younger than me and...'

'Yes, thank you, Ibn Zayd,' interrupted Sahlan ibn Marwan, the president of the tribunal. 'I think we understand your point of view.'

The three plaintiffs having made their case were asked to re-appear again and be cross-examined by the tribunal.

'Afdal ibn Ayyub,' started Ibn Marwan, 'what is your complaint?'

'Well your lordship, my cabbage seedlings were ruined because Abak Bujari stole my water to irrigate his beans. Now I'll have no cabbages to sustain me through the winter and I and my family will starve. He had no need to do it, his allocation would have come around in two days' time.'

He withdrew to be replaced by Abak Bujari.

'What is your grievance, Ibn Bujari?' asked the president.

'I was minding my own business growing my beans,' he started, 'when, one morning, I found my field flooded, the roots exposed and the plants almost ruined. All that day I worked in the broiling sun to try and save my precious crop, but the next morning, your honour, I found them all trampled down and destroyed. What will my family live on for the rest of the year? It's too late to replant a new crop.'

'Who do you blame for despoiling your crop, Ibn Bujari?'

'Why my neighbour, Kamil Zayd, of course! He has a grievance against me.'

'And not Afdal ibn Ayyub?'

'No, of course not. Why would he flood my field and deprive himself of the water he needed for his cabbages on the day of his allocation?'

The middle farmer was recalled.

'Ibn Zayd,' asked the president. 'What do you have to say? It is evident that you lost nothing in this feud between you three farmers.'

'That may be true, your worship,' Zayd moaned, wringing his hands, 'but I feel very aggrieved. I am accused of causing damage to Abak Bujari's beans, and what is more I was very nearly seriously assaulted by him. After all, your excellency, I am a small weak man, and he is young…'

'Yes, yes,' interrupted the president irritably. 'You told us this before. But I ask again, what loss did you suffer?'

'My honour and my dignity, your holiness. I don't like being accused…'

'Very well, Ibn Zayd, you have said your piece. You may leave us. We'll decide what action must be taken.'

The tribunal recessed to another room to deliberate.

'What do you make of it?' the president asked the more senior of his two assessors, who was himself the *acequiero* for nearby Rágol.

'I don't know, Ibn Marwan. I don't know,' he replied slowly, shaking his head and truly perplexed.

'And you, Pedro. What do you make of it?'

'As I see it, Ibn Marwan,' he said in a clear voice, 'there have to be underlying circumstances to cause this feud between the three of them. But are we not permitted to know what these are?'

'No, they're subject to a hearing of the village elders next week.'

'So as I see it, Ibn Marwan,' Pedro continued, 'Abak Bujari had no reason to take Afdal ibn Ayyub's water, since his allocation of water was due in a few days' time.'

'That's correct.'

'Yet Afdal ibn Ayyub clearly believed that Abak Bujari had stolen his water when he found that his beans had been irrigated. So he may well have gone up to his smallholding and trampled on his crops in an act of revenge.'

'Yes, that makes sense.'

'But if Abak Bujari had no reason to take Afdal ibn Ayyub's allocation, then who let the water into his field? It can't have been Afdal ibn Ayyub, who needed the water for his cabbage seedlings, so it must have been Kamil Zayd.'

'You think he perpetrated the act?'

'It could only have been him, Ibn Marwan. After all, he protested his innocence too much for my liking.'

The first assessor, Ibn Din, nodded his head in agreement.

'So what do you think must have happened, Pedro?' asked the president.

'I believe that Kamil Zayd had some grievance against both Afdal ibn Ayyub and Abak Bujari, but we're not allowed to know what this is. I believe that he knew that Afdal ibn Ayyub was planning to plant out his cabbages during his nine-hour night allocation, and in order to divert the blame onto Abak Bujari, he let the water into Ibn Bujari's field, rather than into his own. Doing this would have been too obvious, wouldn't it? The next day, when Afdal ibn Ayyub went to discover who ruined his seedlings he found Abak Bujari's field flooded, but guessed wrongly that he was the cause of the diversion of his water and the loss of his cabbage seedlings. Consequently, he trampled down what was left of Abak Bujari's beans.'

'So you believe the main culprit was Kamil Zayd in the centre smallholding, who suffered no damage or loss?'

'Yes, and Afdal ibn Ayyub fell into the trap set by Ibn Zayd, thinking that Abak Bujari was to blame and trampled his crop. Afdal ibn Ayyub was at fault but it was an understandable error.'

'Hmm. That all makes sense, Pedro. What do you think, Ibn Din?' the president of the tribunal asked the first assessor.

The kindly old man looked thoroughly perplexed, but nodded his agreement. It was all to much for him.

'I am also inclined to agree your assessment of the case, Pedro,' pronounced Sahlan ibn Marwan. 'However, although tribunals have a duty to decide what sanctions should be imposed on those it finds guilty, I am inclined to make a private recommendation to the village elders on behalf of Afdal ibn Ayyub, and let them take this into account when they make their judgement following the hearing next week.'

While the tribunal had reached the right conclusion, the true culprit was not, in fact, Kamil Zayd, but his wife, Jadiya.

The next week the Council of Elders of Ohanes sat together to hear the dispute between the three men. Each was called to appear, as were their wives. Neighbours were called to confirm or refute statements made. The whole proceeding lasted three days as each elder felt duty-bound to ask questions and express his opinion. Now if the 'case of the cabbages and beans' of the previous hearing were rooted in the watering or otherwise of wholesome earth, the 'case of the harlot and two farmers' was rooted in the grimiest muck.

At the end of the three days the leader of the elders summed up the case as follows:

'We have read the transcript of the tribunal over the misuse of *acequia* water by one or more of its users, and we applaud its clarity. We have heard the plaintiffs' attempts at explaining what led to the bitter feud between them which has so soured our community. We have called their wives to give evidence and we regret the ordeal that some of them experienced in appearing before us; likewise with some others villagers from whom we sought corroboration of evidence presented.

'It is clear that the damage done to the crops of Ibn Ayyub and Ibn Bujari results not from the appropriation or misappropriation of *acequia* water, but from revenge by Ibn Zayd resulting from the infidelity of these afore-named farmers with his adulterous wife, namely Jadiya. Not only has this harlot been adulterous with these two men over a lengthy period of time – neither being aware that they were sharing the same woman – but she, Jadiya, has been adulterous with at least a dozen other men in the village, not just during this time but over many years before. She is truly a Jezabel of the first order. Moreover, it is clear from the testimony of neighbours who are all too aware of what is happening nearby, that the wife of Ibn Ayyub – who lost his cabbage seedlings – does not just nag him, but physically abuses him with whatever implement she can lay her hand on in her kitchen, whether of wood or iron. Inevitably, the comely body and bed of Jadiya offered him solace from this vicious wife.

'Unknown to Ibn Ayyub, Ibn Bujari was also the lover of Ibn Zayd's wife, Jadiya. His life seems as miserable as that of Ibn Ayyub. His wife had told her family and friends that she was infertile and was unable to bear children and she received and coveted their sympathy. But the truth of the matter, as admitted by Ibn Bujari at this hearing, was that their marriage was never at any time consummated, not even on their wedding night. Their life together was a sham. Is it any wonder that this man turned to another woman for solace? However, while Ibn Zayd was aware of the infidelity of Jadiya to other men in the community, he himself only discovered shortly before the *acequia* affair that she was adulterous with the two farmers either side of him and with whom he shared the use of the water. At around the same time, and from the same gossiping source, Ibn Ayyub learnt that Ibn Bujari was the lover of Jadiya as well. He was totally besotted with the woman and could not bear the thought of any other man sharing her affections. Jadiya's husband, Ibn Zayd, waited until Ibn Ayyub planted out his cabbage seedlings and then, so as to implicate Ibn Bujari, he entered his land that night and diverted the *acequia* water into it. This flooded Ibn Bujari's field and, at the same time, deprived Ibn Ayyub of the water he needed to water his seedlings. At one stroke the two lovers of his wife were dealt a serious blow to their livelihood and that of their families.

'Of course, when Ibn Ayyub traced the *acequia* back to its source the next day he assumed that Ibn Bujari had taken his water to irrigate his crop of beans and, in a state of fury, having discovered that this man was also a lover of Jadiya, he trampled down his crop, thus destroying it.

'All this because of the nymphomaniacal behaviour of Ibn Zayd's wife, Jadiya, towards other men.'

The leader of the Council of Elders stopped to let the oohing and aahing of those attending the hearing subside. He stood up gravely.

'So these are the sentences we pronounce on those involved in this sorry affair:

'First – since it was Ibn Zayd who caused the loss of Ibn Ayyub's cabbages, he must replant Ibn Ayyub's crop at his own expense to the satisfaction of Ibn Ayyub.

'Second – since Ibn Zayd caused the loss of Ibn Ayyub's cabbages as well as the loss of Ibn Bujari's beans, both of whom are prevented from enjoying the fruits of their labour, he must donate a third of the crops he harvests from his smallholding to each of them.

'Third – since it was Ibn Ayyub who trampled and completed the destruction of Ibn Bujari's beans he must re-cultivate the field. Ibn Zayd, who flooded it the day before, must reseed it at his own expense.

'Fourth – for Ibn Ayyub's adultery with Ibn Zayd's wife, Jadiya, he shall receive fifty strokes of the cane and, if Ibn Zayd so chooses, at his hand.

'Fifth – for Ibn Bujari's adultery with Ibn Zayd's wife, Jadiya, he shall receive fifty strokes of the cane and, if Ibn Zayd so chooses, at his hand.

'Sixth and last – Ibn Zayd's wife, Jadiya, for her adultery with Ibn Ayyub and Ibn Bujari and other undisclosed men in Ohanes, shall be taken to the allotted place outside the town and stoned to death. May Allah forgive her.'

A numb silence descended on the gathering. Pedro was aghast at the severity of the sentence. It was the first time in well over a hundred years that a stoning was to take place in the village. Nobody even knew where the allotted place was. It was beyond belief that the voluptuous Jadiya should be put to death in this brutal way. But this was Islamic law.

Jadiya screamed at hearing the sentence. Until then she had sat impassively, listening to the proceedings and the leader's summing-up as if the case involved someone else and not her. When the sentence was pronounced, she got to her feet like a wild animal, screaming and shouting abuse at the elders, clawing at those restraining her. The three retired soldiers who acted as unofficial keepers of the peace in Ohanes bound a rag around her mouth, tied her hands behind her back and with not inconsiderable force led her away to the village gaol. The two men remained seated, unresponsive, each glancing to see how the other responded to the sentence. They too were escorted to a cell in the gaol.

Justice was swift. Just before sundown the two men were taken to the square, stripped to the waist and the sentence carried out. Ibn Zayd refrained from claiming his right of personal retribution. Afdal ibn Ayyub shrieked in pain and writhed in the bindings which held him. Abak Bujari gritted his teeth against the wadding placed in his mouth to stop him biting off his tongue and flinched only in response to the force exerted in the thrashing. When it was all over, they were released, helped to the ground, and their bleeding backs bathed in clean water and dressed. They had received their punishment and had wiped their slate clean.

Shortly afterwards, still screaming, Jadiya was taken from her cell and dragged out of the village to a raised stone platform in front of a high wall. It had served for years as a loading bay for animals and nobody could remember its original purpose. Her arms were bound tightly behind her to a sturdy post. Immediately after her sentence had been pronounced, donkey-loads of stones and rocks had been collected from the bed of the stream nearby and piled up in front of the platform ready for the stoning. Relatively few villagers assembled at the spot to carry out the sentence of death; among the few were the wives of the two adulterers who had just been caned in the square. Other wives were there too, whose husbands had succumbed to Jadiya's not inconsiderable charms. The only men at the raised platform were those whose conceit led them to have believed that they were the only players in her extramarital life and felt especially betrayed by her wantonness. While the gagged Jadiya squirmed on the post, no one wanted to respond to her glaring challenge to be the first to cast a stone. The nagging, bullying wife of Ibn

Ayyub was the first to pick one up. She aimed it at Jadiya's head but it missed and the stone clattered against the back wall. She had another try and missed again. Abak Bujari's wife tried her hand ambitiously with a heavy rock but it barely reached the feet of the restrained harlot. Other women joined in, then the men. Occasionally a rock would crash into the body of Jadiya with a sickening thud. One, then another, struck her on the head, and another in the face, blinding her in one eye and smashing her teeth back into her mouth.

All this time the stones were piling up against the back wall. It was peppered with holes from the bombardment it had received. After fifteen minutes, one well-aimed stone caught the poor woman on the side of her head and she was knocked senseless, her body slumping in the bindings which held her to the post. By now Jadiya's face had disappeared in a tortured mass of flesh, hair and blood. Her body, arms and legs were etched with welts and the blood which poured from the wounds. People started to drift away, some exhausted with their efforts at the destruction of the back wall, most sickened by the whole spectacle. Still she breathed.

Enough was enough. One of the retired soldiers, disgusted by the whole affair, waved the mob away, climbed up behind the suffering woman and tightened a tourniquet around her neck and the post and put her out of her misery. The stoning left a bitterness in the village which would take years to abate. There would be no such execution ever again.

Pedro would have left Ohanes immediately after the judgement had been made but was asked to stay behind while the leader of the village elders presented him with a beautifully carved ivory box.

'Your clear assessment in the "case of the cabbages and potatoes", Pedro,' the leader said, 'provided the Council of Elders with a basis on which to understand the underlying causes of the antagonism between the three farmers, and we'd like you to receive this as a small token of our appreciation.'

The ivory box dated back four hundred years to the time of al-Matasím. It was barely the size of one's hand but it was a precious gift.

Pedro left the village as the stoning was reaching its conclusion. He was sickened by the unnecessary brutality of it. As he saw the stones raining down on Jadiya, the first riddle of the hermit flashed through his mind:

'When river pebbles fly through the air vacate your sarcophagus.'

The message was clear. It was time to leave Canjáyar and his cave dwelling. Pedro called in to see Jibril Fadl. He described the findings of the village elders and the stoning of Jadiya. Jibril Fadl just shrugged his shoulders. The sixteen-year-old boy explained that he was so disgusted by the affair and his involvement in it that he had to give up his job and continue his journey west. He returned to his *cueva* cut in the rock – the sarcophagus of the riddle – packed his knapsack once more and headed west.

VI: Pedro turns seventeen

November 1490

Events had moved on while Pedro was in Canjáyar. After just a few months in his kingdom in the Alpujarra, conceded to him by the Catholic Monarchs after the fall of Guadix and Almería, *El Zagal* had sold his lands and possessions to one Abu Bakr, and left for Morocco, taking his family and his most loyal followers with him. Impetuous and not noted for his sound judgement, his move to Morocco was to prove a sad and grave error. His nephew, the Sultan Boabdil, at last freed from the spectre of his bitter adversary, ventured out of his Alhambra Palace in the summer of 1490 in a bid to raise the Alpujarran population in revolt.

Starting in the west in Lanjarón, he worked his way eastwards through the villages and towns trying to mobilise a final resistance against the Christians, who were closing in on all sides. He had little success. The people were tired of warring, aware of the divisions between their recent overlord, *El Zagal*, and Boabdil. Moreover, being almost the last bastion of the Muslim kingdom, they had not yet suffered privation at the hands of the Christians. The Sultan got as far as Laujar in the centre of the region and retreated to Granada, humiliated. He knew that his final surrender was not far away. Pedro was totally unaware of this until much later. Indeed, if his friend the Sultan had journeyed just ten miles further east to Canjáyar, they would undoubtedly have renewed their acquaintance from the time of Pedro's sojourn at Porcuna some two years earlier.

After bidding farewell to Jibril Fadl it did not take Pedro long to reach Fondón and the hamlet of Benecid across the river. Irrigated from the fast-flowing Andarax via several *acequias* running at different levels, the valley was a haven of farming activity and prosperity, full of crops of all kinds. Pedro stood on the narrow footbridge over the river in awe of the wealth of produce being grown and the industry of the farmers and their families.

'Admiring my handiwork?' joked a farmer as he crossed the bridge with a hoe over his shoulder.

'Yes, I am,' replied Pedro, caught somewhat off balance. 'I'm just admiring your efforts in growing such a bounty of crops. I haven't seen such a variety anywhere in Almería. It's incredible.'

'We're lucky here, lad,' came the reply. 'The river flows all year around through Fondón, and it's crystal clear with the meltwater from the sierras. As well as that we're sheltered by high mountains on both sides so we can grow quite exotic things such as those date palms over there. And to think that the

Sultan in Granada wanted us to give all this up to go and fight the Christians! I mean, can you believe it?'

'Boabdil?'

'Yes, that's him.'

'He was here?'

'Yes, in the summer. Trying to raise an army, he was. He must have been crazy. Asking us to give up all this.'

'He never reached Canjáyar,' replied a surprised Pedro. 'I was working there and I knew nothing of his being around here.'

'No, he only got this far. He got such a hostile reception from us farmers, he gave up and went back to his palace in Granada. Best place for him, I'd say. He's only a runt of a man anyway. Can you imagine me fighting? I wouldn't know what to do with a lance let alone a sword. Maybe a mace… yes, I could manage a mace.'

'What's that you got there?' he asked, pointing at the hilt of Pedro's sword sticking out from his knapsack which he'd taken off and stood on the footbridge. 'Are you a fighting man?'

'No, no,' laughed Pedro, drawing out his prized sword to show the farmer. 'My father had this made for me when I was thirteen. He said that we lived in troubled times and I needed to have something to defend myself with.'

'Why, it's beautiful, isn't it?' said the farmer examining it closely and turning it over in his hands. 'I've never seen anything as fine as this before. Where was it made?'

'In Lorca, by a master swordsmith called David Levi. He was trained in Toledo where he learnt the secret of making its swords. He showed me how he made it.'

'Well, lad, if you can use this lovely thing, and if this is what I would come up against if I were a soldier, then we did the right thing in giving the Sultan the cold shoulder. I'll stick to farming.'

'You're very wise, sir, if I might say so. There's been too much bloodshed already between Muslims and Christians.'

'But you're not one of us, are you?' commented the farmer. 'You're too tall, and you've got blue eyes.'

'No, my father was a Jewish apothecary and my mother was a Christian with fair hair.'

'You say *was*? Why was?'

'They're both dead. That's why I'm here. I'm wandering through the land, so to speak. A hermit who was a soothsayer told me to spend time with you Muslim people. "Learn of their skills and their crafts," he said. "Soon they'll depart the land."'

'Did he now?… Not too soon I hope,' the man said, and chuckled, although rather uncertainly. He handed Pedro back his sword and went on, 'Well now, lad, if you're looking for work, keen to see our "skills and crafts" as your soothsayer said, then they're starting to harvest the olives around Laujar.

They can always do with help when it's time to pick the olives. It's hard work, but easier than picking turnips on a chilly morning. I tell you, if you're interested I have a cousin who lives in Alcolea, just beyond Laujar. He'll give you a job. Just tell him Yarí sent you. Show him your sword and you'll have a friend for life. He served with *El Zagal* at Ronda – and has scars to prove it.'

'Where is *El Zagal*, as a matter of interest?' asked Pedro. 'The last I heard, he'd been given land in this valley by King Fernando...'

'That was so, but he sold up and left last year. His title was for land over towards Lanjarón, but he was there only a few months, I'm told. Now, if he'd come around here trying to raise an army he might have had more success than his nephew, Boabdil.'

'What's your cousin's name, Yarí, so that I can find him?' asked Pedro.

'Yaruktash Dinar, but most know him simply as Yaruk. Although his house is on the left, you'll find his olive groves on the way out of the town on the right-hand side. Good luck, lad, it's been nice talking to you.'

He swept his arm low across his body.

'*Salaam.*'

'*Salaam,*' replied Pedro, replicating the gesture.

Pedro followed the fast-flowing roadside *acequia* out of the village, crossing the bridge over the river before ascending the long straight slope leading up to Laujar, just a mile or so on. As he expected, he found it a bustling, prosperous town. With a population now greater than Almería, it was the biggest settlement in the Alpujarra. At the entrance to the town a copious spring discharged via a fountain into a stone trough. It brought vividly back to Pedro's mind the fountain which lay against his family house in Vélez Blanco. But worse, he caught his breath at the image which came flooding back of the small square opposite the house, and Zak's sword plunging into his father's chest... and Gaz, trousers down, thrusting into the naked body of Cristina.

The November evening was already drawing in as a bitter wind blew into the town from the high sierras to the west. It was not a good time to continue on to Alcolea so, pulling the hood of his thick *yallabiyya* over his head, he went in search of a bed for the night.

Pedro set off early the next morning. Immediately to the west of Laujar lay a gently sloping altiplano with rich red soil supporting almond, vine and olive. The vines had already been pruned back to black gnarled stubs ready for next year's new growth, yet over half of the almonds and olives remained to be picked. To Pedro's left, the slopes rose gradually to a high barrier of mountains, their crests already powdered white with the first snows of the winter. Two miles further, he reached the watershed of the Andarax, where a deepening ravine marked the start of the River Alcolea, which flowed the opposite way. The village lay a short distance beyond, on a steep slope running down into the valley some way below. Across the valley floor, filled with olive groves, as were all the hills around, interlocking erosion cones of yellow sands marked the desiccated foothills of the high mountains beyond. Alcolea, with its narrow, steep streets and alleys existed for one thing and one thing only: its olives and its olive presses, the *almazaras*.

At mid-morning, Pedro located Yaruktash Dinar in one of his fields beyond the town.

'So my cousin in Fondón sent you?' he said with raised eyebrows. 'I'm not surprised. You aren't the first person he's sent here. He's too mean to employ anyone outside his family, and sending people to me salves his conscience. So you're looking for work, are you?'

'I suppose so, yes. I'm journeying through the Alpujarra, and would like to see how you produce oil from the olives. I've never seen it done.'

'The process is very old indeed, son. But you're a bit early. We've only just started picking the fruit and it'll be a little while before we start milling it to produce the oil. We'll be picking the olives well into February and maybe a bit beyond that. However the trees in this valley ripen first and we're just about to start the picking. I'll certainly need more help by the turn of the year.

'Look, if you stay with me until then,' he offered, 'I'll take you on from now and, what's more, you can help mill and press them. Then you can see how we produce the oil. How does that sound to you?' he asked.

'That sounds fine, Ibn Dinar,' replied Pedro enthusiastically.

'"Yaruk" will do, son. Nobody calls me Ibn Dinar around here. But what's your name? I'm best to know who you are!'

'Pedro, Pedro Togeiro de Tudela.'

'Well, Pedro. I'm pleased to meet you. You look like a lad who'll learn fast. Now, where are you going to stay? You can't sleep in the fields this time of year, that's for sure.' He scratched his head, thinking.

'Look,' he said finally. 'In a couple of weeks' time most of my pickers will arrive and I'll be opening up the dormitory where they stay and then you can live there. But until then you're best to come and live in my house with me and my wives. We've got space enough since my two sons decided to go off to Granada to make their fortune. Little chance of that, I told them, but they wouldn't listen!'

'Your offer's very generous, Yaruk.'

'Think nothing of it, Pedro. I'll enjoy some new company. Now, bring your knapsack with you and we'll start you working. We'll go up to the house at the end of the day and you can meet Mari and Rona. Mari's my first wife and head of the household. Come, there are already some of my workers in the fields. They'll show you what to do. It'll take you all of ten minutes to learn!' he joked.

Pedro was introduced to the three other workers there, a man and two women. He helped spread out the fine-meshed esparto netting around and beneath the trees. While two of them beat the branches with long poles to dislodge the black olives, he helped the elder woman, whose face had more wrinkles than a raisin, to retrieve those which landed outside the net and pick the leaves off others. In this fertile and sheltered valley the olive trees grew to twice the usual size. No pole was long enough to reach the fruit at the top. So, as the newcomer and the most sprightly, Pedro climbed into the middle branches to knock the olives from the upper branches. It was sometimes precarious and always tiring manoeuvring the pole above his head amongst the branches of the trees.

Pedro was greatly relieved when Yaruk collected him from the field at sundown and took him to his house. Mari greeted him coolly but civilly, while Rona, younger by nearly twenty years, welcomed him warmly. She showed Pedro to a large room overlooking the Alcolea valley and the mountains beyond. Buxom, with a round, happy face she was the antithesis of Mari, who was pale and wan. If Mari was in charge of the household it was Rona who ran it. She seemed not to mind as she hummed or sung songs while she cleaned the house, raised the water from the deep *pozo* in the yard, baked the bread in the big oven in the kitchen and cooked the meals. Mari just sat on a stool by the fireside, opposite a heap of olive logs, and grumbled, criticised and chided Rona in her work. Fortunately, the younger woman seemed not to care and busied around unperturbed. Nevertheless, overall, it was a happy household, and Pedro felt privileged to be there while the other workers trooped back up the hill at the end of the day to their modest abodes in Alcolea.

Yaruk had overestimated the time before Pedro would see olive pressing at work. Already a dark brown, foul-smelling liquor, the *alpechín*, was oozing from the bottom of the five-feet high pile of olives in the store.

'Are they going off?' asked Pedro, somewhat concerned.

'No!' laughed, Yaruk. 'We let them stand like this for a few days. As long as the sun and the air can't get to them they won't ferment, and leaving them for a few days reduces the acidity of the oil which we'll make from them. But you're right, Pedro, it's time they were pressed. Come up from the fields at noon and you can start helping me with the milling and pressing.'

Pedro couldn't wait, and soon after midday he returned to the house. Yaruk had been busy all morning cleaning the stone and the pressing equipment. As he hitched his sturdy mule to a long, wooden arm, he explained what they were to do.

'There are several stages in making olive oil, Pedro,' he started, 'but it only requires two pieces of equipment, and neither has changed in centuries. You see here the crushing mill. It's no more than a round stone basin with a flat bottom and a drain hole. That wide millstone stands upright in the basin and is pulled around by old Samson here. I called him that because he's very strong and is used to heaving big stones!

'We feed olives into the trough and the millstone squeezes them as it's pulled around the centre post. It's important that we don't break the olive stones themselves because that makes the oil taste bitter. That's why there's a low rim around the inside of the basin since it stops the millstone making direct contact with the bottom and crushing the olive stones. After Samson has pulled the stone around the trough a few times you can remove the pulp with that wooden shovel and tomorrow we'll start the pressing.'

They continued all afternoon until all the olives so far picked had been milled and the pulp stacked ready for pressing on the morrow. It was already nearly dusk as they returned up the road to Yaruk's house quite close by. Both jumped out of their skins when they heard horrified screaming coming from the house. Pedro reached it first and ran into the kitchen where the screaming was coming from. Mari, Yaruk's first wife, was enveloped in flames while Rona, terrified, was doing her best to smother the flames with her hands – but with little success.

Pedro tore a mat out from beneath the low table on which meals were served, upending it in the process. He ran to Mari and wrapped it around her burning body, flinging her to the floor. Her face was enveloped in flames rising from her thick woollen *yubba*, which had caught in the flames of the open fire. Her hair caught light as Pedro bundled her to the ground. He rolled her over in the mat, beating it with his hands to extinguish the flames. Rona, sobbing uncontrollably, tried to put out Mari's singeing hair with her hands, which were already badly burnt. Yaruk came in, breathless from running up the road. Between the three of them they put out the flames and removed the smouldering mat from around Mari's body. She screamed, sobbed and writhed uncontrollably in desperate pain. Her *yubba* and white cotton undergarment, her *camis*, were burnt to cinders. Pieces of blackened smoking cloth still adhered to her. Her face was barely recognisable. It wasn't just that the fire had removed her eyebrows and eyelashes. Her eyelids, nose, ears and lips were all badly burnt. The skin of much of her body was red and peeling away, exposing red flesh below. Most of the rest of her body was blistered and blackened by the flames and from her calcined clothes. In a while Mari ceased writhing and lay there still. Rona had also stopped sobbing as she knelt on the ground.

Yaruk rose and fetched a pitcher of water to swab Mari's burnt body, but Pedro put his arm out to stop him. He had felt her pulse and had placed his ear to her mouth. She had stopped breathing. Mercifully she was dead. Yaruk found some sheets from another room and placed one over her body. Pedro and he would move her body later.

They eased Rona off the floor and placed her on a low stool. Yaruk swept her hair from her face while Pedro opened her hands to see the extent of her injuries. Both were badly blackened and blistered. With approval from Yaruk, Pedro tore off a few strips of sheeting, soaked one in water, rung it out and gently cleaned off the burnt remains of Mari's dress from her hands. Then, when her wounds were clean, he bound her hands and lower arms as tightly as he dared with clean strips of sheeting. He made two slings, placed them around her neck and put her hands in them. They would be less painful in that position.

Yaruk was badly shaken. Pale and breathless from the exertion, he was distraught at the death of his first wife and mother of his two sons, and anxious over the serious burns suffered by Rona. He held Pedro's hands between his, trying to thank him for what he had done to try and save Mari. But the words did not come. The whole scene in the kitchen was pitiful, made ghoulish by the light of the flickering fire.

'What happened?' Yaruk asked Rona quietly.

She seemed glad that the silence was broken.

'I don't really know. I was drawing water in the yard and heard Mari start screaming. I rushed in here to find her clothing alight and flames shooting up her body. I did my best to smother them, but it did no good, the flames had taken hold. Then Pedro came in and wrapped the matting around her. He acted so quickly. If only I'd done that we might have saved her life…'

She started sobbing again and tried to mop her tears with her bandaged hands.

'You did all you could, my dear,' said Yaruk tenderly, putting his arm around her shoulders. 'You've had a terrible experience and you've suffered severe burns yourself. And you, Pedro – I'm beholden to you for what you did. The speed with which you acted was most remarkable. How did you know what to do? I wouldn't have thought of wrapping the mat around her to try and smother the flames.'

'Instinct, I suppose, Yaruk. As I said to you the other evening, my father was an apothecary – quite a famous one by all accounts – and inevitably I picked things up from him. For instance, I do know that we must keep Rona's wounds dry and clean for the moment. Tomorrow we'll soothe them with some chamomile solution but best of all, if I can find the plants, I'll make up a soothing balm with henbane. This is the best thing for burns. It's getting dark, and I must see if I can find the plants I need in the hedgerows and on rough ground.

'Yaruk, may I suggest you make Rona some very strong and very sweet mint tea, since she's starting to shake like a leaf from her ordeal. I'll go and see what plants I can find.'

Pedro soon found the thyme he needed. Then up on a rocky bank he saw some long stalks of henbane. The thistle-shaped flowers had died away in the late summer but some blackened ones remained, still possessing their seed pods. He collected several of these and a handful of the freshest leaves he could find. In the near darkness of an olive grove he found the lavender and rosemary plants he wanted. They were too tough and woody to pick, so he drew his dagger and cut a few stalks off each plant. He stumbled back down to the road and returned to the house in darkness.

'Have you got any *orujo*, Yaruk?' he asked. *Orujo* was a distillate made from the pressings of grapes.

'Of course, Pedro. It's a bit rough, as I made it myself… but why? Are you in need of a stimulant?'

'No, I want to make a tincture of henbane, and I need something alcoholic to infuse the leaves in.'

Pedro soaked some leaves in the *orujo* and warmed the brew over the fire, stirring the leaves in the liquid periodically to extract their goodness. He decanted the mixture and poured some of the liquid into a cup.

'Take a few sips of this, Rona,' he instructed. 'It tastes terrible but it will dull the pain. Not too much, now. This is one of the deadly nightshade plants and is poisonous and a hallucinogen. You'll feel drowsy, but after all, that's half the idea.'

By this time Yaruk had wrapped the dead Mari in a sheet. Pedro helped him carry her body into another room. While Yaruk hurried up into the village to arrange with the imam for her burial the next morning, Pedro started the more complicated process of making the henbane balsam. He ground up some more leaves of the plant together with some of its seeds, added a few spoonfuls of *orujo*, shook it and left it to stand overnight by the fire.

Pedro got up well before Yaruk the next morning. Taking the jug of henbane from the fireside he added some olive oil and warmed the jar in a basin of water on the fire. It was important that the mixture did not overheat. He decanted the solution, added some crushed leaves of thyme, rosemary, lavender and mint, and let it stand once more. Gradually the mixture thickened as the leaves absorbed the liquid until a thin, greyish-green lotion had formed. It looked and smelt foul but it had miraculous healing powers. While Yaruk left to ensure everything was in order for Mari's funeral that morning, Pedro undid Rona's bandages and bathed her hands in lukewarm chamomile. He dried them and spread the balsam over her hands and arms before re-dressing the burns with clean strips of sheeting.

Her face lightened for the first time since her ordeal. 'My hands already feel better, Pedro. What would we have done if you had not been here?'

'I'm pleased the pain's easing, Rona, but don't be fooled. They will start throbbing and aching again soon enough. Nevertheless, I've done as much as I can for the moment. We must repeat this every day for two weeks, by which time your wounds should be healing satisfactorily. When we get back from the funeral, sip some more of the henbane drink and sit quietly with your hands in the slings. If you act like you're drunk, or think you're someone else, we'll understand!'

Yaruk was in awe of Pedro's healing powers, and each day went off eagerly to collect prodigious quantities of the plants which Pedro needed to make the tincture and the balsam. After two weeks Rona's wounds were healing nicely, and it was time to let the fresh air and sun aid the process. By February, just a few scars remained.

'We must drink to celebrate Rona's recovery,' said Yaruk, 'as well as show our gratitude to you, Pedro, for applying your remarkable medical skills.'

As they stood warming themselves by the winter fire, Yaruk filled some beakers with *orujo* and offered them to the others.

'No thanks,' Rona and Pedro replied in unison. 'It's disgusting!'

They all roared with laughter.

Meanwhile a new pile of olives had accumulated and the two of them squeezed them as they had done days before. The following day they pressed them to make the olive oil.

'I've got three presses here, Pedro, as you can see. They're pretty basic really. They've been here for generations.'

'They look very complicated, Yaruk. How do they work?'

'I'll show you. First we place one of these thick round esparto mats…'

'I might have made these!' cried Pedro excitedly. 'I made dozens of them when I was in Oria.'

'It could well be, who knows,' he replied. 'These came from Níjar, so I suppose it's possible. I soaked a couple of these filters in water yesterday to take away their earthy smell. We place one on this frame over this large circular wooden tub, which is clean and dry… You can shovel in the olive pulp now, Pedro.

'Good, now we place this round wooden cover onto it and fit this short post between it and the main pressing beam above.'

'What next?' asked Pedro.

'Firstly we'll load one of these weights onto the free end of the beam. You'll need to give me a hand when they get heavier later on. You'll see the beam dip as the olives are squeezed.

'Now turn the short threaded crosspiece so that it travels down the screw. That's it, nice and tight. This screw helps keep the pressure on the main beam.'

They changed the weight for a bigger one, then a third, then added the first and second weights again, each time tightening the screw to maintain the pressure until no more oil could be squeezed out.

'How much do you get from a pressing?' asked Pedro as they removed all the weights and loosened the screw thread to pour the oil from the tub.

'Very roughly, fifty pounds of olives will make one gallon of oil,' said Yaruk, 'although by the time we've let it settle, decanted and filtered it, it's a bit less.'

'Shall I scoop out the pulp and dispose of it outside?' asked Pedro.

Yaruk laughed. 'Good gracious me, no,' he replied. 'We've got two more pressings to do yet with this pulp! But first we'll pour the oil into this big tight-necked *tinaja* clay jar to let it settle and put a bung in the top to keep the air out.'

While Pedro removed the pressed pulp from the esparto filter and transferred it to another container, Yaruk boiled some water. A jugful was added to the pulp, which was stirred and returned to the press, on which a new esparto filter had been placed. The whole process was repeated and the resulting oil was poured into another *tinaja*. This was done yet again, but this time sufficient water was added for the olive stones to float to the top. They were ladled out and the last pressing was made of the residue.

'You can see why we have three olive presses here, Pedro,' Yaruk said. 'Pressing the olives takes much longer than the milling, and we've still to clarify the oil. At the moment it's thick and cloudy, but when the impurities have settled out and it's filtered through wads of cotton cloth it will be clear.'

'Is that all you have to do?'

'No, often the second or third stage pressings produce a dark oil and we then filter it through oak charcoal. This removes a lot of the discolouration. Sometimes the oil remains cloudy, and then we shake it up with some white clay and let it settle again. Generally this does the trick.'

'It seems that there must be different grades of olive oil, Yarak?'

'Yes,' he replied. 'The finest oil from the first pressing is called "virgin oil" and is rich golden in colour with a green tinge. The oil we make from the second pressing is poorer in quality and is called "refined oil" since we have to do more to it to clarify it.'

'And the oil from the third pressing?' asked Pedro.

'Some call it "green oil", but it's only really used for animal feed, for making soap and for lubricating wagon wheels and farm equipment. Still, it has its uses, and it does make me a few more maravedís.'

'Which do you sell mostly?'

'The virgin oil is the most expensive and fetches a high price in the big cities. Unfortunately, people around here can't afford it. So what I do is to sell half of the top grade virgin oil as it is and mix the rest with the refined oil to produce one almost as good and at a price ordinary people can afford. In the markets it'll be refined oil which you'll buy.'

Once the other pickers arrived in the middle of December, Yaruk and Pedro were pushed to keep pace with the olives being picked. In fact, extra assistance had to be drafted in to operate the three presses. Old Samson earned his keep turning and turning the millstone to squeeze the fruit. Pedro did not return to the fields to help pick the olives since he was too useful to Yaruk in milling and pressing the fruit and decanting and clarifying the oil produced. Neither did he move into the dormitory with the other workers. His boss was glad to have him in the house so he could continue to dress and treat Rona's wounds.

However, even in the big house, with the growing affection between Yaruk and his young – and now only – wife, three became one too many. By the end of February, with nearly all the olives picked and pressed, and having celebrated Pedro's seventeenth birthday in style, it was time for him to move on.

VII: Raquel of Mecina

February 1491

Using Yazíd's wax crayon to mark his route with the sign of the Rainbow Man, Pedro entered the Granada end of the Alpujarra, taking the long descent down to Ugíjar, where orange picking was in full swing. Then down along the lower road to Cádiar to follow the broad valley of the Guadalfeo which turned south at Lanjarón some forty miles on to reach the sea at Salobreña. The river flowed modestly in a flat, wide channel of grey sand and pebbles. To the south, the 6,000-foot Sierra de Contraviesa formed a high barrier to the sea of mudstones and limestones into which numerous mineral lodes had been emplaced. Opposite, across the line of the structural thrust marked by the valley floor, the more massive dark basement slates and shales rose into the snow-capped Sierra Nevada reaching an elevation of nearly 11,500 feet.

Few tributaries drained the permeable mountains to the south, but many rivers had incised deeply into the northern valley side so that the road along it wound deeply into re-entrants like those at Trevélez and Bubión. For all their massiveness, the basement shales were highly unstable, and Pedro could see many recent landslides which had carried the road away following torrential rain. Such is the way mountains and valleys become as one.

With Lanjarón as his target destination, Pedro stopped a few times overnight. At Almegíjar he turned up onto the steep winding road to join the higher one near the picturesque white hillside village of Busquistar. As he knelt down to mark his change of direction on a roadside stone with his wax crayon, he was startled by the clatter of a horse's hooves as a helmeted *caballero* tried to ride him down. He leapt aside, upending and inverting the marker stone with his knee. As he got to his feet the rider charged past again and the youngster only just evaded the horse and the downward sweep of the sabre as the rider leant forward in his saddle to strike him. Pedro slid the knapsack from his back. He withdrew his gleaming Excalibur from its scabbard, hooking his fingers snugly into its finger guards for extra control and grip.

The rider had turned and as he made his third pass at Pedro with a murderous head-high swoosh of his sword, Pedro ducked and caught the horse with his sword across its hind quarters. The horse shrieked in pain and tumbled, propelling the armed man over its head. He crashed hard into the ground, his helmet clattering onto the road and his mailed shirt cutting a grooved pattern as he slid through the dust. Although badly shaken, he was not to be thwarted. In a rage, he pulled his lance from the fallen horse and, roaring obscenities, he made towards Pedro in a crouched pose with the lance held low in his hands. Pedro stood his ground. He knew that the test for which he had been trained was nigh. But he was ready. Taller and much stronger than when Marco had coached him nearly four years before, he had maintained his sword training several times a week, practising the drills of thrusting, parrying, lunging and withdrawing, always trying to imagine a foe armed with sword, pike, battleaxe or mace in front of him.

In a flash Pedro recognised the soldier. He was the henchman of the loathsome Zaquera who had held his father down as Zak thrust his sword into his chest on the day he returned to Vélez Blanco from his confinement at Porcuna.

'So it's you, you festering cur!' The man spat out the words. 'We promised to get you, and now you're all mine... Don't think you're going to die as quickly as that miserable father of yours did, or your skinny sister for that matter. You're going to be squashed like the toad you are.'

'Just try!' challenged Pedro. 'Let's see how good you are now that you're faced with this tempered blade and not an unarmed and harmless man.'

Pedro stood his ground, taking up a sideways stance, his left arm curved high behind him giving him perfect balance. The soldier approached slowly, feinting thrusts with his long lance, which had a small but deadly point. Pedro watched which way – to left or right – his lance swung as he made his thrusts. He remembered what Marco had told him. A right-handed man advances left side forward with his left hand along the shaft. Invariably as he thrusts, the lance pulls to his left. Pedro studied his opponent carefully, looking into his eyes. They were full of hatred and malice. He knew that those eyes would tell him the instant this stooge of the Inquisition would lunge with his lance. The armoured man approached slowly to within three paces of Pedro and stopped. The lance was barely more than a yard from the teenager's body. Pedro saw his eyes narrow and in that same instant the thrust was made. Pedro sidestepped to his left, knowing that the lance would deviate to his right. As the soldier stumbled forward, having thrust at air, Pedro slashed with his sword, striking the top of the soldier's right arm. The sword sliced into the iron mail shirt and the cotton undershirt. Blood poured from his shoulder. The man turned, looked dispassionately at the blood pouring down his right arm as if it were not part of his body, leered afresh at Pedro and came forward again.

This time the soldier thrust at Pedro's neck. But he could not control his lance, which swung again to his left. Again Pedro darted to his left and this time thrust forward with all his strength as the soldier went past. Pedro's razor-sharp blade, with all his weight behind it, went through the soldier's mail shirt as if he were jabbing at a haystack. The sword penetrated deep into the man's body, and he knew that the man was mortally wounded. But he still had fight left in him. Bleeding from his shoulder and his side, and aware that he was doomed, the soldier made a desperate last attempt to spear Pedro. He could barely raise the lance off the ground. As he thrust for the last time at Pedro, the youngster, his sword held disdainfully out to his side, stamped on the point of the lance, dislodging it from the man's arms. It fell to the ground. The man was defenceless and at Pedro's mercy.

'So,' Pedro jeered, 'you can't cope with an armed adversary, eh? At last I can start to settle some scores.'

'This is for my sister, Cristina, who never hurt a soul in her life.'

Pedro took a step forward and slashed upwards into the man's groin where no armour protection existed. The man was lifted off the ground as his testicles were severed from his body.

'This is for my father, whose medicines saved more souls than all your Catholic popes have ever done.'

This time he slashed sideways at the man's already wounded arm, cleaving it just below the shoulder. The mailed limb thudded bloodily to the ground.

'This is for Alfonso de Castro at Jaén, and all the hundreds of people who the Inquisition has maimed and tortured under the pretext of heresy.'

The third fearful blow fell diagonally, entering the base of the man's neck and cleaving through bone, muscle, rib and lung to halfway down his chest. The two halves of the man, still not dead, fell to the ground alongside the remains of his arm.

'And this is for all the Jewish and Muslim peoples who for centuries you Christians have contemptuously despised, robbed and humiliated!'

Pedro stepped slowly to one side, and with no remorse struck off the man's head with one single blow.

As he did so he heard the sound of horses' hooves approaching around the bend from whence he had come. His blood-smeared sword still in his hand, he grabbed his knapsack and bolted down the bank into some bushes, hiding as best he could. Three riders stopped at the sight of the carnage which greeted them.

'Good Lord!' one shouted. 'Look what they've done to Ado. There must have been at least two of them to chop him up so. He was a mean performer with that spear of his.'

'Where's his horse?' another said. It was Gaz, who had held Pedro down while Zak sodomised him the day before they reached Jaén and who had later raped and killed his sister. 'There's signs of a horse's hooves over here and a lot of blood. The animal must have been injured and run off.'

'Let's go and find them!' It was the unmistakable voice of Pedro's bitter adversary, Zak, who somehow must have survived the blow from Pedro. 'They can't have got too far,' he said, 'I'll prowl around on my horse. You two take a look in those bushes over there.'

They started on the far side of the road, giving Pedro a chance to ease his way through the thicket of bushes until he was a hundred yards away from the road. Then, as he darted across an open space into a cluster of trees, he fell, jettisoning his knapsack as he did so. He fell and fell until he struck the bottom of a deep pit, twisting over on his ankle. His sword, which had plummeted before him, was buried almost up to its hilt in the bottom of the pit. Pedro knew how fortunate he was that he was not impaled on it. He lay there, stunned, seeing nothing around, his eyes unaccustomed to the near darkness. He remained totally still and silent, terrified that his fall might have alerted the three armed men searching for him. He held his ankle. The pain was becoming intolerable and he could feel it swelling by the minute.

He remained immobile for an hour, maybe more. All was quiet. After a while, in the faint light which filtered down, he could start to make out the details of where he was. He had been told that there were scores of old iron and lead mines along the southern flanks of the Alpujarra. Looking up, he guessed that the shaft into which he had fallen was some four or five feet across and at least twenty feet deep. He was lucky it was not considerably more.

Although the sides of the shaft were rough, there were no hand or footholds. Even if there had been, it would be impossible to climb past the five feet of soft friable soil at the top, some of which showered down as he tumbled into the shaft.

He was trapped. There was no way out and no chance of obtaining help. He was miles from the nearest village and a long way from the road. With his knapsack somewhere on the surface, the water skin he had filled earlier in the day and the oranges he had picked by the roadside were all beyond reach. Even his warm *yallabiyya* was rolled up inside his bag.

The hours passed until the daylight started to fade. Pedro sat against the side of the shaft, racking his brains. There had to be a way out. It just required thinking through calmly and logically. People said he was intelligent and quick-witted. Well, let's put it to the test, he thought to himself. It became dark.

Dawn at last broke, and the blackness turned to a grey gloom, but at least he could see something. All through the endless night his hopes were kept alive that somehow he had overlooked an obvious means of escape from this hellhole. It was not to be. There was no way out. He was trapped in the bottom of the mine shaft and would die there. Hungry, soaked through by the overnight rain and shivering with cold, he shouted for help. As the day advanced his voice became a croak. Even the possibility of summoning help faded. Reluctant to admit it, it slowly dawned on him that he was trapped and would perish. The daylight faded into the second night of utter blackness. This time there was no presumption that all would be well on the morrow. As the dawn of the third day came, he lay huddled against the side of the shaft, inert, silent and frozen to the marrow. Starved of sustenance, his mind started to wander. He drifted into semi-consciousness, aware that in his ever-shortening intervals of alertness, sooner rather than later he would fade slowly and painlessly into death.

'Pedro?' a voice called in Arabic somewhere in the recesses of his mind. He was cognizant enough at that moment to know that he was starting to hallucinate.

'Pedro?' the voice called again.

He picked his ears up. Maybe the voice was real?

'Pedro, it's me, Yazíd!'

Pedro could not believe what he heard. His brain was befuddled. He could not focus on what to do.

'Yes, I'm here,' he shouted. But no words came out of his parched throat.

'Pedro, it's me, Yazíd. Where are you? I know you're here somewhere, I've found your knapsack.'

Again, Pedro tried to answer, but he could not utter a single word; not even a croak.

Slowly, his mind started to function again. He knew he had to draw attention to his friend before he went away. He levered himself up onto his good foot, pulled his sword out of the earth and banged it against the side of the shaft.

'Pedro. Where are you? I can hear you. Why don't you speak to me?'

Pedro banged his sword back and forth against two hard lumps of stone. It sounded like a bell ringing.

There was a scuffle then a head appeared over the edge of the shaft.

'Are you down there, Pedro? I can't see you!'

Pedro banged his sword again, this time issuing a croak.

'Yes, it's me, Yazíd. Oh, thank heavens you've come!'

'Pedro, I can barely hear you. Look, I'll throw down your water skin, drink some of that. Ah, good,' he added after a few seconds, 'I can see you now at the bottom.'

Pedro caught the water container and swallowed a few mouthfuls. His relief at being saved from the Inquisition by Don Gonzalo Fernández of Córdoba at Jaén was nothing as compared with this. Unable to calm down, he described to Yazíd in garbled tones what had occurred at the roadside and what led him to fall down the shaft.

'That explains it,' replied Yazíd, leaning over the edge of the shaft, 'I saw a lot of dried blood and what looked like a hastily dug grave.'

'But what brought you here?' asked Pedro, peering upwards. 'How did you know I was down here?'

'You made our sign of the Rainbow Man upside down, didn't you?' he replied. 'I told you before you left María that I'd come and rescue you when you called for me.'

'But I didn't...' Then he remembered that he had knocked over the marker stone with his knee as he evaded the first lunge of the rider.

'But how did you know where...?'

'I just did. I knew you were in trouble.'

'But I'm at least a week's journey away from home. How did you—?'

'I just did. I just kept running...' It was all he would say. 'I'll go and fetch some help. I'll try not to be long.'

'Before you go, Yazíd, will you drop down my *yallabiyya* and some of the oranges from my bag?'

'Better than that, Pedro, you can have the fresh loaf I picked up on the way through Laujar this morning.'

'Laujar? That's miles and miles away.'

'Is it? It didn't seem to take long to get here from there. I'll be off now.'

And he was gone.

It was more than two hours before Pedro heard voices approaching.

'Pedro,' said Yazíd, 'some kind people have come from Mecina to help get you out.'

'Here you are, laddie,' said a man, throwing down a long length of thick and strong esparto rope. 'I've tied a loop in it. Put one leg through it and hold on tight, we'll pull you up.'

'How many of you are there?' he replied.

'Just me, your young friend and my niece. But I think we can manage between us.'

Pedro did his best to provide some assistance by pushing against the irregularities on the shaft wall. Slowly, the three above pulled him out. But it was a struggle. It really needed three adult men. Pedro was showered with soft earth as the rope dug into the soft ground around the edge of the shaft. He was helped out onto the ground. He was not a pretty sight. His swollen ankle still throbbed badly. He was wet and shivering and peppered with brown earth. Yazíd laughed at his sorry appearance.

'It's not funny!' scolded Pedro. 'I could have died down there.'

Then he remembered that it was Yazíd who had found him.

'I'm sorry, Yazíd. There's me telling you off just after you saved my life. You're a wonder, you really are.'

'Don't worry, laddie, we'll soon get you cleaned up,' said a voice behind him.

His eyes, starting to get accustomed to the bright light, Pedro looked around at the two strangers. One was a burly middle-aged man with big, rough hands and wearing a rough rabbit skin waistcoat, a *tasmir* over a long, striped woollen *silhama*. The other was a dark-haired girl of maybe his own age wearing a blue hooded cloak, a *burnu* over her *yubba*. He could not take his eyes off her. With her oval face, black, almond-shaped eyes, lustrous hair and a full figure putting considerable strain on her loose trousers and blouse, she was the most beautiful young woman he had ever seen.

'I'm Salim Almuafiri,' the man said by way of introduction. 'This young friend of yours said that your name's Pedro, yes?'

'Yes, Pedro Togeiro, and like my saviour here, Yazíd, I come from Vélez Blanco.'

'Where's that?' he asked. 'Not around here, I don't think.'

'No, it's a long way away, a couple of days' journey from Almería. Lorca's probably the nearest big town.'

'And where's Lorca?' asked the man again. 'Oh, never mind. I once went to Lanjarón, a whole day's journey from here, so I'm not likely to have heard of any towns you mention, am I!'

He roared with laughter until tears rolled down his face. Pedro immediately took to the man.

'Is this your daughter, Ibn Almuafiri?'

'Ibn Almuafiri?' He looked sideways over his shoulder. 'Oh, you mean me!' he said, doubled up with mirth. He could barely get his words out. 'I thought for a minute you were talking to my father. He died twenty years ago!'

'Just call me Salim, Pedro. Everyone else does.' He burst out laughing.

'No, this isn't my daughter, I was only blessed with three good-for-nothing sons, not a handsome daughter like Raquel here. As I told you, she's my niece.'

He started laughing again. There was nothing stopping the man. Nobody knew what brought this particular bout on.

'They're not good-for-nothing, Uncle,' said Raquel in mock scorn, shoving him waggishly on the shoulder with her hand. 'I know that Turan sits around all day whittling wood and Omar's eyes are so bad that he can't even tie his laces, but Abul works hard enough.'

'Works hard? He'd just as soon tie the mule to the wrong end of the plough,' spluttered Salim, wiping the tears from his cheeks.

'He does try, Uncle,' retorted Raquel. 'He does try.'

'Try! He tries my patience, he does, my dear. That's what he does, tries my patience!'

His own little joke sparked off another round of merriment until they all had to sit on the ground in a circle until the frivolity subsided.

'Now then, you two,' Salim began, 'let's…' He looked around.

'Where's your friend Yazíd gone? He was here just a moment ago.'

'Oh no!' sighed Pedro. 'He's vanished again.'

'Again? How do you mean again?'

'It's too long a story to tell you, Salim. Maybe another time. But Yazíd has this habit of turning up miles and miles away from his home and then disappearing just like a puff of smoke.'

'How did he know you were trapped in the mine shaft?' asked Raquel.

Pedro continued to stare at her. She was gorgeous, and he stumbled over his words in replying.

'I leave signs as I travel across the country. We agreed that if I were in trouble I would make our sign upside down. Three days ago I was attacked by an armed rider and accidentally upended a roadside stone just as I was scratching our Rainbow Man sign on it.'

Uncle and niece both asked different questions at the same time. Again they all laughed.

'What I said, Pedro,' said Raquel, 'was, why did he attack you?' Concerned, she leant over and placed her hand on his arm. 'Were you hurt?'

'That's two questions, not one!' admonished her uncle. 'And what I asked was, "What is your Rainbow Man?"'

'I'd better explain from the beginning,' said Pedro. 'Let's find a shady tree to sit under and I'll tell you. It might only be February but it's very warm.'

Continuously interrupted by questions, it took Pedro a long time to explain what had happened.

'My word, you were brave,' said Raquel, looking at Pedro as if he were a knight in shining armour.

'And is this your sword, Pedro?' asked Salim, examining it admiringly. 'I would hate to be at the receiving end of this. Mind you,' he added, 'I'm a devil with the pitchfork!'

'It's only made of wood!' teased Raquel.

'I know, I'm still saving to buy one with metal tines,' he joked, 'but just think how I could use this!'

He stood up and demonstrated how he would scoop up hay from the field using Pedro's sword as a pitchfork and toss it onto a haystack. He fell down laughing again. Pedro had never met anyone with such an outrageous sense of fun. The man passed his hand down his face, wiping the laugh away and replacing it with a sombre scowl. He could not maintain it and burst out laughing again.

'Is he always like this?' joked Pedro to Raquel, whose hand gently kneaded his arm.

'Nearly always, except when he sees the funny side of things – and then he can't stop laughing.' The girl was nearly as bad as her uncle.

'We must try and be serious, Pedro,' Salim said. 'I see you've got a bad leg. Let's have a look at it.'

'I sprained it falling down the shaft. It's still agony.'

'Hmm, it's badly swollen and very red. Do you think it might be broken?' he asked.

'I don't think so, but it's going to take a long time to heal, and I was hoping to journey on to Lanjarón.'

'That's a good day's journey away, Pedro. I can vouch for that from personal experience! You'd better come back with us and we'll see what we can do with it.'

'And you must come and stay with me and my mother,' said Raquel. 'We've got a room at the back we use as a store. We can clear it out and let you have it.' She was excited at the thought.

'No,' said Salim firmly. 'That wouldn't be right. After all, you're betrothed and due to wed this summer.'

Pedro was stunned. He froze. The blood drained from his face; Raquel noticed.

'No,' said Salim, 'Pedro can stay with me next door. Then you and your mother can look after him... I mean his ankle, of course,' he said with a twinkle in his eye.

'Yes, very well,' agreed Raquel. 'You'll like my mother, Pedro. She's wonderful with cuts and bruises and all manner of things.'

'So was my father, Raquel,' replied Pedro. 'He was an apothecary, and a very good one at that.'

'Right then, Pedro,' said Salim. 'That's what we'll do. Climb on my back and I'll take you to Mecina. Raquel can carry your sword and your knapsack.'

It was a long slog of three miles to Mecina, and such was the strength and stamina of Salim that he only had to put Pedro down twice. While he laboured with Pedro, Raquel skipped on ahead with his knapsack looped over her left shoulder, chopping the heads off tall thistles with his sword with her free hand. Pedro knew that he had fallen hopelessly for this beautiful, bubbling girl. He hoped his ankle would take a long time to recover.

Mecina was a typical Alpujarran village; a seeming jumble of small white houses set around a modest *mesquita* and plaza and joined by a maze of narrow winding alleys. Mecina was the principal village of the six which made up the Tahá group of villages. Pedro recalled a similar group of settlements north of Tabernas, near Almería.

All the houses were small, not least those of Salim Almuafiri and his sister Raghad, who lived next door with her daughter, Raquel. Both houses were located on the edge of the village. Pedro was found a tiny space in the back room where he could bed down. It was close to a back door, which opened onto an alley and this was to prove useful to him in the months ahead.

Raghad felt around the swollen leg, finding no bones broken.

'You must have pulled or torn some of your tendons, Pedro. It's going to take a long time to heal. Raquel said that your father was an apothecary?'

'Yes, he was. But I'm not sure what he would have done for my ankle,' he replied.

'Cold water immediately after you'd done it would have reduced the swelling. Now hot water is best to loosen things up. So what we'll do is to immerse it in hot water morning and evening, and I'll then strap it up firmly.'

'He'll need a crutch to move around on,' chipped in Raquel, who was looking on very concerned. 'I'll get Baka in the square to make one. It'll only take him a few minutes.'

Pedro could not thank Salim and Raquel enough for rescuing him from the mine shaft and for all they were doing for him.

'How can I express my gratitude to you?' he asked.

'You don't need to, Pedro,' replied Raquel. 'However, if you want to you can help me with my worms.'

'You've got worms?' asked Pedro very concerned, recalling some of his father's remedies.

'Yes,' she said mischievously, grimacing as she scratched her backside.

'Are they painful?' he asked in some embarrassment.

'No, not those worms, silly, silkworms!' she chided.

'Silkworms?'

'Yes. Surely you know that this is one of the most important centres in *Al-Andalus* for growing silk?'

'No.'

'But you must have seen the fields of mulberry trees all along this valley?

Three-quarters of all the planted trees around here are mulberries. It's much the same along the Andarax valley too. It's the biggest activity all through the Alpujarra, Pedro! Gosh, you've got a lot to learn. Tomorrow you can come and help me feed the silkworms, but it's best if Uncle Salim tells you all about it first. He's lived here all his life, except when he went to Lanjarón.' She giggled.

The growing of silk, Salim explained that evening after they had eaten, had been assimilated from China by the Arabs at about the time of their migration to *Al-Andalus* and their conquest of Spain.

By the time of Pedro's journey into the Alpujarra, Sevilla had become the major centre for silk with some ten thousand looms and over one hundred thousand workers involved in all aspects of the trade. Granada figured equally. At that time, one tenth of the earnings from silk was paid to the sultanate in Granada, but under later Christian rule a further tenth was allotted to the Church. This was just the thin end of the wedge. Over the next few decades, a variety of sales taxes were imposed which raised to sixty per cent the total duty levied on the sale of silk.

Ten years before Pedro was born, merchants exported nearly three thousand pounds weight of silk to Valencia and thence to Italy. A single bale fetched over sixty English pounds. But it was not just silk that moved to Valencia. By that time hundreds of skilled weavers were leaving Almería to establish looms and workshops there, and sadly, within a hundred years the whole silk industry was in a bad shape. Interference from Castile, excessive duty, increasing foreign competition, epidemics of disease which affected the silkworms themselves and later rebellions by the Mudejares living in the silk-rearing areas of *Al-Andalus*, all led to its decline as a major industry.

After having his ankle re-strapped the next morning by Raghad, Pedro hobbled after Raquel on his crutch to the sheds where the silkworms were reared and where they spun their cocoons.

'This is where we hatch the moths from the pupae which produce the silkworms,' she started. 'Female moths lay between two and five hundred eggs at a time, and once the worms hatch they grow quickly to about the size of your little finger in four to five weeks.'

'And you feed them on mulberry leaves?'

'Yes, and then only fresh mulberry leaves picked the same day. They eat nothing else, and none which are even slightly wilted. It keeps several of us in the village busy picking the leaves and feeding them to the worms. Later, when your ankle's better, you can come and help us. You'll enjoy it; it's almost exclusively the job of the womenfolk, and most of them are young girls my age!'

'But not as beautiful, I vouch!' he said with more seriousness than he wished to convey.

She smiled at him tenderly.

'While they're growing they change skins four times. Then we put them in straw frames where they start to make their cocoons and become pupae. You can see them over here if you hobble over. I'm told that the silkworms inside spin two threads which they weave around and around to make the walls of the cocoons. These are held together with a sticky gum.'

'So how do you separate the thread if it's all gummed up?'

'You can see that later. It's easier than you think. It takes about eight days for the silkworms to make their cocoons. Some we let continue for three or four days to complete the transformation into pupae and then it takes a further fifteen days for the moths to emerge and the whole process starts again.'

'And what do you do with the cocoons?'

'We don't unwind the silk from the cocoons down here in Mecina. That's done up in Pitres. Now,' she said skittishly, grasping hold of Pedro's free hand, 'come and tell me about yourself. I'm dying to find out why you're here in the Alpujarra. I'm sure you've got a lot to tell.'

Pedro was more than delighted to be led out of the shed by the hand to a quiet spot on the edge of the village. His pulse was racing, his breathlessness not being induced by the effort of walking with a crutch. He was totally captivated by this vivacious girl. She made no complaint when he held her hand while he told her about himself; how he came to leave home after Marco was killed; how he was arrested and tortured by the Inquisition and how he came to be orphaned. It was well into the morning when he finished his story. Hardly having left Mecina in all her fifteen years, Raquel was truly in awe of his adventures and his meetings with the Sultan Boabdil and his uncle, *El Zagal*, both of whom she had heard much about. If she had not herself fallen for Pedro earlier, she was smitten by the time he had finished narrating his adventures.

'I've got so much to ask you, Pedro,' she said, 'but I must get back to work and pick some leaves for my little friends. They have voracious appetites.'

'I understand, Raquel, but I've got a lot to ask you too,' he replied.

'I'm afraid mine's not a happy tale to tell,' she replied downcast. 'However, you sit here and rest your foot. You've already been up and around on it enough today. We'll meet here this evening after supper… that's if you can get this far on your crutch.'

'I'll get here even if I have to walk on my hands!' Pedro replied. And he meant it.

With a tweak of her nose and a smile, she slid her hand from his, picked up a big basket in which to collect the leaves and skipped up the road to one of the terraces on which the mulberry trees grew.

It was almost dark when they met that evening. Salim didn't ask where Pedro was going. He had guessed already.

'Do you think you'll meet up with that horrible Zak again, Pedro, and his henchman, Gaz?'

'I hope so, Raquel,' replied Pedro. 'I still have a score to settle.'

'You need to be very careful, my sweet,' she replied. 'They're a pair of murderous villains.'

'Yes, they're no better than scum. But I had the better of Zak when my father and sister died, and if I hadn't been interrupted by Gaz and the one they called Ado, I would have killed Zak. As it was, Zak's lucky to be alive. I struck him a fearful blow across the side of his face and I could tell from his voice when I was hiding in the bushes that it's affected the way he speaks. He must be a hideous sight, since the whole side of his face from his eye to his jaw was sliced wide open. Yes, Raquel, I'm convinced we'll meet up again. But have no fear, dear, I'll be on my guard.' He looked at her and smiled. 'Now how about you, Raquel? Tell me about yourself.'

'There's not much to tell. I was born here and have never been out of the valley. I've been to the market in Laujar a couple of times and to Lanjarón, but that's as far as I've been. When I think of your travels – and you're only just over a year older than me – it makes me very envious. And you with that gorgeous sword. It makes you so manly…'

'Travelling around isn't everything, you know. Not when you get arrested by the Inquisition. As I explained, if it hadn't been for Don Gonzalo Fernández I would still be in one of their dungeons awaiting the *auto-de-fé*.'

'What's that?'

'It's the public trial of so-called heretics, often hundreds of them at a time, in front of thousands of people. Afterwards they're burnt at the stake.'

'Alive?'

'Those who confess their heresy before the pyre is lit are garrotted against the post to which they're tied by the executioner. Relatively few suffer the pain of death in the flames. But either way, it's a frightful way to die when you think that few have any idea of the crime they're supposed to have committed. But enough of that. You were telling me about yourself.'

Pedro barely dared ask her. He almost mumbled the words. 'Your uncle Salim said that you're betrothed to be married?'

The fifteen-year-old fell against Pedro's chest and started weeping. He put his arm around her and held her firm.

'I am due to wed this July,' she sobbed. 'I've only caught a glimpse of my betrothed once and that was three years ago. He already has one wife. By all accounts he's got a violent temper.'

'That's awful.'

'My father betrothed me to him…'

'What's your fiancé's name?'

'Abu Ishar ibn Hakam. He lives in Capilerilla, the highest of the Tahá villages.'

She continued between sobs, 'My father betrothed me to him when I was five. Abu Ishar was himself eighteen then. His family's as poor as ours and my father must have thought his family wouldn't ask much by way of a dowry.'

'So he's now nearly thirty years old?'

'Yes, around that.'

'What dowry was required by his father?'

'I'm not exactly sure. Most of it was settled at that time, and in front of witnesses too as normally happens. It was for house furnishings, bedlinen, carpets – those sorts of things. My family has never been well off, living as we do from week to week, and it totally pauperised my father until the day he died.'

'When was that, Raquel? How long have you lived alone with your mother?'

'It was three years after he arranged my betrothal and just after he…'

She burst into a flood of tears on Pedro's shoulder, sobbing her heart out for several minutes.

'…I've spoken to no one about this, neither to the girls in the village, nor to my mother. She is totally unaware of what happened. When I was eight, soon after my birthday, my father came into my room at night…'

The poor girl could barely speak.

'…and he had his way with me. I didn't know what he was doing, I'd never seen a man before, you know what I mean. Then suddenly there was this stabbing pain and blood running down my legs. He said I mustn't tell anybody otherwise he'd beat me.'

'Was it just the once?' asked Pedro, caressing the nape of her neck.

'Yes. Soon afterwards he died. I think it was Allah's retribution. I'm convinced of it.'

'What happened to him?'

'He was bitten on the foot by a scorpion and the swelling and redness quickly spread up his leg and then up his body. It was a horrible sight. The local surgeon came very quickly to lance the swelling but the poison had set in and he died in agony that very day. It was terrible. I can still hear him screaming even now.'

'That's terrible, Raquel.'

'Yes, but I'm sure it was Allah's way of paying him back for what he did to me. So you see, I'm marrying a man with a bad temper who I know nothing about, who's already got one wife – and I'm not a whole woman. But what can I do? If I admit to what my father did I will be left without a husband, and will effectively be an outcast from this and the other villages.'

It was two weeks before Pedro was able to ascend the road up to Pitres with Raquel. Both of them carried full baskets of silk cocoons for spinning. Several people worked in the spinning shed. Ali, who was in charge, showed Pedro the process.

'Where does the silk go from here after you've spun it?' Pedro asked.

'A lot of it goes to Almería, although most of it is now sent up the coast to Valencia from there. The rest goes to Granada which, in any case, is a lot nearer. We have traders coming here once a week or so to collect the skeins we've reeled off. They deliver it to the weavers in the city where it's dyed various colours and woven into fine silk cloth, satin, brocade or carpets and wall coverings, or used simply as coloured thread for making embroideries and tapestries.'

Pedro and Raquel continued to meet each day as he helped to collect the cocoons so that the silk could be spun from them up in Pitres. After a few weeks when his ankle had healed, Pedro started to work with the men in the fields, inevitably helping with the numerous *acequias* and the distribution of the abundant water down through the terraces. He loved the relaxed life they seemed to enjoy. It was in such stark contrast to the mood he found in Ohanes some months before. But most of all he loved being with Raquel. She was in the forefront of his thoughts all day long. Most evenings they met amongst the tall bulrushes which bordered the stream. But if the two lovers thought that Raghad and Salim did not know that they were meeting secretly they were much mistaken. Both mother and uncle had guessed and although they had not spoken about it to each other, both were greatly distressed by the life which lay ahead for the effervescent and jolly Raquel after her marriage to Abu Ishar ibn Hakam. If she had this brief opportunity in her life so as to experience true and tender love, then they secretly welcomed it. Both of them loved and admired the focus of Raquel's affections but knew that Pedro would continue his travels sooner rather than later. In fact, with Raquel's imminent marriage, he had little option but to do so.

So as the evenings drew out and the days grew warmer, the two youngsters chatted and giggled, petted one another, kissed and cuddled and explored the mysteries of each other's bodies which up to then had remained forbidden fruit. Both knew that their romance could not last and this heightened even more their desire and passion.

It was a few weeks before her wedding day when Raquel pleaded with Pedro to make love to her.

'I know that you'll not be here much longer, my darling,' she said with tears in her eyes. 'It'll be impossible for either of us to live here, knowing that the other is nearby and yet beyond reach. Please make love to me so that I carry your child. When it is born, however despicable my life with Abu Ishar and his other wife is, I will carry in my heart the knowledge that the child isn't his but belongs to you. This will help sustain me through the long years of loneliness which await me.'

It was just four days before the wedding when they met for the very last time in their hideaway in the bulrushes. It was sheltered from the freshening breeze which blew from the high sierras above Pitres.

'Raquel,' Pedro said as they lay in each other's arms, 'I'd like you to have this small carved box which I was given by the elders of Ohanes for helping with their dispute over water rights. It's very precious and goes back several hundred years to the time of al-Matasím, who was one of your greatest leaders.'

She took the treasure and stroked the smooth yellow ivory, flipping the lid open. The inside was lined with cedar wood which was still fragrant.

'And, moreover,' he added, 'I'd like you to have these two jewels which I was given by Yahya al-Nagar, the Prince of Almería, when the King and

Queen received the keys of the city. One is a blue sapphire and the other is a lovely green emerald.'

He placed them in her hand. Both were the size of her thumb-nail. Raquel studied them intently in the breeze, brushing her long hair away from her face. She'd never held precious stones in her hand before. She rubbed them on her sleeve to make them shine and placed them carefully in her ivory box.

'What can I say, Pedro, but thank you with all my heart. You've made me happier in the last six months than at any time in my whole life, and now you've given me these lovely things to remember you by. I'll treasure them all my life. One day they'll belong to your son or daughter...'

'Yes,' she said, replying to his raised eyebrows. 'Your seed is sown. I'm to have your baby. You have no idea how happy I am.'

As she did so a gust of wind picked up the dried rushes beside them, sucking them into a slender whirlwind which scurried up the river bank for a hundred yards before disappearing in front of them.

The second riddle of the soothsayer instantly came into Pedro's mind:

'When your seed is sown lose no time in following the swirling tree.'

He knew that their time together was at an end. They kissed fondly for all too brief a moment and walked back hand in hand to their respective homes.

Salim saw Pedro packing his knapsack but said little. He knew what it signified. With a lot of sadness he embraced the youngster who, with tears in his eyes, walked up through the village in the direction taken by the whirlwind. It would lead him over the mountains to the fabled city of Granada.

VIII: The Final Cut

July 1491

The surrender of Almería to the Christians in December 1489 saw a temporary lull in the visible hostilities between the two sides. Boabdil ventured forth to rouse support in the Alpujarra the following year but he had little success. Both sides were building up their strength for a final showdown, although all knew there could be only one outcome. Granada was the jewel to defend and the prize to be won.

Fernando wasted little time in initiating his campaign of attrition. In March 1491 he took the castle of Padul, some fifteen miles south of Granada. Then in April he and the Queen started to assemble a huge army, eight miles to the north-west of the city near the hamlet of Gozco. By the middle of May a force of forty thousand soldiers and ten thousand horsemen was in place. More soldiers with their sergeants and captains arrived by the week from all over Spain. The encampment stretched for miles in each direction across the flat plain.

While a show of overwhelming strength was part of the royal strategy, the army was not just there for ornament. The road to Granada from the Alpujarra was blocked, as were the roads in from Guadix and Alhama. The city was effectively sealed off. Parties of soldiers and cavalry spread out over the land between the encampment and Granada, destroying farms, trampling down the crops, killing the animals, filling in wells, breaking sluices and razing towers and settlements alike. The citizens of the beleaguered city waited with growing fury and frustration. On June 10th King Fernando, with the Queen and Prince Don Carlos and the Infanta Doña Juana, rode to Zubia, close to Granada and beneath the towering mountains of the Sierra Nevada. They looked out from the upper windows of an abandoned house and contemplated their final goal. Never had they approached Granada so closely before. By chance one day from their high vantage point they witnessed the very last bloody skirmish between the two factions.

Incited by the brazenness of the Christians, the Muslims sallied forth from the south gate of the city, taking up a position opposite their adversaries. In expectation of an attack, the Duke of Escaloña, the Count of Ureña and Don Alonso de Aguiler positioned their forces ahead of Zubia and aside the steep flanks of the sierras, while the Marquis de Cádiz and others faced the city itself. Muslim horsemen started to harass the Christian army. Supported from behind by the discharge from two heavy cannons, their black smoke choking the air, the Muslim cavalry galloped forth to meet the Christians, followed by the foot soldiers, who charged forward with blood-curdling battle cries brandishing their spears, maces and broad scimitars. But as so often had happened in the past, their impetuosity was their downfall. The Christians, disciplined and trained, closed ranks and, with their cavalry making the first foray and breaking open the Moorish line, a rout took place. By the time the short battle was over, one thousand four hundred Muslims lay dead and six hundred were injured or taken prisoner. The powder for the guns was also lost to them. It was a valued prize.

Pedro was unaware of any of this when he set off from Mecina on July 13th after saying his last farewells to Raquel. By midday he had passed through the mountain village of Bubión, choosing to take the northern, more direct route over the mountains, as indicated by the whirlwind, rather than follow the easier but longer route through Lanjarón. By the evening he had ascended to the highest pass over the Sierra Nevada – indeed, by far the highest such pass in Spain. With Granada still over twenty miles away, he bedded down for the night beneath a full moon in a shepherd's circular stone shelter. He had food and drink aplenty for the journey. Raquel had seen to that.

The next morning was bright, still and unusually clear. As he set off he could see in the distance the amber-coloured walls of the Alcazaba with its broad square tower. But what intrigued him most was the sight which greeted him on the plain beyond. It was already shimmering in the morning heat. What was it, or what were they? They appeared as coloured dots, evenly spaced over the plain, stretching each side of the streams which wound amongst them like silver threads. Hundreds of spindly columns of smoke rose vertically in the still air, and here and there clouds of red dust swirled over the ground. Every now and then there was a flash of something metallic glinting in the sun, which lay low in the sky behind him. Despite his keen eyesight, it was all too far away and too indistinct to make out exactly. But his destination was clear.

It was night-time on July 14th when Pedro approached what he could now see was an army encampment of awesome size. He had been walking all day, and although very tired and dusty he was keen to complete his journey. He was a short distance from the encampment which was flanked by an earth bank and ditch, when he entered the small hamlet of Gozco. There were no more than a few dwellings there. Through the cool night air a low buzz of sound came from the nearby camp. Screams came from a large mansion nearby. He ran to where the cries came from and saw flames in an upstairs window.

'Fire, fire!' he shouted. He dropped his knapsack and ran towards the mansion. He reached a side door colliding with a stocky, finely-dressed man who had arrived post-haste in the darkness. A water butt stood in the porch taking the roof drainage, and conveniently a wooden pail stood next to it. The man threw open the door. Pedro dipped the pail in the water butt and tore up the stairs as fast as he could, spilling much of the water on the way up.

'You can't… you mustn't… *Don't you go up there!*' shouted the man as he stomped up the stairs after the swifter youth.

It was too late. Pedro burst into the room which he correctly judged contained the fire. Aware of white-clad figures in the smoke-filled and candlelit room, but not actually seeing them, he rushed to the window and threw the water at the velvet curtains, which were ablaze. The small panes of thick glass in the open window shattered explosively. One corner of the bed had also caught alight. Pulling the top sheet from it, he smothered the flames until only black smoke remained. A tall woman in a cotton nightdress and nightcap, hands to her mouth and whimpering, waved the smoke away with her hands.

'I'm sorry, Your Majesty,' said the man with whom Pedro had collided. 'I didn't know... I...'

Taking her to be the Queen, Pedro looked in horror at the woman in the nightdress. He shook his head, his mouth open speechless in an attempt at an apology. Doña María Manrique de Yllora, the Queen's lady-in-waiting, with one hand still glued to her mouth, shook her head as if to say 'Not me' and pointed to another woman at the other end of the room.

In the light of the single candle and the smoke, he looked around the room for the first time. There were four others there. More were running up the stairs.

'I'm sorry, Your Majesties...' the courtier continued.

Pedro knew his voice. 'Don Gonzalo!' he burst out. 'Don Gonzalo,' he repeated, his voice way off scale. 'It's me, Pedro. Don't you remember?'

Pandemonium broke loose. Everybody started talking or shouting at once.

'Who did you say?' said Pedro's saviour at Jaén, thoroughly confused.

'You must go from here!' chided the lady-in-waiting, Doña María, pushing Pedro towards the door...

'Don Gonzalo, what do you mean by this?' said the Queen sternly.

'I'll need a full explanation from you for all this, Fernández, make no mistake!' came the stentorian tones of the King.

'Get out of here,' shouted the Sergeant-at-Arms, pushing his sword menacingly at Pedro.

'Quiet, quiet!' shouted the King in an imperious voice as he scrambled out of bed. 'What happened, Isabel?' he demanded angrily of his wife.

'I don't know,' she replied defensively. 'I was kneeling by the bedside saying my prayers with you snoring away, and flames started shooting up the curtain. The wind must have blown it against the candle on the dressing table. Then I heard someone outside shouting "Fire, fire!" – and then this young man burst into the room pursued by Don Gonzalo and followed by Doña María and the Sergeant-at-Arms.'

'Do you know this man, Don Gonzalo? He seems to know you,' asked the King of his trusty ambassador to Boabdil.

'Yes, Sire, I do. His name's Pedro Togeiro, and by the look of it he might have saved your lives. A minute longer and both of you might have choked to death in the smoke – that's if you hadn't been incinerated first.'

The King was not well pleased.

'Fernández,' he bawled. 'This is all your doing! I'll need an explanation from you first thing tomorrow morning as to why your curtains and bedding nearly led to our death. We could have died in this house of yours tonight.'

Don Gonzalo Fernández of Córdoba was nothing if not spirited.

'Sire, the curtains and bedding, even the candle, might have been mine. But the flame and the breeze through the open window were not. I shall be here at sunrise tomorrow to receive your gratitude on behalf of this young man who raised the alarm and saved you... At your service, Your Majesties!'

Annoyed by the reprimand, Don Gonzalo turned on his heels and strode out, followed by all the other supposed miscreants.

'Pedro,' he said when they were outside in the darkness. 'I don't know what on earth you're doing here but it's a pleasure to see you again, although of course not under these circumstances. We can't talk now, Pedro. Go with Sergeant Gallardo to the camp. He'll find you a place for the night and get you some hot food. I expect you could do with it. I'll meet up with you tomorrow morning after the King's cooled down.'

'Come with me, young fellow,' said the sergeant, putting his arm around Pedro's shoulder. How do you fancy a bowl of steaming hot venison stew?'

It was not the King who summoned Don Gonzalo the next morning but the Queen. The sun was well above the horizon when he was shown into a downstairs chamber which the Queen had commandeered as her ante-room. Attired, she sat on a stool while her hair was dressed by Doña María.

'I trust you are no worse for wear, Your Majesty?' the courtier asked.

'No, Don Gonzalo. We've got over the trauma of last night, although I can't say that we slept much afterwards. No more than you, I shouldn't think. The sleeping potion which my doctor, Salomón Byton, gave us didn't do us much good. The King's been called away on urgent business, something which he'll wish to tell you about when he returns. He's asked me to express his regret over his outburst to you last night. It was not seemly and was not just. Please accept his apology.'

'Of course, Ma'am,' Don Gonzalo replied graciously.

'My asking you to see me this morning is to thank you and your young friend...'

'Pedro Togeiro, Your Majesty.'

'Yes, you and Master Togeiro, for your speedy action last night.'

'It's Pedro who you should be grateful to, Your Majesty. If he'd not been passing by and raised the alarm I may not have spotted the fire, and you and the King might have perished in the flames.'

'Well, in that case we are indebted to him. It sounded last night as if you know the young man, Don Gonzalo?'

'Indeed I do, Ma'am.'

'How so?'

'It will cause some embarrassment to explain, Ma'am.'

'Why?'

'Because I rescued him from the clutches of the Inquisition in Jaén. From your Inquisitor General, Tomás de Torquemada, to be precise, Ma'am.'

'What was he doing there?'

'Who, Ma'am? Torquemada or Pedro?'

'Both, I suppose.'

'I'll try to explain.'

While the Queen's hair was being brushed by Doña María, Don Gonzalo explained how Pedro, then thirteen years of age, had come to leave his home in Veléz Blanco on the death of Marco; how he lost his mother to slave traders when he was eight and was himself enslaved on board an Arab dhow for nearly two years; how he was arrested for alleged looting after the Almerían earthquake and taken to Jaén where he was imprisoned and interrogated by Diego Rodriguez Lucero… and Tomás de Torquemada.

'Hmm,' she pondered. 'Rodriguez Lucero is already getting a reputation for brutality, Don Gonzalo, but I'm saddened by what you tell me about Father Tomás. I'll speak with him when I see him next.'

She continued. 'It sounds as if Pedro Togeiro has had more than enough adventures for a lifetime. But you haven't explained how he came to be outside our residence here… I mean, of course, your residence.'

'I don't know any more than you, Ma'am. I nearly collided with him outside your door in the darkness and we both ran up to your bedchamber. I haven't yet spoken to him to find out what brings him here to Gozno. I'll catch up with him later.'

'Look,' the Queen said, pulling a jade ring from her middle finger. 'Please give this to your young charge as an expression of our gratitude to him. The gold band is engraved on the inside with my personal insignia. It should guarantee his safety in the future and open doors which would otherwise be closed to him. Moreover, Don Gonzalo, when the opportunity arises I want you to bring him to dine with the King and me. I'm intrigued to meet this young man and learn of his exploits at first hand. In the meantime, find a suitable abode for him in the encampment. With that Toledo sword you say he possesses he will be the envy of my officers here, let alone the ordinary soldiers.'

The township of tents was expanding by the day. The white, red, green or blue tents each accommodated some eight to ten men and were supported on a high central pole and several side poles. The soldiers' heavy arms were stored on adjacent wooden racks. Each tent had a single brazier outside for cooking. While the tents were arranged in close ranks, wide avenues were left between them for the passage of horses, wagons and cannons.

Sergeant Gallardo found room for Pedro in a tent with eight other soldiers. He was judicious in choosing it. Its occupants were a happy-go-lucky but well-disciplined group of men who quickly took to the seventeen-year-old. Amongst the soldiers' tents were others shared by four or five sergeants. Each had the men under his control in adjacent tents. It was a sound arrangement which had evolved over many years of campaigning.

Don Gonzalo found Pedro that morning. He explained how Queen Isabel had shown much interest in his story and wished to meet him. He handed Pedro her jade ring, which fitted snugly on his little finger. He was thrilled with the gift, and the ambassador promised to thank the Queen when he saw her next. Don Gonzalo was distressed to learn of the murder of his father and sister two years before but was heartened when Pedro explained how he had avenged Pedro's father's death by slaying one of the soldiers who murdered him, called Ado. He then entreated Pedro to stay at the encampment. Historic events were about to unfold, in which Don Gonzalo was likely to be a key figure. He wished Pedro well and instructed Sergeant Gallardo to ensure his welfare.

It was a few evenings later at dusk when Pedro and his new friends were grouped around the brazier eating that the young man explained what drew him to the encampment at Gozco. Sergeant Gallardo joined them and listened intently. So did Captain Agustín López, the sergeant's commanding officer. He was a tall, good-looking man in his late thirties with a well-groomed moustache. Until then he had not met Pedro. However, there was general disbelief in the veracity of his story until he showed them the faint scars which he still had on his back from the flogging he had received the day after the 1489 earthquake in Almería, and the marks which remained on his wrists from the *El Strappato* torture at Jaén.

'What do Zaquera and Gázquez look like, Pedro?' asked one of the soldiers.

'Zaquera must be around forty years old. He's thickset and shorter than me. He's got a ruddy complexion and a low forehead. You can't mistake him. Half his left ear is missing and he must have a fearful scar right across his face from eye to jaw. He speaks with a slur, so one side of his face may be paralysed.'

'Anything else?'

'Around his neck will be Sabyán's ruby ring. Oh, and I almost forgot. Immediately after he assaulted me in the barn, he was held down by Sergeant Luque and a giant of a man called Matute and, in the light of a lantern, Captain Ortíz castrated him with his knife. Gázquez, who was screaming for mercy, was given some thread and ordered to sew Zaquera up. The two of them raped a seventeen-year-old Muslim girl in Gérgal the night we stopped there after I'd been taken prisoner. Captain Ortíz said that he had to put pay once and for all to Zaquera's lustings. When I next encountered Zak, the day he murdered my father in Vélez Blanco, he ran at me stiff-legged, so he may be half lame as well as having a paralysed face. He'll also have the marks on his back from the flogging he received after he assaulted me.'

'Most soldiers have got scars from floggings, Pedro,' one soldier chipped in.

'And what about Gázquez?' asked another.

'A bit taller and leaner. Younger. A long nose, and the end of one finger missing on his sword hand, his left hand. He'll also have scars from the flogging.'

There was a pause.

'I think I've seen them here,' a lone voice called out from the other side of the fire.

'Where?' asked Captain López, pricking up his ears.

'The other side of the camp, sir, across the stream which runs through the middle. It has to be Zaquera. The man is truly hideous with a deep purple mark down his face. One side of it is lower than the other. He's gruesome.'

'Was Gázquez there too?' asked Sergeant Gallardo.

'Yes, both of them. But sitting apart from the others.'

'Your chance for justice has arrived, Pedro,' said the captain, inspecting Pedro's sword in his hands while he spoke.

'Sergeant, take Ramírez, Silva and Castaño and arrest them both. Use force if you need to. Bring them back here. I think their days are numbered.'

The sergeant and the three soldiers donned their breastplates and helmets, and with two of them wielding swords and the others short but heavy pikes, they prepared to go.

'Can I go with them?' pleaded Pedro.

'No, you must stay here. You mustn't get involved at this stage.'

It was half an hour later when the four soldiers returned, prodding Zaquera and Gázquez with the end of their pikes. They stumbled along noisily. Both were manacled. Their foul language and cursing could be heard all around. Dozens of soldiers gathered to see what was going on.

'So it's you, you lily-livered cur!' spat Zak when he saw Pedro by the fireside. 'I could have guessed that you'd be behind this. Was it you who chopped Ado up last winter?' he sneered. 'You and how many others?'

'Just me,' retorted Pedro, getting up and tearing the chain from around Zak's neck on which swung Sabyán's ruby ring. 'That's the first thing I want,' he said. 'And the second thing is your life for murdering my father. Release him, Sergeant, so that I can kill him in fair fight.'

'Yes, let me go,' sneered Zak with his horrible, screwed-up face. 'I'll have his guts for garters with one hand tied behind my back – and blindfolded at the same time.'

'Shut him up, Ramírez!' ordered Captain López. 'Let's have no more of his foul mouth. Tie him to that post. Kill him if he as much as moves.'

'Now you, Gázquez. I've got some questions for you. Take him over there to that clearing, Silva.'

'What are you going to do with me?' squirmed Gaz. 'I didn't do nothing, honest. It was him what done it – done him, and the murders.'

'And what about the flogging?' asked Captain López, turning back to Gázquez.'

'I didn't do it. It were done by Sergeant Luque. He pushed Zak and me away so he could give the boy a few feeble strokes of the cat-o'-nine-tails.'

'Is this true, Pedro?'

'Yes. Zaquera and Gázquez were both poised each side of me about to start the flogging but Sergeant Luque pushed them aside and did it himself.'

'So, Gázquez. You can confirm that that's Zaquera over there and that he sodomised Pedro in the barn and that it was he who slew his father?'

'Yes, I told you, it were Zak who killed his father.'

'And do you admit that you raped and killed Pedro's sister, Cristina?'

'Well, I might have…'

'Did you or didn't you?'

'Of course he did, the squirming turd!' shouted Zak through the handkerchief tied ineffectively around his mouth. 'He could never keep his hands off anything in a skirt. Rape his own grandmother, he would.'

Ramírez cuffed Zak hard with his mailed fist.

'You were told to shut up! One more word and your head will feel the sharp points of this mace.'

'Good,' interjected Captain López. 'That's all I needed to know. Come with me, Pedro.'

The officer led Sergeant Gallardo and Pedro a few tents away.

'In view of what you saw with your own eyes, Pedro, and with their own admissions, we have more than enough evidence to hang them both forthwith. Is that how you see it?'

'Yes. They're both vile scum and deserve to die. The sooner the better as far as I'm concerned.'

'Sergeant?'

'Yes, but hanging's too good for vermin like them.'

They returned to the campfire. Captain López announced the sentences in his deep voice. He instructed the soldiers to erect high posts, hooks and ropes from which Zaquera and Gázquez would swing until their lives expired. The sentences would be carried out at daybreak. Pedro's score with the three soldiers who murdered his father and sister would be settled once and for all.

But not like that…

Zaquera, cunning as well as cruel, had tensed his arms as Ramírez had tied his hands behind the post. While Gázquez was being interrogated, he wriggled his arms free of the rough bonds, holding the loosened cord in his hands behind the post, grimacing all the while in abject pain. While the others' attention was distracted by Captain López's pronouncement by the campfire, Zaquera slid from the post unnoticed, snatching a one-handed battleaxe left carelessly on the ground nearby.

The movement caught Pedro's eye. He leapt to his feet and ran into his tent. Advised by the captain not to leave his sword in the rack outside the tent, he drew his prized weapon from its scabbard which, as ever, was tied into the top of his knapsack lying by his bedroll. He charged out of the tent. The others around the fire were already on their feet. Zak, now some twenty yards away, saw Pedro starting to give chase, and hopped off as fast as he could with his grotesque gait. But Zak knew that he was doomed. Twenty yards on, in an open space between some tents, Pedro caught up with him. Zak stopped and turned in a leering crouch. With Pedro just a sword's length away, Zak, the murderous battleaxe in his left hand, swept it to his left across his body, at the same time issuing a blood-curdling curse at the youngster who had so terribly maimed him. Pedro, lithe as ever, pulled away as the curved axe-head scythed past, an inch from his stomach. Then, as the blade swept by, Pedro thrust his sword hard and deep into Zak's belly. As the man's body was propelled around to his left by the momentum of the axe swing, Pedro's razor-sharp sword sliced sideways through the soft tissue below the ribs, almost cutting Zak in half.

Captain López, Sergeant Gallardo, Ramírez, Silva and Castaño arrived on the scene as Zaquera tumbled to the ground, his guts spilling from his wound into a sea of blood. His eyes glazed over as he tried to speak, blood pouring though his disfigured mouth. Amazingly, he was still alive.

'My word, Pedro,' said a panting López. 'That was a mighty thrust you made with that sword of yours! I can see you were well trained by that instructor you mentioned, Marco Arana. He didn't die in vain.'

Pedro had barely listened. As Zak writhed on the ground, he drew his Toledo dagger from its sheath and knelt over the dying man.

'I promised you that I'd catch up with you and kill you,' he said, his mouth set hard and his eyes narrowed to no more than slits. 'This is for what you did to my father.'

Looking up first at Captain López who gave a nod of approval, Pedro buried his dagger slowly into Zak's neck, slicing through his windpipe. A bloody gurgle signified that at last the wretch was dead.

The furious chase after Pedro from the campfire had left Gázquez unattended. He was not going to miss his chance. Manacled though he still was, he saw his opportunity to escape. He tore off into the near darkness, away from the light of the fire. With the protective ditch surrounding the encampment only fifty yards away, Gaz thought he'd made his escape; but he was mistaken. Three young pikemen had seen him bolt and sped to head him off. As Gaz skirted a tent, his goal in sight, he was met by a phalanx of three horizontal eight-foot-long bills. He ran onto them headlong and, without uttering a cry, he was skewered through the throat, chest and groin. The pikemen levered out their spears, nonchalantly cleaned the steel tips on Gaz's clothing, and dragged his corpse through the dust to where Zak now lay dead. Pedro's sister, Cristina, had at last been avenged.

The fire in Don Gonzalo's house at Gozno, earlier on the 14th of the month, provided the spur which the royal couple needed to establish a permanent base for themselves on the plain outside Granada. They had learnt the hard lesson over the years that soldiers have to be kept occupied if serious disorder and internecine fighting in large encampments are to be avoided. Taking the layout of the town of Briviesca near Burgos in northern Spain as their model, the *Reyes Católicos* instructed the Aragón architect, Maestro Ramiro, to plan the building of a brand new city nearby. It was to be called Santa Fe, but it was the total antithesis of the historic city they were now besieging. Small, compact and rectangular, measuring just four hundred yards by three hundred, it would mobilise the immense workforce of semi-skilled men close by. Moreover, no extra cost would be incurred, since they were already being paid to do no more than secure the tent enclosure, make sallies to the walls of Granada so as to arouse the ire of its inhabitants and keep their weapons sharp and oiled.

To build the city, hundreds of soldiers were turned into brick-makers. Kilns were constructed, wood brought from afar to fire them and wooden moulds made by the hundreds. The sandy clay of the valley was dug out, puddled with water and fortified with straw to make the thousands upon thousands of bricks needed. Sawpits were excavated in which to cut the timber needed for the scaffolding and the city gates; foundries were established to cast in damp fine sand the iron bars, window gratings, gate hinges and the miscellany of tools required. Sawyers, carpenters, masons, blacksmiths, hoopers, saddlers and scores of different craftsmen were imported from miles around to speed the construction of the new settlement. The industry was prodigious and the progress remarkable. By the turn of the year the small city was taking shape, and by the following April the four pairs of gates were erected and the King and Queen were ready to move into their new palace – once, that is, it had been suitably consecrated by a bevy of clerics, including the Bishop of Ávila, who was to be the future Bishop of Granada.

Pedro joined the workforce. Captain López, who'd taken a liking to his new recruit, had overheard Pedro say that he had worked on the reconstruction of the Pechina Gate prior to the surrender of Almería to Fernando and Isabel twenty or so months before. So Pedro worked on building the south gate, helping to erect the scaffolding around the burgeoning structure as bricks and mortar were hauled by block and tackle to the working level.

Excitement over the construction of their new city did not cause Fernando and Isabel to take their eyes off their main objective: Granada. In September, negotiations commenced for the surrender of the city to the Christians. The King and Queen charged their able secretary, Hernando de Zafra, to lead the negotiations on their behalf, assisted by the trusty Don Gonzalo of Córdoba and his Moorish scribe, Simuel. As the long-standing ambassador to the Sultan, Boabdil, Don Gonzalo would ensure the latter's confidence in the honourable intentions of the Christian monarchs. Boabdil put his trust in obtaining fair terms in his vizier, Abul Kásim el Muleh, and the Alcalde of Granada, his long-standing friend and advisor, Yusuf Aben Comisa.

The negotiations dragged on. The two sides met with their secretaries and advisors, argued over what had been discussed up until then, possibly agreed certain points and moved on to new issues. They then would retire to their respective camps for consultation and return days later to continue the process.

It was never going to be easy. While the handovers of Málaga, Guadix, Baza and Almería involved just the surrender of cities, the negotiations for Granada concerned the final extinction of Muslim rule in Spain after nearly eight hundred years.

By November 25th the Terms of the Capitulation had been drafted. These contained the Christian sovereigns' demands for the takeover of the Muslim capital and what remained of their empire, plus the concessions sought for themselves by Boabdil and his two negotiators. Indeed, the benefits which Kasím and Comisa sought for themselves, as well as for their sons and nephews, dragged out the negotiations interminably until the King threatened to call the whole exercise off. The Muslims were left in no doubt as to what the consequence of this would be. Yet the sums of money and lands which the two negotiators secured for Boabdil and themselves were immense.

The Terms of Capitulation specified that Granada would be ceded to the Spanish Crown within sixty days, and the remains of the territory, notably the Alpujarra, within ninety days. Five hundred Muslim hostages who had been held by the Christians – not least Ahmad, Boabdil's son and Pedro's friend – would be released in anticipation of this compliance.

Kasím and Comisa won important concessions for their people of Granada: security of persons and belongings; retention of 'booty' acquired during the war; religious freedom, both for Muslims and converts; freedom to use mosques, minarets, and religious objects; retention of the Muslim rituals and slaughterhouses; continuation of the organs of administration for three years; liberty of commerce, especially with North Africa; unhindered emigration to North Africa after the sale of possessions; study of a mixed system of justice for Muslims and Christians; liberation of all Muslim prisoners in *Al-Andalus* within five months, and of all prisoners in Castile within eight months; and retention of arms and horses. In addition, Boabdil was promised title to the lands of the Alpujarra and a considerable financial settlement.

Not having received a reply to the draft Terms from the hesitant and indecisive Sultan, King Fernando sent him a letter on November 29th via Martín of Alarcón, Ahmad's guardian, who was well respected by Boabdil. This demanded the capitulation of Granada within twenty days.

Already starving from the siege of the city which had been in force since the previous spring, and fearful that they might suffer the same awful fate as Málaga just four years before, the citizens sent an urgent deputation to Boabdil December 16th, led by Mohammed el Pequeni, to plead with Boabdil to sign the Terms of Capitulation. Four days later he did so, in the castle of Alfacar, a few miles to the north of the city.

IX: The Jewels of Granada

January 2nd 1492

This was the day the Muslims relinquished their city and lost a kingdom. Across the length and breadth of Christendom flags were flown, bells rung and special Masses held in churches and cathedrals; such was the climactic significance of this single day. For years to come people would ask of their friends, 'Where were you the day you heard that Granada had fallen?'

Granada was founded in the eighth century soon after the arrival of the Arabs in Spain in 711. In the thirteenth century, with the Moorish kingdom shrunk to the regions of Granada, Málaga and Almería, the focus of the Muslims moved from Córdoba to Granada, and the latter city's period of greatness was about to dawn. Two contiguous new precincts were soon added to that built earlier by the Taifas. The Rabad al-Bayyazin stood along the north-eastern edge of the first enclosure, while the Albayzín or Albaicín lay on the crest and northern edge of the hill. A surrounding wall and gates were added to enclose them.

In 1237 on the other side of the river, on the north side of the whaleback hill called Sabika, alongside a new and formidable *alcazaba*, the Nazarí started their glorious palace, the Alhambra, eulogised by the poet Ibn al-Jatib in the following century as a place of stupendous splendour and tranquillity. The cool and peaceful pavilion and water gardens of the Generalife nearby were started eighty years later to complete the triple grouping of structures on the Sabika. While the Alhambra constituted the awe-inspiring palace of the sultans, the city of fifty thousand inhabitants had its own focus. The commercial and administrative nucleus of the Madinat Garnata was centred around the Great Mosque, close to the main gate, the Puerta de Bib al-Ramla, nearly a mile from the Alcazaba. The labyrinth of old narrow streets, alleys and bazaars in this key commercial part of the city was the home of the Granada silk industry and of the Jewish quarter, the Alcaicería. It was here that Julian del Rey – *El Moro*, the great Toledo swordsmith – practised his trade before turning Christian and returning to Toledo. Facing the Alhambra, the hill of the Albaicín provided the luxurious residential district of the city. With some thirty mosques, it was enriched by fine palaces and high-walled villas belonging to the aristocracy and the wealthy.

It was the afternoon of the day earlier, January 1st, when Sergeant Gallardo rode to Santa Fe. The new city was now taking its final form. He found Pedro working high on the scaffolding of the south gate. He told him that Don Gonzalo had been instructed by the Queen to request that he, Pedro, join the

100-strong contingent of the Queen's guard which would lead the procession to enter Granada on the morrow, and that he should take himself post-haste to the officers' quarters on the west side of the camp. The Camp Commandant would be expecting him, but if there were any problems he should show him the Queen's jade ring as proof of his identity. There he would be equipped with the appropriate attire for the auspicious occasion and introduced to his mount, a black mare called La Belleza.

'I don't believe it, Sergeant!' responded a stupefied Pedro. 'Why should Queen Isabel single me out for this honour?'

'The Queen has a long memory,' he replied. 'Cross her and you're an enemy for life. Favour her in some way and she will remember it for as long as it takes her to reciprocate. Don Gonzalo also said to tell you that she hasn't forgotten that you are to dine with her and the King when a suitable opportunity arises; hopefully when Granada is secured for their joint kingdoms of Castile and Aragón.'

At the crack of dawn the next morning, with sparkling hoar-frost on the ground, fearing that even at this late hour the Muslims would renege on the agreement for the handover ceremony, the Knight Commander of León, Gutierre de Cárdenas, secretly led a force of four hundred foot soldiers and five hundred horsemen up the broad valley from the Darro which separated the Alhambra from the Generalife. Arriving by the back route at the iron-studded Puerta de la Justicia, the Christian force was met by the Moorish gatekeeper, Zabí, who on being handed the agreed purse of golden *doblas*, passed over the key of the gate, the only access into the Alcazaba.

Once inside and dividing his force in two, the first to secure the fortress, Gutierre de Cárdenas, led the smaller contingent into the palace to locate the Sultan. Entering the first chamber, the Mexuar, which was the reception salon for visiting dignitaries, he found displayed seventeen standards which had been lost by the Christians in battles in earlier times. Many were in a very poor state. One was over one hundred and fifty years old. Boabdil was then at prayer. On hearing the approach of soldiers, he gathered up his armed men and retreated through a secret door deep into the recesses of the palace. The Knight Commander withdrew his soldiers to the Alcazaba. Leaving a large group as an occupying force, he led the rest out of the fortress and down the long wooded approach to the city. There he took over the commanding Bermejas tower and the adjacent gateway, the Puerta de las Granadas, the only access up from the city to the Alhambra and Alcazaba. Leaving groups of soldiers to hold them, he continued on through the city to take possession from within of the main gate into the city itself, the Puerta de al-Ramla, close to the Great Mosque.

The sun had barely risen over the high Sabika hill to the south-east when, greatly satisfied, the commander headed back to Santa Fe accompanied by just a handful of men. He had fulfilled his mission of securing the peaceful entrance of the King and Queen later that day into the city of Granada and then into the Alcazaba. The privilege of taking possession of the palace itself was for the Monarchs – and them alone.

The Christian occupation of the city gates aroused little response from the inhabitants. Most were relieved that the waiting was nearly over. Their disenchantment with their Sultan was such that they cared little if he relinquished his beloved palace. Soon he would leave with a substantial bounty and, no doubt, they would be left to suffer the consequences of the Christian takeover. They had few illusions about what would happen. Nevertheless, they lived in hope that the infidels would lift the blockade of the city so that desperately needed food might be brought in to abate the starvation and disease which were spreading through the narrow, decaying streets.

All was being made ready at Santa Fe for the Capitulation. For several weeks, the great and the good who held royal favour had been summoned from afar to join the host that would accompany Fernando and Isabel into Granada. Soon after midday on January 2nd, on a bright sunny day the procession got underway.

Led by Gutierre de Cárdenas, the hundred horsemen of the Queen's own guard were given the honour of leading the procession. Riding four abreast on jet-black steeds, they were a stirring sight, with their burnished steel breastplates over royal blue tunics and white breeches. Plumes of feathers adorned the blue caps on their heads. Swords jangled noisily at their sides, while the outside riders held lances aloft from which fluttered blue streamers. Pedro rode in the final rank with his back straight and head held up, as instructed by the cavalry leader. Never would he have dreamt when he watched the royal couple enter Almería two years before that he would be part of this cavalcade. With Sabyán's ruby ring on one hand and the Queen's jade ring on the other, it had to be the proudest moment of his life.

Following twenty yards behind were three horsemen wearing four-sided clerical hats, velvet gowns and long surplices. Aloft in the centre was the large square banner of Santiago. It was under the protection of this patron saint that the King and Queen had fought and won their long war with Granada. To its side were the banners of Toledo and Zaragoza representing the Monarchs' own kingdoms of Castile and Aragón.

Fernando and Isabel followed, with the King wearing a gleaming silver breastplate picked out with gold ornament over a dark red satin shirt and breeches. From his shoulders hung a long heavy dark blue cloak which trailed over the rear of his chestnut horse, nearly reaching the ground behind. He wore the same jewel-incrusted coronet which he'd worn at Almería. The Queen to his left rode astride her faithful white horse as befitted her warrior standing. She wore a green velvet gown studded with pearls and a long cloak held by a gold chain at her neck. Like Fernando, she had on her head a lightweight coronet, but hers had gold pomegranates topping the apices. Fittingly, the coronet had been made especially for the occasion, since *granadas* or pomegranates were the natural emblem of Granada.

Behind the royal pair came the ermine-clad Don Gonzalo Fernández of Córdoba with the group of hostages who had been held by the Christians for many years, including Ahmad, Boabdil's son.

Following the group of hostages came the phalanx of the King's personal guard, two hundred finely attired and disciplined horsemen, picked for their courage, dash and breeding. All rode dapple-grey stallions. All were the sons of noblemen, and all had shown valour in the face of the enemy. They were resplendent in shining brass breastplates over crimson tunics with high-plumed brass helmets secured under their chins with broad brass straps. Unlike the Queen's guards, these riders held long curved sabres held upright in their hands. This was no mean feat, since these were heavy as well as deadly weapons.

Then came the good and the great. Four closed carriages held the religious hierarchy of Spain: cardinals, priests and bishops from all over the land. Each of the thick-wheeled and heavy carriages was pulled by four sturdy horses. Appropriately, in the first carriage, painted red with the motif of Santiago, was the Cardinal of Spain, Pedro González de Mendoza, together with three chosen priests.

The great had been carefully divided by the King and Queen into those closest to them who had shown unswerving loyalty over many years, and those who had opposed them or supported the cause of Juana, the niece of Isabel, in the bitter contest for the crown of Castile and León many years before. Both sovereigns had very long memories.

In the first rank of those most loyal came Juan de Solomayor, the Count of Cifuentes and Assistant at Sevilla and his brother Pedro de Silva. Both had served the Crown through the vicissitudes of the war since 1482 and both had been taken prisoner at the battle of Lucena and held captive by the Muslims for two years. Following was Luis de Santángel, a Jewish convert and close confidant of the King. Then came Alonso, brother of Gutierre de Cárdenas, who was Grand Master of the Order of Santiago, with his squadron of horsemen accompanied by battalions of infantry of the Dukes of Plasencia and Medinaceli. It was these families – the Mendozas, Silvas and Cárdenas – who were the closest and most honoured of the Sovereigns' guests.

Leading the remaining battalions were the redeemed opponents of Fernando and Isabel: first were Diego Fernández of Córdoba, with the people of Gonzalo Mejía; those of the Counts of Cabra, Alonso de Aguiler, and of Ureña came next. Fourth were the soldiers of Pedro de Vera and the Mayor of Morón; fifth came the battalions of the Senior Mayor of Córdoba, Enrique de Guzmán and the Duke of Medina Sidonia. Then the lancers of Rodrigo, Ponce de León, the Marquis of Cádiz. Sixth were the large battalion of the Master of Calatrava and the Count of Cabra.

Of those who once opposed the Queen years before were Diego López Pacheco, with his men; then a beautifully attired squadron of horsemen led by the Duke of Escalona, followed by the foot soldiers with long pikes of the Marquis of Villena; those with swords and maces of Juan de Zúñiga, the Grand Master of the Order of Alcántara. Following were horsemen of Alonso Téllez Girón and the Count of Urueña.

Shrewd as always, King Fernando knew that by the very act of their accepting his invitation to join the celebration of the capitulation of Granada, all these one-time opponents of his and Isabel demonstrated publicly their fidelity to the Crown.

But the mighty cavalcade was not finished. Towards the rear came the battalions of the Duke of Nájera, the Count of Benevente and the Mayor of Atienza, Don Alvaro de Bazón. Soldiers followed by the score from Galicia, Asturias, Navarra and Vizcaya in the north of Spain, flanked by darker-skinned southern men from Sevilla and Córdoba. Further on still came Francisco de Bobadilla, with the men of Jaén and Andújar and of Diego López de Ayala with the contingent from Úbeda and Baeza. Lastly came the artillery, accompanied by even more squadrons of horsemen and infantry commanded by the Master of Alcántara, the Count of Feria, Martín Alonso, the Mayor of Soria, Henao y Lope Hurtado.

All told, some ten thousand horsemen and fifty thousand infantry made up the procession; the whole multitude which had assembled at the vast encampment near Gozno and which, during the autumn and bitter winter months, had laboured to construct the new royal city of Santa Fe. This day, of the Entrance to Granada, was one they would long remember.

The procession passed through the Bib al-Ramla gate then through the narrow streets of the city until they reached the Puerta de Granadas. They then headed up the long slope to the Alcazaba, passing through the double keyhole-shaped entrances of the Puerta de la Justicia. Inside they were met by a procession of Christian prisoners, some symbolically in chains, bearing the image of the Virgin Mary. The King and Queen and the Cardinal of Spain received them with much reverence and ordered that they be accompanied to Santa Fe where they were to be cared for.

In the Torre de la Vela, the Standard of Santiago and the Royal Standard were dipped three times before the Holy Cross. A hymn was sung so all could hear it over the city. Three times the shouts of 'Santiago, Granada and Castilla!' rang out from the high tower. Then, in the presence of the King and Queen, the royal trumpets were sounded from the tower and cannons fired from the battlements. Finally, chanting the *Te Deum Laudimus* Fernando and Isabel descended from the tower to meet the Sultan, Boabdil, for the first time. The small man stood silently outside the Torre de Homenaje with his wife, Moraima, his stepmother, Soraya, and his two principal ministers, the vizier, Abul Kásim el Maleh, and the Alcalde of Granada, Boabdil's close confidant, Yusuf Aben Comisa.

Boabdil came forward sadly but with dignity. The King bowed his head imperceptibly but sufficiently to confer respect to the Sultan. The Queen curtsied commensurately. It was not enough to be seen by those behind but was enough for the Sultan not to feel slighted. With the long sleeve of his purple silk gown brushing the marble courtyard, Boabdil swept his arm low and gracefully across his body in the traditionally more generous Arab salute.

Then, turning to Aben Camisa at his side, Boabdil took the keys from the velvet cushion and handed them ceremoniously to the King. The King acknowledged their receipt with a slow declination of his head and stood back.

The Sultan's eleven-year-old son, Ahmad, who had been held in captivity since the age of three and who had been standing obediently with Martín of Alarcón, ran across the patio to his parents. His mother, not having set eyes on him in all that time, swept him off his feet joyfully, crushing him in a tearful embrace. As she put the youngster down and as he turned towards his father, he spied Pedro standing in the shadows with the ranks of soldiers who were providing the Guard of Honour under the command of Captain López. Ahmad peered a second time and then a third, and with a whoop of glee ran over to his friend, calling out, 'Pedro, Pedro!' as he did so. The seventeen-year-old broke rank and stepping forward impetuously knelt down in his finery to embrace the young prince.

Boabdil, frowning at being shunned by his only son on such an important occasion, saw the focus of the boy's attention and, recognising Pedro, shuffled across the courtyard in his heavy golden brocade *yubba*.

'Pedro… *Pedro Togeiro, be-s-sahh?*' he said in Arabic in a loud voice.

'*Ana howa, sharyib, men Porcuna,*' responded Pedro in the same language.

'*Forsa se ida…* I'm pleased to see you again. Ahmad's never stopped talking about you since you left Moclín with my uncle. You did wonders for him and brought him out of his shell.'

With Ahmad pressed tightly to him, Pedro was led by the Sultan to meet the dumpy Sultana, Moraima, and his father's chief concubine, the gorgeous Soraya. The daughter of the Commander of Bézmar, Don Sancho Jiménez de Solís, Soraya was shortly to be re-baptised as Isabel de Solís.

Fernando and Isabel, who were about to enter the Alhambra to undertake their much anticipated tour of the fabled palace, looked around perplexed at the behaviour of Boabdil's son, and then Boabdil himself.

'Pedro Togeiro?' she mumbled to the King. 'The young man who put the fire out in our bedchamber last July?'

'I think so, my dear,' said the King, himself bewildered.

'How does he know Boabdil and his son?' she asked. 'And how does he come to speak Arabic so well?'

'I've no idea, my dear. I expect Don Gonzalo will know.'

'Yes,' she replied. 'He knows most things. We must ask him when we see him next. Where is he, by the way…?' Her words trailed away as they entered the sumptuous council chamber of the Mexuar.

With the handing-over ceremony finished, most of those present slowly dispersed. Boabdil stayed chatting with Pedro and Martín of Alarcón, whose responsibility for Ahmad had come to an end. Don Gonzalo appeared from nowhere to join them. Boabdil's wife and stepmother stood talking with Yusuf Aben Comisa. Abul Kásim Benegas, being in charge of the Alhambra's substantial treasury, had left to escort the King and Queen around the palace complex.

'It's like old times,' chuckled the good-natured Don Gonzalo to the Sultan and Pedro. His ambassadorial role was almost at an end.

'When I rescued you from Torquemada,' he said to the young soldier, 'I never thought we'd all be standing here together. Regrettably, Boabdil, as you know, I'm charged with escorting you, your family and principals to the Alcazaba.'

'Can I show Pedro around the palace, Papa?' pleaded Ahmad.

'Can you remember your way around?' joked the Sultan. 'It's a long time ago since you were here, and you were only three then!'

'Yes, I'm sure I can.'

'But they'd better go with someone,' chipped in Don Gonzalo, and called to Captain López across the courtyard.

The handsome man came over, still immaculate in his tunic even after the long day.

'I'll go with them too,' volunteered Aben Comisa, overhearing the conversation. 'There'll be doors to unlock if they're to visit the Sultan's private chambers.'

So the four of them set off. Most of the soldiers and cavalry had already left the fortress except the Knight Commander, the Count of Tendilla, who remained there with two thousand horsemen and five thousand soldiers.

The Alhambra palace is a long, lens-shaped system of ornate chambers, shady courts, cool pools and resplendent gardens secured by a high wall with some twenty towers. It comprises three elements: the Mexuar or reception salon, dedicated to the administration of public justice; the Chamber of Comares, the official residence of the Sultan; and the Chamber of the Lions, his intimate family apartments.

With Ahmad skipping ahead, keen to rediscover his childish haunts, the group passed through the Plaza de los Aljibes into the Garden of Machuca with its portico of festooned arches and a garden of low, well-trimmed shrubs surrounding a small pool filled with golden carp. Then on into the Hall of the Mexuar via a modest passageway: 'Here is where the sultans listened to the petitions of their subjects twice a week and held meetings with their ministers,' Aben Comisa explained. At the rear of the Mexuar was a private oratorio or small mosque looking out over the river with its *mihrab* facing the east, where all must face to pray. He translated aloud the Arabic inscription over the niche for Captain López. It said, 'Be not amongst the negligent. Come and pray.' The rear of the hall led into the small ante-room of the Court itself and faced the facade of the Chamber of Comares, with its extraordinarily rich embossed alabaster decoration.

Pausing to absorb the details of the splendour all around them, with Pedro and the captain both expressing stupefaction at the intricacy of the ornamentation, the Arab lord led them through the two doorways where their geometrical symmetry was framed by glazed tile inlays, with panels and friezes of incredible richness. Tripping over each other as they looked up at the intricate ceilings, they passed through the doorway on the left and entered the Court of the Myrtles, as fine as anything to be seen in Damascus and Baghdad. This rectangular courtyard was forty yards long. Dozens of the conquistadores were ambling around the marble terrace mesmerised by the reflections in the pool of the ornate porticos opposite and the massive castellated Tower of Comares overlooking it. Alongside the long pool with its fountains were low myrtle hedges and slim, marble colonnades topped by stucco friezes. This normal scene of utter stillness and tranquillity was disturbed by the buzz of low voices from the visitors, who could not refrain from murmuring their wonderment at the scene before them.

'Good evening, Nasím,' said Aben Comisa cordially as he greeted a man in his forties by the side of the pool. He had strikingly pale skin and thinning fair hair, and concealed his ample girth in a thick, embroidered *yubba* of ruby-coloured brocade. He was Boabdil's eunuch manservant who had served him faithfully through good years and bad.

'Good evening, my Lord Comisa,' he replied in his high voice. 'I've been counselling the ladies of the household. They're very agitated about what might happen to them now that the Infidels have taken over our palace.'

'They have cause to be, Nasím. I'm not sure what will become of them myself. I've petitioned the King that they be treated with respect, but frankly their future is very uncertain. I assume that you'll accompany your master when he leaves here?'

'I gather that is his wish, my Lord Comisa. But I too feel very unsettled.'

'It's understandable, Nasím. You have served your master loyally for very many years and I hope you'll have the opportunity of continuing to do so for many more to come, wherever you and he may be.'

Grateful for the words of encouragement, Nasím bowed low to the Arab lord and passed sedately on his way.

The north portico of the royal court had seven arches above slim columns with stylised stalactites of alabaster which were so real that they almost dripped water. On the walls were poetic inscriptions and verses from the Koran carved into the white alabaster in smooth-flowing, cursive Arabic script on a darker background. Easing past a group of noblemen led by the Duke of Medina Sidonia, with Ahmad still leading the way, Aben Comisa's group entered the Court of the Ambassadors where Boabdil's fate had been sealed when his Grand Council decided to surrender to the Catholic Monarchs.

The third element of the Alhambra, around the Court of the Lions, was built by Mohammed the Fifth. It comprised the private apartments of the Sultan and his harem. Nowhere in the Alhambra surpassed this place for its charm and subtlety. In the centre of the court a marble fountain was supported by twelve carved lions. Flower gardens occupied the quadrants between the paths to the fountain, while around the square court one hundred and twenty-four slender columns supported a facade and ceiling of alabaster tracery to form a cloistered walkway around the garden. No harem in the eastern cities offered such a sublime setting for sensual delights. Today there was little sign of the concubines who dwelt there. Nevertheless, three of them, dressed in colourful silk *durra'as*, their heads concealed in gossamer-thin *jimars*, sat on the edge of the central fountain, clearly embarrassed by the Christian eyes leering at them as if they were creatures from another world.

Still skipping, Ahmad led them around the right side of the court into the Hall of the Abencerrajes, so called because, rumour had it, it was where Boabdil had put to death his most implacable foes, the family of the Abencerrajes. Directly opposite across the garden was the Hall of the Two Sisters, with its central fountain and, most perfect of all, the Hall of the Kings, the sumptuous residence of the Sultan himself. Here the alabaster embossed decoration and tracery reached the apogee of the most intricate detail in the whole palace complex. Between the two adjacent balconies was the Mirador of the Daraxa, or Lookout of the Sultana; this was her dressing room and bedroom. Their backs to the passing throng, two young women, their dark hair rustling in the breeze, reclined on cushions and colourful carpets as they looked out of the low windows over the Darro and the Albaicín on the hill opposite. Pedro noticed two sturdy wooden frames standing upright in the corner of the room and a pile of what looked like carpets beside them. The two young women turned around at hearing Ahmad's Arab voice and smiled at Aben Comisa as one does to a friendly face in a hostile crowd. But being too young, they clearly did not recognise Ahmad.

Seeing their radiant smiles reminded Pedro of Raquel in Mecina. A feeling of melancholy overwhelmed him for an instant as he wondered how she was faring with her bad-tempered husband. She would now be six months into her pregnancy. Would she bear him a son or daughter? Would he – or she – be like him? Had Abu Ishar ibn Hakam discovered that Raquel's baby was not his? How was she, in fact? Indeed, how was the sixteen-year-old coping with carrying the baby? All these questions passed through his mind in barely an instant. Agustín López saw the shadow cross Pedro's face but did not enquire as to what troubled him. He had learnt something of the young man's background while sitting by the campfire at the time Zak and Gaz were arrested, and of the events which led to Pedro losing all his immediate family. He assumed the sudden change in his mood was related to this.

Passing on, they entered the group of rooms making up the Royal Baths. As Pedro discovered at Alhamilla, *baños* were a prerequisite of Muslim life, and of religious as well as hygienic importance. Those at the Alhambra were appropriately luxurious. With coloured tiled walls, marble columns and patterned alabaster frescoes picked out in blues, greens and golds, alcoves surrounded the baths where bathers could relax, be massaged, oiled and perfumed or succumb to the temptations of the harem. The cold baths in the Hall of Immersion came first, with its shallow marbled tanks of cold and hot perfumed water, then the Turkish bath and finally the Hall of Repose with magnificent tile inlay, and where it was said that along the four galleries above blind musicians played sensuous music. Three mature women of the court, fatigued or bored by this day of intrusion into their lives, and whose modesty had been eroded by the passage of time, were perched on the edge of a tiled bench, disporting their ample forms, which sadly had yielded to the forces of nature.

From the Royal Baths, Aben Comisa led Captain López, Pedro and Ahmad down to the palace treasury. It was here that the accumulated wealth of the Sultanate over hundreds of years had been amassed. The first room was the Armoury. Here were lances with broad, narrow, smoothed or barbed tips, single or double-handed battleaxes, smooth or spiked maces and clubs, crossbows with bolts of every type, slender long bows of ash with their flighted arrows, coats of mail, cuirasses and helmets, and leather shields made of oxhide and antelope skin.

In an adjoining room lay well-oiled leather harnesses and double-layered tunics, armour for horses, short-stirruped Arab saddles and high-backed Christian saddles, plus standards, flags and pendants. Around the wall stacked upright in frames were rows and rows of swords, scimitars and sabres of every size, shape and weight to cater for every soldier and any circumstance. Daggers – long, straight, light, heavy or curved – were piled on shelves and alongside, somewhat incongruously, long brass trumpets and the drums of war.

From here they started to descend narrow steps to the repository of the personal arms of the sultans and princes.

As they did so a dusky figure shot past them.

'Who was that?' asked a startled Aben Comisa, as they neared the bottom of the steps.

Captain López and Pedro looked at one another, shaking their heads.

'It was a scruffy young Muslim fellow in a dirty *'imama*,' called out Ahmad in the near darkness. 'I only caught a glimpse of him as he shot up the steps past us. He grinned and winked at me as he went past.'

They reached the bottom. Etched in the dust on the door was a roughly drawn symbol. It was the Rainbow Man.

'Oh no!' exclaimed Pedro loudly. 'It was Yazíd.'

'Who's Yazíd?' they all said.

'My friend from Vélez Blanco. He appears from nowhere and most of the time I never see him go! It's our secret sign. We call it our Rainbow Man. We discovered it on the wall of a cave above our town. We don't know…'

Nobody was listening.

The personal armoury of the sultans was protected by a double-locked, studded, thick oak door. The captain lifted Ahmad up so he could look into the gloom through the small barred window in the door. Inside were the personal arms of the sultans and princes: helmets inlaid with gold and precious stones, swords for combat inlaid with enamel and filigree, bridles, spurs and stirrups, horse bits made of silver for jousting and war, all made and adorned by the best armourers and jewellers in the Empire.

Dragging them away from the lavishness of the weapons displayed, Aben Comisa led them back up the steps to another room for which a different key was needed. Inside were thousands of ostentatious objects for the embellishment of the royal quarters: serving dishes from Damascus encrusted with mother-of-pearl; porcelain vases with dragon motifs from China; tiny cups for sweet mint tea from Mosul; large bowls for fruit from India; a heavy, carved, dark oak dining table and chairs from England; low, carved rosewood tables from Morocco inlaid with ivory, ebony and lapis lazuli; and dozens and dozens of carefully laid out sets of fine porcelain, china and glass. There were ornamental jars of delicate perfumes from Egypt, lamps and candlesticks encrusted with agate and onyx, mirrors framed in silver and gold inlay and surrounded by jewels, while in a small unlocked adjoining room were scores of musical instruments – shawms, cornetti, hautboys, sackbuts, psalteries, rebecs, tambours, nakers and tambourines, plus sets of recorders and crumhorns, each in velvet-lined chests, and beautiful ivory-inlaid lutes. If all this sumptuous splendour were not enough, Aben Comisa led them finally along a corridor and down steps to the final room: the royal treasury itself, containing the accumulated wealth of centuries. Five keys were required to open it, and the Muslim lord had just one.

'Ha!' he remarked. 'I can see that the royal couple and el Maleh have beaten us to it.' He pointed to their footprints in the thick dust around the door. 'Never mind, you can look through the door grating. Here, Ahmad, I'll lift you up. I don't expect you were ever allowed in this room.'

'Oh yes I was,' he replied proudly. 'Papa often brought me down to collect sacks of gold *doblas* when we had to pay the annual levy to the Christians. It always depressed him and he didn't speak to anyone for days.'

They each squinted into the near darkness.

'What's there?' asked Captain López. 'I can barely make anything out.'

'In the centre,' described the Muslim lord, 'is a table made of a single sheet of agate and standing on solid gold legs. On it are engraved glass bowls containing every sort of precious stone imaginable, some cut, others uncut, just as they were removed from the earth; diamonds, rubies, emeralds, sapphires, agates, topazes, tourmalines, amethysts, garnets, aquamarines, olivines, jaspers and tiger's eyes. In spite of the near darkness, it's an incredible spectacle of colour.'

'Over there on the right,' he continued, 'are chests and chests of gold bullion – some in rough-cast blocks, others as polished tablets – and some in newly minted gold coin. Next to them are even more chests of silver – mainly as bars and coins.

'And over there on the other side on that table, but covered in a purple satin sheet, is the jewellery of the Sultan and his wives: diadems, necklaces, bracelets, rings and earrings. It's a pity you can't see them since they're magnificent, and come from all around the world as gifts from foreign princes and kings.'

'So there you are, my friends,' he said, and added with much bitterness, 'that's the total wealth of our Empire... and all of it now belongs to Fernando and Isabel.'

They climbed the steps back into the Hall of Kings and then out into the Court of the Lions. The January afternoon was already drawing in as they stood admiring the symmetry of the court with the twelve lions and fountain centred between the forest of columns beyond. Not even Damascus was graced by such sublime beauty.

'May I visit the Generalife?' asked Pedro, inexplicably drawn to the small isolated palace three hundred yards away across the valley.

'Certainly,' replied Aben Comisa. 'You'll have to leave from the Puerta de los Carros on the other side of the Alhambra and follow the path around to the Generalife Pavilion and its Gardens. You'll need to hurry, since it'll be dark very soon now.'

'However,' he added. 'I need to get back with Ahmad. His father will have business to attend to and will be anxious about his son. Please report to the Alcazaba when you return. Amongst the rooms which Fernando has allocated to Boabdil and his family and followers there will be space for both of you, although it will be a bit crowded!'

Pedro and Captain López hurried off as directed by the Muslim lord. Already the crowds of Christian nobles and dignitaries were starting to thin as they returned to the encampment, or to Santa Fe or to the distant cities from whence they had come.

X: Meeting in the Generalife

'Judging by what you said around the campfire last July, Pedro,' asked Agustín López as they passed through the Puerta de los Carros, 'I imagine that you'll be setting off on your travels again soon?'

'I don't know, sir. It's possible,' replied Pedro. 'It depends on when I see the sign.'

'What sign do you mean?'

'A Jewish hermit I met soon after I left María nearly four years ago posed me four riddles to guide me on my way across *Al-Andalus*. When I recognise the signs I know that it's time to move on.'

'How many signs have you had so far?'

'Just two.'

'What's the next sign you're waiting for?'

'Something about "tears and sapphires". They never make any sense to me until I see something which brings to mind one of the riddles and then I know immediately that it's time for me to move on.'

'Fascinating, Pedro, truly fascinating,' commented the captain. 'I'll be moving on myself very soon.'

'And what's your sign, Captain?' joked Pedro.

He laughed. 'Twenty-five years' service with the King!' No more, no less.'

'That's a lifetime!' commented Pedro.

'Yes, it certainly is. I joined the King as a bugle boy when I was just fourteen and have been in his service ever since.'

'So do you come from Aragón?'

'No, I come from a village near Murcia, called Archena.'

'Do you know Lorca, then, and David Levi who made my Toledo sword? Lorca's not far Murcia.'

'I've passed through Lorca many times but I can't say that I know your swordsmith.'

'And do you know my home town of Vélez Blanco, Captain?'

'No, not really. I know that it's on the way from Murcia to Granada and I've seen your town in the distance high on the hill to the right, but I've never been there. Is it a nice place, Pedro?'

'Oh yes. Yazíd and I especially like the mountains and precipices above the town. You can get away from people up there.'

'Wasn't it your friend Yazíd who made that sign of yours on the door in the Alhambra a short while ago?'

'Our Rainbow Man? Yes, it must have been him, although only Ahmad caught sight of him.'

'Your Yazíd must be an imp, the way you say he appears and disappears.'

'Whether he's an imp or sprite or a genie of the *Arabian Nights*, he's an amazing fellow,' responded Pedro. 'He saved my life after I fell down that mine shaft last year. If he hadn't arrived my bones would still be there.'

'Yes, I remember you saying. He's a useful friend to have, Pedro,' the soldier commented.

'Have you a family back home?' asked Pedro.

'Of sorts, yes,' replied the captain. 'I've a nine-year-old daughter, who my sister's bringing up with her children. Sadly, my wife died in childbirth.'

'If it's not impertinent of me to ask, sir, what will you do when you leave the King's service next year?'

'Actually, Pedro, I'm not sure as yet. Apart from riding and ordering men around, the army doesn't fit you for anything in particular. I'd like to remarry and raise Sonia myself, since I've barely seen her in all these years. My father is keen that I take over the family fulling mill, since he's finding it heavy work now. Maybe I'll do that.'

They passed through the iron gates into the Generalife, also known as the Garden of Paradise. The long garden leading up to the white pavilion lay on several terraces. A sequence of rectangular pools were set on the highest one. Low myrtle hedges, orange and lemon trees, flower beds, tall cypresses and high, square-trimmed fir hedges enclosed the garden. All focused one's gaze on the ornate alabaster tracery which adorned the front of the pavilion at the end of the garden and which looked across at the towers of the Alhambra and the Alcazaba and with the city of Granada below. In reality it was no more than a mirador or lookout tower. The garden was now in deep shadow as they strode along the path to the pavilion. Inexplicably drawn to the building, Pedro ran up the stone steps to the upper gallery. Along it, he turned into a small room lit by the sun. It was now barely minutes away from setting behind Granada.

A woman in a pale blue dress was seated alone on the window sill in deep shadow doing an embroidery. The rose-coloured light of the evening illuminating her intricate work. She leant forward and turned to see who had intruded her solitude. Her face was still in deep shadow, but the sunlight illuminated her golden hair, which reached her shoulders. A fading memory exploded in Pedro's head as she tilted her face towards him.

He ran to her as Agustín López entered the room.

'Mama, Mama!'

The woman put her needlework aside and stood up with her back to the light. She was tall and slim.

'Mama – it's me. Don't you recognise me?'

'Pedro?' she queried. 'Is it you?' she asked in faltering Castilian.

She turned to face Pedro, now nine years older than when she saw him last and no longer a small boy. Her blue eyes, although somewhat sadder now, were as clear and bright as he remembered them. Her smooth, tanned complexion was more mellow and bore just the finest of lines from the passage of time.

'Yes, it's me, Mama. Pedro. You're alive! I can't believe it. We all thought you were dead.'

They fell into each other's arms, neither making any effort to quell the tears that flowed copiously. Captain López looked on, embarrassed, guessing from what Pedro had said previously that mother and son had been reunited. It was a heart-wrenching and touching scene. He withdrew to the gallery and mopped his own eyes with his sleeve, so moved was he by the joyous reunion between mother and son. Pedro and Miriam stayed clasped tightly to one another with the tears flowing unabated. Falteringly, they asked each other, 'What are you doing here dressed as a soldier?'... 'How long have you been here in the Alhambra?'... 'How are Abraham and Cristina?'... 'Are they well?'

It was to no avail. There were simply too many questions to ask after all this time.

'My darling, it's no good, I have to go,' sobbed Miriam, struggling from Pedro's arms as the captain entered the darkened room. 'The Generalife will be locked in a few minutes and I must return to my room in the palace.'

'Yes, and we must go too, Pedro,' said the captain. 'We have duties to perform in the Alcazaba. But rest assured, you can meet again tomorrow.'

Together they set off down the steps into the garden.

'Captain López,' said Pedro, still so excited that he could not wait until the bottom before making the introductions. 'This is my mother, Miriam, who we all thought was dead.'

'Mother, this is Captain Agustín López, one of King Fernando's officers.'

'Words escape me, señora, but I'm truly enchanted to meet you. I know something of Pedro's recent history which, indeed, you may not be acquainted with yourself. But your meeting like this, on this historic day, is nothing less than a miracle. The King must learn of this, for we must all give thanks.'

'To the Virgin Mary – or Allah?' asked Pedro in all seriousness.

'To both. With the help of Aben Comisa and the Christian chaplains we will give thanks to both this very evening.'

With Pedro and Miriam hand in hand, each squeezing the other to check that they were not dreaming, all three walked out of the entrance gate where the gatekeeper was waiting, back through the Puerta de los Carros into the Court of the Lions. Miriam departed to return to her room in the Mirador of the Daraxa, the quarters of the Sultana, while Pedro and his commanding officer found their way back to the Alcazaba.

Miriam and Pedro met the next morning in her room in the Alhambra. It was the same room with the low windows where the two young concubines were seated when Aben Comisa escorted Pedro and the others around the palace the previous afternoon. Neither mother nor son had slept that night. Inevitably, both wanted to ask questions at the same time. Miriam's were the most urgent.

'How's Abraham and my dear Cristina? Are they well? Are you still in our corner house? Is your father still making his herbal remedies? Has Cristina grown into a beautiful young woman? She's fifteen by now…'

They were the questions which Pedro was dreading most of all. How could he tell her the truth?

'No…' he said vaguely. 'They're not there now.'

'Not there? How do you mean "not there"? Have you moved house?'

'No. Oh, I don't know how to tell you this, Mama, but they died.'

'Died? Both of them?' Miriam was stunned. 'How? When? Was there an epidemic in Vélez. Is that what they died of… the plague?'

'No,' said Pedro, again hesitating.

'Well how then?'

'They were killed.'

'Killed? How were they killed? Who by?'

Pedro started to explain what happened when he returned to Vélez Blanco from his captivity in Jaén and Porcuna, but could get no further.

'Returned from where, Pedro? Where did you go? Why did you leave home?'

'Mama… it's all a very long story. Let me first tell you about Papa and Cristina. You must brace yourself since what I've to tell you is too horrible for words. What I can say though is that the three soldiers who put to death Papa and Christina have all met their own end.'

Pedro started to narrate the terrible events of his return to Vélez the day after all the towns and villages around were surrendered to the Marquis of Cádiz after he seized Vera. But he omitted the more unsavoury details of their deaths. Neither did he tell her how much his father had changed so dramatically since her disappearance, and how much Cristina and he had suffered from his vindictiveness. Better that his mother could cherish her memories of the happy times she and Abraham had together. Much of what he said went over Miriam's head as she sat on cushions alongside Pedro, aghast, as the story unfolded. Her dream of one day returning home to her family lay in ruins and she simply could not take it in.

'Where were Abraham and Cristina buried? Did your uncle Joshua know? What happened to the house afterwards? What did you do after you ran away from the soldier who killed Abraham?'

The questions were relentless and Pedro did his best to answer them, but he had still learnt nothing of what happened to his mother.

'What did you and Abraham do when I was taken by the two Africans at Aguilas?'

'Papa told me eighteen months afterwards that he…'

'What do you mean "eighteen months afterwards"?'

Pedro sighed. 'Many things have happened to me since you disappeared, Mama, and they started that day, just seconds after you were kidnapped. Let me explain from the beginning and then you'll know. But first you must tell me your story. You've said nothing of what became of you.'

'Very well, Pedro. I'll tell you my sad tale, but really there's not much to tell.'

She got up, straightened her dress and took up a new position on the cushions.

'As you saw, I was abducted by two black Africans when you and I were standing by the harbour waiting for your father to return from collecting his retort. The two men were slave traders. Their hands were all over me but I was not harmed in any way. They carried me to a boat moored against the wharf on the other side of the harbour and locked me in a dark cabin. There I stayed all that day and all that night until the next morning. I banged on the door and shouted to attract attention, but it was hopeless. I was given nothing to eat nor drink. The next morning the door of the cabin opened and I was literally dragged away by a slave dealer. He was a big fat man with a black beard and a red turban, wearing a filthy striped *yallabiyya*. A curved dagger was stuck in the sash around his waist. He mumbled some things in Arabic at me which I didn't understand but I did pick up the words "Cairo" and "Baghdad" and "harem". He sneered through his broken, discoloured teeth when he said "harem" and leered disgustingly at me. It was awful and I was terrified he was going to… well you can guess. He half dragged and half carried me to another boat, an ocean-going dhow. It set sail soon afterwards, and I thought I was on my way to one of the eastern cities or maybe the notorious Damascus slave market.'

'Did they give you food, Mama?' Pedro interrupted.

'Oh yes. I was given biscuits, dates and figs and fresh water to drink and wash with, so I was well cared for once I was on that boat. However, on the second day the boat put into a harbour. I guessed it was Almería, since it was such a big city and not that far from Aguilas. I knew that we were travelling south from the sun's rays through a crack in the cabin door where I was held. I will always remember the hundreds and hundreds of boats in the bay and the shouting coming from the smaller boats plying to and from the beach with their cargoes.

'I was given soap and water and told to wash myself well and also a brush and comb to do my hair. I guessed that I was to be sold on to another Arab. You see, I was convinced that I'd end up in an eastern city. I was taken ashore in a small boat and handed over to a clean-faced and well-dressed eunuch. He was very courteous and soft-spoken, as most of them seem to be. I was led on foot through the crowded streets up the long flight of steps through the lower gate of the Alcazaba. Then through the Barbican Gate, up through the lovely gardens with their shady trees, pools and marble water cascade, all of which I got to know so well, and into the palace quarters of Salim al-Nagar, the King of Almería. I was taken across the courtyard, which had clearly seen better times, into an ante-room of the court. There I was handed over to the eunuch, Muzo, who was responsible for the concubines. He showed me to a bath containing scented water and I was given new clothes to put on. I didn't appreciate it at the time, but they were the most gorgeous robes made of the smoothest silk: no more than veils, really. All this time people kept speaking to me in Arabic, but I understood little of what was said. As you know, Pedro, I didn't bother much with Arabic at home, since most of the Muslims in Vélez whom I dealt with spoke some Castilian. I wouldn't say that I was frightened but I was very apprehensive as to what would happen to me.'

'Were you taken into Salim's household?'

'Harem, you mean, don't you!' she joked. 'No, worse than that! That evening I was led into the bedchamber of his son, Prince Cidi Yayha al-Nagar.'

Pedro interrupted again.

'He was with his father at the handing over of the keys of the city. I received an emerald and sapphire from him the day before. Did you know that on that very same day he was baptised?'

'No, I know nothing of these things.'

'Yes, he was baptised and took the name Pedro de Granada. I learnt last night that he's to replace Aben Comisa as Bailiff of Granada.'

'That's a pity; Aben Comisa's a nice man whom I respect greatly. He's always treated me very kindly.'

'Anyway, my dear, I was ushered into the bedchamber of Cidi Yayha. Most Christian women have heard tales of such happenings, maybe some dream of it happening to them, but such women's gossip was nothing as to what I encountered.'

'What happened?'

Miriam laughed. Evidently the event was not one that vexed her.

'He was reclined on a low couch amongst soft cushions. He couldn't have been any older than me. In fact, without his black beard, I would have placed him at not much more than twenty. His richly patterned *yubba* covered him loosely and two concubines knelt at his side stroking his hair and generally fussing over him. I must say, they were beautiful girls with figures any woman would be envious of. I have never seen such lovely young women, and I couldn't think why on earth the Prince of Almería would want to bother with a woman in her mid-twenties who's had two children.'

'Mama,' Pedro said. 'You were very beautiful. You are still. Any man would want you for his own.'

'Oh, thank you, my sweet. But you should have seen these gorgeous creatures. They were stunning.'

Pedro thought of Raquel. They couldn't have been more beautiful than his Raquel.

'So what happened?' he asked.

'The two concubines got up and left, looking at me rather curiously. The prince beckoned me over and I had little option but to obey. Without a word he grabbed me rather crudely, as if I was a drunken prostitute in the market place. He threw open his *yubba* as if I were going to prostrate myself before his manhood – the size of which, incidentally, took me aback, I can tell you,' she added with a wink. 'Then he fumbled rather pitifully at my *zihara*. However, I was not going to be treated like a common harlot, and kicked hard at his stiff flagstaff. I was wearing *balgas* and caught him dead centre with the edge of the thick esparto sole.'

Miriam laughed out loud at the hilarity of the scene as she remembered it all those years ago. It was Pedro's mother of old, and he laughed too.

'What did he do?' asked Pedro.

'By this time my ire was well and truly up, although his "thing" was decidedly not! He held it tenderly in his hand as if I had broken it in half and then, finding that it was still in one piece, although somewhat bent, he made another lunge at me.

'This time I was better prepared. I jumped on the couch and slammed my foot into his groin. Looking back it was very cruel of me, since I might have done him permanent harm. I could feel something give under my foot. The poor man was in mortal agony and rolled over the floor, not knowing what to do with himself. By that time Muzo, the eunuch, had entered as well as the two young concubines. For a moment they were at a loss to know what to do. I was led unceremoniously out of Cidi Yayha's room to the harem itself and all the women there looked at me in astonishment. There must have been fifteen of them – all beautiful and all only barely clad. I was still fuming, and they retreated to the corners of the harem as if I was an enraged bull let loose in a street market.'

'It sounds hilarious!' roared Pedro, with tears still streaming down his face.

'I was found a couch for the night,' Miriam continued, 'and had the table of the most exotic food all to myself when it was time to eat. This state of affairs continued for several days, with everyone keeping their distance from the fiery Christian woman. Then, after about a week, I was escorted into Cidi Yayha's room again. It was as if he were breaking in a wild mare and was not going to be beaten. At least, that's how I saw it.'

'Did he break you in?' asked Pedro, now a little concerned in case his mother had forfeited her honour.

'No, much the same happened. I didn't know I could get so mad. He came at me but I slid out of his arms, twisted around and kicked his backside so hard he shot across the marble floor and hit his face against the far wall! He got up with blood literally gushing from his nose, which I think I must have broken rather badly. He was in a really bad way.'

'Were you taken away?'

'Yes, but not before I ran at him and kicked him again. This time he fell to the floor, whimpering and pleading with me not to strike him again. That's the last time I ever saw of him.'

'No!'

'Yes. I never saw him again.'

'So what happened afterwards?'

'Nothing much happened for months. Gradually the other concubines, whom I grew to like and respect, began to accept me. Some were simple village girls, beautiful and enchanting yet not very bright. Others were the daughters of well-to-do people who had fallen on hard times. They were delightful, intelligent and educated, as well as very pretty, and we got on very well.'

'Then what happened?'

'One of them learnt of my interest in weaving and embroidery, and being influential at the court she obtained linen and cotton cloth, plus coloured wools and silks, and I taught her to sew colourful embroideries. Soon, other women, who had been there for many years and were only rarely called upon to satisfy the needs of Ibrahim or Yayha, became interested, and within a year I had a handful of women producing some lovely articles.'

'That's amazing. Did you dye your own wools and silks as you used to?'

'Yes, but this time I had dyestuffs at my disposal from the whole Empire, so we could make lovely bright colours – not just the muted yellows, greens and browns I used to make in our kitchen. Do you remember?'

'Of course. You made some lovely things, and they're all safe in Uncle Joshua's house in María.'

'After about two years my "fame" began to spread, and the Sultan here in Granada – or more likely the people of his court – learnt of our embroideries, which by then were being sent far and wide. So, quite suddenly I left Almería, and was brought here to start a school of embroidery.'

'Did any of your needlewomen come with you?'

'Yes, three or four. As I explained, attractive though they still were, there were many other lovely young women in the harem, who many men would die for…'

'As Cidi Yayha nearly did for you!' joked Pedro.

'No,' she laughed. 'There were truly some gorgeous girls there. I and my team of matrons were not in their league.'

'So how long have you been here in the Alhambra?' asked Pedro.

'It must be six or seven years now.'

'And none of the Sultan's court has molested you?'

'No, never. I think my reputation must have preceded me here!'

'Those two frames in the corner over there which I noticed yesterday must be your embroidery frames?'

'Yes, they are. This is our store, and the room we use in the summer since it's on the cool, north side of the palace. In the winter we use rooms off the Court of Lions since they're sheltered and sunny.'

'There can't be a more perfect setting than this in the whole world to do needlework,' he commented. 'Where do your pupils come from, Mama?' He was immensely impressed by what he had learnt and very proud of her.

'From everywhere. At any one time I might have a dozen needlewomen working here and receiving my instruction. They've come from almost every city in the Muslim world: Jeddah, Baghdad, Riyadh, Damascus, Amman, Cairo. The two seventeen-year-olds who you must have seen here yesterday come from Alexandria and Istanbul. They're very keen to learn and work very hard.'

'I know both those cities, Mama. I've been to both of them.'

'How, Pedro. How could you possibly have been to them?'

'Ah,' he chuckled. 'That's part of my story I've yet to tell you about!'

'So your carpets and mats and wall coverings get to all corners of the Empire?'

'Yes, so I understand. We've become quite famous here.'

'Did you meet Boabdil?'

'Yes, of course, this is his residence. He's shown a lot of interest in what we do and given us a lot of encouragement. But in the last few years, and particularly this last year, the poor man has been weighed down by matters of state and become very withdrawn.'

'Mama,' enthused Pedro. 'I know the Sultan well, as I'll explain later. There's so much to tell you. What I don't understand...' He paused in thought.

'What I don't understand,' he continued, 'is that when I told him and Don Gonzalo – he's the King's ambassador to Boabdil, and he saved me from the Spanish Inquisition – about my travels and about losing you, Boabdil didn't mention that you were here. He must surely have guessed that the tall, fair-haired Christian woman was you.'

Pedro stopped and his brow creased as he struggled to recall what happened.

'Of course, now I remember!' he exclaimed. 'Just before I got onto my story at Porcuna about how you were abducted, his vizier, Abul Kásim Benegas, arrived with an urgent message for Boabdil and he had to leave the room.'

Pedro's face darkened at the memory.

'How terrible, Mama! If Abul Kásim hadn't arrived at that very instant, Boabdil would have heard me tell of your abduction by slave traders and he would have guessed that the fair-headed woman here was you. And we might have been re-united four years ago, and Papa and Cristina would not have been murdered, and...'

'Pedro. I don't understand anything of what you say. The sooner you piece all this together for me the better. Come now, my sweet, tell me what happened to you from the instant I was kidnapped. Don't leave out a single thing. I want to know everything that you've done, everywhere you've been and everyone you've met.'

Before Pedro could begin, Agustín López arrived and interrupted them.

'I'm sorry, Pedro, but it's well past midday and you must take up your guard duties. I'm sorry, señora...'

'Please call me Miriam, Captain.'

'Very well. I'm sorry to break into your reminiscences, Miriam, but Pedro's needed elsewhere. Remember, he's a soldier of the King now! You can meet again tomorrow.'

Mother and son embraced and parted. As they marched to the Alcazaba, Pedro told the captain of his mother's exploits at Almería and her achievements in the Alhambra. López was greatly amused by the happenings in Cidi Yayha's bedchamber. Both he and Pedro had found the man quite repellent.

Pedro and Miriam met every morning for the next few days, catching up on every single nuance of their missing years. Agustín López watched over Pedro with care, impressed by the worldliness of the young man, and still barely able to believe that Pedro should meet his delightful mother in such circumstances.

The perfidious King was not long in exhibiting his true colours yet again. Soon after the taking of the Alcazaba, thirty thousand sacks of flour and twenty thousand sacks of barley were discovered which had been withheld by the Christians from the starving people of Granada. Yet even when released to the city markets, they were a drop in the ocean of what was needed. On the sixth of the month, just four days after the Capitulation, and only a few weeks after the Terms of Surrender had been agreed and signed, the King abrogated the clause permitting the citizens of the city to retain their arms. Food would only be provided to the inhabitants on their handing over their weapons. It was only the start of the unwinding of the agreement, and it explained all too clearly the readiness with which the King had acceded to the many demands of the Muslim negotiators.

The King and Queen did not reside in Granada, choosing to travel each day from Santa Fe, just an hour's ride away, and to return there each evening. During the second week after the surrender of the city, Don Gonzalo passed a message to Agustín López instructing him to deliver Pedro to the royal court on the fifteenth to dine with the royal couple and some of their favoured followers. Don Gonzalo would be there to assist Pedro through what would be something of an ordeal, although the Queen was insistent that everything must be done to put the young man at his ease.

The day arrived. His processional tunic of the Queen's guard had been cleaned and pressed by Antonio Manzano, the equerry to Don Gonzalo, and with new polished boots and with his precious sword polished and gleaming in its scabbard and proudly swinging from his side, he duly presented himself soon after dark at the royal palace in Santa Fe. Although the upper storey was still being constructed, a dining room and kitchen, plus the royal court and ante-room, were finished and were being used by the royal couple. For the while the two monarchs slept in rooms in the simple, two-storey building on the side of the central square which was just finished and was to be used as a hospital for disabled soldiers.

Don Gonzalo introduced Pedro to the other guests who were crowded into the small reception room outside the dining room waiting for the appearance of Fernando and Isabel. Informal though the banquet was intended to be, and frequently though the guests there that evening had dined with the royal pair, there was still a tenseness in the air. On these occasions Fernando and Isabel were not noted for their punctuality. Their closest confidants knew that the delay was intentional so as to permit the royal couple to reprimand those arriving after them and so keep everyone on their toes.

Pedro bowed respectfully to Gutierre de Cárdenas, who had entered Granada at dawn on the day of the Capitulation to secure the city gates. Martín of Alarcón, who knew Pedro from the time he took custody of Ahmad at Moclín, gripped him warmly by the shoulders. Not being sure what to do, Pedro bowed low to the Cardinal of Spain, Pedro González de Mendoza who, whether he expected such homage or not, took the opportunity of placing his hands on Pedro's head and muttered some unintelligible words in Latin. His introductions to Pedro de Silva, Count of Cifuentes and his brother, Juan, were less formal; their years in Muslim captivity freeing them from excess formality. Two learned gentlemen, one elderly and portly, the other tall with a pointed grey beard, both wearing scholar's four-pointed caps, stood rather stiffly in the corner of the poorly lit room. An attendant announced the entrance of the King and Queen before Don Gonzalo could introduce Pedro to them.

Fernando and Isabel were dressed simply and informally in warm velvet gowns which swept the ground. They were aware that the warmth of the blazing fire in the dining room was not sufficient to reach the corners of the room or counteract the residual dampness in the recently plastered rooms. They received graciously the bows of those present as they moved around the small group of their closest followers, welcoming them to the banquet.

'So you must be Pedro Togeiro,' the Queen said to Pedro as he knelt and took the royal hand offered to him. 'I recognise you from the night of that terrible fire in Don Gonzalo's house. The King and I are most pleased that you have come to this banquet tonight which, in all truth, is as much to thank you as to honour Antonio de Nebrija, whom we will introduce to everyone later. May I take this opportunity of thanking you for extinguishing the fire. Who knows what might have happened if you'd not spotted the flames outside?' She looked keenly at him.

'However,' she said, 'I'm still not clear exactly why you were outside our residence at such an hour, and we await your explanation.'

'Well, Your Majesty,' stammered Pedro. 'You see—'

'No, no, later, young man,' she smiled. 'I only jest. I know from what Don Gonzalo has said that you've had some interesting experiences, and we're looking forward to hearing something of them.'

The King approached and took Pedro's hand but his expression of thanks was interrupted by the announcement that the guests should take their places in the dining room. They all entered obsequiously and took their places standing behind the brand new chairs upholstered in red leather with the royal crest carved into the top rail. The royal pair entered without formality and took their seats in the centre of each side, while their guests took their places around them. Pedro, as a guest of honour, sat next to the Queen and alongside Don Gonzalo, while the other guest for the evening sat to the right of the King.

'Gentlemen,' the King announced, 'I must first apologise for our cramped surroundings this evening. The banqueting hall on the first floor is not yet finished so we have to make do with this smaller dining room. It will become the staff quarters of the palace. Nevertheless, I welcome you all here and hope that the simple supper which we offer tonight will not cause offence. Most of you have already met our brave young soldier, Pedro Togeiro, who saved our lives in July and indirectly led us to advance the construction of this new city. Our other guests, who sit alongside me, I'll introduce to you after we've partaken of some food. I expect you're all as hungry as I am.'

For the next two hours a dozen or more servants ferried course after course of the most delectable dishes imaginable.

'If this is a modest offering,' whispered Pedro to Don Gonzalo, 'what's a real banquet like?'

Soup of halibut was followed by turbot in a lemon sauce. Then thin-sliced fillets of veal baked in pastry. Then quails' eggs served in mayonnaise and dressed with chopped parsley. Then roast duck stuffed with chestnuts and braised partridge with redcurrant jelly. Then slices of mutton rolled around ham pâté and roasted to crispness in deep fat. Then the main course: hunks of wild boar, hunted and killed in the hillside woods above Santa Fe three days before and spit-roasted over a slow fire since dawn. Then, for those with sufficient room, hard, strong mature cheeses from Manchega, softer white cheeses from Galicia and the finer-flavoured, local goat's cheeses from *Al-Andalus*. Then last of all the pastries: small cakes with chopped almonds or caraway seed or flavoured with freshly picked oranges from Almuñécar, crusty pastries with chopped dried dates and sultanas from Almería, and thin flaky pastry soaked in honey. All the time the courses were being laid before the guests their silver goblets, acquired from the Treasury of the Alhambra, were being filled and refilled with fruit juices and different red wines from Valencia, La Mancha and Rioja.

'Eat your fill,' advised Don Gonzalo with a wink at Pedro's left elbow. 'But stick to fruit juice and water. Remember, you have to earn your supper with your life story!'

When the meal finally came to an end and all were replete to the point of bursting, the King asked Pedro how he came to be outside Don Gonzalo's house on the night of the fire.

'The Queen tells me that you come from Vélez Blanco, a Muslim town. How so? What brought you here? Have you Moorish blood?'

'No, Sire,' answered Pedro. 'My father was a Jewish apothecary and my mother was a Christian seamstress...'

'Was? Pedro, why do you say was?'

Pedro took a deep breath and told the gathering his story. The cardinal nodded off noisily. Gutierre de Cárdenas, sitting directly in front of the fire, fidgeted uncomfortably in his thick tunic dripping with medals and honours, while the two brothers de Silva listened attentively, particularly to Pedro's seizure by soldiers of the Inquisition after the Almerían earthquake and his incarceration at Jaén.

'And you never saw your mother again? Oh, that's a terrible thing to happen to young children,' commented the Queen when Pedro narrated how his mother was abducted at Aguilas.

'Ah! Now we know where you learnt to speak Arabic so fluently,' interrupted the Queen when Pedro told of his captivity aboard the Arab dhow.

'So that's how you came to know Boabdil!' said the King when Pedro reached his being taken to Porcuna by Don Gonzalo.

'And it was Inquisition soldiers who murdered your father and sister?' queried the awakened cardinal, not altogether happy with the reported activities of the overzealous quasi-religious order.

'However, Your Majesties,' concluded Pedro after his lengthy discourse. 'You won't believe this but on the very day you received the keys of the city, I found my mother.'

'What!' they all exclaimed.

'Yes, alive and well, in the Alhambra.'

'It was a miracle, Ma'am,' interrupted Don Gonzalo. 'A true miracle.'

'How wonderful, Pedro,' exclaimed the Queen, genuinely pleased. 'But what was she doing there? You said she was dead.'

Pedro explained the circumstance of their meeting and what had become of his mother since she was abducted by slave traders nine years earlier.

'*God moves in a mysterious way, his wonders to perform,*' chanted the cardinal in a monotone, touching his fingers together lightly across his chest.

'You are so right, Your Eminence,' replied the Queen. 'From the time when my Lord Gutierre secured the gates at dawn it was truly a day of miracles. But nothing surpasses this, Pedro, to be reunited with your mother after all that time. I have heard of the Muslim School of Embroidery at the Alhambra. It's famous. And to think it was established by your own mother. That's amazing beyond words.'

'Tell me. What will she do now?' she added.

'I don't know, Your Majesty,' he replied. 'I think she'd like to return home to Vélez Blanco, but our home might be no more after all this time.'

'Hmm,' thought the Queen for some moments. 'I have an idea. Come to me with your mother tomorrow morning. Ask Captain López to accompany you.'

'Yes, Ma'am. I will,' replied Pedro.

'Now,' said the King, wanting to draw Pedro's sagas to a close. 'Time is moving on, and I can see that the rich food, good wine and warm room are starting to take their toll. So before we all find our beds I'd like to introduce someone who will help make Spain the greatest nation in all Europe. To my right is the noted scholar, Antonio de Nebrija.' The studious man nodded with just a trace of a smile. Antonio had held the Chair of Rhetoric at Salamanca University for eleven years.

'I believe you have brought a book of great import with you today?' asked the King.

'Yes, Sire,' replied the learned man, pointing to an immense leather-bound tome on a side table behind him.

'Preparing my earlier Latin grammar,' he said enunciating his words very carefully, 'opened my eyes to the great need which exists in our country for a codification of our language, specifically Castilian. You know as well as I that we have no established spelling of words. Verbs as such, both when spoken or written, are almost unrecognisable, and what with that and the many different languages and dialects spoken here, proper discourse, even between learned people, is difficult. So over the last ten years I've been preparing a *Gramática de la Lengua Castellana* which I'm pleased, Sire, to be able to present to you this day.'

'I took the liberty of looking through it earlier this evening,' said the King, 'and it's certainly a monumental work. You are to be applauded, Señor Nebrija, on a magnificent achievement. No other language in Europe has been set down in this way. I am certain that it will now make Castilian the dominant language of our united country, help bring our peoples together, and even supersede Latin in our churches and cathedrals so that ordinary people may savour fully our blessed Lord's teachings and commandments.'

'Would you not concur with that, Your Excellency?' asked the King of the Cardinal of Spain, who had nodded off and missed much of the discussion.

'Of, course, Your Majesty,' he spluttered. 'The quality of Latin has improved immensely since Señor Nebrija wrote his Latin grammar.'

Miriam was flabbergasted to be told by Agustín López early the next morning that she was to ready herself for an audience with the Queen at Santa Fe that very morning with himself and Pedro. It was a long time since she had ridden a horse but, nevertheless, the group arrived promptly at the palace at midday and waited in the ante-room adjacent to the Queen's study. Miriam was smartly attired in a long high-waisted blue woollen *zihara* and a very dark red, thick woollen cloak and hood or *burnu*. Both were needed. It was a bitter January day and an icy wind blew down from the north. Snow was building up thickly on the 11,000-foot mountains to the south of Granada. The three were shown into the warm panelled study of the Queen.

'Señora Togeiro – or may I call you Miriam?'

Miriam curtsied and assented.

'Miriam. Your son here has told us much about himself, and the King and I have thanked him for raising the alarm over the fire which swept through our bedchamber last July. You are fortunate to have such a fine son.'

'Yes, I know, Ma'am. He's—'

'The King and I were astonished and overjoyed when he told us how you and he were united by chance in the Alhambra the day of the Capitulation. It had to be the work of God and I gave thanks to him in my prayers this morning.'

'Thank you, Ma'am.'

'We were particularly struck by the tale which Pedro told of your "encounter" with Cidi Yayha al-Nagar several years ago in Almería.'

Miriam blushed.

'You know that we've appointed him Bailiff of Granada?'

'Yes, Ma'am. Pedro told me.'

'Would you like to meet him again?' joked the normally stern and humourless Queen. 'Have no fear,' she added before Miriam could reply. 'I'm sure that he'd hide under the table at the very sight of you!'

'But now to serious business, Miriam. You suffered grievous wrongs at the hands of the Moors when you were abducted, and later when you were held against your wishes in Almería and the Alhambra. Worse, you have lost a husband, daughter and possibly your home because of the wickedness of Christian soldiers bearing the insignia of the Inquisition. For this we crave your forgiveness. We must make amends.

'You cannot stay at the Alhambra, that's clear. What I plan to do, with your approval, is to see you safely returned to your home in Vélez Blanco. To ensure your safe return I am asking Captain López to accompany you there and to see you reinstated in your home. Whatever needs to be done to make it habitable and comfortable he will arrange and pay for. Moreover, as a token of goodwill to help make amends for your "lost" years, I am giving Captain López two hundred and fifty thousand maravedís to place in your name with a registered moneylender in your town or a neighbouring town.'

Miriam was too overcome to reply.

'Does this meet with your approval, Pedro and Captain López?'

'Yes, Your Majesty. It's wonderfully generous,' replied Pedro.

'Of course, Ma'am,' replied Agustín López. 'I'm always at your service, as you know. May I ask, however, if I may take the opportunity while accompanying Miriam, I mean Señora Togeiro, to Vélez Blanco, to return to my own home since it's barely two days' journey from Los Vélez. It's nearly two years since I saw my daughter last.'

'Very well, Captain. I know that you've been at the encampment since it was established last spring. You thoroughly deserve some leave. I think I'm right in saying that next year you're due to leave our service?'

'Yes, Ma'am. That's correct. I'll have served the King twenty-five years by then.'

'And we cannot persuade you to stay with us? You know how much we value you.'

'Thank you, Ma'am, but no. The army has been my life since I started as a bugle boy when I was fourteen and I'd like to try my hand at something else.'

'We understand. Be sure that you have our very best wishes for the future.

But we do expect to see you back from Murcia until next year when you take your leave of us.'

'Of course, Ma'am. As soon as Señora Togeiro is settled comfortably and I've seen Rosa.'

'You'll be coming with us, won't you, Pedro?' pleaded Miriam.

'I fear not,' interrupted the Queen. 'As a member of my personal guard, Pedro has one more duty to perform for me before he returns home to you.'

XI: A World to the West

January 25th 1492

On this day, in the third week after the surrender of Alhambra and in accordance with the Terms of Capitulation, the former Sultan of Granada, Abu 'Abd Allah Boabdil, titled Mohammed the Twelfth, left the Alcazaba in exile with members of his family, his household and a hundred and fifty or more of his closest associates.

For three days after their audience with Queen Isabel, Pedro used his free mornings to help Miriam pack her belongings. Her clothes and personal possessions fitted easily into a couple of large leather saddlebags. On the Queen's suggestion, knowing that Miriam's embroidery school would inevitably be wound up, Miriam rolled into waterproofed canvas sheets many of the exquisite products she and her team of needlewomen had made. On the morning of the fourth day, bubbling with excitement at the prospect of seeing her home again, she and Agustín López rode out of Granada with a spare mount plus three packhorses. She and Pedro embraced briefly knowing that in just a few weeks' time they would be reunited in their home town in the mountains of the Sierra de María. Pedro shook hands cordially with the captain. His mother could not be in better hands, but he doubted that he would ever see the officer again.

Knowing of Pedro's friendship with Boabdil and Ahmad, the Queen appointed Pedro to the squadron of fifty horsemen which would conduct the Muslim party into exile. Martín of Alarcón was in charge. For the weeks before, Boabdil and his family had been packing their personal effects, storing them in the Alcazaba until their day of departure. Others of his party, living under close guard in their villas on the Albaicín hill across the Rio Darro from the Alhambra, had been doing likewise. Everything was closely supervised by senior army officers. They were under strict instructions from the King to prevent other than personal possessions being removed.

Accompanying Boabdil was his loyal and long-suffering wife, Moraima, who was heavy with child; his eleven-year-old son, Ahmad; his plain and stocky mother, Fátima; his brother, Yusuf, with his deformed hand; Nasím, the eunuch, his personal manservant; Faiz, the elderly gardener to whom Boabdil had confided his boyish secrets and who chose to see out his days in exile; Ibrahim, the family doctor who would see Moraima through her pregnancy; and not least, his stepmother, the beautiful temptress Soraya, who had displaced Fátima in the household of his father, Muley Hasán, and had born Hasán two sons, Cad and Nazar, both of whom were accompanying the party. Like their mother, they had been baptised just weeks before into the Christian faith, taking the names Fernando and Juan.

Accompanying the members of Boabdil's family was his long-serving minister, the former Alcalde of Granada, Yusuf Aben Comisa, and his son Mohammed, and his former vizier, Abul Kásim el Maleh, and his two sons, Hamet and Mohammed. All three sons of these dignitaries, like their fathers, were substantial beneficiaries of the Terms of Surrender conceded by Fernando, and between them they acquired lands, farms, olive groves, salinas, and mills.

Setting off after midday on a clear and sunny day, and strung out for miles on horses, in carriages, on foot or perched on baggage in the wagons, the party made slow progress down through the city, out through the Bab al-Ramla Gate and southwards towards Lanjarón and their eventual destination in the Alpujarra. In due course Pedro rode forward to join Boabdil, who was riding alongside Soraya. It was a long, hard slog up to the top of the pass over the sierras and they did not reach the summit until after sunset. The constellation Orion stood proudly in the darkening sky to the south-west.

With the party drawn out for a couple of miles behind, Boabdil and the others dismounted. He looked back at Granada and his beloved Alhambra, the deep shadows of evening picking out the city in sharp relief. Boabdil, overcome by grief at the loss of his kingdom, heaved a great sigh and wept.

The sharp-tongued Soraya turned and mocked him. '*Weep like a woman – you, who could not defend your kingdom like a man!*'

Boabdil did not reply. He just looked down on the fabulous city. He would not set eyes on his beloved Granada again.

'Pedro,' he said eventually, turning his reddened eyes to the young soldier. 'You've been a good and faithful friend to Ahmad and me ever since we met at Porcuna. I'd like you to have this dagger as a measure of our love and esteem for you. There's little else I can give you now. Most of what I own has been taken from me.'

He pulled from his belt a curved dagger, its silver hilt and gold sheath studded with hundreds of small sparkling sapphires.

'This ornamental dagger belonged to the great Mohammed the Fifth who ruled here one hundred years ago, and which was itself a gift to him from the Caliph of Baghdad. Please take it, and remember us kindly by it.'

As he spoke his tears dropped onto the exposed bright steel blade. Looking up to the distinctive group of stars in the constellation of Orion, Pedro instantly recollected the third of the hermit's riddles:

'Follow the hunter's sword when tears fall on twinkling sapphires.'

He knew that it was time to move on. He took the dagger from Boabdil's hands as the small man stood on tiptoes and kissed Pedro on both cheeks. Ahmad ran forward and put his hands around Pedro's waist, burying his face in the soldier's tunic. Although sad that he could not follow his mother home to Vélez Blanco immediately, Pedro knew that his destiny continued to drive him westwards across *Al-Andalus*. Remounting, the leading group started down the other side of the pass, reaching Padul a short while later. There, they stopped the night.

That evening Pedro explained to Martín of Alarcón his predicament and, knowing something of Pedro's journeying, the Constable of Moclín released Pedro from his obligations so that he could recommence his travels. Pedro handed back his military apparel, and the next morning, after saying farewell to Boabdil and his family, to Martín of Alarcón and his former comrades-in-arms, he set off alone and on foot, going westwards. Boabdil's exiled party would continue on to Lanjarón at the eastern end of the Alpujarra, then press on the eighty or so miles into the Andarax valley and the district of Laujar which lay at its headwaters. A castle there would be the new home for him and his family. Others in his party, Abul Kásim and Aben Comisa and their sons and families, would travel on to their respective estates assigned to them in the surrender treaty.

For Pedro, it was a wonderful relief to be on his own again, free to go where he liked and travel as rapidly or as slowly as he wished. Since arriving at the Christian encampment near Gozco the previous July his life had been action-packed and at times stressful. Now he could savour some solitude. So he took his time. He had some six months' wages concealed in the pocket in his knapsack. He had his Toledo sword and dagger to provide protection, and the Queen's jade ring to help extricate himself from any difficulties which he might encounter. Westwards lay Sevilla, some two hundred miles away. It was by far the largest city in *Al-Andalus*, and indeed in Spain, and it was to there that he set his course, deciding, however, to take the southerly, coastal route via Almuñécar, Nerja and Málaga. Then he'd cross the sierras to Antequera to pick up the Granada road to Sevilla.

It was in Almuñécar in February that Pedro reached his eighteenth birthday. It was from here that he had sailed to Aguilas after *El Zagal* had accompanied him from Moclín. After exploring the great man's summer palace, now largely deserted, he journeyed on slowly to Málaga. The city was still in ruins from its sacking by the Christians five years before. It was a dead, silent place, inhabited by old men, old women and cripples, many limbless or mutilated. There were no children; there was no laughter. The absence of beggars signified that the cupboard was bare and there was nothing to be had.

Pedro did not linger there and turned north to Antequera, set in the northern shadow of the precipitous limestone crags which traversed southern Spain. There in the *plaza mayor*, he read the earth-shattering proclamation of King Fernando. Signed by the King on May 1st, but thought to be the handiwork of Queen Isabel herself, it gave the Jews in Spain just three months to be baptised into the Christian faith or leave the country. The repercussions on the fabric and prosperity of Spain would be far-reaching and felt for centuries to come.

Jews resided in small communities of dozens or hundreds in every town and city of Spain: some twenty communities in Fernando's kingdom of Aragón, and over two hundred in Isabel's kingdom of Castile. For hundreds of years they had been persecuted and victimised in all countries of Europe. In Spain, increasing numbers had opted to be baptised as Christians, although for many it was no more than a token gesture and they continued to practise their religion secretly in the confines of their homes.

The *Exigit Sincerae Devotionis* authorised the establishment of the Spanish Inquisition in 1478 and also required that Jews live in closed communities or ghettos and wear yellow patches on their clothing. The appointment of Tomás de Torquemada as Inquisitor General of Castile initiated the second stage in the organised drive against the Jews. The third and final act against them was the King's 'convert or leave' proclamation of May 1492. Most Jews chose to leave. But they were prohibited from taking with them gold, silver or money, and could only take those belongings which they could carry or load into carts. The Jews were city dwellers, being essentially craftsmen and tradesmen, and did not own land to bequeath or sell. So their houses and their contents, not being transportable, became forfeited. Many crossed the border to neighbouring Portugal. In *Al-Andalus* most of the eight thousand remaining Jews were ferried across to North Africa from Cádiz, Almería and Málaga. Those leaving the Mediterranean ports also migrated to Naples, Genoa and Marseilles. Those leaving northern Spain travelled to countries in northern Europe. All told, in the three months, as many as one hundred and fifty thousand Jews left Spain, taking with them their supreme professional skills, business acumen and craftsmanship.

Pedro entered Sevilla one scorching afternoon in the middle of July. A heat haze shimmered over the city. As he passed through the portal of the west gate, a round-faced rider with a ruddy complexion galloped by, brushing past Pedro as he did so and careering into a donkey laden with straw. The donkey stumbled and regained its footing, but not before its elderly owner was knocked to the ground and trampled on by the animal. The horseman glanced back at the bundles of straw strewn across the road and galloped on. Pedro went to help the old man, who shouted and waved his fists at the rider, now lost to view. Neither man nor donkey seemed much worse for wear, and once the bundles of straw had been tied back onto the animal, the two continued on their way. As Pedro started to follow them he noticed a long brown leather roll which had fallen from the back of the rider's saddle and lay on the lee side of the gateway. He picked it up, brushed off the grit and pushed it into his knapsack. He stopped in the nearby Plaza de Giraldillo to inspect its contents. He undid one of the leather ends and spread out three parchment maps onto the steps. They were all sea charts. The first two were large-scale maps of local coastlines. One covered the narrow straits between Gibraltar and Tangier and the other covered the coast to Cádiz and Huelva, close to the Portuguese border. Pedro had seen such charts before. However, it was the third and largest chart which caught his eye, and he studied it with growing excitement.

It showed what he deduced to be the African coast running down from the Straits. The coastline itself was almost obliterated by finely written notes written diagonally against the coast. Standing out from the coast of Africa were groups of islands with the same fine detail annotated around each island. But what grabbed his attention was the left-hand side of the map. A rather vague coastline was shown, together with islands here and there, but all were devoid of annotation. Ali, the captain of the dhow in which Pedro had been enslaved as a cabin boy, had told him of alleged 'lands beyond the sea' as well as reports, always third or fourth hand, of mariners who had returned from them. Pedro knew immediately that the sea charts were of great significance and that the rider who dropped them must have been on an important errand. He had no hesitation as to what he must do.

Faced with a myriad of narrow, tortuous streets and culs-de-sac, which still reflected the ad hoc growth of the former Muslim city, Pedro followed the city wall around until he hit the wide, fast-flowing Guadalquivir. Hundreds of boats of all sizes plied their way up, down and across it. Such sights always stirred him. Resisting the temptation to lean against the wall and gaze at the hypnotic scene, he carried on along the riverside, spying in a short while the tower of the Giralda.

Across from the Giralda were the low walls surrounding the *alcázar*, and it was to this former Muslim palace that he directed himself. Smaller than the Alhambra in Granada, it was nevertheless a fabulous assemblage of arched courts, shady gardens and royal chambers.

At first the guard at the main entrance to the *alcázar*, the Puerta del León, would have nothing to do with Pedro, telling him in no uncertain terms to go and bother a lesser mortal than he. He was hardly less dismissive when Pedro persisted by showing him the leather roll in his knapsack and his explanation of how he came by it. However, when Pedro stood his ground and showed him the jade ring of Queen Isabel, the guard's attitude changed dramatically, and addressing Pedro with a mixture of 'sir', 'my lord' and 'sire', he was conducted through the narrow gateway into a small garden beyond containing shrubs and trees. Told to wait, he was eventually met by a portly court attendant.

'Are the King and Queen in residence?' Pedro asked politely.

'No, they're not,' replied the attendant in a surly fashion. 'And what if they were?'

'I found this leather roll containing sea charts, and I think they might know something of them. They seem very important.'

The attendant listened impatiently to Pedro's explanation of how he came by the leather roll and the maps it contained.

'Well, the royal couple aren't here. We're not expecting to see them this year. Now if you give me the roll I'll see that the maps are returned to their rightful owner.'

'No, I want to hand them personally to whoever's in charge here,' replied Pedro firmly.

'The Duke of Medina Sidonia is resident here currently in the absence of the King and Queen,' came the reply.

'Well, may I see him, please. These charts are important.'

'No,' the attendant replied dismissively. 'The duke's not here today, although he's expected back tomorrow. If you care to call here then I'll try and get you an audience with him, but I can't promise it. He's a very busy man.'

The attendant turned away.

'Sir,' called out Pedro. 'Wait a minute. Please will you tell the duke when he returns that I bear this jade ring of Queen Isabel which she gave me soon after the surrender of Granada in January. Please tell the duke this. Tell him that I have something very important to hand to him and it might be urgent.'

'You were at the surrender of Granada?' the attendant asked, startled.

'Yes, I was. And I was a member of the Queen's personal guard which entered the city ahead of the monarchs themselves. Please tell the duke this. I saw him in the cavalcade riding behind them.'

Pedro returned the next day and the next, sitting with growing frustration with many other aspirants in the gilded splendour of the Salón de Embajadores adjacent to the former sultans' private rooms waiting for an audience with the duke. Unknown to him, soldiers were scouring the streets searching for the leather roll dropped by the rider. On the third day, late in the afternoon, Pedro was ushered in to the duke's presence.

The elderly man looked up slowly from the pile of state papers through which he was working his way.

'How can I help you?' he said wearily.

'My name's Pedro Togeiro, Your Grace,' replied Pedro, keen to establish his credentials. 'I bear the Queen's ring for rescuing her and the King from the fire in Don Gonzalo's mansion at...'

'So you're the young man who saved them?' the duke exclaimed. 'Well, well!' He got up from behind the leather-topped desk and came round to Pedro.

'I'm delighted to meet you. You were at Granada, weren't you? I seem to remember seeing you talking to the Sultan and his son in the Alcazaba?'

'Yes, Your Grace, I got to know Lord Boabdil when I taught his son, Ahmad, Castilian when he was at Porcuna.'

'Well, well,' exclaimed the duke slowly, shaking his head in disbelief. He stood there, rather stooped, holding Pedro's hand between his, squinting in the poorly lit room at the Queen's jade ring on one of Pedro's finger and Sabyán's ruby ring on another.

'Well, my boy,' he continued. 'What brings you here to this court? You're a long way from home.'

'Your Grace, I picked up this leather roll containing sea charts when I entered the city three days ago. It was dropped by a rider passing through the

Puerta del León, when he collided with a donkey, knocking over its owner. If he'd stopped to enquire if the man had been hurt he might have seen the roll in the road. As it was, he continued without stopping.'

'That sounds like one of Colón's men,' the duke replied, with a sigh. 'They're all tarred with the same brush; always impetuous and always in a rush to do things.'

'Colón, Your Grace?'

'Yes, Cristóbal Colón,[2] the navigator. It's his sea charts which you found. We've had men out searching for them for days now… and you found them and brought them here!' he exclaimed again, truly dumbfounded. 'My, you certainly seem to have a knack of being in the right place at the right time.'

'Is Señor Colón here, Your Grace? I'd like to hand them back to him personally if it's possible.'

'No, he's supervising the provisioning of his ships. But be assured, he'll be mightily relieved to know these charts are safe and to have them returned to him. I'll despatch a rider with them this evening. But first, young man. Let's take a look at them. I've never seen these precious charts of his which he's always talking about. Or have you seen them already?'

'Yes, Your Grace. I took a look at them to see what was in the leather roll. When I saw them I knew that they had to be important. That's why I came to the palace with them straight away, and why I didn't want to hand them to the court attendant at the gate.'

'Quite right too, my boy. Always see the man in charge – or the woman, of course!' he chuckled mischievously, referring to the Queen.

He pulled the charts from the roll and weighted them down across his desk. Both men pored over them intently, the duke chortling to himself as his finger wandered over the places which Cristóbal Colón had talked to him about for several years.

'So there you are, my boy, Colón's treasured charts,' said the duke after they had examined the charts for fifteen minutes. 'I'll roll them up and get them sent to him right away.'

'Where is he, Your Grace?' asked Pedro.

'Where is he?' repeated the Duke. 'Why, across the estuary from Huelva at Palos de la Frontera. If you want to see something historic you should go there right away. He'll be sailing very shortly. I'd be there myself, but matters of state, you know…'

---

[2] Known as Christopher Columbus in the English-speaking World.

XII: *The* Niña, *the* Pinta *and the* Santa María

August 3rd 1492

After the signing of the *Capitulaciones* in Santa Fe in April, Cristóbal Colón left Granada on May 12th for Palos de la Frontera armed with his royal warrant for the chartering and victualling of three ships. In the parish church of St George in Palos he told the Mayor, registrars and public notary what he needed. Then he went to the nearby town of Moguer de la Frontera where he chartered three ships. However, the sailors there, and in nearby Palos, which was a substantial maritime community of three thousand souls, refused to enlist for the voyage. Colón sought the help of the friar, Antonio de Marchena; he was Guardian of the convent of La Rábita y Párroco de Palos, and also the friend of Martín Alonso Pinzón, a rich and influential sea captain who admired Colón. They canvassed the help of Martín's brother, Vincente Yáñez Pinzón, and between them the brothers recruited the crews Colón needed, including the Pinzóns' brother, Francisco, who would join Martín's ship as master. Undoubtedly, without the Pinzóns' considerable local influence, Colón's historic voyage of discovery could not have taken place.

On the brothers' advice, the ships which Cristóbal Colón had located in Monguer were deemed unsuitable, and were replaced by the *Niña*, *Pinta* and *Santa María*. The *Niña*, the smallest of the three and originally called the *Santa Clara*, was the property of Juan Niño, from whose name the boat was taken. Changing the name of the boat to that of the owner, captain or locality was then common. The *Niña* was a caravel, and was the smallest ship, displacing only sixty tons. Each of its three masts was rigged for triangular lateen sails. The *Santa María* was by far the largest. It was a three-masted *ñao* of nearly two hundred tons. It was chartered from the owner and mariner, Juan de la Coas, from Santander in northern Spain. The *Santa María* had previously traded to Flanders from Bayona in Galicia. The third ship, the *Pinta*, like the *Niña*, was a caravel, weighing seventy tons, and like the *Santa María* was square-rigged on the fore- and mainmasts but lateen-rigged on the rear mizzenmast. It was a mere seventy feet long and little more than twenty feet wide. It displaced just seven feet of water. All three boats were solidly constructed of oak, and the sails made of strong hemp canvas.

The Pinzón brothers, Martín and Vincente, scoured the local towns to enlist the crews for the three ships, eighty-six men in all. Most were local sailors, but there were a dozen from Galicia and the Basque country. Others came from Portugal, Genoa, Venice, Sevilla, Cádiz and Córdoba. Between them they spoke Arabic, Greek and Hebrew. There was a notary, a royal auditor, three surgeons and a couple of painters. Significantly, there were no soldiers or priests.

Pedro arrived post-haste at Palos from Sevilla in the early morning of August 3rd. Fearing that he might miss the sailing of the three ships, he had sped as fast as he could through the fierce heat and dust of midsummer to get there. The road was crowded with horsemen and those travelling on foot, all with the same intent of witnessing something historic. Palos de la Frontera, lying on the east bank of the Rio Tinto estuary and across the water from Huelva, was at the far western end of *Al-Andalus*. It was the very end of the road as far as Pedro was concerned. After the ships had set sail he would turn tail and take the long road back home to his mother in Vélez Blanco through Sevilla, Granada and Almería. It would take him some six weeks to get home on foot.

Somewhat wearily, Pedro walked up to the small castle in the centre of the town. A lot of people were milling around. Many were heading for the promontory at the mouth of the estuary a couple of miles further on for a better view of the departure. This was clearly imminent. Not being sure where he was, Pedro wandered in the direction of the river, past Martín Pinzón's house in the main street, then up to the left to the squat brick church of St George. This was only a stone's throw from the sandy bluff which abutted the estuary. As he rounded the front of the church with its arched doorway of red and yellow brick, the stocky figure of Cristóbal Colón and his older friend, Martín Pinzón, left after attending morning Mass. They were followed by Vincente and Francisco Pinzón and the rest of the crew. They had just received their wages for the voyage, which comprised four monthly instalments paid in advance on the instructions of the Crown. Although paid in gold *doblas*, the wages, as set out in the *Capitulaciones*, were equivalent to nearly seven hundred maravedís per month for a cabin boy, a thousand for the seaman, two thousand for the officers and four thousand for Martín Pinzón. For the cabin boys, some twenty in all, the wages were unusually generous, and had regard to the risks involved in this epic voyage into the unknown.

Pedro leant against a wall watching the high-spirited sailors with their canvas kitbags slung over their shoulders ambling along with their characteristic rolling gait. They were making their way down towards the wooden staging from where they would be rowed across to the three ships moored some hundred yards away across the water. The mainsails of the two larger ships fluttered gently in the morning air. One cabin boy, a couple of years younger than Pedro, deviated down a narrow, shady passage close to where Pedro stood.

Pedro turned with a start as a scream ran out along the alley. Fifty yards on he saw the cabin boy fall to the ground as a rough-looking man removed a long knife from the boy's chest. Pedro chased along the alley at the man with the knife, at the same time drawing his sword over his shoulders and shouting to raise the alarm. The man was searching through the boy's pockets for the leather purse containing his four months' advanced wages, but the man, seeing Pedro charging at him with a drawn sword, ran off and disappeared around a corner out of sight. Arriving at the youngster, Pedro knelt down at his side, supporting his head in his hand. Blood was gushing from the deep wound in the boy's chest and he was frothing at the mouth. He looked up at Pedro, his eyes glazed. The poor boy was dying. Pedro laid the boy's head gently on his knapsack, wondering what, if anything, he could do. Suddenly, standing by his side was Yazíd. Pedro looked up at him in astonishment.

'What!… How…?' he stammered.

'You haven't left any of our signs for a month now, Pedro,' scolded Yazíd. 'I was getting worried about you so I came to find you.'

'But how…?'

'I don't know,' he said. 'I keep telling you. I just follow my instincts.'

'Pedro!' he cried, pointing with his hand. 'Look at the boy's kitbag. What's it got written on the top of it?'

'Pedro Tegero,' replied Pedro, looking at it again, not comprehending.

'But that's your name?'

'No, mine's Pedro Togeiro,' the elder boy replied, looking up at his friend, confused.

Beyond Yazíd, over the wall of the passage, Pedro spied the *Pinta* in the estuary. A stork stood on the top of the tall central mast with its wings outstretched over the limp sail which was lit by the morning sun. The sail was emblazoned with the huge red cross of Santiago. The fourth and last riddle of the hermit flashed into his mind:

'You have reached both the end and the beginning of your journey. You must choose your destiny now as you look down on yourself with wings spread over a blazing cross.'

Pedro looked at the *Pinta*, then at the cabin boy's kitbag and then back at the *Pinta*.

'You have to go, Pedro,' urged Yazíd. 'It's a sign. Don't you see? You have to go and join the ship in this boy's place. You've got his name!'

'But I'm returning home directly I've seen these ships set sail. I can't…'

'You must,' insisted Yazíd. 'Look, leave this boy with me. There's nothing we can do for him. I think he's stopped breathing.'

Pedro looked at the *Pinta* again, lying at anchor in the still water of the estuary close to the *Santa María* and the *Niña*. His pulse started to race at the sudden prospect of the voyage to far-off lands.

He made up his mind.

'Very well, Yazíd. I'll go in this poor boy's place.'

Little time could be lost. His head was filled with a hundred and one things to arrange.

'Yazíd,' Pedro said, delving into the bottom of his knapsack for the remains of his wages for serving the Queen. 'Take this money. I shan't need it on board ship. Use it to get home with.'

'What about this boy's purse with his four months' wages for the voyage? What shall we do with that?'

'Tuck it safely back in his pocket. If they find you with the money, they'll think you killed him. Best to leave it where it is, Yazíd.'

Pedro pulled the two rings from his fingers.

'Do you remember the beautiful young woman, Raquel, who came with her uncle after you found me in the mine shaft at Mecina?'

'Don't I!' he exclaimed. 'What a stunner – and what a figure!'

'Well, I'll explain when I return, but we fell in love afterwards and she'll have had my baby by now. She's married to a bad-tempered man a lot older than her. They'll be living in the village of Capilerilla, on the hill high above Mecina. Please will you go through the Alpujarra on your way back home and see if you can find her working in the fields? Give her this ruby ring. Give her my love and tell her that I think about her all the time. Tell her I'll see her when I return. Have you got all that?'

'I think so, Pedro.'

'Lastly, please give this jade ring to my mother. She's already seen it. It was a gift to me from Queen Isabel.'

'Your mother? Queen Isabel?' Yazíd exclaimed. 'Is your mother alive, then?'

'I've no time to explain properly, but yes. I found Mama alive and well in the Alhambra the day Boabdil surrendered the city to King Fernando and Queen Isabel. It was a miracle, truly a miracle. Mama will help fill in some of the details for you when you get back. One thing more, Yazíd. Please will you take my knapsack back home with my sword and this beautiful ornamental dagger. I won't need them on board ship. But I'll hold on to my Toledo knife. I'm sure I'll find that useful.'

'Yes, of course, Pedro. But where did you get this gorgeous dagger?'

'The Sultan Boabdil gave it to me when I accompanied him and his family from Granada. It belonged to the great Mohammed the Fifth and was a gift to him from the Caliph of Baghdad.'

Yazíd's jaw dropped and he shook his head in disbelief.

'Shall I hide your sword in our cave?' he managed.

'No, leave it with Mama, please, or Uncle Joshua. Now, Yazíd,' Pedro went on, 'help me into this boy's clothes. Maybe there's a clean shirt in his kitbag. I can hardly wear the bloodstained one he's got on.'

With great haste, Pedro changed clothes, putting on the cabin boy's trousers and spare shirt and donning his red sailor's cap on his head. They were a bit tight but they would do. He swung the bag over his shoulder.

'How do I look, Yazíd?' he asked.

'Like a proper seaman, Pedro. Now be off, before the last boat leaves from the staging.'

'Good bye, Yazíd. I'll see you in Vélez when I return in a few months' time.'

'No, Pedro. I'll meet you on the shores of Cathay!'

Pedro glanced back at his friend as he started down the road. *Was he serious?*

Pedro tore back past the church, down the slope towards the water, past the shallow well with its brick surround which had been used to fill the enormous water barrels in the three ships, and then around the corner to the wooden staging which ran out into the water. The last of the seamen and cabin boys were already clambering over the seats of the boat past the oarsmen, throwing their kitbags into the bows. Pedro was the very last to clamber aboard.

The Al-Andalus Chronicle
Part III: Ignominy and Glory

Part III: Ignominy and Glory

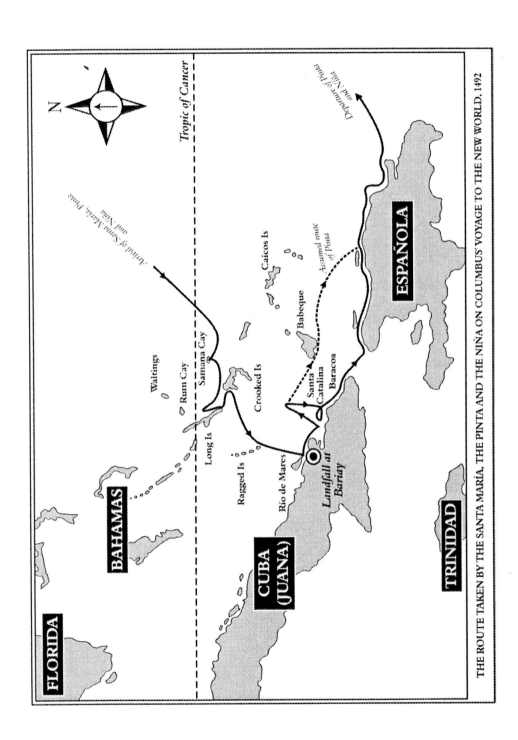

THE ROUTE TAKEN BY THE SANTA MARÍA, THE PINTA AND THE NIÑA ON COLUMBUS' VOYAGE TO THE NEW WORLD, 1492

I: Pedro Joins Ship

Friday, August 3rd 1492

He sat at his small desk in his poorly lit cabin surrounded by his sea charts and nautical instruments. He started a letter which he had composed in his mind a long time before:

> *In the Name of Our Lord Jesus Christ*
>
> *Most Christian, exalted, excellent, and powerful princes, King and Queen of the Spains and of the islands of the sea, our Sovereigns: It was in this year of 1492 that Your Highnesses concluded the war with the Moors who reigned in Europe. On the second day of January, in the great city of Granada, I saw the royal banners of Your Highnesses placed by force of arms on the towers of the Alhambra, which is the fortress of the city…*

Unaware of the historical significance of this day, the eighteen-year-old, a canvas kitbag slung over his shoulder, had run down to the waiting boat, leaving behind his friend Yazíd to tend the dying cabin boy. It was before seven in the morning and the sun was only just glinting over the horizon. The kitbag had roughly marked on it the name 'Pedro Tegero' and this was the name which the boy, Pedro Togeiro, had now to adopt. He had half run, half slid, down the steep gravely path to the boat which was waiting close to the water's edge below the bluff, tucking his shirt into his trousers at the same time. Both were a bit tight. Seamen manned the three sets of oars, impatient to set off. Others were jostling each other boisterously on the several rows of benches. Their kit was already stowed aboard. A stocky, bearded man stood by the boat on the landing stage. He was Juan Quintero, the bo'sun of the *Pinta*, which lay a short distance out in the estuary, its mainsail starting to flap in the burgeoning breeze. He waved the boy to him vigorously.

The boy reached the boat, panting.

'*¿Y tú, chico, quien erés? ¿Como te llamas?*' asked the bo'sun, in his rough and ready Castilian.

'*Pedro Tegero, señor,*' answered the boy in the same language. He was decidedly nervous.

The man scowled and peered at the list of the ship's complement in his hand. His eyes were more suited to scanning a distant horizon than reading print in twilight.

'Who?'

'There, sir,' replied Pedro, looking over the seaman's shoulder. 'There it is,' he said with noticeable relief – "Pedro Tegero".'

The list contained twenty-six names:

Martín Alonso Yáñez Pinzón – captain
Francisco Martín Pinzón – master
Cristóbal García Sarmiento – pilot
Juan Quintero de Agruta – bo'sun
Cristóbal Quintero – owner and seaman
Goméz Rascón – co-owner and seaman
Juan Reynal – master-at-arms
García Hernández – dispenser/steward
Maestro Diego – surgeon
Francisco García Vallejo – seaman
Juan Rodríguez Bermejo – seaman
Alvaro Pérez – seaman
Antón Calabrés – seaman and servant to the captain
Gil Gutiérrez Pérez – seaman
Juan Verde de Triana – seaman
Sancho de Rama – seaman
Diego Martín Pinzón – seaman
Juan Veçano – seaman
Pedro de Arcos – cabin boy
Juan Arias – cabin boy
Fernando Médel – cabin boy
Francisco Médel – cabin boy
Alonso de Palos – cabin boy
Juan Quadrado – cabin boy
Pedro Tegero – cabin boy
Bernal – cabin boy and servant to captain

'Ah, yes,' said the bo'sun. 'Where have you been, lad? We've been waiting for you for days. You should've been at Mass an hour ago in St George's church. Everyone was there except you to receive the advance on their wages. The Admiral wasn't too pleased, I can tell you.'

'I turned up as the service was ending, sir. I...'

'You can call me "Bo'sun", lad, which is what I am. I'm not one of them officers.'

'I'm sorry, Bo'sun, but I was delayed. My mother was not too well and I had to...'

'Huh, likely story,' he replied, but with more humour than malice. 'More likely you couldn't bear to leave your girlfriend behind, eh! Well, jump to it. Throw your bag into the boat and jump in. The wind's picking up and the captain will want to set sail shortly. We've got a long way to go. A very long way!'

Pedro threw his kitbag to the sailor at the prow who let it fall into the boat indifferently. None of the Palos men budged to make room for him. A voice hailed him from the third bench and the sailor there made space for him.

Poor Pedro Tegero's mind was in a whirl. So much had happened in the last hour he could not take it all in. He had come to Palos de la Frontera simply to join the gathering crowds and to see the three ships set off on their voyage of discovery and with the clear intention of returning to his mother, Miriam, in his distant home town. Yet here he was joining the crew. Should he not scramble overboard now and wade ashore before it was too late?

The longboat quickly reached the *Pinta* and the crew scrambled quickly up the rope ladder onto the main deck. Pedro was the last but one to board. A helping hand reached down to take his kitbag from him. There seemed to be men everywhere, all rushing around with great purpose. The last man on the boat threw lines up to men on the low foredeck at the bows. The lines were passed through two pulleys, and six men hauled the heavy longboat on board, lashing it safely in place on the foredeck. The last man in the longboat clambered nimbly up the ladder. Pedro, still standing there perplexed, was pushed aside and the ladder was pulled in, a rope tied around it and secured to the side.

'Heave-ho, heave-ho!' groaned a dozen men rhythmically as they raised the anchor from the shallow water with the thick cable. Feeling hopelessly inadequate, Pedro ran to help, but he was elbowed aside. This was man's work. And indeed it was. Pedro's hands were simply not strong enough to grasp the thick cable. To keep out of the way, he went to the corner of the low quarterdeck at the stern of the ship where there was the least activity – or so he thought.

'Make the anchor fast, now!' came a resonant order from above him.

'Lower the mainsail, Francisco, otherwise we'll make too much headway in this breeze.'

'Aye, aye, Martín,' replied his brother, mustering six men from the anchor party.

'Raise the mizzen, Bo'sun. That'll give us just enough headway. We've got nearly an hour to wait to get across the bar.'

'Aye, aye, Captain,' replied the bearded man.

He shouted across to four sailors.

'Up on the quarterdeck and raise the mizzen. Look sharp!'

'Pilot,' shouted the captain above Pedro's head. 'Get the ship under control and bear to the centre of the river.'

Cristóbal García Sarmiento, a tidy, dark-featured man in his forties, called two men and passed Pedro as he entered the dark open space below the quarterdeck.

'You, lad, you can come and help!' he shouted to Pedro.

'Juan,' he shouted across the boat to the master-at-arms. 'Keep a look out at the bows, if you please.'

All was activity. The crew were everywhere. Amazingly, none got in each other's way. All had a purpose. As Pedro dived into the low space at the stern which housed the tiller, he managed to catch a glimpse of two ships ahead of him. Three hundred yards ahead and in the centre of the half-mile wide estuary was a large be-castled ship, the *Santa María*. Behind it on its starboard quarter was a smaller, sleeker ship, the *Niña*. Both were moving slowly against the current.

The relief felt by Cristóbal Colón on the *Santa María*, as he completed his letter to King Fernando and Queen Isabel of Spain, in seeing his small fleet setting off at last was overwhelming. He was the Admiral of the expedition and the greatest navigator of his age. The whole enterprise had been too long a time coming. Finding and equipping the ships was the easiest part.

The three boats moved slowly down the estuary with the *Niña* in the lead; she was the nimblest of the three. Wisely, the pilot of the *Santa María*, Pedro Niño, had kept her longboat in the water to help give the ship steerage, and the six oarsmen in the longboat were kept busy keeping it on course through the deepest channel. The River Odiel joined the Tinto on the right bank, and soon after eight o'clock the three boats reached and crossed the sandbar at Saltres where the rivers, charged with winter sediment, dumped their load as the rivers' spate abated against the open sea. The journey proper had begun.[3]

---

[3] The details of the voyage were faithfully recorded by Colón in his ship's log or *diario* and the following descriptions are derived from the modern word-for-word English translation given in Robert Fuson's *The Log of Christopher Columbus* (1987).

II: All at Sea

It was time to get fully underway. With the commands of the officers and the chants of the seamen in the *Santa María* carrying across the open water, the yardarm of its mainsail was raised and its sail struck. The *Pinta* and *Niña* followed suit with the pilot Cristóbal García Sarmiento chanting, as was customary, from the elevated afterdeck at the stern:

'Larga la vela mayor en nombre de Santísima Trinidad, Padre, Hijo y Espíritu Santo, tres personas y un solo Dios verdadero, que sea con nosotros y nos dé buen viaje a salvamento y nos lleve y vuelva con bien a nuestras casas.'

'Let go and raise the mainsail, bo'sun!' then cried the *Pinta*'s master, Francisco Pinzón, from the rail of the quarterdeck, his brother Martín Pinzón standing by his side. The bo'sun, Juan Quintero, called four men to him. They released the ropes which kept the part-raised yardarm clear of the deck, lowered it and untied the lashings securing the furled sail. This forty-foot heavy yardarm, which more than spanned the boat, was made of two lengths of round pine lashed together. Then, joined by some of the cabin boys – who were, in reality, apprentices – the seamen took hold of the four hemp lines which passed through pulleys set into the top of the thick stubby, seventy-foot-high mainmast, and which were attached through more pulleys to the yardarm, one at each end and two along its length. The *Pinta* was not a large ship, but nearly one hundred pulleys or blocks, some with one internal sheave and some with two to make the ropes run freely, were needed to support the fixed and running rigging. These themselves comprised several miles of hemp rope, sometimes as thick as a man's forearm.

'*Heave, heave!*' the men cried in unison, as the heavy main yardarm was raised and the 1,200 square feet of hempcloth mainsail unfurled noisily. The *Pinta* came to life and sprung forward as the Cross of Santiago caught the wind. Several of the crew were pitched backwards with the thrust.

'Trim the yardarm and mainsail lines, Alvaro!' shouted the bo'sun to one of his men. 'Keep it tight to the wind.'

'Now the foresail and spritsail, Bo'sun, please!' shouted the master from above. The slanted lateen sail on the mizzenmast was already raised in place.

'Very well, Master. Look to it, lads!' instructed the stocky, bearded man, a short length of rope with knotted tails in his sturdy fist to encourage compliance. 'The sooner we get the boat under way, the sooner we'll eat!' he added.

'Aye to that!' shouted the men heartily around the boat. It was well past their first meal of the day. Nobody had eaten since the previous evening.

The operation was repeated with different sailors and cabin boys taking on the less arduous task for these smaller sails. Using the same procedure as for the mainsail, the yardarm at the foremast was lowered to the deck, the sail unfastened and then raised on high by means of the cables passing through the masthead pulleys. The 500 square feet of foresail caught the wind. The spritsail followed suit.

But not all was done. The ship's caulker, the Basque, Juan Pérez, took on the duty of lighting the fire in the iron hearth placed inside the low open deckhouse below the quarterdeck, while García Hernández, the steward, who had the onerous duty of dispensing the daily rations, assembled sufficient food for all the officers and crew from his locked store. His was never the most popular post on board ship, particularly towards the end of a voyage when provisions were meagre. But today would be a veritable feast. There was plenty of fresh meat, bread, fruit and vegetables on board and the Admiral and three captains had ordered a special ration to be issued due to the late hour and to celebrate the start of the journey. It was now well into the morning and the steward had been instructed to bring forward the midday meal. Not until the crew were fed would the ship's watches be set and duties allocated.

Although Pedro was mystified by all the ropes swinging above his head, he was nevertheless not idle.

'Set a course to the south-east, Cristóbal, or better, two points to the north of that!' shouted the captain, standing at the rail of poop deck. 'I see that the *Santa María* is looking to follow the coast to Cádiz for the while.'

'Aye, Martín.'

The *Pinta* was not steered by a wheel but by a long tiller which swept much of the space in the open deckhouse below the quarterdeck at the stern of the ship. The thick oak tiller ended with a cast-iron sprocket which fitted tightly over the square top of the oak rudder post. Moving the eight-foot-long tiller was heavy and tiring work, even for several men. To reduce the effort involved, a clever mechanism was used in which a closed line was looped from the end of the tiller and passed through pulleys at the side of the cabin, the floor and ceiling. By drawing down the left-side or right-side line, the tiller was swung left or right and the rudder rotated. Even then it was heavy work, and the helmsmen were changed frequently. To direct the helmsmen, the master-at-arms, Juan Reynal, as assistant to the bo'sun, shouted instructions from the bows, with the pilot, Cristóbal Sarmiento, checking the compass bearing from the stern. Pedro was commandeered by Samiento to assist the helmsmen and the youngster was only too glad to have a task to perform.

As Pedro bent forward to enter the deckhouse, two cabin boys skipped past noisily, knocking him forward. They looked identical. One pulled the red cap from Pedro's head, poking fun of him, chanting, 'Mama's boy, mama's boy.' Clearly, what Pedro had told the bo'sun when he joined the longboat had been passed around the seamen. Pedro tried to grab his cap but they ran around the deck throwing it back and forth to each other, with Pedro caught as piggy in the middle. When he was breathless and thoroughly humiliated, the second boy stood cockily over the open main cargo hatch and casually dropped Pedro's cap into the hold. Both boys skipped away, laughing and making faces at Pedro.

The pilot had seen all this. 'Uh, those damned Médel boys,' he said to Pedro. 'I don't know why they're still on this ship. They're always up to mischief. One day they'll get their just rewards. Take no notice of them, Tegero.'

'Are they twins, sir?' asked Pedro. 'I can't tell one from the other.'

'No. Fernando and Francisco Médel are brothers, but very close in age. Come, Tegero, we must turn this ship to the south-east, otherwise we'll lose the *Santa María* and incur the captain's wrath.'

Slowly the boat came around from its southerly course to run along the Spanish coast some ten miles distant and in view. The *Santa María* lay half a mile ahead, with the *Niña* three hundred yards to starboard. Cristóbal Sarmiento advised Pedro to retrieve his cap and pointed the way to the stairway into the hold. With all the crew above deck the hold was empty and Pedro was able to explore. Not that he could see much; it was so dark it took several minutes before he could make out the plethora of objects which lay below decks. He retrieved his red cap. Then, with the ship rolling uncomfortably from side to side, he eased his way forward in little more than six feet of headroom towards the bows. Only in the centre of the hold reserved as accommodation for the crew was there any space to move.

Running down both sides of the ship were dozens of massive, chest-high, oak barrels stored securely on their sides, the biggest of them holding over one hundred and seventy gallons of water. There were smaller ones holding vinegar and oil, and yet more narrow-topped upright casks of wine bound in wicker frames with two carrying handles. All told there were over 160 vessels holding seven hundred gallons, some eighty tons all told. They were the lifeblood of the ship and were deemed sufficient for a journey of thirty days. Never an opportunity was lost in topping up the water in the barrels. Then there were lines of smoked hams and sides of cured bacon, casks of salted beef and pork, strings of onions, garlics and peppers, rounds of hard cheese, baskets of dried fish, clay pitchers of olive oil, large sacks of flour, rice and vegetables, honey, dried figs and almonds, and suspended nets filled with fresh fruit, sadly, all needing to be consumed in the first week or so.

Everywhere there were coils of rope of different sizes looped onto hooks, dozens of iron-hinged chests, spare pulleys, plus fishing nets and copper cooking pots. Several crossbows with bundles of bolts hung on hooks, as did the seamen's' canvas kitbags. At the stern on the starboard side lay the ship's lombard cannon of 3½-inch calibre with its wooden frame, shot and closely-sealed casks of powder. Opposite it on the port side lay the smaller, 2-inch calibre falconet which, with a charge of powder, would launch bits of scrap iron in the general direction of its target. Both could be mounted on deck later. Sets of tools for the carpenter, sailmaker, caulker and cooper lay tidily at their respective stations.

Staggered by the scale of stores carried by the ship, Pedro made his way to the bows, banging his head more than once on the curved deck beams above. At the narrow end of the ship was a stack of olive logs for burning on the hearth. On the floor of the hold, beneath the open main hatch, there was a second hatch. Curious as ever, Pedro raised it, believing it to conceal a lower hold. He could see little but a glint of light very close to him which moved to port and starboard with the motion of the boat. It was water! Pedro stretched his arm down and touched it. What was it doing there? How deep was it? The boy lay down on his stomach and stretched his arm down into the darkness. At elbow length he could feel the massive oak keelson, the internal keel which ran down the centre of the ship to strengthen the main keel. Almost nine inches of fetid, cold sea water lay over it. Pedro had little time to ponder.

'Who goes there?' came a stentorian voice from the foot of the steps.

Pedro jumped to his feet and lowered the bilge hatch. He moved shame-facedly from the darkness.

'Oh, it's you, is it!' accused the steward, García Hernández. He seemed more formidable than Juan Reynal, the master-at-arms.

'I could have guessed it was you. I've been watching you loafing around the ship while everyone else was working. What are you doing down here? You know you need permission to be down here at this time of day? What have you stolen? Come on, show me?'

'Nothing, sir,' stammered Pedro. 'I've taken nothing. I came down here to retrieve my cap. The pilot, Mr Sarmiento, told me to. The Médel brothers threw my cap into the hold and—'

'Well, you've no right to be here and the pilot knows that. Now get back on deck and do something useful.'

Then, feeling a little guilty for bawling out the youngster who he could see was distressed, he said remorsefully, 'Well, all right lad, while you're here you can bring up one of those hams hanging there. But no slicing off a piece for yourself, now.'

Chastened, Pedro returned to the deck. The ship was still running along the Spanish coast and was now a couple of miles behind the *Santa María*. The wind was gusting while the three sails flapped noisily. The sea was choppy and becoming rough. With the ship's master, Francisco Pinzón, in command of the ship, ably assisted by the bo'sun's deputy, the master-at-arms, Juan Reynal, plus a handful of men, the officers and crew were eating their midday meal. The rest would eat later. The officers were seated around a pull-down table at one side of the low deckhouse and all were attended by Antón Calabrés, the Italian servant to Martín Pinzón. Judging by the noise which they were making they were in high spirits. But so were the crew. Ravenously hungry, they were seated cross-legged here and there around the deck, some on coils of rope, some on the steps to the afterdeck, a couple against the mast and some under the low, five-foot-high foredeck, sheltering from the stiff breeze. Each had a plate of some sorts, mostly a platter of wood but some of pewter, each laden with a hunk of fresh bread and ship's biscuit, a thick slice of pork, a large dollop of overcooked beans from the stewpot and an orange or apple. All ate with the aid of a spoon, their pocket knife and their fingers. By their sides were large earthenware mugs of red wine – part of the crew's daily ration of a quart of water and a quart of wine each day.

Pedro searched for and retrieved the kitbag of the dead boy whose identity he had adopted. It had been kicked unceremoniously beneath the foredeck. It was time to look inside it. Evidently the crew were eating off their own plates and with their own knife and spoon and using their own mugs. He pulled out its crumpled contents. There was another clean, broad-sleeved white shirt, a spare pair of brown breeches which extended to just below the knee, a grey fleecy, waist-length jacket with a hood for cold days, and two pairs of long woollen socks. Also a pair of soft shoes – more like slippers. Sure enough, at the bottom was a tarnished metal spoon, a round wooden plate with a high rim, and a chipped earthenware mug with another pair of socks stuffed inside. Pedro worked his way across the deck between the men towards the iron hearth, now almost out. There was no galley or designated cook as such on the ship. Except on this first day, every man and boy prepared his own food or that of himself and his mates. Nevertheless, the iron hearth, placed mostly inside the deckhouse but sometimes pulled out onto the open deck, provided a focus for meals. Some of the seamen looked up nonchalantly at Pedro; most did not. No one nodded acknowledgement. No one smiled. No one waved even a spoon in friendly recognition. He might not have been there. He ladled himself some beans, took a hard biscuit – the last of the fresh bread had long past gone – cut a slice of pork and looked around for a space to sit. None was evident.

'Over here,' came a voice from across the deck. It was the sailor who had found room for him on the longboat and who had helped him up the ladder onto the ship.

'Over here, lad,' he repeated warmly, waving Pedro to him.

'Pedro, isn't it?' he asked when Pedro had sat down cross-legged beside him.

'Yes, sir, Pedro Tegero.'

'No need for the "sir", Pedro,' the man laughed. 'I'm just a member of the crew. My name's Juan Rodríguez Bermejo, but for some reason everyone here calls me Rodrigo de Triana, so that will do. Call me Rodrigo.'

'Thank you, Rodrigo,' answered Pedro, already tucking into his meal. 'And thank you for making room for me on the longboat. There don't seem too many friendly faces around.'

'You're right, Pedro. It's a problem you'll have to face until you earn their respect. I have the same problem too, but I'm a seaman and you're just a cabin boy and new to the ship.'

'Why is that, Rodrigo? I don't understand.'

'It's very simple, Pedro,' the friendly seaman replied. 'You see, eighteen or more of the crew on this ship come from Palos: the captain, his brother who is master, the bo'sun, the master-at-arms and most of the other officers. The Pinzóns know most of the crew and their families personally and most have sailed with Martín and Francisco before. Palos is a very close community.'

'So where do you come from, Rodrigo?'

'Me? Oh, I come from Lepe.'

'Lepe!' Pedro exclaimed. 'But Lepe's only seven or eight miles from Palos!'

'I know,' laughed Rodrigo. 'But it's the other side of the river from Palos and over an hour's walk away. I might just as well have come from the moon!

'So where do you come from, Pedro?' he continued.

Pedro did not know what to say. Questions would surely be asked if he admitted that he did not hail from Palos or Moguer, its twin town. But to lie and say that he came from either of these towns would invite a lot of awkward questions which he could not possibly answer.

'I come from a small town called Vélez Blanco, Rodrigo,' he answered honestly.

'And where's that, Pedro?'

'It lies on the north-east corner of Almería, close to the region of Murcia.'

'My!' retorted Rodrigo. 'That sounds a long way away. Your town must be in the kingdom of the Sultan?'

'It was, Rodrigo. It was. But the Muslim kingdom is no more, and the people in my town, those of whom are Muslims, are now deemed Mudejares.'

'Converted Muslims?'

'Yes.'

'But you're not a Moor, Pedro?'

'No, I'm a Christian… well, half Christian.'

Pedro was desperate to change the subject. His background and life story were too complicated to want to describe them while eating a meal cross-legged on a rolling ship.

'Have you sailed on the *Pinta* before, Rodrigo?' he asked in a high tone.

'Changing the subject, eh, Pedro! Got something to conceal, eh! Never mind. There's plenty of time to get to know one another.' He paused for a moment. 'I think I'll get to like you, young man. You're "deeper" than these other seamen here and you speak Castilian beautifully. You've obviously moved in the right circles.

'But to answer your question. No, I haven't been on this ship before, but I've spent a life at sea, ever since I was a cabin boy like you, inexperienced and vulnerable. Mostly I've sailed from Sanlúcar, but sometimes from Sevilla and sometimes from Palos too.'

'Rodrigo, even now I don't understand…'

But Pedro's next question about Palos was cut short by the bo'sun who summoned the crew with his shrill whistle, a sound which Pedro would get used to soon enough.

'All hands to the mainmast!' shouted Juan Quintero in gruff voice. He was every bit a bo'sun. The ship's master, Francisco Pinzón, stood at the rail of the afterdeck, a list in his hand.

'The captain, pilot and I have agreed the following duty rosters,' he announced without ceremony. You all know the procedure. Most of you have sailed with us before. Isn't that right, men?' he challenged.

'Aye,' cried the crew, in fine humour after the best meal they had eaten all summer.

'And you know why we're here, don't you?' cried Francisco.

'Aye, to find gold!' came a voice from the rear of the assembled men.

Francisco looked around at his brother, Martín, who smiled and raised his eyebrows innocently.

'No, to find new lands, you landlubbers! To find a new route to China and the Great Khan. Now here's the roster. Read it out, Bo'sun, please.'

Juan Quintero held the list well away from his face so as to focus on its content.

'As usual there will be six four-hour watches during the day, rotating after eight turns of the sandglass, which will be called by the cabin boys. The first watch will start at first light, then late morning, then mid-afternoon and then at vespers at seven, when after prayers we'll take supper. Then before midnight and then during the night. Is that clear?'

He was not looking for a response.

'Three seamen and two cabin boys will take each watch, the first and the fourth, the second and the fifth and the third and the sixth, with one of the officers in charge. The night watches will take particular care. The watches will rotate each week.'

The bo'sun called out the names. The first two groups meant nothing to Pedro. Then:

'Francisco Vellejo, Rodrigo de Triana, Diego Pérez, Juan Arias and Pedro Tegero. They will serve under the pilot, Cristóbal Sarmiento.' But, of course, the pilot was always on call.

Pedro jumped when his name was called. But he caught the eye of the pilot, standing to the side, who winked at the youngster. Pedro felt a bit taller. He had found an ally. Moreover, he would work alongside Rodrigo.

'The seamen can start their duties. The cabin boys can stay behind. The master will instruct them.'

The crew dispersed, muttering amongst themselves. Some were happy with the rosters, some were not. The cabin boys stood around while the captain's brother came down from the afterdeck.

One of the Médel brothers standing behind Pedro pinched his backside. The other boys sniggered.

'Most of you know your duties,' announced the ship's second-in-command. 'You'll take your watches, sweep and scrub the deck each day and, most important of all as we sail south, you'll water the deck morning and afternoon. We don't want the planks shrinking, do we. You'll carry errands for the officers and help prepare the meals and call the crew to eat. The steward will instruct you in the chants you'll use. You'll turn and call the hourglass every half-hour and woe betide any of you who turn it an instant too early or an instant too late. While on watch you'll help raise and lower the yards, shin up the shrouds to tend the sails as needed, help lower and raise the auxiliary and keep the deck and hold shipshape. You'll take your orders from the bo'sun and from the master-at-arms. Is that clear? Good. Now go to your duties. Remember,' concluded the master, 'you need fear no retribution if you do your duty and show respect.'

Pedro commenced his duties, glad to know at last what they involved but totally unprepared for life on board and all that that entailed.

By late afternoon, having sailed some forty-five nautical miles, the *Santa María* turned south. The other two ships followed suit. At sunset, they turned to the south-west by south. Destination – the islands of the Canaries.

III: Canaries

For the next two days the *Santa María*, *Niña* and *Pinta* held their course to the south-west by south, making over one hundred and twenty nautical miles on the Sunday.[4] It was a familiar route for Colón as well as his captains and pilots, but often a stormy one.

While not on watch on the fourth morning Pedro was on his knees scrubbing one side of the pine deck using a pumice block, as did another cabin boy, Juan Quadrado, on the other side. It was tiring work but the sea air was bracing and sun warm on their backs. Two seamen were high in the starboard shrouds splicing in a ratline to replace one which had broken away. Suddenly an iron marlinspike, used to separate the strands of rope when splicing, hurtled down from the rigging, bounced loudly on the deck a foot from where Pedro was working and brushed past his arm. Pedro jumped to his feet, but with the sun in his eyes he could not make out who the men were who were working above him. Before he could call the officer on watch, there was a loud cry from the stern. Men were on their stomachs in the deckhouse trying to peer through the foot-high hole in the transom beyond which the tiller was attached to the rudder post.

'Captain, Captain,' they shouted anxiously, 'the rudder's come adrift!'

There was a great commotion. Martín Pinzón, relaxing on the quarterdeck, ran down the steps to the main deck and went stooping into the low deckhouse, only 5½ feet high. The rear end of the tiller was wedged tightly at an angle into the top of the aperture, the rudder clearly having risen several inches. He rushed back onto the quarterdeck. His brother, the pilot and the bo'sun were already leaning out over the rear rail, while the ship rolled strongly in the sea.

'The rudder pintles have jumped out of their gudgeons, Martín!' they shouted. In this state the ship was not capable of being steered.

'What do we do, Martín?' they shouted.

'Lower the mainsail,' he ordered. 'We must lose headway. Slacken off the mizzen and foresail.'

'All hands on deck!' shouted, Juan Quintero, realising that speedy action was needed. He gave the necessary orders. Pedro was swept along in the emergency. The marlinspike was grabbed off the deck by a callused hand.

'Signal to the Admiral on the *Santa María*, Francisco, that we have a problem. But he'll see our mainsail lowered soon enough.'

---

[4] In Spain in the fifteenth century nautical distance was measured in leagues of some 17,130 feet. A league equalled about three nautical miles. Here, following Robert Fuson's *The Log of Christopher Columbus* (1987), distances are expressed in modern nautical miles of 6,076 feet.

'Bo'sun, fetch Sancho de Rama, the carpenter, and Juan Pérez, the rigger. We might need to fix up a platform to lower over the side to see what can be done.'

'Look to it, Bo'sun!'

Francisco looked over the stern rail as far as he could. This time the pilot held his arm.

'Martín, it looks as though part of the lower iron gudgeon has broken away, allowing the rudder to swing free, and this has forced the upper pintle up from its own socket. There's no way we can get the rudder back in place and secure it. I think all we can do is straighten it out using the tiller, secure it in place, and pass a rope through the ring on the back of the rudder and then pull the rudder tight against the boat from each quarter. At least then we won't lose it. I know we can't steer the ship with the rudder as it is, but if we don't use the mainsail we should be able to maintain steerage with the mizzen and the foresail.'

Gil Gutiérrez Pérez, the person who was most expert in rigging and splicing ropes on board, volunteered to go over the stern on a rope to effect the repairs. Gil swung himself down on the rope on which he was held and passed another rope through the iron ring, carrying the free end back to the deck. Both ends were passed through pulleys, pulled very tight by half a dozen men and secured.

By this time the *Santa María* had lowered sail and fallen back to the *Pinta*, but the heavy sea prevented any assistance being provided. Martín Pinzón called across to Cristóbal Colón and explained what had happened and what action they had taken. The Admiral was furious, blaming the *Pinta*'s two owners.

'Deliberate sabotage by Quintero and Rascón!' he fumed across the water. 'They did everything from the outset to delay the voyage. And now this. But you've done well to make the repairs, Martín. We'll continue under light sail until we reach the Canaries and make a proper repair there.'

It was fortunate that sailors as experienced as the Pinzóns and the pilot were on board to navigate the ship. In any event, the *Pinta* was a caravel and easy to manoeuvre. The caravel had been developed by the Portuguese and had been quickly copied by the Spanish. Both held their own secrets of the ship's design very closely and no design plans survived to later centuries. Nevertheless, the ship was based on the figure '7' in ratios of 1:2:3, with seven for the beam, fourteen for the rounded keel and twenty-one for the overall length. This led the *Pinta* to be seventy-four feet long, excluding the bowsprit and stern post, the keel fifty-two feet long. It was only twenty-one feet in the beam. When loaded with its eighty-odd tons of cargo it displaced a little over six feet. By careful use of the fore-and-aft sails, with the bowsprit used as needed to provide more sideways 'leverage', the ship could be steered to the left or right of the prevailing wind. But it was tiring work for the officers and crew and the watches were double-manned to cope.

Eighty-seven miles were sailed that day, being both day and night.

The following day, August 7th, the wind blew very strongly and the ropes holding the *Pinta*'s rudder in place snapped. Gil Gutiérrez repeated what he had done the previous day, this time passing a thicker rope through the iron ring on the rudder and placing knots tight up against each side of the ring. This prevented the rope from chafing inside the ring and held the rudder in place more securely.

'Martín!' shouted the bo'sun, clambering quickly up the steps from the hold. 'We're leaking badly. Water's come up through the bilge hatch and is starting to lap over the floor of the hold.'

'Holy Mother!' cried Martín, opening the main hatch in front of the mainmast and peering down into the near-darkness. 'That's the last thing we need. When did you last inspect the bilge, Juan? You're meant to do it every day! Organise the crew to man the pumps. We must get the water down below the floor level in the hold otherwise much of our stores will be ruined.'

The ship had two manual pumps. These lay between the mainmast and the quarterdeck on each side of the ship. Essentially octagonal wooden tubes some nine inches across, they extended from the deck down into the bilge. By raising and lowering a crosspiece handle at deck-level, a flexible leather valve, shaped like an inverted cone and attached to a wooden piston, pulled water up the tube to discharge it over the deck and through the scuppers into the sea.

Juan Quintero ordered two seamen to man each pump. Up, down, up, down, up down. It was strenuous work. After ten minutes the team was replaced. At each pull a quart of brown noxious water squirted out over the deck and spilled into the sea. In half an hour the water had left the hold and lay below the bilge hatch.

'Well done, lads!' shouted the bo'sun. 'You can stop now. From now on we'll man the pumps for five minutes on each turn of the glass. That should keep it under control until we get to Lanzarote.'

The *Santa María* approached close to the *Pinta*. The *Niña* was two miles ahead, sailing smoothly.

'I see you're manning your pumps, Martín?' shouted the Admiral across the water.

'Aye, Cristóbal,' replied the *Pinta*'s embarrassed captain. 'We've sprung a leak, but we've got it under control now.'

'What?' commented Colón bitterly. 'Four days into the voyage across the western ocean and you're already manning the pumps!'

'We'll be all right when we get to Lanzarote,' replied Pinzón. 'Then we can beach the ship and re-caulk her with oakum. We must be approaching the island now on the port side. Lanzarote can't be too far away now.'

'No, Martín,' shouted Colón into the wind, cupping his hands to his mouth. 'We're making for Gran Canaria. Las Palmas provides a better anchorage and there are better facilities there.'

'But Lanzarote's a lot nearer, Cristóbal. Gran Canaria is at least another day's sailing beyond.'

'Maybe, Martín, but, nevertheless, we're making for Gran Canaria. You seem to have the *Pinta* well under control.'

Martín Alonso Pinzón, the Captain of the *Pinta*, was a man in his early fifties. A disciplinarian and also an impetuous man, he was used to getting his own way. He had been at sea all his life, trading around the Mediterranean and then down the west coast of Africa under a Dieppe navigator. He became a hardy sailor and skilful pilot. On one such voyage it was said that they got carried far to the south-west and discovered a new land and a mighty river. Yet Martín's conduct was so mutinous that he was dismissed from the maritime service of Dieppe. Rebellion was in his soul. He had returned home to Palos and retired from active life as a sailor, starting a shipbuilding business with his brothers. Then Martín had become acquainted with Cristóbal Colón. Martín had inspected the eleventh-century Vinland map of the Vikings on an earlier visit to the Holy Office in Rome and became an active supporter of Colón's project. Queen Isabel sought his opinion concerning the project, and it was Martín's influence which took Colón to Palos to commission the ships for the journey. It can truthfully be said that without Martín Pinzón, Cristóbal Colón's journey of discovery would not have taken place.

Seventy-five miles were made, sailing both day and night.

Pedro was starting to get his sea legs and becoming accustomed to the hard life on board. The problems with the rudder and the continuous changes to the sails and yards which resulted, plus the regular manning of the bilge pumps, kept the whole crew busy, and few had time to rest and relax. Meals were irregular, and few managed to get much sleep.

During inclement weather the crew slept in what space they could find below deck, but its dampness and the stench from the bilge below, the smell of rotting food, the foul air, the incommodious inclination of the seamen to belch, fart, vomit and swear, plus the incessant activities of lice, fleas and rats, persuaded many to seek the open deck and suffer the wind and rain. Pedro, who had become used to sleeping outdoors during his long journeyings across *Al-Andalus*, avidly took Rodrigo's advice and sought a place on the open deck, or under the foredeck. Even then, the exercising of the bodily functions of the crew over the side of the ship, the exorcising – not always privately – of their sexual frustrations and the noisy venting of their corporeal gases, meant that one's nights were never peaceful. But such was life on board.

The next day, August 8th, with the three ships sailing close by, all on reduced sail because of the problems with the *Pinta*, the three pilots could not agree on their location. Each had assessed their position from dead reckoning and each placed the flotilla in a different place.

'We'll carry on to Gran Canaria,' insisted the Admiral, overriding the views of his three pilots. None was a better navigator than Colón. 'Lanzarote and Fuerteventura are twenty to thirty miles over the horizon on our port beam,' he said. 'You can see the clouds over the islands. We should be in Las Palmas by nightfall.'

Midday arrived. One of the cabin boys on watch called the officers and crew to eat in the customary way:

'Tabla, tabla, Señor Capitán,
y Maestre, y buena campaña,
tabla puesta, vianda presta,
tabla en buena hora,
quien no viniera que no coma.'

'Pedro,' said Rodrigo de Triana, as they sat together against the ship's side. 'I think you'd better go and check. There's a kitbag floating inside the open bilge hatch, I think it's yours. I'll guard your plate. Take care now, Pedro.'

The kitbag was indeed his. His clean clothes, as well as the kitbag, were soaked in brown, stinking water.

Thursday, August 9th saw the three ships reach Gran Canaria. The Admiral ordered Martín Pinzón to remain there and make the necessary repairs to the *Pinta*. The *Santa María*, with the *Niña* under the captaincy of Vicente Yañez Pinzón, the second brother of Martín, sailed on to Gomera, one of the seven islands of the Canaries. This lay beyond Tenerife, the largest island in the group, and one hundred miles to the west of Gran Canaria.

'I'll try and find a replacement ship for the *Pinta*,' said the Admiral to the *Pinta*'s captain, not concealing his fury at the unseaworthiness of the ship. 'Then I'll return here. In the meantime, Martín, see that the rudder is repaired and the ship made watertight. I shall be back within a week.'

However, with contrary winds and then becalmed, the *Santa María* and *Niña* did not reach Gomera for three days.

The *Pinta* was beached at high tide on the sands near Las Palmas and the ship pulled over by block and tackle, with the hawsers anchored by deadmen dug deep into the sand so that the leaks in the hull planking could be located. The internal structure of the ship, such as the keel, keelson, stempost and sternpost, were all made of oak, but its sides and decking were made of pine which, with its natural resin was better able to withstand prolonged immersion in sea water.

Martín Pinzón ordered the *Pinta* righted so that the problem with the rudder could be addressed first. But soon, having given instructions to the bo'sun and the ship's carpenter, Sancho de Rama, as to what had to be done, he set off with his brother, Francisco, for Las Palmas. For several days little was seen of him. With limited guidance proffered from the remaining ship's officers, the ropes holding the anchor in place were removed but scant progress was made in dislodging the anchor, which remained jammed in the aperture by the tiller; to do so might have caused the whole heavy structure to fall into the shallow water in which the men were working. Lack of direction, indifference and the attractions of a semi-tropical island, led to little or no progress being made with the rudder. Cristóbal Quintero and Goméz Rascón, although joint owners of the ship, but not its builders, seemed indifferent to its fate, while Martín Pinzón, convinced that Cristóbal Colón intended to replace the *Pinta* anyway, was content to let things drift and to socialise – and some said womanise – in the city.

With no watches to be kept, few officers to maintain discipline and with time on their hands, the men of Palos had a field day. García Hernández was bullied into issuing more rations than were budgeted and leg-pulling and horseplay amongst the crew turned to squabbles and fighting. Those of the crew not from Palos – that is, Juan Peréz, the Basque caulker, Antón Calabrés from Italy, Juan Verde from Sevilla as well as Rodrigo de Triana from faraway Lepe, and not least Pedro – were all subject to some form of abuse. At least Pedro was in good company.

From the outset of the journey, his beautiful Toledo knife with which he cut his food was coveted by many of the crew. The finely-tempered long steel blade with its horn handle had been crafted along with Pedro's fabulous sword by David Levi in Lorca when Pedro was thirteen years old. Indeed, it had been his birthday present from his apothecary father, Abraham. 'We live in troubled times, Pedro,' he had said. 'You'll need to be able to defend yourself when you get older.' And so it had proved. Pedro had left his sword for Yazíd to return home with.

Good old Yazíd, what a friend he's been, thought Pedro to himself. How is he getting on? He must have passed through Sevilla by now. A year younger than Pedro, his Muslim friend, darker and more thickset, could run like the wind and do so for hour after hour, such that, on occasions, he would find himself in totally unfamiliar surroundings, miles and miles from home. Pedro had left the dying boy in Yazíd's care, asking him to report the killing to the constable in Palos and to hand over the boy's purse, which the robber had tried to snatch. Pedro also left with Yazíd his Toledo sword, since it was the last thing he needed aboard, plus Queen Isabel's jade ring bearing her coat of arms, Boabdil's ornamental curved dagger and the ruby ring Sabyán gave him for saving her children's lives in the flood.

Pedro was alone one evening towards sunset sitting on the beach, eating, when Juan Verde approached him. The seaman had several days' growth on his scarred face and his disfigured brown teeth showed through his leering grin.

'Well, there's a thing!' he started as he approached Pedro. 'All alone. Don't like the ship's company, eh?'

A short stiletto knife clicked open in his hand. He advanced towards the cabin boy, who was rising to his feet.

'A boy like you shouldn't be carrying a knife like that,' he threatened, pointing to Pedro's dagger in his hand. 'Them's too dangerous for small boys like you. Hand it over and you won't come to no harm.'

A small boy no more, Pedro was tall for his age and indeed taller than Juan Verde, but the latter was stocky with powerful arms like knotted cords. Pedro stood his ground. With his sword in his hand he would have feared no one, but he was no match for a hardy seamen bearing the scars of many a knife fight on his face and body. Pedro retreated in front of the short stiletto blade. Skipping around the corner of the ship appeared the Médel boys, seemingly unaware of the approaching confrontation… or were they? Were they in league with Verde? Pedro saw the Médel boys through the corner of his eye. One darted at him. A blade flashed through the air catching Pedro on his bared forearm, as Fernando Médel, the elder of the two, tried to grab the dagger from Pedro's hand, knocking Juan Verde over. But the Vélez boy was stronger than he looked, and his courage had never before found wanting. Blood poured onto the white sleeve of Fernando Médel from Pedro's wound. Pedro ran to the ship holding his bleeding arm, waded through the shallow water and climbed the rope ladder.

'What happened, Pedro?' asked Rodrigo, looking over the side. No one was to be seen.

Pedro, breathless, explained.

'You'll have to take great care, Pedro. From now on I'm going to keep a close eye on you. Luckily you've only got a scratch,' he said as he bound Pedro's arm with a clean piece of cloth. But that, by no means, would be the end of the matter.

The *Santa María* and *Niña* reached Gomera at last on Sunday, August 12th, and Cristóbal Colón sent the ships' auxiliaries ashore. They returned the next morning and Juan de la Costa, the *Santa María*'s owner and master, told the Admiral that no ship was available with which to replace the *Pinta*.

'However,' he said. 'the good news is that Doña Beatrix de Peraza y Bobadil was expected to return from Gran Canaria very shortly.'

'Ah, I know of Doña Beatrix,' replied Colón, perking up. 'She's the young widow of the former Governor of Gomera, Hernández Peraza. There was a rebellion by the natives here not long ago,' he continued, 'and on the death of Hernández, Doña Beatrix became Governor.'

'Yes,' replied de la Costa, 'I understand the vessel she is travelling in is some forty tons and is owned by a man from Sevilla named Grajeda. The ship would be a bit smaller than the *Pinta*, and even the *Niña*'s sixty tons, but it could be ideal.'

'Well, at the very least,' concurred Colón, 'it's probably a good sailer, not like this two-hundred-ton monster we've got here – which is more suited to carrying coal from Bilbao!'

What Colón did not tell the *Santa María*'s master was that Doña Beatrix was reputed to have been a former lover of King Fernando and was said to be stunningly beautiful. Colón was therefore as keen to meet her as to acquire her ship. Moreover, a ship of just forty tons would not require a crew the size of the *Pinta*'s, and he could leave behind some of its more awkward members – not least the two joint owners, who would have no place on a different ship. Yes, it all sounds very promising! he thought to himself.

Doña Beatrix's ship did not arrive the next day and on the Wednesday the Admiral sent Antonio de Cuellar, the *Santa María*'s carpenter, on a brig leaving Gomera for Gran Canaria with a letter for Martín Alonso Pinzón telling him that he, the Admiral, was awaiting the arrival of Doña Beatrix's ship, and that he was sending Antonio de Cuellar to help with the repair of the *Pinta*'s rudder.

By the Friday, the crews of the *Santa María* and *Niña* were getting restless and there was no sign of the expected ship, nor of the *Pinta*. The next day Colón went ashore and confirmed that no other suitable ship was available. On Sunday a special Mass was said for the safe arrival of the island's Governor, and the Admiral determined that he would wait just three more days for news of the *Pinta*. Three more frustrating days went by with the crew increasingly restive. It was already three weeks since they had left Palos, yet the voyage of discovery had barely begun.

At dawn on Friday, August 24th, the *Santa María* and *Niña* set sail for Gran Canaria and by chance overtook the brig which had set sail on the 15th from Gomera. It had been delayed by strong headwinds. The *Santa María*'s carpenter, with the Admiral's letter to Martín Pinzón, returned on board. The ships made good progress and that night skirted Tenerife to witness an incredible and rare pyroclastic display from Mount Teide, the 11,000-foot volcano which dominated the island. The sky was alight with the eruption of red-hot molten lava hurled thousands of feet into the air in great thundering spasmodic explosions. Lumps of magma, bigger than a man, cascaded down, turning as they cooled into rounded volcanic bombs and crashing to the ground, to become absorbed into the incandescent lava flowing like treacle down the mountainside, venting a cloud of poisonous sulphurous gas and steam, and re-digesting its hardening crust into a scabby goo. Bombs fell noisily from the sky into the sea, sending up spumes of steam.

Some of the ships' crew looked at the spectacle awe-struck. Many were simply terrified, never having experienced the Devil's Inferno before, and they ran around the ships shouting and wailing that it was a sign sent by God to warn them of the folly of their pending voyage across the western sea. They must return to Spain forthwith. Cristóbal Colón calmed their fears, going around his ship telling the crew that he had seen similar eruptions from Mount Etna and Stromboli in Italy, and they were not to be frightened.

Pedro Tegero's fracas with Juan Verde and the Médel brothers on the beach at Las Palmas did not end with the soothing words of Rodrigo de Triana. When Fernando Médel climbed back on the *Pinta* he had run across the deck to the master-at-arms, Juan Reynal, holding his bloody sleeve.

'What's the matter with your arm, boy?' the master-at-arms had asked.

'I was attacked with a knife by Pedro Tegero, Sergeant,' he had wailed, crocodile tears running down his face. 'He came at me with his knife. If it hadn't been for Juan Verde and my brother he would have killed me.'

'That's right,' Juan Verde had said, just reaching the deck. 'That new boy's a menace and needs to be taught a lesson.'

The master-at-arms had found Pedro leaning against the quarterdeck, his sleeve rolled down over his bandaged arm, apparently none the worse for wear.

'So you've been fighting with another cabin boy, eh, Tegero?'

'No, sir,' he answered, 'I was attacked by that sailor over there, I don't know his name, and…'

'That's not what he told me, Tegero,' said the master-at-arms, 'I think this is a matter for the captain,' he had concluded.

Pedro was summoned before Martín Pinzón on the quarterdeck an hour later.

'So,' the captain had said sternly. 'You turn up late for the voyage on some flimsy excuse, lounge around the boat hiding in corners, go poking around the hold without permission – oh yes, I heard about your escapade down there from the steward – and now you attack Fernando Médel with a knife. It's lucky his father isn't here or he'd break you in half!'

'But sir,' Pedro had stammered, too startled by the turn of the events to defend himself cogently, 'it was me who was attacked by Juan Verde. He came at me with a knife while I was on the beach. Then the Médel brothers arrived and blood from the cut on my arm must have got onto Fernando's shirt. I was the one who was wounded, not Fernando.'

Pedro had rolled up his sleeve and removed the bandage from his arm. The blood had dried but his arm was red and swollen.

'That's your story, Tegero,' the captain had retorted, his mind already made up. 'Fernando's got a nasty cut on his arm and Juan says that it was your own knife which got deflected onto you as he and the Médels struggled to get it out of your hand. Who do you expect me to believe? A boy who I've never seen before, or a man who's sailed with me for many years before and an apprentice from a Palos family which I've known for years?'

'I'll spare you the *tratos de cuerda* this time, Tegero, but any more trouble from you and you'll be strung up by your wrists on the yardarm.'

'Master-at-arms!' he had called. 'See that this boy is tied to the foremast. He can enjoy the view from there for twelve hours. And no food or drink now, do you understand?'

It could have been worse. Twenty-four or forty-eight hours tied to the masthead on a heaving ship at sea was not uncommon. As it was, the boat had been grounded and the weather had been benign. Moreover, after nine hours, after representations by Rodrigo, who repeated Pedro's side of the story to Juan Reynal, Martín Pinzón had relented.

The *Santa María* and *Niña* arrived back at Gran Canaria at nine o'clock the next morning. Cristóbal Colón was aghast that no progress whatever had been made with the *Pinta*'s rudder. He was more convinced than ever that the ship's owners, Juan Quintero and Goméz Rascón, were reluctant to make the journey and had done everything to delay it. He was appalled at the unkempt state of the *Pinta* and the unruliness of the crew, who were unshaven and unkempt.

'By Saint Fernando, Martín,' he said angrily, using the strongest expletive in his armoury, 'you've done nothing in the sixteen days since I departed for Gomera. You've done absolutely nothing to repair the rudder, which is still wedged up against the tiller housing, and judging by the state of your ship, your crew, and your run-down stores, you've all had a field day. What's been going on?'

'Well, Cristóbal,' Martín stammered, not usually short for words or at the receiving end of a dressing-down, 'you see…'

But the Admiral was having nothing of it.

'I'm putting Maestre Diego, my bo'sun, in charge of the rudder. I've spoken to him and Antonio de Cuellar, my carpenter, and we see no alternative but to construct a new one. Your man, Sancho de Rama, can help. At least,' he conceded, 'it seems that your Basque, Juan Pérez, has re-caulked the leaks. He seems to have done a good job.'

'Indeed so, Cristóbal,' replied Martín. 'He and some seamen worked hard on that after we'd let the water drain out of the ship. We pumped the remainder out and the bilge is now totally dry.'

'Excellent, Martín. I've also spoken to your brother, Vicente. He's not at all keen, but I think we should re-rig the *Niña*. In the more southerly latitudes we'll be in, we'll have following winds and the *Niña* would be better square-rigged on the mainsail and foresail and not rigged with three lateen sails as it is now. She'll make much better progress and it will be much easier for the crew.'

'That makes sense, Cristóbal,' replied the *Pinta*'s captain. 'I'll try to persuade my brother. But have no fear, once he's convinced of an idea, he'll throw his support behind it wholeheartedly.'

And so he did. Progress with both the *Pinta*'s rudder and the *Niña*'s re-rigging were rapid.

Later, the Admiral went into the city to learn that Doña Beatrix de Peraza y Bobadil had sailed for Gomera five days earlier and should have reached there before the *Santa María* and *Niña* departed. It was worrying news; and moreover, he mused bitterly, he would miss the opportunity of meeting Gomera's ravishing Governor.

Within four days all the repairs and changes had been made and at midday on Friday, August 31st, the three ships set sail for Gomera, and with a following fresh breeze, they arrived there on the Sunday. In Gomera, Cristóbal Colón had left behind Pedro Gutíerrez, the representative of the Royal Household and King Fernando and Queen Isabel's eyes and ears. With twelve other men and much help from the people of Gomera he assembled all the water, wood and other provisions, such as salt, wine, molasses and honey, necessary for Colón's estimated twenty-one days' voyage, although twenty-eight days' supplies were assembled. Finally, on September 4th, dried meat, salted fish and fresh fruit were loaded on board.

None the worse for wear, Doña Beatrix had arrived safely back at Gomera.

Cristóbal Colón, dressed in his best blue silk doublet, black breeches, white stockings and buckled shoes was made welcome by her and her island court and treated royally as befitting an Admiral bearing a Royal Warrant for an historic voyage. Although her renowned beauty might have faded a little, Colón was enchanted by her courtly bearing and grace and bewitched by her flashing smile and sparkling black eyes.

On the evening of September 5th, with all three ships seaworthy and fully re-provisioned, a special service of thanksgiving was held. The ships would sail on the morrow.

IV: Deep Water

Thursday, September 6th 1492

Before noon at the last half-hourly turn of the sandglass, a cabin boy on the *Santa María* marked the end of the second watch by chanting:

> '*Al cuatro, al cuatro,*
> *señores, marineros de buena parte;*
> *al cuatro en buena hora*
> *de la guardia del señor piloto,*
> *que ya es hora;*
> *leva, leva.*'

And with this cue, cabin boys on the *Pinta* and *Niña* chanted the same refrain. It was time to set sail. The three ships raised their mainsails, cleared the southern point of Gomera, and followed a compass bearing due west. The journey proper had at last begun, more than a month after they left Palos.

'Martín! Vicente!' the Admiral called across to his two captains not far away across the water, 'I heard a rumour before we departed that a squadron of three Portuguese caravels is in the vicinity with the intention of preventing our leaving the Canaries. I doubt if there's any basis to the rumour but please keep a good lookout from your mast tops. We bear the King's Warrant, and the Portuguese have no right to interfere with our passage on the high seas. Moreover, we are journeying westwards towards lands which have been designated ours by Treaty. Nevertheless, gentlemen, please keep close by until we're clear of these islands.'

'I expect King John of Portugal is annoyed that you turned to King Fernando to support your venture, Cristóbal!' jested Martín.

'You might be right, Martín, you might be right. But he had his opportunity eight years ago. It was Spain which backed this journey and I trust we'll bring back many riches for King Fernando. However, I doubt if John is behind this, Martín. More likely it's just a group of captains looking to make trouble. They're as mischievous as the English. Nevertheless, we must keep a close watch.'

'Aye, we will that. Have no fear!' shouted the brothers to the Admiral on the *Santa María*.

But both the Admiral and the captain of the *Pinta* were right. King John of Portugal had rejected Colón's plans for a expedition to the west. Moreover, any lands discovered to the west of the African coast were assigned by papal bull to Spain. The Admiral's plans for a voyage of discovery were a very long time in the making.

Cristóbal Colón was born in Genoa in 1451, the son of Domenico Colón, a weaver, and Suzanna Fontanarossa. Genoa, like Venice, was one of the great trading cities of the Mediterranean, and for hundreds of years its ships had traded along the coast of Spain, often repelling local competition. The loss of Constantinople to the Turks in 1453 blocked off their eastern markets, and in consequence the Genoese were obliged to look more to the west.

As a sailor Colón had visited Flanders and England where, in 1476, the fleet with which he sailed was attacked by the French. His ship was burnt and it is alleged that he swam six miles to shore. He had remained in Portugal for some ten years and from there he had sailed to Ireland and maybe Iceland. He was familiar with the northern Atlantic and with the Norse tales of lands far to the west. He had voyaged extensively down the west coast of Africa to Guinea and the Gold Coast. While in Portugal in 1479, Colón had married Doña Felipa Perestrello y Moniz, and the following year she had borne him a son, Diego. Sadly, Doña Felipa died just a few years later. Colón had returned to Lisbon but later in 1485 settled in Córdoba. There he had taken a lover, Beatriz Enríquez de Arana who, in 1488, bore him his second son, Fernando.

…The ships made little progress that Thursday with little wind, drifting between Gomera and Tenerife, twenty miles away. The following day they were becalmed all day and night…

Several factors had stimulated Colón's interest in the 'lands beyond the sea'. Beatriz's brother was a cosmographer, and Colón's younger brother, Bartolomé, was a map maker who was to become famous in later years. Moreover, Colón was friendly with the Florentine astronomer and mathematician, Paolo del Pozzo Toscanelli. Through all these contacts he was very aware of the existence of distant lands.

At that time Spain and Portugal were competing aggressively to develop trade routes around Africa to India, the Spice Isles, China and Japan. To settle their bitter differences, the Treaty of Alçaçovas in 1479 had fixed their respective zones of influence, with Portugal winning the prize of the west coast of Africa, the Azores and Madeira, and Spain the Canaries, the Africa coast down to a headland opposite the Canaries, and lands, as yet unknown, to the west.

In 1484 Cristóbal Colón had sought the backing of the King of Portugal for a voyage westwards, but to no avail. Later, Colón's brother, Bartolomé, sounded out the King of England, where he held the office of cartographer, but again without success; the Wars of the Roses were still in full swing. Finally, thoroughly frustrated and depressed, Colón had approached King Fernando of Spain. His proposal for a voyage of discovery to the west was assessed in 1486 in Salamanca by Hernando de Talavera, the Bishop of Avila.

The basis of Colón's conviction that it was feasible to sail westwards from Spain to China and Japan was, in fact, erroneous. Colón believed that the earth was a lot smaller than it really was, and that Asia lay a lot closer to Europe. He reinterpreted the astronomical measure of the Arab, al-Farghani, and reduced Ptolemy's value for the length of a degree at the equator by 25% making the circumference of the earth only 20,400 statute miles. According to Colón, Europe and Asia were then separated by only just over four thousand miles, and this placed China and Japan within striking distance. If Colón had known the magnitude of his error it is doubtful that he would have contemplated the voyage and the New World would have remained undiscovered for some time to come.

...At three o'clock on Saturday morning a north-east wind picked up and the ships again set course for the west. With a choppy sea on the starboard quarter, the *Santa María* took on a lot of water and this impeded its progress...

For several years afterwards Cristóbal Colón had been racked by doubt over his project, despairing of ever getting approval and financial support for the voyage. Around 1490, he had obtained the support of a Franciscan friar who was the confessor to Queen Isabel. Slowly but surely, powerful voices in the royal court had joined his cause, in particular the Duke of Medina Sidonia and the all-powerful Cardinal Mendoza. Queen Isabel had sought the views of the mariner, Martín Alonso Pinzón, who had also backed the venture wholeheartedly. The royal duo of King Fernando of Aragón and Queen Isabel of Castile – los Reyes Católicos – had finally supported Colón's plans. Nevertheless, they made clear that their priority was the overthrow of the decaying Moorish kingdom of Granada under the then Sultan, Boabdil, against whom they had waged a holy war since 1483.

...On Sunday, September 9th, they finally lost sight of land. Many of the crew wept for fear that they would never return. After assessing the distance sailed by the *Santa María* after each watch, as did the pilots of each of the three ships, Colón decided to declare a smaller distance for the flotilla's daily progress, and to keep to himself the true distance which he determined. Already, after setting out from the Canaries only a few days previously, he feared the reaction of the crews to being taken thousands of miles across the open uncharted sea. Overnight the ships progressed ninety miles. But the *Santa María*'s helmsman steered the ship to the north of their westerly course and Colón had cause to reprimand him...

With the fall of Granada on January 2nd 1492 the way was clear for the Monarchs to negotiate with Colón the terms of his long-planned voyage. On April 17th of that year, the two parties had signed an agreement, known as the *Capitulaciones*. This was registered in the chancery of Aragón, and not Castile, and indicated Fernando's personal commitment to the voyage. The agreement accorded Cristóbal Colón the title of Admiral, Viceroy and Governor General of new lands to be discovered. Of the 2 million maravedís which Colón had estimated for the whole venture, the Monarchs put up half. The Admiral had put up one-eighth of the cost, that is, 250,000 maravedís, and would receive one-tenth of the gold, silver, pearls and spices found, jurisdiction of the products grown in the new lands, and one-eighth of the benefits. Martín Pinzón had also put up one-eighth of the cost of the venture and had provided the three ships, while the rest came from the aforementioned noblemen of the realm.

For several days the *Santa María*, *Pinta* and *Niña* made good progress on their westerly course, sailing between a hundred and one hundred and eighty nautical miles each day in good weather and with a following wind. Cristóbal Colón only declared some four-fifths of these distances. On the Tuesday they passed a mast floating in the sea which must have come from a ship the size of the *Santa María*, but the crew were unable to haul it aboard. Its pilot, Pedro Niño, checked the compass and found that the compass needle did not point to the Pole Star but declined or deflected to the north-west at sunset and to the north-east at sunrise. Thoroughly baffled, he failed to understand the Admiral's simple explanation of this phenomenon.

When the three ships left the Canaries on September 6th, it was time for the ships' masters and pilots to establish a much tighter routine for their navigation than hitherto when they were sailing on a familiar course from Spain to the Canaries. Cristóbal García Sarmiento, the *Pinta*'s pilot, finding in Pedro a ready pupil, was glad to use him during the cabin boy's watches to help him with his measurements.

'We've all got our own ways of doing this, Pedro,' he explained, 'but what I've done is to place marks on the starboard side of the ship at the bows and the stern. I'll want you to go to the bow mark and drop pieces of wood into the sea. I'll note the time when they pass me in the stern.'

'But how, sir? How do you record the time? We've only got the sandglass and that runs for half an hour.'

'It's as much a black art as science, Pedro!' he laughed. 'Every pilot's got his own method, and that's why two pilots will never agree on the distances their ships have travelled. In our defence, though, keeping a true course is more important than knowing how far we've sailed each day. But on this journey the Admiral is insistent that we measure the ship's speed every turn of the sandglass and total it up for each watch and then for each day. That's why I need your help.'

'So how do you do it?' asked a persistent Pedro.

'Basically, Pedro, I count the number of chants it takes for a piece of wood thrown into the sea at the bows to travel to the stern. Now I've counted my chant against the small sand-timer my wife has in the kitchen for timing eggs and cakes she makes, and I've timed this kitchen timer against the half-hour sandglass on board the ship here. So I know how many chants make up the turn of the glass. Do you follow me so far?'

'I think so. So by counting the number of times you say your chant during the passage of the float along the boat, you can work out the speed of the boat.'

'It's crude, I know, but it works sufficiently well. I've produced this table which shows the distance travelled per turn of the hourglass in *pasos* or the equivalent distances for the whole four-hour watch in *millas*[5] and *leguas*.'[6]

Cristóbal Sarmiento showed Pedro his neatly written table of figures.

'What chant do you use, sir?' asked Pedro.

'My chant happens to be the first couple of lines of the Lord's Prayer, but everyone has their own. It works so long as you do it steadily and rhythmically and know how many chants make up the sandglass timer. Generally I do three runs each time and take the middle one.'

'And what about setting course and knowing your bearing?' he asked after a pause.

'That's less difficult. I'll tell you about that tomorrow.'

For the next week or so the three ships made good and steady progress westward across the ocean, achieving eighty to a hundred miles or more each day. Seamen on the *Niña* saw a tern and ringtail one morning, which they perceived as a good sign. Such birds, they asserted confidently, do not venture more than seventy-five miles from land. The next night, on the Saturday, a shooting star flashed brightly through the sky, falling into the sea to the south-west, maybe only ten miles away. Superstitious as always, many crewmen saw this as an omen of impending doom, while Cristóbal Colón noted enthusiastically in his diary that evening that it was the closest he had been to a falling star.

On Monday, September 17th, with favourable current and winds they made a record one hundred and fifty nautical miles, although Colón announced nine miles less. They encountered lots of weed in the sea with long grassy stalks and fruit like the mastic tree.[7] The crew of the *Santa María* found a live crab, which clearly indicated that land was not far away since, they believed, crabs were never found more than two hundred and fifty miles from land. Colón noted that the sea was less salty and he was confident that land was not far away. The *Pinta* sailed ahead to spot land first; the first of their false dawns. Men in the *Niña* spotted a school of porpoises and succeeded in harpooning one to add variety to their diet of ship's biscuit, rice, beans and salted and dried meat. The sea became smooth and calm. 'Like the river at Sevilla,' noted the Admiral.

The next morning the *Pinta* lay to for the *Santa María* to approach. Martín Pinzón informed the Admiral that he saw a large flock of birds flying westwards, a sure sign of land nearby. Moreover at sundown he said he saw land forty-five miles to the north beneath a bank of cloud. That evening the Admiral recorded his growing concern about Pinzón's independence and keenness to be the first to spot land. Fine and resourceful captain though he

---

[5] The lengths of the Colombian pace or yard, mile and league are not known accurately but were roughly 4.7ft, 4,300ft and 17,600ft respectively.

[6] Later, once the distance of a minute of longitude was established, navigators used a knotted cord to determine their speed through the water, the 'log' being let out from the stern and the knots counted.

[7] They were entering the Sargasso Sea. The ocean depth was well over a thousand fathoms.

was, Cristóbal Colón was uneasy about the *Pinta*'s captain and his growing ambition. The Admiral refused to change course to the north. With the winds freshening that night, he ordered the topsails on the *Santa María* taken in.

By now Pedro was carrying out his duties of cabin boy to the full. He got on well enough with Juan Arias, the other cabin boy, and Francisco Vallejo, the seaman, both of whom came from Palos or Moguer, but, in truth, both suffered him rather than warmed to him. Rodrigo de Triana continued to be his truest friend, while the pilot, Cristóbal Sarmiento, was showing a growing interest in the Vélez boy.

It was into the second week after leaving the Canaries, and three weeks after the affair with Juan Verde and the Médel boys, during the third watch of the day on a hot afternoon, that Pedro, shirtless, and Juan Arias were scrubbing and watering the main deck. Fear of the deck drying out and the pine planks shrinking was ever on the mind of the bo'sun, Juan Quintero. Unseen by Pedro, as he hauled a pale of water from the sea, Martín Pinzón had descended to the main deck from the quarterdeck and was making his way forward to where the master-of-arms was keeping his usual lookout.

Swooooosh! Sea water cascaded over the deck from Pedro's wooden pail. Pedro looked around in horror at the cry from the captain a few yards away.

'You cursed boy!' he shouted. 'Look what you've done!'

Martín Pinzón's best soft leather shoes with brass buckles were soaked, as were his white stockings. Pedro looked up, his red cap falling from his head.

'Oh, not you!' exclaimed the captain. 'I could have guessed it was you.'

'I'm sorry, Captain,' blurted out Pedro. 'I didn't see you behind me.'

'Didn't see me?' bawled Pinzón. 'Cabin boys are meant to have ears as well as eyes. You should have heard me walking across the deck.'

'Master-at-arms!' he shouted to the man at the bows who had heard the commotion. 'Do something with this boy. He's getting on my nerves. A thrashing, keelhauling, the yardarm, a spell in leg irons, the masthead, I don't care what. But do something and keep him away from me.'

The captain stormed off, water squelching from his shoes.

Juan Reynal, a disciplinarian by duty but not an unfair man, took Pedro to the side. He noted the faint lines across Pedro's back. He guessed what they were, but did not ask.

'I saw what happened, Tegero. Obviously it was an accident. That I could see. Nevertheless, I'm obliged to do something with you.'

He had second thoughts about the use of the lash, even a token dozen strokes.

'You can do a stint of lookout from the yardarm of the mainmast until sundown. I'll make sure you get your supper, but I'd stay well away from the quarterdeck if I were you. Now put your shirt and cap back on, take a good draught of water first and get yourself up the starboard shroud... You've been up there already, I take it?' he asked.

'Yes sir,' replied Pedro a little nervously. The boat was rolling in a beam swell. Standing on even the deck without a handhold was not that easy.

On Wednesday, September 19th, the three ships were becalmed and sailed only seventy-five miles between day and night. Colón noted only sixty-six. Terns flew over the ship to indicate that land was not far away. Soundings were taken with the lead, but the bottom was not reached with twenty fathoms of line. Martín Pinzón continued to press the Admiral to take a northerly heading. The Admiral knew from his charts that islands lay to the north and south but wished to continue between them westwards to the Indies.

Colón ordered the three pilots to calculate their position. Juan Niño in the *Niña* reckoned that they were 1,320 miles west of the Canaries, Cristóbal Sarmiento in the *Pinta* with his chant of 'Santa María' believed they were 1,260 miles away, while Sancho Ruíz on the *Santa María* itself said they were 1,200 miles on. The next day, with more terns and smaller birds flying over the ships, Colón ordered a course shift to the west-north-west. Rafts of thick weed stretched to the north, and the seamen, ever apprehensive, feared that the weed would engulf them. But with so many birds seen, land could not be far away.

For several days more the sea was calm and the winds light to variable. Progress was modest, just forty to sixty miles per day. The rafts of weed were thick and worrying. Later in the day of the 23rd, with no wind, the sea became rough – an unusual phenomenon. The restlessness of the crews, increasing by the day, only abated when the wind picked up strongly from the west-north-west.

That night and the next day on the *Santa María* the agitation of the crew grew. Seamen huddled in groups, their muted voices carrying across the open deck.

'…It's madness to go on…'

'…The wind and currents are taking us for ever westwards. We'll never get home…'

'…That's right. We'll never see our families again…'

'…The man's a foreigner, he can't be trusted…'

'…He's just in it to further his own ambition…'

'…Yes, and to line his own pocket…'

'…I say we throw him overboard…!'

'…I say "aye" to that. Martín will see us home safely…'

'…Aye, that he will…'

And so it continued.

But not all the men on the ship were from Palos. Indeed, four were criminals granted an amnesty to participate in the voyage. They owed Colón their freedom. They told the Admiral of the hostile and ugly mood of the crew. They warned him that one or two of the militants were planning to push him overboard that night while he was taking a star fix on the Pole Star from the poop deck.

V: To Catch a Thief

Tuesday, September 25th 1492

Cristóbal Colón took his leave of Juan de la Costa, the *Santa María*'s owner and master, and Pedro Niño, the pilot, and retired early to his cabin. He wanted to be left alone. Every venture, every project had its ups and downs. This was no exception. The Admiral had felt angry and frustrated by the delays which occurred in the Canaries but now for the first time he felt down, depressed: no sign of land, the crew rebellious and his principal lieutenant questioning his every decision. He sat at his small table lit by a lantern and re-examined his charts. He knew in his heart that land must lie much further to the west of their present position, but the expectation of his officers and crew were becoming too high.

He sighed wearily, the burden of responsibility weighing on him, and opened his ship's log, his *diario* of the journey. But it was more than a detailed daily record of the voyage which recorded the ship's position, bearing, distance sailed each day, the state of the sea, current, wind and sails; indeed everything pertaining to the ship's progress across the ocean. No, it was also a letter to the King of Spain, whom he had promised faithfully to inform of all aspects of the journey. But what could he say about Martín Pinzón? If he were to be too critical of his actions and attitudes, the Admiral's own judgement would be questioned as to why he chose the Palos man in the first place as his second-in-command. Yet was the selection of Pinzón wholly his? No, the Queen and King themselves promoted the cause of Pinzón and the seamen of Palos as the best for the planned voyage of discovery. Moreover, Palos fell within the jurisdiction of his greatest supporter, the Duke of Medina Sidonia, who was more than keen to direct Colón to the seafaring town on the banks of the Rio Tinto. So what could he say about Martín Pinzón? What could he write in his log?

The truth about the men of Palos lay much deeper than simply the case of Cristóbal Colón arriving there in May that year and seeking the assistance of the Pinzón brothers, which he had to admit was proffered generously. But the role of the Monarchy in this saga had not been wholly without blemish. The Crown had actively encouraged boats from Palos and Moguer to fish and trade around the African coast so as to combat the Portuguese, who considered these fishing grounds their own. Never slow to protest, the Portuguese had complained that the fishermen from Palos were not respecting the treaty, and after the Palos men attacked the Isle of Antonio Nolli in 1486, the Spanish Crown had imposed a sanction on Palos. This required the town of three thousand inhabitants to provide two caravels fully provisioned at the town's own cost for two months. While Cristóbal Colón could not have found more suitable ships or experienced blue-water seamen anywhere else in Spain, it was nevertheless true that by his going there the Crown had saved itself two-thirds of the cost of the voyage. Moreover, it had compromised the men of Palos in a royal affair. They had felt insulted and humiliated with the signing of a peace treaty, which ceded to Portugal the colonial zone of Africa for which they had fought and which was vital to the economy of their community.

Colón chewed over all this as he pondered what to write. Should he express in his log his growing distrust of Martín Pinzón and the crews he had hand-picked for the three ships? It was evident to him that the *Pinta*'s captain wished to claim the glory for the voyage for himself. He was forever running his ship ahead of the *Santa María* so as to be the first to sight land, fully aware that King Fernando had offered an annuity of ten thousand maravedís to the first person to spot land. Yet despite Pinzón's independence, the Admiral knew that Pinzón needed him in order to return home safely. He dipped his pen in the ink pot. Discretion dictated caution. He would keep his inner thoughts to himself, at least for the while.

Finally he closed his ship's log for the day. Then he called his servant, Diego de Salcedo, to his cabin, washed and put on his night clothes. Together they knelt down and said their prayers. Both were devout. The Admiral climbed into his narrow bunk against the starboard side of the boat behind a dark red velvet curtain. Dutifully, Diego tidied the Admiral's desk and replaced the *diario* in an oiled leather folder. He placed the Admiral's quadrant, dividers and sandglass in their respective positions on the table. He placed the compass sitting in its square box against the port side so that it would not get knocked over, blew out the candle in the lantern and himself turned in on the floor next to his master.

The next day was bright and the sea calm all morning. Martín Pinzón was convinced they were close to land. Using a line strung between the ships, he returned the charts which Colón had passed him three days earlier with the position of islands marked. At sunset, Pinzón, standing at the stern of the *Pinta*, shouted across to Colón in great joy that he had sighted land and claimed the King's reward. When the Admiral heard this he fell on his knees and gave thanks to God. Martín Pinzón called his crew to the mainmast and together they said, '*Gloria in excelsis Deo.*' The Admiral followed suit with his officers and crew. The crew of the *Niña* climbed the rigging on the fore and mainmasts, all claiming that they could see land. The Admiral believed it lay seventy-five miles to the south-west.[8] The sea was calm and smooth and many of the men from the ships went swimming, joyful that their goal was in sight.

After sunrise on the next morning, the 26th, Colón realised that what they

---

[8] Only an island more than 2,500 feet high would have been visible from the masthead of the *Pinta* at this distance.

had thought was land was nothing more than storm clouds on the horizon. The ships returned to their original westerly course. With the sea calm and 'like a river', and the air sweet and balmy, they made over ninety miles both day and night.

Although not having yet earned the crew's respect and therefore still largely ignored, Pedro Tegero was well integrated in the *Pinta*'s day-to-day routine; chanting the turning of the sandglass and the ends of the watches, calling the men to eat, scrubbing and watering the deck, and helping keep the boat shipshape; but most pleasurable for him was helping Cristóbal García Sarmiento, the pilot, navigate the ship and determine its speed through the water.

It was mid-morning on the 26th, with the midday meal in the offing. The sun was shining in a clear blue sky and the sea calm. The ship's foresail, mainsail, slanted mizzen and spritsail were all billowing in a light breeze and carrying the ship steadily westwards. Most of the crew were able to relax, the disappointment of the previous evening behind them. With cards and dice prohibited on board because of the arguments they could cause, some of the more agile seamen and cabin boys were leaping for the last apple suspended from the yardarm. Others lay on their stomachs, elbows on the deck, arm-wrestling boisterously. Others sat around chatting. Two men were up to no good in the deep shadow below the foredeck, their trousers around their ankles. One or two picked lice from their heads and bodies. Some hung their clothes overboard on ropes to wash in the sea. Martín Pinzón, always one eye on the distant horizon, looked down from the quarterdeck at the scene of tranquillity. Um, how long will it last? he wondered.

'Pedro, I promised to tell you how we take bearings and set a course,' said the pilot. They were both standing on the port side against the afterdeck.

'Are you familiar with the stars, Pedro?'

'Yes, Cristóbal.' Unlike the other cabin boys, he was now on first-name terms with the pilot. 'I can find the Pole Star from the Plough and know most of the constellations in the sky, like Auriga, Gemini and Orion and the triangle of bright stars of Vega, Altair and Deneb, and I can find...'

'Good heavens, Pedro, where did you learn all this?' asked the pilot, dumbfounded.

Not for the first time while on board, Pedro was unsure what to say.

'I learnt about the heavens from an Arab captain,' he stammered.

'When was that?' asked the pilot.

'A long time ago, Cristóbal,' was Pedro's guarded reply.

'So you've been to sea before?' probed the pilot.

'Yes, but on a smaller ship than this.' It was as much as Pedro wanted to say. The events of all those years ago were still painful to recall.

'Well, let's see,' pondered Sarmiento. 'Determining time is difficult at sea. It doesn't matter much on land where we have church and city bells ringing on the quarter, but at sea timekeeping is very important.'

'That's why we have the sandglasses?'

'Of course, and that's why it's so important to turn them on the half-hour. Fortunately at this time of year around the autumn equinox the rising and setting of the sun gives us a good twelve-hour fix and we can judge midday to within a quarter to half an hour at the most.'

'What about at night?'

'We still have the sandglass, of course, but we then have the pointer stars of the Plough.'

'The two at the left?'

'Yes, these swing around during the night with the rest of the stars in the heavens, and if you keep a good watch on them you can judge your time quite well. They move in the opposite direction to the shadow of a sundial by a quarter of a revolution in six hours.'

'And the quadrant tells us our latitude?'

'Yes, I'll show you how to use it one night. But by measuring the angle of the Pole Star above the horizon at dusk or dawn, when it's sufficiently light to see the horizon, we can determine our latitude.'

'What about our…?' Pedro's question about taking bearings was cut off by a scream.

He and the pilot looked around as Fernando Médel, the cabin boy, crashed to the deck from the rigging. He lay in a heap, semi-conscious, his left arm bent back on itself under his body. Pedro ran across the deck to him. He was there in an instant. The surgeon, Maestre Diego, somewhat worse for wear after quaffing his midday quota of wine too speedily on a warm day, staggered across the deck and fell over.

Pedro knelt by his adversary's side and straightened him out on the deck. He saw immediately that his left arm was broken. Pedro removed his own shirt and as gently as he could he laid the boy's arm on it by his side. Taking advantage of the boy's semi-conscious state he straightened out the broken arm, manipulating the broken bones with his fingers so that they were properly aligned. The pilot and the captain's brother and ship's master looked on, as did many of the crew, including Francisco Médel, Fernando's younger brother, who was surprisingly subdued.

'Cristóbal,' said Pedro to the pilot, as much an order as a request. 'Please fetch me two short lengths of wood and some cloth.'

The pilot descended rapidly into the hold, searched around amongst the carpenter's tools and equipment and returned post-haste.

'Your shirt man, quickly,' he said to the inebriated surgeon. If he could not do his duty and help the injured boy, he could donate his shirt. He tore off a sleeve, tore it into strips and passed these and the splints to Pedro.

'Please hold these to each side of his arm,' he said to the pilot, 'and I'll bind it up.'

It all took only a few minutes. The pilot tore up the surgeon's other sleeve and made a sling. By the time Fernando Médel came too, his arm had been set and he was sitting up against the quarterdeck. The steward, García Hernández, handed him a flask of brandy from his locked cupboard below decks to lessen the shock and deaden the pain.

'My word,' asked a flabbergasted Cristóbal Sarmiento when those watching had dispersed. 'Where did you learn to do that, Pedro?'

'My father was a renowned apothecary and I learnt much about medicines and healing from him.'

'Was, Pedro?'

'Yes, he's dead. He died four years ago,' was all the youngster was willing to say.

But if Pedro's star seemed to be in the ascendancy, it was soon to be occluded by other events.

An hour later, as the crew relaxed with half their daily quota of wine after eating their midday meal, they were summoned to the mainmast by the bo'sun, Juan Quintero.

'Sancho de Rama's leather purse with his wages for the journey is missing from his kitbag,' he shouted angrily. 'All you men are to bring your belongings on deck this minute to be searched, and woe betide whoever has stolen it.'

He pulled the knotted ends of his lash through his hands.

'And officers will accompany you to see you don't get up to any funny business.'

Muttering angrily, the seamen and cabin boys trooped below to collect their belongings, followed by the master, pilot, the two owners of the *Pinta* and the steward.

VI: Mutiny and Landfall

The wages for the officers and crew for the voyage were not insubstantial. At the insistence of the King they had been specified in the *Capitulaciones* to have regard to the uncertainties and risks inherent in a voyage into the unknown. For the seamen the wages comprised four monthly instalments paid in advance to provide security to their wives and families in the event that they failed to return. Paid in gold *doblas*, they were equivalent to 1,000 maravedís per month, with 700 maravedís per month being the worth of the cabin boys. The officers received 2,000 maravedís, while Martín Pinzón received twice this amount. For the cabin boys in particular the wages were unusually generous and were the same as for shore-based skilled craftsmen such as carpenters, shipwrights and builders. The crew received other benefits from the journey. Food and drink were included as part of their salary, and each crewman was entitled to a share of the booty or cargo returned home.

Like many of the seamen, Sancho de Rama had left three-quarters of his four months' allowance with his wife for herself and their three children, but the remainder, 1,000 maravedís in gold coin, had stayed untouched in his tie-up leather purse placed safely in a pocket deep inside his canvas kitbag.

Angry at having their midday meal break interrupted and their honesty questioned, the crew returned on deck with their belongings. Most had canvas kitbags – grey, oily and soiled from years of wear – while others had their belongings tied up in sheets. Pedro retrieved his kitbag from beneath the foredeck. His thoughts were still on the Médel boy's broken arm, wondering if he had bound the splints too tightly. Despite three lengthy immersions in the sea his holder was still discoloured from its soaking in the bilge. One at a time the crew poured their motley belongings onto the deck to be searched by Juan Quintero or Juan Reynal, the master-at-arms. Most of them stood around indifferently to the proceedings, taking it to be one of those tiresome chores imposed on them by overzealous officers. Fernando Médel still sat against the foredeck, a bit woozy from the brandy, while his brother, Francisco, proffered both his and his brother's bags to the bo'sun and then sloped back stiffly to his brother's side. One at a time the seamen bundled their clothes, shoes, purses, crucifixes and good luck charms back into their bags. Pedro's was next.

'What's this?' exclaimed the master-at-arms, feeling something leathery at the bottom of the boy's bag.

'So *you* stole it, did you?' he said, loudly enough for all to hear, holding Sancho de Rama's purse up for all to see. Sancho grabbed it and tipped out the coins onto the deck. He counted it out.

'Is it all there, Sancho?' asked the bo'sun.

'Yes, it seems to be,' he replied, swinging a fist at Pedro, who was also on his knees, but missing.

'You good-for-nothing thief!' bawled the ship's carpenter, his face red with fury and eyes narrowed. 'I'll see your guts spill out over the deck for this. You mark my words.'

'Oh, no you won't, Sancho. This is a matter for the captain. He'll decide what's to be done with this boy. Thieving is serious business, make no mistake, and he'll get his just rewards.'

'But I didn't take Sancho's purse!' protested Pedro. 'What would I want with it on board this ship? Someone must have planted it in my bag.'

He scanned the deck. The Médel boys were not to be seen.

'The captain will be the judge of that. Take him below, Juan,' ordered the bo'sun. 'Put him in the leg irons at the bows.'

Pedro was marched, protesting, down the steps into the near-darkness below. Half a dozen hands cuffed him hard on the head as he was pushed past the crew. He was undoubtedly safer below deck. On deck, backs would have been turned and he would have been pitched into the sea.

It was midway through the night watch, after the third turn of the sandglass:

'Tres va pasada
y en la cuatro muele;
más molerá
si mi Dios querrá,
a mi Dios pidamos
que bien viaje hagamos;
y a la que es Madre de Dios y abogada nuestra,
que nos libre de agua, bomba y tormenta.
!Ah, de proa, alerta, buena guardia!'

Thus chanted Pedro de Arcos, the cabin boy. And from the bows came the 'All's well' reply of the lookout, Alvaro Pérez: *!Alerta!*

All was quiet as the *Pinta* rolled gently across the flat ocean, only the noise of the gently flapping sails, the sea gurgling under the bows, the snores of the seamen and the rustle of their straw-filled palliasses carried across the sea. The *Niña* sailed smoothly four hundred yards away on the port quarter with the *Santa María* a mile behind.

In bare feet, Rodrigo de Triana tiptoed across the deck and down into the hold, feeling his way through the darkness, careful not to trip over the legs of those seamen sleeping there. He made his way to Pedro who was lying awkwardly against a sack. A chain passed through the leg irons clamped to his ankles to rings on the side of the ship. Rodrigo put his finger on Pedro's lips to warn him not to speak. He was taking a fearful risk in visiting Pedro. If he were to be caught he would be flogged, or worse, drawn through the sea from the stern on a rope bound around his wrists. Rodrigo passed Pedro a ship's biscuit, some lumps of bully beef and a beaker of mixed water and wine. He would need the latter to soften the rock-hard and indigestible biscuit. The seaman squeezed Pedro's shoulder for a few moments, muttered some words of encouragement into his ear, and disappeared as silently as he had come.

Sunday, September 30th saw the ships push through a lot more weed. The Admiral believed land must be close. That night the compass declined to the north-west of the Pole Star but at dawn it pointed true north. Not for the first time Colón explained to his pilots that the Pole Star did not lie at the true celestial pole but some degrees away and rotated around the true pole as the night progressed, as did all the other stars in the heavens.[9] But his pilots failed to comprehend this and preferred to find fault with the compass or chose to believe in some supernatural cause. The following morning, the first of October and almost two months after they had left Spain, it rained very hard, the first proper rain they had received. They made seventy-five miles more. Pedro Niño, the pilot of the *Santa María*, calculated they were 1,734 nautical miles west of the Canaries, similar to the Admiral's declared figure of 1,752, although his personal figure which he had not revealed was over 2,120 miles.

That evening after prayers and the crew's supper on the *Pinta*, Pedro was brought before Martín Pinzón. He had remained in semi-darkness in irons for five days and had to squint as he encountered the muted evening light. The captain was seated at a table on the main deck in the lea of the open deckhouse; there was insufficient height for Pedro to stand before him inside the deckhouse and the quarterdeck above was too breezy. Martín's brother Francisco, the ship's master, sat alongside him. The bo'sun stood watch to keep the crew away.

'So, Tegero,' Pinzón began, 'we meet again. This time on a serious charge of theft. You're clearly a troublemaker. Firstly you pick a fight with Fernando Médel, in which if you hadn't been forcibly restrained by Juan Verde you would undoubtedly have done him a lot more harm than you did. Then you wilfully soak my feet as I walked the deck, ruining my buckled shoes. And now, it seems, you've been secretly rummaging through my seamen's possessions and stole Sancho de Rama's money purse from the inside pocket of his kitbag. The master-at-arms tells me that you have old scars on your back from a previous flogging. This tells me plainly enough that you've been in trouble before. What have you to say?'

'Sir,' replied Pedro, 'I have not been rummaging through the crew's belongings, nor did I steal Sancho de Rama's money. What would I do with his money on board this ship? Why is none of his money missing from his purse? As I've explained before, neither did I attack Fernando. It was he and Juan Verde who attacked me while I was on the beach at Las Palmas.'

---

[9] In Colón's time the Pole Star had a declination of 3½° and lay well away from the celestial north pole, equal to some seven moon diameters, compared now with less than 1° or two moon's diameters.

'So what was the money doing in your kitbag?'

'I don't know, sir. I didn't know it was there. Someone must have put it there.'

'Why should anybody do that?' reproached Martín Pinzón caustically. 'I've seen you around the boat, aloof, always looking around, not talking to the seamen or other cabin boys…'

'But, sir,' replied Pedro, almost breaking down, his voice shrill, 'it is they who won't talk to me! I do all that is asked of me to the best of my ability on this ship, and yet I'm made to feel like an outsider, like a criminal.'

'And so you are, Tegero. I don't know what you're doing on this boat or where you come from, but there's no doubt in my mind that you stole this money – and you will pay for it.'

'Martín,' interrupted his brother, who up until that time had remained silent. 'Cristóbal Sarmiento wants to say something on the boy's behalf.'

'Ask him to step forward then,' instructed the captain.

The pilot was ushered from the deckhouse. He had overheard much of the hearing.

'Well, pilot, what is it you want to say?'

'Martín. I've got to know young Pedro pretty well in the last couple of weeks and I find him a hard-working, likeable and conscientious young man, quick and eager to learn. Did you know that he can read and write Latin as well as Castilian, and is familiar with Hebrew and Arabic? You can tell from the way he speaks that he's not like the other members of the crew here. He's deeper, more studious. I don't believe for one minute that he stole Sancho's purse.'

'I'm grateful to you for your comments, Cristóbal, but nothing you've said convinces me that the boy is innocent. I know a mischief-maker when I see one.'

'Bo'sun,' he instructed without any more ado. 'Return him to the irons. I'll spare him a lashing, but tomorrow at noon you will see that he suffers three *tratos de cuerda* from the yardarm. That should teach him a lesson. Have all the crew present.'

The punishment of *tratos de cuerda* hoisted the miscreant from the deck by his wrists with a rope passed over the yardarm, and then let him fall violently while tensing the rope so that his feet would not touch the deck.

'But,' protested his brother. 'Three *tratos*? That could cripple him for life! The boy's only eighteen.'

'In that case he'll have a lifetime to get over it,' Martín Pinzón commented callously. 'That's my judgement. I'll hear no more.'

He got up from the table, climbed the six steps up onto the quarterdeck and went to the stern rail. Pedro was led back down to the hold and the irons were replaced. He knew exactly the nature of the punishment he was to receive.

With only a quart of stale water by his side in the darkness and the malicious jibes of the seamen rolling out their mattresses for the night, warning him of the pain that he would endure on the morrow, Pedro slept not a wink that night. Etched on his mind for ever were the four long winter months, five years before, when he had been incarcerated in the dungeons of the Spanish Inquisition, and his nightmarish interrogation at the hands of the Inquisitor General of Castile, the notorious Tomás de Torquemada. Only the intervention of Don Gonzalo Fernández of Córdoba while he dangled from the *Strappato* saved him from having dislocated shoulders and possibly permanent disablement. The *tratos de cuerda* was essentially the same punishment.

The ships held course to the west and made one hundred and seventy miles both day and night. Colón declared only ninety. The sea continued to be smooth and favourable and much seaweed was encountered.

At midday the next day on the second turn of the sandglass during the second watch the bo'sun's whistle called the crew to the main deck. Pedro was led up onto the deck. Crews were generally subdued on these occasions, invariably taking the side with the victim, with each man thinking, 'There for the grace of God go I...' But there was some muttering and sniggering. How would the boy cope with this ordeal?

Cristóbal Colón stood on the poop deck of the *Santa María* sailing close by, and seeing the commotion on the *Pinta* and the assembled crew, shouted across to Martín Pinzón. 'What's ado, Martín?'

'A cabin boy is to be punished with three *tratos de cuerda* for stealing money from the kitbag of one of my sailors.'

'That's a bit harsh, isn't it?' questioned the Admiral. 'What's the boy's name?'

'Tegero. Pedro Tegero,' replied the *Pinta*'s captain. 'He's got to be taught a lesson. This isn't the first thing he's done on this ship.'

'Well, if you say so, Martín,' replied the Admiral. 'I just hope you know what you're doing. The *tratos de cuerda* is a terrible punishment for a youngster.'

'One's got to have discipline on one's ship, Cristóbal,' replied Pinzón. 'Otherwise one's asking for trouble. You mark my words.'

The *Santa María* drifted away. Not wanting to be party to the punishment, the Admiral turned his back on the *Pinta*, although many of his crew watched from the starboard side.

Pedro was led to the yardarm, his shirt removed and his wrists tied tightly with rough hemp rope. The rope was thrown up to Juan Verde de Triana, who was straddling the yardarm high above the deck. He passed the rope through a pulley suspended from the spar and dropped the loose end to the deck. All the officers lined the rail of the quarterdeck, including the pilot, Cristóbal Sarmiento. He was gripping the rail so hard his knuckles were white. Three sailors took the rope, waiting for the instruction from the captain to proceed with the punishment and hoist Pedro from the deck. A deathly silence had descended over the ship.

Suddenly, Fernando Médel, his arm still in a sling, broke ranks and ran into the centre of the main deck.

'*Stop, stop!*' he cried. 'It wasn't Pedro who did it. It was me and Francisco and Juan Verde. We stole Sancho's purse and put it in Pedro's holdall so that he'd get the blame.'

There was silence for a few seconds and then an uproar.

'Verde, get down here at once!' shouted Martín Pinzón to the man on the yardarm. Bo'sun, untie Tegero and disperse the crew!'

Rodrigo de Triana and Cristóbal Sarmiento ran to Pedro to help the bo'sun free him from the rope around his wrists and to console him. Juan Quintero himself was full of remorse and sympathy and immediately instructed the steward to bring forward a quart of wine and some food. The youngster had eaten nothing except what Rodrigo had illicitly given him during the night. Sancho de Rama himself went to Pedro and offered his sympathy.

The captain, red-faced with embarrassment and fury, shouted to the Médel boys and Juan Verde to attend him and his brother immediately. The Médel boys showed genuine remorse, but the seaman showed none, unconcerned that an innocent member of the crew could have been punished for something he had not done.

'All of you deserve the punishment which Tegero was to suffer,' declared Martín Pinzón. But he was mindful of the fact that the father of the Médel boys worked in his shipyard as a sawyer standing in or above a saw pit, cutting tree trunks into planks using an enormous two-man, coarse-toothed saw. The man was a veritable giant and towered over him. His temper matched his massive arms and shoulders. Some prudence was merited.

'Bo'sun. Three dozen lashes for Juan Verde now. Then confine him below and put him in irons for seven days on a diet of biscuit and water.'

'Master-at-arms!' he called, 'see that these Médel boys are securely tied to the foremast for thirty-six hours. And nothing but biscuit and water. Do you understand? But first they can witness the punishment of their partner in crime. Maybe the sight of his bleeding back will teach them a lesson.'

Wednesday, October 3rd saw them make over one hundred and forty miles with a lot more weed evident. Cristóbal Colón calculated that the three ships had journeyed almost two thousand four hundred miles. For three more days they continued in calm seas and in pleasant weather, making four hundred and sixty miles, although the Admiral declared less. On the 6th, Martín Pinzón shouted across to the Admiral to try and persuade him to steer to the south-west by west to reach the island of Japan, which was marked on Colón's charts, but the latter insisted on maintaining a westerly course for the mainland of China. The murmurings of the crew on the *Santa María* resurfaced, with the men becoming more and more agitated. They were being carried relentlessly westwards by wind and currents against which they knew they could never return.

'…It is madness to continue…'

'…We'll never return to Spain…'

'...Why doesn't he listen to the advice of Martín Pinzón...?'

'...And make for Japan. Martín's sailed these waters and discovered new lands to the west with a mighty river...'

'...Why should we continue to listen to this foreigner...?'

'...I say throw him overboard and make Martín the Admiral...'

The mutterings became more vocal and the voices louder. The seamen started to form into some six groups around the boat, each egged on by a ringleader, fomenting dissent, stirring up the remainder. Fists were raised and threats directed at the Admiral and his officers. Bartolomé García, the bo'sun, and Diego de Arana, the *Santa María*'s master-at-arms, did their best to quell the growing mutiny, but to no avail. They were Palos men and deep down had some sympathy with the support being expressed for the *Pinta*'s captain. The position of Cristóbal Colón was becoming more and more precarious by the minute. The rumpus on the *Santa María* carried across the water to the *Pinta*, sailing a hundred yards away.

'What's afoot, Cristóbal?' shouted Pinzón across to the Admiral. He could tell by the tone of the voices on the Admiral's ship that a serious disturbance was brewing. Indeed, his own crew, his own Palos men, were starting to join the rebellion.

'The crew are mutinying, Martín!' shouted Colón above the noise of the rebellion. 'They say they want me to take your advice and turn three points to the south to make for Japan.'

'You must stand firm, Cristóbal. You've made your decision and you must stand by it. I told you before that you must maintain discipline on board.'

'You mean flog the six ringleaders?'

'No!' he shouted as loudly as he possibly could so that all could hear him on the three ships. 'Don't waste your time with that. Be rid of them. Throw the mutineers into the sea. Do it now. I'll back you if questions are asked when we return, have no fear.'

With Pinzón's strong words of advice there was a sudden quietening on the *Santa María* and *Pinta*. Heads down and muttering to themselves, the groups of crewmen dispersed and shuffled back to their posts. But defiantly two or three of the ringleaders held their ground. Cristóbal Colón, against his better judgement, and with the whole of his long-planned voyage of discovery at risk, foolishly agreed to their demands. If no land were sighted in eight days they would turn back.

All the crew remained on tenterhooks, expecting to discover land whenever they raised their eyes to the horizon. Every distant cloud, every mat of weed, every flock of birds and every change in the colour or state of the sea indicated that land was not far away.

The next morning, on the Sunday, land was spotted once again on the horizon, but yet again it proved to be a false alarm. Colón ordered that henceforth the three ships should rendezvous at sunrise and sunset when conditions were clearest. He told the captains to warn all their crews that the

10,000 maravedís annuity offered by the Catholic Sovereigns would be forfeited by any officer or crew member who falsely claimed to see land, even if afterwards he did actually then sight it.

That morning the *Niña*, being the swiftest of the three ships, ran ahead. It fired a cannon and hoisted a flag to indicate that land had been seen. Alas again, by sunset, no land was seen. But the ships maintained their west-south-west bearing and made eighty-four miles by day and night.

For the next three days Colón took the ships to the west-south-west and south-west making speedy progress across a placid sea – 'like the river at Sevilla' he wrote again. Some eight hundred leagues had been traversed since the mutiny and no land had been sighted. Once again the agitators got to work on the crew of the *Santa María*, cursing the Admiral as a foreign ignoramus out for his own glory, tricking them with his false promises of wealth and fame. Once again Cristóbal Colón needed Martín Pinzón's help to quell the uprising, with dire threats of stringing up the mutineers over the sea from the main yardarm or throwing them in the sea behind the ship.

It worked, but the *Santa María*'s crew had not forgotten the Admiral's promise to them four days before. If land were not sighted in that time the ships would return. But what would Colón say to the King? How would he excuse his return to Spain when possibly he was within just days of making a landfall? Indeed, would he survive the journey home with a hostile crew who would need to justify their turning back? The Admiral, fretful and withdrawn in his cabin, or looking out to sea from the afterdeck, brooded. Wisely, he avoided putting his thoughts on paper. One day the King would read his *diario*, success or no.

The day after this second insurrection, on Thursday, October 11th, the ships passed through a mat of fresh green weed, with reeds and sticks, one of which was carved. They sailed eighty-one miles from sunset the previous day to sunset this day. The officers and crew were all certain now that land was not far away.

Vespers that evening, said on each ship, had a special solemnity. Even the most recalcitrant members of the crews joined in the prayers. On the *Santa María* it was led as always by her master, Juan de la Costa, praying that new lands would be found and a landfall made:

'*Salve, digamos*
que buen viaje hagamos.
Salve, diremos
que buen viaje haremos.
Mostremos tierras nuevas en su Nombre.
Rueguemos a nuestro Señor Jesucristo nos dé una recalada.'

In the middle of the fourth watch that evening, around 10 p.m., the Admiral said he saw a light to the west. The moon was in its third quarter and rose in the east shortly after midnight. Pedro Gutiérrez and Rodrigo Sanchez were keeping a lookout on the principal ship. The *Pinta* had sailed ahead as was usual. Pedro Tegero had a rough throat and could barely croak and was on night watch with Rodrigo de Triana. Both were on the foredeck, their eyes peering through the salty spray to the moonlit western and south-western horizons. It was two hours after midnight.

'Look,' croaked Pedro excitedly, pointing westward with his arm.

Rodrigo shielded his eyes with his right hand and followed Pedro's hand. He jumped in the air with joy and ran and hugged the cabin boy.

'*Land ahoy! Land ahoy!*' he shouted for all he was worth.

The *Pinta* fired its cannon. The *Santa María* and *Niña* came up to the *Pinta*. The Admiral was informed that it was Rodrigo de Triana who had first seen land.[10] It lay just six miles to the west. All the sails but the mainsails were hauled in and the ships lay to until the morrow.

After a journey of some 3,200 nautical miles and some thirty-three days from the Canaries in calm seas and propitious winds, Cristóbal Colón had finally made his momentous landfall.[11]

---

[10] Rodrigo did not receive the King's annuity. It seems that Cristóbal Colón claimed this himself as having first seen a light (or a vision) two hours earlier. Years later Rodrigo did receive a reward and the honour for first sighting land.

[11] Colón's dead reckoning was remarkably accurate. His landfall was, in fact, 3,100 nautical miles from the Canaries.

VII: Samana Cay

Friday, October 12th 1492

At dawn the crews saw naked people on the island. At midday, Cristóbal Colón went ashore in the *Santa María*'s longboat, followed by Martín Pinzón, the captain of the *Pinta* and Vicente Pinzón, the captain of the *Niña*. The Admiral unfurled the royal banner. The two brothers raised a flag which displayed a large green cross with 'F' marked on one side and 'I' on the other, the letters denoting King Fernando and Queen Isabel. Above each letter lay their personal crown; that for the kingdom of Aragón over the 'F' and that for the kingdom of Castile over the 'I'. After a prayer of thanksgiving, Colón ordered the two Pinzóns, Rodrigo de Escobedo, the secretary of the fleet, and Rodrigo Sanchez of Segovia, the comptroller of the fleet, to bear witness that he was taking possession of the island in the name of the Sovereigns. Colón recited the required declarations and these were recorded faithfully by Rodrigo de Escobedo. As well as those present with the Admiral, all the ships' companies bore witness to this announcement. To this island Cristóbal Colón gave the name San Salvador.[12]

No sooner had the formalities been concluded than people came down to the beach. All were totally naked. All were young. None appeared over thirty. They were tall and well-built with fine faces, although their appearance was marred by their very broad heads and foreheads. With their light olive skin they were no darker than the people of the Canaries or peasants in the fields of Andalusia. They had straight, coarse hair, worn short over their eyebrows, with a long ponytail at the back. Many of the natives had painted their eyes or noses or faces, while some had painted their whole body black, white or red. They were very friendly. They called themselves the Guanahaní[13] and although they spoke fluently, they were of course not understood by the explorers. Their only weapon was a short wooden spear pointed with a fish tooth.

Colón showed one man his sword but so ignorant were the natives of iron artefacts that the man cut his hand while grasping the blade. The Admiral was overwhelmed by the friendliness and openness of the islanders who, as he expressed to the King in his *diario* that evening, would readily and freely convert to the Holy Faith. He presented some of the natives with sailor's red

---

[12] Watling Island in the Bahamas bears the title *San Salvador* as Colón's first landfall in the New World, but Robert Fuson in his book *The Log of Christopher Columbus* (1987) supports the view of Captain Gustavus Fox, Assistant Secretary to the US Navy in 1861 and endorsed by *National Geographic* in 1985 after extensive research that Samana Cay, 70 miles to the south, was the true landfall of Colón.

[13] The Taíno Indians on Guanahaní belonged to the Arawakan-speaking peoples and had a Neolithic culture, practising sedentary agriculture, fishing and hunting.

caps and some with necklaces of glass beads which they hung around their necks. Many of the natives bore scars on their bodies. By signs they told the Admiral that other people came to their island and took them away. The Admiral told his captains to instruct their crews to take nothing from these people without giving something in exchange, and this they did.

While the six oarsmen of the ship's auxiliaries stretched their legs on the white coral sand, others swam the few hundred yards ashore to join them and celebrate their historic landfall. Pedro was amongst them. The island was small and flat with many bodies of open water. A lagoon lay in the centre. The island was very green with trees extending right down to the beach.

The next morning the natives came paddling out to the ships in dugout canoes, many bearing just one man but some canoes were so large as to carry forty or fifty men. They brought balls of spun cotton, spears and parrots. No other animal life was seen. With much fun and laughter on both sides, the officers, seamen and cabin boys delighted in showing the natives around every nook and cranny of their ships. The natives' innocence and lack of coyness with respect to their nakedness was matched by the embarrassed curiosity of the crew. After over two months on board ship, this grew to excitement and arousal when later on young women and girls swam out to the ships.

Colón found that some natives had pieces of gold hanging from holes in their noses. In what was to became an obsession, he learnt by signs that much gold was to be found by going south. One seaman exchanged three almost worthless small Portuguese coins for some twenty-five pounds of spun cotton.

At daybreak on Sunday morning Colón took his three ships along the coast to the north-north-east. Dozens of canoes followed. He passed many villages whose inhabitants swam out with gifts of water and food, but the ships did not stop. The whole island of San Salvador was surrounded by a reef with deep, clear water inside. Seven islanders were taken on board the *Santa María* so as to act as guides and to return them to Spain so that they might learn Castilian. Three of them were transferred to Martín Pinzón's ship. Hundreds of small islands lay round about. All seemed inhabited. Colón searched for a suitable location to build a fort but none was found since the island was so flat. In the evening they headed for another island fifteen miles away to the south-west, but lay to during the night for fear of running their ships onto a reef. The island turned out to be somewhat further than expected, and with contrary tides they did not arrive there until noon the next day. The island was large, some thirty miles long, with coasts running north-south and east-west. Colón named it Santa María de la Concepción.[14] They lowered the sails and anchored at sunset. During the night one of the natives escaped and swam home.

At dawn on the next day, Tuesday, October 16th, Colón went ashore in the small boat and was met by more natives, again totally naked. After two hours,

---

[14] Now thought to be the coast of Acklins-Crooked islands, not Rum Cay as was thought, and which lies closer to Watling Island.

with no gold evident, the ships sailed on, but as they were leaving a second native from San Salvador jumped into a dugout which had come alongside the *Niña* and escaped. Andres de Huelva and Francisco Niño from the *Niña* tried to catch a second dugout, which outran their ship's boat. Instead they brought back another native they found on the beach who had come to trade a ball of cotton. Colón sent for him and gave the man a red cap, some green glass beads on a string and two hawk's bells which, being of metal, became greatly favoured by the natives. With news that on a large island to the west the people there wore gold on their arms, legs, ears and in their noses, and with the weather threatening and the wind veering, the Admiral ordered the native freed to return to the beach in his canoe.

They had been sailing westwards to this other island for three hours when they came across another native paddling there across the open sea from Santa María de la Concepción. Colón ordered that the man be brought abroad. He had with him a lump of bread and a gourd of water, but also a lump of 'bright red earth' which was kneaded from a powder, as well as some dry leaves which Colón had seen at San Salvador.[15] The native was given bread and honey to eat by the crew. At sunset with the sea calm they hove to and took in their sails just a couple of lombard shot's distance offshore but in a great depth of water. The native they had taken on board was allowed to paddle ashore.

The next morning at first light they moved closer inshore and anchored off a small village. Colón named it Fernandina.[16] The native whom they had taken on board the previous day came from this village and must have given a good account of the voyagers, since many dugouts came to the ships, bringing water and all manner of things. Everyone was given honey when they came aboard as well as a dozen or so glass beads and even eyelets used for lacing shirts. All were worth no more than pennies but were prized by the islanders. With Pedro for the first time being entrusted with an oar on the *Pinta*'s longboat, each of the ships' boats went ashore to fill the ships' water casks.

Like all the other islands which the crews had seen, Fernandina was flat with no mountains. It was very green and fertile with a great variety and abundance of trees which were quite unlike those of Castile. Here and there were small plantations of a tall crop resembling millet. The grain was evidently ground into flour when ripe.[17] The fish were totally different too and of all the colours of the rainbow. The people of this island were like those encountered before and had the same customs and spoke the same language. They went about naked as did the earlier islanders, but some wore a form of tunic made of cotton, while the married women and those over eighteen years of age wore small pieces of cloth at their fronts which scarcely concealed their modesty.

'One of my natives told me,' said Martín Pinzón to the Admiral, 'that

---

[15] The bread was made from maize; the 'bright red earth' was probably dough made from a variety of sweet potato and the dry leaves were tobacco.

[16] Long Island.

[17] The crop was maize and was unknown in Europe.

there's an island nearby which they call Samoet, or something which sounds like that, where we can find a lot of gold.'

'I've heard the same thing, Martín,' replied the Admiral. 'I'm aiming to turn south and head there shortly.'

'Hum. I think we might be better following the coast around to the north, Cristóbal. My native says it'll be easier to navigate around the island in that direction, and we've the advantage of a wind from the south and south-west too.'

'Good idea, Martín. Tell your Cristóbal Sarmiento to steer that course. We and the *Niña* will follow you.'

However, after sailing just six miles from the cape where the ships had been anchored they discovered an excellent harbour wide enough for one hundred ships. Ashore they were met by ten men. While seamen from the three ships filled their water casks in water-filled hollows, Colón and his party were taken to the nearby village. The houses were tall and conical like Moorish tents and possessed chimneys, but no village had more than a dozen or so dwellings. One man was found who had a piece of gold in his nose but he would not relinquish it to the visitors. Cabin boys from the three ships visited the village and looked inside people's homes. The Médel boys and Pedro, who were now friends, reported that the houses were made of thatched palm fronds and that they were very clean inside. They were furnished simply with beds made of nets of cotton.[18] Enchanted by all he had seen on this island and the other islands, but with the weather worsening and the wind blowing from the north-west, the ships turn around and head south-east. It rained very hard from midnight to daylight. Indeed, it had rained every day since their landfall five days earlier.

Not surprisingly, life on board the *Pinta*, as well as the other ships, had changed since their landfall.

'I don't understand it,' commented Pedro to Rodrigo de Triana during an evening watch when they were 'in charge' of the ship, then at anchor.

'All the way here the crew have been worried about being taken further and further from home, or worried about the constant westerly wind, or the weed in the sea, or our not ever finding land. Now that we're here, they seem equally unsettled. Why is that?'

'You know, Pedro, a seaman's life is totally predictable. We spend our lives at sea from the age of twelve or thirteen, raising the yards, unfurling the sails, swabbing and scrubbing the decks, eating the same monotonous food. Although we grumble, we don't really like change. For many of us our whole life is spent on the same ship with the same officers and the same shipmates.'

'That's why the crews are so loyal to the Pinzóns?'

'Yes, of course. And the constant westerlies and all that weed we pushed through, as well as the expectation of seeing land due to all the seabirds we saw, unsettled them.'

---

[18] The first appearance of the hammock.

'But they're not always at sea, Rodrigo. Much of the time they're ashore.'

'Yes, but on shore what do we do!' laughed Rodrigo. 'We return to our wives who nag us all day for being away so long and not giving them our wages. Then after a short spell ashore we have the back-breaking task of loading water and provisions onto the ship for the next voyage.'

'But there must be some pleasures in their lives, some breaks in the routine?'

'Yes, there are. When we get a share of some unexpected booty or when we visit a port of call and can find a noisy tavern with a buxom barmaid!'

But Pedro was right. The landfalls to the islands which they had visited had an unsettling effect on the crew. For a while they adhered to the instruction from the Admiral to deal with the natives honourably and fairly. Mostly, in fact, they did. For the most part the crews were restricted to the ships unless they were fortunate to row the officers ashore in the auxiliaries. The ships were generally anchored well offshore, outside the reefs which surrounded the islands, and only the brave or the rash sought to swim ashore when inquisitiveness, or a sense of adventure, or the lure of the native women made the risk worthwhile.

After the weather cleared on the Thursday the three ships sailed around the island until dark and then anchored. At dawn the next day they raised anchor and split up in search of the island to the east. The *Pinta* went to the east-south-east, the *Niña* to the south-south-east, with the *Santa María* taking the middle course to the south-east. Within three hours land was sighted and before midday the three ships met up at the northern end of a small island. The natives on the *Pinta* confirmed that this was the island of Samoet. Colón christened it Isabela.[19] The island was more beautiful than those they had seen before with the coast surrounded by a sandy beach. It was a little higher with a hill in the centre and fine harbour. The trees and vegetation were luxurious. Colón was convinced that many plants and trees would be found which would be worth a lot in Spain for use as dyes, spices and medicines. So fragrant were the flowers that their smell could be savoured even as the coast was approached. According to the Indians, as now Colón referred to the islanders, there was a village inland where a king ruled all the neighbouring islands and who possessed much gold. However, the Admiral was becoming suspicious that there was no substance to these assertions by the Indians.

The next morning, Saturday, October 20th, the three ships weighed anchor and sailed around the island to the north-east in search of this village but the sea was too shallow to approach it. Rounding a cape to the south-west which the Admiral named Cabo de la Laguna they turned and headed northwards along its western coast. With their shallower draughts, the *Pinta* and *Niña* managed to anchor close inshore, but the *Santa María* had to lie to offshore under a light sail since the sea deepened rapidly away from the coast and lowering the anchor was impossible.

---

[19] Southern Crooked Island.

At mid-morning the next day, it being Sunday, the *Santa María* and the other ships stopped at the Cabo de Isleo[20] and, after eating, the other captains and the boat parties went ashore. Others of the crew swam ashore. The Admiral reminded the men again that nothing was to be touched. But they found the villages deserted, the Indians having fled. The island was green and fertile with great groves of beautiful trees and fruits of a thousand kinds. There were small lakes with thickets at the water's edge. The flocks of coloured parrots were so dense as to darken the sky. Conscious that they could not identify the trees and plants which they encountered, samples of all of them were collected to return home for the King to see. A six-foot serpent[21] was killed and its skin removed to take back to Spain. There were many such serpents and the people ate them. The meat was white and tasted like chicken. They found aloe trees in great profusion.[22] Because this fragrant resinous wood is used for incense, Colón ordered that a thousand pounds of it should be taken to the ships. Two miles inland they came across a village. Again the people had fled, but some men did approach and they were given glass beads and hawks' bells which made them very happy.

It was nearly three weeks since Pedro's ordeal before the mast and the subsequent flogging of Juan Verde for placing the purse belonging to Sancho de Rama in Pedro's kitbag in order to implicate him as the thief. After seven days in irons, Juan Verde was released but under his breath he swore to take vengeance on Pedro whom he blamed for his punishment. Despite the dousing of his bleeding back in sea water, and despite salt being rubbed painfully into the lacerations, his confinement below decks in a fetid atmosphere prevented the wounds from healing and within a short time his back was swollen and purple. Maestre Diego, the ship's surgeon, became the butt of Juan's foul tongue as he tried one remedy after another, but to no avail.

'What do you suggest, Pedro?' he said. 'I've seen what you're doing for Fernando Médel. His arm looks to be healing really well now. I expect you'll be able to remove the bandage soon. I heard that your father was an apothecary...'

'Yes,' replied Pedro enthusiastically. The years had softened his view of his morose and miserable father from whom he had fled in fear after the fatal accident to Marco Arana, his sword master.

'People said that he was one of the finest apothecary for miles around. He didn't believe in leeches and secret potions but in the use of herbs and medicinal plants, and it was my uncle Joshua who supplied him with these from the mountains and forests above our town.'

'That's fascinating, Pedro,' declared the surgeon. 'So can you help with Juan? I know you've no cause to do so after what he's done to you, but...'

---

[20] Cape of the Island, probably on Fortune Island.
[21] An iguana.
[22] But more probably agave, a close relative of the aloe.

'Of course I will,' replied Pedro. 'Why don't we go ashore next time we reach land and see if we can find some suitable plants? I'm sure the Indians who we've got on board will be able to help us.'

And so they did. When they landed on Isabela, Maestre Diego, Pedro and two of the *Pinta*'s Indians from San Salvador, went ashore in the longboat and foraged deep in the thick forest. The Indians showed them several likely plants, but Pedro found the one he wanted when they pointed to a spindly plant with greenish-grey leaves which resembled chamomile. He had suffused its antiseptic healing properties on more than one occasion in the past. Back on board, with the Indians poking the brew with sticks, Pedro heated the feathery leaves in water to extract the goodness from them. When the brew had been concentrated by boiling and then allowed to cool, Maestre bathed Juan's oozing wounds with the fluid. Within days his wounds were dry and the swellings had reduced. From then on Maestre and Pedro made many sorties into the forests to search for medicinal plants, but this did not stop the malicious Juan from vowing to get his own back on the cabin boy.

Still intent on meeting the islands' king, Colón was told by the Indians about another island which they called 'Colba' and which Colón believed to be Japan, and where lay many great ships, as well as about a second island which they called Bohío. This island was much larger. However, the Admiral had already decided to head for the mainland and to the city of Quisay[23] in order to pass Fernando's letter to the Great Khan and to seek a reply from him.

Monday saw the ships remain there all day awaiting the arrival of the king and the gold which he had promised. Many people came to the ships and happily exchanged the pieces of gold they had in their noses for hawks' bells and glass beads. As usual they were all naked, with some painted white, red or black.

They brought spears and balls of spun cotton which they traded with the sailors for pieces of glass or broken cups or clay bowls. While waiting, Martín Pinzón killed another serpent with his sword, and much aloe was collected.

Cristóbal Colón determined it was futile to spend any more time exploring these islands, not least because the winds and currents were so variable that navigation around and between them was difficult, if not hazardous. He wished to set sail for Cuba[24] forthwith, but despite the heavy rain there was no wind and the sea was dead calm.

At midnight on the 24th they did set sail from Isabela for Cuba. The Indians said it lay to the south-west and that much commerce was to be had in gold and spices. From his charts the Admiral surmised that Cuba and Japan were one and the same. They sailed all night in the rain with the *Santa María* under full sail, comprising the mainsail, the bonnet, which lay above the crow's-nest on the mainmast, the foresail, spritsail, mizzen and topsail. Even

---

[23] Hangzhou in China.
[24] Colón's first reference to Cuba, one of the few Indian place names to survive.

the sail of the small boat on the poop deck was set. So they continued until dusk. During the night, unable to anchor and not knowing their position, they lowered all their sails except the foresail, but with rain and threatening weather they made uncertain progress, sailing no more than six miles that night.

The next day their progress was equally erratic but by mid-afternoon they spotted seven or eight islands in line some fifteen miles distant which Colón called the Islas de Arena.[25] Despite being a considerable distance away they anchored in very shallow water. On Saturday, October 27th, they set sail again to the south-south-west to what Colón took to be Japan, making fifty-one miles during the day. Just before sunset they saw land, but it rained so hard that the ships had to beat about all night.

---

[25] Ragged Islands.

VIII: Cuban Landfall

Sunday, October 28th 1492

Pedro, being the cabin boy on watch at daybreak, was standing on the foredeck, his arm around the mast. The island of Colba, or *Cuba* as the Admiral now referred to it in his ship's log, his *diario*, lay just a few miles away. Pedro droned the daybreak chants in a clear voice:

> 'Bendida sea la luz
> y la Santa Veracruz,
> y el Señor del a Verdad
> y la Santa Trinidad;
> bendita sea el alba
> y el Señor que nos la manda;
> bendito sea el día
> y el Señor que nos lo envía.'

Then the master, Francisco Pinzón, from the rail of the *Pinta*'s quarterdeck, recited aloud the Lord's Prayer and *Ave María*. It being Sunday, he continued, asking the Lord for a good day and a good voyage for the captain and crew:

'Dios nos dé buenos días; buen viaje; buen pasaje haga la ñao, señor capitán y maestre y buena compaña, amen; así faza buen viaje, faza; muy buenos días dé Dios a vuestras mercedes, señores de popa y proa.'

The ships approached the coast and entered a beautiful river which was free from dangerous shoals and other obstructions.[26] The water along this coast was very deep and clear right up to the shore. The river mouth itself was twelve fathoms deep and wide enough to beat about in. The ships anchored inside. The land was flat and exceeded in beauty the other lands which they had discovered. The river's margin was choked with trees, beautiful and green and different from those of Spain, each with their own flowers and fruit.[27] There were many birds of all sizes which sang sweetly and many varieties of palm trees. Some were of medium height with large leaves and devoid of bark near the ground.[28] The Indians covered the sides and roofs of their cabins with their fronds, tying them on to the poles which made up the frames of the cabins and securing them in place with strong twine made of strips woven from the dried palm fronds.[29]

The three auxiliaries took Colón and his captains ashore. They approached

---

[26] Bahía de Bariay on the north-east coast of Cuba. Colón's much-lauded landfall was made there.
[27] Mangroves.
[28] There are 80 species of palm in Cuba, the tallest and straightest is the Palma Real.
[29] *Bohíos* – these palm cabins are still a feature of rural Cuba.

two dwellings but the inhabitants had already fled in fear. Inside they found a dog which did not bark,[30] nets made of palm threads, cords, fish hooks made of horn and harpoons made of bone. The cabins also had fire hearths. Nothing was touched by the visitors. The grass around was very high and they found purslane[31] and wild amaranth.[32]

The captains returned to their longboats which they rowed upriver, past the dense mangroves along the water's edge and the tall palm trees behind them. Beyond, in the distance, were high mountains. The Guanahaní had told Colón that there were ten large rivers on this island, which took twenty days to circumnavigate in their canoes.[33] They had told him that gold and pearls were to be found in abundance and that large ships from the Great Khan in China visited this place. From here to the mainland was ten days' journey. Colón named the river and harbour San Salvador.

The next morning the ships weighed anchor and sailed westwards, passing around two big promontories extending to the north-west and east. By vespers two more rivers had been encountered, the latter being very large.[34] With birds of all sizes in the trees, the crickets singing at night, the deep, clear rivers, the mountains in the distance and the cool soft breezes at night, Cristóbal Colón thought the land was paradise. One mountain in the distance had a distinctive mound on the summit while to the south-east, beyond the river were two very rounded hills. The next morning they departed Río de Mares and sailed forty-five miles to the west to another cape.

'My Indians tell me, Cristóbal,' shouted the *Pinta*'s captain to the Admiral, 'that beyond this cape is a river which is only four days' journey to Cuba.'

'Cuba?' questioned Colón.

'Yes, they say that Cuba is a city and lies on the mainland to the north. They tell me that the King of Cuba is at war with the Great Khan, whom they call Cami.'

'Very well, Martín,' replied the Admiral enthusiastically, 'we will approach this river and send a present to the king as well as my letter from the Sovereigns. I'll send Jocamél Rico from my ship. He comes from Genoa and has been on a similar mission in Guinea. I'll also send some of the Indians from Guanahaní. Afterwards they might choose to return home. We must try and go and see the Great Khan at his city in Cathay. I was told before we left Spain that it's a big city.'

That night Colón took a sighting on the Pole Star and found their latitude to be 21° north of the equator.[35]

---

[30] Undoubtedly Colón could identify a dog when he saw one. This reference to barkless dogs has baffled scholars over the years but it is thought that the Guanahaní might have bred a dog which did not bark for use in hunting.

[31] A herb used in salads.

[32] Pigweed or *bledo*, an edible plant native to Cuba.

[33] Derived from the Arawak word *canoa*.

[34] Río de la Luna and Río de Mares.

[35] This was remarkably accurate. The actual latitude at this point is 21° 18'.

On the Thursday, November 1st, one of the Indians from the *Santa María* went ashore to speak to the natives at Río de Mares to assure them that the visitors meant no harm. The river was very deep and the ships could approach close to the river bank. Three miles upstream the water in the river was fresh. Sixteen canoes came to the ships with spun cotton and other small objects. Still no gold was seen, although one Indian had a piece of silver hanging from his nose. By signs the Indians indicated that merchants would arrive to buy objects from the Christians and would bring news of their king, who was four days' journey away. The Indians were naked, as were those before them. They spoke the same language and had the same customs. They were very friendly and indicated that they were at war with the Great Khan, whom they called Cavila. Colón was now certain that they were on the mainland of China, three hundred miles from Zayto[36] and Quinsay. That evening Cristóbal Colón calculated that they had travelled over three thousand four hundred miles from Hierro in the Canaries, and he was certain now, based on his charts, that he had indeed reached the mainland of Asia.

The next day, parties from the ships went upriver in the auxiliaries to explore the forest, which was thick and verdant. As much to stretch their legs as to explore, Pedro Tegero and Maestre Diego, the *Pinta*'s surgeon and apothecary, roamed amongst the trees, eagerly searching out likely herbs. Both were keen to preserve them, and they carried a lined bag in which to collect their specimens. The undergrowth was very thick. Pedro, roaming around on his own, broke off a palm frond, sliced off its enormous leaf with his knife and used the stick to probe around amongst the ground plants, the shade and dampness around trunks of fallen trees offering the most propitious spots. Some distance away through the forest Pedro heard raised Castilian voices and the shrill cries of Indian women, followed by angry shouting of Indian men and a scuffle. Then it went silent. Suddenly, minutes later, running out from between the trees brandishing a knife was Juan Verde.

'Now I've got you, my little sweet!' he whispered breathlessly, aware that others were around. 'There's nobody to protect you this time and nobody will find the slivers of your measly body in this jungle after I've done with you.'

He came forward and lunged at Pedro with his knife. Pedro sidestepped, failing to make contact with him with his own Toledo knife. If only I had my sword with me, he thought to himself. An image flashed through his mind of the loathsome murderer, Zak, in his shabby soldier's tunic, squirming on the ground, his face sliced open by Pedro's sword. The enraged seaman turned and came at Pedro again, this time screaming profanities at the youngster. Again Pedro, moving quickly aside, the other way this time, avoided the sweeping blade. But his foot caught in a tangle of undergrowth and he pitched headlong onto the ground, his knife jarring from his hand.

'Now you're all mine!' leered Juan Verde. 'Lying there all ready for cutting up like a pig in a slaughterhouse!'

---

[36] Zaytun (possibly modern Zhao'an) derived from Marco Polo and was on fifteenth-century charts.

This time he came at Pedro more slowly, more deliberately, his knuckles white around the grip of his knife which he held in his upturned hand. He took one step forward and leapt onto the boy, thrusting his knife at Pedro's chest. With his stick still in his left hand Pedro parried the blow, rolled over on his side and jumped to his feet, picking up his knife as he did so. Juan lay sprawled on his stomach in front of him, his knife embedded deep in a rotten branch which was covered in yellow fungus. Pedro kicked the blade away, half of it remaining in the rotten wood. He stamped the killer in the neck and stood hard on his back, his foot between his shoulder blades, pinning him to the ground.

Running from amongst the trees came the surgeon, followed by two naked Indians, one with his upper body and upper arms painted black and with black stripes across his face. He held a five-foot spear in his hand and looked fearsome. The other Indian Pedro knew well. He was one of the two from the *Pinta* and he called himself Caritao. They quickly guessed what had happened. Pedro released his foot from the seaman's back and he turned over and stood up, looking thoroughly perplexed.

'So you're up to your tricks again, Verde,' declared the ship's surgeon. 'Caught red-handed, I'd say.'

He turned to Pedro and the Indians.

'Why don't we leave him here for the ants and beetles? They'll soon find his tender back to feast on.'

'Grab hold of him,' he said, signalling to the Indians, 'Find some creepers and we'll tie him to one of these rotten tree trunks. That one looks good,' he added, pointing to a fallen palm tree crawling with red termites.

'Oh no, please, Maestre!' pleaded Juan Verde, 'I wouldn't have done him no harm. I just saw him on his own and got carried away. Look. You can see my knife is broken. So I couldn't have done nothing to him anyway.'

It was obvious to everyone why the blade of his knife was broken. Half of it still lay in the branch.

'I promise I'll be good, Maestre, honest. Just give me another chance. I'll do anything this boy wants. But please don't tell the bo'sun or the captain what I done. They'll flay me this time.'

'Well, what do you say, Pedro? It's up to you.'

'Let him be,' he said with magnanimity, 'after all, no harm was done.'

Pedro knew now that he had the measure of this killer. Juan Verde would never threaten him again. If he were to do so, one word from Maestre Diego would, at the very least, see him strung from the yardarm.

That day many canoes came to the ships still anchored near the mouth of the Río de Mares, bringing more balls of spun cotton and the nets they used for sleeping in. Ashore the next day, on Sunday, November 4th, in great excitement, Martín Pinzón brought to the Admiral two pieces of cinnamon, a spice which was greatly prized; he had seen Indians carrying bundles of it. The bo'sun, Juan Quintero, said that they had found cinnamon trees, but on examination the Admiral found this not to be so. Nevertheless, the Indians stated that cinnamon and pepper, samples of which Colón had brought from Castile, could be found in abundance to the south-east of Cuba, as well as much gold and pearls. They also said that close by there were men with one eye and others who had dogs' snouts who, on capturing a man, cut off his genitals, beheaded him and drank his blood.

However, the peoples on Cuba were very gentle, naked and without weapons of any consequence. The lands were very fertile and full of *niames*.[37] They resembled carrots and tasted like chestnuts. The Indians planted beans and a great deal of wild cotton was collected in the mountains at all times of the years.

At dawn the next day, Colón ordered the *Niña* to be beached at the Puerto de Mares, which formed a magnificent harbour at the estuary of the river, so that the hull could be cleaned. The *Pinta* and *Santa María* would follow. For safety reasons, two ships had to remain in service at all times. While the *Niña* was beached, Bartolomé García, her bo'sun, approached the Admiral very excitedly to say he had found mastic, and claimed a reward.[38] Maestre Diego and Rodrígo Sanchez located the tree and brought a little mastic and a piece of the tree for the Admiral to return to the King. Enough existed in the vicinity to harvest fifty tons a year, a priceless cargo for a ship such as the *Niña*. That evening, envoys sent to the Indians, Rodrígo Sánchez and Maestre Diego, returned and reported back to Cristóbal Colón. The Pinzón captains joined him in the Admiral's small cabin on the *Santa María* to hear their story.

'We must have gone thirty-six miles inland to a village of fifty cabins and a thousand inhabitants,' started Rodrigo. 'A great many people lived in one large hut. The villagers received us with great solemnity, as is their custom, and all of them came to touch us and kiss our feet in wonderment, since they thought we'd come from heaven!

'They then carried us on their shoulders,' continued Rodrígo, 'to the biggest building in the village and we were given chairs to sit on which they call *dujos*. They're shaped like a short-legged animal and have a back which folds down. They were very comfortable to sit on. The women as well as the men seated themselves around us, kissing our hands and feet and pleading with us to stay. We showed them the cinnamon and pepper which you gave us to take and they told us by signs that there were many spices like them nearby. However, because we hadn't seen signs of any rich cities we decided to come back to the boat.'

'That's most interesting, Rodrígo. And you brought back three more Indians with you?'

'Yes, Admiral, one of the village elders, his son and one of his men; but more than five hundred would have come if we'd let them.'

---

[37] A variety of sweet potato.
[38] Mastic was a much-prized arromatic, astringent resin exported from Greece and of great commercial value. What Colón discovered was something similar but inferior.

'Did you see anything else of interest, Rodrígo?' asked Martín Pinzón, ignoring his ship's surgeon.

'On the way there, Martín, we met many people going to different villages carrying charred, hollowed-out wood in their hands, and herbs packed inside which they were smoking. We found no village with more than five cabins, and we saw many geese.[39] But the only four-footed animals we saw were these peculiar barkless dogs. We saw an immense amount of cotton, which had been gathered and spun. In one house there must have been over twelve hundred pounds of it.'

'And were they similar people to those we've met here?'

'Yes, Martín, they're all quite light-skinned, and all naked apart from the small piece of cloth the women wear in front of them. They're all very meek and gentle and kind.'

I have to say, Most Serene Princes, he declared in his *diario* that evening, *that if devout religious persons knew the Indian language well, all these people would soon be Christians. Thus I pray to our Lord that your Highnesses will appoint persons of great diligence in order to bring to the Church such great numbers, and that they will convert these peoples just as they have destroyed those who would not confess the Father, Son and Holy Spirit…*

It took several days to finish the cleaning and re-caulking of the three ships. It was hot, dirty and tiring work – beaching the ships, careening them onto one side and then the other, scraping off all the barnacles and growths and repacking the seams with oakum to keep out the water. The *Pinta* was the second ship to be cleaned, but little re-caulking was necessary since it had been done at Las Palmas. Nevertheless, Pedro was assigned the task of helping Juan Pérez, the caulker, by unravelling yards and yards of worn rope to make the fibrous filler. With a blunt-ended steel tool and a mallet, Juan drove the oakum deep into those seams which still needed to be made watertight. As time would show, the cleaning and re-caulking of the *Pinta* and *Niña* was well worth the trouble taken. Without it, the ships might never have returned safely.

With the imminent departure of the flotilla, five youths from the village came aboard. Colón ordered them held so that they could return them to Spain. Later seven women and three children were brought aboard from the village. That night the husband of one of the women and the father of the children came and asked that they might come too. This was agreed. All the Indians then on board were content and evidently must have been related.

Colón had heard of two islands to the east, one called by the Indians Bohío and the other Babeque,[40] and it was to the latter that he headed when they set sail from Río de Mares at dawn on Monday, November 12th. They sailed to the east-by-south along the coast for fifty-four miles to a cape which Colón

---

[39] They were more likely to have been turkeys.
[40] Bohío is Hispaniola and Babeque is the island of Great Inagua off the north-east coast of Cuba.

named Cabo de Cuba.[41] All night they stood off the coast, beating to windward but making little headway. Next day they sailed south-east towards a large gulf between two high headlands and to what appeared to be a separate island across the gulf, making sixty miles all told. For several days Cristóbal Colón and his three ships sailed along the coast, first to the south-east and then back to the west, battling against contrary winds, searching for a safe anchorage in the heavy seas. He found that the offshore reefs ran continuously along this stretch of coast for hundreds of miles, sometimes formed lines of low, tree-covered coral islands, and it was truly hazardous to try and sail between them. Nevertheless, in his *diario* he eulogised to the Sovereigns about the beauty of the land he encountered, the depth of the sea and the rivers and harbours he had found:

Your Highnesses will have to pardon me for repeating myself concerning the beauty and fertility of this land, but I can assure you that I have not told a hundredth part. Some of the mountains appear to reach Heaven[42] and are like points of diamonds; others of great height seem to have a table on the top; the sea is so deep that a ship can approach some of them right up to the base. They are all covered with forests and are without rocks.

On Saturday, October 17th, Colón took the ship's boat and sailed between the islands, observing that the tide was the reverse of Palos, being low when the moon was south-west by south, whereas in Palos it would have been high tide.[43]

For several days the Admiral attempted to sail the three ships to the north-east and east, searching for the island of Babeque. But with contrary winds and rough seas they made little progress, being blown back from whence they had come. Twice the ships found themselves not far from the harbour they'd set out from and to which the Admiral sought eventually to return, named Puerto de Príncipe. Some frustration began to appear with the officers, particularly his second-in-command.

'I thought we were making for the Island of Babeque?' shouted Martín Pinzón across to the Admiral when they anchored at sunset on the 20th.

'We are, Martín, but the winds, tides and currents along this coast are not helping us.'

'But we're going around in circles and spending too much time exploring these small islands,' he added, trying to conceal his frustration and anger over the delay.

'These islands are most interesting, Martín. The King will be most pleased to learn of all we've found and that we've planted crosses everywhere we've been.'

'But the King will be more pleased to learn that we've found gold, and my Indians assure me that there's gold on Babeque.'

---

[41] Punta Lucrecia.

[42] The Sierra del Cristal inland of this point reach 4,040 feet.

[43] An extraordinary piece of correct observation. Some six hours elapse between high and low water. At a longitude of 76°W Puerto de Príncipe lies nearly five hours behind Palos at 7°W.

'They've been saying that ever since we landed at Guanahaní,' retorted Cristóbal Colón.

'That may be so, Cristóbal, but they're so certain this time that I'm inclined to agree with them. I say that we should go there forthwith and find out.'

'We will, we will, after we've...'

The last few words of the Admiral's response were lost in the breeze. Very disgruntled, and kicking wildly at a piece of rope attached to the poop rail, Martín Pinzón stormed down the steps onto the main deck towards the deckhouse.

'Martín!' the Admiral shouted again across the water. 'I've been looking through the crew manifests. Am I right in saying that you've got a cabin boy on board named Pedro Tegero?'

'Yes, Admiral,' replied Martín, still angry, and stirring the pot by referring to Colón by his title. It was a long-standing source of irritation to him. 'The boy's a troublemaker. Why? Do you want him?'

'Wasn't he the boy you were going to subject to three *tratos de cuerda*?'

'Yes, it was, but...'

The *Pinta*'s captain stopped. He was reluctant to finish the sentence and admit that he had erred in sentencing Pedro so hastily.

'Well, Martín. I'd like to see him and talk with him. Would you send him over in your longboat?'

'Most certainly, Admiral,' he replied.

'Bo'sun!' he shouted across the deck to Juan Quintero. 'Take Tegero across to the *Santa María*. Tell him to take his belongings with him. With the weather as uncertain as it is, it may not be possible for him to return immediately. In any case, maybe the Admiral wants to make him an officer on the *Santa María*!'

And maybe, he thought to himself, I've got other plans...

IX: Meeting the Admiral

Tuesday, November 20th 1492

Cristóbal Colón sat behind his desk in his cabin which was situated at the stern of the *Santa María*'s poop deck. He was wearing a simple white blouse with wide sleeves, tight at the wrist, and over that a black woollen doublet with its gashed sleeves picked out in grey and gold. He was wearing a floppy black bonnet on his head. With his sunburnt face tired and drawn, he looked every bit an Admiral weighed down with the dual task of making fantastic discoveries for the King and returning eighty-seven men safely to Spain. The cabin was sparsely furnished but commodious; indeed, it was the only place on the three ships which offered any privacy. He sat facing the cabin door, which lay to his left. On his desk were his trusty navigation instruments. To his side stood his compass box and on his right, against the starboard side, lay his couch behind a red curtain.

Diego de Salcedo, the Admiral's personal servant, showed Pedro into the cabin. Cristóbal Colón lowered his pen, ensuring that he did not leave a blob of ink on his precious *diario*.

'Come in, lad. Offer the boy a chair, Diego, and bring us some wine, if you will.'

Pedro's legs were shaking. He had no idea why he had been summoned to see the Admiral. Was it the affair with Juan Verde in the forest, or even the problems with the Médel boys? Surely all that was forgotten now... Gingerly Pedro sat down, perching himself on the edge of the chair.

'Your name's Pedro Tegero?' the Admiral started.

'Yes sir.'

'The same Pedro Tegero whom Martín Pinzón punished with the *tratos de cuerda*.'

'No sir. As I was about to be hauled up on the yardarm the Médel brothers owned up that it was they and Juan Verde who placed Sancho de Rama's purse in my kitbag in order that I'd get the blame and be punished. Juan Verde received lashes and was placed in irons for a week.'

'So you weren't implicated?'

'No sir, not at all.'

'So why did they pick on you?'

'I don't know, sir. Rodrigo de Triana...'

'The man who spotted Guanahaní first?'

'Yes sir. He and I. Rodrigo said it was because I didn't come from Palos or Moguer.'

'Ha!' laughed the Admiral. 'That figures!'

He paused a while, looking into Pedro's face which was lit by the light from the windows opposite him.

'Pedro, I was looking through the crew manifests the other day and was struck by your name. I'm sure that this is total coincidence but I have a recollection of a lad, apparently your age, with a somewhat similar name – Pedro Togeiro.'

Pedro literally jumped out of his skin. His face must have paled noticeably in the rosy light coming through the stained-glass windows set in the transom.

'Yes,' the Admiral continued, tapping the tips of his fingers together lightly, 'this Pedro Togeiro retrieved my roll of sea charts from the streets of Sevilla last July and saved this voyage. These charts here,' he said, pointing to them on the table. 'If this boy hadn't done this we'd never have set sail.'

'Yes sir, that was me,' answered Pedro quietly.

Cristóbal Colón sat back in his chair dumbfounded.

'Well, well,' was all he could say. He stared into Pedro's face, his face lightening noticeably.

'Pedro, you'll have to explain. I must have made a mistake with your name, but how did you come to be aboard the *Pinta*?'

'Sir, it's a very long story and some of it you may rather not hear. But you are right, I picked up your roll of charts in Sevilla in July. As I entered the city's main gate a rider with a ruddy complexion swept past careering into a donkey laden with straw, and knocking over its elderly owner. As he swept past a leather roll fell from his saddlebag. The rider didn't stop.'

'Ah, that would have been Rodrigo de Escobedo, the Secretary of the Fleet. He's on this ship here and you'll meet him. He was always very impetuous.'

'I undid the leather roll and quickly realised that they were sea charts of distant lands and I immediately took them to the *alcázar*, since I knew they must be important. I asked to see the King or Queen but they were not there...'

'No, they were – and, I assume, still are – in Barcelona...'

'I waited a couple of days and finally obtained an audience with the Duke of Medina Sidonia. He recognised the charts immediately, of course, and told me that you were soon to set sail from Palos de la Frontera on your voyage of discovery across the western ocean. So, I decided that before returning home—'

'Where is your home, Pedro?'

'In Vélez Blanco, sir, in Almería, near the border with Murcia.'

'Yes, I know of it but I've never been there. Please continue, Pedro.'

'I decided that I'd travel to Palos and see your three ships set sail. It would be a truly momentous occasion. Great crowds were already making their way there.'

'But how did you come to be on the *Pinta*?'

'Sir, this is something you may not wish to hear, but I arrived in Palos as you, your officers and crew were leaving St George's church. I saw you there. One youngster broke away and ran down an alleyway from the church, near to where I was standing. I heard a scream and saw the boy fall to the ground bleeding profusely, and a thief trying to steal his purse containing his wages for the voyage. I shouted and the thief ran off, but when I got to the boy he was bleeding badly and clearly dying. Yazíd, my Muslim friend—'

'Who's Yazíd?'

'It's too long a story to explain, sir, but my friend Yazíd arrived from nowhere and persuaded me to join the *Pinta* in the dying boy's place. You see, what happened, was predicted in the last of the riddles of a soothsayer many years ago.'

'That you would join the *Pinta*?'

'That I would reach both the end and the beginning of my journey and that I would see a stork with outstretched wings sitting over a burning cross. Looking out over the estuary that instant I saw the *Pinta* emblazened with the Cross of Santiago on its mainsail lit by the morning sun. There was a stork on the yardarm drying its wings in the morning air. I knew then that the last of the soothsayer's riddles had been fulfilled. So I donned the boy's clothes and ran down to the boat at the water's edge.'

'Amazing, truly amazing!' said the Admiral, trying to untangle the events which Pedro had described. 'So your proper name is Pedro Togeiro?'

'Yes sir, Pedro Togeiro de Tudela.'

'But the name of the cabin boy who died was Pedro Tegero?'

'Yes sir. His name was written on his kitbag. The similarity of our names was part of the soothsayer's prediction and it was why Yazíd persuaded me that I must join the *Pinta*.'

'And you'd never been to sea before?'

'Yes sir, I have. As I explained to Cristóbal García Sarmiento the other week, many years ago I spent time on an small Arab sailing ship…'

'A dhow?'

'Yes sir, a dhow.'

'But how?'

'It's another long story, sir, but when I was eight I was taken by slavers at Aguilas when my mother and I accompanied my father there to collect a retort…'

'A glass retort?'

'My father was an apothecary, sir, and the retort had been sent to Aguilas from another city. I don't know where.'

'So it's you who have been collecting plants and herbs amongst the trees with Maestre Diego?'

'Yes sir, they were the basis of my father's potions and ointments and…'

'Please carry on, Pedro. I'll try and keep up with you!'

'I had just seen my mother grabbed by two black men and carried away screaming. I never saw her again – well, that is…'

'And you were taken aboard this dhow?'

'Yes sir, and for some eighteen months the boat's captain, who was called Ali, traded around the ports of the Mediterranean: Venice, Constantinople, Alexandria and others.'

'Heavens! I've never been to Constantinople!'

'Well sir, I was on an Arab boat.'

'So how did you escape?'

'Ali was a kindly man and I learnt much from him, not least Arabic. It wasn't he who put me on his boat. Eventually he felt sorry for me and released me on the coast of Almería and I returned home.'

'Well, well,' said the Admiral again. He was then silent for a while, trying to pull the loose ends together in Pedro's story.

'It was the Duke of Medina Sidonia,' the Admiral continued. 'He wrote to me before we departed about your returning my charts. He was most impressed by your self-assurance and maturity. But he also said that you wore Queen Isabel's ring, without which he would not have agreed to see you.'

'Yes sir. I gave it to Yazíd to return to my mother...'

'But you said she was dead?'

'Yes sir. I thought so for ten years, and then...'

'How did you come to wear the Queen's ring? Very few people are so honoured.'

'Well you see sir, I saved her and the King from a fire.'

'That wasn't you, was it?' exclaimed the Admiral. 'Surely not! I heard about the fire from Don Gonzalo Fernández of Córdoba.'

'Yes sir, I know Don Gonzalo well. It was he who followed me up the stairs of his mansion outside Granada to where we saw this fire in an upstairs room. We burst into a room and I put the fire out, the curtains were ablaze, and it turned out it was the bedchamber of King Fernando and Queen Isabel who were using Don Gonzalo's house. They were as startled as I was!'

'You said you know Don Gonzalo. When? How?'

'It was Don Gonzalo who rescued me from the torture chamber of the Spanish Inquisition in Jaén.'

'Not that butcher, Diego Rodríguez Lucero, the Inquisitor of Jaén?'

'Yes sir, he and Tomás de Torquemada.'

'Tomás de Torquemada?' You've met that scoundrel?'

'Yes sir. It was he who strung me up on *El Strappato* with my hands bound behind my back, and it was then that Don Gonzalo burst into the chamber and rescued me and took me to the castle at Porcuna. Another minute or so suspended on that hook and my shoulders would have been dislocated and I would have been maimed for the rest of my life. I owe Don Gonzalo a great deal. I love that man, sir, as if he were my own father.'

'Yes, he's a fine man. Someone to whom both the King and Boabdil owe a great deal. But tell me, Pedro... Porcuna... Wasn't that where Boabdil was imprisoned?'

'Yes sir, but several years before. His son Ahmad was interned there and Don Gonzalo was keen that I should teach him Castilian. That's why he took me there.'

'So I presume you got to know his father, the Sultan, Mohammed the Twelfth.'

'Very well indeed, sir. We became close friends, and for all his faults I admire Boabdil. I think he did the best for his people. I accompanied him when he left Granada after its fall to the... I'm sorry, sir, after the Royal Sovereign's glorious entry into the city on January 2nd this year.'

'Yes, Pedro, I was there. It was indeed a great day for Castile.'

'I was there too, sir. The Queen allowed me to ride with her personal guard. It was a great honour...'

'And fully justified by the sounds of it! Well, well... well, well!'

The Admiral was silent for quite a while digesting Pedro's story. Pedro sat there, very still. After a while the Admiral stirred and sat forward in his chair.

'But how did you find yourself in the cells of the Inquisition, Pedro? You'd done nothing to cross their path, surely? When was this?'

'It was when I was fourteen, sir. I had run away from home after two terrible things I'd done. I entered the city of Almería the evening of the earthquake...'

'That was five years ago, wasn't it, in 1487?'

'Yes sir, five years ago this month, almost to the day in fact. I was helping an elderly jeweller to extract his treasure box from the ruins of his shop when I was pounced on by some rough-looking soldiers in uniform. I was imprisoned overnight with other men and the next day flogged. Then I was ridden through the snow-covered mountains behind Granada for several days to a city a long way away.'

'Jaén?'

'Yes sir. It was only later that I was told that I was in the cells of the Spanish Inquisition. And there I stayed through the bitterly cold winter months until I was taken to be examined by the two inquisitors. I'd already heard about Tomás de Torquemada by then from a poor man in a cell next to me, so I was utterly terrified when I recognised him sitting there behind the desk.'

'So would I have been, I assure you, Pedro. I've met the man. He's quite forbidding.'

'You say you did some terrible things which made you run away from home? Are you able to tell me what they were?'

'They are the most shameful things that I have ever done, sir. I still have the most terrible nightmares over them, seeing their faces in the dark, hearing their voices and the screams. You see, I accidentally caused the death of a man on the way back from obtaining my Toledo sword.'

'A Toledo sword?'

'Yes sir. My father had it made for me in Lorca when I was thirteen. It's a beautiful sword, sir, made by a true Toledo craftsman. Months later, my sword master, a wonderful old soldier who fought at the fall of Constantinople, was teaching me to use my sword against all sorts of adversaries, armed with lance, axe or sword, when he slipped forward on my unsheathed blade and died. I was so terrified of my father's reaction that I ran away from home. I knew then that I was cursed and had to expurgate my sins, however long it took and however far I had to travel. It was weeks later that I witnessed the earthquake in Almería. I ran there from the Baños to help but I was set on by the soldiers of the Inquisition. I still don't know what they were doing in the Moorish city of Almería.'

'Torquemada's men believe they have the right to go everywhere. To be honest, Pedro – and maybe I shouldn't say this – but his appointment as Inquisitor General of Castile has been one of the most unsavoury aspects of the Queen's rule.'

He sighed, pushing his chair back. 'So after this voyage, you'll return to your parents in Vélez Blanco?'

'To my mother, yes sir. My father's dead. He was killed by the same soldiers who arrested me after the earthquake. One of them, named Zak, was a true monster. He was apprehended with his henchman, Gaz, in the encampment at Santa Fe and they both died. I had the satisfaction of personally avenging my father's death with my sword.'

'Well, that's a truly amazing story which you've told me, Pedro. For a young man of just eighteen years you've been through a great deal. Now, I gather that you've brought your belongings with you. I'll get Diego to find you somewhere to bed down for the night. We can return you to the *Pinta* tomorrow.' He smiled.

'Thank you for telling me your story. And thank you for finding my charts. I will find a way of rewarding you.'

Pedro did not return to the *Pinta*. Other events prevented it.

X: Española

Wednesday, November 21st 1492

At sunrise, with a southerly wind, the three ships sailed to the east along the north coast of Cuba. But with a contrary sea they made little progress, making only eighteen miles by vespers. Then the wind shifted to the east and they made another nine miles by sunset, but this time to the south by east. Colón took another fix with his quadrant.

'This can't be right!' he complained to his pilot, Pedro Niño. 'Twenty-one degrees? Surely, we must be further south than this? By the Holy Cross,' he exclaimed angrily, 'this quadrant must be wrong.'

If Cristóbal Colón was not very impressed by his quadrant, believing that it was faulty, he was equally unimpressed by the *Santa María*. To him she was slow, awkward and difficult to manoeuvre, and totally unsuited for exploration. From the very outset, Colón's favourite ship was the *Niña*.

That evening, Martín Pinzón in the *Pinta*, without warning, and without seeking the consent of the Admiral, or even informing him, sailed off on his own to the Island of Babeque which he believed lay to the east. For several hours the *Santa María* had the *Pinta* in sight until the caravel finally disappeared from view when twelve miles away. The *Santa María* lowered her sails and posted a lantern so that the *Pinta* might return, but it was to no avail. To Colón, the action of Pinzón was an act of utter treachery and he never forgave him.

Colón knew that Pedro, the saviour of his sea charts in Sevilla, could not now return to the *Pinta*. The morning after the *Pinta*'s departure, from the rail of the poop deck, he shouted down to Bartolomé García, the *Santa María*'s bo'sun, 'It seems young Pedro Tegero is now a member of our crew, Bartolomé. So please add him to your duty roster. But first, be so good as to show him around the boat.'

'Aye, aye, Admiral. I will,' replied Bartolomé.

'Look lad,' he said, after he had taken Pedro aside. 'You've been serving on the *Pinta* so there's no need for me to show you around this ship. But tell me, as a matter of interest what ship did you serve on before the *Pinta*? Was it a Palos ship?'

'No, Bo'sun. A dhow. A large one with two lateen sails.'

'For how long and where?' asked the bo'sun, flabbergasted.

'For some eighteen months and mainly around the eastern Mediterranean, Bo'sun.'

'Well, I never!' was all Bartolomé could say. But why would that make the Admiral brighten up? he pondered. Huh, it beats me!

Pedro wandered around the boat. Apart from its size, it held no surprises except that it had a poop deck on top of the quarterdeck at the stern of the ship, beneath which was the Admiral's cabin. It was steered the same way as the *Pinta* with block and tackle used to pull the tiller one way or the other. The space under the fo'c'sle was sufficiently large to stand up in, and the anchor was raised from the bows using a capstan with four sturdy wooden spars. Eight men were needed to raise the heavy anchor via a cable stretched along the whole length of the main deck. Seeing this cumbersome arrangement, Pedro understood why Cristóbal Colón chose to lay to in sheltered harbours where he did not need to lower the anchor, or chose to beat about off the coast at night, rather than try and moor where the sea was very deep. Pedro descended into the hold. He found it much more spacious and roomy than the *Pinta*, containing many more barrels of water and casks of oil and wine. Also, there were many more chests at the stern of the boat, no doubt the source of all the trinkets which the Admiral handed to the Indians so freely. Were these meant as gifts for the Great Khan in China? Pedro thought to himself as he scanned the chests. A country with the finest porcelain, carved jade, ivory, inlaid wood and scented sandalwood? Surely not!

The next morning, the Admiral, with a couple of seamen, plus Pedro and the other cabin boys, sailed the ship's auxiliary along the coast finding a river which cascaded down from the mountains. Amongst the stones on the stream bed were some which glistened like gold and he instructed the boys to dive into the water to gather some for the Sovereigns.[44] On the mountains in the distance the boys spotted pine trees, straight and tall, thick and slender. They saw oaks and other trees. The Admiral realised that, with a sawmill located by this fast-flowing river, everything existed to provide the timber and masts for the largest vessels of Spain. While there, they cut a spare mizzenmast and lateen yard for the *Niña*.

I cannot express to you, my Sovereigns, the Admiral confirmed in writing that evening, *what a joy and pleasure it is to see all this, especially the pines, because there could be built here as many ships as desired… I have not praised* [this land] *one hundredth part it deserves and it pleases Our Lord to continually show me something better, for always in what I have discovered up to the present it has been a matter of going from good to better, as well in the trees and forests and grasses and fruits and flowers as in the people… and the same is true with regard to the harbours and waters.*

Earlier that morning, Pedro and the Indian whose name sounded like Ta'hí, left the others collecting the gold-looking pebbles and swam upstream, turning into a small tributary where the long grass and tall canes on each bank almost reached across the narrow stream.

Laughing and shouting to one another, they splashed around in the water,

---

[44] In truth he must have known that the stones were not gold, otherwise he would have collected all he could find. They were evidently fool's gold (pyrites).

reaching down to collect the golden stones, throwing them onto the bank. They had accumulated a small pile before it dawned on Pedro that they had better return to the ship's longboat since the sun was already well past its zenith. However, when they reached the spot where the boat had been tied, they found it gone. They chased along the bank coming out into a clearing near the river mouth just in time to see the longboat reach the *Santa María*. They waved and shouted but it was in vain, The ship was a good mile beyond the line of breaking surf. They stood there watching as the *Santa María* and *Niña* weighed anchor, hoisted their sails and slowly got underway.

Pedro sat on the river bank distraught, his head in his hands. He did not know what to do and he was utterly drained. He felt as he had when he had tumbled into the disused mine shaft in the Alpujarra nearly two years before with absolutely no hope of escape. Ta'hí tugged his arm, pulling him to his feet and scratched some marks in the sand with a stick, pointing to the coast to his right.

'*This is the coast, yes?*' he indicated in his native language, pointing to the coastline to their right. He drew a boat and scratched two stick men and a line running to the right.

'Yes, of course, Ta'hí,' Pedro exclaimed, guessing what he had meant. 'We can meet up with the ships further along the coast!'

Ta'hí nodded and grinned.

Barefoot and both naked, Pedro set off with his Indian friend who loped along in a long-strided run, neither fast nor slow, something he could do for hours on end. Soon they were in the thick forest. Their problems had started in earnest.

The next day the *Santa María* and *Niña* sailed due south, but the current prevented them from reaching land. By Saturday morning, despite a favourable east-north-east wind they were as far from land as the previous day. Beyond a cape in the far distance to the east Colón believed he could see other land which the Indians called Bohío. They told him that it was inhabited by a people with one eye in their forehead, as well as others they called cannibals.[45] All the Indians aboard were terrified of going there and pleaded with the Admiral not to do so.

They sailed through the night and the next morning reached land at a low island where they had been several days before on the way to Babeque. The coastline was protected by raging surf and, unable to land, the two ships continued on westwards, finally reaching La Mar de Nuestra Señora, where they had been a week earlier. Aware now that the time spent exploring this coastline had been a root cause of Martín Pinzón's precipitate departure, Colón turned tail and sailed eastwards finding a harbour between some islands.

---

[45] The people of Caniba who eat people, a Taino Indian word.

Once in the forest, with coconut, banana, mango and every variety of palm tree surrounding them on all sides, Pedro and Ta'hí found a path and ran along it, but it twisted and turned until they had totally lost their bearing. Pedro peered through the canopy of trees but could not pinpoint where the sun was since there was just a bright, diffused glare through the foliage. They picked up another well-used path used by villagers and came to a fast-flowing stream which Pedro assumed flowed northwards to the coast and they set off across it, supposedly heading east or south-east. By now Pedro's feet were in a terrible state, cut, scratched and bruised. Ta'hí shredded some palm fronds and bound them around his feet. They set off again. All this time Ta'hí kept up a rhythmic loping.

Soon darkness began to descend on the forest. Ta'hí searched around and eventually led Pedro to an empty thatched hut and made him rest there. He disappeared into the near darkness and soon returned with some fruit from the trees around. Exhausted and dejected they stayed there the night.

The *Santa María* and *Niña* were not able to drop anchor in the deep water beyond the reef, and during the night of November 26th the coastal current had carried the ships some fifteen miles south-eastwards along the coast. Continuing on that day, they passed seven or eight rivers in the space of fifteen miles, most of which discharged into tree-bordered sandy coves with narrow openings into the sea. Soon they saw the largest village which they had seen in Cuba, and a short while later encountered a most remarkable harbour set in some incredibly beautiful land surrounded by mountains. A high, distinctive, isolated flat-topped mountain lay inland to the right and the land around was intensively cultivated. Captivated by the beauty of the place, which exceeded everything he had seen so far, Colón ordered the ships to be anchored offshore and he took the longboat into the harbour to take soundings. Like nearly all the bays or coves along this stretch of coast, it was hammer-shaped with a narrow entrance from the sea widening rapidly into a broad sheltered bay hundreds of paces across. Inside the harbour on the south side, rather concealed, they found the entrance to a river which could accommodate even a galley and was more than five fathoms deep. Colón and both crews were enchanted by the verdant forests and greenery, the clear water and the colourful birds. The vegetation grew right down to the water's edge, with the high river banks cut into here and there where Indians had slid their canoes down into the water. Huts could be seen in clearings between the trees. Dense mangroves with exposed twisted roots competed at the water's edge with rushes with pinking feathery flowers almost ten feet tall offering a surfeit of strong canes, while behind lay varieties of different alms, bananas, mangoes, breadfruit, almonds and yaggruma, and low trees with broad canopies with glossy, round, red-veined leaves. Towering over all of these in the forest behind were the most magnificent palm trees in Cuba with dead straight smooth grey trunks.[46] Besotted by all he saw, Colón told his men how he would describe to the King in his *diario* what they had seen:

A thousand tongues would not be sufficient to tell it, nor my hand to write it, for it looks like an enchanted land... Such was his captivation with all that he saw around him. He noted later:

Your Highnesses will order a city and fortresses built in these regions, and these countries will be converted. And I certify to Your Highnesses that it does not seem to me that there can be more fertile countries under the sun, or any more temperate in heat or cold, with a greater abundance...

Pedro and Ta'hí were up at first light. The Indian cleaned and re-bandaged Pedro's feet and they set off once again. Before the cloud and mist came down, Pedro caught sight of the sun and, getting his bearings at last, he and Ta'hí continued their way to the south-east. The coast appeared occasionally through the murk. It lay many miles to the north of them.

Once, in the forest, close to a village, they came across a native of around middle age. He lay on a stretcher, neither dead nor alive. Puzzled, Pedro approached the man but he was angrily dragged away by Ta'hí. The Indian stooped and walked like an old person, then lay on his side with his eyes closed and his head on his hands, pretending to be dead. Evidently the man had been put out in the forest to die. Pedro thought to himself, No wonder we never see any people over thirty years old!

The two continued all day making slow progress over difficult ground. Both preferred to be in the open than in the clammy, dripping forest, yet the Indian seemed unperturbed by the weather, But Pedro started to shiver, and with his feet and scratched legs starting to cause him real distress he was glad when they found shelter for a second night.

For the crews of the *Santa María* and *Niña*, the next four days were wet and blustery with a strong easterly wind preventing the ships' departure. So with time on their hands Cristóbal Colón ordered that a large cross be placed at the south-east entrance of the harbour.

Sunday, December 2nd, saw the weather no better; yet it was evident to the Admiral that whether the wind blew from the sea or the land, the harbour provided an excellent safe anchorage with the shoal at its entrance abating the strength of incoming waves. Fittingly, he named this magnificent harbour Puerto Santo.[47] More stones appearing to contain gold were found at the river's mouth by the cabin boys. The next day they hoisted the sails on the longboats and went to the south-east from Puerto Santo across a more open bay to the next headland and entered another large river. Nearby they found five large

---

[46] Palma jardin, palma cocotero, palma real (the tallest and straightest). The rushes were *caña brava*.
[47] The beautiful enclosed bay of Bahía de Baracoa.

canoes, all beautifully carved, and later a thatched boathouse containing one canoe hewn from a single tree trunk with seventeen benches for the rowers. They followed the path through the forest and climbed the distinctive, steep-sided mountain with a flat top which lay five or six miles inland.[48] They found a village at the top, but with no gold evident, the party returned to the ships, leaving the villagers unmolested.

When they returned to where they had left their boats, some native men approached. One stood in the water, raising his hands to the sky and shouted, seemingly inciting the villagers to attack Colón's men. But Colón's Indian grabbed one of the sailor's loaded crossbows and approached the Indians, showing how far the crossbow bolt flew when released, and the villagers fled in fear. Some of the crew went up river to the Indians' deserted village where they found a large hut which had several rooms divided by woven mats and strings of shells hanging from the ceiling.

In the middle of the afternoon the next day Pedro and Ta'hí entered a clearing. Some dozen cabins lay in a circle with smoke rising from many of them. With Ta'hí supporting him, Pedro staggered into the clearing. Some of the women ran to them, helping carry Pedro to one of the cabins and leading Ta'hí to another, chatting with him excitedly in their own tongue. Two young women – girls really – laid Pedro down on a raised couch covered with a roughly-woven cotton sheet. They removed the palm-frond bandages from his feet which were lacerated, blistered and swollen. One of the girls went to the fire and removed a pot sitting on the stone hearth and brought the hot water over to the couch. They bathed Pedro's feet and then his legs and thighs, cleaning and soothing the wounds with balls of raw cotton. Exhausted though he was, stirred by the attention of the girls, the manhood of the eighteen-year-old youth rose, standing up as straight and as strong as a palm tree in the forest. The two girls, maybe fourteen or fifteen years of age, with their firm, black-pointed breasts and brown bodies, giggled and joked as they quite deliberately brushed the backs of their hands across Pedro's erect penis while they soothed the wounds on the sides of his thighs. Pedro tried to sit up but they eased him back on the couch while they continued bathing and cleaning his wounds. Then one girl, giggling and egged on by the other, climbed onto Pedro, straddling him as she took him inside her. After a few gleeful jerks she was pushed off by the other girl, who wasted no time in doing the same, leaning forward to roll her youthful body back and forth across his chest while she heaved up and down energetically on top of him. Voices were heard as the men returned to the village and in a flash the two girls had gone, holding a hand to their mouths as they scooted, giggling, out of the doorway.

Pedro remained in the village for that day and the next, recovering his strength, but still running a fever. News had travelled through the forest of the

---

[48] Known as El Yunque de Baracoa.

two big ships which had arrived from across the sea and the men in the village guessed that Pedro had come from them. Ta'hí appeared laughing from one of the huts, hand in hand with an attractive young woman. He indicated to Pedro by signs that he would not return to the *Santa María* with him but would return to his home. Pedro shook Ta'hí's hand to thank him for his friendship and for guiding him through the forest. Six men from the village led Pedro down to a river and hauled a dugout from a thatched boathouse. It took them a full three hours to reach the coast. Pedro got out of the boat, stiff and cold. His relief was overwhelming for there, in the bay, lay the *Santa María* and the *Niña*. Pedro stumbled along the sandy beach in the rain, waving frantically to the ships, half a mile away.

Diego Bermúdez, on duty in the crow's-nest, was keeping a lookout for Pedro on the instructions of the Colón. He relished the thought of the gold *dobla*, promised by the Admiral to whoever spotted the youngster on the beach. He shouted down from the mast:

'I think he's arrived, Admiral! There's a naked white man on the beach waving to us. It must be him.'

Colón ran to the starboard rail of the poop deck. A golden *dobla* clattered noisily onto the main deck below the main mast. He waved to Diego Bermúdez as the seaman climbed down from the ratlines onto the deck and retrieved it. Within a half hour Pedro was returned to the *Santa María*, shivering and shaking with fever, and with his legs and feet red and swollen.

The next day, on Tuesday, December 4th, the two ships departed from Puerto Santo, reaching the cape of Cabo Lindo[49] at the eastern end of Cuba. They beat about all night so that they could see in daylight the country which stretched to the east. The Indians had told the Admiral that the island of Babeque lay to the north-west[50] but with the prevailing wind from the same quarter it was impossible to go there. However, in the distance to the east he saw a very great land which was the land the Indians called Bohío and of which they were so fearful. With a good breeze behind them, the sea calm and a strong current running in the passage between the two islands of Cuba and Bohío, the *Santa María* and *Niña* made rapid progress to Bohío. As darkness approached, Colón ordered the *Niña*, being the better sailer, to run ahead and find a harbour for the night. This she did, but with her ship's light going out the *Santa María* was unable to follow her into the harbour, and the larger ship had to remain offshore until morning.

At dawn on Thursday, December 6th, Cristóbal Colón found himself twelve miles off a land which he knew from the Indians on board the *Santa María* to be Bohío.[51] Several headlands faced him to the east and to the south-east. A high, level island lay some distance away along the northern coast

---

[49] Now known as Punta Fraile.
[50] Some sixty nautical miles away and over the horizon.
[51] Colón named this island *La Isla Española*, which is now Haiti and the Dominican Republic.

which Colón later named Isla de la Tortuga.[52] Many fires had been seen that night as if the islanders were guarding their coast with watchtowers. At the hour of vespers in the early evening the *Santa María* and *Niña* entered a harbour which Colón named Puerto de San Nicolas.[53] Along this coast, which was free of reefs, the water was clear and extremely deep right up to the land. Even at a boat oar's distance from the land it was still five fathoms deep. The harbour was the finest they had seen with a deep and narrow inlet running inland for nearly two miles. The land around was high and level, with trees and grasses similar to those of Spain. Many large canoes were seen but the natives had fled. The Indians on the *Santa María* were terrified of the people on this land but worse, they had grown suspicious that Colón did not intend to return them to their own people. On his part, Colón was becoming anxious, if not paranoid, about securing some trade in gold before his return to Spain.

The day before, when Pedro was helped up onto the deck of the *Santa María*, he was in a sorry state after his headlong seventy-mile chase with Ta'hí through the dense forest from La Mar de Nuestra Señora to Puerto Santo. His feet were cut, blistered and swollen and his arms and legs lacerated by the branches and brambles which he had brushed past. Moreover, whether it was the exposure to the persistent rain in the dank forest, or the water which he had drunk from the streams, he was running a high temperature.

'The boy seems in a pretty bad way, Diego. Make a cot up for him in my cabin,' Colón ordered his servant, Diego de Salcedo. 'I'm looking to you to care for him and return him to good health.'

'Yes, Master, That I'll do.'

Colón turned to the ship's physician, Juan Sánchez, who was a short, rotund and jovial man in his forties with a thick rim of curly brown hair around his shiny bald head. 'Juan, please tend to his wounds. See that they are clean and dry.' He added, 'What can you give him for his fever? He's very hot.'

'We must keep him cool, Cristóbal. During the day I think it'll be best to bring his cot out onto the quarterdeck so he can benefit from the sea breeze. In the meantime I'll make up a tea with cinnamon, garlic and honey. That should help his fever.'

Even the fresh sea breeze on deck did not improve Pedro's fever, although his wounds were starting to heal. He was very hot and becoming delirious, twisting and turning in his cot. The Admiral was becoming worried.

'Can't we try something else, Juan? He's not getting better.'

'I can try bleeding him. That usually…'

'Bleeding! Bleeding! He's not a sucking pig ready for the pot. What does it say in your medicine book for fevers?'

'Well,' Juan replied slowly, stooping down and turning his head to one side as if expecting a clout. 'It mentions bleeding and hot poultices…'

---

[52] Now Ile de la Tortue.
[53] Now Baie du Môle lying at the western tip of the island.

'Ugh – physicians!' exclaimed the Admiral. 'Find out what the Indians say. I'll wager they'll have a remedy.'

Pedro's nightmares were as bad as those he had experienced just before the Almería earthquake five years earlier. Then, a night of charcoal blackness and cotton-wool stillness was followed, almost in an instant, by hurricane-force winds and, the next morning, by the violent earthquake. He saw in a jumbled succession of terrible happenings; the face of poor Marco, as the old soldier stumbled on the wet cobbles, wide-eyed with a mixture of surprise and horror as Pedro's sword passed through his neck; the look on his father's face as he peered out of their kitchen window at the commotion, and from which Pedro fled into the mountains; but worst of all, far worse, the Dantean scene of flames and molten metal shooting into the sky as the furnace exploded; of the men writhing and screaming on the black cinder path with smoke rising from their chests, embedded with molten iron; of Rodriguez, and the giant iron-master's white-knuckled fury over the horrendous deaths of two of his men. Pedro had lived with his shame to this very day for not owning up to the accident. And all because of that sword…

The Indians told Colón that this island of Española was larger than Cuba, the island from where they had just departed.[54] Their fear of the Caniba people convinced Colón that these warlike people belonged to Great Khan of China and that he must therefore be close by. More crewmen were sent ashore. They found more cotton trees, trees producing mastic, but for which the resin did not coagulate as it should, and many aloe cactus plants with their fleshy toothed leaves containing the strong medicinal purgative. Dace, salmon, hake, mullet, eels and shrimps were caught in the sea in abundance. They planted a cross at the entrance to the harbour to commemorate the acquisition of the island on behalf of the Sovereigns and in the name of the Lord. Some men explored further inland and brought back to the ship a beautiful young woman, as naked as those before her. She and the Indians on board conversed in the same tongue. She was clothed by the crew and given gifts aboard and then returned safely and unmolested to her village.

The next day, December 13th, nine crewmen went to her village twelve miles away and found it to have over a thousand houses. Following the good reports which the young woman had evidently given to her people, more than two thousand villagers assembled, many placing their hands upon the seamen's heads as a sign of reverence and friendship. The people were taller and paler than the olive-skinned Indians whom the Christians had encountered previously, and they had more handsome faces. Colón had discerned from the Indians on the *Santa María* that the rather ugly Guanahaní Indians on San Salvador and the Indians on Cuba bound the tops of their infants' heads when they were small, causing their faces and particularly their foreheads to be unusually wide.

---

[54] This is what Colón recorded at the time. In reality, Española is approximately 76,000 sq km and Cuba 114,500 sq km.

The villagers brought fish and bread made from the radish-like *niame* roots, some of them as thick as your leg. These roots were grated and, after soaking in water to extract a poison, they kneaded the dough-like mass and baked it in a fire. Unlike the Cuban Indians, who also cultivated maize, this was the islanders' staple diet and was grown in fields around the village where it was planted as small shoots. A river ran through the middle of the valley and, via ditches, the villagers watered their fields. The trees had shiny, dark green foliage, the fruit trees were laden, the plants were in flower and the nightingales sang in the trees; but still no gold.

Hearing from those on board the *Santa María* about Pedro's plight, three Indians from the village came by a canoe to tend to him. They carried a basket containing a number of their small red peppers,[55] slivers of their spiky aloe plant, some of the dried leaves which they smoked in hollowed-out tubes, and many other roots, berries and leaves which no one on board recognised. The Indians crushed them all together in an earthenware bowl, then boiled the mixture in water on the ship's hearth and finally strained the broth into a small bowl through a fist of cotton cloth. Then, donning a feathered headdress and a coloured knee-length apron, one of the Indians raised the earthenware bowl above his head and, after loudly intoning some incantations to his gods, he ceremoniously passed the noxious-smelling remedy to Juan Sánchez, indicating by gestures that it should be given to Pedro.

'Drink this, lad,' Juan said, helping Pedro sit up. 'The Indians have made it from some of their plants. They say that in a few days it'll reduce your fever.'

'Ugh!' Pedro said sipping it. 'It must be good – it tastes foul! Are you sure it's not poison?'

After seven days the ships left Puerto de la Concepción and sailed across to the Isla de la Tortuga, just six miles across the strait between the island and the mainland. The explorers found the high but flat land totally cultivated. After returning to Española they departed on the 16th, reaching a village twelve miles on where they anchored very close in. Five hundred men came to the beach with their king. They paddled across to the two ships in their canoes. Many of them wore small grains of gold in their ears and noses.

I ordered that everyone be treated honourably because they are the best and gentlest people in the world, and above all because I have great hope in Our Lord that your Highnesses will convert them all to Christianity and they will all belong to you, for I regard them as yours now, wrote Colón that evening.

The Indian king was a young man around twenty years of age. He was accompanied by several ministers or courtiers. They, as well as all their womenfolk, were naked. Many were notably lighter in colour. The whole country around seemed to be planted with *niames*. The king came on board the *Santa María* with his courtiers and many of his subjects. They could not believe

---

[55] Chilli peppers.

that the ships came from a distant land called Castile, instead believing that they had descended from heaven. The king was served some ship's food, which he barely tasted before passing it to his courtiers to savour.

'Feeling better, Pedro?' asked Juan Sánchez, as for the first time in nearly ten days, Pedro swung his legs over the side of the cot and sat up.

'Yes, I feel a lot better, thank you. But what day is it? Where are we?'

'It's the 17th. You've been delirious for ten days now, Pedro, and we're just offshore from a big island which the Admiral has named La Isla Española, after our own country.'

'So we've left Bahía de Baracoa?'

'In Cuba? Yes, ages ago. We're on a different island now, bigger, cooler, and with many more people.'

'I remember nothing except the awful nightmares I had and that horrible drink you gave me.'

'That's what saved you, Pedro,' Juan Sánchez said, laughing, 'or maybe it was the prayers they said to their gods! Whichever it was, it's they you have to thank for your recovery… and the Admiral, I might add. You've been sleeping in his cabin ever since we lifted you aboard. You were in a terrible state, I can tell you.'

'But now it's time for you to take up your duties again.'

'That I'll be only too glad to do,' replied Pedro.

The Indians mixed freely with the officers and crew on both ships. They brought with them some arrows which belonged to the Caniba, the *Canibales*.[56] These were as long as spears and tipped with hardened sticks. Two of the Indians claimed that the *Canibales* had bitten chunks of flesh from their bodies. The Indians showed the crew pieces of gold which they had flattened into thin leave. Some pieces were as large as one's hand and the seamen traded worthless glass beads for them. One man whom they called the Cacique or tribal leader, came forward and indicated to Colón that much more gold was to be found on the Isla de la Tortuga across the straight. This island lay closer to the island of Babeque and was where, unknown to the Admiral, Martín Pinzón headed when he deserted the *Santa María* and *Niña*. The Indians on both Cuba and this island of Española had said it possessed much gold.

The two ships remained at anchor the next day due to lack of wind but, in truth, because the Cacique had promised to bring more gold. At dawn the crews decorated the ships with the arms and banners for the feast of the Commemoration of the Annunciation. Many lombard shots were fired. Four Indians bore the Cacique from his village to the beach on a litter and two hundred of his subjects followed. He came on board as Colón was eating breakfast in the deckhouse below the quarterdeck. He seated himself beside the Admiral. Despite his nakedness he had a regal demeanour. Two of his

---

[56] The first time Colón had referred to this much-feared tribe as 'cannibals'.

courtiers sat at his feet while his subjects remained outside on the deck. After eating with the Admiral, the Cacique's servant brought an encrusted belt and some pieces of wrought gold for Colón. The Admiral felt great love for this mild-mannered man of such noble bearing, and presented him with the string of amber beads which the Admiral wore around his neck, plus some red shoes and a flask of orange water. The Cacique expressed a liking to the bed cover in the Admiral's cabin and this was presented to him too.

I called for my gold coin on a pendant, Colón wrote that evening in his *diario, with the images of your Highnesses engraved upon it and showed it to him. I again told him that Your Highnesses command and rule over the best part of the world and that there are no other such great Princes. I also showed him the royal banners that have a cross on them which he greatly admired.*

The Cacique was conducted ashore that evening with great honour and the lombards on both ships were fired in salute. He and his son were borne back to their village on litters, as they had come.

During the night of Wednesday, December 19th, the *Santa María* and *Niña* set sail, eventually clearing the straight between Española and Tortuga and, after passing many capes, headlands, fine bays and high mountains, they anchored in a magnificent harbour some forty-five miles to the east, near a small island which Colón named Santo Tomás. Inland, Colón recorded, were mountains higher than the volcano of Tenerife which had erupted when they passed it in August.[57] The next morning, moving the ships closer inshore, they were met by scores of Indians bringing *niame* bread, nuts and five or six varieties of fruit which the Admiral ordered to be preserved to return to the Sovereigns. Many of the women, all naked, without even the scant loincloths worn by their kinfolk on Guanahaní, were exceedingly beautiful and light-skinned, with fine bodies and white teeth.

For the first time since his adventure with Ta'hí, Pedro went ashore, accompanying some of the sailors who went armed, as had become customary when making a new landfall. As they reached the trees bordering the beach, Alonso Chocero spied a young beauty peeping at them from behind a tree, with an Indian, presumably her brother or husband nearby. Drawing his sword, the Palos man chased the Indian away, ran and grabbed the girl, and dragged her screaming into the trees. Hearing her cries, Pedro, still weakened by his illness, ran up the beach.

'Leave her alone!' he shouted. 'You've heard what the Admiral has said. The Indian women are not to be harmed.'

Other seamen followed Pedro. One, a dark and swarthy man, a Basque named Chachú, and fleet of foot, ran ahead and drew his sword as he reached Alonso Chocero, who already had the terrified girl on the ground, his body between her legs. But if Pedro thought that the Basque was going to intercede on the girl's behalf, he was mistaken.

---

[57] Mount Teide on Tenerife is 12,200 feet, while the highest mountain in Española is 10,400 feet.

'Oh no you don't!' Chachú shouted, threatening Alonso Chocero with his sword. 'This one's mine. You got the better of me with the ones in Cuba but you're going to take second turn with this one!'

Chachú clouted Alonso on his bared backside with the flat of his sword and shoved him off the girl with his foot. He then made a grab for the girl himself as she got up to run away. Alonso, rising to his feet incandescent with rage, with one hand trying to yank up his trousers above his knees, was not to be thwarted. He struck the Basque a hard blow across his back with the cutting edge of his blade. Chachú tumbled, blood starting to stain his white shirt. But as the enraged Alonso stepped forward, his sword above his head ready to make the fatal strike, Pedro bundled into him, knocking him over, the sword spilling from the Palos man's hand. Two other seamen following behind fell on him, pinning him to the ground. The girl ran off into the forest, screaming. The wounded Chachú was led off by the seamen and helped back to the *Santa María*'s longboat, which was pulled up onto the beach. Alonso, swordless, careered off along the beach. Although Juan Sánchez, the physician, stitched the deep gash in Chachú's back as best he could, he could not stanch the bleeding, and two days later the Basque died. Chachú was buried at sea while the ship was at anchor, his shroud weighted with stone ballast. Amazingly, as it turned out, his was the only death amongst the crewmen during the voyage.

Cristóbal Colón yet again ordered that at no time must the Indians be maltreated or molested, particularly the womenfolk; but in relation to the Palos men especially, it was a vain hope.

Indians came to the shore begging the Admiral to visit their Cacique who was waiting to see him. He warmly greeted Colón and his party, offering food, brightly coloured parrots and many other objects. In return Colón handed them glass beads, brass rings and hawks' bells from his bottomless chests.

The next day at dawn the ships set sail to visit the islands of Tortuga and Babeque, which were said to be the source of much gold, but due to lack of wind they returned to their earlier anchorage. This time more than a thousand Indians came to the ships in their canoes. Five hundred more swam the three miles from the shore, including women and children. Colón sent the secretary to the fleet, Rodrigo de Escobedo, and five others along the coast in the longboat to meet the Cacique in his village. He was the greatest of all the tribal chiefs whom they had met and was called Guacanagari. Guacanagari showered Colón and his men with gifts, paying them great honour, but the Indians from the *Santa María*, being Taínos from Río de Mares on Cuba, experienced difficulty in understanding them.[58] From the information he gleaned, Colón now knew for certain that a great quantity of gold was to be found on this Isla Española. Guancanagarí treated Rodrigo de Escobedo and his party with great friendliness, lading them with gifts made of cotton, carved masks, and many things from their cabins. The chief pleaded with them not to depart when it

---

[58] They were close to the linguistic boundary of the Taino people.

was time for them to leave. One Indian in particular was exceedingly friendly, and with a companion eagerly joined the *Santa María* to show the Admiral where gold could be found further along the coast. Amongst these lands was one further to the east named Cibao which Cristóbal Colón surmised was Japan – where, it was said, that the inhabitants carried banners made of beaten gold.

The next day, Monday, December 24th and Christmas Eve, the two ships set sail with a land breeze behind them. Colón noted that the people of this island of Española, which they called Bohío, were of greater stature, lighter-skinned and of milder manner than those of Cuba, although like them, they painted themselves, sometimes black or mixed colours, but mostly red, which they said was to protect them from the rays of the sun.

The next day, in a light wind, the two ships sailed to Punta Santa, as Colón named it.[59] At eleven o'clock that night, the Admiral was asleep in his cabin after two very hectic days. The ship was some distance offshore in a dead calm sea. Juan de la Cosa, the owner and master of the *Santa María*, held the watch with two seamen and a cabin boy named Maestre Juan. However, totally contrary to orders, Juan de la Cosa and the two seamen were asleep, inexcusably leaving the youngster in charge of the helm. Although the sea was calm, the current drifted the ship towards a coral reef over which the sea could be heard breaking, even at a distance of three miles. Suddenly, poor Maestre Juan felt the rudder ground and heard the noise of the sea against the ship. Cristóbal Colón, feeling the ship shudder, was on the deck in an instant, even before Juan de la Cosa and the other two seamen on watch could rouse themselves.

Colón immediately ordered the rest of the crew mustered and that the small boat be launched in order to take the heavy anchor from the bow and cast it into the sea at the stern to prevent the ship grounding further. With the tide ebbing, the ship swung broadside in the ever-shallowing sea and, having eluded the reef, settled on a sandbank. To lighten the ship Colón ordered the mainmast cut down and the ship lightened as much as possible. However, with the tide ebbing further, the *Santa María* settled into the sand and rolled over partly onto one side. Although the ship remained intact, the hull, under its own weight and not being supported by the sea, became stressed and its seams opened. The *Santa María* was lost. Using the two auxiliaries the Admiral ordered the crew to be ferried across to the *Niña* for their safety.

---

[59] Now Pointe Fort Picolet.

XI: A Gift of Gold

Christmas Day, Tuesday, December 25th 1492

With the *Santa María* aground and lost, Cristóbal Colón and his crew were ferried to the *Niña* and, uncertain over the extent of the sandbanks, the small ship remained at sea and beat about all night. The next day Diego de Arana, the master-of-arms, and Pedro Gutiérrez, the representative of the Royal Household, sought the help of the Cacique whose village lay several miles away and whom the Admiral had received aboard the *Santa María* three days before. The Cacique wept when he heard about the disaster. Forthwith, he came with many canoes and with hundreds of his men, and in no time they had unloaded everything from the stricken ship and carried it ashore and thence to their village, placing guards so that nothing might be removed. Two large dwellings were set aside for the seamen to use.

I certify to your Highnesses that in all the world I do not believe there is a better people or a better country. They love their neighbours as themselves… and are always smiling… The King by his manner of eating, his decent behaviour and his exceptional cleanliness, showed himself to be of good birth.

The next day the Cacique came to the *Niña* again, offering Colón everything he possessed to make up for the lost ship. Other natives paddled to the ship in their dugouts trading pieces of gold for hawks' bells which they valued above all else. The Cacique assured the Admiral that much gold existed on their island of Bohío, although the Admiral was beginning to suspect that the chief was not being wholly truthful with him with regards to the gold that might be found. The two dined together on the *Niña*. Later they went ashore to the village and ate a meal comprising several different types of *niame* served with shrimps and game, plus other dishes, including the bread they called *cazabe*.[a] Afterwards they rubbed herbs into their hands to soften them.

After one of the Admiral's crew demonstrated the power and range of a Turkish bow, a lombard cannon and musket were fired and the Indians fell on their knees in fear. A large mask with gold was placed on the Admiral's head. Other gold jewellery was placed around his neck. Colón knew for certain now that it was God's will that the *Santa María* should founder so that he might get to know these kind and gentle people and establish a settlement there. With many of his crew requesting to remain, the Admiral ordered that a tower and fortress be constructed with timbers from the ship.

On December 27th an Indian messenger arrived with the news that the

---

[a] The *niame* was sweet potato (not to be confused with the common potato later brought back to Europe from South America); the game was possibly turkey and the *cazabe* was cassava or manioc bread.

Pinta had been spotted further along the coast. Immediately the Cacique dispatched a canoe there. Pedro Niño, the pilot, accompanied it. Pedro pleaded with the bo'sun that he be sent too, but he was told in no uncertain terms that he was to stay on the ship.

The Admiral had been brooding for some time about the fate or whereabouts of Martín Pinzón's ship, growing more concerned by the day that Pinzón might already be returning to Spain with news of their discoveries. While relieved to hear the news that the *Pinta* was safe and close by, he made up his mind that he would return home post-haste, since it was his duty to report the news of their findings to the King and not that of Martín Pinzón.

The next day, still bitter over the desertion of the *Pinta*, which left him with just one ship after the loss of the *Santa María*, Colón instructed Bartolomé García and as many men as he could muster to start the laborious task of ferrying out to the *Niña* wood and other essential supplies in anticipation of the ship's imminent departure for Spain. The following day, January 2nd, a year to the day after Granada was taken by Fernando and Isabel, the Admiral went ashore to take his final leave of Guacanagari, for whom he had developed such a deep and genuine affection, presenting him with one of his shirts. Aware of the fear which the Cacique and his subjects had of the much feared Cariba, and in an attempt to inculcate a sense of aggression into these mild people, a lombard was brought ashore and fired at the stranded *Santa María*. Guacanagari saw how far the shot travelled and how it passed easily through the side of the ship. Then a mock battle was organised between the seamen on the beach using the Indians' own arms, so that not only might the Indians fear those of the crew who were to remain but also that they might consider the Christians as friends and allies in their conflicts with the Cariba.

Diego de Arana, the *Santa María*'s master-at-arms, being a soldier, was put in charge of the party which was to remain at Villa de la Navidad[61] with two other officers. Pedro Gutiérrez, the representative of the Royal Household, was to be second-in-command, and with him was Rodrigo de Escobedo, the secretary of the fleet. In addition, thirty-six seamen from the *Santa María* and *Niña* volunteered to remain with them.

'Shall we leave Pedro Tegero behind with Diego de Arana, Admiral? If he's as resourceful as you say he might be quite an asset to Diego.'

'I've thought about that, Bo'sun,' replied Colón. 'However, he's been away from his home now for a considerable time and I know he's anxious to return to his mother.'

'But that will mean raising the *Niña*'s complement by three overall.'

'Maybe, Bartolomé. But keep in mind we have to accommodate several of the Indians we're taking back, so our including Tegero will make little difference. Anyway, who's to say that we might not need his resourcefulness during our return journey?'

Cristóbal Colón called all the officers and men together who were to

---

[61]The name Colón gave to the fort which was to be established.

remain at Villa de la Navidad and addressed them as to what their duties and conduct must be. They were: first, to consider what a blessing God had bestowed on them and to pray for the Admiral's speedy return; second, to obey their captain, Diego de Arana, in all things; third, to respect the Cacique, Guacanagari, and his chiefs, avoiding annoying or tormenting them, and to be honest and gentle of speech; fourth, not to injure or use force against the Indians, man or woman, and not to injure, harm or molest the women; fifth, to stay together and not leave the dominion of the Cacique who loves them so much; sixth, to suffer their solitude, which is little less than exile; seventh, to beg the Cacique to send canoes with them to find the gold mines along the coast and to find a more suitable location for a village. Finally the Admiral promised to petition the Sovereigns for special favours to bestow on them on his return.

Left behind for them was a year's supply of biscuit and wine, seeds for sowing, much artillery and the ship's boat. After the *Santa María* had been split open, all the casks and cargo were removed. Of the ship's contents not a leather strap nor nail was lost.

At sunrise on Friday, January 4th, the *Niña* weighed anchor and departed in a light wind. Sailing eighteen miles that day past reefs and coastal shoals and banks, the ship anchored off a mountain which Colón called Monte Cristi. He was more convinced than ever that La Isla Española was none other than Japan and that it would yield a great deal of gold and a great quantity of mastic, and rhubarb, the juicy red stems of which they had already encountered. They continued on the next day, sailing eastwards along the coast passing many beautiful mountains and flat cultivated plains. While the sea was generally deep and clear, shoals and reefs continued to threaten the unwary pilot.

On Sunday, January 6th, Francisco Niño was on the masthead and spotted the *Pinta* sailing towards them from the east. It came up alongside the *Niña*, but with the sea only a few fathoms deep, Colón returned the way he had come to a safe anchorage thirty miles to the west.

Martín Pinzón came aboard the smaller ship.

'I thought you and your caravel were lost, Martín,' started Cristóbal Colón coldly.

'I'm sorry, Cristóbal,' replied the *Pinta*'s captain, spluttering in a highish voice, a rare occurrence for the hardened seaman. 'We got caught in a current which took us away from you and with the westerly breeze it was impossible for us to turn and—'

'That's abject nonsense, Martín, and you know it! There was a light breeze from the north-east. We lowered our mainsail and hung around well into the night. We also placed a lantern on the mizzen so that you could find your way back to us. Your disloyalty to me was tantamount to treason and put our whole voyage in jeopardy. The King shall hear of this.'

'Nevertheless,' Colón continued, his voice softening in a gesture of reconciliation, 'we must now work together as comrades if we are to return our ships and crews safely to Castile. We both have much to report.'

'But where's the *Santa María*?' asked Pinzón.

'This is why your despicable action threatened our whole venture. We lost the *Santa María* on Christmas Day, nearly two weeks ago. While I was asleep, the officer on watch, Juan de la Cosa from Santoña…'

'A Basque man!' interjected Pinzón with relief.

'Yes, a Basque man. Quite inexcusably he was asleep, together with the two seamen who were supposed to be on watch with him, leaving the ship in the hands of a boy. With little wind the ship drifted in the current between some reefs and grounded on a sandbank, where it opened up and was lost.'

'What became of your crew? They can't all be on the *Niña*?'

'I'll tell you about our adventures later, Martín, but I left thirty-nine behind at Villa de la Navidad under the command of Diego de Arana and Pedro Gutiérrez with instructions to construct a fort and await my return later this year.'

'Well, well!' commented Pinzón slowly, the awareness dawning on him of how his thoughtless action in sailing off in the *Pinta* on November 21st might have imperilled the whole venture.

'You'd better come inside the deckhouse and tell me what became of you, Martín. For all I knew you were already on your way back to Palos.' He turned aside. 'Diego, bring us some wine, if you will, and some *niame* bread.'

The Admiral and his deputy were now more relaxed following their confrontation.

'When I left you,' started Martín Pinzón in his explanation, sipping a glass of wine…'

'What's that spotty rash you've got on your hands, Martín?' interrupted Colón, seeing Pinzón's hand around the goblet.

'I don't know, Cristóbal. I've got them on my feet too, as well as aches in my joints. It must be old age, I suppose!'

'I hope it's only that, Martín, and that you haven't caught something nasty while you've been here. I hope the sores aren't serious. But I'm sorry to have interrupted you. Pray continue.'

'After I left you, we sailed to the island of Babeque, where the Indians had told me there was much gold to be found. We spent a week or so there but we found none.'

'Huh! I think half the time they've been misleading us purposely so that we'd leave them alone and go elsewhere.'

'…We could see the mountains of this island in the distance so we sailed here, anchoring in a river mouth. It's around forty miles east of here. There we traded with the natives for a considerable amount of gold, some in the form of—'

'I hope that you and your crew traded for it honestly, Martín, and didn't steal or threaten the Indians to obtain it!'

'No, of course not,' replied Pinzón, diverting his gaze from the Admiral.

'We learnt that there's an island the other side of the one which you call Juana or Cuba which the Indians call Yamaye,[62] ten days' journey away by canoe, where they say there are many gold mines. And they say that there's another island to the east of here which is inhabited only by women. I planned to go there. My crew were very keen.'

'Yes, we've heard of this island many times.'

'How much gold did you find, Cristóbal?' asked Pinzón innocently.

It was the question the Admiral was dreading. He put on a brave face.

'We found several rivers in Juana and also here in La Isla Española with gold in the stream beds mainly the size of rice grains. I have a few dozen pesos to take back to the King but I determined that, since this land already belongs to him, later expeditions can come to extract it at their leisure.'

'Did you find much, Martín?' Colón asked, trying to appear indifferent, praying that the answer would be equally negative.

'Yes, quite a bit, Cristóbal. I'd say around nine hundred pesos in all;[63] some as small lumps and grains we found in the river beds, but mainly as pieces which the Indians had hammered flat or made into crowns and small ornaments.

Whether serious or not, he added charitably, 'It's all yours to do with as you will, Cristóbal.'

'Thank you Martín,' the Admiral replied, endeavouring to conceal his envy, 'that's most generous of you, but you and your crew found it so you must keep it.'

After pumping out the bilge and re-caulking the *Niña* the next day, the two ships departed, freshly stocked with water and wood. The Admiral was determined now to return forthwith to Spain and not put up any more with the rebellious and conniving Pinzón brothers. Many tortoises with shells like great curved shields were encountered swimming in the sea as well as three sirens, their faces more manlike than shown in paintings.[64] On January 10th the *Niña* and *Pinta* reached a fine anchorage at a river which Colón named Río de Gracia,[65] unfairly and spitefully overruling the name Río de Martín Pinzón which, quite properly, the *Pinta*'s captain had bestowed on it as its discoverer. The *Pinta* had remained there for sixteen days while the crew traded for gold with the Indians. Contrary to the conditions of the *Capitulaciones* signed in Santa Fe between the King and Cristóbal Colón the previous April, and having assumed that the Admiral would have filled by now his own treasure chests with gold, Martín Pinzón had ruled that he would retain half the gold found by him and his men, with the remainder being divided equally between them. He had made his crew swear that they had only been at the Río de Gracia for

---

[62] Jamaica. Also then inhabited by the Taino people.
[63] Equal to some 900 ounces or 56 lbs or 26 kilos.
[64] The references are to turtles and manatees.
[65] River of Grace. Now Puerto Blanco.

six days, but Colón soon learnt of this lie. While there, Pinzón took by force four Indian men and two young girls to serve his and his officers' diverse purposes, but later, on hearing of this, the Admiral ordered them clothed and returned to their homes.

The two ships sailed on eastwards along the coast of Española, noting many headlands, rivers, harbours and anchorages, while being very wary of the shoals and sandbanks which layed along it. On the 13th, amazed at the size of La Isla Española, they anchored in a deep, nine-mile-wide bay to the east of Cabo de Enamorado[66] and at the north-east tip of a large promontory forty miles long which jutted out like a ragged tongue from the coast. Beyond this appeared to be a separate island which Cristóbal Colón took to be the land of the feared Cariba, the tribe of cannibals.

Several men went ashore from the *Niña* to collect *niames* for the ship. They encountered an ugly, naked man with his face smeared with charcoal and with his coarse hair pulled back in a ponytail. He was invited aboard the ship. His different speech and manner indicated that he was one of the Cariba who, it was alleged by the Taínos Indians, ate their captives.[67] This aggressive tribe was evidently composed of daring people since they travelled around all the islands of the Indies, including the island of Matinino, farther to the east.[68] This was the island inhabited only by women where a great deal of copper-rich gold existed.

The *Niña*'s men took the Cariba Indian ashore where fifty-five of his tribe with thick, long hair and wearing headdresses of colourful parrots' feathers were assembled. Pedro had pleaded with Bartolomé García to go too. It was his last chance to go ashore before they departed and he wanted to take something back for his mother.

'Very well, Pedro. You can go. But no running off, now! Keep close to the men. And you'd better take some of the hawks' bells with you from the chest below. They're what the Indians seem to like most.'

The seamen traded for some bows and Pedro managed to obtain an ornamental mask carved from a piece of cedar wood and polished brightly with beeswax. His mother would like that. However, after the seamen had obtained the bows, the Indians suddenly withdrew, preparing to attack and capture the seven seamen. But the seamen were ready, and when the Cariba approached, the *Niña*'s men ran at them, giving one of the Cariba a great cut on the buttocks and injuring another in the chest with an arrow. Sancha Ruíz, the *Niña*'s pilot who was in charge of the small party of seamen, withdrew them to the caravel before they could run after and harm any more of the Cariba, who had fled. Colón was not displeased to hear of this skirmish since this small demonstration of force by his men might prove advantageous to his small

---

[66] Lover's Cape. Now Cabo Cabrón.
[67] They had encountered the Ciguayos Indians on the cultural border with the Taínos Indians.
[68] Martinique.

colony of thirty-nine souls at Villa de la Navidad if they were to encounter these Cariba. They were only some hundred miles distant.

'What did you obtain from the Indians, Pedro?' asked the Admiral when the cabin boy arrived back on board the *Niña*.

'I traded two hawks' bells and a red seaman's cap for a small mask made of cedar wood. It's very well carved.'

'Well, I think you need something else to take back to your mother. In any case, I still have to reward you for finding my sea charts. Come up to my cabin.'

'Now,' Colón said when Pedro had shut the door, 'are you by any chance betrothed back in Castile?'

Pedro was taken aback. His mind raced to Raquel in the village of Mecina in *Al-Andalus*. How was she and the child – his child? How was she coping with the violent, middle-aged Abu Ishar ibn Hakam, to whom she had been betrothed and to whom she would now be married? Did Yazíd manage to see her on his way home?

'Pedro?'

'Oh, I'm sorry, Admiral. I was miles away. Yes, I am betrothed,' he replied, 'to a beautiful girl in the Alpujarra. Her name's Raquel.'

'That's good,' Colón answered.

'Here,' he said, bending over the chest containing his personal effects, 'please take this sheet of wrought gold which I was given by the Cacique.' It was the size of his hand and as thin as a sheet or two of card. 'There's enough there to have rings made up for your mother and your Raquel.'

Pedro was overwhelmed. He did not know what to say. The Admiral laughed.

'Think nothing of it, Pedro. From what you've told me, Queen Isabel would be the first to approve of this gift. I shall tell her how you came to be aboard the *Pinta*. She'll be amused to hear of it, although not altogether surprised, I'll warrant!'

The next day, January 14th, none the worse for the skirmish, several of the Cariba Indians paddled out to the ships. They were given honey and biscuits to eat as well as red caps, beads and a piece of red cloth. Their king promised the next day to bring a gold mask, repeating that much gold existed on their island and Matinino. But worryingly, the two caravels were leaking a great deal of water at the keel due to the poor work of the caulkers at Palos before they had set off.

The next day, the crown of gold arrived from the king, and for the very last time on the voyage, cotton, *niames*, and bread were obtained by the crews in exchange for caps, bells and beads. Four young Indians, who appeared to have a great deal of knowledge of the islands to the east, were taken on board to return voluntarily to Spain.

Much seaweed lay in the bay where they were anchored, similar to that which the ships encountered crossing the ocean. Believing that this weed was derived from shallow coastal waters off islands running to the east, the Admiral concluded that they must now be less than twelve hundred miles from the Canaries, whence they had come.[69]

The next day, January 26th 1493, the *Niña* and *Pinta* departed the Indies, one hundred and seventy-six days after they had left Palos.

---

[69] Colón was optimistic. He was still some 2,700 nautical miles from the Canaries.

XII: Lisbon

Wednesday, January 16th 1493

'Bendita sea la luz
y la Santa Veracruz,
y el Señor de la Verdad
y la Santa Trinidad;
bendita sea el alba
y el Señor que nos la manda;
bedito sea el día
y el Señor que nos lo envía.'

At the first tiny glimmer of light on the eastern horizon, Rodrigo Monte, a cabin boy on the *Niña*, chanted with gusto the daybreak oration. Before a westerly breeze and taking a heading to the north-east, the *Pinta* and *Niña* set off for home. For the crew, if not the officers, it was not a day too soon.

At one time or another, some twenty-three Indians had been on board the *Santa María* and *Pinta* to be taken back to meet the King. Most had been released or had escaped. Remaining were three Taínos on the *Pinta* from Río de Mares in Cuba and seven on the *Niña* with the Admiral and Vicente Pinzón. Four of these were Ciguayos from Puerto de Flechas in Española who joined the ship the day before they departed. One of the Ciguayos was the father of the Cacique, Guacanagari, with whom Cristóbal Colón had become very close. Three were from Guanahaní. They had been with the Christians almost from the start.

After forty-eight miles, one of the Ciguayos pointed to the island lying to the south-east which they said was inhabited only by women but, after just a few miles, and despite this compelling lure, the *Niña*'s crew made clear their preference to return home forthwith. With both ships leaking badly, Colón saw the wisdom of this, and the ships' bows were turned once again to the north-east.

For twenty-seven days the two ships sailed east-north-east or north-east, sometimes being pushed by the wind more to the north and sometimes more to the south. Every day the pumps were manned for an hour to prevent the sea, which was seeping into the ships, from welling up from their bilges into the holds. At times the *Pinta* dragged behind the *Niña*. Unfairly, the Admiral berated the loyal Vicente about the inability of the larger of the caravels to sail close to the wind.

'If only your brother had taken the trouble to replace that defective mast of his, and not spent so much time searching for gold, we might be able to take the course we choose.'

Martín Pinzón's acquisition of so much gold still irritated Colón beyond measure, but the latter at least still had his health. The pains in the Pinzón's joints grew worse, as did the rashes on his hands and feet, and he became more prone to fatigue.

In light to moderate seas, encountering many tuna and at times great rafts of weed, the ships made good progress, sailing eighty or more nautical miles per day. On February 6th they made an astonishing two hundred and twenty-three miles in the day, the greatest for the whole voyage. But it was too good to last. Using dead reckoning, Colón placed the ships at over two hundred miles to the south of the island of Flores, the most westerly island of the Azores group of islands. They were Portuguese possessions. These nine widely spaced volcanic islands stretched in a line roughly from the north-west to south-east across the ships' route to Spain, and they lay some nine hundred miles due west of Lisbon in Portugal. The capital of the Azores, named *Santa María*, was the most south-easterly of the islands. Pedro Juan Niño, the *Niña*'s pilot, Vicente Pinzón, the ship's master, and Bartolomé Roldán, the apprentice pilot, all placed the ships in and around the approaches to the Azores, and very much closer than the Admiral.

On Wednesday, February 13th, the wind picked up and the sea became grey and stormy with high waves. Lightning flashed across the sky to the north-north-east, presaging a great storm. Immediately, the two captains ordered everything moveable above and below decks to be firmly secured. As far as possible the decks were cleared of all objects and the hatches were checked for being watertight. All but the main entrance hatch onto the main deck were closed and sealed. There was no chance of using the open hearth in a storm so this was moved back and tied to the side of the deckhouse. From now on there would be no hot food nor hot drink. Ropes were fixed in place along the centre of the deck to provide a handhold and also along the side rails for the same purpose. Below decks, everything was made doubly shipshape: the crews' kitbags were tied well above the floor to keep dry, all lids were tightened on containers and all perishable provisions placed in canvas sacks. All that could be done was done.

The wind increased that night and the waves were frightful, coming in opposite directions, trapping the ships so that while still in the trough of one, another wave would come from the side to crash over them. The mainsail on the *Niña* was set very low to escape the worst of the wind, which increased in fury as did the sea. Seeing the great danger which the ships were in, Colón and Martín Pinzón ran before the storm, letting the gale carry them where it would. In no time, the *Pinta* disappeared from sight. The *Niña* showed a lantern, but in a short time the *Pinta* was lost to sight.

Conditions aboard the two ships were both dreadful and dangerous. To venture out onto the open deck was to run the risk of being swept overboard with not the slightest chance of rescue. The two pumps, one each side of the mainmast and a yard in front of the deckhouse, needed almost constant manning, each by two men, night and day. Just standing in the low deckhouse controlling the massive spar of the tiller using the rope and pulley assembly was difficult enough. Those of the crew not needed on deck mostly remained below deck, in near total darkness, since the hatches onto the deck had to remain closed. No lantern could be lit. It was unhygienic, airless, humid, fetid and cramped. Fear kept the peace amongst the men. The Indians aboard, clothed and barefoot now like the rest of the seamen, took their turn to man the pumps, but otherwise they wisely kept to themselves and out of mischief.

Many of the seamen aboard the two ships had spent the greater part of their lives at sea but they had never experienced a storm so awful or so continuous before. Many were too sick to go on deck to help run the ship or even to retch over the side. Amongst those badly affected was Colón's servant, Diego de Salcedo, who remained curled up below deck at the prow for days. Sea water dripping down through the deck hatches, stinking bilge water surging up into the hold through the bilge hatch, vomit and excreta all added to the awfulness of the conditions below decks.

For Pedro it was an experience he would never forget. The stink and squalor were worse even than his months-long incarceration in the dungeons of the Inquisition. At least the dreadful conditions there were of his own making. As during that nightmare, this, his latest birthday, his nineteenth, passed unnoticed; but to be sure, his mother Miriam would have remembered and marked it in some way. Fortunately, Pedro avoided sickness and now, fully recovered from his fever, he took every opportunity to go up on deck and help out. His willingness and good humour to do double turns on the pumps and help the pilot unstintingly did not go unnoticed by Colón, Vicente Pinzón or Bartolomé García, the bo'sun.

The next day, knowing that all was lost in the worst storm he had ever experienced in all his years at sea, the Admiral ordered that a pilgrimage to Santa María de Guadalupe be pledged, during which a candle weighing five pounds should be carried by the chosen pilgrim. Every man was given a chickpea, one of which was incised by a knife with the sign of the cross. Every man took one pea from those shaken in a cap. Colón was the first to draw and by chance picked out the marked pea. He pledged himself to undertake the pilgrimage if they were to survive the terrible storm. But still it increased in strength.

And as before, Colón wrote in his *diario* that night, *I have committed myself to God and have conducted my enterprise for Him, and He has heard me and given me all that I have asked, and I believe that God will fulfil what has begun and that he will deliver me safely.*

Writing down everything about the voyage which the evening light permitted, the Admiral placed a parchment in a sealed barrel and cast it into the sea, beseeching whoever might find it to deliver it to the Sovereigns.[70]

---

[70] It was never found.

After sunset the sky cleared from the west although the sea was still very high. A small sail was placed on the mainsail and the ship ran before the wind. The next morning, the 15th, land was seen off the prow some fifteen miles distant. The pilots and sailors believed that they were already off the coast of Spain. All the next day, and the next, in heavy seas and fierce winds they tacked one way and the other, trying to reach one of the two islands which were then in sight. That night, after skirting one of the islands, they dropped anchor in a bay only to lose it. They set sail again and beat about all night finally anchoring on the north side of the island. The ship's boat was sent ashore. The island was Santa María in the Azores. The islanders marvelled that the ship had survived the storm, which was the worst they had experienced in living memory, and they indicated a harbour where the ship might anchor safely. That evening three islanders came down to the shore and were rowed across to the *Niña*. They brought fowls and fresh bread.

The captain of the island, Juan de Castañeda, promised to come at dawn with more provisions. In compliance with the vows which the officers and crew of the *Niña* had made during the peak of the storm four days earlier, Colón sent half his men ashore to fulfil their pilgrimage to a small hermitage or chapel near the shore, but which was concealed from view from the ship. Three messengers also went ashore to the village to ask a priest to come to the ship to say Mass. The first half of the crew went in their shirts as vowed but while praying they were attacked and seized by the villagers and by the captain of the island. By eleven o'clock the men had not returned and, suspecting foul play, Colón weighed anchor, taking the ship to a point where the hermitage was visible. Suddenly a body of horsemen appeared on the shore, dismounted and rowed out to the *Niña* in a boat with the evident intention of taking the Admiral prisoner.

'Will you give me safe conduct to come aboard?' Juan de Castañeda, shouted across the water.

'I will. I give you my word,' replied Colón, but nevertheless felt no compunction about holding the man and his crew in the light of his arrest of the *Niña*'s men.

But Castañeda had second thoughts about going aboard the ship.

'By what right are you detaining my people?' demanded an angry Colón. 'Your action in arresting my men will surely annoy your King Juan of Portugal, since his people are well treated in Castile and can come and go where they please. My men ashore will have told you that we have just returned from our voyage to the Indies. My Sovereigns, King Fernando and Queen Isabel, have given me letters of recommendation for all the Princes and Lords of the world, and these you can see if you wish.'

'They are of no concern to me or my King,' Castañeda replied, dismissively.

'I remind you that I am King Fernando's Admiral of the Ocean Sea and Viceroy of the Indies, and have a warrant signed by him and bearing his royal seal.'

'Huh! What is that to me,' the island's captain repeated.

'What it is to you, my dear sir, is trouble. There is much love between our two Kings. I have sufficient crew to return on board my ship here to Castile, and when my Sovereigns and your King hear of your insolence in arresting my men, you and your people here will be severely punished. Have no fear.'

'Do what you will, you blackguard!' the island's captain replied tersely. 'This is Portuguese territory and I do not recognise your King or Queen, nor their letters.' He stood up in the bows of his boat. 'Bring your ship into the harbour before it sinks in this high sea.'

'I will,' replied the Admiral, 'but rest assured that I will take a hundred of you Portuguese to Castile before I leave my ship.'

With the weather and sea showing no signs of abating, the *Niña* entered the harbour and they filled the empty water and wine casks with sea water to improve the ship's stability. But the harbour offered little shelter on an island which was skirted by high cliffs. The next morning, Wednesday, February 20th, the anchor broke and Colón had little choice but to sail on to the island of San Miguel, fifty miles to the north-east.

They beat about all that night in a mountainous sea, the storm still raging. With San Miguel not visible in the heavy rain, they returned to Santa María at daybreak so as to recover their men and the lost anchor and cables. That evening, having returned to the same harbour in which they had been two days before, a boat came with five sailors, a notary and a priest seeking a guarantee of security, which was granted. Since it was late they slept on board. The next morning they examined the letters of authority from the Spanish Sovereigns and, satisfied, returned ashore, finally releasing the *Niña*'s men, who returned to the ship unharmed.

The next morning, Saturday, February 23rd, unable to find a suitable spot along the coast to take on wood and stone ballast, they turned to the east and headed for Spain, driven by a strong south-westerly wind. For a week or more they ran before the incessant storm, sometimes going to the north-east and sometimes to the south-east.

When the *Pinta* separated from the *Niña* on the second day of the storm ten days earlier, Martín Pinzón's caravel was in an even worse plight than the smaller ship. She was taking on an inordinate amount of water, both through the side planking and over the deck, and her mainmast was showing signs of serious strain and was not able to carry full sail even in a moderate wind. Driven by the gale, the ship bore to the north-east, passing between the islands of Santa María and San Miguel. For fourteen days more, under a foresail and barely any mainsail, the ship crashed and rolled in the heaving ocean. The crew stayed below decks, save those manning the pumps on a half-hour rota and those helping Cristóbal Sarmiento, the pilot, handle the heavy tiller and its steering assembly. By now there was little fresh water to drink on board and no hot food. Martín Pinzón's physical condition worsened and his brother,

Francisco, as master, took over responsibility for the running of the ship.

By an act of God, on the first day of March, the officer on watch, Gómez Rascón, spotted land on the starboard bow through the spume and driving rain. The helm, which had given them so much trouble on the journey out, was hauled over to the port side and within hours the *Pinta* limped pitifully into the sanctuary of the northern Spanish port of Bayona in Galicia. Bayona, known as the Villa Real, was the most important port in all Spain. With neighbouring La Coruña it enjoyed a maritime monopoly for trade with Portugal, France, England and Flanders in fish, skins, oil, wine, sugar and wool.

As the first ship to bring news of the voyage, Martín Pinzón, his brother, and the remaining officers and crews were fêted. They were treated to much needed hot meals with fresh meat, vegetables and fresh bread as well as with lodgings for the duration of their short stay in Bayona. Soon after the arrival of the *Pinta*, hundreds of excited townsfolk, well used to welcoming home ships from long voyages at sea, rushed down to the quayside to see the olive-skinned Indians from Guanahaní with their peculiar broadened heads and all the miscellany of objects which the *Pinta* had collected in the Indies: cotton, plants, seeds, chilli peppers, cobs and roots of maize, *naime* or sweet potato, medicinal and aromatic plants. There was cinnamon bark, stone axe heads, bows and arrows with fish bone tips, the skeletal bones of the fish they had caught, dried skins of the big lizards which they had caught, cotton sheets, hammocks and nets, and green amber. However, the gold they had obtained at Río de Gracia in Española was kept well out of sight. This did not prevent rumours circulating through the town that the ship was so laden down with this coveted cargo that it was barely able to reach port.

That very day Martín Pinzón wrote to the Sovereigns with news of his return and of their fabulous discoveries, craving an audience.

Delayed unavoidably by the four days in the Azores, the *Niña* encountered another terrible storm on March 3rd, which rent its sails in two. Lots were drawn for another pilgrimage, this time for the lucky winner to go in his shirt on their return to Santa María de la Cinta in Huelva. Miraculously, for the third time the Admiral chose the incised chickpea.

Struggling on bare masts, the *Niña* approached land and on March 4th it turned into the broad harbour of Lisbon on the Río Tajo, Portugal's principal city. Colón was informed that the storm which had so nearly claimed his ship, and must surely have taken the *Pinta* and all its crew, was the worst in living memory in the western Atlantic. Twenty-five ships had been lost in Flanders alone and many more had been unable to depart for months.

Colón wrote to the King of Portugal who was in residence only twenty-seven miles away at Valle de Paraíso. The next morning Alvaro Dama, the captain of Portugal's greatest ship, which carried more cannon than Colón had ever seen on a ship before, paid a visit. Dressed as befit a lord and admiral of the Portuguese fleet, he boarded the *Niña* to the sound of drums, pipes and trumpets. When he had inspected the letters and warrants from the Spanish Sovereigns, he offered generously to do all that the Admiral requested.

The next day, Friday, March 8th, Don Martín de Noroña, a distinguished nobleman, arrived on horseback and delivered a letter from King Juan. The Portuguese Sovereign would be pleased to be attended by the Admiral. Colón thought hard. Vicente Yañez Pinzón was needed to clean up the ship and re-provision it with sufficient water, wine, wood and fresh food to complete their voyage to Palos. Moreover, while he had remained loyal to Colón throughout the seven months of the voyage, he was still deemed by the Admiral to be as tainted as his brother, Martín. Sancho Ruíz, the pilot, who, more than anyone, had seen the *Niña* safely through the storm, deserved to go with him. And furthermore, as the Sovereign's Admiral of the High Seas, it was fitting that Colón should be accompanied by a servant.

'Bo'sun!' he called to Bartolomé García. 'Find young Pedro Tegero and send him to me.'

'Yes, sir, right away. By the way, Admiral, you were right,' the bo'sun added, 'nobody aboard this ship worked harder or more willingly than Pedro during the storm. He was always there when I called for more hands on deck.'

Pedro arrived breathless from helping mop up the mess still sloshing around the hold. The Admiral was buttoning up his best silk doublet.

'Pedro, you are to accompany me and the ship's pilot to meet King Juan of Portugal. With poor Diego still incapacitated, you're to act as my personal servant. We're departing shortly with Don Martín of Noroña.'

'But what shall I wear?' asked Pedro, indicating his worn and filthy clothes.

'Don't worry, lad,' replied the Admiral, almost euphoric after the trauma of the last few weeks. 'Have a look in Diego's chest. I'm sure you'll find a clean white shirt and breeches and stockings and shoes. And, of course, a seaman's red cap... I think we might just have one left.' He laughed.

'By the way, can you ride a horse?'

'Yes, sir, but I haven't been in a saddle for quite a while.'

'No, nor have I, Pedro. Regrettably, there were no horses in Cuba or Española, were there!'

With the weather still windy and wet, Don Martín's small party only got as far as Sacavem and, after staying the night, arrived at the King's palace the following evening. Thirty-eight-year-old King Juan II received them with great honour and respect. The King had been on the throne for twelve years. Being an astute politician and statesman and patron of Renaissance art and literature, he was known as Juan el Bueno.[71]

'Welcome once again, my Lord Admiral, The noble Don Martín brought me news of your arrival.'

---

[71] John the Good. In 1494 he signed the Treaty of Tordesillas, setting the bounds for Spanish and Portuguese colonial expansion.

'Thank you, Your Majesty,' replied Cristóbal Colón, bowing low and sweeping his arm across his chest.

'How many years is it now since you came here seeking my support for your voyage?'

'I think five, Sire.'

'Well, how I misjudged your will and determination, Señor Colón! I take my hat off to you. But it was a miracle that you survived that frightful storm. Did you not have another ship with you?'

'Yes, Sire, the *Pinta*, under the command of Martín Alonso Pinzón…'

'What! That rascal from Palos?' chipped in the King.

'Yes, Sire. His brother, Vicente, is aboard the *Niña* with me as master.' He went on without pausing, not wanting to get distracted about the notorious activities of the men of Palos over the years. 'Unfortunately, the *Pinta* got separated from us when we were approaching your islands off the Azores. I have no idea whether Martín Pinzón or his ship survived the storm.'

'Have no fear, Admiral, for all his faults he's a great sailor. I expect he made land somewhere along this coast. I expect he's already on the way to see your King Fernando with your news!'

Cristóbal Colón blanched visibly.

'Now sit down beside me, Admiral, and tell me all about your voyage.'

It was an honour to be seated in the presence of a sovereign, a privilege which the Catholic Monarchs themselves rarely granted, and never to Colón. Sancho Ruíz and Pedro Tegero remained standing, behind the Admiral.

'I see you have a servant with you!' the King commented. 'Your Spanish ships are clearly better endowed than ours!'

Stung, the Admiral replied, 'No, Sire! He is a young apprentice seaman on my boat, who through his diligence and spirit did as much as anyone to see us through the storm. He deserved to accompany me. His name's Pedro Tegero, Sire. By amazing fortune he is acquainted with King Fernando and Queen Isabel, whom he saved from a fire…'

'Not the fire at Santa Fe?'

'Yes, Sire. You know of it?'

'Of course, I heard of it within days. If it had been as calamitous as reported to me I might now be the sovereign of our two countries!'

He turned to Pedro. 'Well, well! So you're the culprit… But pray continue, my Lord Admiral.'

Relaxed and put at ease, and for nearly an hour without interruption, Colón described in detail their journey and the islands and peoples whom he had discovered.

'Truly fascinating,' commented the King. 'But you do realise, Admiral, that all the lands you discovered are mine.'

'Sire?' replied Colón, totally startled.

'Yes, my Lord Admiral. Under the terms of the *Capitulaciones*, I understand that the Indies which you found belong to Portugal.'

'Sire, replied Colón, regaining his composure, 'the Catholic Monarchs expressly forbade my journeying to La Mina and Guinea on the African coast, these being your lands. With this I wholly complied. As I've explained to Your Highness, our voyage took us westwards across the Ocean Sea to new lands – which I proclaimed there as belonging to Castile.'

'Very well, Admiral. Have no fear! This matter can be resolved amicably between our two kingdoms. We have no need to dispute the issue now.'

'Tonight,' the King went on, changing the mood, 'you're to be the guest of the Prior of Clato. I'm sure he'll honour you fittingly for your courage and tenacity in venturing so far beyond our shores.'

The next day after Mass, it being Sunday, the King spoke again at length to Colón about the voyage, promising to help in whatever way he could with the final stage of his voyage.

The day after the *Pinta*'s arrival in Bayona, and with Juan Quintero supervising, the caravel was moved to the boatyard of Pero Arroyo and Pero Enríquez. There it was taken out of the water. After the bilges had been pumped dry, the ship was recaulked and then fitted with new masts and sails. While there the bo'sun saw to it that the crew gave the ship a thorough scrub and clean, particularly below decks, which were in a disgusting state. Back in the water the ship's boat was used to ferry fresh water from a quayside well to the *Pinta*. Wine and fresh food followed. Martín Pinzón was fully aware that the designated port for the departure and the arrival of Colón's small flotilla was Palos de la Frontera.

Then on March 8th news arrived that the *Niña* had arrived at Lisbon and that the Admiral was the guest of King Juan. Pinzón's pride demanded that he must arrive in Palos first to announce the news of the ships' safe return. He speeded up the repairs and re-provisioning of the *Pinta* and on the March 10th, ten days after his arrival home in Spain, he left Bayona and headed south to Palos. Some of his crew had departed to return to their homes in other parts of Spain, but most of his crew were from Palos, Moguer and Huelva and they rejoined the ship for this last journey.

Martín Alonso Pinzón was dreading the meeting with Cristóbal Colón and his worry over this was affecting his health. The acrimony between the two was deep and bitter and had grown progressively through the voyage. He knew that the Admiral believed that his action in abandoning the *Santa María* and *Niña* on November 21st when they were in Cuba was both treacherous and treasonable and he feared that Colón intended to seek redress through the Sovereigns. But he, Martín, believed that Colón had become bogged down at Río de Mares, sailing pointlessly hither and thither amongst the small coral islands. He had expressed his disquiet to the Admiral, who had ignored his overtures; and finally, through pure frustration, he had sailed off to Babeque in search of gold. Martín felt bitter that the Admiral had not appreciated that it was he, Martín, who through his forceful intervention and wholehearted support for the Admiral, had prevented the mutinies on the *Santa María* on

October 6th and 10th. As it was, if they had not found land soon afterwards, the Admiral would have been obliged to concur with his precipitate promise to the mutineers and would have had to return forthwith to Spain. Martín was also resentful that Colón did not acknowledge that it was he who had first discovered the island of Española, and he felt that it was an act of pure spite on Colón's part to change the name of the Río de Martín Pinzón to Río de Gracia.

On January 10th the Admiral had demanded that Martín release the four Indian men and two girls whom he had taken aboard the *Pinta* to return to Spain. Yet, just before they departed Española, four Ciguayos joined the *Niña*. Was not this the action of a mean-spirited and spiteful man? Finally, Martín had offered to hand over all the gold which he had found at Río de Martín Pinzón to Colón, but jealous of Martín's success in amassing the one thing above all else he craved, Colón had rejected his generous offer. Martín desperately needed to arrive at Palos first and send a second letter to the Sovereigns in Barcelona expressing his point of view. His headaches and aching joints continued.

The day after Martín Pinzón's departure from Bayona, the Admiral took leave of the Portuguese King and, accompanied by Don Martín de Noroña and a score of cavaliers, they rode to the monastery of San Antonio where the Queen was staying. She had insisted that the Admiral paid his respects to her before he rejoined his ship. The following day, as Colón was about to return to the *Niña*, a squire arrived from the King to offer overland transport by carriage to Spain, but the Admiral politely declined. On behalf of the King, the squire gave Sancho Ruíz, the pilot, twenty gold coins and Pedro ten.

The following morning, March 13th, surprisingly still wholly unaware of the safe arrival of the *Pinta* in Galicia, the *Niña*, cleaned and re-provisioned, weighed anchor and in a heavy sea and a wind from the north-west, sailed for Palos, some three hundred miles distant. That same afternoon news arrived in Lisbon that the *Pinta* was safe and in Bayona, but the news was too late to reach Colón. At noon on March 15th, the *Niña* crossed the sandbar at Saltes and dropped anchor in the place from whence it had departed on August 3rd the previous year.

Thus, the writing is now completed… Cristóbal Colón wrote in his final *diario* entry *…and I have given a full account of my voyage, which Our Lord has permitted me to make, and for which He inspired me. His Divine Majesty does all good things, and everything is good except sin, and nothing can be imagined or planned without His consent. This voyage has miraculously proven this to be so, as can be learnt from this writing, by the remarkable miracles which have occurred during the voyage…*

Amazingly, that very same afternoon the *Pinta* sailed into the river and dropped anchor close to the *Niña*. The ship had been spotted as it entered the estuary and the people of Palos were there on the bluff overlooking the anchorage near St George's church to welcome home their illustrious captain and their kith and kin. But with the exception of two sailors from the town who had volunteered to keep watch aboard, the *Niña* was totally deserted. There was no welcoming cheer for the *Pinta*. No lombard was fired in salute.

XIII: A Letter from Don Gonzalo

March 1493

Pedro Togeiro de Tudela, adopting his real name once again, wasted no time in setting off from Palos for home. He had a journey of nearly five hundred miles ahead of him. Most of the crew of the *Niña* were keen to do likewise, although many were faced by the same journey but expressed in yards not miles. Pedro said his goodbyes to Vicente Pinzón, the *Niña*'s captain, Pedro Niño, the pilot and Bartolomé García, the bo'sun, but especially to Cristóbal Colón. The Admiral shook his hand warmly, saying that he was sure that he would hear of the young man's exploits again some time in the future. With his trophies of the voyage in his kitbag, including the thin sheet of gold given to him by the Admiral and the ten gold coins from the King of Portugal, Pedro collected the remainder of his wages on the completion of the voyage. Wobbling uncertainly on his feet after being so long at sea, he headed up past St George's church, through a throng of excited townsfolk already gathering there, past the alley where the cabin boy was slain and down the main street of the town, passing a long row of houses on his left, amongst them one belonging to Martín Pinzón.[72]

Pedro was in desperate need of some sturdy shoes and some new clothes, so he stopped off in a shop just down from Pinzón's house near the town square and bought what he need with some of his wages. As he left the store he heard cheers billowing up from the waterside and, reaching the rise beyond the southern edge of the town, he caught sight of the *Pinta* lowering its sails as it approached its mooring close to the *Niña*. Loud cheers went up from those gathering on the water's edge and a puff of bluish smoke rose into the air followed a second or two later by the dull detonation of a lombard cannon being fired from the *Pinta*. The ship's arrival was the first Pedro and the *Niña*'s officers and crew knew of the *Pinta*'s survival after the two ships had separated a month before off the Azores. Pedro was thrilled beyond measure that Martín Pinzón and his crew, and especially his friend Rodrigo de Triana, had arrived home safely. Resisting the temptation to return to the wooden jetty where ships' crews disembarked, Pedro turned back up through the town towards nearby Moguer to join the main highway from Huelva to Sevilla, some fifty miles distant.

He did not get very far. The whole town of Palos was ecstatic. Months and months of worry and pent-up anxiety by the townsfolk over whether their

---

[72] Now a small museum dedicated to the town's most famous son.

loved ones would return from the ocean voyage was released in one explosive outpouring of rejoicing. Everyone in the town was connected in some way with the sea. Many had husbands, sons, nephews, cousins or boyfriends on one or other of the returning caravels. The crews from the *Niña*, already celebrating with their families in their homes, came back out into the streets and joined the happy throng in greeting their co-explorers disembarking from the *Pinta*. Now, with the *Pinta*'s safe return, every seaman had at least two women around his neck or hooked tightly onto each arm, or had children's faces buried deeply against his body. Palos had seen nothing like it ever before, and that day became part of the folklore surrounding this seafaring community. Caught up in the tumultuous euphoria, Pedro's tears of joy joined those of everyone there of whatever sex, age or disposition. Eventually the throng evaporated as the seamen drifted at last to their homes. Those with homes in Moguer, Huelva or other nearby towns had left earlier. With one final wave to those remaining in the town square, Pedro set off for his home. Although soon to be shattered, his spirits had never been higher. In a couple of weeks time he would be reunited with his mother in Vélez Blanco. Yazíd would have explained everything to her.

Good old Yazíd, what a friend he had been! A year younger than Pedro, dusky-skinned, stockier and always scruffy, he had once saved Pedro from a lingering death. Even now Pedro did not understand his friend's capacity to cover great distances in impossibly short times, whether by supernatural power or simply by sheer stamina. Maybe Yazíd was a sprite after all – an afreet. There was the time, for instance, when Yazíd had searched for and found Pedro lying with a twisted ankle at the bottom of an old mine shaft near Mecina into which he had fallen days before with no hope whatever of escape. But what an unexpected outcome there had been to his rescue! Then there was the time when Yazíd appeared at the handover of Almería, and finally by the side of the dying cabin boy in Palos, persuading Pedro to join the *Pinta*.

Pedro strode on, whistling loudly. All would be well. Yazíd would have told Pedro's mother, Miriam, everything. Particularly, how the fulfilment of her son's last riddle induced him to join the *Pinta* and from which he would return to recount to her his exploits and experiences.

How impatient would his mother be for her son's return! Miriam, fair-haired, tall, slim, with her beauty barely fading as she passed her thirty-sixth birthday, was overawed to have been invited to meet Queen Isabel of Castile and to have spoken at length with her. This had been soon after the fall of Muslim Granada to the Christian forces on the January 2nd 1492, some fourteen months before. Later accorded by the Pope the title 'The Catholic Monarchs', Fernando and Isabel made a formidable pair, and through their diligence, guile and hard endeavour, they steered Spain into its glory days which were soon to follow. Miriam had been discovered by Pedro in the Sultan's quarters in the lovely Generalife pavilion and gardens which faced the towering walls of the Alhambra, the Sultan's magical and ornate palace.

For some nine years Miriam had languished in the harem of the Sultan, having earlier been captured by black African slavers when visiting the Almerían port of Aguilas with her husband, Abraham, and eight-year-old Pedro. Miriam had violently resisted the overtures of the lascivious Prince of Almería, Cidi Yayha al-Nagal, and subsequently the Sultan himself in Granada. But through her handiwork using fine silks, she was encouraged to found an embroidery school in the Alhambra, to which young women of noble family from Cairo, Baghdad and Damascus could come to learn the skill. Miriam was sitting at the open window of the Generalife with the golden rays of the setting sun illuminating her handsome face when fate led Pedro to her on the very day of the liberation.

Through her courtier, Don Gonzalo Fernández of Córdoba, Queen Isabel had promised Pedro that he must dine with her and the King as a reward for his saving their lives in the bedroom fire at a mansion belonging to Don Gonzalo himself. Six months later, Pedro was invited to ride with the Queen's personal guard at the fall of Granada. It was during his exploration of the Alcazaba, the Alhambra and the Generalife later that very day with the Captain of the Queen's guard, Agustín López, and under the supervision of Boabdil's close confidant, Yusuf Aben Comisa, that he had discovered Miriam. Pedro and his father – now, of course, deceased – had heard nothing of her since that accursed day at Aguilas all those years before. Both had assumed her dead, or worse, far worse, sold in the slave market of Baghdad. It was only the day after her joyous reunion with Pedro that she learnt from him of the death of Abraham and Cristina. As it was, Pedro kept the brutality and horror of their murder from her.

Queen Isabel learnt of this miraculous reunion between mother and son when Pedro dined with her and the King in the Sovereign's unfinished palace in their new city of Santa Fe, outside Granada. Much out of curiosity, the Queen invited Miriam to an audience with her. Finely dressed and looking fit and bronzed, Miriam explained to the Queen the tragic events which caused her to spend almost half of her adult life imprisoned in the Sultan's quarters, although fortunately not as a concubine. As she laughingly explained to the Queen, 'There were already in the harem the most gorgeous, sultry young women from all corners of the Muslim empire. The Sultan hardly needed the attentions of a matron like me in her mid-twenties who had had two children!'

Decisive as always, the Queen appointed the handsome Captain Agustín Lopez to accompany Miriam back to her border town of Vélez Blanco. The Queen handed the captain, dressed in his smartest tunic, 250,000 maravedís to deposit with a registered moneylender in the town to secure Miriam's future, and as recompense for the ordeals which she had endured. As a final duty for him, the Queen instructed Pedro to accompany Boabdil, the Sultan, on his tearful departure from his beloved city. It was as Pedro was leaving the Sultan to journey on to Palos de la Frontera that the Sultan solemnly bequeathed the great Mohammed the Fifth's sapphire-encrusted ornamental dagger to Pedro as a token of their friendship and in recognition of Pedro's companionship of his then young captive son, Ahmad, in the tower of Porcuna.

Agustín López had been in the service of the King since the age of fourteen and, after twenty-five years' service, he was due to retire. His home lay at Archena, near Murcia, and thus on the Christian side of the former Muslim kingdom. Archena was barely two days' ride from Miriam's hilltop town, but he had seen scarce little of his home over the years. A widower, he then had a nine-year-old daughter called Sonia, who was cared for by his sister. His ageing father considered that it was Agustín's filial duty to take over the running of the family fulling mill on his retirement from the army. But this had little appeal to him. The cleaning, shrinking and thickening of woollen cloth in troughs of hot water, piped from a nearby thermal spring, using the brown cleansing clay from nearby pits, was not high on his agenda. After an uneventful journey on horseback across the now subjugated Muslim kingdom of *Al-Andalus*, the couple arrived at Miriam's home a week or so later. It was the first time in years that Miriam had been in proper masculine company – and not that of bejewelled and obsequious eunuchs – and she adored every minute.

Cristóbal Colón, above all else, had two pressing tasks to perform on his arrival in Palos. But first he placed the seven Indians aboard the *Niña* in the hands of his faithful manservant, Diego de Salcedo, in whom he had complete faith, with the instruction to find them safe accommodation and look after them. Bartolomé García, the bo'sun, always dependable, was entrusted with boxing-up securely the miscellaneous gold booty, most of it in the form of gifts from the Cacique, Guacanagari, together with the green amber, dried plants, fruits and tobacco leaves; the chilli peppers, cobs and roots of maize, *naime* or sweet potato; the aromatic herbs, cinnamon bark, dried animal skins, skeletal fish remains; and the cotton hammocks and nets, plus bales and bales of spun cotton. With the help of a couple of the more mature seamen, such as Rodrigo de Triana, the precious hoard was transported to the nearby monastery of La Rábita for safe keeping, prior to it being sent on to the Sovereigns, then in Barcelona.

Within an hour of his arrival, Colón went to La Rábita, overlooking the mouth of the Río Tinto estuary, and where he had received so much support for his venture several years before from the prior and cosmologist, Pedro de Marchena. With the blessings of the resident Franciscan prior there, he attended Mass and gave thanks to God for the safe return of his ship and crew, humbly praying for the safe return of the *Pinta*. Then, conducted to a quiet and comfortable room, he wrote a letter to Luis de Santángel, a principal financier for the voyage, for onward transmission to the Sovereigns. He was desperate to do so in case Martín Pinzón had survived the voyage and had already written to them. (Unknown to the Admiral, Pinzón had already done so while the *Pinta* was being repaired in Bayona.) As Colón started writing he heard the familiar sound of a lombard being fired and prolonged cheering, and knew then that his prayers had been answered and that the *Pinta* was safely delivered.

Later translated into Latin, the letter started:

Because my undertakings have attained success, I know that it will be pleasing to you: these I have determined to relate, so that you may be made acquainted with everything done and discovered in this our voyage. On the thirty-third day I departed from the Canaries,[73] *I came to the Indian sea, where I found many islands inhabited by many men without number...*

He wrote and wrote, amplifying the things which he had scribbled in the hurried note which he had sealed in a barrel and thrown into the sea at the peak of the storm. It took him the remainder of the day and well into the night to write this epoch-making letter to his patron. Finally, with a sense of relief and satisfaction, he finished it, signing it simply:

Cristóbal Colón, admiral of the Ocean fleet.

Now he was ready to face his recalcitrant captain, Martín Pinzón. Struggling with aching joints and with a sickly, blotchy skin, Pinzón arrived soon after sunrise the next morning to give thanks for the safe return of his ship and crew. Whether the two explorers made up their differences now that they were all safely returned, or whether Colón persisted with his threat to charge the Palos man with mutiny, remained locked within the sanctuary of the monastery.

Sometimes walking and sometimes hitching a ride on a wagon, Pedro arrived in Sevilla the following day. Boarding a ferry boat, he was rowed across the fast-flowing Guadalquivir, flushed by the winter rain. He soon found himself within the city wall and inside the Jewish quarter, or what had been the Jewish quarter. Pedro was staggered by what he found. Of course, the tight, interlocking network of narrow streets, alleys and culs de-sac remained; but the bustle and vitality of the ghetto had vanished. Metalworkers and tradespeople had gone. Most of the houses were deserted and boarded up. The white houses and swept streets were no more. Paint was flaking from walls, windows and doors and the blustery winds from North Africa had dusted the roughly rendered walls with their reddish patina. Emaciated dogs wandered around searching for scraps, or roamed through empty houses hunting for rats. Granted, a few houses remained occupied, as did a few shops selling vegetables or fresh fish or old clothes, but the ambience of the close-knit Jewish community had vanished. Yet this was the scene in nearly every town and city in Spain, particularly in the south. Following the royal decree of April the year before, which gave the Jews three months to leave the country, up to one hundred and fifty thousand departed from Spain's shores.

---

[73] In the official Latin version printed in Rome and published on May 3rd this was incorrectly translated as 33 days after leaving Cádiz. The first folio edition of four pages was published in Spanish and printed in Barcelona in April.

Shocked and saddened by what he had found, Pedro hastened through the city, finding himself inevitably, as did all visitors, at the cathedral and the Giralda tower which once had been the minaret of the Muslim mosque. Opposite lay the dark red walls surrounding the former *alcázar*, now the royal palace. It was here nine months earlier that Pedro had brought Cristóbal Colón's sea charts after they had fallen from the saddle-bag of a passing rider by the main city gate. Pedro strolled to the portal of the palace which was guarded by two formidable armed guards. On the studded door between them hung a wooden notice board on which messages could be left. One in particular caught Pedro's eye because, although the writing had faded and the paper was discoloured, the writing of the addressee was beautifully scribed.

'Stand back!' ordered one of the guards, as Pedro peered at it between the pikes they carried.

'Please can I take a closer look?' he asked politely.

'Why? Do you think Don Gonzalo has written to you?' The two guards roared with laughter. One, good-humouredly, prodded Pedro in the chest with the staff of the pike.

'Don Gonzalo Fernández of Córdoba?' asked Pedro, unperturbed.

'Yes, who else? There's only one Don Gonzalo we know of. He's a regular visitor here.'

'I know him too. Please can I see who the letter's written to?'

The soldiers relented and one of them picked it out from between the cross-strings of the notice board.

'There you are, young fellow. Now, is it addressed to you?'

Pedro brushed the dust off the name with his thumb.

'Yes it is. It's addressed to me!' he exclaimed. 'Pedro Togeiro from Vélez Blanco. Can you see?'

'And that's you?'

'Yes, sir.'

'Well you'll have to prove your identity before I'll give it to you.'

Pedro thought hard. What did he have with him? He unhitched his ship's kitbag from his shoulder. It was all he had.

'There you are. You see? Pedro Tegero.'

The guards looked at the name. They could barely read but the roughly-written name on the canvas bag started with a big 'T' and had a 'g' and 'r'.

'Um. Very well. But you'll need to sign for it inside. But before I let you in, tell me what Don Gonzalo looks like? And what's his personal attendant called?'

Martín Pinzón was as equally keen as the Admiral to secure the booty which the *Pinta* had brought back from the Indies. After hearing Mass in La Rábita, he returned to his ship after collecting several of his crew on the way. From there the bags of alluvial gold from Río de Gracia and the golden ornaments he had acquired by diverse means from the natives, weighing some nine hundred ounces in total, were placed in sturdy lidded boxes and taken to his house. He was committed to distributing half the gold amongst his crew, and this he set about doing with the help of the village apothecary and his set of brass scales. All the remaining miscellaneous objects were transported for safe keeping to La Rábita.

A couple of days later a letter arrived in Palos for Martín Pinzón from Queen Isabel. In it she thanked him for the letter which he had sent to the Sovereigns from Bayona announcing the ship's return and for all the services which he had rendered. More significantly, at about the same time orders were sent by the Sovereigns to all the trading ports in northern Spain – in Galicia and Cantabria – forbidding any ships from sailing to the Indies.

Having satisfied the guard, Pedro opened the letter. It was written in beautiful Castilian of which Antonio de Nebrija, the humanist and author of the *Gramatica de la Lengua Castellana*, would have been proud. The letter said:

Letter from Gonzalo Fernández to Pedro Togeiro, lately of Vélez Blanco lying in the former kingdom of the Sultan, Mohammed the Twelfth. Written this day, December 15th 1492.

Firstly, I hope that you are able to convince the guards outside the palace of your identity. If they remain querulous as you open this letter, you can describe to them what happened in my house in Gozco on the night of the fourteenth of July. That should convince them of your authenticity!

Although possibly in vain, I am writing in the hope that you will receive this letter in due course. I have some disturbing news to impart to you concerning your Muslim friend, Yazíd. But it is better that I try and explain events in the order in which they occurred. Please bear with me.

A month ago while conducting business with the Duke of Medina Sidonia here in this palace, I chanced upon the repository of items confiscated from convicted criminals and other miscreants. A jade ring of Queen Isabel, bearing her personal coat of arms on the inner rim, immediately caught my eye (it should never have been placed amongst these other objects), but alongside it was a beautifully crafted Toledo sword with a distinctive haft with alternating white and red brass oval rings and I immediately recognised it as yours. A ruby ring I did not recognise, but the curved, sapphire-encrusted dagger I knew to have belonged to Boabdil as an heirloom of his illustrious predecessor, Mohammed the Fifth. I knew for certain, then, that these objects had been taken from you. I feared the very worst.

The palace treasurer could throw little light on how your belongings came to be there, except to say that they had been sent to Sevilla from Palos de la Frontera. Boabdil, whom I met in the summer in his new residence, told me that you were heading there after you left him and his party on the hill overlooking Granada, on his tearful departure from the city. On learning this, I sent Antonio Manzano, my trusted attendant whom you know well, to Palos, to try and discover what became of you, since by then I was convinced that you must have suffered some tragic fate. Antonio met the sergeant of the town who said that on August 3rd, the very day Cristóbal Colón set off on his voyage with his three ships (and we all pray daily for their safe return), a Muslim boy, around sixteen or seventeen years of age, was arrested for the killing of a youngster who was to be a cabin boy on the *Pinta*. The sergeant had difficulty understanding the Castilian spoken by the young Muslim, who was very agitated and dressed very poorly. The sergeant said that the Muslim boy told him that he, the Muslim boy, was accompanying a tall white boy, older than him, named Pedro, and that this Pedro arrived too late to save the life of the young cabin boy after he was knifed by a thief. The Muslim boy said that his friend Pedro boarded the *Pinta* in the dead boy's place – something to do with a prophecy – and asked the Muslim boy to look after his belongings. You must understand that all this was pieced together by Antonio only after his lengthy interrogation of the sergeant, who became more and more uncomfortable and defensive as the facts were disclosed.

With little further attempt by the sergeant to get to the bottom of the incident, the Muslim boy was sent here in chains, and in the Felons Court he was found guilty of the murder of the cabin boy. Little assistance was given him in order that he might explain what must have happened. Even his name of Yazíd was incorrectly transcribed as Yusuf, a common enough Muslim name. This whole incident is a travesty of justice and reflects shamefully on the attitude of many of His Majesty's subjects to the Muslims following the conquest of Granada. Your poor Yazíd was sentenced to serve three years on a galley, where presumably he now is.

As soon as I found this out I had his sentence suspended and had the court bailiff dismissed from his post, as I have also done with the sergeant in Palos who is now serving in the ranks in some dusty corner of Castile or on the snowbound borders of Navarra. But more importantly, I am taking steps to locate Yazíd and to have him released from slavery forthwith. I don't need to tell you that life on the galleys for criminals is extremely harsh, and few survive the ordeal for much more than a year. So I have sent letters to the constables of all the major ports from here to Marseilles and on to Genoa to locate your friend. I pray to God that we will find him soon. Please rest assured that I will leave no stone unturned until I have found him and had him released. Pray it will not be too late.

Pending your safe return from across the seas, or in the event of you not doing so (in which case this letter is, of course, superfluous) I took possession of your belongings, and am arranging with Martín of Alarcón, who you remember from your Moclín days, to have them returned to your mother, since

I have guessed that this is why you left them with Yazíd. I know that Martín or another trusty officer will be able to locate your mother, Miriam, in your home town without any difficulty. I am writing a letter for them to pass to her which will inform her of these happenings.

In closing therefore, Pedro, I continue to pray for your safe return and that of all your fellow explorers. I hope one day soon we shall meet again.'

Signed

Gonzalo

PS: If you do collect this letter on your way home from Palos, you might find it quicker to go from here by sea to Almería rather than by road through Granada. Granada is not a nice place to be at the moment since there's a lot of civil unrest in the city. To this end I attach a Letter of Credit which will allow you to sail to any port in the kingdoms free of charge. Any captain can convert this credit note into maravedís in any port of destination.

XIV: Girl with Blue Eyes

Pedro stood there transfixed by the news about Yazíd. Poor Yazíd! For him of all people to be immobilised by being chained to a bench in a slave galley was unimaginable.

'Bad news?' asked one of the guards, impressed that the young man in front of him should have received a letter written personally by the eminent knight of the realm.

'Yes! Don Gonzalo tells me that a very close friend of mine has been sent to the galleys for something he didn't do. He says he's put out feelers to find out where he is.'

'Well, have no fear then. If anybody can find him and save him from a fate worse than death, Don Gonzalo can. I'd trust that man with my life.'

'How right you are in your judgement, Sergeant. Five years ago he saved mine from the hands of the Inquisition in Jaén!'

The two guards stood there open-mouthed.

'Goodbye, gentlemen,' said Pedro, grinning and then staggering away as if he were a cripple. 'Thank you for passing me the note.'

There was nothing to do but to return home with all haste. Nevertheless, he would take Don Gonzalo's advice and travel by sea using the Letter of Credit. How thoughtful the man was.

He paused, thinking to himself, If poor Yazíd didn't make it home, he couldn't have called on Raquel to see how she was. Heavens! I must go there first! Throwing his kitbag over his shoulder he lengthened his stride and headed off purposefully through the city. He needed to proceed downriver to Sanlúcar at the mouth of the Guadalquivir, from which most ships of any size sailed. However, rather than walk the fifty miles to Sanlúcar, Pedro took a small boat leaving on the hour from below the floating bridge. There was enough of a current for it to drift downstream without problems.

Leaving the city to tramp the two days to Sanlúcar were several Muslim families and groups of families: riding in wagons, pulling handcarts, or simply moving along in their colourful robes, heads down, resigned. They were leaving Spain for good. Clearly, they were not prepared to be baptised into the Christian faith and thereby become Moriscos, or retain their religion as Mudejares and keep some semblance of their former existence within the Christian community. This sorry picture was being repeated all over the country, and would continue for many years more.

Pedro arrived in the bustling port of Sanlúcar late afternoon. It was low tide. Dozens of ships of all sizes were moored some hundred yards out in the broad, flat estuary. The wetlands of Doñana, shielded by a line of tall bullrushes, lay across the water. Sanlúcar was a hive of activity, with seamen coming ashore noisily from voyages searching out wives or whores on the quayside; small boats, loaded down, transporting goods to and from the moored ships; and fishermen paddling around in the soft muddy sand unloading their catches into baskets from their small boats lying on their sides with long ropes tethering them to the shore.

Pedro entered a waterside tavern to enquire about ships sailing to Almuñécar or Motril. Both were the key ports for Granada, some forty miles inland from them. Either would do. He tucked his kitbag tightly under his arm, but it was not enough. Barely had he got inside the door when a buxom barmaid, carrying two full tankards of ale in each fist, carelessly barged into him, pitching Pedro to the floor. It was a set-up job. An ageing sailor of fearsome countenance, a mop of black hair, black beard and a black patch over one eye, but nevertheless showing amazing agility, rose from the nearby table, grabbed Pedro's bag from the floor and shot out through the door. The barmaid looked around innocently, cocking her nose at Pedro, while the whores at the bar with their broken teeth, painted faces and dyed hair, on the lowest rung of their chosen calling, nudged their clients in the ribs and cackled.

Unperturbed, Pedro got up and tore out through the door. The months on the high seas had kept him nimble and had made his grip strong. Moreover, he had lived cheek by jowl with some pretty uncompromising characters on board. The thief was no match for him. As Pedro caught up with him twenty yards along the quay, the sailor turned, brandishing a knife, expecting Pedro to cower and flee. Pedro stopped, withdrew his own Toledo dagger from his belt, its long, mirror-like blade glinting in the afternoon sun. Pedro grinned, confident in his own strength and dexterity, inviting the sailor to come at him. He rolled the dagger around lightly in his hand. The sailor, just a few yards away, looked into Pedro's eyes. They were relaxed but menacing and he saw that he had met his match. Pedro feigned to leap at him. The sailor threw the kitbag at Pedro's chest and ran, slipping and falling over in the process. He looked around, terrified, as Pedro made to lunge at him again. This time the sailor got up and ran for all his life along the quayside. Pedro stood there watching with amusement, and witnesses to the incident avoided Pedro's gaze as he picked up his kitbag. It was still intact. He strolled nonchalantly back to the tavern. He went in, looked around slowly at the staring faces and sat down calmly at the table vacated by the thief. The place was deathly silent. Politely he asked the barmaid for a tankard of ale and a slice of bread and cured ham. It came on a sparkling china plate and with a sharp, clean knife.

Pedro arrived at the turn-off along the Guadalfeo river four days later. At about the same time Cristóbal Colón departed La Rábita and Palos de la Frontera to travel home to Córdoba via Sevilla to be re-united with his wife, Beatrix de Arena, and his two sons, Diego and Fernando. On horseback it would take him little more than a day. The Admiral had settled all his affairs in Palos, entrusting the *Niña*'s bounty to the prior of the monastery and also ensuring the safety and well-being of the ten Indians.

The *alcázar* at Almuñécar, for centuries the summer retreat of the Sultans of Granada, had changed little since *El Zagal*, the Muslim lord and noted warrior, had accompanied Pedro there from Moclín, over five years before.

Throughout the voyage to the Indies, and particularly during the blackest days when he was confined below deck accused of stealing, Pedro had thought endlessly about Raquel, reminiscing over their short love affair; remembering her beautiful face looking down into the dark mine shaft in which he lay. Yazíd had found Pedro there and went to summon help from a nearby Alpujarran village. And what help it turned out to be! This beautiful fifteen-year-old Muslim girl with shining black hair and a disarming smile, arrived with her fun-loving uncle, Salim Almuafiri. For several months, while his twisted ankle healed, he was cared for by Raquel and her mother, Raghad. Pedro stayed next door with Salim, Raghad's brother, but each day to their quiet amusement, Pedro secretly slipped out of the back door to meet Raquel on the river bank amongst the tall rushes. Raquel was then betrothed to a thirty-year-old man named Abu Ishar ibn Hakam, who lived in a village higher up the valley side, and to whom she was very soon to be married. But Ishar already had a wife – and a violent temper. Poor Raquel was dreading the marriage. Before Pedro departed, following the fulfilment of the second of the soothsayer's riddles, she pleaded with him to give her a child to remember him by, believing that she could pass the baby off as Ishar's. For almost two years now, in his mind's eye, he had pictured Raquel with a young toddler living a bruised and battered existence with her stern husband.

It started to drizzle as he skirted the puddles which lay along the gravel path towards Mecina when a thought struck him like a hammer blow. Raquel might not be living there any more! She might have died during childbirth, or his 'son' might not have survived, or 'he' might be crippled or handicapped. Pedro's blood froze. How did he not think of these things before? Should he not turn back and leave her unmolested, however she might be suffering? It might be kinder for her in the long run. If her husband, Ishar, were to learn of Pedro's existence now, what consequences might befall Raquel? He sat down on the side of the bank, in two minds as to what to do. Should he go on? Should he go back? He made up his mind. He would carry on, but he was worried beyond belief as to what he might discover.

Later that day Pedro reached the outskirts of the small whitewashed village on the floor of the valley. At first nothing much seemed to have changed, but he noticed that many of the orchards of mulberry trees on the hillside, used for rearing silkworms, were riddled with weeds, and the white houses, once radiant, now looked distinctly shabby. Grass grew amongst the cobbles of the narrow streets, once carefully swept. What had happened?

The conundrum was soon solved. Coming along the path towards him was a file of fifteen to twenty villagers, carrying babies, manhandling carts, leading pack mules or just bearing heavy bundles over their shoulders. The villagers filed by, barely aware of the bystander moving aside to let them pass. The weather had turned cold and the drizzle had given way to light rain driving into their faces. Most of the men were wearing ankle-length white cotton *camis* and, on top, thick camel-haired *yallabiyyas* with their ample hoods pulled up over the maroon or dark blue *'imamas* which were wound tightly around their heads. The women were wearing long silk or cotton *milhafas* over their heads and shoulders. Their free hands clenched the shawls tightly under their chins to shield their faces from the rain. On their feet both men and women wore leather sandals or *balgas* made from woven esparto grass.

The file of people, carts and mules continued on without speaking. Then a smallish woman who was leading a toddler by the hand, her girth and slight stoop suggesting someone of middle years, paused and peeped through her bright red *milhafa* at Pedro. She moved a step towards and stopped again, wiping the rain from her eyes with the back of her hand. The woman leant forward and restrained her taller companion by the arm who was carrying a heavy bundle. The younger woman stopped and peered at the stranger. Pedro's heart jumped, but he looked away. He had to be careful about declaring himself.

'*Pedro?*' the elder woman asked uncertainly.

'*Pedro? Entsa howa?*' she asked in Arabic. 'Is it you?'

Pedro opened his mouth to speak but remained silent, not knowing how to react. He looked at the group moving on along the path. There were men there but none seemed attached to these two woman.

'*Smah li, sidi,*' the women said. 'I'm sorry, sir.' She pulled her shawl across her face and continued on along the path. Pedro ran to her. He had to be certain.

'*Entsi hiya Raghad?*' he asked in Arabic. '*Entsi hiya Raquel?*'

Yes, yes,' they replied in their own language. 'It's us!'

The two women drew the shawls away from their faces and ran to Pedro. Each buried her face against his wet coat, throwing her arms around his neck. Unsupported, the toddler fell over into a puddle and cried. Through the women's sobs Pedro felt their bodies relax and soften. They pulled themselves away, looking up into his face. Raquel reached to his chin but he could have tucked her mother under his arm. Tears of joy were streaming down their faces, and their noisy sobs stopped the party ahead in its tracks. All the time Pedro's eyes were searching amongst them for Raquel's husband, Abu Ishar ibn Hakam. Raquel, her beautiful features flushed by the cold rain, guessed Pedro's concern.

'It's all right, Pedro,' she said reassuring him. 'You have nothing to fear. I'm alone now.'

'No, you're not. You have your child… and me!' retorted her mother loudly, scolding her daughter.

'Pedro,' Raghad said very formally, 'we want you to meet Raquel's daughter, Zara.'

'*Your daughter, Pedro. She's your daughter!*' whispered Raquel not wishing the party ahead to hear.

Pedro picked the little girl up into his arms. She was wet through and cold. She had her mother's lovely features and dark hair, but her complexion was a little lighter and she had blue eyes, just like him. The three adults had so many questions to ask. Each was silent for a moment trying to decide where to start. Pedro jumped in first.

'Where's your uncle, Salim?' he asked Raquel. 'Isn't he leaving with you?' Pedro had already guessed that the party was departing the village for good.

'He stayed behind,' interrupted her mother.

'Come,' she ordered, 'let's return home out of this rain. We'll all catch a death of cold. The house is all shut up and... no matter. We can soon get it straight. You can tell us how you come to be here, Pedro, and we can tell you our news, little though it is.'

While Raquel, Pedro and little Zara held each other tightly, not wanting to let go even for one minute in fear that it might all be a dream, Raghad ran forward to the remainder of the villagers who were patiently waiting for them some fifty yards along the path. The rain had intensified and they were looking cold and bedraggled. She returned to the happy couple. The group would continue without them. They had several days ahead of them to get to Adra on the coast. There would be plenty of time for Raghad and Raquel to catch them up, if needed.

'Come,' Raghad said with no more ado. 'Let's give that silly old fool brother of mine a surprise!'

The women retraced their steps back to the village, no more than half a mile away. Nobody spoke. Raghad's house was locked up and boards were nailed across the small, deep-set windows. The sound of them unlocking and entering the house brought Salim Almuafiri scampering around from next door.

He got down on his knees and peered around the foot of the door.

'Who goes there? Friend or foe?' he growled in a deep voice.

'It's us, you imbecile!' chided Raghad. 'Who do you think it is?'

'Uncle! called out Raquel, running to her fun-loving uncle and leading him by the hand affectionately into the house. 'Look who's come!'

The robust man, with the strength of an ox, who had carried Pedro on his back all the way to the village from the mine shaft without barely pausing, put his hand over his eyes.

'Who is it?' he whimpered. 'I can't see.'

He stumbled forward and fell over a chair.

'Oh, get up!' roared Raghad. 'Why can't you be serious for one minute. You're always playing the fool.'

Pedro roared with laughter, remembering the crazy antics this loveable man played while he was staying with him. He shook the man warmly by the hand.

'*Kif mashya el-amor, forsa se ida,*' he said. 'How are you, it's lovely to see you.'

'*Selam, Pedro, la bas alik…* Hello, Pedro, how are you doing?'

Barely wanting to let each other out of their grasp, and certainly not out of their sight, Pedro and Raquel helped Raghad and Salim to put the house in order and to light a fire in the hearth. Raquel explained, while they were putting furniture back in its place and sweeping the floor, that two months after her marriage to Ishar his sleeve had got trapped under the rolling stones of an olive press and his right arm was drawn under them and crushed. An excellent surgeon was called from Orgiva, the nearest big town, and he arrived on horseback the same day, but he had no choice but to amputate Ishar's arm below the shoulder. Such was the loss of blood, the pain and shock that Ishar died soon afterwards.

'Ishar didn't treat me badly during our short marriage,' Raquel admitted, 'but I could never love him, not after you. Whatever the reason he soon seemed to tire of me.'

'But didn't his family "claim" Zara after she was born?' asked Pedro.

'I was only three months pregnant, Pedro,' Raquel explained, 'and neither Ishar nor his family were aware that I was with child. Being a mere woman I would have just been another mouth to feed if I'd stayed with them, so I returned here to my mother…'

'And me!' chipped in Salim from across the room.

'…Yes, and you, Uncle. I explained to my mother and Uncle Salim that I was expecting your baby, Pedro, and that you'd return to me one day as you've miraculously done.'

Broom in hand, she leant across and gave him another hug.

'Enough of that! There's work to be done!' came a stentorian voice from the kitchen.

Soon the house was warm and cosy. Salim went next door and returned with some bread, olive oil and fruit and warmed some red wine with spices on the fire.

'You make yourself comfortable now, you two… not you,' – she glared at her brother – 'you can get some more wood in… Now you two… no telling her your news, Pedro… I don't want to miss a single word… do you understand!… Not one single word now… I'm going into the village… Tonight we're going to have a banquet… It'll be fit even for that no-good Sultan of ours… and then afterwards, and not before, you can tell us what became of you!'

All this time Raghad was rushing around the house organising everyone's life. Then she shot off through the door with an empty basket. Pedro took Raquel into his arms again and swept little Zara off the ground. What a family! How wonderful to be back amongst them again.

Soon Raghad was back and with Raquel's help she set about making a mouth-watering meal. Pedro had not been treated to such a sumptuous feat since he was dined one evening by Boabdil and Don Gonzalo in the tower at Porcuna: the very evening he told how he had been enslaved on an Arab dhow when eight years of age, and confessed for the very first time to anyone the terrible things which he had done which caused him to run away from home when he was thirteen; and so very much more. While the womenfolk prepared the meal, Pedro was able to play with his young daughter in front of the fire, aided by Salim, who was a born entertainer. On Raghad's orders, his news was to wait until after they had eaten and settled down comfortably. But Salim was allowed to explain why he decided to remain in Mecina.

'You see, Pedro,' he started in his native tongue, serious for once. 'I've never been further than Lanjarón in my life, and then only once or twice for market. Granada to me is a lifetime away – although I'm told it's only a couple of days away, even on foot. So far the Christians have left us in peace in this valley since Granada fell to them last year. I haven't been "converted", and neither am I classified as what they call a Mudejar. So I decided that I'll just stay here and see out my time.'

His face cracked open in a wicked smile and he said in a loud voice, 'But now that insufferable and bossy sister of mine has come back home to plague me, I think I'll pack my bags and leave!'

'Where to?' Raghad shouted from the kitchen. 'You can't even find your shoes in the morning, let alone the path out of the village!'

And so the banter continued.

In due course they all sat around the table. The first course was *salata baladi*, being a salad made with cucumbers, tomatoes, onions, watercress, parsley, green peppers and mint leaves. This was followed by *kishk bil firakh*, pieces of boiled chicken braised in a gravy made of yoghurt, chicken broth, onion and butter. Finally, to round it off, they finished with *baklawa*, a treat which Pedro once received at the hands of the lovely Sabyán in Oria. The *baklawa* comprised thin layers of pastry filled with nuts, almond and pistachios and steeped in syrup.

'Raquel,' he asked. 'Do you still have the sapphire and emerald I gave you before I departed?'

'Of course, my darling,' she replied laughing. 'I looked at them every day to keep you in my thoughts. And the small four-hundred-year-old ivory jewel box you gave me.'

'Belonging to the great al-Matasím?'

'Yes. I keep the two stones inside it. They were all I had to remember you by after you left.'

'Except for the little matter of Zara!' quipped Salim.

They all laughed. Raquel skipped off to retrieve the ivory box and the two jewels.

'How did you say you came by these, Pedro?' asked the elder man.

'I've told you many times, Uncle. You don't listen,' said Raquel.

'What? What's tha – tha – that you said?' stuttered Salim, holding his hand to his ear.

'Oh, you!'

Raquel leant forward and gave him a friendly cuff.

'The sapphire and emerald were gifts of sorts from the Prince of Almería, Yahya al-Nagar,' Pedro explained. 'Before the entry of the Catholic Monarchs into the city of Almería in December, three or so years ago, I joined a party of workmen helping to reconstruct some of the city walls which had collapsed in the earthquake two years before. In a fit of rare generosity, Yahya, a lascivious man, threw the foreman a handful of jewels to pass to us workmen. I heard him say that we might just as well have some of his treasure chest before the Christian monarchs arrived and confiscated everything in the palace.'

'And the ivory box?'

'Some months later, before I fell down the mine shaft and you rescued me, I was asked to assist in a dispute over water rights in Ohanes. It's a village high, high above Canjáyar in the Almería end of the Alpujarra, beyond Laujar. I was helping the main landowner there, Jibril Fadi, to administer the water rights in his various smallholdings down by the river. As you know these are highly regulated. Because I was new to the area, the village elders in Ohanes thought I'd be a useful independent member of their tribunal.'

'And they gave you this box?'

'Yes, they said my assessment of the petty squabbles between three farmers gave them the solution to the problem.'

'So what was the outcome?' asked Raghad.

'Not what anyone expected, Raghad,' answered Pedro. 'The dispute between the farmers turned not to be about their water rights, but about the infidelity of two of them with the third farmer's wife. In fact this Jezabel had been sleeping with half the village!'

'So what happened to her?'

'She was stoned to death. It was so utterly barbaric that I packed up and left Canjáyar that very day.'

'How absolutely terrible,' commented Raghad. 'What happened to the men?'

'They didn't escape punishment, Raghad. They were stripped and severely flogged in the village square, and they were required to replant and tend the other farmer's crops which they had destroyed. It was all very complicated.'

'But they lived!... Huh! Nothing changes. One law for you men and one law for us women. Nothing changes.'

The two women removed all the plates and dishes and piled them in the kitchen. They could keep until the morrow.

'Now Pedro!' Raghad said, as they reseated themselves around the fire. 'Little Zara's sleeping peacefully in Raquel's room, so we're all ready to hear of your adventures. Promise me that you won't miss out a single thing.'

It took Pedro well into the night to tell them what had become of him after he had left them in June, nearly two years earlier; of his rescue of the King and Queen from the fire and his later dining with them; of his revenge of Zak and

Gaz at the Christians' encampment on the plain outside Granada; of the grand state entrance of Fernando and Isabel to the city and his incredible discovery that very day of his mother Miriam, amazingly alive and unscathed in the Sultan's harem of the Alhambra; of the tearful departure of Boabdil and his retinue from the city and his journey to Sevilla and then to Palos; of the events leading to his joining the crew of the *Pinta*; and finally, his adventures on Colón's voyage of discovery to the Indies. His near-fatal traverse across Juana or Cuba with the Indian, Ta'hí, particularly enthralled them.

'Gosh, I nearly forgot to show you the things I brought back!' Pedro exclaimed after he had finished. The fire had nearly gone out. He retrieved his wet kitbag from inside the front door where he had dropped it and pulled out his crumpled spare clothes. Raghad swept these up, promising to wash them the next day. Amongst the little bits of cinnamon bark, miscellaneous dried leaves, now disintegrated, a crumpled tobacco leaf or two, maize cobs and *niame* roots, Pedro found the small ornamental mask carved from cedar wood which he had bartered for with the coloured glass beads. He passed it around. But pride of place went to the piece of wrought gold.

'And this is what Cristóbal Colón gave me for finding his sea charts in Sevilla and returning them to him via the Duke of Medina Sidonia. The Admiral said that the gold was to make a ring for my mother and for my…' he paused, not wanting to say 'fiancée' '…and for my girlfriend in the Alpujarra.'

'You told him about me?' exclaimed a delighted Raquel, clapping her hands together in glee.

'Yes, and how you pushed him down the mine shaft, I expect!' chipped in Salim.

'Yes, I told him about you, Raquel,' answered Pedro, smiling. 'There's enough gold here for two rings and more, and as soon as I return home I'll have them made up for you and my mother. You can choose which of your two stones, the sapphire or the emerald, you'd like placed in the centre.'

'And the other stone's for your mother's ring?' asked Raquel. 'Oh, I do hope I'll meet her soon.'

'No, I have a ruby for my mother's.'

'A ruby?' asked Raghad. 'How many more precious stones do you have!'

'Just the one, Raghad!'

'And who was that a gift from? Did you get it in the Indies?'

'No. From Sabyán. I'm sure I told you about Sabyán when I was here last.'

'Not me, Pedro,' said Salim. 'You didn't tell me.' He leant forward and sobbed his heart out, his head buried in his arm.

'Oh, stop it, you old fool!' reprimanded his sister. How did she cope with him all these years?

'So how did you come by it?' she asked.

It was given to me by this beautiful and graceful woman when I was thirteen. It was the ring belonging to her husband, who was killed at Lucena fighting alongside the Sultan. Hundreds if not thousands of your people died that day. A few weeks earlier I'd run away from home and happened to be staying in Oria with a wonderful, learned man, Abu Bakr al-Jaldún, known as the Mullah. During a thunderstorm one night the dry river bed across the road became a raging flood. I saw two children clinging to a tree trunk in the middle of the torrent and I carried them back safely. Their mother, Sabyán, gave me the ruby ring as a token of gratitude. I adored her. Yes, she was a Muslim woman, but there was much about her poise and serenity which reminded me of my mother, who you must remember, disappeared when I was only eight.'

'Can you show us Sabyán's ring?'

'No, I'm afraid not, Raghad. As I explained, Don Gonzalo collected all the things which poor Yazíd had with him when he was arrested, to take back to my mother. The ruby ring was amongst them. In his letter to me', Pedro dug out the letter from his bag, 'Don Gonzalo promised to return them all to my mother. She may already have them by now.'

'And you'll be returning to her soon?' said Raquel.

'Yes, very soon now.'

Raquel's face clouded over and tears started to well up into her eyes at the prospect of losing her Pedro again so soon.

XV: Boabdil Beleaguered

March/April 1493

Pedro stayed with Raquel and her family for ten days. He removed the boards from the windows, whitewashed the outside walls and helped Salim sow seeds and plant vegetables in the garden. It was spring. The soil was warm. The timing was perfect.

On his second day, while Raquel was in the village, Pedro took Raghad aside and asked for Raquel's hand in marriage. Raghad needed no persuasion. She reached up on tiptoe and threw her arms around his neck, hugging him for all she was worth.

'Of course, Pedro! Raquel needs a husband and little Zara needs a father. Raquel was convinced that you'd return to her. She never lost faith in you. She loves you dearly, Pedro, and I know that you feel the same way towards her. However, you're Christian and she's Muslim…'

'In truth, Raghad, I'm half Jewish and half Christian. This means that baby Zara is one-quarter Jewish, one-quarter Christian and half-Muslim!'

'Of course, I hadn't realised that. But it presents no problem. With her life before her, and if she is now to remain in Andalusia, she may just as well as "convert" to Christianity and be done with it. I'll probably do the same, but I can't speak for Salim, he's very entrenched in his ways.'

'And devout?'

'No, no, he has no strong views on anything. Your God, Allah or Jehovah – it makes little difference to him.'

'But what will you do, Pedro?' asked Raghad seriously. 'I know you want to return to your mother. I'm sure she's as anxious to see you again as we were.'

'Yes I do, and I must set off soon. My plan is to visit Boabdil…'

'That good-for-nothing!'

'He's not good-for-nothing, Raghad. I know he's a weak man, but unlike his uncle, *El Zagal*, who kept fighting until the bitter end, Boabdil had the sense to see that he couldn't resist the overwhelming might of King Fernando and Queen Isabel. The whole of Christendom was supporting them. I know him well and intend to call on him on the journey home. His residence can only be a day or so away from here.'

'So you'll leave Raquel and Zara here?'

'Yes and no. I'd like to take Raquel with me to meet my mother, and maybe your brother would like to come with us as far as Laujar and meet the Sultan.'

'And Zara?'

'If you and Raquel are agreeable, maybe she could stay with you? When I've got everything arranged at home, you and Salim can come over for the wedding. Salim can give Raquel away.'

'Give her away? You mean free?' asked Salim, when the plan was unfolded to him and Raquel that evening. 'I doubt that. I'll need a sapphire, emerald or ruby to fix to the end of my hoe! No – of course I will,' he continued in his usual style. 'And I'll give her mother away free too for that matter. I'd donate a big bag of turnips to give her away!'

The plan was agreed. Salim found a sprightly young chestnut mare left grazing in a field by one of the departed families, and a saddle and bridle inside an abandoned barn. Several days later, with Salim and Raquel taking turns riding the mare (who was 'christened' Indy by Raquel, after Pedro's adventures), the three set off for Laujar, Boabdil's abode.

At about the same time, Cristóbal Colón set off from his home in Córdoba on a triumphal journey to the Sovereigns' court in Barcelona. The journey would take him through Murcia and Valencia. Before the month of March ended Martín Alonso Pinzón died, aged fifty-two. It was thought that the contagious disease he caught from native women in Guanahaní, exacerbated by the stress of the terrible storm and the threatened action by Colón, all went to bring about his untimely death. He was buried in La Rábita. The following year, in 1494, this contagion spread across the world, and in Naples it became known as 'the French disease'.

When Granada fell to the Christians on January 2nd the previous year, Mohammed the Twelfth, Abu 'Abd Allah Boabdil, known colloquially as *El Chico*, the boy, on account of his small stature, was confined with his followers in the Moorish fortress of the Alcazaba which lay alongside his glorious former palace, the Alhambra. On January 25th, with his family and retinue, he was forced to leave Granada for good. The party numbered several hundred in all. Boabdil was accompanied by his long-suffering and pregnant wife, Moraima; his twelve-year-old son, Ahmad; his plain and dumpy mother, Fátima; his brother, Yusuf, with his deformed hand; Nasím his faithful servant and eunuch; Ibrahim, his doctor; and not least his stepmother, the vivacious temptress and his former concubine, Soraya. She had displaced Fátima in his father, Muley Hasán's household, and borne him two sons, Cad and Nazar. Like their mother, they had been baptised weeks before into the Christian faith, with Soraya taking the name Isabel de Solís. Accompanying the family members were Boabdil's long-serving minister, the former Alcalde of Granada, Yusuf Aben Comisa, and his son Mohammed; and his former vizier, Abul Kasim el Muleh, and his two sons, Hamet and Mohammed. Like their fathers, all three sons were substantial beneficiaries of the Terms of Surrender agreed by Fernando. Between them they acquired lands, farms, olive groves, salinas, and watermills.

Knowing of Pedro's friendship with the deposed Sultan, Queen Isabel had appointed Pedro to her household cavalry to accompany the party out of the city. It had been a long hard slog out of the Bab al-Ramla city gate up to the top of the pass over the sierras leading down to Lanjarón, the turn-off into the Alpujarra, and on the warm sunny day the party got strung out for miles. The Alpujarra is the name given to a near-straight, east-west valley some seventy miles long. The western 'Granada' end of the Alpujarra, in which Raquel's village of Mecina lay, was wetter and flanked by higher, smoother mountains than the eastern 'Almerían' end, where desiccated, angular yellow hills with deep gulleys, ravines and isolated buttes, descended in terraces to the river valley below. The town of Laujar at the headwaters of the Andarax was by then much larger than the city of Almería, which had not recovered from the disastrous earthquake in 1487. It was to Laujar, some fifty miles away, that Pedro, Raquel and Salim headed when they left Mecina.

When Pedro had accompanied Boabdil to the crest of the hill overlooking his beloved city, the little man stopped, looked back and wept. The sharp-tongued Soraya turned and mocked her stepson cruelly, saying, 'Weep like a woman – you, who could not defend your kingdom like a man!' There, Boabdil's gift to Pedro of the sapphire-encrusted dagger helped trigger the third of the soothsayer's riddles which had guided the youngster's long journey across *Al-Andalus*. He knew then that it was time to move on and take the long road westwards to Sevilla.

Bells had greeted Boabdil as he entered the Alpujarra at the town of Lanjarón, already famous for its copious springs. In due course his party made the long and gradual ascent from the bustling town of Ugíjar, surrounded by orange groves, up to the high altiplano and Laujar, and on down a slope for two miles more, following the course of the burgeoning River Andarax, to what remained of an *alcazaba* at a settlement called Codbaa, later dubbed Fuente Victoria. This run-down fortress and the extensive estates around had been the home of *El Zagal* before his departure to Orán three years before. High mountains lay to its north and south, but a re-entrant to the south of Codbaa allowed access through the sierra to Berja and Dalías, and it was on these southern slopes that Boabdil went hunting on occasions.

Perhaps it stemmed from the complaint to the King the previous December from his 'eyes and ears' now resident in Codbaa – Hernando de Zafra – about Boabdil hunting in territories outside his jurisdiction, but by the turn of the year the King was becoming concerned about the former Sultan's potentially disruptive presence in the area. The enclosed nature of the Alpujarra region had kept the Muslim communities there largely isolated during the ten years of the Christian offensive. A revolt was always threatening, and one erupted six years later, demanding the attention of Queen Isabel; although it took seventy years more before the biggest and final rebellion exploded, with disastrous consequences for the Muslims and economic ruin for the Alpujarra region. With the threat of a Boabdil-inspired revolt in mind, Fernando had instigated negotiations for Boabdil's departure from the Alpujarra, and therefore from Spain, with Boabdil's long-standing advisors, Abul Kasim el Muleh, his former treasurer, and Yusuf Aben Comisa, a member of Granada's Muslim aristocracy, acting on the Sultan's behalf. The Sultan himself travelled to Barcelona in January to meet the Catholic Monarchs, and from then on El Muleh and Aben Comisa regularly met Hernando de Zafra to progress the negotiations.

Pedro turned into the former *alcazaba* at Codbaa. Much of it was semi-derelict but one wing had been renovated and was inhabited by Boabdil and his family. Aben Comisa, El Muleh and their sons owned property elsewhere in the valley, and between them and Hernando de Zafra there were constant comings and goings to the Sultan's residence. But the place seemed deserted as Pedro, Raquel and Salim led Indy through the half-broken studded door in the stone portal and entered the gravel forecourt. But they had not entered unseen. A door in the wing to their right swung open and out shot a youngster in a flowing, ankle-length *camis* and a blue *'imama* wound around his head. He was followed by a small boy.

'Pedro, Pedro!' he called, as he ran for all he was worth across the yard.

'Ahmad!'

'I thought I recognised you when you came into the yard!' cried the excited young prince in remarkably good Castilian.

The thirteen-year-old had grown a lot since Pedro saw him last. He had filled out and grown in confidence. No more a wan little boy too shy even to say his name. Pedro leant forward and wrapped his arms around the youngster and kissed him on both cheeks. The two had become very close during Pedro's internment in Porcuna castle while he was recovering from his ordeal at the hands of Tomás de Torquemada.

'It's wonderful to see you again, Ahmad, and your Castilian is almost perfect now.'

'Thank you, Pedro. I've plenty of chance to practise it, since we see a great deal of Hernando de Zafra these days. Do you know him? He's Queen Isabel's secretary and he acts as her representative here.'

'I don't think so, Ahmad, although I expect he was at Granada when you were reunited with your parents after your nine years as hostage. They must have been terrible years.'

'They could have been worse, Pedro, but I did have you there for several months to play with and to learn your tongue.'

The two continued reminiscing for several minutes.

'Ahmad,' said Pedro. 'I've been very rude and have not introduced you to my fiancée, Raquel, and her uncle, Salim Almuafiri. They don't understand Castilian so we must speak in Arabic.'

Ahmad bowed very low, sweeping his hand low across the ground in a fulsome gesture of welcome.

'*Kayf haalak, Raquel, wa anta, Salim, tasharafna be-moqaabelatek,*' he said. 'How do you do, Raquel, and you, Salim. It's a pleasure to meet you. But I have failed to introduce you to my young brother, Yusuf, who insists on following me everywhere.'

'Please come into the palace,' he continued in Arabic, leading them to the door from which he had come. Pedro could not get over the prince's poise and royal bearing as, in his flowing gown, he ushered them to the door.

'My father's due back from hunting later today,' he said. 'I know he'll be absolutely delighted to see you again, Pedro. We speak about you very often.'

Ahmad led them up a long flight of steps into a comfortable though sparsely-furnished room. Through a window looking out to the west they could see the high sierra to the left. Snow still capped its northern ridge. The sun shone strongly through the window, splashing a bright yellow patch on the stone floor and warming the room. Clapping his hands, Ahmad called for a jug of fresh pomegranate juice. Soon, four earthenware goblets and olives and dried dates arrived on a silver tray. Continuing in Arabic for Raquel and Salim's benefit, Ahmad brought Pedro up to date on what had transpired since Pedro had left his father's party after his departure from Granada. Taking longer, Pedro described all his adventures and his plans to marry Raquel later in the year.

'And you say you have a daughter, Raquel?' Ahmad asked, drawing her into the conversation for the first time.

'Yes, she's called Zara and she'll be a year old soon.'

'How is your mother, Ahmad?' asked Pedro.

'You'll meet her soon, Pedro. She's resting. But she's not well. The trauma of all the changes we've endured in the last fifteen months, and now her pregnancy, have taken a toll on her health. I'm afraid Abrahim has to attend her daily.'

A twinkle came into Ahmad's eye as he retrieved a small golden *dobla* from a pocket in his *camis*. He winked at Pedro. Pedro grinned and winked back. He guessed what was coming. Ahmad's planned little game of sleight of hand was the very first thing Pedro had used at Porcuna to draw the shy prince out of himself.

'Now, Salim,' Ahmad challenged. Pedro had told him about Raquel's fun-loving uncle. 'Which hand is the coin in?'

'That one!' answered Salim, slapping his hand.

'Wrong. It's in this hand!'

Salim frowned and looked perplexed, but was always willing to have some fun. His face lit up as Ahmad repeated the sleight of hand several times more, sometimes sliding the coin into his right hand and sometimes letting it fall into his left hand. There was simply no way of telling.

'Let me play, Ahmad,' pleaded Raquel.

So the little game continued between them all, with Pedro testing if his hands were as dextrous as they were five years before.

It was dusk when Boabdil rode into the yard accompanied by the two sons of El Muleh, Hamet and Mohammed. It had been a successful foray. Over the front of Hamet's saddle was a young hind, while his brother had several brace of partridge hanging from his. There was just sufficient time for the household cook to prepare the venison for the meal that evening. The birds were better left mellowing for a few days. The deer was skinned, drawn and mounted on the iron spit over the fire. The hind would take several hours to baste and roast, but no matter; it gave time for Pedro, Raquel, Salim and Ahmad to settle down comfortably with the Sultan, a very pregnant-looking Moraima and Boabdil's grumpy mother, Fátima.

Poor Boabdil was the sultan left holding the flickering kingdom of Granada together, and he had paid the price. Taken prisoner by the Christians after the battle of Lucena in April 1483, he was imprisoned at Porcuna for a few months. However, he was more useful to Fernando as the vassal king of Muslim Granada, and by demanding three-year-old Ahmad as hostage in his father's place, Fernando had the Sultan totally in his grasp. Prince Ahmad, accompanied by the older Cidi Hamet, spent nine years at Porcuna, and he was not reunited with his parents until the very day Granada fell to the Christians.

It was getting late when the Sultan, his immediate family and guests finished eating. Raquel and Salim retired to the rooms which had been prepared for them. Boabdil and Pedro were left alone to continue talking, this time reverting to Castilian.

'I think Ahmad has told you that Fernando and Isabel are now determined to drive me from my lands?'

'Yes, he did.'

'First they destroy my kingdom, then they force my capitulation over Granada, and now this! Why can't they leave me in peace here? This is my homeland, not Morocco. *Al-Andalus* has been the country of my forebears for nearly eight hundred years.'

The poor man was clearly very distressed, and Pedro did not know what to say. There was no point in repeating the mantra about 'the overwhelming might of the Christians'. It was Boabdil himself who had admitted this to Pedro years ago.

'El Muleh and Hernando de Zafra are arriving here in two or three days time to give me the draft agreement which they've negotiated with the Sovereigns in Barcelona. So, sadly, my days here are numbered. Aben Comisa has been in contact with the Sultan of Morocco about where I might live if I return there. But I don't trust that man and I've heard some terrible stories about the maltreatment and atrocities which have been inflicted on my people who were forced to emigrate there after Granada fell.'

Pedro thought of the poor villagers of Mecina whom he had met as he approached the village. And that could have been the fate of Raghad and Raquel if he had not arrived in time.

'Pedro, I know that you want to return to your mother as soon as possible now: she must be desperate for news of you, particularly with your friend, Yazíd, not returning home with news of you. But I would be honoured if you were able to stay here until Jusuf Aben Comisa and Hernando arrive. I'm sure you know Aben Comisa.'

'Yes, Boabdil, I do. If you remember, with Ahmad he showed me and Captain Agustín López around the Alhambra after you handed over the keys of the city.'

'That was when you discovered Miriam in the Generalife?

'Yes it was, but even now I don't know what drew me to that small palace, since it was already close to sunset and the gates were being locked.'

'*Ojalá*, Pedro! If only we knew.'

'Good, that settles it,' he concluded. 'You'll stay!'

Aben Comisa and Hernando de Zafra arrived as predicted three days later, having arrived by boat at Adra, the nearest port, just a day away on horseback over the Sierra de Gádor. They were closeted with Boabdil the better part of a day discussing the terms of the settlement for the sale of the estates of the Sultan, plus those of his ministers and their sons to the Christians. On April 10th Boabdil signed the agreement for the sale of his estates in the Alpujarra. The agreement for his expulsion from *Al-Andalus*, for that of his family and hundreds of his supporters was signed by the Sovereigns on June 15th and by Boabdil himself on August 7th. Fernando and Isabel bought Boabdil's estates for nine million maravedís, those of El Muleh for one and a half million, and those of Aben Comisa for one million. But for transport from Adra to Morocco in ships provided by the Sovereigns, Boabdil was obliged to pay the colossal sum of eleven million maravedís. Even in this final act of humiliation to the Muslim lord, the Sovereigns had to twist the blade one more time.

'Pedro, I know that you are leaving tomorrow. You have been a good and loyal friend to me for several years and I shall never forget what you did for Ahmad, who is growing into a fine young man. Will you do one more thing for me?'

'Yes, of course, Boabdil. If I'm able.'

'Will you accompany me and my family from Adra when we finally leave? The ignominy of my final departure is more than I can bear, and having you and some other dear friends with me will be of great comfort to me.'

'I promise I will.'

'Wonderful, that makes me feel so happy. Rest assured I will get a message to you in Vélez Blanco as soon as I know when it will be.'

XVI: Reunited

On April 20th 1493 Fernando and Isabel accorded Cristóbal Colón a triumphal entry into Barcelona. From a balcony of their palace, bedecked for the occasion with a gold-braided canopy and a crimson velvet front-piece bearing their royal coats of arms, the Royal Family watched the procession approach. On the balcony with the King and Queen were four of their children: Juana, 14, later to succeed Fernando to the throne of Castile; Juan, 15, who died a year before Isabel; María, 11, who later married Manuel of Portugal; and Catalina, 8, later the wife of King Arthur of England in an all too brief unconsummated marriage, and then on his premature death, becoming Catherine of Aragón, as the long-suffering wife of Henry VIII.

The Admiral, maximising his triumph, strode past, waving to the crowd. He was dressed magnificently for the occasion in black doublet and hose picked out with white and silver, a waist-length black velvet cloak, lined with dark grey silk, and a black floppy bonnet on his head topped by a white ostrich feather. With him were his two sons, Diego, 13, and Fernando, just 5. They were accompanied by several of his principal lieutenants from the voyage: Cristóbal García Sarmiento, the pilot of the *Pinta*, who hailed from Pontevedra in Galicia and who had brought the ship and its crew safely back to Spain; Pedro Juan Niño, the owner and master of the *Niña*; and the two bo'suns, Juan Quintero of the *Pinta* and Bartolomé García of the *Niña*. The brothers of the deceased Martín Pinzón – Francisco of the *Pinta* and Vicente of the *Niña* – were notably absent, as was Rodrigo de Triana, who first sighted land and surely merited recognition. By then, however, the Admiral had convinced himself that his vision of seeing land several hours before the seaman on the night of October 11th was genuine. However, what caused the people of Barcelona to line the streets in their thousands was not just another procession of the wealthy, the brave or the good, but six of the Indians following on foot directly behind Colón. Copper-skinned, bare of chest and of foot, they were clad in colourful skirts and high, garish headdresses. Shiny brass necklaces hung around their necks and they wore multicoloured grass amulets around their upper arms and around their ankles. Several of them carried red and green parrots on their arms, and two of them led frightened, four-foot-long iguanas on leads, the poor animals sliding and skidding around, unable to get a foothold on the shiny cobbles. Bringing up the rear were two wagons drawn by mules loaded with all the things which the two ships had returned to Spain. However, pride of place went to the Indians. They were meant to be a spectacle and they were – and they loved every minute.

The procession stopped at the palace steps to which the Sovereigns and their children had descended. Colón approached their majesties, bowing low and long in homage. Diego came forward and handed his father his treasured *diario* of the voyage which was secured in a new oilskin wallet. Very formally the Admiral presented this to the Queen. It was the very fulfilment of his voyage of discovery; a public demonstration that he had successfully achieved what he had set out to do in accordance with the *Capitulaciones* of almost exactly a year before. The Queen received the heavy tome from Colón with gratitude and passed it to a notary at her side. Within months the precious ship's log would be copied word for word in its entirety. With this formality over, and while Colón chatted to the Monarchs, their children ran down the steps to merge with the crowd, who by then were swarming around the Indians, touching their bronze skin and petting the parrots. For everyone there, and not least the Indians, it was a day to remember.

The Catholic Monarchs were the phenomena of the age – and indeed, before and after it. By then they were at the peak of their power, with Isabel of Castile forty-three years of age and Fernando of Aragón forty-one years of age. They were married in 1469 when Isabel was nineteen and Fernando two years her junior. Isabel assumed the crown of Castile five years later on the death of her stepbrother, King Enrique IV; but it was not until five years afterwards that Fernando became king of Aragón on the death of his father, Juan II. Castile, with the historic cities of Toledo, Salamanca, Leon, Segovia, Burgos, and Valladolid gracing its windswept plains, dominated the heartland of the Iberian peninsula. Aragón to the east had its capital in Zaragoza on the banks of Spain's largest river, the Ebro; but the kingdom included the principalities of Valencia and Cataluña, for which Barcelona was its capital. Fernando also enjoyed the title King of Naples.

Both inherited jealous and feuding nobles who were self-serving and semi-independent lords of their domains. Fernando and Isabel quickly set about bringing order to their kingdoms; placing their own nominees in charge of the many provinces; appointing compliant bishops and competent and loyal captain-generals to the regions; putting their kingdoms' finances on a proper footing; raising taxes and levies. It was a monumental task and they did not spare themselves one jot. While Valladolid was the seat of Castile's court, the royal couple were rarely there, choosing to move continually around their kingdoms together from one city to another, staying just a few weeks or months in each. For instance, from Barcelona, where they had arrived in May the previous year, they spent a week in Córdoba, fifteen days in Extremadura, two weeks in Valladolid and three weeks in Zaragoza, before returning to Barcelona in the October. In each city they held court, heard petitions, approved budgets, resolved difficulties and put down local insurrections and discord. It was a punishing routine. Devout in their faith, devoted to each other and dedicated to their royal duty, they laid the foundations for Spain's greatness to come. Poor Boabdil could not have confronted a more formidable duo.

Nothing better illustrates Isabel's devotion to duty than her weekly routine. On every Thursday and Saturday one hour was dedicated to signing briefs and documents; mails and petitions were handled promptly every evening; Monday afternoon was allotted to her secretary, Hernando de Talavera; Tuesdays to cabinet meetings; Wednesday to the royal auditor; Thursday to memorials and Friday to fiscal matters. Aside from signing documents for an hour, Saturdays were left free.

Hernando de Zafra and El Muleh kindly accompanied Salim most of the way back to his village while making their own journey back to Adra, to return to Barcelona with Boabdil's comments on the draft agreement for his ultimate departure. Salim had declined taking Indy, feeling more secure on his own feet – that is, after he had managed to tie his laces. So, late in the morning on the same day, Pedro and Raquel set off for Almería and then on to his home town. One or other, or both, rode the sprightly mare, Raquel snuggling up close to Pedro on the saddle in front of him when the road took a long descent. With his arms tightly around her waist while she held the reins, she loved it. It was what she had dreamed of during all those lonely nights when he had gone.

The road followed the course of the River Andarax, and with few hills to ascend they made good progress. The mulberries and almonds of the western Alpujarra gave way to olives, then vines and then oranges as they descended to lower, warmer climes. Neat rows of market crops occupied the tilled reddish-brown soil in the valley floor, and water gurgled cheerfully along the narrow earth channels, irrigating the crops with the meltwater from the mountains. Pedro was surprised how little had changed since he had passed along this road two years before. The ground between the trees in the orchards was still kept free of grass and weeds with saucer-shaped hollows dug neatly around each tree to trap the rain; the farmers still toiled dressed in their traditional way and in bare feet or esparto sandals; and the villages were clean and newly white-washed for the spring. Happily, they showed little sign of abandonment. It was a friendly and heartening scene, and confirmed how little affect the conquest had had on the Alpujarra mountain region. A few miles on from Codbaa, the road climbed to Canjáyar, and Pedro showed his fiancée the roadside cave-house he had occupied during his stay there with Jibril Fadi; and he indicated to her the village of Ohanes high in the mountains above where Jadiya had been stoned to death.

The couple stopped the night in Alhama de Almería, a spring-fed village on the slopes of the right bank of the valley. The owner of the tavern and his wife made them very welcome, showing them to a tiny upstairs room with a single creaky bed. The travellers dined bounteously that evening on roast chicken, with Pedro making a start on teaching Raquel Castilian, something which she had urged him to do. It was the first time the couple had been alone since Pedro's return, and the bed did more than creak that night as they liberated their pent-up passions.

The next night saw them nearly fifty miles further on at Sorbas, a village perched precariously on the edge of a deep gorge. Earlier, Pedro had rejected the option of following the Andarax all the way down to Almería, since he shuddered at his memories of the city where he had gone to help out after the earthquake. His nightmare at the hands of the Inquisition started on that day. Their third night was spent in a roadside hostelry near Huércal Overa. The next day Pedro would be reunited with his mother, and following a rich stew of steaming mutton, carrots and onions, the couple retired to their room to savour their last night together alone.

The following day they took the short cut over the 5,000-foot-high Sierra de Las Estancias and that afternoon Pedro pointed up to his home in the distance as he and Raquel ascended the road from the hamlet which had sprung up below the hilltop fortification of Velad al-Ahmar. With peace descending at last on this border region, and given its strategic position guarding the highway between Murcia and Granada, the hamlet would in due course grow into the large town of Vélez Rubio. Pedro's home of Velad al-Abyadh, alias Vélez Blanco, lay much higher up, and was the principal settlement in the area, with its houses clustered around an imposing *alcázar* on the summit of the hill. The town was protected by an enclosing wall with three entrance gates. Another wall ran across the upper part of the town, dividing it in two. This one enclosed the *alcázar*, a mosque and a rock-hewn *aljibe*. While desperately looking forward to returning home after so many years, Pedro did so with trepidation, if not foreboding.

Eleven years before, when he was little more than nine years old, he had found his way home after eighteen months as a slave on an Arab dhow. Then he had entered the east gate and ascended the street to his home, bubbling with excitement at the prospect of seeing his mother again whom he loved dearly. He knew with absolute certainty that she would be sitting in the sunshine outside their corner house, doing her needlework, waiting patiently for his return. But she was not there. She never returned. His apothecary father, Abraham, now bad-tempered and cantankerous, showed no interest in his son's return and said little about Miriam other than he had searched for her in Aguilas for days and days after her abduction by slavers, but to no avail.

Yet Pedro's recollection of this event dimmed when set against that which occurred five years later. Then, returning home and up the very same street after *El Zagal* had seen him safely onto a boat at Almuñécar, Pedro had seen uniformed soldiers holding down his father over the stalls which he erected in the small open space outside their home, slitting his throat and then running him through with their swords. In the same instant before Pedro charged up the road with his Toledo sword in his hand, he had seen a soldier holding down his sister, eleven-year-old Cristina, with another raping and then strangling her. It had happened in a nightmarish blur. Two of the soldiers, dirty, unkempt and with the foulest tongues were Zak and Gaz, agents of the Spanish Inquisition, at whose hands Pedro had suffered twice before. Zak, recognising the youngster whom he had once sodomised, had run down the street to complete his bloody intent, but Pedro had caught him across the face with his sword, maiming the cur for life. With Zak's partners in crime bearing down on him, Pedro had had little choice but to flee to his cave retreat on the mountain slopes above the village. Soon afterwards his family home had been locked and boarded up.

Leading Indy, Pedro and Raquel entered the east gate and up the street to his home. He could see ahead of him the open space on the left where Abraham and Cristina had died, and on its right his house, with water spouting into the stone trough on the outside wall. Raquel could sense Pedro's tenseness beside her as they approached his house. Hearing the clatter of hooves approaching, a tall, fair-haired woman came to the door. The afternoon sun lit up her face. It was his mother! Totally forgetting Raquel, Pedro ran up the street and fell into Miriam's arms. Joy, happiness, the release of tension, all dissolved in a cascade of tears. Now nineteen, manly, hardened by a life's worth of experiences, Pedro still could not contain himself and he wept and wept and wept, his shoulders heaving in great sobs. The relief he felt knew no bounds. It was the same for Miriam, even more so. Raquel led Indy up to the house and tied him to an iron ring on the wall by the water trough. She had failed to grasp the intensity of Pedro's longing to return home but she could not contain herself either, joining them in their tearful reunion.

It took a long while before the tears abated, even then every attempt to speak finished in more spluttering and more heaving sobs. For Miriam to see Pedro coming up the road was an enormous, though wonderful, shock, since with Yazíd's arrest at Palos no message had reached her of Pedro's where-abouts. When Pedro had left her in Granada to accompany Boabdil, he had promised to return to her immediately afterwards. He should have been back within weeks, at the latest a month, yet fifteen months had elapsed.

As introductions and explanations were made during the next few hours, Pedro's fiancée and his mother, so different in so many ways, warmed to one another, and soon were chatting and giggling in Arabic while they prepared the evening meal together. Pedro stood in the doorway of the kitchen enchanted by the happy scene.

'Now, my dears,' Miriam said a little later, pondering where they should stay. 'You're best to have my room, since it has a large bed. I'll move into the room at the back. It's plenty big enough for me.'

Raquel and Pedro looked at each other, surprise written over their faces. Miriam laughed.

'You thought I'd insist on you having separate rooms until you're married, didn't you! Oh no. Life's too short. You must enjoy each other now. After all, you've been apart long enough. And besides you'll have your Zara with you soon, and you'll need the space for her little bed.

'Raquel, my dear,' Miriam continued, placing the younger woman's hands in hers, 'as far as I'm concerned you're one of the family now. Many terrible things have happened here and it's time for a new beginning. A fresh start. Seeing you two together and so much in love makes me more happy than I can express. Anyway, soon…'

Miriam did not finish her sentence then, but did so later when Pedro asked after Captain Agustín López.

Miriam's face flushed. Then all the words just poured out in a jumble.

'Agustín – I mean Captain López – oh, I mean – Agustín… He and I see quite a lot of each other. You see, he lives not that far away.'

'In Archena, doesn't he?' interrupted Pedro. 'I remember him telling me when we were exploring the Alhambra together. In fact, that was just before we stumbled upon you looking out of the window at the setting sun!'

'You're quite right,' continued Miriam, excitedly. 'His family's business is running a fulling mill near Archena. His father's insisting that Agustín should take it over now that he's retired from the Queen's service. But he's not a bit keen, and he's looking around for something else to occupy himself with.'

'So did he see out his last year as an equerry of the Queen?'

'Yes, he did, and that finished just two months ago, so he's a free man now.'

'But he's a widower isn't he, Mama? And doesn't he have a young daughter?'

'Yes his dear wife died in childbirth several years ago. Sonia is ten now, and such a lovely girl…'

'So you seen them from time to time?'

'Oh yes, Pedro,' Miriam confessed, blushing again. 'Agustín comes over every week or so. He's just a day's ride away, albeit a long one, but he's used to long distances.'

'That's wonderful,' chipped in Raquel.

'Yes, and he'll be here tomorrow, so you can meet him. Sonia's coming too.'

'Oh, you will love him, Raquel,' Miriam enthused. 'He's so tall and handsome in his uniform and he's very kind and considerate.'

Raquel had been looking into Miriam's eyes as she was speaking. Her woman's intuition was not found wanting.

'You love him, don't you, Señora Tog – I mean, Mir – No, I'll call you "Mama" from now on,' observed a perceptive Raquel.

'Yes, I do, and "Mama" will be lovely. But I do love him dearly, Raquel,' she admitted, 'and I think he does me. I fell for him when he escorted me home from Granada at the instigation of Queen Isabel. He was so manly and I felt so safe riding alongside him. And it was such fun to be with a real man again… Well, you know what I mean,' she said with embarrassment, remembering the hand-wringing eunuchs in the Alhambra.

'So you'll wed?' asked Raquel. Her dark eyes pleading for an affirmative response.

'Yes, I'm sure we will.'

'So we can have a double wedding!' Pedro said. 'Oh how wonderful that will be.'

Agustín López had the shock of his life seeing Pedro again. They had met for the first time at the Christian's encampment at Gozco during the vast build-up in their forces before the fall of Granada – an event achieved, in fact, without bloodshed. Around the soldiers' campfire one evening a soldier had said that he had spotted two scruffy soldiers in the camp resembling Pedro's description of Zak and Gaz. Immediately Agustín, the officer-in-charge, had despatched a heavily armed party to arrest them. The two renegades had met their end that night. Agustín and Pedro had been escorted around the Alhambra by Aben Comisa the day of the handover, and the captain was with Pedro when Pedro discovered his mother in the Generalife garden pavilion. She was so graceful and so beautiful in the soft amber light of the setting sun that Agustín had fallen for Miriam then and there. Their destiny must have been sealed when the Queen instructed him to accompany Miriam home and 'without delay'. She had suffered quite enough.

With young Sonia and Raquel getting on so well, despite the language difference, it was a wonderful and joyous occasion, and Pedro was delighted after dinner that evening to assent to Agustín's request for Miriam's hand in marriage. To see his mother happy again was all he wanted. Agustín and Pedro discussed possible wedding arrangements, and it was concluded that the end of the year was most appropriate, in the light of Pedro's promise to Boabdil to accompany him when he finally left Andalusia.

A few days later Pedro and Raquel, riding Indy alternately, went to the village of María, four miles up the road from Vélez Blanco, so that Raquel could meet Pedro's uncle, Joshua. He was such a contrast to Abraham, affectionate and kindly, and being childless he and his wife Ana had treated Pedro and Cristina as their own. It was to them that Pedro had fled when he ran from home after the death of Marco, and it was good old Joshua who had come down to reopen Miriam's boarded-up house on her 'miraculous return from the dead', as he described it, and to work with Agustín López to make the house shipshape. On Miriam's return, Joshua had retrieved from below his floor the chest which he had buried after Abraham's and Cristina's deaths. The chest contained the family's savings and valuables, and he returned these to her. So Miriam, with the considerable sum given to her by the Queen as recompense for her years of confinement, was now more than comfortably off. Sadly, Ana had died after a prolonged illness, and Joshua had decided to move down to Vélez Blanco to be near Miriam, since they were both on their own. The house alongside Abraham's little market square was now empty and Joshua had bought it. So with Joshua's horse and two pack mules and Indy, it was a relatively easy matter for Pedro and Raquel to help him move down from María.

'What will you do with the business now?' asked Pedro.

'I still have my teams of youngsters collecting herbs from the mountains and it's enough for me to go up to María each week to supervise them and lay the herbs out in boxes to dry. But I don't travel so far and wide these days,

Pedro. You'll find that the town here has changed quite a lot since you left home five years ago. That was, if you remember, just after all the Muslim communities for miles and miles around were surrendered to Rodrigo Ponce de León, after his threat to take Puerto Lumbreras by force. All but one or two of the Jewish families have left now, and they, as well as me, have been baptised as Christians. Frankly, it was the only thing I could do. I was never as devout as your father, and I saw no sense in uprooting myself and moving abroad. In fact, you'll find that the whole town has become Christianised. Moreover, many Christians families have settled here and the town has become very prosperous. All this has been good news for me, since it's given me a lot more trade locally.' He paused. 'But what will you do, Pedro, now that you've come back? Will you become an apothecary like your father?'

'I'm not sure, Uncle. My father was instructing me in the preparation of his medicinal cures before he died and all his equipment is still intact in the dispensary. I also learnt a great deal from the physicians on the voyage and, indeed, helped one or two of the crew who had ailments. So with you being nearby, I might re-establish the practice.'

Some weeks later, while Pedro was giving Raquel a lesson in Castilian, a surprise visitor arrived at Miriam's house. It was Martín of Alarcón.

'Greetings, Pedro,' the round and ruddy-faced visitor said, when Miriam showed him into the house. 'Do you remember me? I've brought the things which Don Gonzalo retrieved of yours from the treasury at Sevilla.'

'Of course I remember you, Martín! If you recall we met last the day the King and Queen entered Granada. The first time was when Don Gonzalo and Boabdil brought me to Moclín when you were Constable there.'

'I still am, Pedro, although I don't get there too often now. Yes, I remember that day very well. It was when *El Zagal* arrived to take you down to the coast. I'd never met the man until then and he quite terrified me!'

'He also terrified a couple of Christian soldiers guarding the strategic pass at Ventas de Zafarraya, Martín. It was the funniest thing I've ever seen when he sent them packing with the flat of his sword. He's truly awesome when he's aroused! But he did get me to Almuñécar safely.'

Martín unclipped a bundle from his saddlebag.

'I've got here your prized Toledo sword for you, all shiny and bright and still as sharp as a razor.' He removed a leather pouch from his pocket. 'And here's Queen Isabel's jade ring, Pedro. You're very honoured to have one of her rings. She must think very highly of you. Possession of it will open up all sorts of doors for you across the kingdom. Don Gonzalo is the only other person I know who wears her ring. You must take great care of it. But do wear it. It's a lot safer on your finger than in a jewel box, and with your sword at your side you'll never be threatened. After all, I saw how you despatched that devil, Zak, at Gozco!'

'Is there any news of Yazíd, Martín?'

'Yes, some. At least we know he's alive. Don Gonzalo has discovered that he's in the Adriatic with a naval squadron of biremes. You know, the big fighting ships with two banks of oars? We're making every effort to get him released, but these things take time. Don Gonzalo says that you're not to worry, though. Yazíd has been traced and the ship's captain knows that Yazíd must not come to any harm.' He smiled and went on, 'Here also is this exquisite sapphire-encrusted dagger and your ruby ring. Don Gonzalo thinks that the dagger used to belong to Boabdil.'

'Yes, it did. Originally it was a gift to Mohammed the Tenth by the Caliph of Baghdad a hundred years ago and it's very precious. And the ruby ring belonged to a Muslim who was killed at Lucena.'

'I was there that day, Pedro. It was sheer slaughter. The Moors lost thousands upon thousands on that battlefield, foot soldiers and cavalry. But they were appallingly let down by their leaders. Only Boabdil put up any resistance, but the little man got surrounded by our men and was captured.'

'And then he was imprisoned in Porcuna for three months,' added Pedro. 'That's when everything started to go wrong for him.'

By June, Raquel was becoming homesick and longing to see Zara, whom she missed greatly. Joshua, finding there to be a great demand in the local markets for dried fruits, such as figs, raisins, plums and apricots, agreed to accompany Raquel home, and collect these provisions on his return through Pechina. Pedro had no worry about entrusting Raquel to Joshua's care. He was accustomed to travelling far from home selling his sachets of dried herbs. Moreover, with the cessation of hostilities between Muslim and Christian, the land was much safer than it used to be.

Pedro accompanied them through the town in order that he and Raquel could visit Aaron, the jeweller, who, like Joshua, had remained and 'converted'. Pedro handed him the flattened piece of wrought gold from the Indies which Cristóbal Colón had given him and the sapphire and emerald stones from Cidi Yahya al-Nagar's treasure trove in Almería. Pedro asked Aaron to make two gold rings and insert the stones into them. Raquel had chosen the sapphire as her preferred stone and Pedro already had ideas for the emerald. Lastly, he handed Aaron the beautiful ruby ring which Sabyán had given him and which had belonged to her husband. It was a man's ring, and much too heavy for Miriam. Moreover, the mounting was of low-quality gold with a lot of copper in it. Pedro asked the jeweller to polish the ruby afresh and reset it in a new pure gold ring.

XVII: Morocco

Summer 1493

The season passed largely uneventfully. As much as a reward for finally extinguishing the Muslim kingdom of Granada as delight over Colón's discovery of 'lands beyond the sea', a papal bull was issued on May 3rd giving Fernando and Isabel jurisdiction over all lands discovered in their names in the Indies. In August, Boabdil's wife, Moraima, died in childbirth, as did her baby daughter. But the year had seen the deaths of many important dignitaries. The ten years of unremitting pressure on the Muslim Kingdom of Granada eventually took its toll on those supporting the Monarch's cause. In February, soon after the surrender of the city, Pedro Enrique, the Mayor of Andalusia, died in Antequera on the way to Sevilla; in August the same year the Duke of Medina Sidonia, to whom Pedro had passed Colón's sea charts, passed away, and within three days so did the Marquis of Cádiz. Then, that very June, while Pedro awaited news from Boabdil, Alfonso de Cárdenas died. He was the Master of the Military Order of Santiago.

Whether derived from the bullion brought back by Martín Pinzón or Cristóbal Colón, the Catholic Monarchs sent sufficient gold to Pope Alexander VI to cover with gold leaf the roof of St María the Great in Rome. The ceiling was also so covered in the Sala Real de Palacio de la Alifafería in Zaragoza, the seat of Fernando's kingdom in Aragón. A large lump of gold of considerable value was also donated to the cathedral in Toledo, the seat of the principal archbishop of Castile.

Raquel returned with Joshua to be reunited with her mother, Raghad, and her daughter, Zara, now into her second year. The travellers were only just in time. Raquel's fun-loving and leg-pulling uncle Salim had contracted pneumonia a month after his return from Codbaa and despite the loving care administered by Raghad, the infection had spread from one lung to the other. Two days after Raquel's return, he passed away. Both Raghad and Raquel were devastated. Joshua stayed on for a while, staying in Salim's house next door to Raghad, helping her put Salim's affairs in order, offering comfort and support to the grieving women. In many ways, Joshua and Salim had much in common: both were good-natured and kindly, and what Joshua might have lacked in tomfoolery, he made up for in robustness and worldliness. But with few families now remaining in the dying village of Mecina, it was evident to all of them that there was no future there for mother, daughter and granddaughter.

Half-heartedly, Pedro reopened Abraham's dispensary, using Joshua's herbs and what he could recall of his father's remedies, and provided palliatives and cures to those who called. The memory of the events in the small square adjacent to his house were still too painful for him to contemplate erecting Abraham's stalls. But in reality he was becoming bored, waiting for the return of Raquel and waiting to receive a message from Boabdil. This came in September when a Moorish horseman clattered to the door on a black stallion. Sporting a full black beard, he was magnificently attired in a scarlet *gilalas*, polished black riding *ajfafs*, and a long white *burnu* flowed from his shoulders. With his large black *'imama* wound around his head, he cut an imposing figure. If he bore arms, they were well concealed.

'Do you remember me?' he thundered at Pedro in Arabic after Miriam had shown him into the house.

'Porcuna? No?' the rider continued. 'I was with my lord Boabdil when he arrived once to see young Ahmad,' he said, switching to faltering Castilian, 'when you were impris – I should say, staying there, with his lord Gonzalo.'

'Of course. You're Yusuf, aren't you?' replied Pedro, a big grin extending from one ear to the other. He clapped the man on the shoulder.

'And you rode off with Don Gonzalo's man, Antonio Manzano…?'

'Yes, to find Abu Abdalá and bring him to Moclín.'

The two continued reminiscing for a while over a glass of cool water from the spring outside the house. Miriam surveyed the tall, handsome man, so erect and full of latent power. Yet these were the Moors whom my dear Agustín fought for so many years? What a shame that two such fine men should have to oppose one another. How wonderful that these days are over now.

'Mama, you seem in a dream?' asked Pedro. 'Is there anything wrong?'

'Oh, not at all, my dear. Quite the opposite, I was just musing how glad I am that hostilities between the Muslims and Christians are at an end.'

'Pedro,' the bearded rider said getting to his feet. 'I bring news from my lord. He and his family and many of his followers are making ready to leave Codbaa and the villages in the Alpujarra and ride to Adra to embark for Morocco. I've come to inform you that he'll await you there.'

'Excellent, Yusuf,' replied Pedro enthusiastically. 'I've been waiting months to hear from the Sultan. Give me a day or so to put my things together and I'll ride back with you. It will be nice to have company on the way. My mare, Indy, could do with a bit of exercise too!'

'Very well, Pedro. I'll be back the day after tomorrow at dawn. We'll ride together then.'

Such was the enthusiasm with which Queen Isabel greeted the news from Cristóbal Colón in April of his discoveries in Cuba and La Isla Española that she immediately sanctioned preparations for a second voyage. On September 25th, as Pedro and Yusuf passed through Almería taking the coastal highway to

Adra, Colón's second voyage commenced from Cádiz with sixteen ships and a complement of fifteen hundred men. Amongst the ships was the *Niña*, and amongst the crew were Cristóbal García Sarmiento, who had piloted the *Pinta*; Juan Quintero, its bo'sun; Juan Reynal, its master-at-arms; Cristóbal Quintero, the *Pinta*'s owner; and several of the *Pinta*'s seamen, including Antón Calabrés and Juan Verde de Triana. More significantly, the cartographer, Juan de la Cosa, and many nobleman accompanied the voyage, such as Sebastián de Ocampo, who eventually showed that Cuba was an island, and Juan Ponce de León, who was the first to see the coast of Florida. As with the first voyage, most of the crew were from *Al-Andalus*.

Pedro and Yusuf arrived at the small port of Adra soon afterwards. Set tight against the barren and rugged brown mountains of the Sierra de Gádor and only some thirty miles from Almería, it was a notably inauspicious port for Boabdil's ignominious departure from Spain. For the eleven million maravedís which Fernando demanded as payment from Boabdil for his departure were twelve ships, amongst them two mighty carracks and two caravels. Over six thousand two hundred people from the villages in the Alpujarra and from the city of Granada were starting to gather there to accompany Boabdil, his ailing mother, Fátima, and the princes Ahmad and Yusuf to Morocco. Amongst them also were Yusuf Aben Comisa and Abul Kasim el Muleh and their sons and families.

Boabdil and Ahmad greeted Pedro warmly when they met in his campaign tent which had been erected, amongst scores of others, to accommodate such a gathering. The bustle, noise and dust reminded Pedro of the Christian encampment at Santa Fe exactly two years before.

'We're delighted that you are able to accompany us to Fez, Pedro. How are your beautiful Raquel and your lovely mother?'

'Raquel returned to Mecina to see little Zara again, and my uncle Joshua went with her. I received a letter last week to say that her uncle Salim died of pneumonia and that her mother has decided to leave Mecina and move to my home town on the borders of Murcia. Mecina and many other villages in the valley are becoming deserted as scores upon scores of your people depart.'

'Yes, it's very sad, Pedro. Very sad indeed. Still,' he continued, brightening up, seemingly not greatly concerned by the plight of his kinsfolk, 'I've some good news for you. Don Gonzalo and Martín of Alarcón are here to see us off. If you ride with me, I'll take you to the hostelry where they're staying. It's a mile or two out of this dusty town.'

'So you got my note then, Pedro?' Don Gonzalo started after the pleasantries were over.

'Yes, I did, but it came as a terrible shock for me to learn about Yazíd, and to find that he couldn't have returned to Vélez Blanco to tell my mother that I'd embarked on the *Pinta*.

'Is there any news of Yazíd?' Pedro asked.

'Yes, good news, I'm glad to say,' replied the courtier. 'The captain of the galley on which he's serving has written to say that he'll be releasing your friend as soon as they finish their current tour of duty in the Adriatic.'

'And when will that be, Don Gonzalo?'

'Oh, very soon. He might even be ashore by now. I've sent an authorisation for Yazíd to obtain a berth on a ship sailing to Spain and with a bit of luck he should be home here before too long.'

'That's great news, Don Gonzalo. I can't thank you enough for all you've done for him.'

'Think nothing of it, Pedro. That's what I'm here for. If I can't help to right some of the wrongs in the badly run corners of this kingdom, I might just as well accompany Boabdil to Morocco.'

'You know that you'll be more than welcome if you do, Gonzalo!' chipped in the Sultan, more buoyant than Pedro had ever seen him, the burdens of his kingdom, which he had borne since he was a young man, lifting from his shoulders.

The fleet of ships waited at anchor for weeks in the shallow waters off Adra for the hot easterly levanter winds, dominant in the summer months, to give way to a *poniente* blowing strongly from the west or south-west. In mid-October, on Boabdil's thirty-first birthday, they weighed anchor, and within two days had crossed the hundred or so miles of open water, straggling across the Mediterranean into the port of Melilla directly opposite. Always an emotional man, Boabdil was in tears as he looked at the receding brown mountains of Almería from his ship.

'Do you know, Pedro,' he said, as they stood at the stern rail of the caravel on which they were sailing, 'my people in Granada are now obliged to wear a yellow hood and a blue tag on their right shoulder! Fernando has completely rescinded the agreement which we signed when I agreed to concede my city to him.'

Pedro thought of the army of fifty thousand or more soldiers which had amassed at the Santa Fe encampment on the plain outside Granada, and how the Muslims were impotent in the face of the Christian blockade which almost throttled the life of the city before the surrender.

'And those who have remained,' continued an increasingly indignant Boabdil, 'have been treated despicably and with the utmost cruelty. Contrary to our agreement, they're not allowed to enter mosques or attend the Friday orations. Moreover they're being expelled now from the city and being forced into the suburbs, which are impoverished and run-down.'

Pedro remembered the appalling state of Almería after the earthquake and how so little had been done by its Muslim inhabitants to repair the damage caused by it during the two years leading up to its surrender to the Monarchs two years later. Who was not to say that the citizens of Granada had not neglected their own city similarly?

'And I gather,' continued Boabdil, gathering a head of steam as if he had relinquished his kingdom voluntary for the health and well-being of his subjects, 'that Bishop Cisneros has mounted bells in our minarets and crosses and images in our mosques. If anyone rebels against this sacrilege they are tortured until death! I'm told that between December and June last year, seventy thousand of my people were baptised. It's scandalous, Pedro, scandalous!'

Pedro remained silent.

It was a difficult journey of well over a hundred miles from Melilla to Fez, and particularly arduous for Fátima. The barren, red-brown land was hot, rocky and inhospitable. The multitude of over six thousand Muslim refugees could not have chosen a worse time to emigrate to Morocco. Theirs was an enormous throng which represented twice the population of the city of Almería, and it exceeded in number the size of all but a few cities and towns in *Al-Andalus*. Moreover, while Morocco and *Al-Andalus* shared much of the same history, with the same waves of Phoenicians, Carthaginians, Romans, followed by the Muslim Caliphate, the Taifa and the dynasties of the Almorávides and Almohades colonising Iberia, Boabdil's Nazarí dynastic family was wholly of *Al-Andalus* descent, and they did not consider Morocco their homeland. So the multitude which disembarked from the ships at Melilla were little more than foreigners who happened to speak the same language, share the same religion and possess similar customs.

Morocco shared few of the natural assets of *Al-Andalus* which had been so assiduously marshalled by the Muslims over a period of seven hundred years. The clear blue skies of Spain were pushed south in the winter by the westerly winds sweeping across Europe from the Atlantic bringing the country – and particularly *Al-Andalus* – much-needed rain. Less frequently did this climatic belt push south into North Africa. With its rugged, mountainous terrain of the High Atlas, the land was rocky, dusty and infertile. Only along the rivers draining northward to the sea from the Atlas, and those draining southwards to be swallowed up in the sands of the Sahara, was any cultivation possible.

If this underlying situation were not bad enough for Boabdil's émigrés, that which they encountered was far worse. For seven or eight years, Muslims, rather than convert to Christianity, had been leaving *Al-Andalus* in increasing numbers, swelling to tens of thousands after the collapse of their kingdom in 1492. Some had gone to Algeria, Tunisia and other Muslim countries bordering the Mediterranean, but most had taken the easy option of Morocco. However, what they encountered was a country suffering from a prolonged drought, with imports of food and manufactured goods from Muslim *Al-Andalus* drying up. Severe famine threatened. Many emigrants did find sanctuary in benign communities in Morocco. Others were less fortunate, and were persecuted and beaten, with women and children violated and taken as slaves. Many returned to their homeland in *Al-Andalus*, accepting the shame of conversion in a Christian kingdom which did not want them back. It was very tragic since, inevitably, those who returned to *Al-Andalus* were no better off than those who chose to remain in Morocco. And if this situation for Boabdil's emigrating party were not bad enough, bubonic plague was sweeping across Morocco from Tunis.

Through contacts with the Moroccan Sultan, and on behalf of Boabdil, Aben Comisa had secured a wing in the Royal Palace in Fez as well as other property in the historic city for himself, El Muleh, their sons and families. But, except where some of the émigrés had made their own arrangements, the bulk of those arriving on the twelve ships at Melilla had to fend for themselves. Experiencing the harsh natural environment of northern Morocco, the famine and the plague, rejected by an indigenous population on the verge of starvation who had barracked themselves into their villages for fear of contagion, many turned tail and returned to Adra.

For several hours Boabdil watched dispassionately while his kinsmen disembarked slowly from the ships carrying what meagre possessions they had been allowed to take with them. Bulky items such as furniture were, of course, impossible to bring; besides, the Christian administration in Granada had confiscated anything of any value from those leaving, while soldiers in Adra had robbed those arriving at the port from the Alpujarran villages under the pretext of 'spoils of war'. As the sun set below the western horizon, with several of the ships still to arrive and several others still disgorging their passengers, Boabdil summoned his family and immediate friends and rode inland. Pedro looked back at the pitiful refugees, contemplating what would become of them; thinking again that this might have been the fate of Raquel, Raghad and baby Zara if he had not intercepted them as they had left Mecina.

The party, numbering some two hundred in all, including doctors, body-guards and servants, arrived in Fez two days later. Fez, the oldest city in Morocco, was founded in 790 when King Idris I started a settlement on the right bank of the river; while his son, Idris II, who ascended the thrown at the age of twelve, settled on the left bank in 808 just four years into his youthful reign. Ten years later, eight thousand families arrived from Córdoba who had been expelled from the emirate by Christians, and two thousand more arrived from Kairwan seven years later. These peoples settled on both sides of the river and thereby united the city. With the refinements and skills they brought with them, Fez became a spiritual and intellectual centre, and a university was founded there in 859. But the city of Fez which Boabdil and his party reached had declined from its heyday two hundred years before in favour of the city of Marrakech.

Boabdil's party found its way past the cemeteries and tombs on the hills ringing the city, down into the tangle of narrow alleys and streets. Once prosperous, with merchants, shopkeepers and the tall narrow houses of low-ranking officials, the city had seen better times, and it was evident that many properties had been recently abandoned with the plague threatening a foothold in the city. The heart of the city was the holy Medina quarter, protected by tall, crimson parapets linking numerous square towers. The narrow streets inside the Medina's walls inexorably led to the magnificent, blue-tiled Quarawiyin mosque with its tall minaret. It was the oldest mosque in North Africa. On one side of the mosque lay the university and on the other the Royal Palace. The Sultan of Morocco was absent on business, and it was to a wing of this palace that an attendant led the visitors.

Pedro remained there two days helping Boabdil, Fátima and Ahmad settle in. The complex of rooms occupied two storeys of the palace wing and was arranged around a secluded, marble-floored courtyard within a shady, colonnaded arcade. An ornate fountain in the centre, spouting water piped from the river, fed water to several orange trees set in their marble kerbs. It was a scene of peace and tranquillity. Although tufts of grass sprouted from between the marble slabs of the patio, Pedro guessed that it would take little more than a week for gardeners to bring it back to pristine condition. A few more weeks of concerted effort would see the palace restored to a similar condition. However, this did not stop Boabdil complaining about the run-down accommodation which he had been bequeathed. After two days there, and becoming rather irritated by Boabdil's constant complaining and lack of consideration for those around him, Pedro determined that he had done his duty by the former Sultan of Granada, and that it was time to leave for home. For Fátima, who had yet to reach fifty, the journey from Adra was one step too far, and she died within weeks of their arrival in Fez. So Pedro said his last goodbyes to Boabdil and Ahmad. His five years of friendship with the Sultan had run its course. Ahmad, now thirteen and so tall and handsome, accompanied Pedro to the outskirts of the city. They hugged each other for a long while, before Pedro mounted Indy and rode away.

'Oh, by the way, Pedro!' Ahmad cried out, running along the road to his friend. 'For your information I've heard a report that a beggar claiming to be the King of Almería is to be found in the villages around Tlemcen. I'm told that nobody there knows who he is.'

'Umm, thanks for the information, Ahmad, but where's Tlemcen?'

'I think it's a hundred or so miles to the east of here towards Oran, but it's not that far from Melilla.'

'In that case I might make a detour and see who this fellow is.'

Pedro enquired in each of the villages he passed through on the way to Tlemcen but to no avail. It was on the second day, when some dozen or so miles from this town, that a villager said that he had seen such a beggar that afternoon and indicated the direction he was heading. The man, he said, was very scruffy, and despite the warm weather was dressed in a striped *yallabiyya* with the hood pulled over his face. Riding Indy, Pedro did not take long to catch up with him. Pedro dismounted and approached the beggar from behind. He was dressed in no more than rags, and his *yallabiyya* was filthy and torn. He wore sandals on his feet but they were trodden-down at the heels, the straps were broken and he would have been better-off walking in bare feet. The man was stooped, stumbling along with the aid of a staff. He was spat on as he passed a bystander. A small boy, no more than seven or eight, threw something in front of him and the beggar stumbled over it, falling untidily to the ground. He got up slowly and stood erect for a moment before he tilted his head to one side and continued on his way. It was at that instant that Pedro recognised who it was. He ran to the beggar, pulling Indy behind him.

'My lord Abu Abdalá?' he said as he reached him.

Pedro came around to face the man. A grubby bandage was tied around his eyes. The man was blind.

'My lord Abu Abdalá, known as *El Zagal*?' Pedro repeated, switching to Castilian. He recognised the old warrior's strong jawline through his grizzled beard and dusty weathered features.

The beggar turned to face the person addressing him.

'What if I am?' he answered gruffly in rusty Castilian.

'Sire, I know you – from Moclín.'

'Who are you, speaking to me in Castilian? Cannot you see that I'm blind?'

'Sire, my name is Pedro Togeiro. Several years ago you secured safe passage for me from the castle of Moclín, past Christian-held Granada, to Almuñécar on the coast.'

'Ugh! I don't remember. Be off, before I strike you with my staff.'

Pedro laughed.

'That sounds like the *El Zagal* I knew of old! Don't you remember, Sire? Your nephew, Boabdil…'

'That good-for-nothing scoundrel!'

'…And Don Gonzalo Fernández summoned you from Granada to take me to Almuñécar to find a ship. Don't you remember the Christian soldiers guarding the pass near Alhama whom you chased away?'

'Aye, cowardly good-for-nothings they were. They were lucky to get away with their lives!'

'So you remember then? You remember me?'

'A tallish lad, with brown hair and blue eyes?'

'Yes, Sire. That was me. But I'm a bit taller now.'

El Zagal ran his hands over Pedro's face, studying the youngster through blank eyes.

'Yes, and now a man, I can tell.'

Boabdil's uncle, the old warrior who had led, almost single-handedly, the Muslim resistance to the Christian takeover, pulled back the hood of his *yallabiyya* and lifted his head up proudly.

'Yes, I'm *El Zagal*,' he said defiantly. 'And if I'd had my way I'd still be Lord of Granada, and the infidels would be back in their hovels licking their wounds.' He coughed. 'So what brought you here? Pedro, you said, didn't you?'

'Yes, Sire, Pedro. Maybe we can sit in the shade of this tree and you can also tell me how you came to be as you are.'

'A beggar, you mean?

'Well… yes, I suppose.'

El Zagal listened attentively, just nodding and grunting acknowledgement as Pedro narrated the recent events in the former Muslim kingdom of Granada.

'And you say that my nephew is here, in Morocco?'

'Yes, Sire, with Aben Comisa and El Muleh and their families. They are ensconced in the Royal Palace in Fez where I left them a couple of days ago... Now, Sire. Please tell me what became of you and how you came to be in such plight.'

The old warrior edged deeper into the shade of the tree and leant forward, locking his hands around his staff placed in front of him.

'I decided to leave my estate in the Alpujarra three years ago. I knew then that our kingdom was doomed. So I came here. But little did I know that the Sultan here was in league with Muley's son!'

'Boabdil?'

'Yes, of course. Him. I despise him too much even to want to speak his name.' The old man spat on the ground.

'Soon after I arrived in Oran I was arrested by the Sultan's men here and thrown into a dungeon. But I didn't stay there long. I was dragged out and pushed onto a stool and my head bound fast against a post. All this time a furnace was belching green flames. Then an iron ladle with a long wooden handle was thrust into the flames and filled with red-hot molten copper. Before I knew it, the ladle was swung slowly in front of my face, searing my flesh and burning out my eyes. I screamed in agony – yes, the mighty *El Zagal*, vanquisher of Gentile and infidel alike – screaming in agony! Through all the battles I've fought in every corner of *Al-Andalus*, never, never have I experienced pain such as that.'

'What happened then?' asked Pedro.

'I was pushed out into the street. A placard was placed around my neck pronouncing, "This is the King who surrendered Granada".'

'But that's not true!' cried Pedro. 'It was Boabdil who surrendered Granada, not you. You had left *Al-Andalus* two years before!'

'Of course, but nobody wanted to listen. From that time on I've been a beggar, wandering hither and thither through village after village, not knowing where I was going: spat on and mocked by everyone, the butt of every practical joke which every street urchin could play on me. Occasionally a kindly soul would give me a crust of bread or an apple to eat, and sometimes I came across an old barn where I could rest my head for a few days. But this has been my lot for two years or more and now I just wish to die. Die with some dignity. Die like a warrior, not like a wretched beggar!'

Pedro's heart went out to the man. *El Zagal* might have been treacherous, scheming and devious, but he was strong and brave and a great leader of men. Not for nothing had the Catholic Monarchs themselves dubbed him *El Zagal*, the Valiant, and held him in awe. Not for nothing did they buy him off at the surrender of Guadix by the grant of an estate in the Alpujarra, and not for nothing had they identified Boabdil as the weak link whom they could twist around their little finger.

'No, not like a wretched beggar,' the man repeated.

'You shall not die like a warrior or a beggar. Not if I can help it.' Pedro was silent for a minute, thinking.

'Would you return with me to Almería, my lord?'

'Thank you for your offer, young man, which is appreciated. But I cannot. If I return to *Al-Andalus* the King's men will eventually hunt me down and kill me. Fernando constantly fears a revolt by my people. I must remain here, I have little choice.'

'Yes, I understand. What's the name of the village ahead, Sire?' asked Pedro.

'I think it's called Jerada,' answered *El Zagal*.

'Well, kindly wait here in the shade of this tree. I'll be back before sunset. Here, take my water skin from my saddle. It was filled with fresh water this morning. I'll be back as soon as I can.'

Pedro climbed back on Indy and rode hard into the village two miles up the road. He rode around between the small whitewashed dwellings for nearly half an hour. Their walls were thicker and the windows even tinier than those in the villages of *Al-Andalus*. Eventually he found what he was looking for in the village square.

'How much for a comfortable room with clean mattress and linen?' he asked at the single hostelry in the village... with a full pitcher of water a day, and a good meal at sundown,' he added.

'In Castilian money, one hundred maravedís a day,' the man answered, after a few moments' thought.

'Hum,' answered Pedro. 'At four hundred and fifty maravedís to a golden *dobla* that will make forty *doblas* for the room for six months. That will give me time to try and find a more permanent arrangement. My friend is blind and has fallen on hard times. But he was the greatest warrior which *Al-Andalus* has seen since the time of Mohammed the First. So please honour him as is his due. I'm giving you fifty *doblas* in good faith, but I'll be back within six months and if I find that you have evicted my friend or mistreated him you will know the edge of my sword.' Pedro withdrew his sword partly from his scabbard. 'Is that clear?'

'Yes sir, of course. Have no fear,' the landlord replied indignantly. 'You have no cause to threaten me. Though poor, I am an honourable man. Your lord will come to no harm while he is under my roof.'

'Good, many thanks.'

'And could your wife care for him?' said Pedro, suitably vanquished. 'Wash his clothes and bath him?'

'I have no wife, sir. I live alone. But there is a kindly widow named Eva across the square. She was once well-to-do, but has now fallen on hard times. She was married to Ismael, the scribe in the mosque over there. The poor man was taken by the *peste* two months ago, God rest his soul. I'm sure that for a small sum she would care for your lord; wash his clothes, accompany him to the *baños* next to the mosque each week, trim his beard, and ensure his general well-being. She is a lovely woman and a very caring soul.'

'Excellent. I shall speak to Eva on the morrow. Lastly, my man, can I have a room for myself for two days? This will give me time to get Abu Abdalá settled in with some new clothes.'

Pedro returned along the road. He helped *El Zagal* into Indy's saddle and led him into the village. The next day he took him to the *baños* where he was scrubbed clean; his hair was cut and his beard trimmed short in the fashion which Pedro recalled; he was bathed in scented water and rubbed with fragrant oils. While that was being done, Pedro visited the *zoco*, the street market, and bought a new soft woollen *yallabiyya*, darkish blue in colour, not a coarse one made of camel hair; a maroon *yubba* or tunic with broad sleeves; two ankle-length, white cotton *camis* with a broad leather belt and curved dagger; under-clothes; two *'imamas* for his head, one white, one black; a pair of black, polished, calf-length leather *ajfaf* for his feet, and woollen socks; and a solid pair of leather sandals. He also bought some strips of white cotton which would act as a blindfold, since bright sunlight hurt the nobleman's eyes. With winter around the corner, he bought a couple of thick woollen blankets for his bed and several soft cushions. Lastly, he bought a steel razor and whetstone, a whalebone comb, soap, and whatever toiletry items he could find to pass to Eva.

When *El Zagal* was finally groomed, presentable and freshly attired, he introduced him to his new landlord and Eva. The change in *El Zagal* was remarkable. Blind though he was, some semblance of pride had returned, and he stood erect, with his head turned into the fresh morning breeze blowing down from the mountains. His jaw was set firm and resolute. With one hand on the brass pommel of the new dagger placed on his belt, and the other holding Indy's bridle, Pedro walked him to the mosque, to the *oratorio* where he might listen to the mullah's Friday orations, to the *baños*, to the fountain in the square and its stone bench under the shade of the gnarled olive tree, up and down between the stalls of the *zoco*, then back to the hostelry. Everywhere Pedro went he introduced *El Zagal* to the local people who, not recognising the freshly clad, upright figure, gave him the respect and homage which Allah demanded.

When Pedro was sure that the Mohammed Abu Abdalá ibn Sa'd, the former King of Guadix and the King of Almería, known as *El Zagal*, was safe and secure, he paid his last respects to him and departed.

XVIII: The Ambassador

November 1493

Pedro arrived back in Vélez Blanco in the middle of November. Snow had already powdered the high sierras around, etching the gulleys and crests, ridges and cornices, into a winter wonderland. He sat for a while on Indy admiring yet again the imposing 5,000-foot sentinel of la Muela – the Molar – which stood guard over his home town from across the valley. How many times had he and Yazíd sat cross-legged in their cave hideaway together watching the last rays of the setting sun rise up its slopes, changing from amber to crimson to violet.

He arrived home to a joyous gathering. Little Zara rushed to the door to greet him, as did Raquel, and he swept his daughter up into his arms for a long embrace with both of them. Raghad had returned from Mecina a month earlier with Raquel and Joshua. Raghad had moved in with Miriam while Raquel had moved across Abraham's small square to stay with Joshua. Agustín López and his daughter Sonia had arrived the very morning of Pedro's arrival home. Agustín was especially glad to see Pedro so that they could discuss the final plans for the double wedding. Already he and Miriam had made all the preliminary arrangements. Now that Pedro had returned they could finally fix the day. It would be December 26th, four years to the day after the handover of Almería by *El Zagal* to Fernando and Isabel – and, as it happened, soon after Cristóbal Colón had returned to Villa de la Navidad on Española on his second voyage to the Indies.

The month that remained before the wedding was full of activity. Nobody revelled in it more than Miriam and Raghad, so close in age but physically so different; one tall, slim and fair and the other dark, small and rotund. They were both born organisers and got on famously. Pedro and Joshua made arrangements with the pastor in the small church of Magdalena situated close to the walls of the *alcázar*, which only a couple of years ago had been a mosque. Now it was replete with crosses, an altar, pulpit, font and pews. In a few years' time a new church would be constructed adjacent to the central gateway of the town, conveniently using its cut stone for the purpose.

While Pedro and Joshua were so engaged, Agustín took Miriam, Raghad and Raquel to Lorca in Murcia to have gowns made for the wedding. Lorca had been a Christian town for over two hundred years, and many ecclesiastical foundations were established there: abbeys, churches, monasteries and convents. These had spawned a flourishing industry for the making of ornate church vestments and regalia, in silk, brocade and velvet and in white, red, purple, green and gold. While the womenfolk were gone, Pedro called on Aaron Levi and collected the ruby, emerald and sapphire rings which the jeweller had made for him using Colón's sheet of gold. Aaron had done a wonderful job and the stones sparkled brilliantly in their settings. Some gold remained and Pedro, commissioned a medallion and chain for himself shaped like the outline of the *Pinta*, and a small gold pendant cross for Raquel, both for delivery in three weeks' time.

The great day arrived. At ten in the morning the small party of eight – the six adults, plus baby Zara and ten-year-old Sonia – entered the church. Snow was starting to fall outside. They gathered around the stone font at the rear of the church where the pastor, Alonso Bernáldez, baptised Raquel and Raghad into the Christian faith. Zara cried as she was sprinkled with the icy water and was given the name Sarah. Miriam could not recall whether Pedro had been baptised, such was the sensitivity between herself and Abraham over whether Pedro and Cristina should be brought up Jew or Christian, and so Pedro was likewise baptised.

Raquel looked radiant in her white silk wedding gown with a silver tiara set with wild purple irises and snowdrops, picked early that morning, pinned onto her shoulder-length raven hair. Pedro's long-abiding memory of his mother, through all the years of her disappearance, was of the blue dress she was wearing the day she was snatched by slavers. He was thrilled beyond words when, having kept it as a surprise, Miriam appeared from her room in a gorgeous pale blue brocade dress. In it with her golden hair and the gold earrings which Agustín had bought for her, she looked utterly stunning. By contrast, Raghad had chosen a simpler long green gown which matched her darker skin and, in keeping with her former faith, she wore a pink silk shawl over her head.

It was winter, so flowers were difficult to come by, especially in and around the 3,000-foot-high town of Vélez Blanco. But Joshua's teenage herb collectors had come down from María for the wedding and brought bunches of rosemary, thyme and germander to adorn the church, placing them on the altar, at the foot of the pulpit and around the font. If their winter colours were muted, their fragrance was delectable.

True to his lifelong profession, Agustín López was resplendent in the dress uniform of the Royal Guard. He removed his heavy sword as he entered the church, placing it on the table inside the door. Pedro had fitted himself out with grey doublet and hose, with the insets to the slit sleeves – then in fashion – in royal blue. He wore white woollen stockings and black buckled shoes. His black floppy bonnet had a white feather, much like the one Colón wore for his triumphal procession through the streets of Barcelona the previous April. Raquel had insisted that he wear his Toledo sword and dagger on his belt, but like Agustín he was obliged to leave it at the doorway. Joshua was dressed more simply, with a dark red woollen cloak helping to keep the chill from his bones on a bitterly cold day.

Several guests had been invited to the weddings. Amongst them were Miriam's neighbours, who had washed and dressed the bloody bodies of Abraham and Cristina after their brutal murder; Yazíd's father, Yakub ibn Hayyan, and his family; half a dozen of Joshua's herb collectors from María; Aaron Levi, the jeweller; and several of Agustín's former comrades who had ridden over for this special day. With the bell in the small tower of the church thudding its dull invitation to attend the ceremony, the guests took their place in the pews.

Pedro, Agustín and Joshua sat alongside one another in the front pew. At the rear of the church Miriam stood quietly with Raquel. Both were nervous. For Raquel, the church surroundings, the language and the proceedings were quite alien. Startled, Raquel found her mother standing beside them.

'What are you doing here, Mama?' she whispered. 'You should be at the front of the church?'

'No! I'm joining you and Miriam here.' A twinkle appeared in her eye. 'Didn't you know! Joshua and I are getting married too!'

Interrupting the guffaws of astonishment from Miriam and Raquel, the pastor, Alonso Bernáldez, called the three brides-to-be forward to the front of the church, while at the same time beckoning forward Pedro, Agustín and now Joshua to stand together in front of him at the chancel steps.

Pedro stepped forward and placed Raquel's sapphire wedding ring and Miriam's ruby wedding ring on the open pages of the pastor's order of service. Embarrassed that the turn of events had caught him off guard, Pedro fumbled around in another pocket and found the tiny velvet-lined box holding the emerald ring. It was meant as a gift for Raghad after the wedding. Now it would serve admirably as her wedding ring.

'Dearly beloved brethren. We are gathered here today in the sight of God...' Alonso intoned.

There was a commotion at the back of the church as the west door was flung open. Snow swirled in from outside carried on a freezing gust of wind. Everyone looked around, startled. Several figures entered, silhouetted darkly against the light outside. They strode down the aisle noisily, their leather riding boots resounding on the stone floor. Halfway down the aisle a square of light from a window high in the wall illuminated the becloaked central figure.

'Don Gonzalo!' Pedro cried out, 'And Antonio Manzano!... and Martín of Alarcón!'

Beneath the central figure's right arm, shielded by his thick, ermine-lined cloak, was a hunched, dusky figure, his face sallow, his hands clenched and callused.

'Yazíd!' Pedro cried.

Under Don Gonzalo's other arm, also with the courtier's cloak over his shoulder, was a handsome, olive-skinned and richly dressed young man, his white turban no match for his sparking white teeth.

'Ahmad!' cried Pedro in total disbelief.

'…to join these men and these women in Holy Matrimony…'

Nobody took any notice. Pandemonium reigned. Yazíd ran to Pedro and Joshua, flinging himself at his soulmate and at Pedro's uncle, who had always treated the Arab boy as his own; Agustín ran down the aisle to greet Gonzalo, Antonio and Martín, his former comrades-in-arms; while Ahmad ran to Raquel, so beautiful in her white silk dress, whom he had fallen for when they met at Codbaa.

'If anyone here present has just cause or impediment why these persons should not be joined together in Holy Matrimony…'

The pastor had done his very best. He touched his fingers together lightly as only priests can, and with a tilt of his head, a smile which would have graced Archangel Gabriel, and with a 'tut-tut' in Latin, he joined the happy throng. Introductions were made all round. Don Gonzalo had heard so much from Pedro about his long-lost and beautiful mother, but he was enthralled by her radiance, unable to keep his eyes off her as he filtered through the group. Poor Yazíd, so recently chained to an oar of a galley and clearly not recovered from his ordeal, took Raquel in his arms, recalling her contagious laugh when she and her uncle Salim had run back with him to the mine shaft where Pedro was trapped. For poor Yazíd, the relief at being home at last amongst his friends after all he had been through was all too much, and the eighteen-year-old broke down, soaking Raquel's shoulder in his tears. Raquel comforted him tenderly, trying to comprehend the ordeal which he had been through. Martín of Alarcón had not seen Ahmad since he relinquished his charge to Boabdil inside the entrance to the Alhambra on that fateful day nearly two years before, and he grasped the thirteen-year-old tightly to him. The bond between them was still very strong. Martín pushed the Arab prince away from him at arm's length, looking at how proud and confident the youngster had become: so different from the shy little boy whom Pedro had taken under his wing at Porcuna.

'I told you that I'd bring Yazíd back to you, didn't I!' cried Don Gonzalo gustily to Pedro. 'He arrived at Cartagena only three days ago and my good man, Antonio here, met him and brought him to me in Murcia.'

'And Ahmad?'

'You must have told Ahmad when you were in Fez about your plans to marry…' he turned to Raquel… 'to marry this delightful young woman. Ahmad made his own arrangements to come here and despite the risk he was running in coming back, he made contact with Martín of Alarcón, his protector all those years ago at Moclín. Martín met him at Aguilas and brought him here today.'

After all the introductions had been made and the merriment had subsided, Alonso Bernáldez recommenced the wedding service, which ran its traditional course. Agustín picked the ruby ring off the pastor's book, placed it on Miriam's finger and then, following the prompt from Alonso, said in a firm voice:

'With this ring I thee wed. With my body I thee worship…'

They kissed.

Then Joshua did the same with Raghad's emerald ring and kissed her on the cheek gently. Lastly, Pedro placed the sapphire ring on Raquel's and did likewise.

'I hereby pronounce Agustín and Miriam, Joshua and Raghad, and Pedro and Raquel man and wife. For those whom God hath joined together in Holy Matrimony, let no man put asunder…'

Alonso brought the ceremony to a close:

'In the name of the Father, the Son and the Holy Spirit…'

The service closed and the registers were signed, with Don Gonzalo and Aaron acting as witnesses.

For days before the wedding Raghad and Raquel had been preparing a wonderful spread, of which even Sabyán in Oria would have been proud. As mother and daughter had busied themselves in the kitchen, Pedro and Joshua had moved the furniture out of Miriam's living room to make more space. Her beautiful wall tapestries, which had been carefully stored by Joshua after the house was shut up following Abraham and Cristina's death, had been re-hung on the walls; thick Níjar rugs covered the stone floor. A big fire had been kept burning in the grate for days and the house was warm and snug. Now the food was laid out on the big oak table pushed back against the wall. Two large earthenware jugs of spiced wine sat warming on the hearth, and an iron cauldron with vegetable and mutton broth hung over the fire from a hook and chain. All was ready for the celebration.

The party hastened down from the church through the streets to Miriam's house. Don Gonzalo and those on horses rode down, and Antonio and Martín led them away to old Moses' stable lower in the town to be fed and cared for out of the snow.

The womenfolk, helped by Joshua's youngsters, for whom it was a wonderful day out, served their new husbands and all the guests with steaming bowls of broth and goblets of mulled wine. There were also plenty of delectable dishes to choose from on the table. As a special treat for Pedro, Raghad had made his very favourite dessert, the honey and nut-filled pastry called *baklawa*.

On occasions such as this Don Gonzalo was in his element, and he became the life and soul of the party. Beneath his thick ermine-lined cloak, he had on a calf-length robe in gold brocade with broad sleeves and a gold chain with an emerald medallion around his neck. On his right hand he wore Queen Isabel's jade ring. Once inside the house, he removed his riding boots and slipped on a pair of black slippers over his white woollen stockings. He was every bit the King's man.

Antonio Manzano returned with Martín, each carrying a large chest. While they prised off the lids, Don Gonzalo took up a position with his back to the fire, tapped a spoon on the fireplace and called order.

'It goes without saying,' he began, 'that this is a very special day for our three happy couples. Nothing has given me more pleasure in years than being able to come here today with Martín and Antonio to be amongst so many friends and happy people. I ask you to join me in a toast to our newlyweds. May God protect them, care for them and grant them health and happiness.

'With your permission, I would like to start by apologising to Yazíd for his ordeal at Christian hands. The incompetence of the State officials of Castile in casting him into slavery was inexcusable, and I have endeavoured to ensure that it cannot happen again. But he has survived, and given time his body and soul will recover. Yazíd, on behalf of Queen Isabel, please accept our sincere apologies.

'The toast is particularly apt for Joshua and Raghad, Agustín and Miriam, and Pedro and Raquel, since each of them, in some way or other, has seen suffering. No more so, of course, than in the case of Pedro's charming and beautiful mother, Miriam. Her ordeals from the time she was taken by slavers at Aguilas, through her years of internment in the *alcazaba* in Almería and then in the Alhambra in Granada, were quite sufficient. But then to find that her husband, Abraham, and her eleven-year-old daughter had been murdered. It truly beggars belief.

'Agustín,' he said, turning to the Queen's former equerry. 'You have a special duty to make up for all of Miriam's lost years. Knowing you as I do, I know that you won't be found wanting in this regard!

'About Pedro, what can I say? The burden which he carried around following the accidents at Bédar, and soon after in the back yard of this very house, were more than a grown man could bear – let alone a thirteen-year-old; and I cannot imagine what his fate would have been if I hadn't plucked him from the hands of the Inquisition at Jaén. He and I were fated to meet again when he rushed up the steps of my mansion at Gozco ahead of me to the Sovereigns' bedroom to save them from the fire. That single event more than anything changed his fortunes… maybe even more than the four riddles of his hermit!'

Don Gonzalo turned to Pedro and they both laughed.

'Today has been a wonderful day for all of us here. But it is not yet over! Antonio, please remove the items from the chests.

'As a gift for you, Miriam, and for you, Agustín, as her faithful officer over many years, the Queen would like you to accept this table. It comes from China and I'm told is over a thousand years old.'

Antonio placed on the floor an exceedingly heavy eight-sided polished serpentine table. The fluted pedestal and the three carved feet on which it sat were also made from the same dark green polished stone, figured with red and black veins.

Martín placed the next objects on the stone table.

'As a gift to you, Pedro and Raquel, the King would like you to accept this solid silver tureen, a dozen silver goblets and serving ladles. Whether for cool fruit drinks in the summer or warm spiced wine in the winter, they should serve you well. They were made by the finest craftsmen in Italy.'

Everyone gathered around the octagonal table, running their hands over the smooth serpentine and down the fluted pedestal. So heavy was the solid silver tureen that Raquel could hardly lift it off the table.

Don Gonzalo banged the spoon on the fireplace once again.

'And lastly, I am honoured to read the following announcements...'

'Before you go on, Don Gonzalo, may I say a few words?' interrupted Miriam.

'Yes, of course, my dear.'

Miriam stepped forward into the centre of the gathering, her hands placed in front of her. Her natural gracefulness was never more evident.

'I couldn't let this occasion pass,' she started coyly, 'without thanking you all for coming to celebrate this, our very special day.'

She became a little flustered as tears formed in the corners of her eyes. Her shoulders relaxed into a softer line and her hands went up to her flushed cheeks.

'Oh dear, I knew this would happen. What I really want to say is... well... How happy I am to be home again... How happy I am to have my Pedro back home... How happy I am to see him so happy with Raquel and little Sarah. I love them both dearly... How happy I am to find true happiness again with Agustín... and how happy I am to be able to cherish and care for him and young Sonia... Just think of it... I've now got a new husband, two new daughters and a granddaughter!' She paused. 'There! And how happy I am to have remembered to say all these things!'

Everyone laughed.

She turned to Don Gonzalo, addressing him directly, her voice becoming softer, lower and more serious.

'Don Gonzalo, during our brief reunion after Pedro found me in the Generalife gazing out of the window, and many, many times since, Pedro has spoken to me about all the things you've done for him: saving his life, healing his wounds, arranging his return home, and many, many other things. You've been his saviour and benefactor, steering him safely through adolescence into manhood. You've been a second father to him, and I know he loves you and reveres you. Please accept my humble gratitude for all you've done for him. We're greatly honoured that you were able to be with us today, and we're all truly blessed by your presence.'

Miriam went across and kissed Don Gonzalo tenderly on the cheek. But she did not get away that lightly. He took her in his arms and, cheek to cheek, held her close to him, remembering all the tragic things which had befallen her and her family.

'It's all past now, Miriam,' he whispered to her. 'Thankfully, it's all behind you.'

She eased away from him.

'Now,' he said, lightning the mood and addressing the whole gathering. 'As

I've said, I've got some important announcements to make. I didn't just come here for the mutton broth and the mulled wine, you know… or even Raghad's *baklawa!*'

Antonio passed him two documents, each bearing the Sovereigns' seals.

'The first one comes from Queen Isabel and is addressed to Agustín. It reads:

'"To Captain Agustín Jaime López Marín:

'"For your loyal and devoted service to me over many years it gives me great pleasure to appoint you Bailiff of Los Vélez. In due course, Pedro Fajardo Chacón, now only fifteen years of age, will assume the title Marquis de los Vélez. But he will need an able administrator, and it is to this end that your appointment of Bailiff is made. As Administrator of the many settlements and communities which make up the district of Los Vélez, your duties will be to oversee justice and equity in the application of the laws of my kingdom; to collect my taxes and tithes; to support the bishop in seeing that our true faith is obeyed in every household, whether Christian or Mudejar; and, above all, to promote the commerce and prosperity of my subjects, whatever their walk of life. As Bailiff of Los Vélez you will be entitled to reside in the small but beautiful castle of Xinquena. The costs of the staff of five there, including two retired and trusty soldiers, will be borne by the Crown through the taxes you collect. These duties will start with immediate effect."'

'"Signed: Isabel. Queen of Castile."'

Antonio Manzano handed Agustín a bunch of large keys. Agustín and Miriam were now the proud occupants of a castle.

The room was abuzz. Agustín looked across the room at Miriam, rattling the keys at her. Both were completely taken aback. Agustín had been looking for a suitable occupation on his retirement from the army, but he had never dreamed of this.

'Is that the imposing red castle on the way to Lorca?' asked Raquel.

'Yes, it's only half an hour's ride from here,' answered Pedro. It was built originally to close-off the valley. You can see it from the top of the road.'

Don Gonzalo banged the spoon on the fireplace again.

'I've one more announcement to make. Then we can settle down and enjoy the reception!'

'This one is directed to Pedro and Raquel, and it comes from the King.'

The courtier broke the seal and unfolded the second document. 'It says:

'To Pedro Togeiro de Tudela:

'It is with pleasure that I confer on you a new appointment, that of Ambassador to Morocco. Relations between the Sultan of Morocco, Mohammed ibn Nazar, and the kingdoms of Aragón and Castile, have become strained due to the Muslims of Granada leaving our lands because of their unwillingness to convert to the true religion, by falling trade, by the economic plight of Morocco, and by the pestilence which is sweeping across North Africa. Your appointment offers an opportunity to set our relations with the Sultan in Morocco on a sound and proper footing for the future well-being of our two kingdoms. Your youth, fluency in Arabic, and experience well beyond your modest years gained from tragedy, adversity and exploration, make you particularly suited to this new post.

"'Posts of Ambassador usually carry a title, and this is no less important for our links with our Arab neighbours than with the courts of Europe. Consequently, I am pleased to confer on you a Knighthood, and in keeping with your action in saving the lives of myself and Queen Isabel, it appears entirely appropriate to us that you adopt the title Don Pedro of Gozco (it being the location of Don Gonzalo's residence in which we were staying at the time). Your new ambassador's residence is already being furnished in the beautiful city of Marrakech and I will expect you and Doña Raquel, an equal and essential partner in this venture, to take up your duties by the month of May or, as necessity determines, later, when the pestilence in Morocco has subsided.

"'However, you will need a trusty messenger to conduct official documents and messages from your embassy to my Court, wherever that resides. Yazíd, son of Yakub ibn Hayyan, appears ideally suited to this role, and you have my blessing to appoint him as your official Envoy.

"'I will be pleased if you will attend our court with Doña Raquel to be invested as Knight of the Realm and to receive your official Letter of Appointment as Ambassador to Morocco.'

"'Signed: Fernando, King of Aragón, King of Naples and Sardinia.'"

Don Gonzalo went across to Pedro.

'Welcome to the club!' he said. 'And to you, my dear, Doña Raquel! In the diplomatic circles in which you'll now move, you'll make a dashing couple. Dress in sumptuous clothes, flaunt your beauty, but remember, you must always do what is right for our Kingdoms of Castile and Aragón.'

'Oh, we will, we will,' she replied.

'Where's the King and Queen's court at the moment?' asked Pedro of Don Gonzalo.

'They'll be in Valencia until April, and then they'll travel to Toledo on the way to Valladolid for June. The journey to Valencia from here, whether by sea or road, is not difficult; either will take about five days. So I suggest you make that your target. But you need be in no rush. You can help your mother and new stepfather settle into Xinquena. The rooms there have been unoccupied for a year or two, and they'll need some attention to make them homely.'

The wedding reception extended well into the evening, the cauldron of mulled wine having been filled and consumed twice more. The snow had ceased, but with it lying ankle-deep on the ground it was impossible to go far. The thick Níjar rugs and the warm room were as commodious as any Gonzalo, Antonio or Martín had experienced in their campaigning days, and they were content to make themselves comfortable in front of the fire.

In early March, with the sun now warming the land and the pink almond blossom aglow on the mountain sides, Pedro, Raquel, two-year-old Sarah and Yazíd set off for Valencia. Their new life lay before them.

Historical Postscript

On his second voyage, Cristóbal Colón returned to Villa de la Navidad on Hispañola in December 1493 but no sign remained of the thirty-nine men whom he had left there to construct the fort. He returned from this voyage in May 1496, almost three years after his departure. Colón made two more voyages to the New World: in 1498 when he discovered Trinidad and the mainland of South America, and in 1502 when he visited Honduras and the Panama isthmus. He was sent home from his third voyage in irons due to serious disputes amongst the settlers on Hispañola. He died in Valladolid in 1506 at the age of fifty-five.

In November 1499, Martín Pinzón's younger brother, Vicente, sailed from Palos and reached the coast of Brazil the following January where he explored the mouth of the Amazon river. In 1505 he was made Governor of Puerto Rico from where he surveyed the coast of the Yucatán and Venezuela.

No trace of Colón's original *diario* of his first voyage exists. Queen Isabel's copy, which became known as the 'Barcelona Copy', survived until around 1544 and then was also lost. Luckily, by then Friar Bartolomé de las Casas had pieced together the original log both from the notes he himself had made from it, much of it verbatim, and from notes Colón's son, Fernando, had made of what his father had told him as well as from discussions which the friar had with Fernando. So what is today called the 'Log of Christopher Columbus' is the faithful reconstruction of the *diario* by Bartolomé de las Casas.

Queen Isabel died in 1504, aged fifty-four, twelve years before Fernando. Her kingdom of Castile, being quite separate and distinct from Fernando's kingdom of Aragón, passed to their eldest surviving heir, Juana ('Joan the Mad'). Juana married Philip of Austria ('Philip the Fair') and although their union was short-lived, as Philip died at the age of twenty-nine, the marriage linked Spain to the House of Hapsburg, covering Germany, Austria and the Low Countries, and it set in motion through Charles I of Spain (Charles V of the Holy Roman Emperor) Spain's domination of continental Europe and the creation of its vast empire, which stretched from California to Tierra del Fuego and across the Pacific to the Philippines. The wealth from gold and mainly silver returned to Spain between 1505 and 1650 financed the fleets and armies which built and defended this empire. This reached its zenith around 1590, after which the profligacy of Philip IV and the growing maritime might of protestant Holland and England began to erode its power.

Boabdil died in 1533, aged seventy. He was buried in Fez. It is not known whether he ever returned to Spain. His rival, *El Zagal*, died some years before and was buried in Tremecen, also in Morocco. Christian Spain endured two major revolts amongst the indigenous Mudejares (Muslims who converted to Christianity). The second of these in the Alpujarra in 1568 caused the death of tens of thousands and the forced expulsion of over 90,000 inhabitants to other parts of Spain. In their place came people from the north of the country who were wholly unsuited to farm the dry lands of *Al-Andalus*, and through their mismanagement caused an ecological and economic disaster. The region, as well as Almería in general, went into a decline and for centuries became the backwater of Spain.

The continent of Africa continued to grind against *Al-Andalus* with destructive earthquakes in 1495, 1504 and 1518. The most serious of all for Almería was in 1522, when the city was ruined. From the seventeenth century on they became less catastrophic but nevertheless they have continued to this day.

Don Gonzalo Fernández of Córdoba continued to serve the Crown loyally. In 1496 he led coalition forces from Castile, Austria, Milan and Venice to drive the French out of Italy, and it was in this and subsequent campaigns there that he earned the title 'The Great Captain' by which he is now best known. He created compact, self-contained, highly mobile *tercios* of two thousand paid volunteers, which became the model for regiments and fighting units years later.

Appendix

Historical Events at the Time of the Conquest of Granada

1478 The Spanish Inquisition created.

1482 Fernando and Isabel declare a holy war to oust the Muslims finally from Spain.

1483 Tómas Torquemada appointed Inquisitor General of Castile and Aragón.

1483 The four months' imprisonment of the Sultan Boabdil in Porcuna after the battle at Lucena.

1483 Boabdil's son Ahmad held hostage in Porcuna until 1492.

1487 The surrender of Málaga in May and the plight of its citizens.

1487 Almería earthquake in November.

1488 Ponce de León takes Vera and some forty Muslim towns and fortresses.

1488 The surrender of Guadix by *El Zagal* on December 3rd to the Catholic Monarchs.

1489 The surrender of the city of Almería by *El Zagal* on December 26th to the Catholic Monarchs.

1491 From April the build-up of the Christian encampment outside Granada.

1491 The bedroom fire on July 14th in the bedchamber of Fernando and Isabel at Gozco, outside Granada.

1491 The start in September of the construction of Santa Fe.

1492 The surrender of Granada on January 2nd to the Catholic Monarchs by Boabdil.

1492 Boabdil's departure from Granada on January 25th.

1492 The degree for the expulsion of the Jews from Spain promulgated on March 31st.

1492 The publication in August of Antonio de Nebrija's *Gramática de la Lengua Castellana*.

1492 The signing on April 17th of the *Capitulaciones* by the Monarch and Colón.

1492 The departure on August 3rd of Cristóbal Colón with the *Santa María*, *Pinta* and *Niña* on his first voyage to the Indies.

1492 Colón's historic landfall at Samana Cay on October 12th.

1492 The foundering of the *Santa María* on December 25th.

1493 Departure of the *Pinta* and the *Niña* from Hispañola on January 16th.

1493 The arrival of the *Pinta* at Bayona on March 1st.

1493 The arrival of the *Niña* in Lisbon on March 4th.

1493 The arrival of both the *Pinta* and *Niña* at Palos on March 15th.

1493 Cristóbal Colón's triumphal entry into Barcelona on April 4th.

1493 The start on September 25th of Colón's second yoyage.

1493 Boabdil's departure in mid-October from *Al-Andalus*.

1496 Don Gonzalo Fernández of Córdoba, the Great Captain, leads his tercios against the French in Naples.

1499 Serious revolt by the Muslims in the Alpujarra.

1502 Final expulsion of the Muslims from Spain pronounced.

1504 Queen Isabel dies.

1516 King Fernando dies.

Bibliography

Albarracín Navarro, Joaquina, *Venta de bienes rústicos que pertenecían al Rey Zagal*, Agricultura y regadio en *Al-Andalus*, Actas del Coloquios, Instituto de Estudios Almeriense, 1996.

Alonso, Jorge, *Historia de Almería* (cartoon book), Instituto de Estudios Almeriense, no date.

Anon, (*About olive presses*), Larouse Enciclopedia Ilustrado, vol. II, pp.25–40.

Anon, (*About silk production*), Larouse Enciclopedia Ilustrado, vol. LIV, pp.1393–1401.

Anon, (*About the rearing of silkworms*), Larouse Enciclopedia Ilustrado, vol. LIV, pp.1367–1382.

Anon, (*About the use of mulberry trees for rearing silkworms*), Voz de Almería.

Anon, *The Letter of Columbus*, Lenox Library Reprint 1493–1893, printed by Order of the Trustees of the Lenox Library, New York, 1893, Second Edition.

Anon, *El agua en al agricultura de Al-Andalus*, Junta de Andalucía, 1995.

Anon, *The Routes of Al-Andalus*, Granada, 1995.

Anon, *Una lectura del paisaje agrícola andalusí en Níjar y Huebro*, Agricultura y regadio en *Al-Andalus*: síntesis y problemas, Actas del Coloquio, Almería, Instituto de Estudios Almeriese, 1995, pp.229–258.

Anon, Revista Velezana, *El parque natural. Sierra María*, Ayuntamiento de Vélez Rubio, 1996.

Anon, *El legado andalusí*: Porcuna (Jaén), Ayuntamiento de Porcuna, 1998.

Arié, Rachel, *España Musulama* (Siglos VIII–XV), Barcelona, 1982.

Barrionuevo, Lorenzo Cara, *Un capítulo casi olivado en la historia de Ahemeña*, El Eco de Alhama, 1985, pp.9–14.

Barrionuevo, Lorenzo Cara, *La civilización islámica. Historia de Almería*, Instituto de Estudios Almeriense, 1993.

Bromhead, C.E.N., *Geology in Embryo (up to 1600 AD)*, Proc. Geol. Assoc., Ciencias Sociales, 1945.

Del Valle y Díaz, Félix, *La espada de Toledo*, Junta de Comunidades de Castilla-La Mancha, 1995.

Dennis, Amarie, *Seek the Darkness*, printed in Madrid by the Successors of Rivadeneyra Press, Inc, 1961.

Díaz-Plaza, Fernando, *La vida cotidiana en la España de la Inquisición*, Cronicas de la Historia, EDAF, 1996.

Dunn, O., and Kelly, J.E., *The* Diario *of Christopher Columbus's First Voyage to America, 1492-1493*, University of Oklahoma Press: Norman and London, 1991.

Eléxpuru, Inés, *La cocina de Al-Andalus*, Alianza Editorial, 1994.

Fuson, R.H., *The Log of Christopher Columbus*, International Marine Publishing Company, Camden, Maine, 1987.

Gala, Antonio, *El manuscrito carmesí*, Planeta, 1990.

García de Cortázar, F., y González Vesga, M., *Breve historia de España*, Alianza Editorial, 1995.

Garrido Atienza, Manuel, *Las capitulaciones para la entraga de Granada*, Diputación Literaria Paulino Ventura Graveset, Granada, 1910.

Glick, Thomas F., *Islamic and Christian Spain in the early Middle Ages*, Part 2, Movement of Ideas and Technologies, The Library of Iberian Resources.

Gómez Díaz, Donato, *El esparto en la economía almeriense*, Diputación de Almería, 1985.

Jacobs, Michael, *A Guide to Andalusia*, Penguin Books, 1990.

Jíminez Jurado, María Isabel, *Palabra en el tiempo de la industría de la sed en Almería: un caso insólito de trabajo femenino*, Revista de Humanidades y, pp.159–168.

Maniatis, N., Herz, N., and Basiakos, Y., *The Study of Marble and Other Stones used in Quarrying*, Trans. 3rd Int. Symp. of Assoc. for the Study of Marble and other Stones used in Antiquity, 1995.

Marín Fernández, Bartolome, *Almería y el mar*.

Martín, José Luis, *La edad media en España*, Biblioteca Básica de Historia, 1990.

Navarro Espinach, Germán, *La sed entre Génova, Valencia y Granada en la época de los Reyes Católicos*, Istituto di Storia del Medioevo, 1993.

Pastor Medina, Ginés, *Los maestros de cantera*, Oficios Artesanos, 1990.

Pastor Mines, Ginés, *Macael y las canteras de mármol. Su aportación al patrimonio monumental de España*, Arte y Cultura, 1998.

Peinado Santaella, Rafael, *La repoblación de la tierra de Granada*, Los Montes Orientales, 1990.

Posadas Chinchilla, A.M. and Vidal Sanchez, F, (Editors), *El estudio de los terremotos en Almería*, Instituto de estudios Almeriense, Diputación de Almería, 1994.

Renwick, W.G., *Marble and marble working*, Crosby Lockwood and Sons, London, 1909.

Roth, C, *The Spanish Inquisition*, W.W. Norton and Co., London, 1996.

Sáez, A.F. y Belén, A.S., *Los Baños de Sierra Alhamilla*, Diputación Provincial de Almería, 1998.

San José, Carmen Trillo, *Los diferentes aprovechimientos del agua en la alquería del reino de Granada: la Mahah, del distrito de Quempe*, Agricultura y Regadio en Al-Andalus: Síntesis y Problemas, Actas del Coloquio, Instituto de Estudios Almeriense, Diputación de Almería, 1995, pp.215–228.

Sánchez-Albornoz, Claudio, *La españa musulmana, según los autores islámicas y cristianos medievales*, España-Calpe, Madrid, 1973.

Segura Del Pino, María Dolores, *Las fuentes de Alhadra. Abastacimiento urbano y regadío en al Almería, muuslmana y morisca.* Agricultura y regadio en *Al-Andalus*, Síntesis y Problemas: Agricultura y Regadio en *Al-Andalus*, Actas del Coloquios, Instituto de Estudios Almeriense, 1995, pp.453–463.

Sierra Fernández, Avelino, *La carabela Pinta y su arribada a Bayon*, Diputación de Pontevedra, 1997.

Thomas, Hugh, *El Imperio Español*: de Colón a Magallenas, Planeta Historia y Sociedad, 2003.

Vidal, César, *Enigmas y secretos de la Inquisición: el libro prohibido*, Ediciones de Bolsillo, 1999.

Vincent, Bernard, *Andalucia en la edad moderna; economía y sociedad*, Diputación Provincial de Almería, 1990.

Vincent, Bernard, *1492: El año admirable*, Drakontos, 1992.

Waelkens, M., Herz, N. and Meons, L., *Ancient stones: quarrying, trade and provenance*, Leuven University Press, 1992.

Wert, Juan Pablo, *El reino nazarí de Granda*, AKAL Historia de Mundo para Jóvenes, Serie Historis de España, 1994.

Printed in the United Kingdom
by Lightning Source UK Ltd.
102132UKS00002B/1-30